# THE LION OF DJIBOUTI

BY

## LINDSEY D. LINDEN

Title: The Lion of Djibouti

Author: Lindsey D. Linden

Genre: Historical, mythical fiction.



ISBN: 978-0-9863482-0-4 Electronic epub format
ISBN: 978-0-9863482-1-1 Trade paperback
ISBN: 978-0-9863482-2-8 Electronic mobi format
Format: Trade paperback and e-book
Publishing Date: February 1, 2015

Description: A war-torn Ethiopia and an America in the throes of social unrest provide the backdrop for poignant story of loss, famine, war, faith and love. Guided by spirit elephants, haunted by hyena-men, The Lion of Djibouti is the quest of two brothers to reunite across two continents after a brutal lion attack.

Audience: Adventurers, conservationists, naturalists, anti-poaching organizations, sociologists, students of history, lovers of fiction, seekers of faith and the mystical.



Edited by Nicole R. Klungle

Cover Design and Formatting by Damonza

# THE LION OF DJIBOUTI

THE HAUD REGION

# ETHIOPIA 1948

"TAFARI! TAFARI! LEAVE the goats! Come! Come to me! Time for you to become a man!"

Darting through an opening in the tiger bush, side stepping a clump of savanna grass, Tafari hurried to where his Father stood.

"Yes, Father?" he asked, catching his breath. "How may I serve you?"

Tafari searched his father's deep brown eyes for a reply while his shifting feet stirred small clouds of dust that swirled around his ankles.

"Tell me how I will become a man," he half asked, half demanded, his dula planted firmly on the ground before him.

"Patience," his father told him, his brow furrowing as he studied his eldest son's face, "is the beginning."

Tafari's father looked to where the score of goats was loosely grazing. Noting each one's place, he searched for any dangers that might be near. His two younger sons, Menelik and Teimbaka, were at the far back of the herd, shouting at each other in some game he could only shake his head at. As of yet, they were of little use as herdsmen.

"Can you not show me this *patience* then? I very much think it is time for me to become a man."

Tafari's father kept his gaze upon the family's goats for a moment more before looking back to his son. Adjusting his shamma over his lanky frame, he said, "Like a tool it is Tafari; different for every man. Like a dula," he explained, holding out his own thick, gnarled walking stick for his son to study. "Each hand must be content with the feel of it, the shape of it, before you become comfortable with it. Before it is of any use to you."

Tafari scrunched his face, struggling with the words of his father.

"But if—"

"Enough," his father softly said. "There is work to do. Firewood we will need for camp, and much of it. This task I give to you," he told him, lifting his gaze back over the small herd. "And take your two brothers. We will need enough wood for two days."

The goats began to bleat, the bell of the lead animal clanging in protest as the goat moved quickly away from the two young boys who were chasing each other through the grazing area.

"Enough, Menelik! Enough, Teimbaka! Come here. Now!"

As one, the boys lowered their walking sticks to their sides and raced to see who could stand before their father first.

"I am here, Father!" gushed Menelik.

"No, I am here!" shouted Teimbaka.

"Be still," he commanded. "Tomorrow we will offer sacrifice for the belg. The goats must be kept at peace. They must not be uneasy when I choose which among them will bring the blessing of rain."

He shook his head and chuckled.

"You see now why patience is the beginning, Tafari?" he asked as he studied the blank expressions on the slender faces of his two youngest sons. "How can you explain knowledge before knowledge is present?"

Lovingly, he patted Menelik on the head and then did the same to Teimbaka.

"Keep these two from harm. Keep their feet pointed in the right direction. And you two," he said to the two smiling faces fixed upon him, "listen to your brother and keep to what must be done. No games when there is work to do. Yes, yes? You understand?"

"Do not worry, Father," Tafari said before either of his brothers could reply, "no harm will come to them while they are with me. I will take them to the dry riverbed and we will gather all the firewood we will need."

"It is settled, then. Pile the wood there, where there is a break in the brush," he instructed, pointing to an area some distance away, far past where the goats were grazing. "There, there, you see the place I mean? Where the two leafless trees stand apart?"

Tafari followed his father's eyes and pointing finger. He nodded.

"When your mother and I have settled the goats and have made camp, I will return with the donkey, and we will load what you have gathered. We will need to be back at camp long before the sun begins to set."

"Might we find wood nearer to where—"

Tafari fell silent as his father's attention shifted to what lay behind them.

"What do you see, Father? The bad soldiers?" he whispered, turning to scan the horizon for any columns of dust.

The bell of the lead goat abruptly jingled. Tafari turned back around to see his mother leading the donkey away. The lead goat fell in behind them, the rest of the herd ambling after it.

"I see your mother is set to make camp sooner then her dawdling family," Tafari's father observed. "We would both be wise to be about our tasks."

Clasping Tafari firmly on his shoulder, he said, "Take care of your brothers and be quick about your work. I will be back sooner than you think."

"Do not worry, Father. I am ready to be a man now."

But if his father heard him, Tafari did not know, for his father was already hurrying to catch up with the goats, his dark silhouette cloaked in a swirling cloud of dust and the shifting folds of his tattered shamma.

*

"WHEN WILL FATHER return?" Menelik wearily asked his older brother as he dropped an armload of branches down on the pile they were making.

"Soon," Tafari replied. "Patience, patience, young brother," he added with a knowing nod.

"Away with you, thieving soldiers! I, Teimbaka command it! Do my bidding or I will strike you down!"

His dula grasped tightly in his hand and raised aloft as though it were a long spear, the youngest of the three brothers challenged his invisible foe with glaring eyes and a grimacing expression. With a swoosh, he swung the dula down and to the side as though he were blocking an enemy's sword from being raised against him.

"Take care and do not laugh at me," he warned his two snickering brothers. "For I do the emperor's bidding!"

"You will be doing goat turd's bidding if you do not help us gather wood," Tafari scolded, swinging his own dula out to make contact with Teimbaka's.

The meeting of the wood produced a sharp crack. To Teimbaka's dismay, his dula fell from his grasp.

"Gathering wood is not a task for an emperor's warrior," he protested, bending to snatch up his weapon.

"Ha! The smell of goat—"

The widening eyes of Teimbaka silenced Tafari. Staring steadfastly over Tafari's shoulder, Teimbaka began to shake. Tafari studied his youngest brother's face with a mixture of amusement and annoyance.

*"Negusa negast,"* Teimbaka urgently whispered.

He looked to each of his brothers, tears welling up in his eyes.

"What game are we playing now?" Tafari sighed as he half-heartedly looked back over his shoulder.

An enormous male lion greeted Tafari with a menacing roar. Instinctively, he crouched down and thrust his dula outward.

"Away!" he screamed.

The great male shook his head, bared his teeth, and snarled. Entranced, Tafari watched as the mane of the beast began to move in several directions at once. Legs sprouted, and new sets of piercing, yellow eyes appeared as several lionesses began to move past. They took to the trail of the goats and his parents. The lead male looked at Tafari and roared.

"Be gone!" he shouted, swinging his dula.

Effortlessly, the great male leaped across the few yards that separated them. With a swipe of a giant paw, he raked the dula from Tafari's hands. As blood sprayed out from Tafari's shredded forearm, he heard his own scream.

*

MENELIK PUSHED AWAY from Teimbaka and ran up the dry riverbed. Focused on nothing but escape, he sprinted away, leaving his brothers behind. But the screams and roars chased him. They seemed to be right behind him. He ran faster. He closed his eyes. The screams went quiet. He surged ahead.

Beginning to tire, his legs numb, his body slick with sweat, he still could not bring himself to stop or find the courage to turn his head. Afraid of what he might see if he did, he continued to run, pressing forward, following the path of the sand in the riverbed. Not until the sun turned his shadow tall and thin did he begin to slow. Even then, several minutes passed before he found himself standing still.

Catching his breath, shaking with fatigue, he tried to blink away the image of Tafari's death. But he kept seeing the jaws of the lion clamp down around his older brother's neck. When he tried to clear his head of the image, he saw instead the face of his younger brother, Teimbaka, frozen with fear.

The calls of a pack of hyenas erupted, breaking into his thoughts. Drifting up the dry riverbed, the chilling cackles made him shiver. Staring in the direction he had run from, he bowed his head.

"Father! Mother!"

He didn't know if he had shouted for them out loud or had only screamed for them in his head. The thought of his parents brought a sudden ache to his chest. He gasped and choked, wondering if they were alive. The goats and the donkey were gone, he knew. But he hoped that his mother and father had heard or seen the lions before they struck. He shook his head. The notion that his parents might be gone was unsettling.

Again, he saw Teimbaka staring blankly at the lion, shaking.

What would his parents say to him when he found them, if he found them? How could he tell them that he had run off and left his younger brother to fend for his own life? They wouldn't accept his fear as an excuse, he knew. The needs of the family came first. It is what they had both preached to all of them from the time they were able to understand. They would not forgive him. Trembling, wringing the fabric of his robes with his hands, he began to cry. He had no choice. He would go back to find Teimbaka.

But the dry riverbed beckoned, enticing him to rest. Suddenly overcome with exhaustion, he felt himself slowly drifting downward. The sand felt soft beneath his body. Eyelids fluttering, he struggled to stay awake. But sleep came swiftly.


Menelik awoke to a night devoid of stars. Shivering, he peered in all directions, searching for the inhuman shapes that had invaded his dreams. But he could not find the shapes within the darkness that enveloped him.

Scared and confused, he pushed himself to the safety of the thickets that lined the banks of the dry riverbed. He fell back asleep only to awaken a short time later to the bewitching sight of his parents and Tafari passing by. As they moved past the spot where he was lying, he tried desperately to push himself up, to run to them, to embrace them, to tell them that he was alive. But his arms and legs would not move.

"Have you nothing to say?"

The voice of his father was at once calm, accusatory, and forlorn. Menelik looked out at his family and saw Tafari pointing his dula to the spot where he was hiding. He tried to answer, but found that he had no voice. His eyes filled with tears.

"We must go, then," his father stated.

They moved on.

Once more, thrashing against the forces that were holding him down, Menelik strained to get up. But he still could not move. Near panic, his eyes clinging to the figures that were drifting farther away, he screamed, "Don't leave me!"

"Be still, brother," Tafari bade him, his fingers gently brushing across his brow. "You must be strong now, if only for Teimbaka. Find him. Find your brother."

Menelik stared up into Tafari's black-brown eyes.

"I must go now," Tafari whispered.

Tafari began to recede, his words, his voice, and his body melting into a void that Menelik could not fathom.

"Tafari!" he gasped, his hands struggling to find an opening between the branches of the thicket. "Tafari!"

But Tafari was gone.

*

THE COMING OF the day brought the sudden explosion of life. Birds began to chatter and squawk, insects buzzed, and not far off, a group of Vervet monkeys screamed an urgent, unified warning. Menelik rubbed the sleep from his eyes and pulled his earth colored shamma close about him. He shivered and slid his hands across his arms. His fingers came away with traces of blood from scratches caused by the thorns of the bushes. He wiped the blood on his robes and crawled out of the underbrush.

As he stood and stretched, he took in his surroundings and the sounds of the various wild voices that clamored about him. Off in the distance, far down the river of sand, he heard a lion roar. A moment later it roared again. This time, however, the voice of the lion was followed by the ranting cackle of hyenas.

Shadows began to race toward the sounds of the lion and the hyenas—formless, swift gliding patches of darkness sweeping down the riverbed as if they had been summoned. Dazedly, Menelik looked up and saw that the shadows were from vultures gathering above. Despair grew darker within him even as the sun's first rays sparkled on the particles of sand at his feet.

*What will you do, oh great warrior emperor Menelik?* he chided himself.

He closed his eyes, hoping the answer would come. The faint *cling clang* of a small bell drifted to him. Without hesitating, he moved to follow it.

As he hurried down the river of sand, the calls of the beasts grew louder. But he was mostly numb to their growls and cackles. Only the faint *cling clang* of the tiny bell was he holding on to—that, and the echoing words of Tafari. Even when the winged shadows grew denser and darkened the way ahead in a circling swirl, he still was not aware of what the dark mass implied.

Air suddenly beat down upon him, his neck, head, and cheek assaulted with feathers and a rush of wind. Instinctively, he ducked and swung his dula. But his hands were empty. Startled, he took stock of where he was. What he saw made him squirm.

Some fifty yards ahead of him, three hyenas were charging and dodging each other, nipping and yelping around a dark stained lump. With a loud, menacing snarl, one hyena chased the two others away. Menelik watched as it hastily took a bite out of the clump they were fighting over. But the others quickly returned to nip at the haunches of the first. Jumping away, the hyena glared and yelped, its muzzle stained with blood. Its jaws were firmly clamped upon a jagged section of sinewy bone. Menelik shut his eyes and screamed.

A short distance away, off to his left, a single lioness calmly watched him from the shade of a tree. She answered his scream with an echoing roar.

"No!" he shouted back as he opened his eyes and saw her. "No!"

The lioness rose. Menelik bent and picked up a large branch and swung it over his head. He charged. The puzzled lioness watched him race toward the hyenas.

"Get away!" Menelik screamed at the scavengers, wielding the branch as a club. "Get away!"

The hyenas separated as he drew near, two moving off to flank him while the other held its ground. Menelik swung his weapon down with all his strength and caught the lone hyena on the snout. With a snarling squeal, the animal dropped the section of bone and retreated. Menelik pressed forward. Closing in, he swept the stick out in front of him.

"Be gone!" he commanded.

The retreating hyena turned and snarled. Menelik could see the blood dripping from its teeth. Enraged by the sight, he lunged at the beast.

Pain shot up through his entire body as powerful jaws ripped into his calf. As he barely registered the attack from the second hyena down at his leg, the first one leaped upon his chest. He flailed at the beast with the branch and tried to knock it away, but the animal clamped its jaws around his forearm. Menelik sank to the ground in agony. Warm, foul breath came snorting across his neck. He readied himself for what was to come.

A thunderclap exploded right above him. Moisture splattered his face. It felt thick and hot. The hyena atop him jerked away, crying out in agony. Then another blast erupted. A second hyena wailed. He felt dizzy. Voices drew near. Winged shadows fluttered about him as another blast rang out. Menelik fell into a misty dimness and closed his eyes.

*

"ARE WE TOO late?"

Martin looked over his shoulder at his wife as he ejected an empty shell casing from the rifle and slipped another bullet in the single-shot chamber.

"Are we in time?" she pressed, her tone urgent. Then, brushing by him with a reproachful glare, Patricia Mathis bent to the boy and flipped open the lid of the first-aid kit.

With a practiced fluidity, Martin raised the single-bolt-action rifle to his shoulder, squinted into the sight, and let off another round. The bullet exploded sixty yards down the dry riverbed, splintering the trunk of a dead tree a half-second after the remaining hyena jumped out of sight.

"Damn. Missed."

The boy twitched and moaned as Patricia dabbed rubbing alcohol on his wounds. She gave her husband the briefest of glances.

"How many do you think there are?" she asked, glancing quickly about. "You know, just the three we saw, or do you—"

Martin looked at the carcasses of the two hyenas he had killed. He ejected the spent shell case from the chamber and reloaded.

"Not what I would have hoped for as a trophy," he observed.

"What *are* you rambling about?" Patricia asked as she ripped long strips of gauze from the roll wedged between her knees.

"I said, not what I would consider trophy-hanging material." He added with a laugh, "I was hoping to do better today."

"Don't talk like that."

"Like what?"

"Like you're some idiot who is above having any feelings whatsoever for someone you have just saved."

She gave him a sharp look. He flinched.

"Oh, Pat," he began, his tone holding a bit of an apology, "it's only a little Negro boy. It's not as though he's anyone of consequence."

"Not as though he's anyone of consequence?" she repeated, her voice rising in pitch with each word. "What an ignorant thing to say. You're beginning to sound like our guide. Awful man; where did the agency find such a— Such a—"

"I think that's stretching it a bit," Martin replied before she could finish, his attention drawn to what he could see through the sight of his rifle.

"Is it?" she challenged. "Then why is it you haven't even offered to lend me a hand? Why are you preoccupied with squinting through your sight when there's a young boy fighting to keep his life here at your feet?"

Martin sighed and raised his eyes skyward. The vultures were multiplying. Their calls were becoming more numerous and shrill. He glanced quickly about, searching for any other threats that might be lurking nearby. Without a word, he shouldered his rifle and went around to the other side of the boy's body and took to one knee.

"Hold the end while I wrap the roll around his wrist," Patricia instructed him with a trace of a smile. "We'll do his leg next."

Martin took the end of the roll of gauze without saying a word.

"I do love you, you know," she added with a wink.

"So I've heard," he replied, trying his best to seem gruff.

"Mathis! Come! We must go! We're wasting time!" The voice of Peter Gunstard boomed up the dry riverbed with authority. Patricia looked her husband square in the face, her lively green eyes flashing with anger.

"Don't," was all he said to her.

Martin let go of the gauze he had been holding and rose to his feet. He looked back down the dry riverbed to where their safari guide, Peter Gunstard, stood waiting with the six bearers they had enlisted for the week's hunting excursion.

"The boy's still alive!" he called back. "He needs attention!"

"Leave him!" Gunstard instructed as he swung his own rifle from his shoulder. "He's not worth the trouble!"

"Not worth the trouble," Patricia hissed under her breath. "I'd like to take a pair of shears and cut—"

"Cannot comply!" Martin yelled back. "We'll have to take him with us!"

The tall, broad-shouldered safari guide definitively shook his head and then said something to the six bearers standing behind him. He slipped the large pack he was carrying off his back, cradled his rife in the crook of his right arm, and made his way to where the Mathises were.

Martin could sense a confrontation with every step that brought Gunstard closer. *It was inevitable*, he thought. It had seemed one was bound to pop up somewhere along the way ever since they had begun their sojourn a little over two days ago.

Although World War II had been over for a few years, for some—for men like Peter Gunstard—the war had not ended. Germany had not lost. Had not surrendered. And never would. For him, the conflict still existed, taking place in some form, on some front. The fact that Martin and Patricia had both served as officers for the United States during the war only seemed to fuel that particular resentment within the man. It was something that Martin and Patricia had both picked up on when they had been introduced to him in Mogadishu. It was just a hunting trip, they had reminded each other, and he had come highly recommended.

But as Martin watched the German approach, he was fairly certain that the former colonel from Rommel's North African command was used to having his orders followed without question. He sensed that this had not changed with the war's end. The notion gnawed at him as Gunstard drew near.

"I said, leave him," Gunstard stated, stopping an arm's length from Martin, his pale blue eyes showing no hint of emotion.

Martin held Gunstard's gaze for several seconds. Neither man flinched or spoke.

"Why bother with him?" Gunstard's tone was softer now, almost compromising. He shifted his rifle, removed his broad-lipped bush hat and ran his fingers through his short-cropped, blonde hair before placing back atop his head.

"A little darky boy isn't worth holding up a hunting safari, is he, Mathis? Especially if it's a black rhino you're after. There are still many kilometers to make before we cross over into Kenya. Leave him to the hyena that got away," he chuckled, offering a weak half-smile. "It would be no loss," he added, glancing down at the boy. "He looks dead anyway. Same as that fly-infested pile," he said, nodding to the bloody, torn robing that hid the remains of another child.

Patricia whirled round and glared at the man. Martin could see the emotion in his wife's face, the fight in her eyes. He spoke up before she could.

"I cannot judge this boy's worth; nor can you, Mr. Gunstard. Hard to say anything at all about him before we get him cleaned up and have his wounds attended to."

Gunstard looked at the circling, squawking vultures.

"He does deserve our admiration and respect, wouldn't you agree?" Martin asked.

"And just how do you figure any filthy native boy from this backward land deserves anyone's respect?" Gunstard spat back.

"His courage, of course," Martin was quick to say. "Did you not see him charge those hyenas with just a tree branch? Surely you must be swayed by courage. Does it not remind you of what you must surely have witnessed during the war from the men you served with?"

"Don't speak to me of the war." Gunstard's voice was harsh and cold. He squeezed the stock of his rifle between his hands. "What you call courage, I call stupidity, undisciplined ignorance, a wish to die. So let him." Gunstard glanced back at the bearers before saying, "Even they would leave him. They know death when they see it. It is the way here. The boy is done, and we are wasting time."

"I don't agree," Martin countered. "That blood-stained pile of robing and what remains of whatever poor unfortunate soul lies beneath it was probably the reason for this boy's actions. I don't see that as being stupid."

"Stupid," Gunstard spat, "is wasting time talking about a dying native boy when the day is getting shorter. This is a hunting trip. I am in command. Leave him. It's time to move out."

The boy heaved and gasped, then groaned in a loud, wailing pitch.

Gunstard swung his rifle to ready and slid the bolt to load the chamber. He took aim at the boy.

"Dear God, man, no!" Patricia screamed, scrambling to her feet.

As Gunstard's finger found the trigger, Martin thrust the butt of his rifle into the man's face. Gunstard fell backward off his feet. Martin pounced on him, hoping to wrestle the loaded gun from his hands. But Gunstard kicked out and up into Martin's stomach, pushing him back. Martin fell to one knee. Gunstard scrambled to his feet and raised his rifle.

A shot rang out. The vultures shrieked as a bullet flew skyward.


"Drop the rifle!" Patricia held a Colt .45 service revolver with both hands, her left palm supporting the butt of the pistol, her right hand gripping the stock, finger on the trigger. She pointed the gun squarely at Peter Gunstard's head.

Gunstard twisted his face into a snarl.

"I said, drop it."

At five feet, five inches, Patricia was a good eight to nine inches shorter than their guide and a good deal slighter in build. If she had been asked to guess, she would have ventured that Peter Gunstard outweighed her by some seventy-five to eighty pounds. But she had learned many things during her four years of service in the military. And one of the lessons that she had been taught was that a loaded weapon in the grasp of a steady hand was a great equalizer.

Gunstard glared at her, but made no move to drop the rifle. With a grim smile curling about the edges of his lips, he jerked his weapon into firing position and swung the barrel at Martin. Patricia's shot was immediate and on the mark; the bullet deftly grazing the meaty flesh behind the thumb of Gunstard's shooting hand. The bullet's impact forced him to release the trigger and take his hand off the stock of the rifle. Martin lunged and grabbed the Remington's barrel and yanked it away from him.

"Excellent shot, dear."

If Patricia heard her husband speak, she did not show it. She stood frozen in the ready position, the Colt .45 aimed once more at Peter Gunstard's head.

Nose and lips bloodied, his left hand squeezing the wound below his right thumb, Peter Gunstard stared at Martin before slowly turning his attention to Patricia. Suddenly, he burst out laughing. Patricia and her husband exchanged confused looks. Gunstard slapped his thighs and bellowed his crazed pleasure skyward. The vultures shrieked back.

"What on earth?" said Patricia.

"Stupid Americans!" Gunstard howled. "Look around. What will you do? Will you shoot me now?" he challenged Patricia, taking a stride toward her.

Patricia steadied herself. Her aim did not waver.

As quickly as it had erupted, Gunstard's laughter abated. He caught his breath and said, "Well, will you, Mrs. Mathis? Will you shoot me? I think not."

He stepped menacingly toward her. She placed a bullet in the dirt by his boot tip.

"Don't tempt me," she hissed, raising the gun back up to his face.

Gunstard raised his hands, his face contorted in mock fear. The boy groaned anew; louder and more agitated. Patricia glanced worriedly at him.

"Yes," Gunstard laughed, "what will you do? You have your *boy* to take care of now. And look where you are," he continued, prompting her to take in her surroundings with a sweeping gesture of his arm. "Where exactly are you, by the way, Mrs. Mathis? Do you have any idea?"

With a smirk, Gunstard turned his back on the Mathises and began walking toward the six bearers.

"Where are you going?" Patricia demanded.

"I'm going to find some black rhinos," he said over his shoulder. "Where are you going, Mrs. Mathis?" he added with a howl. "Do you even have a clue?"

Patricia heard the bolt action on Martin's rifle. She looked over at him as he took aim at Gunstard's back.

"Martin—no."

For longer then she felt comfortable watching, Martin held his gun sight on Gunstard's retreating body, his trigger finger tensed. Slowly, he lowered his weapon, exhaling as he did, and looked over at his wife.

"You should have let me."

Patricia watched as Peter Gunstard slung his pack up onto his back. Again, he said something to the bearers. One of the men immediately bent and rummaged through a large duffel bag. A moment later, the man handed him another rifle, a second pack, and what looked to be a box of ammunition. Adjusting the straps of the rifle and the two packs, Gunstard looked back at the Mathises, smiled widely, and doffed his hat.

"Enjoy the bush!" he called out.

With that, he turned and walked off.

"Dear, God. He can't just leave," said Patricia.

"I'm afraid he already has."

"But we—"

"No, we don't need him," Martin said.

"But how—"

"We just will," he reassured her. "We've got a compass in our gear. Water. Food if we need it," he said, slapping his rifle. "And it looks as though we still have our six men with us."

Martin nodded in the direction of the bearers. They had gathered up what gear Gunstard had left and were moving up the dry riverbed toward them.

"The one you've been calling Anthony seems to understand a smattering of English," he remarked.

The boy on the ground whimpered and shook.

"We'll get by, then," she offered.

"Of course we will, Pat. Of course we will."

*

BLOOD. BLOOD WAS all that filled Teimbaka's senses. He did not think to move, did not think to run, did not heed the panic that swirled within him. He did not think to look away even as the *negusa* lion slashed and ripped his brother apart with his massive teeth and jaws. And when the beast was finished with Tafari, when the lion looked at him and roared and seemed ready to strike, he still saw nothing but blood. Heard nothing but the blood-curdling cries of his brother. Felt nothing but the blood that had splattered upon his face and blurred his vision. And when he wiped the blood from his eyes, he saw that the great lion was gone.

He stood frozen, statue-like. Only when a trickle of urine ran down his legs did he find some sense of awareness. And only when he began to shuffle away, to step aside from the small puddle forming at his feet, did he start to comprehend what had taken place.

The wave of nausea was quick and overpowering. He fell to his knees and violently threw up. Gasping for air between fits of heaving, he crawled on his hands and knees, moving forward and backward and side-to-side. The smell of death filled his senses. He choked on it. Clasping a hand over his mouth, he scurried away on two knees and one hand. That's when he latched on to Tafari's dula.

Grasping the thick walking stick, he caught his breath and planted one end of it into the ground. Pulling himself up, he leaned heavily upon it, taking strength and comfort in the feel of the wood.

Fresh sounds of death drifted to him from a good distance down the river of sand. Lions were roaring. A woman screamed in fear and then fell silent. A man loosed a warrior's call of vengeance. Lions roared. The air seemed rife with panic. Then suddenly all was quiet. The air became still.

"Shall I tend to the goats?" he heard himself ask Tafari. "I do not need to wait for Menelik. He is no good with the goats. He doesn't know them like I do."

He waited for Tafari to reply. Minutes passed. Many minutes. The sun made Teimbaka's shadow long, but still Tafari would not answer. Teimbaka became annoyed.

"It is not yet time to sleep," he lectured his older brother. "We have not even had the evening meal yet. Why are you so tired? Are you not hungry?"

With each question left unanswered, his annoyance grew toward anger. *Why does my brother not answer?* he wondered. *Why is he sleeping when there is still work to do? Mother will need the wood for the fire. The goats will need tending.*

"I will eat your portion, then. You do not need it if you are asleep. Mother and Father will see that I deserve it. Tending to the goats is not easy. It isn't, you know!" he angrily shouted. "I will tell them that you want me to have your food! You don't deserve it! You are lazy!"

Teimbaka started to turn away, but then thought better of it. He stretched the dula out toward Tafari.

"Come, brother," he said softly, offering the end of the walking stick for his brother to grab hold of. "Tafari, please. Tafari, it's time we go."

But Tafari remained silent. He did not move.

With a shrug of resignation, Teimbaka left his brother. Using Tafari's dula to steady his footing, he ascended the shallow bank of the dry riverbed and began walking in the direction his parents had taken.


Teimbaka's steps were labored and uncertain. Twilight had fallen. *Where are my parents?* he wondered. *Surely they could not have traveled farther than where I am now. And why is Father not looking for me, calling for me?* It was father's strictest of rules: to be within the light of the fire before darkness. Yet it was almost dark. Where were they? And why could he not hear the small bell of the lead goat?

The unsettling calls of hyenas interrupted his thoughts. Even though their laughter seemed very far away, it still made him shiver and wonder. He wondered what they were hunting, what they had found. He wondered if they had come upon Tafari sleeping, or if they had picked up on *his* scent and were now following him.

Startled by the thought, he picked up his pace.

*Certainly I will find my parents' campsite soon and smell the evening meal cooking over the burning wood. Certainly my father and mother will receive me with joy and forgive me my lateness and my shirking of duties. I will gather double my share of firewood in the morning, I will tell them. And I will tend to the goats in earnest, and obey and listen to all I am told to do.*

With these thoughts spurring him forward, he began to run.

With the coming of night, sweat dripping from his brow, eyes focused on nothing but the path he was following and the hypnotic motion of his feet hitting the ground with each stride, he did not see the thick, twisting, low-hanging vine that looped across the trail before him. It caught him just below his chin, throwing him harshly backward. He sat up, gasping for breath. The air was thick, moist, and close. *Something is different. Something has changed*, he thought.

Grasping the dula, he looked around. It was dark, darker then he could ever remember. And the sky was gone. There were no stars or clouds above him; no moon lit the sky. There was only the dark. And sounds: odd sounds, close sounds, eerie sounds, sounds that moved, sounds that stayed. All of this made his spine tingle, his body tremble. He sprang to his feet.

Blinking his eyelids, trying to focus in the lack of light, forms began to take shape all around him, looming in from the sides and above. Branches sprouted in all directions from countless tree trunks that seemed to be of one, the canopy of leaves and branches creating a ceiling where there should have been sky. Birds and monkeys and other creatures he knew nothing of called and squabbled, warned and enticed, hunted and hid, pounced and retreated, scurried and became still.

*It must be the forest where water always falls.* It was as his father had described to them. But he, like his brothers, had not been able to under-stand what his father had told them. Only the open had they always known: semi-arid grasslands and steppe and plateaus where the goats would graze for a time before they would move on. Or mountains. Some near, some far, some nothing more than ridges, some that reached up and touched the clouds; these they knew of. But the idea of a forest where rain always fell they could not comprehend.

*This must be where he had been leading us.* They would skirt the edge of it, he had told them. It would provide them with food and water on their journey away from war, away from the bad soldiers, away from *ferenji*, away from the Ogaden, away from Somalia.

Something buzzed close to his ear. He batted the sound with his free hand. A rustling erupted from behind. He jumped and turned to face it. A screech came out of the darkness from ahead. He jumped and turned again. Another screech erupted from somewhere off to his side. The buzz-ing grew louder around his ears. He took a step forward. Fluttering wings battered his ankles before flying up to his face. He started to run, but the same low-hanging vine stopped him. He stepped back and brought his dula crashing down onto it. Tears welled up in his eyes. He pushed the vine upward, bent, and scooted through. An animal he could not see hooted some blaring, echoing call. He swung his dula out ahead of him and ran and ran and ran.

When the dirt beneath his feet began to change, he stopped run-ning. When the loose dry sand he had been traveling on became slick and wet and then changed to mud, he allowed himself a respite—a chance to breathe, to look around, to take a moment to think.

Stars, brilliant and glittering with their white-blue light, beckoned his eyes upward. There was sky! Not far from where he stood, the surface of a small pool of water shimmered with the glimmering reflection of that which existed above. *A clearing,* he realized. Trees ringed the area some twenty yards off in every direction. *Like some holy place,* he mused, *an oasis. Perhaps my family is here.*

It was within that thought that he came to face the sudden, aching realization that he was alone. Hungry, exhausted, thirsty, scared, lost, and with little hope, he felt his tears return. He began to shake.

*What have I done?* What sins had his family committed that the Mother would punish them so, punish him? How could he make up for it? What sign would She give to him so that he could make everything right? He raised his dula to the stars.

"Mother, show me what I must do. Help me. Give me some sign," he pleaded in a whisper.

A breeze stirred. Ripples formed on the surface of the water. The wavering starlight drew him closer. He bent and touched the edge of the pool; the water was cool. He tasted it from the tips of his fingers. He cupped his hand, filled his palm with it, and drank. Eagerly, he repeated the motion a dozen times. *She provides me with water. I am here for a reason.* He nodded. *She wants it to be so.*

The deep, strong purring of a big cat seeped into his awareness. Instinctively, he willed himself to stiffness. The purring was steady and calm, methodically moving from one side of him to the other. He balled his muscles tight. He waited. The pool became still. He let his eyes drift upon it. A shadow crossed over the water's surface. All was quiet. Finally, after what seemed like many minutes, he turned his head ever so slightly to venture a look.

A sinewy leopard met his gaze with harsh, yellow-green eyes. Teimbaka blinked. The leopard's tail twitched. Teimbaka's gaze drifted to the trees. Safety was twenty yards away.

A ghostly howling erupted from within the treetops, drawing the leopard's attention. Teimbaka sprang to his feet. The leopard's head snapped back to him, snarling, fangs exposed. Teimbaka leapt across the pool, his feet splashing at the edge. He raced for the forest. The leopard growled and gave chase.

He had once run after a stray goat that had been spooked by a boom of thunder. The goat had been at the back of the herd, and the chase had taken them away from the rest of the goats and his family. They had run through a sliver of a mountain pass. Rain had begun to fall, lightly at first, but then gradually becoming steady, then hard. And then, in an instant, it had blown into a raging torrent. The water had swelled with the run-off from the rocks, rushing after him in a wave. He had run as fast as he could, he remembered, determined to catch the stray goat. He had finally reached the frightened animal at the edge of a deep ravine. The water had risen, swirling around their knees, threatening, pulling and pushing, before it flowed past them and cascaded some forty feet below.

He revisited this memory as he raced the leopard to the forest. But as he reached the nearest tree, his strength evaporated. The trunk was too large to place his arms around. He looked up in a panic; there was no branch low enough for him to grab hold of. Defeated, he turned to face the onrushing leopard. Placing his back against the tree, he clasped his dula with both hands and held it before him. The leopard was almost upon him.

"Tether the rope about your waist!" his father had yelled to him from above as a wall of water careened down the floor of the mountain pass toward him. "Quickly, Teimbaka! Do as I say!"

Teimbaka had peered up through the downpour and found the dangling rope and his father's face. The huge drops of rain had hidden the tears he did not want his father to see. He placed the woven hemp around his waist as he had been told and felt himself lifted. He remembered, as he always would, watching the goat's wide, terrified eyes as it was swept over the ledge by the onrushing wave.

The leopard coiled to pounce. Teimbaka closed his eyes.

"Hold your stick tight, boy!"

The claws of the big cat tore into the wood of the tree just as Teimbaka was jerked upward. He could hear the razor sharp nails scratching and scraping as the animal let loose an angry, startled growl as it tried to reach him. Teimbaka watched it drop to the ground and ready itself for a leap as he ascended from the forest floor. The massive hand that had taken hold of his dula now clamped around his wrist and pulled him higher. The leopard sprang up the tree, snarling with rage, claws raking off jagged pieces of bark as it climbed after him.

Enormous hands encircled his waist and threw him upward. Just as he felt as though he was about to fall back, other hands grabbed his arms and yanked him to safety. Below him, the leopard slid off of the tree trunk and deftly landed on the forest floor. Teimbaka could see its eerie yellow-green eyes as the animal sought him out.

Soft laughter blew against the side of his cheek, its warm, foul smell making him wince. He glimpsed two blurry points of white inside the opened mouth next to his face.

"Father?"

"No noise," a voice hissed.

Then something hard struck him on the back of the head.

*

"YOU LIKE THE teeth of Bawa?" the man asked him, his mouth open wide, his forefinger and thumb sliding over his two incisors. "Ivory."

The word *ivory* slid from the man's gaping mouth as though it were floating on a slow moving cloud. Deep, dark eyes—almost black—peered down at Teimbaka with a glazed look. Murky red rivulets spread outward from the iris, giving the dark orbs an aura of bedevilment. The man laughed, but there was no humor in the sound. Teimbaka cringed at the odor from his mouth. When he tried to turn his head away, the man held his chin so tight that he could not move.

"Bawa's reward," he whispered, tapping the two ivory teeth. "Reward for harvesting the most tusks!"

Bawa released Teimbaka and with a clap of his hands jumped up.

"Four dozen in one day!" he howled, his body spinning. "Many, many elephants!"

Bawa unsheathed a broad machete from his side.

"Much blood," he went on, speaking in a hushed tone, placing a finger up over his lips as if to tell Teimbaka to be silent. "Many elephants, much blood," he repeated in a far-off voice.

"You speak like a crazed jackal, Bawa. The boy will wish he had died the other night if you keep babbling your insanity."

Teimbaka smelled the burning wood of a campfire and the enticing aroma of food. He rubbed his eyes, felt the lump on the back of his head, and winced. The quiet laughter of men prompted him to raise himself up on his elbows.

Intensely dark were the faces of the four men around him. Not brown or deep brown or brownish-black, but a deep blue-black that he had never seen before. One man was enormous, with a huge chest and stomach that connected to massive arms and upper legs that looked like barrels used to store rainwater. Another looked to be almost as powerful, but his body was lean and defined, where the other man's was more layered with fat. A third man also looked to be very strong—thickly built and compact, like a formation of rock. And the fourth man, the spinning one who called himself Bawa, moved like a one-horned antelope might. For that is how Teimbaka perceived him, turning as he was on spindly, muscular legs and holding his machete aloft by an arm that seemed to form some sort of misshapen antler.

"Is he, boy?" the huge man asked as he took a large mouthful of food from the bowl he held. "Do you think he is a jackal?"

Than man chortled, licked his fingers, smacked his lips, and then slapped the top of his bare, protruding stomach. Teimbaka looked at him dumbly. He had never seen anyone so large.

"I tell you it was a day to behold." Bawa was bending to him now, the blade of the machete held close to Teimbaka's face. "Reta Basa knows," Bawa hurried to add, spinning to look at the compactly built man. "Reta Basa knows Bawa speaks the truth. He was there. He was there."

He waved his machete at the man. Reta Basa shook his head and smiled.

"You were there!" Bawa shouted, his voice rising. "Forty-eight tusks! Twenty-four elephants! One blade! One man! Much blood!"

Reta Basa nodded, then bent to the task of eating. The other two did the same.

Bawa sheathed his weapon and grew silent. He hung his head and whispered, "Yes, much blood—much."

"Maybe on this run we'll all get lucky and one of them will fall on you and crush your jaws," the big, heavy one offered with an amused laugh.

"So much the poorer you would be then," Bawa replied coldly. "Little payment would there be for all of you if Bawa's blade was not there to work," he added, slapping the hilt of his weapon.

"Little payment there is anyway, for the work. With or without you,

Bawa," said the leaner strong one, though he did not venture to meet the other man's eyes as he spoke.

The others grunted their agreement at this, their flat, wide faces suddenly taking on a somber appearance.

"Yes, Untello, so little money for so much ivory. If only we knew where and who to take it to once—"

Reta Basa silenced them with a sharp wave of his hand. Only with his eyes did he tell them that someone or something was approaching. As if some unspoken command had been given, each of the men stood and reached for one of the long-shafted spears stacked in a line on a crude wooden rack behind them. Securing their machetes to their waists, they disappeared into the forest. Teimbaka watched them go, wondering what was happening. He listened intently for a moment, but heard nothing.

The smell of the food quickly pushed aside his question of what Reta Basa might have had heard and, without a care, he went to the nearest bowl of food and began to eat. He consumed the food as quickly as he could. When he finished with the first bowl, he went to the next. It was when he was eating from the third bowl and looking about for some source of water that he heard footsteps nearing the camp. A few moments later a tall, broad-shouldered man—a *ferenji*, a white-skinned man—dressed all in faded brown and wearing a dull green, broad-rimmed hat, stepped into the campsite with a rifle cradled in one arm. His pale blue eyes flickered over Teimbaka before moving to search the rest of the campsite. He fiddled with a white bandage that was wrapped around one of his hands as he surveyed the scene.

"So you have taken over here, boy? Killed the great brute Matula with your bare hands?"

Teimbaka smiled at the man and kept eating. He eyed him warily as he stepped farther into the campsite and slung the backpack off his shoulders. Before Teimbaka could blink, the man had pulled the bolt lever back on his rifle and pointed the barrel right at his face.

"Where are the others, and why are you here?"

Teimbaka's smile left him. He stared at the rifle barrel while trying to gulp down his last mouthful of food.

"A darky boy is no use to me. Especially one who steals food and can't talk."

"I am not a thief!" Teimbaka shouted, jumping to his feet and slapping at the rifle barrel.

"Then what are you?" the man stonily demanded.

Teimbaka began to tremble, startled by what he had done. Even so, he glared at the man with defiance. The man glared back. He raised his rifle again, took aim at Teimbaka's face, and placed his finger on the trigger.

With the sound of slicing air, one of the long-shafted spears the men had taken struck and pierced the ground between the man and Teimbaka. Teimbaka jumped sideways and dropped the bowl of food he was holding. The man, however, showed no sign of alarm. He simply kept the aim of the rifle at Teimbaka's face.

"Save your bullet, Gunstard," a deep, clear voice commanded.

"Ah, Untello. I might have known this was one of your brats," Gunstard replied with an air of familiarity, though he kept his finger on the rifle's trigger.

From three sides of the campsite, Reta Basa, Bawa, and Untello stepped out of the forest. Untello strode over to Peter Gunstard and pushed the barrel of the rifle toward the ground. Loosening the spear from the soil, he gave Gunstard a look of disdain and said in a similar, casual tone: "I would not dishonor a child of mine by bringing him to a place where *you* are."

He examined the tip of the spear, wiped the dirt off with the bottom of his sleeveless undershirt, and eyed the sharpness of the metal edges. Satisfied, he nodded his head and grunted.

"Then why is he here? He is of no use to us." Gunstard removed his hat and wiped the sweat off his brow with the sleeve of his shirt. "Might as well just let Bawa slice his throat and be done with him," he said, grinning first at Teimbaka and then winking at Bawa. "What say you, howling monkey-dog; does your steel thirst for blood today?"

Bawa rubbed his ivory incisors and laughed.

"Howling monkey-dog," he repeated, seemingly overjoyed by the sound of the phrase. "Two nights past; did you hear it? It was me! Had to howl to get the leopard to look away."

Bawa stared at Teimbaka. He furrowed his brow before saying, "They had given him passage up till then. Until he took water from the pool." Bawa tilted the tip of his spear and placed the blade to Teimbaka's cheek. "Why did you do that? Did you not know?" he asked, giving the boy an odd, perplexed look. "That's why he came. Because you drank."

"See what you've done, Gunstard?" The booming question came with massive arms that encircled and squeezed Gunstard's chest and lifted him off the ground. "Now he'll talk gibberish all night."

"Matula," Gunstard struggled to say.

As though he was holding a child, Matula threw the man to the side with ease. Gunstard landed awkwardly, fighting to keep his balance. He brought his rifle up and aimed it at Matula.

"Enough!" Untello stepped to Gunstard and took hold of the rifle barrel. "Enough from both of you!" he shouted, looking between Matula and Gunstard. "And you too, Bawa!"

Bawa looked away.

"We've been waiting for you for two days, Gunstard," Untello stated accusingly. "We are tired of waiting. Why are you late? Why should we not just take your gun and kill the elephants ourselves? Kill *you?*"

"You could, Untello. You could take my rifle and try to shoot an elephant, maybe even bring one down." Gunstard pulled his rifle from Untello's hands and shouldered it. "But the first time something goes wrong—a bullet gets jammed, the loading bolt gets stuck—you're out of luck. Aren't you, you great black beast?" Gunstard chuckled and shook his head.

"And then what would you do? What? Throw one or two of those at a bull," he taunted, nodding at the spear in Untello's hand, "and then run around and follow it for days with the hope that it might, *might* lose enough blood to where you could actually get it to the ground to let Bawa do his hacking?"

"No good you are late," Reta Basa said. "We have been watching. The herd is edgy. It is perfect where they are now."

"Are the trucks close by?"

"Close enough," Reta Basa told him. "Hidden."

"How much petrol? Enough to make Nairobi?"

"Why there?" Bawa protested. "Too far, too many roads, too many *thieves!*" he howled, laughing at his own words.

Reta Basa gave Untello a wary glance. Untello nodded.

"Enough, yes, to Nairobi."

"We were hoping for some sea air," Matula half-heartedly complained. "A day or two in Mogadishu: hashish, beer. Whores," he added, clutching his crotch.

"The Italians are coming back, I hear," said Gunstard. "And the Brits and the Frogs are sticking their noses in everything. The port is crawling with customs agents, troops, and spies. Nairobi is easier and cheaper. Planes fly in," he explained using a hand to simulate an airplane landing, "we load them up, they fly off. Our payoff is bigger."

"How much bigger?"

"Why don't we just leave it at bigger, Untello. And if you object, we can discuss it then. Of course," he went on, offering a smile and a nod to Teimbaka, "all of you will have to factor in the extra cut that is going to the boy, here. I expect you've taken that into account."

Matula looked at Bawa and grimaced.

"Damn you, Jackal. I told you we should have let the leopard have him."

"No, no, no," Bawa hurried to say, "you will see. The Mother looks after him. It would have brought us Her wrath if we had let him perish."

"Then he gets paid from your cut if he gets paid at all," Matula growled. "I don't know what he can do anyway. He is so puny."

"You will see his worth," Bawa assured them, looking to each of their faces. "Bawa sees it."

"We can send him ahead," Untello offered, "to scout. He can get closer then us. He is so small that they will not think anything of him. The bulls may think he is a dik dik."

"Can he help carry an eighty-pound tusk?" Gunstard pressed. "Can he wield a machete and hack off a tusk? Can he crawl between the beasts' legs and cut their dick and balls off for the yellow slants?" He said the words acidly, eyeing Teimbaka.

"He can be your *boy*," Reta Basa stated. He smiled when Gunstard gave him a withering glare. "He can carry your bullets and learn to load your gun."

"Yes, yes!" Bawa agreed with a sense of urgency. He moved to where

Teimbaka stood, grasped him by the shoulders, and moved him to stand before Gunstard. Bawa's face broke into a wide smile. He touched his ivory teeth. "Yes, teach the boy. The gun," he said, extending a finger toward the rifle, "how to use it, take care of it, kill with it."

Peter Gunstard stared into Teimbaka's eyes.

"You have a name, boy?"

Bawa poked the back of his shoulder when he was slow to answer.

"Teimbaka," he heard himself say.

"Teimbaka," Gunstard repeated with a chuckle. "You best learn to forget you were ever called that. And forget who you were before you ended up here."

He stepped away from Teimbaka and placed his rifle against the wooden rack where the spears had been lined up. He took off his hat and hung it on the rifle barrel, unclasped a canteen from his belt, and took a long drink of water.

"Tomorrow we kill elephants," he told Teimbaka. "We kill as many as we can and then butcher them for their ivory. All of us will have blood up to our elbows." He gave Teimbaka a withering look. "You ever kill, boy? You ever see anything die?"

It had been a long, difficult climb down the ravine to reach the fallen goat. His father had been silent the entire way. Teimbaka remembered the look on the animal's face as his father extracted the long-bladed knife from within his robes and slit its neck. *If I had saved it, had run faster, kept it with the herd, the animal would not have broken a leg in the fall and would not have to be slaughtered,* he had told himself. But he had not been fast enough. He had not saved the animal. The goat had stared at him as it had bled out.

"No matter. Tomorrow you will see more than you would have ever thought. And you best have a stomach for it. You are with Gunstard now. You will learn to kill." He paused to let his words sink in. "Or the one who kills will kill you."

Gunstard raised an invisible rifle to his shoulder, yanked the bolt back, aimed it at Teimbaka, and pulled the trigger.

*

**"I** PRAY TO GOD that we're doing the right thing, have done the right thing."

"A little late for second thoughts now."

Patricia ran a hand over the back of her head, twirling the tresses of her somewhat frizzy, long auburn-brown hair. She looked out the porthole of their cabin, scanning the horizon for some sign of land. It had been well over a week since they had departed Djibouti. Time had passed slowly.

"If you've changed your mind …"

"No, no I haven't," she assured him, though her tone lacked conviction. "I mean, I know I've done the right thing. *We've* done the right thing," she quickly added, turning to face him. "He'll be so much better off. Won't he?"

Martin chuckled while his fingers fidgeted with the rim of the felt hat he was holding. He sat down on the edge of the bed.

"You've asked me that nearly every day since we took him out of that hospital in Addis Ababa."

Patricia's eyes flared with an unspoken *so?*

"You're pretty funny sometimes."

"He would have died in that hospital." Her tone was sharp. "You saw. They couldn't have cared less. Just another poor, orphaned child with no money and nowhere to go once he was well enough to be released. I got the distinct impression of that when we brought him in, that they wished we had done just what that bastard Peter Gunstard told us to do. Damn doctors; they would just as soon we left him in that dry riverbed to die."

"A harsh statement coming from a former nurse."

"War-time nurse," she corrected him. "Entirely different from these peacetime practitioners who seem to only want to treat those who have money."

"Now, don't go besmirching the good reputations of physicians just because the ones in Addis Ababa rubbed you the wrong way. It's not like you to pigeonhole an entire profession like that."

"Oh, I know, I know," she agreed, a bit exasperated. "It's just that it made me so mad. God help us if this is how doctors are going to be in the future. Turning people away because they can't pay for help. Ridiculous."

She laughed a nervous laugh as she looked for his reaction.

"I doubt very much if that day will ever arrive," he finally said, staring at the floor.

A moment later, he looked at her and grinned.

"But if it does, I'm sure you'll be right up front speaking out against it."

"Goddamn right, I will!"

"Now, now, not very wise to take the Lord's name in vain when we've been asking so much of him lately."

"God forgive me," she corrected herself, making the sign of the cross against her body.

She smiled and gave her husband a wink.

"He knows I didn't mean it. He'd have to if He's taken any kind of notice of what we've been doing lately."

Martin returned her smile but said nothing. He held her gaze for a time. He wondered if she was having the same conflicting thoughts that he was.

Patricia stepped to the porthole again. She looked out once more, squinting against the midday sun as it reflected off the surface of the waves.

"You're certain there'll be no snafu when we disembark? Customs, immigration … You're sure your buddy at the State department took care of everything? I mean, what if—"

Martin put down his hat and moved off the bed. He gently took hold of Patricia's shoulders, turned her toward him, smiled, and put a finger to her lips.

"You're pretty funny sometimes. You do know that, don't you?"

Patricia sighed and fell against him. Martin pushed her lightly away until her back came to rest on the wall.

"Don't go playing the weak and helpless now," he joked. "Won't do. Can't have it. Might not pass you through customs. Might be labeled an undesirable."

"Undesirable. Hmmph! Undesirable, indeed."

He leaned forward and stole a kiss from her before she realized what he was doing.

"Cad," she lovingly scolded him, her bright green eyes sparkling.

"Why, Madam, a married man cannot be labeled a cad when he kisses his own wife in the privacy of their stateroom. A scoundrel, perhaps; yes, that would fit."

"Mother will be shocked when she hears of it: a scoundrel in the family, indeed. Newcastle will be all abuzz with the gossip."

They both laughed.

"I know I'm being silly, but I'm worried that not everything will go well. I mean, I know your position in the State department allows you certain privileges, so to speak, but are those privileges enough to get Gabriel into the U.S. without all of us going through utter hell?"

Martin looked past her, saying nothing. She wondered if he'd heard anything she'd said.

"Look," he said.

She turned and squeezed her body close to his so she could peer out the cabin porthole.

"Is that—"

"New York."

"God it's beautiful. So good to finally be home."

She hugged him dearly and put her head against his shoulder.

"Yes, it's good to be home, but—"

"But what? Martin, what is it?" she asked, lifting her face to his. "You're not happy to be home?" she pressed, squeezing his upper arms. "Look at me. Tell me what's wrong."

Martin stepped away.

"Martin, really, what in the—"

"Oh, nothing's *wrong*," he finally confessed, though Patricia was anything but convinced. "It's just that, it's just—"

"Just what? Come on, out with it."

Suddenly seeming very weary, Martin sat back down on the edge of the bed. He grabbed the felt hat and fiddled with the crease. Patricia noticed a few flecks of grey in his dark brown hair.

"I guess it's just the realization that it's over," he sighed. "Our adventure has come to an end."

"Over? Nothing's over, dear. It's really just starting, don't you think?"

She stepped across the small room and sat down next to him. She placed his hand in one of her own and gently squeezed it.

"The beginning of what, though? I wonder what problems, what adjustments lie ahead of us. Bringing the boy to America—"

"Is the best thing we could have done," she confidently stated, finishing his sentence.

She squeezed his hand a bit harder.

"And let's not worry about any problems unless we need to. We've—*you've*—smoothed things over with the State Department, and Mrs. Tate has agreed to help bring the child up."

She stood up and walked to the porthole. She could see the top of the Empire State building.

"And I think that will do her the world of good," she continued. "I know her life has been empty since her husband was lost at Anzio. And then to have her boy stricken with leukemia; well this will be the best medicine for her. I doubt taking care of our house and our needs is a very fulfilling life. Don't you agree?"

Martin toyed with his hat for a time before answering.

"It's not us that concerns me. It's him." He looked at her then, hoping she understood what he meant. "It's *him*."

Patricia crossed to the bed, sat down, and lightly brushed his cheek.

"I'm not sure I know what you're saying," she told him.

"I mean, it's all fine and well what we've put in place, what we've done to try to make this as smooth as possible, but what I'm worried about is what *he* will want. Will he want to be here in America with us, with Mrs. Tate? What happens if and when he remembers? Do you think he'll just want to forget where he is from? What if he resents us, hates us, for taking him away from Africa? What then?"

Patricia parted her lips as if to reply, but then pursed them together. She sighed.

"He doesn't even know who he is," she ended up saying. "What did the doctor call it? Acute shock? We don't know that he'll ever remember anything."

"I know. 'The bite marks will heal in time,'" he said, trying to mimic the doctor's deep voice and British accent, "'but his mind may never want to remember.' But I wonder."

"What?"

"The boy's, what, five, six, seven? Somewhere down the road he's going to stumble upon the memory. And then?"

Patricia got up from the bed and began to pace back and forth. Suddenly, she stopped and turned toward him.

"The truth," she stated. "That's what your *then* will require. The truth."

"And what will that be? What is it now?"

"That we found him on safari being attacked by a pack of hyenas, that we saw him fighting the beasts off with just a club and his bare hands. That we buried the remains of another child—his brother, a friend—near to where we found him."

Martin pinched the bridge of his nose and took a deep breath. Patricia could see that her husband was not convinced.

"What more can we do, dear? What more?"

They were interrupted by three crisp knocks on the cabin door.

"Yes?" Martin inquired in a loud voice.

"Steward, sir! I'll be 'round to gather your bags to take up on deck shortly. Just wanted to give you and Mrs. Mathis notice."

"Thank you, Mr. Epps. We'll be ready."

"Very good, sir!"

Martin smiled at his wife and placed his charcoal-grey hat snugly on his head. Out of habit, he smoothed the little red and white feather that was stitched to the outer band.

"I'll look after the bags. I suppose it's best you go to the infirmary and see to Gabriel."

Patricia took hold of Martin's forearm as he started to turn away.

"We'll be fine. He'll be fine. You'll see."

*

T
HE DULA GLOWED *within his hands. He clung to it as if there was nothing else to his world. Clouds thickened, grew dark, and moved toward him, jagged fingers of lightning shooting out from their depths. Thunder erupted and roared in his head. Raging currents of wind whipped him around, bearing him aloft. A torrential squall erupted. All was confusion. All seemed lost. He clenched the dula tighter as he began spiraling downward. He was falling out of the clouds, out of control. He screamed.*

Gentle hands grabbed his shoulders and steadied him. Menelik heard a woman speak. Her voice was soothing and calm.

"The boy's dreams are tortured," Eleanor said. "Has he been this way since you found 'im?"

"Off and on. There are days when they tell us he's been resting comfortably, and others—" Martin shrugged.

"We know it's a lot to ask of you, Mrs. Tate. But we would have never forgiven ourselves if we had left him in Ethiopia," Patricia added, glancing at Martin.

"Well, let's all hope that this shock business the doctors talked 'bout passes quick-like. 'Specially if this is what it's doin' to him. Looks to me like he be needin' some home cookin' and some peace and quiet."

"Then, does this mean …? I mean, we're the ones who will adopt him, but we think you will be instrumental in his upbringing. That is, if we're not asking too much of you."

"He's a fine-lookin' boy."

"We had hoped you'd take a liking to him, Eleanor. We thought it would be so much easier, I mean, better—"

"I think what my wife is trying to say, Mrs. Tate, is that—"

"I know very well what you be sayin', Mr. Mathis. The boy's Negro, I'm Negro, and you two be white. Might confuse the child greatly when he does wake up to be told that *you all* are his parents, no matter if he 'members his real ones or not. And that just wouldn't be right after what you told me he's been through."

Eleanor Tate adjusted the thick-lensed, black-framed glasses that had slid down the bridge of her nose.

"Wild animals, you say," she said, shaking her head. "I just can't 'magine a child that young havin' to fight wild dogs or hyenas or whatever they were with his bare hands."

She fussed with the brown lace doily that was pinned to her hair, her fingers making certain that her hair bun was still intact.

"But the Lord must have His reasons. Fittin' that you gave him the name of Gabriel, the Lord's archangel." She turned her attention to the boy. "Gabriel," she said to him, resting one of her small, lightly wrinkled hands on his forehead. "A fitting name indeed. Gabriel, the messenger of the Lord."

Menelik absorbed the word *Gabriel* and used it to block the confusing dreams that sought to entrap him once more. Endless had they been. Endless and ever tormenting with their dark corridors and empty swaths of wastelands that led to nowhere. *Gabriel,* he wondered. *What if?*

"Gabriel."

He heard voices. Someone placed a hand gently atop his forehead.

*Brilliant was the light from the dula now. His eyes fluttered against the glare. It edged away from him, drifting upward. He watched it levitate until he no longer held it. He reached out for it. His fingertips caught hold. Fingers intertwined with his. He heard a word whispered above him:* Gabriel. *He looked up.*

A woman held tight to his fingers and caressed them within her own. She looked into his frightened, light-brown eyes and smiled. Bending closer to him, she spoke to him in the kindest of voices. He understood nothing of what she said.

She took his hand and touched it to her chest.

"Eleanor," he made out. He watched her lips move as she spoke more words he didn't know. "Eleanor," the woman repeated before falling silent.

Menelik stared at her in silence.

"Gabriel," she told him, touching his hand to his own chest. "Gabriel."

"Gabriel," he weakly repeated.

The woman looked over her shoulder to where two other people were standing. He followed her gaze and saw she was looking at two *ferenji*. He watched her smile and nod her head. He wondered where he was.

*

THE FLAMES OF the fire conjured up an array of mystical imaginings, from rows of armor-clad warriors doing battle to a massive water buffalo preparing to charge. Large moths, drawn by the light of the fire, fluttered about, their wings turning a reddish-gold. Teimbaka stared at them, mesmerized, for the moths were fire-eagles to him, ancient birds soaring over glorious, ever-changing mountains.

Sparks exploded, spreading a fiery trail. Eyes wide, heart racing, he watched as the particles of flame sought to reach and bring down the fire-eagles. But the winged ones were too elusive and too quick. Dipping and dancing, they flitted away, taking refuge in the darkness before they could be caught. When they reappeared moments later to reclaim their domain, he exhaled with an impish grin.

"It is not yet time to dream. That is for when your eyes are closed. Your blade won't sharpen on its own."

Untello spoke to Teimbaka in earnest. Holding the boy's gaze, he ran the sharpening stone along the edge of his gleaming machete. Something in the man's eyes made Teimbaka shiver. It was the same look he had given him when they were facing each other at the mouth of the cave where the ivory was kept. The recollection unnerved him. He tried to block it out, but it did no good. He remembered.

Death was there. He felt it all around them as soon as he stepped into the entrance of the cave. But there was also something more: anger and hostility and a presence he could not readily identify. He stared at the piles of bloodied tusks, some with muscle and flesh still attached. Looking at them, he could almost hear the blades hacking into the elephants' jowls. It wasn't hard to imagine that the spirits of the murdered beasts had followed what had once been theirs. He had tried to run from the cave, but Untello had grabbed him and held him still.

"So you feel them," he stated, his voice emotionless. "Not many do."

His grip had tightened as he'd waited for a reply.

"Will they harm us?" Teimbaka finally asked.

Untello looked around the enclosure, his eyes slowly passing from one pile of tusks to the next.

"Often, I have been awakened in the night by the sounds of a charging herd. The ground would shake, and I would be jolted from the earth and roused from my sleep. I would scramble to my feet and look to the others to warn them—only to see that they were fast asleep, unaware that anything was happening."

Untello paused, a darkness passing over his features.

"I have since come to know that the beasts that charge the camp, that come for me, are not of this life."

He fell silent for a time. Teimbaka said nothing.

"On those mornings when the beasts have haunted my sleep, I have searched the ground around the camp."

"What did you find?" Teimbaka gently pressed when Untello seemed to fall under some sort of spell.

"Tracks where there had been none before. Sometimes one set, sometimes hundreds."

"We should leave before they come," Teimbaka hurried to suggest, his eyes darting to the innards of the cave to the places he could not see.

"They have never harmed me, though," Untello relayed with an odd, short-lived laugh. "Perhaps they are just waiting."

"Waiting?"

"For me to pass from this world into theirs," he told Teimbaka, nodding at his own observation. "Where I will be trampled for eternity for the killing I have done."

Teimbaka witnessed a sadness come upon him then. It was strong. The man looked as though he had lost something he cherished.

"Why do you do it, then? If you know the elephants are angry with you and will crush you when they can, why do you not let them be?"

"It is not enough to be a warrior, a hunter, any longer. What was once free—from the land, the waters, and the sky—is free no longer. Men like Gunstard are everywhere. The days of my father and the elders before him are gone. The whites brought a world to Africa that She was not prepared for. They care nothing of Her. They only take. Take, enslave, and kill."

Teimbaka could feel his anger.

"Protect the Mother!" Teimbaka shouted. "Kill the takers!"

"Many have," Untello told him. "Yet, when one is killed, two come to take his place. I have seen this."

"Will there never be a time, then, when a man of Africa can again be a warrior for the Mother, Her protector?"

"I cannot see that answer, Teimbaka. I only know that I am not that man. She must look for another."

"But you are strong, Untello. Even Matula—"

"No, Teimbaka. I, as well as Matula, have walked with the likes of Gunstard for too long. The riches of the *ferenji* have become ours. Our families—even they expect sugar and flour and machine-made clothes now. Where the meat and hide of a hunted impala was once treasured—"

He left off, shaking his head in disgust.

"Now it is machetes and sharpening stones and lamps that burn oil. Sharpening stones," he spat. "This they expect for my time away. Soon it will be guns," he lamented. "Sharpening stones and sugar." He spat again with a shake of his head. "Each time I run the stone across the edge of my blade, I hear the Mother cry."

Teimbaka gazed upon the tusks in dismay. He felt shame. He could have sworn he heard a young elephant wail from the depths of the cave.

"Now you will become like me, like Gunstard. I am sorry, Teimbaka. I am sorry."

The fire crackled and spit. Teimbaka found he was still staring at Untello. A fire-eagle swooped low into their vision. With a sudden flash, an eruption of sparks engulfed it. It vanished as if it had never been. Untello grunted and bent to his work.

*

"**T**O THE LEFT, boy! Move to your left!"

The rhinoceros turned with Teimbaka's movement, hooves scraping the dirt, its horn lowered, pointing toward him.

"Excellent, boy! Your usefulness has now become apparent to me! Draw the beast a little more the same way so I can get a better shot! Shuffle left!"

To Teimbaka, the orders Peter Gunstard shouted to him sounded as though they had come from some distant mountaintop, so enraptured was he with the magnificent, ancient animal before him. Spellbound by the beast's snorting, the twitching of its ears, and the tiny black eyes that bore into him from behind its menacing, arcing horn, he did not notice its massive body moving forward or feel the ground beneath his feet begin to shake.

"Idiot! You're drifting right! Go left! The other way, idiot!"

Teimbaka jump-hopped to his left, lost his footing, and fell. The rhinoceros's horn dipped lower. The earth rumbled. A rifle shot erupted behind him, rattling his head.

The bullet hissed by him before ripping into the soft tissue just inside the right shoulder of the charging beast. The rhinoceros crashed to the ground, its horn gouging the earth. Teimbaka covered his head with his arms as the animal careened toward him, spewing dirt into the air and showering him with stones and clods of earth. The sound of the two-ton animal sliding headlong against the unforgiving soil was unnerving. The wounded rhinoceros came to a shuddering stop inches from where he lay.

For a moment, there was no sound or movement. And then he heard footsteps running towards him. Strong arms lifted him up.

Through the settling dust, Teimbaka heard the fallen animal gasp and choke. A figure swept past him. It was Bawa, his machete raised. The tiny, dark eyes of the beast looked to Teimbaka. It struggled to move its head. Bawa swung his machete into the base of the animal's horn. The rhinoceros wailed and blinked its eyes. With his booted foot, Matula placed the weight of his body upon the beast's head and positioned the tip of his spear at the animal's neck in case it tried to get up. Teimbaka started to cry and tried to look away. But massive hands held his head still, forcing him to watch. Bawa swung his blade twice more. The animal wailed with each severing blow. Teimbaka writhed.

"What is wrong?" Untello demanded. "You have seen ivory cut out before."

The tiny, dark eyes of the rhinoceros blinked rapidly, then closed. Frothy red bubbles gurgled forth from its mouth as blood-laced mucus streamed from its flaring nostrils and mingled with the blood oozing down from the base of its horn. The massive body quivered. Bawa savagely swung his blade once more.

"Stop, idiot! You won't be able to cut it loose from just one side! Reta, get some rope from the truck!"

Gunstard was beaming as he strode next to the fallen rhino, admiring the dying beast from head to tail with every footstep.

"A nice bonus, yes, howling monkey-dog?"

Bawa rolled his eyes back into his head and nodded.

"Good money. Big money. Horn, hooves, tail, and balls!" he cackled. "Maybe ears and prick too! Whatever the yellow slants want in their soup!" he howled with glee.

He raised his blade to strike. Gunstard reached out and grasped his wrist.

"No! Wait. Wait until Reta comes with some rope. Matula can lift the head so you can get the horn from both sides."

Bawa's face flashed with anger.

"We don't want to leave any part of it, do we?" Gunstard hurried to add. "One perfect rhino horn is worth ten elephants."

"Ten." Bawa repeated in awe. He looked at the bloody base of the horn and nodded. Lowering his machete, he said, "We wait for Reta Basa, then." He looked at the dead beast for a moment as if seeing it anew. "Ten," he repeated, saying the word as though it were holy.

"And you, boy," Gunstard said to Teimbaka, "I see now why Bawa said to keep you."

He smiled at Teimbaka. Teimbaka would not meet his eyes.

"What? You don't want the credit for leading us to this prize?"

He leaned down to the boy so their faces were close.

"You may even be able to buy some real clothes now with the extra money from this kill." He fingered Teimbaka's shamma as if it were diseased. "And get rid of this filthy rag."

Teimbaka stiffened at Gunstard's touch, but held his tongue. Reta Basa returned from the trucks with a spool of heavy rope.

"Loop it around the snout and then again behind the second horn. Between you, Matula, and Untello, you should be able to lift the beast's head off the ground so Bawa can cut away from all sides."

As Reta Basa began to unwind the rope, Teimbaka felt Untello's grasp loosen. He pushed the man's hands from his chin and wiggled free.

"Leave him," Gunstard ordered when Untello started after him. "We have work to do. And boy!" he called out to Teimbaka.

Teimbaka stopped walking but did not turn his head.

"You still need to find elephants. The day is early yet. Earn your keep."

Teimbaka looked out over the terrain, his eyes seeking nothing. He did not want to find anything else, anything that Gunstard and the others would kill and butcher. Why the rhinoceros had been there, just standing, almost waiting for him to find it, he could not understand. *Why didn't it run when it saw me? Why did it just stare at me until the others had come?* He shook his head. Bawa howled behind him. He heard the others laugh. The dull slicing and hacking of the machetes followed.

The sky above him was pale blue with wisps of high, white clouds. Far off in the distance, he could see the peak of a snow-capped mountain. But what mountain it was, he did not know. He had lost grasp of where they were, where they had been, where they were going.

Amidst the chest-high grass, thickets of brush and pockets of trees dotted the landscape as far as he could see. *It would be easy to run and hide from them,* he thought. *But then what? Where would I go?*

He did not notice the movement at first. And when he did, when the pocket of brush some fifteen to twenty yards ahead of him swayed and shook, he immediately thought it was a lion or a lurking hyena. But the brush rustled and bent with too much commotion. No predator would be so careless, he knew. When the animal emerged from the cover of the brush, he felt sick to his stomach.

The rhinoceros calf walked toward him, moving slowly, as if it were lost or bewildered. Before he could shout to it to warn it away, he heard the bolt of Gunstard's rifle slide open and closed.

"No," he whispered, looking to the hunter.

"You're a good-luck charm today, boy."

"No!" he screamed.

Teimbaka covered his ears as Gunstard pulled the trigger. The rifle seemed to jump in his grasp, but the powerful German kept the barrel level and absorbed the recoil of the weapon into his muscular shoulder. Almost instantaneously, the calf crumpled into the grass. Bawa was already rushing to it, his bloodied blade held high.

Teimbaka blinked and held his breath as another form walked out from behind the brush. It was another calf. But it wasn't a rhinoceros.

"Elephant," he murmured aloud.

"Where?" Gunstard demanded, his tone animated, excited. "Where do you see them, boy?"

The German ejected the shell casing from his rifle and slipped another one into the chamber. He slid the bolt to load it.

"Don't shoot it. It's only a baby," Teimbaka pleaded, his eyes welling with tears.

Gunstard surveyed their surroundings.

"Where is it?" he hissed, raising the rifle to his shoulder and sweeping the area. "I don't see any elephant, boy. Where?"

The baby elephant raised its trunk and flapped its ears. It glanced over to Bawa, who was already hard at work hacking the hooves from the rhino calf. With a piercing wail, the elephant pinned its ears close to its head and charged. Teimbaka screamed.

"What is it, boy? What do you see?"

Gunstard twisted him sharply round by the shoulders and glared into his face. The elephant was nearly upon them. Teimbaka began to shake. He struggled to free an arm and stick his hand out from his side to protect himself. The pink-red eyes of the tiny beast locked onto his eyes. They bore into him, filled with rage. With a final trumpeting, the elephant lowered its head and plowed straight into him.

Teimbaka slumped to his knees. Gunstard slapped him hard across the face and flung him to the ground. Franticly, Teimbaka felt along his body for the injuries the young beast had inflicted. But he was unhurt. The baby spirit elephant wailed once more and then vanished. Teimbaka buried his face in his hands and cried.

JANUARY 15, 1951

*Dear Martin,*

*It's morning right now. Eight a.m. to be exact. Sunrise was pretty. The sun changed when you left. Did you know that? I see more of you in it now. Makes daybreak even more special, knowing the sun was with you while I slept—or tried to sleep, anyway. It's been that way since you were called back to duty, all six months and fifteen days ago. At least, that's what*

PATRICIA PLACED THE pen on the paper and tried to rub the weariness from her eyes. She stretched and yawned and checked the kitchen clock again: 8:05. Mrs. Tate would arrive in twenty-five minutes.

"Coffee in twenty-five," she said aloud with a sigh. Out of habit, she reached for the cup of coffee that wasn't there. "You could make it yourself," she muttered.

She sighed again.

The pen found its way back between her fingers as her husband drifted back into her thoughts. She was tempted to write *Korea, go away* or *Korea, disappear,* but she didn't. There was no sense in doing that, she knew. It would only make the loneliness worse or make Martin even more aware that he was on the other side of the world.

*I do every morning when I see the sun come up. I say, "Good morning, darling."*

*Did I tell you that Mrs. Tate is teaching me how to make coffee? I'm sorry; is that you I hear laughing out loud? Well, you'll see. Breakfast, you ask? Hmm, let's see how the coffee lessons go. That might take some more time.*

Patricia pinched the bridge of her nose and closed her eyes.

"Be strong," she whispered. "Be strong."

With a deep breath she looked anew at the letter she was writing. Her tears made the words blurry and out of focus. Annoyed, she wiped the back of her hand across her eyes, jerking her head back when the pen poked her cheek. She laughed and checked the kitchen clock again. It was 8:15.

*Speaking of Mrs. Tate, she and Gabriel are doing wonderfully. She tells me he's taken to English and school like he was born to it. She said his teacher thinks he is excelling at his bookwork but still has a little trouble interacting with the other children. Eleanor says she thinks he's just shy. That it's just a phase.*

Patricia put her head between her hands and propped her elbows on the edge of the table. A lone tear slid off her cheek. With her thoughts beginning to spin, she didn't realize she was already writing the next sentence.

*Sabre jets, Thunder jets, B-45s, B-47s, B-36s; it really does confuse me, Martin. Are they really as fast as they say? I can't imagine if they are. They frighten me. I know how good a pilot you are. And I know you went through extensive training on jets before they shipped you out. But it all seems like it's going too fast. We're learning to kill at such a lightning pace. I thought Hiroshima was the ultimate. How wrong I was. Now there's talk of hydrogen bombs carried by planes that go faster than the speed of sound! What if the Chinese had that capability right now? What would happen to Korea—to us in Korea? And God help us if Joe Stalin and all those Red crazies decide they want to drop one just to see how it works. What the hell has Harry Truman gotten us into? I want you home! I want this stupid, senseless war to stop! And may Joe McCarthy and his little-minded worms hear me loud and clear: I don't give a damn about Korea or President Rhee or the Chinese or the Russians! I care about you! You!*

A blast of cold air blew in from the kitchen door and swept over the back of Patricia's neck.

"Mornin', Mrs. Mathis."

Eleanor quickly closed the door behind her and stepped into the kitchen. She eyed Patricia with concern.

"You ready for your coffee lesson?" She paused before adding, "By the look of you, I'd say you'd be needin' some."

"Coffee," Patricia repeated with a slight nod of her head.

"You writin' Mr. Mathis again?"

Patricia looked at the letter on the table.

"Trying to," she offered with a slight shrug of her shoulders.

"And how's that goin'?" Eleanor asked as she hung her overcoat on the coat stand by the door.

Patricia stared at the letter for a moment before crumpling it into a ball.

"I'll fill the percolator," she said as she pushed away from the table. "It will go better," she added with a nod to the ball of paper she was stuffing into the pocket of her blue terry cloth robe, "after I have some coffee."

THE RAIN—MORE OF a drizzle or a mist—had been falling steadily since before dawn, soaking everything it touched, including Eleanor's shoes. Even her ankle socks were soaked through, leaving her feet clammy. But she hardly noticed. It was the names on the headstones that commanded her attention: the names as well as the memories that went along with them.

She bent and fooled with the placement of the red roses she had laid upon the two side-by-side graves, a grateful smile complementing her fingers' work. The rain would keep the flowers fresh for a bit longer, she knew. The thought made her happy.

Her eyes drifted over the lines of the various headstones that filled this part of the cemetery as she searched for Gabriel. Inhaling the smell of the fresh-mown grass, she nodded her head with satisfaction. Old Mr. Brown, the caretaker, did a fine job. The striking green color of the newly mown lawn seemed a paradox to her, however; the lush, vibrant hue seemed somehow out of place among the graves that held so many.

"Where is that child?" she quietly asked out loud.

She adjusted her worn raincoat and made certain her clear plastic hair bonnet was still sitting properly atop her head.

"George," she inquired of her late husband's grave, "you see him anywhere about?"

She caught a blur of movement up the hill from where she stood. It had to be him, she thought. She had seen no one else in this part of the cemetery since they had arrived.

"You'd like him, George. There's somethin' special about him."

She sighed and leveled her gaze at her late husband's headstone.

"Don't let me mislead you none. He's got his troubles," she went on with a shake of her head. "Something eating at him from inside." She paused. "Don't at all know what it is, though. Don't think he's got a clue himself. Headaches, visions," she muttered. "Causin' us some trouble at school. Teacher calls him disruptive. Says he started a fight with some older boys. But he wouldn't tell me why."

Some new movement made her look up the hill.

"Gabriel Tate! You best not be soilin' your good clothes!"

She inwardly winced when she saw him roll from one headstone to the next and raise the closed umbrella she had given him up to his shoulder like it was a rifle. As if he could read her thoughts, Gabriel waved a hand from his neck to his knees, a signal that all was good. A wide smile was etched upon his face.

"See what I mean, George," she chuckled, her eyes drifting back to the chiseled name in the stone. "Got an answer for everythin'."

Taking a white handkerchief from her coat pocket, she wiped some of the moisture from her face. Her expression grew pensive.

"Save for those scars on his arm and leg. I see him rubbing 'em all the time. Says he hardly notice 'em, though." She shook her head and looked up the hill. "Coulda fooled me."

She absently tugged at her coat sleeves, her thoughts drifting between her late husband and Gabriel's up-the-hill mischief. After a moment, she closed her eyes and raised her face toward the gray sky.

"Mrs. Mathis is losin' faith. Little by little, losin' faith. Oh, not in you, Lord," she hurried to explain, opening her eyes so she could address the clouds and what lay beyond. "In herself, I mean. And the war, and Washington, and Gabriel's school, if you be wantin' to know the truth." Pausing, she fingered the top button of her raincoat. "And, of course, you be wantin' to hear the truth, Lord," she added, making the sign of the cross against her body as she did. Her fingers pulled at the edges of the handkerchief clutched in her other hand before continuing. "Guess you'll be pleased that he be goin' to a Catholic school soon, what with his incident with that big loose dog and his teacher bein' so mean about how he bein' too much trouble and not fittin' in and all. I mean, Lord almighty, Lord, the boy just done blacked out. Weren't his doin'. Why that teacher blame him for that?"

The misty drizzle started to fall a bit harder. The strength of the raindrops gave her pause. She looked for Gabriel again, but couldn't find him. Somber headstones, rain, and green grass were all she could see.

Death reached up and touched her, its sudden presence giving her a start. She shivered even though she was not cold. She fought to keep her gaze upon her late husband's name. But the pull of someone who had left her world too soon turned her to him. Her lips formed the letters of each word as she read the engraving.

ABRAHAM THOMAS TATE

1938–1948

*God Bless the Soul of the Child*

She had openly wept when she had first seen the inscription the stone carver had placed on her son's grave. A very generous and thoughtful act on his part, she had realized later on; later, when the pain of her loss had somewhat numbed. She had barely been able to afford the headstone at the time. An inscription had been far beyond her means. She dabbed at her eyes with the handkerchief.

"I've been meanin' for you two to meet," she whispered, glancing up the hill to see if Gabriel was there. "I hope you know that no one could ever replace you. You always be my boy, Abraham, my son."

She bowed her head and shuddered. It was a short while before she found her voice again.

"He's good for me," she told him, though it sounded like an apology. "He needs me. You'd like him. Lord, it's so hard sometimes," she managed to get out before her throat closed up.

Her lips mouthed the words, "I love you."

A rumble of thunder echoed across the dense, rain-filled sky. Eleanor looked up with wonder.

"I'm here." Eleanor gave a slight start as Gabriel placed his hand inside of hers. His smile was wide and engaging, his eyes bright with life.

"Do the spirits answer you, Mother? Do they hear your voice?" Gabriel glanced between the headstones and Eleanor's face.

"I believe they do," she told him after a long pause. "And I believe they hear me. Even if they be far away from this place, I know the good Lord sees to it that they get my words. And as for answerin'—well, I think we has to listen very hard to hear 'em. And sometimes, I believe that when they do answer, we don't realize that they are."

"Why is that?"

Eleanor smiled at the question while her gaze lingered over the graves in front of her.

"Because I think, Gabriel, that they sometimes answer us with a sign, 'stead of with words. Just like the Lord answers our prayers with signs. And sometimes His answer is down the road a piece, ain't it, 'stead of right away? And I think that's how it is for the souls of our loved ones, too."

She looked at the child, wondering if he understood any of what she was saying to him. Her smile turned to a frown.

"Oh, Gabriel. Look at you! I thought you promised me."

Gabriel dropped her hand and stepped back.

"Don't step away from me. Come back here, young man."

Head bent, eyes downcast, Gabriel did as he was told. Eleanor ran a hand over his close-cropped hair and shook her head in dismay.

"Your head be soaked," she scolded, bending to him so her voice wouldn't carry. "Why didn't you use the umbrella?"

She looked at the grass stains on the knees of his pants and the elbows of his raincoat.

"Where's the umbrella? Did you lose it?"

Gabriel sheepishly glanced up the hill and nodded his head that way before saying, "It has guard duty. It's keeping watch over us, keeping us safe."

"Keepin' watch—what? You usin' it as a gun? In a cemetery, of all places? Lord, have mercy. You go and fetch it right now."

Gabriel bolted up the hill so fast it made her gasp.

"And be respectful of where you put your feet!" she called after him. "Lord, have mercy," she muttered.

Another rumble of thunder made her laugh.

"I'll take that as a yes, or at least that you be thinkin' about givin' me some, Lord."

"Beggin' your pardon, Mrs. Tate."

Eleanor gave a start and turned to find the caretaker, Mr. Brown, standing a few feet behind her.

"Didn't mean to startle ya none," the aged, overall-clad man was quick to add.

Mr. Brown held his cap between his weathered, brown hands and offered Eleanor a polite smile. Though he was permanently bent at the waist due to the nature of his job and gruff in appearance, with soiled clothes and a full, unkempt gray beard and wild, curly locks of ashen hair, Eleanor was at ease with the man's presence. It had been that way since the first time they had met, when she had taken notice of his soft, engaging hazel eyes, his forgiving tone of voice, and his polite manner.

"Land's sake, you are a quiet one, Mr. Brown," she said. "I didn't hear you at all."

Mr. Brown glanced over his shoulder to where he had left his wheelbarrow on the gravel pathway. The wooden handles of a pick, a shovel, a hoe, and a steel-toothed rake lay out the front end.

Eleanor followed his gaze and shifted a little at the sight of the tools resting in the metal bed. Mr. Brown smiled and bent his head a little lower.

"Yes, ma'am. Thunder musta—"

"What can I do for you, Mr. Brown?"

"It be Mrs. Mathis, ma'am. She be on the white side of the cemetery with her car. Told 'er I'd come tell you and the boy she be here, since there be no road on this side. She say she knew you here. Say she be takin' you both to lunch."

"Lunch!" Gabriel shouted as he ran up to Mr. Brown and Eleanor. "What's for lunch?"

"Hush now, Gabriel. Where be your manners? Can't you see Mr. Brown and me is talkin'?"

Gabriel looked at Mr. Brown's grubby overalls, muddy work boots, and dirty hands and asked, "You dig all these graves?"

"Gabriel Tate! For goodness sake! What kind of question is that to ask somebody you ain't even met yet?"

To Eleanor's great relief, Mr. Brown burst out laughing so hard he slapped his cap against his thigh a few times before he could catch his breath to say anything.

"That be all right," he told Gabriel as he tried to stop laughing. "Kinda goes with how I look, I s'pose. Don't it, boy?"

"I apologize for the boy, Mr. Brown. He just full of mischief, he is. Gabriel, say hello to Mr. Brown and then tell him you sorry for bein' so—"

"Hello, Mr. Brown."

"Pleasure's all mine, son," he replied, extending his weathered and work-worn right hand.

Gabriel looked at the dirt-caked fingernails and the little lines of mud on the man's wrist for a second before accepting his hand and shaking it.

"And, yeah, over this side, least ways, I be puttin' many a soul in the earth."

"Do you ever hear their spirits cry?"

Mr. Brown gave Gabriel a thoughtful look, but said nothing.

Off in the distance, a car horn honked three times.

"That be Mrs. Mathis, I'm thinkin'," he said, looking at Eleanor. "She probably thinks I forget. You best be on your way."

"Mrs. Mathis is here?" Gabriel asked excitedly. "Is she taking us to lunch, Mother?"

Mr. Brown looked at Eleanor, the two headstones, and Gabriel, his expression questioning.

"That's what Mr. Brown here was sayin' to me before you rushed down here like some windstorm whistlin' through a tree."

"You think she's taking us to Jack's again? Cherry Coke, hot dog, and fries! Let's go, Mother! Let's go!"

Gabriel pulled on Eleanor's arm and tried to drag her away.

"We'll leave in a minute, Gabriel," Eleanor told him sternly. "After I tell Mr. Brown how nice everything looks round here and what a real fine job he does."

"Why, thank you, ma'am, nice of you to notice. I tries to keep it that way so everybody can find a little peace when they here—'specially the ones stayin' for good."

"Mother."

"Hush, Gabriel."

The car horn sounded again. Eleanor sighed heavily and offered Mr. Brown a smile.

"Guess we'll be takin' our leave, then, Mr. Brown."

She looked at the headstones of her late son and husband and crossed herself.

"You ever had a Cherry Coke, hot dog, and fries at Jack's, Mr. Brown?" Gabriel asked as he pulled on Eleanor's arm once more.

"Jack's?" He eyed Eleanor with a raised brow. "You mean that nice diner over in Fair Haven?"

Eleanor nodded. "That be the one."

"Didn't know they be lettin' our kind in there, 'cept if you be a cook or warsh dishes."

"They don't."

"Then?"

"'Cause Mrs. Mathis is with us and she pretend that we ain't what we are. Mr. Jack okay with it long as we sit in the back. But we've had some looks and stares and grumblin' and such. Can't say I like it. But Mrs. Mathis say it's time. Say she just dare somebody to say somethin'."

"Well, I'll be," he said with a shake of his head.

"You should go too, Mr. Brown. Best hot dog and fries I ever had."

"I'm afraid I can't be pretendin' what I ain't, Mr. Gabriel," the man replied good naturedly. "But maybe I meet you there someday."

Mr. Brown put his cap back on his head and smoothed out his beard as Gabriel and Eleanor took their leave.

"You enjoy your lunch," he called out after them. "And you take care of your … your mother, young one."

Gabriel animatedly waved goodbye. Mr. Brown watched them walk away for a few moments before shuffling down to where he had left his wheelbarrow and tools. With the rain beginning to fall a bit harder, he carefully raised the wheelbarrow up on the single wheel and trudged off to dig a new grave.

MARTIN WATCHED THE sun do its slow slide into the water. The brilliant reds, yellows, and violets he saw in the sky were the same, he reasoned. Yet, there would be no call of a passing gull gliding out over the Shrewsbury River on this evening, nor the ringing of a tugboat's bell as it nudged a barge up to the Sea Bright dock. And he wasn't going to hear the hoots and hollers from the kids playing kickball in the street in front of their house. Or feel the smile forming on his face when he heard the smack of a bat on a baseball from the empty lot a block over. The smell of garlic and fresh-baked bread wasn't going to be wafting to him from his neighbor's kitchen on this night. And worst of all, he wouldn't be seeing the gleam of his wife's smile or the twinkle in her eyes when he handed her a happy hour vodka martini—two olives, if you please.

Still, all the hopes and dreams and silent prayers he had invested in so many sunsets before this one remained intact. No amount of time or distance would change who he was or what he believed in. If his tour of duty in Korea had accomplished anything, it had cemented the faith he had in himself and in those he cared for.

Even now, as he watched a blood-red Asian sun sink into the Yellow Sea with his thoughts halfway around the world, his will to bring right where wrong was running rampant was pushing him to the brink of both physical and mental fatigue.

"No time to fall apart," he would tell himself more of late, when calamity seemed bent on ruling the day.

The sound of metal hitting asphalt roused him from his thoughts. Immediately, he scanned the score of Sabre jets on the tarmac, scrutinizing each individual plane until he spotted the mechanic who had dropped his tool.

Martin raised a finger to the setting sun and silently sent his wife his love. He would wait for hers and her greeting when the sun rose again on the morrow. So it had been for the sixteen months since he had received his call-up orders. And so it would be again on this night. He shrugged and took a deep breath.

Korea had seemed like such a piece of cake for a while. Once MacArthur had organized the various U.N. and South Korean troops under his command and had driven the North Koreans to within miles of the Manchurian border, victory—a swift and decisive one—had been all but assured. But no one had foreseen the avalanche of the Chinese. Even MacArthur had been taken off-guard. The endless waves of bugle-blowing, screaming infantrymen with their tanks and mortars had turned everything around. And now MacArthur was gone. But the hundreds of thousands of Chinese soldiers remained. How would it all end? He didn't know. Maybe no one did, he thought.

Sunset was turning into twilight as he stood thinking of everything and nothing. Another hollow, unsettling night to be endured, another day of war marked off on the desktop calendar with a line of black ink from a pen. And then tomorrow, he would rise before dawn, as he always did, and wait for Patricia's greeting on the morning sun. He wondered if she slept as little as he did. He hoped that that was not the case. He also hoped that she could now make a good cup of coffee, and maybe even breakfast. He smiled.

"Colonel Mathis, sir?"

Martin whirled round at the voice.

"Sorry to disturb you, sir. But two communiqués from Headquarters were just unscrambled."

"At ease, Gregory."

The teenager relaxed his stance and gave the folded sheets of paper to Martin.

"Good news or bad?" Martin asked the young corporal.

"Why, I wouldn't know, sir. Not for my eyes."

Martin gave the nineteen-year-old a mischievous grin.

"Probably the newest scuttlebutt on base already. Probably sweeping through the ranks as we speak."

"I can assure the colonel that no one has laid eyes on or been privy to what Headquarters relayed in those messages, sir."

"I'll hold you to that, son," Martin replied, stifling a chuckle. "That will be all for now."

The two exchanged salutes. The corporal turned smartly on his heels and left.

"What now?" he mumbled, looking at the papers in his hand.

With a sigh of resignation and a last glance toward the western horizon, Martin left the perimeter of the airfield and headed back to his quarters. His orderly looked up from the filing cabinet when Martin entered the outer office.

"Call it a day, Steve," he said, tapping at the pages of paper in his hand. "Probably an early day tomorrow. Get some shut-eye while you can."

"But, sir, if those—"

"Then I'll come find you," he told him as he opened the door to his office.

Martin closed the door behind him and went to his desk. He turned on the desktop lamp and sat down. Unfolding the papers, he smoothed the pages with his palms. With a deep sigh, he began to read.

"Panmunjom," he whispered, a trace of a smile brightening his face. "May wisdom reside."

He quickly read through the entire message before shuffling it beneath the next. At once, his smile disappeared. He shook his head as he read and re-read the message. His brow furrowed with deep wrinkles of concern while his glazed eyes searched for any kind of answer within the corner of the room. His tired hand pushed through the bristles of his silver-speckled hair.

The bottle of Scotch he kept in the bottom left-hand drawer found its way to the top of his desk. He let his eyes linger over the drawing of the fully rigged sailing ship on the bottle's label for a moment, imagining that he was on it, sailing the great oceans of the world, instead of sitting where he was. He unscrewed the cap.

"Silent night, holy night, I wish I may, I wish I might."

Martin raised the bottle, eyeing the liquid inside through the hole in the top before taking a sip. He closed his eyes and savored the liquor's burn.

"Lord give us strength," he said to the bottle. "We war to find peace."

He briefly laughed.

"Does it make sense to you?" he asked the replica of the old clipper ship.

Martin took another sip of the Scotch before putting it back into the drawer. As the alcohol began to work its powers within his weary body, he reached for pen and paper. The need to communicate with Patricia was suddenly paramount.

*Dear Patricia,*

*It is good to see you, even though you still have to be a creation of my imagination. I know that sounds crazy, but then again, maybe you of all people know it isn't. Don't let this beginning throw you. I'm well. A bit tired, as usual, but nothing more serious than that. Just miss you, you know. And I couldn't help but feel sorry for myself. I hoped to be home for Thanksgiving. Now Christmas looks very doubtful. Actually, there is no chance at all for Christmas. Sorry—again.*

*I've just gotten word that a cease-fire line has been tentatively agreed upon at Panmunjom. I am both happy and discouraged by this. Happy, because it brings me closer to being home with you; discouraged, because it means we have given up on the purpose that brought us here in the first place. I can't swallow the idea of not outright winning this war. Nor can I swallow how many people*

*have lost their lives over what is looking more and more like a
tragic stalemate.*

*Yet, the war in the skies continues. In fact, beginning tomorrow,
the air battle will escalate. I don't tell you this to worry you. (You'll
probably find out before this letter ever reaches you anyway). If this
makes you scratch your head, don't feel you're the only one. But
ours is not to reason why, is it?*

*This war is nothing like the one we fought in together. Clearly
there was a need then, a cut-and-dry case of good versus evil. But
Korea just isn't as clear. There are veils and layers and shadows
and mists of what is right and what is wrong here. President Rhee
seems no better than who we fought against in WWII. Even the
people themselves—those who are supposedly on our side—seem
not to care for our efforts or even appreciate our being here. There
are many, I believe, who would just as soon kill us as extend us a
helping hand.*

*Death, as well, seems crueler here. I know that may sound odd.
But it is a mocker here, a mischief-maker, striking blindly like some
enraged lunatic before running away to hide or hurl insults. Great
piles of rotting flesh, carnage everywhere, poverty and filth and*

Martin crumpled up the letter to Patricia and tossed it in the
wastebasket.

"Jesus Christ, man, you can't send her that."

He placed a new sheet down in front of him and began again.

*Dear Patricia,*

*I hope Gabriel is adjusting to the rigors of my old alma mater,
Annunciation. It is hard to believe that he is in second grade—or*

*is it third? When I read in your previous letter that you and Mrs. Tate were having a devil of a time getting him to go, I thought back to when I was nine or ten (I know we'll never know for sure his real age) and remembered feeling the same way. It was hard for me to go off to a private Catholic school when most of the neighborhood was going to public. Tell him I know how he feels. But he'll adjust. Just takes a little time. It did for me.*

*Nice to hear that you think Gabriel has, in your words, brought Eleanor back to the living. It makes me feel that we did do the right thing in bringing him with us to the U.S. and adopting him. I can only hope that he feels the same way. I suppose, since he is now following in my footsteps, that a progression to St. Augustine's and Yale must also be in his future.*

The impact from the explosion of an incoming mortar round shook his desk. The second blast loosed the pen from his fingers' grip.

"What the hell?"

Small-arms fire erupted as the warning sirens blared across the compound. Martin yanked open the top right-hand drawer of his desk and grabbed the Colt .45 and holster he kept there. He calmly strapped it about his hips and then pulled down an M1 semiautomatic carbine from the rifle rack on the wall behind him. He shoved a magazine clip into it and stuffed another clip into each of his pants pockets. The door to his office flew open. He pulled the Colt from his holster.

"It's me, Colonel! It's me! Don't shoot."

"Dammit, Steve! What the hell are you doing? You know better than that."

"Sorry, Colonel. I was—."

"Report, man! Report! What the hell is going on?"

"I— I— I'm not sure, Colonel. Just wanted to make sure you were okay."

"Jesus! I'm fine! Get over to the pilots' quarters and tell them to move those planes out of danger! Tell 'em to take to the air if need be! Then get on the horn and let Headquarters know that we're taking small-arms fire and mortar rounds! Go!"

Another explosion rocked the roof over their heads. The sound of semiautomatic rifle fire followed.

"Go, Steve! Go! You have your orders!"

As the man raced out the door to carry out his orders, Martin was right on his heels. The night exploded in a wash of reddish-orange light as a flare arced across the sky overhead. Two more flares followed. He caught a glimpse of tiny blue-white flashes fifty or more yards west of his position. Bullets scraped and pinged off the cement close to him. Martin aimed his M1 and returned fire.

Two jeeps raced down the runway toward the infiltrators' position. Martin could make out the MP armbands of the soldiers riding in them. An incoming mortar round hit the lead jeep dead center. The vehicle lifted off the ground and burst into flames. The screaming of the wounded men was barely audible over the screeching brakes of the second jeep. Martin gave the enemy position another burst from his M1 and raced toward the jeeps.

"Get this vehicle out of here!" he shouted as he drew near. "You're sitting ducks!"

"There might be wounded!" came a hurried reply.

The four soldiers jumped out of the jeep and crouched down in unison as a burst of bullets whizzed around them.

"Who's in command of this squad?" Martin yelled as he slid down to take cover behind the second jeep.

"I guess I am," came a shaky response. "Sergeant Morrel was in the lead jeep."

He recognized, Gregory, the young corporal who had given him the message from Headquarters.

Another flare lit up the sky right above them. The men Martin looked upon were more like boys: their eyes wide and blank, their faces twisted in doubt.

Martin took a quick look over the jeep to the burning wreck ten yards away.

"Well, Corporal, the dead won't be needing to be moved anytime soon, and the wounded—if there are wounded—can't be moved if we get ourselves blown up too. So on my signal, we're going to give you cover fire and you and you two," he nodded to the next two in line, "are going to get this jeep moving so you're not going to end up like them over there. Got it?"

"But what'll you do, Colonel?"

"Once you get going, move away from the airstrip and come back around on their position. Make sure you zigzag. No need for anyone to be a hero, but we have to get those bastards concerned about us instead of blowing up our jets. Private," he hurried to say, looking at the last soldier.

"Ramone, sir."

"Ramone and I will take a quick recon over to the wreck and then see what kind of hell we can give our visitors."

He looked at the young faces staring at him, wanting to say more. But there wasn't time.

"Kick some ass, men. On three: one, two …"

Martin and Ramone stood on three and blasted round after round into the area where the enemy was positioned while the others climbed into the jeep. The young corporal gunned the engine, pumped the clutch, shifted gears, jumped the vehicle forward, and sped off. Immediately, Martin and Ramone raced across the cement and dove close to the burning jeep. The smell of charred and burning flesh was immediate and overwhelming. Martin heard Ramone gag.

A mortar shell exploded behind them in the spot where the other jeep had been parked. Martin pressed his body as close to the shuddering cement as he could and covered his head with his hands. When he felt it was safe enough, he raised himself up to a crouch and took stock of the situation. Everyone in the first jeep appeared to be dead.

"Looks like no survivors; is that what you see, Ramone?"

Ramone didn't answer.

Martin turned and saw Ramone lying face down. Blood was gushing from a deep wound that looked to have taken most of one side of his neck away. He knew by the amount of blood around Ramone's head that there was no hope; Ramone was dead too.

"Goddamn it."

Slapping a full clip into his M1 and then smacking the butt of his Colt .45 strapped to his hip, Martin raced around the burning metal and the dead it held and sprinted toward the ROK position. Twenty-five yards in, another flare brightened the night. Instead of sliding for cover, he began firing the M1 and kept firing until his magazine was empty. When the clip automatically ejected, he slapped the other spare in without breaking stride.

In the eerie red-orange glow of the flares, he thought he could make out the shapes of the enemy. He concentrated his fire. An enemy form slumped over, and then another. The ammo clip ejected. His M1 was empty.

As he reached to draw his revolver, he caught sight of the two mortars the commandos had set up. They were fifteen yards ahead to his left. He could see the teams of men operating them. Feeders were sliding new rounds into them. Martin stopped, took aim, and shot one of the feeders in the chest. The man dropped to the ground, the mortar round rolling off to his side. He swept his aim, locked on to the other feeder, and pulled the Colt's trigger.

A searing pain exploded on the side of his head. More pain erupted above his left knee. He fired one last round before he crumpled to the ground in a wave of utter darkness.

*

A GREAT SMILE CAME to Teimbaka as the massive herd of spirit elephants moved easily about him. *So vast are their numbers now,* he thought. *Ten-fold or more have they grown.* No longer did their presence alarm him. He had overcome his fear of them some time ago. Not since the little one had charged at him those many years in the past had any shown hostility toward him. It was as if there was a peace between them now, or some sort of understanding. For his part, he looked forward to their presence.

As for killing real elephants and leaving their hacked-up carcasses strewn about the land, he was not so troubled by this aspect of his life that much anymore. He supposed it was due to a mixture of the money he made from the elephant's ivory and his own growing insensitivity to their deaths. And as they had touched upon in passing conversations through-out the years—Untello, Matula, Reta Basa, Bawa, and even Gunstard—the beasts were so numerous, so seemingly infinite in number, that the hundreds they killed each year were surely just a trifling. There was no need for concern, Teimbaka had reasoned, and he doubted there ever would be.

And yet, even though they were all in agreement that the elephants' numbers would never diminish, the herds, especially of late, had become harder to find.

The continuing hunt for ivory had forced them to travel endless miles through many more countries than they had ever traversed in the past. Their new, semi-nomadic way of life had also changed the way in which they carried out their business. No longer did they store their harvest in the spirit cave or wait until they had truckloads of ivory before transporting it to the docks of Djibouti or Mogadishu as they had done in the past. Gunstard had changed all that. Now they sold to the nearest buyer wherever they happened to be, by whatever means was available, be it a port, an airfield, a helicopter landing pad carved out of the jungle, a caravan going to market, or a boat going one way or the other on a river. They now harvested and sold as quickly as they could, oftentimes utilizing many of these modes of transportation on the same day.

Their travels had taken them to Kenya, Uganda, Tanganyika, Rhodesia, Mozambique, Ethiopia, South Africa, Eritrea, French Somaliland, Somalia and all the various smaller pockets of sovereignty that would materialize for a year or two at a time before disappearing again. And on occasion, when Gunstard had told them to lie low for a while, Untello had taken him to explore the Congo and parts of Angola and Sudan.

This had given Teimbaka the opportunity to meet many different peoples and different tribes. The Zulu, the Maasai, as well as the Samburu of northern Kenya—those who had taught him the use of the arrow and the bow—were but a few of the peoples that he had spent time with and had grown to respect.

As the passing of the years had brought Teimbaka from childhood to the brink of manhood, so too had that same passage of time changed the countries in which he had traveled. Much turmoil and unrest had he witnessed, and there was more that he had heard tales of. This upheaval had intensified when European rule had ended and the doctrines of Africans had begun. The struggle to rule, to reap the rewards of wealth and power, had quickly followed the Europeans' exit. It had become a never-ending, unyielding plague that had swept across the continent. The quest for independence was not without violence.

The seemingly constant struggle for power and independence throughout much of Africa had caused Teimbaka and the others a good deal of trouble. For oft times, where the elephants were to be found, so were revolution, war, or just blind tribal hate.

It was during such days—of men killing men, when the air carried the scent of decaying flesh and spilled blood—that Peter Gunstard would talk of taking leave of their ivory venture for a chance to participate in some bloody conflict. The years had brought little change to the man. He was still hard, cold, ruthless, and unfeeling. The only instances Teimbaka could ever remember a glimmer of emotion in him were when he would bring down a charging "big tusker" or come across the mutilated bodies of men who had just done battle. These were the only times Teimbaka had ever seen Gunstard smile.

Teimbaka shivered when he thought about Gunstard. How he would examine each fallen body they would happen upon, taking whatever possessions he found and fancied, or putting a bullet through the forehead of any who still might have the will to live and the wish to keep the possessions that Gunstard desired. Only disdain did the wounded ever receive from him, never mercy.

"There are no wounded. Only those who aren't dead yet," he would say as he loaded a bullet into the chamber of his gun.

And he would make them dead, always.

A sudden shifting within the herd of spirit elephants roused Teimbaka from his thoughts. The animals nearest him began to part. In the pre-dawn darkness, he strained to see the cause.

Two orbs of a red-pink appeared, floating in the twilight air some thirty feet above the ground. They seemed to be swaying from side to side, spaced a good ten to twelve feet apart. Teimbaka felt the ground beneath his feet begin to shake as the orbs drew nearer. He stood erect, balanced his weight, and readied the steel-tipped spear he carried. The ground shook with greater force. He held his breath and tensed.

An enormous bull spirit elephant suddenly towered above him as the darkness of night slipped into the half-light of daybreak. Though he was little more than a silhouette at the moment, Teimbaka could see that he was an ancient beast with tusks so big and aged that the bottom of the curves scraped the ground before curling skyward, ending in tips shaped like regal crescents.

The bull lowered his scar-laden head and tried to push him. Though he could feel nothing, Teimbaka sensed the urgency in the beast's action. When he didn't move, the bull stepped back and then repeated the motion. But this time, along with the push, the bull turned his head and used one of his tusks to try to move him off to one side. His skin tingled where the ghost ivory moved through him.

"I don't understand," he said to the spirit beast.

The gigantic bull stepped back and peered down at him. Slowly, his eyes lifted away to look past where they stood. Teimbaka turned to look with him.

Although he had seen numerous prides on the hunt in the years that followed his brother's death, Teimbaka had forgotten what it felt like to be so close to a single lion without the buffer of others standing next to him. The piercing stare of the lion's yellow-brown eyes bore into his own, holding him with a hypnotic intent. Teimbaka leveled his spear and bent to a crouch. The young male, its mane not yet fully grown in, stood and took one step toward him.

The call of a solitary bird brought with it the first red-gold ribbon of light on the eastern horizon. The lion opened its jaws. The hint of a breeze rustled the tips of the grasses. The lion coiled. Teimbaka felt his heart racing. The lion sprinted forward and leapt. The spirit elephant charged. Teimbaka thrust out his spear.

The ghost tusks caught the side of the lion while the predator was still in mid-leap. The lion snarled in pain and fell sideways as the spirit elephant pursued it and raked a ghost tusk along its exposed side. Blood oozed from the wound. Teimbaka moved closer, his spear held firm and tight.

The retort of Gunstard's rifle boomed across the plain as a bullet hit the ground by the lion's head.

In an instant, the lion was gone, disappearing into the grasses. So too, were the spirit bull and the great herd of spirit elephants.

"Damn it!" Gunstard cursed as he strode up to Teimbaka. "Such an easy shot to miss. Too bad you didn't finish it off with the spear."

Teimbaka looked at Gunstard and then looked at his spear: the steel tip was dripping with blood.

"I don't—"

"You should have thrust it into him the second time instead of raked,"

Gunstard chuckled. "Pissed him off to no end, to be sure. We'll have to look out for him the rest of the day. Might hang around to get even."

Gunstard eyed Teimbaka for a moment before breaking into a smile.

"You surprise me, darky. You showed courage. Not many would take on a lion in the grasses with just a spear. I will remember this."

"I don't— I mean— What did you see?"

"What did I see?"

Gunstard repeated the question as though it were an accusation.

"I saw a stupid darky boy who strayed too far from camp almost become breakfast. Why were you out here, anyway?"

Teimbaka looked back out across the plain where the spirit elephants had been. The first rays of the sun gave the steppe some color and depth. He studied the area where the many beasts had walked. He wondered if Gunstard could see their tracks as he did.

"We heard the shot. What is it?" Untello, long spear in hand and broad machete tied about his waist, joined Gunstard and Teimbaka.

"Lion," Gunstard stated, glancing at Untello. "The boy," he went on, nodding toward Teimbaka, "was playing tag with it. I made the mistake of getting involved."

With that, Gunstard took his leave. Untello stepped closer to Teimbaka.

"So they were here."

Teimbaka continued to gaze out at the plain. After a long pause, he told him, "There were hundreds. More than I have ever seen." Teimbaka turned to him, his expression a mixture of confusion and awe, and said, "A great bull protected me. The lion—it was not me who wounded it. He was ancient, enormous. I have never seen—"

Untello shook his head. His face was long, his eyes sad.

"Have you never seen?"

"Many years has it been since they have come to me," he relented. "I wish it were not so."

"But you have told me—"

"Yes. I have told you different. I did not want you to know."

He held Teimbaka's gaze, hoping he would find some understanding when he admitted, "It hurt when they no longer wished me to be a part of them. Though I had feared them at first, I had—"

He hung his head, shrugged his shoulders, and left the sentence unfinished.

"Untello! Teimbaka!"

The two turned at the sound of Reta Basa's call. They both smiled as they watched his stocky, compact frame hurry toward them.

"Perhaps we can buy him longer legs when we are finally done with taking ivory," Teimbaka remarked in jest.

"Don't forget the arms," replied Untello.

"How would we know him, then?"

They shared a laugh.

"What is your hurry, Reta? It is too early to sweat."

"It's Bawa. And Gunstard," Reta Basa replied to Untello, though his eyes were fixed upon the bloodied tip of Teimbaka's spear. "A dream—a vision, he calls it. He's told Gunstard he knows where a great herd is. They're breaking camp."

"What so? Bawa has had many a dream. Why is this one any different?" Teimbaka asked.

"Gunstard believes; that is why. Bawa says that his ivory teeth feel something when he faces west. It is the way his dream told him to go."

"The years have finally—"

"There is a look about him. Gunstard believes," Reta Basa stated. "I saw it in Bawa as well."

"What does Matula say?" Untello replied. "Surely he does not want to change plans just because of some dream the howling monkey-dog has had."

Reta Basa looked squarely at Untello.

"You have seen the years take the will from Matula. Too many wives, too many children to care which direction we go. Only that the ivory is much, that his share is big."

Reta Basa looked back across his shoulder, back to where camp was set up.

"And in the end, is that not what all of us really care about?"

Untello grunted and looked toward camp. Without another word, he pushed by Reta Basa and Teimbaka to make his way back.

"A lion you have fought this morning," Reta Basa said in a hushed voice.

Reta Basa looked at Teimbaka as if for the very first time.

"You are a man now. Come," he said as he cuffed the back of Teimbaka's shoulder. "Let us go."

ON THE ELEVENTH night after they had broken camp on the promise of Bawa's vision, a great calm settled over Teimbaka. Up until then, he had been uneasy and out of sorts, for the journey had been fraught with grumbling, petty arguments, and open frustration. There had been no sign of a great herd of elephants anywhere. No trail of bent or broken saplings to follow, no mature trees with their bark rubbed off, no wide swath of trampled grass to tell of the herd's passage. And where they would have expected to find a multitude of dung piles left by the beasts along the way they were traveling, they found none, nor the smell of any such fecal droppings wafting upon the air.

Everyone was tense and quick-tempered. They had traveled far—too far, according to Matula, after the first few days of their sojourn had turned into several. But Bawa would almost on the hour reassure them with the re-telling of his vision of an endless herd. And Gunstard would slap his rifle butt and simply state that they would keep moving.

And so they had kept on, the routine never varying. Rise at dawn, break camp, travel west, search for signs of a great herd, listen to Bawa rant and Gunstard talk of killing, find nothing all day, set up camp, go to sleep. To Teimbaka, it had become tedious and boring. His uneasiness had grown. The fact that the spirit herd had not appeared to him since their journey had begun had only added to his unrest.

However, on this night, he lay down without the burden of the day's struggles tugging at him. He drifted off to an early, peaceful sleep.

Some hours later, well before dawn, he was awakened by the sensation of his face being touched. He was both happy and surprised to find a baby spirit elephant standing over him, beckoning him to rise. As quietly as he could, he gathered his spear, tied his machete to his waist, and fixed his bow and arrow sack to his back. After checking to see if the rest of the camp was still asleep, he motioned the young spirit beast to lead the way. With no other gesture, the young spirit elephant turned and walked into the night. Dutifully, Teimbaka followed.

At first, he tried his best to mark the terrain the ghost beast was leading him through, hoping he might be able to find his way back. But the darkness made it difficult to see. And when a dense fog suddenly formed around them, the notion of remembering any landmarks that would bring him back the way they had passed left him altogether. There would be no way back this time, he realized. He was at the mercy of the ghost beast. He suddenly wondered where it was leading him and why.

Soon, he found that the boundaries of time and distance had lost their meaning, as nothing else existed within the fog but the baby spirit elephant and himself. How long and how far they traveled in that manner, he could not say, for as soon as he placed a footstep within the imprint made by the young ghost beast, it would vanish, swallowed up by the dense mist that surrounded them. He found himself struggling. The notion that the baby spirit elephant was leading him to his doom began to creep into his thoughts.

Finally, the reassuring touch of a cool breeze stirred upon his face. Directly ahead of him, the baby spirit elephant stopped, raised its tiny trunk, and let loose a call. Their journey, it seemed, had come to an end.

With the trumpeting from the young spirit beast, the mist began to swirl and then lift altogether. Teimbaka found that they were standing on the peak of a mountain. Below them, stretching as far out as he could see, was a vast, gray plain. As he looked on, the ashen area began to shift. To his confusion and delight, the plain then began to sparkle, the gray mass he was staring at suddenly transforming into shapes that took on a luminous aura. His eyes widened.

An uncountable herd of spirit elephants moved lazily across the horizon-wide expanse, the near perimeter dotted here and there with enormous, tusk-laden bulls. Speckles of glittering gold and ivory reflected up into his eyes from their massive, ethereal bodies. Between what few gaps there were between the roaming elephants, the shimmering water of a lake, as large as the plain itself, reflected the light of the coming day. He gazed upon the scene in wonder, for it seemed that the plain and the lake existed at the same time, sharing the same space where the spirit elephants walked. He blinked his eyes and shook his head. He had never seen anything so beautiful and astonishing.

Without warning, from within the midst of the herd arose a bird of sheer, radiating white. He turned his face sideways and shaded his eyes. Yet, all the while, he strained and squinted to keep the bird in view. Though it was not large, when the bird stretched its wings, the light that emanated from the feathers enveloped the entire plain and the sky above. As the glowing aura fanned out and washed over the forms of the spirit herd, each elephant raised its trunk and bellowed a resounding, earth-rattling call.

Teimbaka fell to his knees. Placing his spear, bow, and arrows upon the ground, he closed his eyes and bowed his head. The trembling of the earth ran through him. The sensation filled him with a mixture of fear and calm.

"So you have come."

The sound of the voice touched every part of him. At once he was filled with a sense of both contentment and peace.

"Look upon me."

Teimbaka opened his eyes. A pure, pulsing light filled his vision.

The bird hovered before him for a moment and then vanished. In its place stood a man.

"Where did it go?" he whispered.

The man said nothing for a time. Teimbaka eyed him with suspicion. Slowly, however, he began to sense that there was something familiar about him. Perhaps it was his earth-colored shamma or his square chin or his black-brown eyes. In the end, he could not quite decide.

"The spirit takes the form of the bird, and sometimes, others. Do not always rely on your eyes to find what you seek."

Teimbaka paid little heed to what the man was saying, as he was looking past him for the radiant bird.

"They have chosen you."

The man waved a dula out toward the endless herd of spirit elephants as he proclaimed this. His face held both pride and strength. Yet, as Teimbaka continued to watch him, he saw the expression on the man's face grow somber, almost forlorn.

"Much will be asked of you. Endless will your task be."

The man then looked upon Teimbaka with tears in his eyes.

"Thousands will you need, but there will only be you. May the Mother keep you safe now that I cannot."

"Who?"

The man gathered his shamma close about him.

"Perhaps you will remember when the dula of Tafari replaces the spear you carry."

"Tafari?"

Teimbaka spoke his brother's name and felt a chill.

"Father?" he whispered.

Behind him, Bawa cackled and howled. Startled by the sounds, Teimbaka whirled around.

"Shh! Keep quiet lest they hear," Bawa hissed, a finger pointing toward the plain. "You babble much, for one so young. Have these few years already rotted your brain?"

Teimbaka staggered back.

"How did you—?" he heard himself ask as he looked wildly about for the man he had just been speaking with.

"It is as I envisioned," Bawa gushed in a hushed tone. "Now all will believe, all will know, all will say it was me."

He looked at Teimbaka with the eyes of one half mad.

"I could not tell them, though. Or you, boy—that you would be the one to lead us to them. That part I kept to myself." He chuckled, touching one ivory tooth and then the other. "Now we will all be rich!" he howled, a touch of lunacy in his tone. "Gunstard will be pleased! The harvest blades will sing!"

He cupped one hand over his mouth while using the other to motion for quiet.

"Shh, we must not disturb them," he urgently whispered, wagging his pointing finger. "They must not know we are here. Not yet, not yet."

Teimbaka turned and followed Bawa's finger. The great herd was still there. *How could that be?* Bawa had never before told him that he could see spirit elephants.

A swirling cloud of dust rose into the air over the head of one of the enormous bulls as it raked its tusks along the ground.

"The ivory of three of the beasts," he heard Bawa gasp.

Confusion became despair as Teimbaka realized that the elephants beyond them on the plain were no longer spirits, but were real: made out of flesh and blood and bone and ivory.

"Where did they go?" he asked.

"Where did they go, boy? Why they are there, there before us. Why look so pained? You should be happy, proud, excited." Bawa hopped into the air and twirled once around. "Ready your blade!" he proclaimed with a lifting of his face to the sky. "Shh, shh, shh; if they hear or smell us— Which way is the wind from? Which way?"

Teimbaka's heart grew heavy as he looked out upon the herd. For where they had once seemed so grand and endless, they now appeared neither infinite in number nor majestic in appearance. And the great sentry bulls, those whom he had initially gazed upon in wonder when the mist had first cleared, now looked tired and old, with tusks no bigger than what he had cut upon many times before. Even the lake, whose shimmering surface had so captivated him, no longer glittered. The water, what little there was of it, had turned brown and murky.

"They will be here soon."

"Who will be here?"

"The others, boy, the others. They broke camp after I left to follow you. As soon as they come, it will begin."

"We'll have to climb off this mountain first."

"Mountain? Are you sick, boy? What mountain?"

It was only as Bawa spoke of it that Teimbaka saw that they were not on any mountain peak. It was only a small hill on which they stood. And the plain below, that which had only a short while ago seemed to be far beneath them and endless, was now just an open stretch of sunbaked steppe that could be crossed with a few minutes' run.

"We should leave here. Something is not right. These elephants, they are—"

"The fulfilling of a dream," Bawa chuckled, while his fingers played upon his two ivory teeth. "We will be rich. Rich, rich, rich! Shh!"

The trumpeting of a single elephant made them both look back to the herd. An aging bull stood glaring directly at them. The beast shook its head back and forth.

"I told you to be quiet," Bawa hissed with anger. "If they leave because of you …"

"They won't leave here. Surely this place must be—"

"Must be what?"

"Special, holy, because—"

"Foolish talk," Bawa spat.

"The spirit elephants."

Bawa reached out and grabbed Teimbaka by the cloth of his tunic. A wild look took hold of his eyes.

"Do not talk of them," he warned. "They do not exist." He jerked Teimbaka to him so their faces almost touched. "They do not exist, I say," he repeated with vehemence as he began to pull and push Teimbaka by the material of his shirt. "Only bad will come of it, evil. I know! I know!"

He began to shake.

"Then know that they were here, Bawa. Thousands of them, filling a plain to the horizon's ends."

"Lies! Lies! Lies!"

Bawa stepped away from Teimbaka and covered his ears with his hands.

"I do not hear this! I do not hear! Let the lion you wounded find you and slash your tongue from you!"

"It was not I who wounded the lion, Bawa," he shouted back in anger. "It was a great spirit bull. Three times the size of any you or I have ever seen."

"Serpents and scorpions walk in your head! You lie! You lie!"

The bull elephant bellowed and took a few menacing strides forward before it abruptly stopped and gave another ear-splitting warning.

"Bawa, we must leave this place now! We can go before any of the others arrive. No harm will—"

"No!" Bawa screamed with defiance. "My vision! It is my vision!"

He glowered at Teimbaka, shaking with rage, his fists clenching and unclenching.

"There are no spirit beasts! They do not exist! They cannot hurt me!"

Teimbaka stepped away as Bawa raised his machete out before him.

"One hundred, two hundred, I will harvest it all! Ivory teeth! Ivory blade! Ivory eyes!" he howled.

Again, the bull trumpeted a warning and rushed several yards closer to them.

"He will send us to the spirit world! Then you will see! Then you will see the endless spirit herd as I have!"

Bawa sliced his machete through the air in a menacing arc. He glared at Teimbaka with gritted teeth.

"I will kill you first."

Before Bawa could move, the bull elephant charged. Teimbaka smiled as the ground beneath their feet began to tremble and crack. Bawa began to shake with the fear.

The explosion of the rifle pierced Teimbaka's heart as if a spear had been thrust into it. Suddenly feeling weak and dizzy, he turned to watch the charging bull stumble, then crash to the ground as its legs crumpled beneath him. Teimbaka cried out in despair at the sight. But his cry was lost within the crazed howling of Bawa.

"Gunstard is here! Gunstard is here! Let the killing begin! Let the harvest begin!"

As Teimbaka had witnessed him do so many times before, Bawa raced down the sloping mound they stood upon with his machete held aloft. And although the body of the bull elephant was still heaving, Bawa began to wildly hack away at its face, his blows spraying blood and sending chunks of flesh into the air above his head.

Teimbaka looked away from the morbid scene, unable to stomach any longer the butchering that he had come to accept as part of his existence.

But even though he had averted his eyes, he could not block out the haunting, pain-filled cries of the felled animal.

"No!" he shouted to the sky above. "No more! Please, Mother, no!"

Pain burst across the small of his back as Gunstard smashed the stock of his rifle into it. He sank to his knees.

"I have no more use for you," the German spat. "Go blubber on your own, boy. And hope that we don't cross paths again."

As if to accentuate his point, Gunstard slammed his rifle into Teimbaka's shoulder, sending him sprawling. As Teimbaka rolled off the small hill, the blade of his own machete cut open a gash on his upper thigh.

The loosing of his blood awakened his rage. Leaping to his feet, he grabbed hold of his spear. Hefting it to his shoulder, he readied to throw.

One of Matula's massive fists came bashing against the side of his head. Teimbaka fell to the ground with a thud, his spear flying harmlessly to the side. As he fought to keep hold of his senses, the side of his stomach withered from a hard, swift kick. He gasped, fighting for breath. Matula stood above him and cursed him. He felt spit splatter on his forehead.

"So you are the one."

It was the voice he had heard before. It reverberated throughout his entire being. Again, it calmed him, easing the pain that wracked his body. And then the bird was suddenly there, a brilliant white. He reached for it.

"You are back," he whispered.

"Never did I leave," the voice softly told him, though it was not the bird that spoke. "Never will I."

"Then it was not," Teimbaka fought for air. "Some dream I had? Something I imagined?"

"Lie still and catch your breath. You struggle to say words that are spoken to no one."

"Untello?"

Teimbaka heard him laugh.

"Open your eyes and see for yourself. That is, if Matula has left you able to see."

As Teimbaka opened his eyes and tried to focus, Untello bent and helped him to sit up.

"You are lucky that your head is still connected to the rest of you," he chuckled.

The clear, resounding echo of another rifle shot brought a new wave of pain to Teimbaka. He flinched.

"It is only Gunstard," Untello relayed, seeing the shudder in his body. "You have heard the sound so many times before. You should not be surprised."

"Stop him," he implored. "Stop him now, Untello. Stop him before it's too late."

"What are you saying? What gibberish has Matula's blow loosed? Why have we traveled all this way?"

Teimbaka looked into Untello's questioning eyes and said, "You know why. There is something here."

"What are you saying?"

Rifle shots began to fire in precision, the cry of a dying elephant filling the measured gaps between each one. Teimbaka trembled as the wails of death began to mount.

"Where Gunstard kills; it is a spirit place."

Teimbaka looked to see if Untello understood.

"I saw—"

"What?" Untello pressed when Teimbaka seemed to drift into some kind of trance. "What did you see?"

"I saw— It was—"

"Untello! Come! Leave the boy."

Reta Basa strode over to them, his expression tense and serious.

"There is much to do. Leave him."

"A spirit herd," Teimbaka told Untello. "Greater than you or I have ever before seen. There," he motioned with a nod of his head, glancing up to Reta Basa, "where Gunstard kills. They *were* the plain. There were thousands."

Untello jerked Teimbaka to his feet and roughly shook him by his shoulders.

"Enough, Teimbaka! Enough!"

"I wait for you no longer, Untello" Reta Basa stated as he spit upon the ground. "This madness does not concern me, or you."

Teimbaka grasped Untello by his upper arms as Reta Basa strode off.

"I am not mad. You know what I have seen and what I speak of. But it was nothing like either of us has ever seen before. There is a power here. I fear it will punish us."

Untello opened his mouth to speak, but said nothing. He took Teimbaka by his wrists and pried his hands away. He took a few steps away, and then turned back around.

"It is too late for me to stop," he stated, though there was a hint of pleading in his voice. "Don't you see that? It is too late for me to believe."

"No!" Teimbaka screamed when he realized Untello was going. "It is not too late! It is not!"

But Untello had gone. Teimbaka watched as he strode across the plain. He cast his eyes to the ground.

The feather seemed to loom up at him, as if it were bigger than it actually was. Enraptured by the sheer whiteness of it, he bent to it, but then hesitated, taking a step back. The more he gazed upon it, however, the more he was drawn to it. Tentatively, he reached for it again and clasped it between his fingers. Slowly, he lifted it to his eyes. The feather shimmered for a moment before vanishing. Teimbaka touched the air with his fingertips.

"They have chosen you. Why are you not with them?"

The words echoed through his head, displacing all the confusion that was there. He gazed out at the plain and absorbed all that was occurring. After a moment, he lifted his face to the sky, stretched his arms out wide, and gave a knowing nod of his head.

With the desperate wail of another dying elephant filling his ears, he retrieved his spear, gathered his arrows and bow, and made tight the belt that sheathed his machete. With a final glance at his surroundings, he walked down the small hill and crossed to the open steppe and the plain beyond.

The smell of blood and gunpowder, the sound of Gunstard's rifle and the crazed laughter of Bawa, the sight of dozens of dead or dying elephants besieged his senses. Blood-smeared harvest blades flashed, gleaming crimson in the rising sun, their reflections shining into his eyes as they moved in precise, striking motions. Already he could see small piles of tusks had been made. Bawa, Matula, and Reta Basa were spread apart and hard at work. Teimbaka could see the white T-shirts they wore were now mostly red.

A rifle shot boomed across the plain. Teimbaka was drawn to it. Another elephant fell. This confused him, because he could see that the elephant had no tusks. It was then that he realized that some of the carcasses he was passing had not been touched. These, he saw, were also tuskless. Gunstard was just killing, just shooting and killing any elephant that he could.

"Why are they not running?"

He asked the words aloud, as if there were someone who would hear them and reply. But there was no one to hear his words but himself. *I am alone.*

He cupped his hands around his mouth and yelled, "Leave this place! Leave now! I cannot save you! Run!"

Even as his shouts left him, he saw another elephant fall to Gunstard's marksmanship.

"Scatter!" he screamed. "You must not wait for me! Run!"

A gigantic red-eyed bull suddenly appeared next to him.

Teimbaka placed his hands over his ears as the great beast unleashed a trumpeting call that rumbled across the plain like a wave of thunder. At once, the herd responded in kind, then took flight. Teimbaka smiled at the sight of Gunstard frantically reloading and firing on the run while trying to keep pace with the stampede that was swiftly moving away. He turned to thank the enormous bull. But the elephant was no longer there.

"The spirit bull from the morning of the lion," he murmured.

"Stupid boy!"

Bawa's face was contorted with rage, his blood-drenched machete pointing directly at Teimbaka.

"Look what you have done! Fool! You have cost us all! I will kill you!"

Teimbaka waited for Bawa to strike, but no blow was delivered. In its stead came a gurgling chuckle that evolved into full-blown, crazed laughter. Bawa looked away and surveyed the field behind him.

"Come boy," he called back over his shoulder. "Earn your keep. There is too much for me to do myself. Start stacking the ivory."

Teimbaka stared at the back of the spindly man before casting his gaze to the retreating herd. He nodded, satisfied that they were safe.

"Hurry, boy. Come. You do too much of nothing lately."

Teimbaka looked out over the plain and saw Matula heading his way. He hurried to join Bawa while sneaking peeks at Matula out of the corner of his eye. He breathed a sigh of relief when he saw the large, powerful man stoop and pick up a bulky tusk.

"Have you forgotten what to do, boy?" Bawa asked him as he placed a booted foot on a freshly harvested tusk. He eyed him with dismay before adding, "Must I re-teach you everything?"

Teimbaka glanced around quickly for Matula's whereabouts.

"Where do you want them piled?"

"Find an open spot, away from the swarming flies and the rotting carcasses. Start with this one and then hurry back."

Reluctantly, Teimbaka laid his spear down and lifted the tusk by its blood-less end.

"If the wind had not changed," he heard Bawa mutter. "We would have gotten them all."

"The wind," Teimbaka scoffed.

"Yes, boy, the wind," Bawa called over to him. "The wind. The wind. The wind!"

Teimbaka could not help but laugh at Bawa's lunacy. With a last heave, he lifted the tusk up and trudged away, the ivory perched precariously upon his shoulder.

"Gunstard will not claim all the glory! Hi-eee! He is not the only elephant hunter here! I claim my right! I claim it!"

Teimbaka smiled and shook his head on hearing Bawa's rant. Dropping the tusk at his feet, he let his gaze wander over to the little mound of earth where he had stood just minutes before. He wondered if he should not run across it and just keep on running.

"I will be swift! My blade will sing! I will be known to all!"

"Howling monkey-dog," Teimbaka said, stifling a laugh.

The soft, forlorn cry of a baby elephant found its way to him.

Turning, he murmured, "Do not let it be so."

Teimbaka whimpered at the sight of Bawa's raised machete.

"No, Bawa, no!" he screamed.

He set off running, drawing his own blade from his side.

"By the Mother, no!"

But there was no stopping the howling monkey-dog. He was filled with the killing urge.

Bawa swung his blade into the face of a baby elephant with all his strength, the steel slicing through the flesh of the animal at the base of its trunk. The animal reeled backward with a hideous gurgle. Teimbaka raced to it. The sound of his pounding heart filled his ears.

"Hi-eee! A great hunter am I! A hunter! Hi-eee! Bawa! Bawa! Bawa!"

Teimbaka scrambled to the side of the young beast. Horror stricken, he tried to cover the bloody wound with his hands. Locking his fingers together, he pressed his hands against the gaping cut. But blood flowed through the cracks of his interlaced fingers and around his palms no matter how hard he pressed or where he placed them. He felt the death-shudder of the animal run through him. The tiny eyes in the trunk-less face blinked several times before turning a pinkish-red.

"You are the spirit," he realized.

The tiny eyes stared into his.

"All those years ago, it was you."

"Piece it back together, boy!" Bawa cackled. "Hi-eee! Or wear it!"

When Bawa laid the severed trunk of the baby spirit elephant across his shoulder, reason left him. Trembling with rage, he grasped his machete. And as the torment of Bawa's maddening laughter droned on, he whirled round and swung it upward with all the strength he possessed.

As he watched Bawa's faceless body topple to the ground, he threw the blade down and staggered back. A patch of earth and grass exploded near his feet, the sound of the gunshot reaching him a split second later. Slowly, he heard distant voices screaming his name. With a surge of panic shooting up from his bowels, he searched for his spear. His mind an empty blur, he leaped for it and grabbed it in one fluid motion. Without looking back, he sprinted across the crest of the little hill and ran and ran and ran.

*

FAR OFF IN the distance, the unmistakable call of a hyena sent a shiver across his shoulders. Stopping to listen, he crouched and held his breath. The evening quiet brought the faint ringing of a tiny bell. Straining to locate it, he stood with his hands cupped behind his ears.

It had been two days since he had left the plain of dead elephants. He had had little water, no sleep, and no food during that time. His senses were muted. And now the light of the day was beginning to fade. Had he imagined the bell, he wondered? The jingle drifted to him again. He looked in its direction.

Silhouettes moved across his sightline, far enough away from where he stood that their shapes were muddled in the dim light. Undeterred, he started out after them with a quickened pace. As he drew near, he could make out the figures of people and animals. He began to sprint. When he could see that the animals were goats and that the people were a man and a woman and three children, a cry of warning rose up amongst them. One of the children brought the lead goat to a halt. The animal shook its head and looked toward him. The tiny bell tethered around its neck jingled.

"Are you a highwayman come to rob us?" the child holding the lead goat called out to him.

"A highwayman?" Teimbaka repeated, confused. "I know nothing of highwaymen!" he hollered back.

"Father!" another of the children called out. "He is hurt! There is blood!"

Teimbaka looked down and found that the gash on his thigh had opened up again. Fresh blood darkened the brown robe he was wearing. Teimbaka saw the woman in the group shuffle close to the man and whisper something to him. Teimbaka straightened his shamma and wiped the dust from his shoulders.

"How were you hurt?" the man called over to him.

Teimbaka touched his shoulder where Gunstard had smacked him with his rifle.

"I fell," he replied with a pause, "and landed on something sharp."

"I am John," the boy who held the lead goat proclaimed, taking a stride toward Teimbaka. "If you are a highwayman, I will make short work of you."

"John, be still," the man said.

The youth stepped back.

"I am no highwayman," Teimbaka repeated, holding his arms out from his sides. "You can see this, can you not?"

"Why is it, then, that you carry a bow and—?"

"Be still, John," the man ordered with a forceful tone. "Tend to the goats with your brothers."

"Yes, Father," John replied with a slight bowing of his head.

"These are dangerous times. A family traveling with goats is at risk," the man said, turning his attention to Teimbaka. "We have no money," he was quick to add. "That is what the goats are for—to sell at the markets in Nairobi."

Some memory tugged at Teimbaka as the man spoke. But he could not quite bring it to the forefront of his mind.

"Joseph is my Christian name," he offered when Teimbaka did not readily reply. "My wife is Mary; our sons, John, Mark, and Thomas. We are of the Christian faith. Which faith do you practice?"

"Faith?"

Teimbaka thought of the spirit elephants and how he had betrayed their trust. His shoulders slumped.

"I have no faith," he murmured, averting his eyes from Joseph as he said the words.

"The tale of these times," Joseph replied. "Kenyan fighting Kenyan.

Those who want to remain a British colony and those who seek to destroy all things British. Countryman against countryman, and all of us caught in between. Many have lost their faith."

Teimbaka pictured Bawa's face twisting in the air.

"Independence, revolution, a new age," Joseph sighed. "Just words to cover up killing and robbing. Do you not think this is so?"

"As captured birds we are," Teimbaka responded, though his voice seemed foreign to him. "Both mercy and death in the power of those who hold us."

"Please? It is all that we have." Mary's voice was soft, endearing, soothing. Teimbaka had not noticed her approach, as her steps had been taken in silence. She stood next to him, her head slightly bowed, a wooden cup and a crust of bread balanced within her opened hands.

A strong feeling tugged at Teimbaka's heart.

"Water and bread," she said to him, risking a glance at his face.

The kindness Teimbaka found in Mary's eyes stirred feelings he did not understand. Not knowing what to say, he gratefully accepted the bread and water. In turn, he bowed his own head.

"What are you called?" she asked, drawing her hands away at the touch of his.

"Teimbaka."

"Eat and drink, then, Teimbaka," Joseph instructed. "For we must still travel a ways. It would not be safe if darkness finds us still out in the open." His face lined with worry, he added, "Predators of all kinds would be upon us then. Men, as well as beasts."

He looked over at his three sons, who were dutifully tending the half-dozen goats.

"Nothing suits a hungry lion better than goats."

"Will he die, Mother?" John called out.

Mary shook her head and did her best to cover her amusement.

"How can one tend to goats, John, when one's eyes look elsewhere?"

John smiled as a reply to his father.

"Your wound, is it bad?" Joseph asked. "Have you lost much blood?"

The sound of cloth being torn drew both men's attention. Mary had turned her back, but it was clear she was ripping some of her inner robing from her garments. When she turned back to them, she looked upon her husband in earnest.

"What is it, Mary? What is it you ask of me?"

With the slightest tilting of her hands, she motioned toward an earthen jug resting on the side of the dirt track they were following.

"But we have so little," Joseph said.

Mary furrowed her brow while again her hands asked for the jug.

"You are right, of course."

"Sit," Mary bade Teimbaka, motioning him to a place on the ground.

Joseph brought the earthen jug and placed it in his wife's hands, saying, "To share what we have is God's will. It is His way that we follow."

With great care, Mary tipped the earthen jug until some of the water it held trickled onto the strip of cloth she had fashioned. She bent and began to cleanse Teimbaka's wound. Her kindness brought tears to his eyes.

"We travel to Nairobi. Are you headed the same way?"

Although Teimbaka's thoughts were lost in the motion of Mary's hands, Joseph's question brought a troubled look to his face. He realized he had no notion of where he was headed.

"Home, perhaps?" Joseph offered. "I can see by the look of you that you are not Kenyan."

"Yes, home."

"Sudan? Somalia? Ethiopia? You are far from all of them."

"I— I have been far away."

The tiny bell jingled. Joseph's features awoke at the sound.

"I fear that old Babar is right. We have tarried too long for safety's sake. Mary, please finish. And Teimbaka, do you wish to travel with us? Your arrows, bow, and spear would be welcome if we were to come across danger."

Teimbaka reached behind his head and stroked the feathered ends of the arrows. He looked tenderly into Mary's eyes as she arose from his side. A feeling of loneliness overcame him as she moved away. He quickly wiped away the tears welling in his eyes before anyone noticed they were there.

"You are welcome to join us," Joseph said again. "The main road that will take us there is not far ahead."

In the brief silence that lay between Joseph's question and Teimbaka's reply came the lone call of the hyena that Teimbaka had heard before. Babar, the lead goat, immediately shook his head. The tiny bell rang with urgency.

For a moment, Teimbaka lost himself in the sound of it.

"I must go another way."

The words left him before he realized he had spoken. He listened to them as though another voice had offered them.

"God's blessings on you, then," Joseph said. "John! Start Babar on his way. We will follow momentarily."

"Yes, Father!"

"And keep a close eye on your brothers!"

"I will not fail you, Father!"

Joseph smiled and stifled a chuckle.

"Mary, we must go now," Joseph said as he reached out for his wife's hand. "We have done what we can."

Mary stepped close to Teimbaka and took the empty cup from his hand. Before she turned to join her husband, she looked into his eyes and said, "Go with God, Teimbaka. He will not forsake you."

Her words and voice swept through him as those of the white bird had done. He looked longingly after her, suddenly lamenting his quick decision not to travel in her company. But as Mary took hold of Joseph's hand, the moment of regret passed.

"And to you," he called out after them, "may your God keep you well and safe."

Mary turned at his words, her face filled with concern.

"He is not *our* God, Teimbaka. He is *yours* as well. As He is of everything and everyone."

Mary raised her hand in farewell, then turned and walked with Joseph to catch up to her sons and the herd of goats.

The hyena hooted once more. The animal was closer. His head beginning to throb, Teimbaka placed his palms to his temples and pressed. Closing his eyes, he welcomed the blankness he found there.

"For you."

Startled, he jerked his head back and blinked open his eyes. John stood before him, holding a long, thick stick in his outstretched hands.

"Mother said to bring this to you. She said you might need it to walk with."

Before Teimbaka could reply, John thrust the stick into his grasp and then sprinted away. Teimbaka's eyes went wide.

"Tafari's dula," he whispered. "But how?"

Looking up from the dula, he sought out John to ask him how they had come to find his brother's walking stick. But the boy was already far away. Teimbaka slid his fingers over the smooth, worn wood.

"Be on guard, John!" he yelled. "Lest lions appear out of nothing and take everything away!

T HE TWENTIETH NIGHT of Teimbaka's journey found him sitting next to a small campfire of his own making. The flames drew his thoughts into it, and more. Moths flitted about the fire as if they were engaged in some arcane right of passage, while other insects of various shapes and sizes zigzagged across the wavering heat. He watched, detached, not wishing to be lured back into a memory he did not wish to relive. So instead, he crouched next to the flickering blaze and stared into the blues and yellows and shades of orange, trying his best to think of nothing at all.

Although the fire was a source of comfort to him, it was also one of misgiving. For he had seen a cluster of lights from a village no more then a mile away and had heard the voices of people as they hurried to reach them before the fall of darkness. He knew that, if he could see the lights, so too could his fire be seen. The flames were a lure. So he had taken precautions in building it where it might go unnoticed. He hoped they would be enough.

Teimbaka ran a hand over the smooth wood of Tafari's dula and nodded to the fire. He had understood, as soon as John had handed him the walking stick, what lay before him. There would be no other course for him to follow now. He would find Menelik, and they would be a family again.

Abruptly, he stood and cupped a hand behind each ear. He reached for an arrow and nocked it to the bow. The eerie whistling he thought he heard was growing stronger. As he listened to it, he could make out some odd twanging accompanying it. He lowered the bow when voices began to sing. Captivated and intrigued by the sounds of song and melody, he did not realize until it was too late that those who were singing and playing were almost upon him. He bent to the fire and gathered dirt into his hands to douse it.

"Greetings to you!" came a friendly voice from the cover of the trees. "There is no need to cover your fire."

The music stopped. There was a slight pause.

"There is nothing to fear from us. We are just three azmaris. Perhaps a song could be traded for some of the cooked meat we have been smelling for the past mile."

Teimbaka said nothing.

"It is so, stranger," a different voice offered in a friendly tone.

"We seek nothing more then a place to rest for the night. And possibly a bite of food to fill our empty stomachs."

"*Azmaris?* I am not familiar with the word," Teimbaka replied. "Is that what tribe you are from?"

From behind a cluster of trees, three men emerged. Each held an instrument that was as odd as their clothing. The eldest, an elderly man with a bearded face, dressed in robes of yellow, red, and white, took a step forward and bowed his head. With an engaging smile, he addressed Teimbaka.

"We are musicians. If that be a tribe, then it is so that we are a part of it."

Extending an arm so his robes flowed about him, he continued.

"But surely, one such as yourself is familiar with musicians. You have no cause to fear us." With a nod to Teimbaka's bow and arrow, the man added, "Surely that is evident."

Teimbaka studied his weapons for a moment.

"I intend you no harm," he stated. "It is just that I was—"

"Our sincerest apologies for interrupting your time of reflection," the elder offered apologetically as he sat himself down next to the small fire. "Adiam! Gather more wood! We cannot expect this good man to yield all of his warmth to us!"

Teimbaka watched the youngest of the three—a youth no greater in age than himself—lay some object down, then disappear back into the darkness of the woods.

"Be wary of lions!" Teimbaka called after him. "They lie in wait, in the night!"

"You have seen lions about?" the third man inquired, his eyes darting about the campsite. Visibly frightened, he took a few steps toward the seated elder.

"Father, we must go back to town. No matter what they said they would do—"

The elder quickly raised a hand. He eyed his son with a stern and unforgiving expression.

"Be silent, Yolyos! Your fear is without cause. If lions were about, then surely we would have been their dinner before now. But perhaps we should be thankful of your krar playing."

The elder man smiled. And when he spoke next, his voice was light-hearted and filled with mischief.

"Even lions cannot stand to listen to badly tuned and badly played krar. So the strings of your instrument, Yolyos, have saved us all." He laughed. "Be it for once that your lack of practice has done us all some good."

The elder addressed Teimbaka.

"My name is Susenyo. My son, Yolyos," he said, motioning to the still fearful-looking man whose dress was a flowing robe of deep blue. "And Adiam is the other of our little group."

"Adiam!" he called out with annoyance, "Where is the wood? This fire grows cold!"

Almost at once, Adiam appeared as if out of nowhere. So silent was his return that even Teimbaka was caught off guard. Without a word, the yellow-and green-robed youth stepped to the dwindling fire and deposited an armful of sticks and small branches. Then, without speaking a word, he bent to the task of resurrecting the flames.

"The meat we smelled on the night breeze cast a spell over us all," Susenyo continued, his tone of voice exceedingly flattering. "Antelope of some kind, ah—? I am sorry, I did not catch your name."

Teimbaka stared at the man for some time before replying.

"Teimbaka is my name. And your nose must need cleansing. Can you not tell the difference between bush pig and antelope?"

Susenyo slapped his thighs and laughed.

"Bush pig! Why, of course! It has been so long, though, since I have smelled one roasted out in the open. Not often enough have I—*we*—had the fortune of tasting the sweet, succulent meat of the bush pig," he said with a wink and a broad smile.

Teimbaka remained silent. Susenyo took the respite to admire the bow and arrows in Teimbaka's possession.

"Hunting has fast become an art of the past, Teimbaka. Rare is it, to come across one so skilled as to bring down a bush pig with but a bow and a few arrows. Scarcer still to find one who can even track the elusive beast. Come," he beckoned with a sweeping gesture of a robed arm and a smile that glittered in the reflection of the fire. "Come and sit by the fire, if you would, and tell us of the tale of your hunt. It will be as soothing music to our ears after days of travel on the road. Yolyos, Adiam—a true tale will you be privy to. Listen to a true hunter, the last of a forgotten breed. Wonder at his skill. And keep silent as he speaks, so that we may all hear the arrow as he nocks it to his bow when he prepares for the shot."

Teimbaka sat at the newly rebuilt fire and sheepishly looked at his three visitors.

"But before you begin, Teimbaka," Susenyo tentatively added, "might we taste a morsel of your prize so that we may fully appreciate what you have accomplished?"

As he weighed the notion of agreeing or saying no, the face of Mary materialized before him. Though she said nothing, her appearance beckoned him to share what he had with those without. He stared into her imaginary eyes and nodded.

"I will share what I have," he said.

"Do you hear that Yolyos, Adiam? Here, out in the wooded darkness, there lives the spirit of goodwill."

Susenyo kept his gaze upon Teimbaka as he stood and moved away from the fire. His eyes followed his every movement.

"Sad it is that the spirit of good no longer flourishes in the towns and cities. What is it that has made people of those places so cynical and untrusting? Perhaps all would be better served if more time was spent in the wilds. Perhaps a few weeks sleeping beneath the trees, with a star-filled sky to nourish one's visions and dreams of heaven, would rekindle that which has been lost."

Susenyo's eyes briefly met with those of Yolyos and Adiam before he continued.

"Have you not witnessed this yourself, Teimbaka? Is it not so, that the people of the cities and towns have grown hard, even cruel?"

Teimbaka did not reply. The three watched him as he dug deeply into the soil with his hands.

"Dirty meat," Yolyos whispered to his father with disdain. "This is what we came for, what we have come to?"

Susenyo put a finger to his lips and gave his son a pointed, angry look.

"The trees can sometimes be filled with creatures one cannot hear or see," Teimbaka said as he lifted a hide-bound bundle from the earth. "Until you awaken and find your food has disappeared, you do not know that you have erred in choosing one for storage. You at least know there is no beast under the earth that wants to carry your food away. And if one comes to dig for it, you can at least choose to fight for it, or flee."

Teimbaka returned to the campfire with his bundle.

"You see, Yolyos," he said, unfolding the hides so that the man could look upon what was wrapped inside. "No beast or soil has touched the meat."

Teimbaka allowed himself a pride-filled smile.

"Eat and you shall see, Yolyos. The Mother was kind to me—to us— to have given us such a delicious meal as this."

"How true are your words," Susenyo gushed with praise as he took the bundle of meat from Teimbaka.

Though Teimbaka had offered the food to Yolyos, Susenyo hungrily pulled a large strip of the bush pig from the mound and stuffed it into his mouth. His eyes bulged with pleasure at its taste.

Taken aback by the abrupt action of the man, Teimbaka stared at him as he continued to feed himself. It was then that he noticed his plump hands and fleshy cheeks.

"Is it not your custom to eat together?" he blurted out. "Are not those you travel with as hungry as you?"

Barely pausing long enough from his meal to reply, Susenyo met Teimbaka's piercing look with one of indifference. With a smacking of his lips, he said, "What I leave for them will be plenty. You need not concern yourself, Teimbaka."

Teimbaka looked at Yolyos and Adiam. He could see their hunger in the way their eyes followed each morsel of food that Susenyo placed into his mouth.

"What I give is of my concern," he stated forcefully. "I give this meat to all. Not to one."

A look of hostility flashed across Susenyo's face. But just as quickly, it disappeared, replaced by one of benevolence.

"I do only as they have bade me to do, Teimbaka. As I am the eldest, they insist that I eat my fill." When he saw that Teimbaka was not convinced, he said, "Look, I will show you."

He held the bundle of meat out to Yolyos and then to Adiam. And although Teimbaka could see each man's desire to take from the offering, neither would accept any from Susenyo's hands.

"You see. Our ways are different from your own. But if it is your strong belief that we follow your will, we will break the custom which our kind has followed for centuries."

"My apologies, then. I did not mean to offend. It is only—"

"Please do not trouble yourself with our ways," Susenyo said in earnest. "So many different customs and rituals are there amongst the peoples of these lands. Strange and odd ones we have encountered ourselves," he went on with a nod, as if to revisit some memory. "Troublesome they can be sometimes, yes? Yet, we must respect the ways of others." Susenyo swallowed a mouthful of the bush pig, smacked his lips and wiped the grease from his lips with the back of his hand. "Do you not agree, Teimbaka?" he asked.

"Yes—the ways of others," Teimbaka replied half-heartedly.

*The ways of Peter Gunstard,* he thought. *Cruel, brutal, harsh, uncaring; were these ways to be respected too?* He shook his head. He eyed Susenyo anew.

"Many places have I been. Many customs, different ways, different tongues have I witnessed. Not all are worthy of respect. Not all should be accepted. Not all should be left to endure."

In the uneasy moment that ensued, Susenyo was quick to partake of another piece of bush pig while shrugging his shoulders.

"It is as you say, Teimbaka," he concurred, though his tone was light. "We ourselves have seen as such. But, who is it that should decide what is acceptable and what is not? You, perhaps? Are you the sayer of such things?"

"No," he was quick to reply, the flames of the fire bringing him the vision of Bawa's faceless corpse. "But neither am I blind to cruelty and those who would practice it."

Teimbaka was taken off guard by someone's laughter. It was the youth, Adiam.

"How is it one laughs at this?" Susenyo barked with irritation. "Do you wish to bring shame upon us, Adiam, for ridiculing the words of your host?"

Adiam cowered under the angry glare from Susenyo.

"Please forgive me. It was not my intent, Teimbaka, to—" Adiam lowered his face so that the shadows cast by the fire would shroud him from the others.

"Do not trouble yourself, Adiam. No offense was taken. Your laughter caused me no harm."

"I found no humor in what you spoke," Adiam explained, his voice close to sadness. "It was more … irony that I found."

"Be silent, Adiam, so Father may eat in peace," Yolyos interjected with an air of disdain. "Perhaps, if his meal is tranquil, he will be more giving of what still remains."

"Let the youth speak," Teimbaka responded as he grasped his dula and rested it on his knees.

Adiam's eyes darted from face to face with uncertainty. It was only when Susenyo gave a subtle nod that he continued.

"You speak of injustice and cruelty, Teimbaka. It has been my observation that these exist wherever I have been. One might think that they would only be found in places of ignorance and want. Yet, they flourish equally within the doors of higher learning and wealth. And while cruelty and injustice might fester within the realm of the needful, simply as a way to survive, they are used and honed by those who are learned and rich as a means to gain more power—a tool, if you would. The bitter humor I found was in the fact that, out here," he explained with an expansive spreading of his arms, "in the solitude of darkness and fire, there is one who speaks of these affronts as though there is a force strong enough to thwart them."

"Is that energy not within you, Adiam? Is there not a part of you that becomes angry when wrongs are committed in your presence? Is there not a natural feeling you hold inside of you that urges you to do right when you are a witness to these acts?"

Adiam opened his mouth as if a ready response was on the tip of his tongue. But instead, he shook his head as he lowered it.

Barely audible, he mouthed, "If it is there, I no longer feel it."

"Say again, Adiam? What is it you say you feel?"

"He said," Susenyo interrupted, "that the feeling of which you speak resides within all of us. Alas, for some, it is buried so deep that it might not well exist at all."

Susenyo met Teimbaka's gaze with a wide, sparkling smile. "Were it to be that all men held true to themselves, to their neighbors." Susenyo shook his head in lament and let his voice trail off.

A pocket of trapped air burst within the fire. Red embers rose into the darkness above the flames in a broken trail. Teimbaka was reminded of another fire and another time.

Susenyo was quick to read his changing expression.

"Where do the embers take you, Teimbaka? From where you have come, or to where you have yet to go?"

Scattered pieces of spirit elephants and hyenas, lions and goats, Gunstard and Bawa, Untello, John, and Mary flew into his recollections. But none would remain. It troubled him that he could not picture any of them intact.

"Flames seem always to draw one's mind to reflection; dreams that are wished for or ones that have been lost. Both soothing and disturbing can the flames of a fire be. And each one brings its own mood; anger, hope, sadness, desire." Susenyo shrugged his shoulders as he finished speaking. He, too, was drawn into the hypnotic flicker of the flames.

"Where is that you go, Susenyo? Where is it that a musician travels in the darkness of the night?"

Susenyo's reply was quick, and came with a smile and a wink.

"Perhaps the very place to which you are bound, Teimbaka. Perhaps fate has brought us together so that we might travel as one. Think of the prospects! A fine team we could make!"

Taking a final mouthful of bush pig, Susenyo passed what was left to Yolyos, then lifted his arms.

"The company of the three of us for what must be a lonely journey for you, Teimbaka! Music, laughter, philosophy; all this we can provide! And from you," he went on excitedly, bending forward as if to speak in confidence, "we could learn the ways of the land. You would not need to teach it. No, of course not. It would be by our own keen awareness that we would become privy to the ways of a great hunter such as you. And the food you would provide for us at the beginning our journey would be the food that we would be able to provide for ourselves once we part ways. Your tutelage would be invaluable." With a pronounced nodding of his head, he proclaimed, "Consider! The possibilities are endless!"

When Teimbaka made no immediate response, he was quick to add, "But perhaps I err in my assumption that you would want company."

"But, Father," Yolyos added, his lips slick with the grease from the meat, "we cannot—"

"Silence, Yolyos. Do not try to sway Teimbaka with any more words. The decision is for him to make."

Susenyo gave his son a knowing glance.

"Where is it that you travel to, Teimbaka?" Adiam asked with sincerity. "What makes one to travel as you do—alone, and keeping to the forest?"

"Home."

"And where is home?" Susenyo prodded.

The question brought the memory of the dry riverbed to him. He saw it clearly: the pile of wood he and his brothers had gathered and the edge of the forest his father was taking them to. He barely remembered his father saying the name of the land.

"Ethiopia."

"Ah, Ethiopia! A beautiful land it is. So varied. The terrain, the people, the cultures."

Susenyo's voice was like the purring of a tamed cat.

"From Addis Ababa on the high plateau to the port of Assab; a hard way for travelers such as ourselves. But the rewards are plentiful. Your home has always treated us well, Teimbaka. Always very hospitable."

"A wife awaits you there?" Adiam asked.

Teimbaka laughed.

"Now there is humor in my words? Or is there more irony about?" Adiam asked.

"Only the irony of being unwed. The humor is that I have not even thought of such a time."

His smile faded and his face grew solemn as he continued.

"I go in search of a brother. Many years have we been apart. It is my hope that not too many have passed for us to be reunited."

"A brother," Susenyo stated with a furrowed brow. "What name was he given? Perhaps I—we—have crossed each other along the many paths we have traveled."

"Menelik," Teimbaka replied, looking at the three light-brown faces around him for any glimmer of recognition the name might spark. "I know him by nothing else. If there is more to his name or mine, I do not know what it is."

"Do not let your face be pulled by sorrow, Teimbaka. The name you say has some familiarity to me."

Susenyo rubbed his bearded chin as he thought. "It is the exact placement of it though, that is elusive."

"Yolyos!" he exclaimed an instant later, his voice filled with excitement. "Surely you recall our meeting with a young man that went by the single name of Menelik, do you not? Where was it, though? Perhaps the train we rode out of Addis toward the coast."

Yolyos seemed puzzled by his father's urging, but was quick to recollect the meeting as he studied Susenyo's face.

"Yes. Yes! I believe it was on that very train. I do not recollect much of what we spoke about," he said, shifting his attention to Teimbaka. "But I do recall his kindness. Was he not the very young-looking man, Father, who was caring for some children whose parents had fallen to the small-pox? Was he not taking them to their relatives and bearing the burden of the expense on his own?"

"I believe he is the very same, Yolyos. Indeed! Yes, now I remember clearly!"

"He is alive, then," Teimbaka said with a sigh.

"Did you doubt that he was?"

Teimbaka blinked the vision of Tafari and the lion from his eyes.

"There is always doubt, wonder, when one has been away, Susenyo. If you imagine and dream, then you must see not only the light, but the darkness as well. The Mother divides Her blessings and her curses equally; do you not see this as truth?"

"The Mother?" Adiam asked, perplexed. "What mother do you speak of?"

Teimbaka looked at Adiam as though he had asked him to explain what the sky was.

"Africa, Adiam. From Her is where all begins; to Her is where all will return when Her breath carries our spirits from our flesh."

Teimbaka searched the depths of Adiam's light-brown eyes. The flames of the fire flickered within them.

"Africa, the Mother; we are all of Her, as were all who came before us and as will be all who will follow us. You are Hers, Adiam. Have you not known this?"

"The land as my mother is something that my eyes have not seen, Teimbaka. True though it may be, my heart has not felt it so, either," he said with some sadness in his voice.

"Still, you are of Her, Adiam," Teimbaka softly replied. "You are her son."

"Menelik, your brother, is Her son as well," Susenyo remarked with a hint of irritation in his tone. "What fate do you think She has given him? Does it not interest you that Yolyos and I have crossed his path?"

"That Menelik was alive when you saw him is enough to satisfy me. A great worry has been lifted. But what more is there to say of him, Susenyo? That he traveled on a train heading toward the coast tells me little. From where did his journey begin and where did it end? Did he return to where he began or stay where the train left him?" He shrugged. "It is before me to find out all of these answers now. Yet, even on this night, word of him has come to me, unexpected, but welcome. I am closer to him now than I have been for some years."

"Yes, closer," purred Susenyo. "And closer will you be if more eyes, more ears, are focused on his whereabouts. Think how we may be of help to you and your brother: four to look, to seek, to inquire. Your search could be greatly shortened with our help. And while we all undertake this endeavor on your behalf, Teimbaka, your help to us would be but a small burden to shoulder. So simple would the journey of four men become. This you can see for yourself, yes?"

The light of the fire danced across the men's features, both highlighting and masking each of their pensive faces.

"Four different ways of thinking, four different opinions. Stopping to rest, stopping to eat, these are the burdens of traveling in company." Teimbaka slid four of his fingers along the wood of the dula, his eyes following their movement. One by one, he removed three of the fingers and looked back up at Susenyo. "Alone," Teimbaka said with resolve, nodding to the lone finger resting on the wood, "one travels as one wishes."

"Knowledgeable of the ways of the cities, are you then?" Susenyo countered. "Friendly faces are often a disguise of the deceitful."

He smiled anew and smoothed his robes.

"I have made many true friends in the villages and towns and cities of Ethiopia, Teimbaka. Many eyes, many ears," he told him, gesturing to his own eyes and ears as he spoke, "to see, to listen, to find; alone, one can only look in one direction at a time, and hear only the sounds and words from those who are directly near. Is there not logic in a search where hundreds seek, rather than one?"

He waited for Teimbaka's reply. But when none was forthcoming, he continued on.

"The whereabouts of a kind man such as your brother will be known to many. How many days, weeks, or months are you willing to let slip away while you search on your own, while you try to decide what faces speak the truth to you and which are only telling tales for their own selfish reasons? At any time, your brother may well be walking on an adjoining street or be in the next village ahead, and you would never know. Is this something you wish to leave to chance?"

Without waiting for an answer, he pressed on.

"This is where we would be invaluable to you. Many villages, houses, and inns are open to us. Because of our trade, we are welcomed and received in good trust. And with each new home we enter or village we travel to, there lies the prospect that Menelik will be sitting there, waiting for Teimbaka to find him, wondering why it has taken him so long to do so."

In the silence that followed Susenyo's speech, the flames of the fire dimmed. Grey smoke snaked lazily into the darkness above them.

"Four is better than one," Yolyos offered lightly, licking the grease from his fingertips.

Teimbaka grunted, then looked to Adiam.

"And what say you, Adiam?"

"The youth—"

"I have asked him so that I may hear him, Susenyo," Teimbaka stated firmly, shifting his dula so that it stood erect by his side.

Adiam nibbled at the small portion of food that had finally made its way to him. He ate slowly while his eyes darted between Susenyo and his son. Only when Susenyo grunted and raised an eyebrow did he venture to speak. With a slight shrug of his shoulders, he said, "If it is meant to be, your brother and you will be united. If it is not, then ten thousand eyes would be of no help."

"The boy speaks of fate. And what do any of us know of it? How does one know what fate has in store for us? I will tell you how, Teimbaka. It is only when we turn back to look at the past that we see what fate had in store. Many times—"

"Enough words, Susenyo. Sleep shall we need for tomorrow."

Teimbaka stretched his body to the ground, positioning his back toward the fire. Pulling his dula close and laying his spear, bow, and arrows within easy reach, he heaved a deep breath and closed his eyes.

"Wonderful! Wonderful! You have made the right decision, Teimbaka," Susenyo gushed. "Of great service shall we be to you. Great service! You shall see."

Susenyo waited for a response, but received none. His smile was wide and filled with satisfaction as he looked to his son and then to Adiam.

"Food shall we have now," he whispered excitedly. "At least for a time."

The call of a single jackal drifted to them from the depths of the trees. Susenyo's smile waned at its presence. In the silence that followed, the soft, wind-blown tones of Adiam's washnit floated through the campsite.

"Cease your endless flute-playing," Yolyos hissed. "Let it be quieted for once."

"The sound of it will keep the jackals away, my son," Susenyo whispered softly, bending closer to Yolyos. "Plus, while he plays, he is awake."

"What of blankets and pillows, Father?" Yolyos whispered in return. "I cannot rest pleasantly without them."

Susenyo put a finger to his lips to silence his son. Nodding toward Teimbaka, he said in a louder voice, "Your jokes will make for happy dreams, Yolyos. Now rest. Dawn comes early in the wild."

*

AND SO IT came to pass that Teimbaka became part of a group once again. For several days, they headed eastward. The group traveled as Teimbaka was accustomed to, keeping to the forest when they could, staying away from the roads and the villages, doing their best to keep their distance from people.

Being close to the same age, Adiam and Teimbaka shared much of those days in each other's company while the group made their way to Ethiopia. In that time, Adiam taught Teimbaka to play the kebero and tsenatsel, so that he might accompany the melodies of the washnit. In turn, Teimbaka instructed the youth on the skills of the arrow and the bow. But Adiam did not take to the ways of the weapons as Teimbaka had taken to the drum and the rattle. Perhaps it was the killing, Teimbaka came to realize, for Adiam would become sad and distant when the blood of a felled animal pooled around the wound of an arrow. And with each new, successful kill, Adiam would find reason not to be a part of it, until finally, Teimbaka stopped seeking out his company when he would set out on a hunt.

On the morning of the eighth day, Teimbaka led Susenyo, Yolyos, and Adiam into Ethiopia, crossing the border from Kenya through the area between the lakes of Turkana and Chew Bahir. Teimbaka purposely took them this way because he knew the land to be sparsely populated, with few settlements to be concerned about. And as he had traveled this way before with Gunstard and the others, he also knew there would be no government checkpoints to deal with, either Kenyan or Ethiopian. Gunstard had spoken often in the recent past of certain governments beginning to take stricter measures against the flow of ivory across their borders. And while he was no authority on the specific laws regarding the flow of ivory between the governments of Kenya and Ethiopia, he knew well enough to want to steer clear of any possible confrontations with armed policemen or border guards.

As it was, the crossing into Ethiopia went without instance, save for the complaining of Yolyos. Teimbaka had come to understand that this was just a part of the young man's nature. But on this day, Susenyo voiced his displeasure as well.

"Yes. When, Teimbaka? As Yolyos has said, it has been over a week since we have seen another living soul, much less had the comfort of a roof over our heads or a blanket to throw over our sleeping bodies," Susenyo griped. "When will we enter Ethiopia so that we might begin our search for your brother? Or look forward to an evening spent entertaining a group of hard-working townspeople?"

Teimbaka kept on walking with his head directed forward, hiding the smile on his face. But when the huffing and puffing of Susenyo and Yolyos became too much to bear, he stopped and turned with outstretched arms.

"Do you not recognize the country you have so often traveled, Susenyo? We have been walking in Ethiopia for some hours now."

"Then when may we seek out a town and rejoin civilization?" Susenyo inquired in a tone that held both exhaustion and exasperation. "When will we see the faces of others?"

"And when will I have a pillow and a blanket for my sleep?" Yolyos added.

"Has the Mother not provided you with everything you have needed, Yolyos? Has She not been kind to us on our journey thus far? We have had food and water and fair weather; what more does one need?"

"A back that does not ache from sleeping on the ground, Teimbaka, and pillows so my rump may rest without the bruising from stones. And even more," Yolyos continued, amused by his next chosen words, "the chance to inhale the perfume of a beautiful woman who might be inclined to allow one such as myself to steal a kiss, or more!"

Yolyos laughed heartily, but ceased abruptly when no one else joined in.

"Patience, Yolyos," Teimbaka responded. "Have not the ways of the Mother shown you this?"

"Patience is not a virtue either my son or myself, to a great degree, possesses, Teimbaka. I too must confess that I desire more than we have had these past several days and nights."

"The river Omo is not far from where we stand," Teimbaka relayed without sympathy. "Along its banks there will be dwellings. There, perhaps, you will find some degree of satisfaction."

Without waiting for a reply, he turned and walked onward at a hurried pace. Without stopping for rest or food, they came in sight of a village by late afternoon. This brought much joy and relief to Susenyo and Yolyos. Yet, when Teimbaka sought to press ahead, they stopped him.

"Why do you wish me to stop, Susenyo, now that we are in sight of what you have so longed for? This makes no sense to me."

"It is as much for your benefit as it is for ours, Teimbaka," Susenyo explained. "We always send only one of us to enter a town when we first arrive. Surely you can see the logic. We do not wish to make some grand spectacle of ourselves, with our fine robing and instruments. No, we have learned to be more sensitive to the ways of the town and their customs before we announce ourselves." With a nod to Yolyos and Adiam, he expounded, "Over time, we have come to know the ways of the city dwellers. Just as you have come to know the ways of the open and the wild."

He took a step toward Teimbaka, offering a gracious nod and an engaging smile.

"You have brought us thus far. And we have been well while in your care. We have trusted you and your ways. Now, it is you who must give us our due in these matters. You will see that we are adept in the ways of the people. Soon we shall find your brother. Or at worst, word of his whereabouts."

Reluctantly, and with a fair amount of bewilderment, Teimbaka acquiesced. Susenyo went into the town alone.

Soon after his departure, Adiam put his washnit to his lips, and to

Teimbaka's surprise, began to play a joyful, lively melody instead of the eerie, forlorn tunes that Teimbaka had become so accustomed to him choosing. Immediately, Teimbaka joined him, pounding out a rhythm on his kebero. Even Yolyos joined in, strumming his krar when his pleading looks of disdain failed to halt the impromptu concert of his two companions. And as it can be with those who possess music in their hearts, a good deal of the late afternoon passed in this manner as each lost himself to the flow of the music and the passions which it stirred.

"Stop!"

Jolted out of their stupor by Susenyo's sharp command, the three men stared at him blank-faced, uncertain as to what they had done to cause the plump, round-faced, bearded elder to be so agitated.

"What are you doing?" he hissed. "What idiocy prompted this? Do you wish to give the entire town a concert for free? What need would they have for us then? How would we get paid? Stupidity! Yolyos, you should know better!"

"But the town is far away," Teimbaka pointed out. "Even if they could hear some of the music, certainly they could not feel it, embrace it."

"What do you know of music?" Susenyo asked sarcastically. "You are no azmari. 'They could not feel or embrace it,'" he scoffed, grunting his displeasure.

"What is there to *know* of music, Susenyo, save that it be pleasing, or not? Why would the people of the town expect any more from it than that?"

The anger upon Susenyo's face suddenly dissipated, replaced by one of mischief. His heartfelt laughter soon followed.

"It is my error to have lost sight of the simple truth of which you speak, Teimbaka. My apologies for having been so indignant," he said with a slight bow, the words flowing smoothly from his lips. "This is no place for an angry face. No, we exchange all the veils of anger and exhaustion for the happier outlook that lies ahead. It may only be a farming village we will enter, but it is a prosperous one," he told them, with a twinkle in his eyes as he rubbed his hands together. "A fine household is there, as well. And some wealth with the family that dwells in it, I have been told.

It will serve us well in preparation for the city of Omorate, which is not too far north, I have learned."

"And what name does this village go by?" Yolyos asked.

"Why," Susenyo laughed, "how foolish I have become in my later years, Yolyos. I forgot to ask!"

With his bright, engaging gaze falling to each of them, Susenyo spread his arms wide, then motioned to the village with a nod of his head.

"But regardless of what name she may go by, our lady awaits us! So let us go to her with smiles on our faces and joy in our playing. Come! We go!"

*

TO TEIMBAKA, THE hours that passed from late afternoon into nightfall were as a time spent in a dream. All the people of the village, it seemed, had come out upon their arrival, their faces brightening with delight at the appearance of the azmaris and the music that they played. The crowd danced and sang and chanted all about them, following them in this manner all the way to the household Susenyo had been told about. And when they stopped in front of a fine-looking stone house that had a small courtyard at the entrance, the people surrounded them in a half-circle, urging them to play on, shouting their desire for the music not to end.

Mesmerized by the accolades and attention, Teimbaka found that he was filled with a joy he was not familiar with. That there could be so much happiness in one place, among so many, and that he was partly responsible for it, made him laugh freely as he pounded out the rhythm that the people danced and swayed to.

In the midst of the festivities, the door to the courtyard opened behind them, a finely dressed man, woman, and several children stepping through it. When Susenyo glanced over his shoulder and saw their arrival, he nodded to his companions and shook the tsenatsel he had in his hand with a renewed vigor. Then, with a whoop and a wink, he urged Teimbaka, Adiam and Yolyos to play with more energy and passion. As the family stepped closer, Susenyo turned and greeted them with a wide engaging smile while bowing deeply with his free hand held to his heart.

Having glimpsed Susenyo's actions, Teimbaka looked across his shoulder, nodding his own greeting toward the family as they positioned themselves at the near edge of the festive crowd. And when he saw that one of the family members was a young woman who he thought might be close to the same age as his, he bent to the kebero in earnest, his hands suddenly seeming to take on a life of their own. Deftly, and with great enthusiasm, his palms and fingers pounded out a vibrant, intoxicating beat. Closing his eyes he began to sway, losing himself to the rhythm and the timbre of the drum.

When Susenyo finally gave them the signal to cease playing and informed them of an invitation to share dinner with the family of the house in return for a more intimate recital, Teimbaka sagged with exhaustion. And as he rubbed his stinging hands together, he looked upon Adiam's swollen lips and Yolyos's bent and inflamed fingers and concluded that to be an azmari was a hard way to make a living indeed.

As Susenyo lead them through the courtyard of the stone house, it was as if they were entering a realm far removed from the village just outside. Instead of mud and hard-packed dirt, their feet walked upon bricks that had been laid in an image of the sun, complete with flaming edges that licked out toward a row of small green shrubs that lined each of the inner walls. Teimbaka marveled at the bright colors of the paint that had been used to decorate the brick, for whomever the artist was, he had used many shades of yellow and orange and red, so that when one looked down, one's eyes became lost within a shifting, mesmerizing haze of multi-hued flame.

The stone of the house itself and the walls of the courtyard had been sanded smooth and stacked with great precision before being mortared and painted white, he could see. And the roof, shining brightly with a coat of clear varnish, was made of a rich-colored wood whose timbers seemed to all have been cut from the same tree. So beautiful was it to look upon, Teimbaka thought. He wondered what the people of the village must think of their own houses of dried mud and roofs of straw when they passed by.

Teimbaka inhaled deeply, almost tasting the sweet pungent aroma that wafted on the air of the courtyard. The smell was heady, almost hypnotic. He let his senses linger in it for a time, relishing its pleasure, happy to be removed from the stench of oxen and goats and donkeys that permeated the village.

"They burn incense," Adiam said to him in a low voice. "I have never trusted those who practice the burning of the spice."

"It is a sweet smell, nonetheless," Teimbaka casually replied. "Is it always like this?" he asked Adiam with a sigh as they sat themselves down on a smaller inner wall that separated the courtyard from the house.

"Like what?"

"To be both drained and exhilarated. Exhausted but renewed by the energy that existed for the past hours."

Teimbaka turned to look at Adiam, but the youth seemed preoccupied.

"Perhaps all this is old for you. Though it would seem hard not to be touched by the people's joy. Do I sound foolish?"

Teimbaka sensed Adiam struggling to find the right words to say. When he did speak, Teimbaka was as much troubled by the tone of Adiam's voice as by what he said. In a sad, almost forlorn manner, Adiam said to Teimbaka: "Never do I tire of the music. For it is in those times when the feeling of the melody runs through me that I am what I wish to be. If I could only play forever without stopping to eat or drink or wonder where it is that I will sleep or if I will have to— But, it cannot be that way, can it? When we stop playing, the life that I am tied to rushes back in. It is as if the music is mocking me. This life is cruel. More often than I would wish it to be."

"I do not understand what you say, Adiam. The music has ended, yet we sit here in comfort waiting to be served a fine meal. I do not see the cruelty in this. You must show me, if I am not looking where I can see this."

Adiam heaved a sigh and closed his eyes for a moment.

"What is still to come is yet to be," he told him in a voice that was barely audible. "You will come to know this for yourself, Teimbaka. I wish it could be otherwise."

"The tone of your conversation does not do justice to your music. I have often imagined that musicians speak in melodies. I see now that I have mislead myself." The sound of the female voice brought Teimbaka and Adiam to their feet. A veiled and scarfed young woman, dressed from head to toe in a simple black robe, stood before them. She stared at Adiam and Teimbaka for a moment with dark, smoldering eyes, and then nodded to the tray of food she had brought to them.

"We beg your forgiveness," Adiam said with a slight bowing of his head.

"Please, it is I who should apologize for interrupting without announcing myself." In a soft gentle tone, she told them, "I am called Yeshie." She added, "I asked that I might serve you your meal so that I could meet two gifted players such as yourselves."

At this, Yeshie bowed her head while extending the tray of food toward them. Her hands and wrists were slender and smooth, her skin the color of sun-darkened sand. Upon handing Teimbaka the polished wooden tray, Yeshie allowed her touch to linger, letting her fingers slide along the side of his wrist.

"You are the drum man, are you not?" she inquired with a slight flutter of her eyelids. "Your playing was admired by all."

She paused, staring briefly into Teimbaka's eyes. He felt a surge of excitement and strength.

"As was yours—"

"Adiam."

"Adiam, your flute was like that of a dozen songbirds," she offered with an audible sigh.

"I thank you for your gracious words, kind lady. If only I could actually play like a dozen songbirds," he told her with a laugh.

"Please, eat," she said to them. "Do not let me keep you from your food."

"Will you not join us?" Teimbaka quickly asked. "Taking a meal with a woman—"

He glanced away, suddenly feeing very foolish. But Yeshie eased his anxiety almost at once, giggling lightly while, again, grasping his forearm with her soft, sensuous hands.

"I had my evening meal some time ago, drum man. But your offer is most enamoring. Is there more to you, then, than just your talents with a drum?"

Teimbaka looked to Adiam for help with a reply, but the meal Yeshie had served to them had Adiam's full attention. Somewhat perplexed and at a loss as to how to respond, Teimbaka looked sheepishly back to Yeshie.

"The kebero I have just learned," he managed to say. "I am barely familiar with it."

"Your humility is charming, drum man, but not necessary. The beat that your instrument pounded out is still strong within me. I can barely wait for the sound of it again."

Before he could stammer a reply, Yeshie whirled and went back into the house. Teimbaka squatted down across from Adiam and stared after her.

"It would seem you have gained an admirer," he remarked as he tore off a piece of injera from the tray of food placed between them.

"What do you mean?"

"What do you mean, what do I mean?"

Teimbaka looked at Adiam with a blank expression on his face.

"Did you not hear her say that the beat of your instrument was still strong inside of her?"

"Yes, but—"

"Teimbaka, she is a female and you are a male. What more do I need to say?"

Adiam gulped down a mouthful of food as he waited for him to respond. He began to laugh when Teimbaka remained silent.

"So the prospect of you lying with her tonight is almost a given. What holds you back that you cannot speak of it?"

Teimbaka stammered and swayed before finally blurting out: "But she is just a girl!"

"Hold there, drum man! Now you are a judge of when a girl is a woman and a woman, a girl? Do you think she sees you as man or boy? What folly will you confess to next?"

"I do not— I mean— I didn't— I mean—"

"Yes, you said that," Adiam chided in good fun. "You do not, you did not; a very concise statement. I must remember to use it myself on occasion."

Teimbaka shifted his position so he could use the small wall as a backrest. He looked skyward for a moment, and then shook his head and sighed.

"What troubles you of this? Surely you have been with a woman before…. Oh, my, now it is my folly to have judged. Is this so, Teimbaka? You have grown to the threshold of manhood without having tasted the fruit of a woman?"

At a loss as to what to say, Teimbaka looked dumbly at Adiam. When

Adiam burst out in laughter, he didn't know whether to be angry or perplexed.

"Is this so funny?" he demanded to know. "Must I be mocked for this if it is so?"

"You do not see the humor as I," Adiam struggled to say between his fits of laughter. "Whatever you do, do not let her find out that you are a virgin."

"Why?" Teimbaka asked, indignant that Adiam was carrying on so. "Will she parade me through the streets like I am some bizarre beast? Will she laugh at me as you do?"

"I do not mock you, Teimbaka. That you think I mock Teimbaka, the man, is not my intent. It is simply a word of advice that I offer to a friend."

Adiam paused to let Teimbaka speak, but then thought better of it and continued.

"She will feast upon you if she were to find out. And you would revel in her appetite. Too much so, if you were not careful. Bound to her, you might become ensnared by her tendrils of pleasure. Delightful as they may be, they would still be shackles of a kind. And do not be fooled, drum man, shackles of passion and lust are often stronger than those forged of wood or iron."

Adiam took a mouthful of food, contemplating his words as he slowly chewed.

"I would hope that you would partake of this woman, my friend. But I caution you if you do. If it is truly your brother that you seek, then be aware, be cautious, and do not fall into the trap of what your bodies desire."

Before there could be any further exchange of thoughts on the matter, Susenyo came hurrying out of the house, rubbing his palms together.

"Do not linger over your food, you two. The family awaits our playing. And, of course, we will not disappoint them."

Susenyo's chest heaved with excitement as he glanced back into the house he had just left.

"Such a fine house it is," he told them with relish in his voice. "Many valuable items that would be cherished by others in other cities and towns."

He looked cautiously at Teimbaka and added, "Of course, anyone might admire another's possessions. The beauty of art and jewelry and sculpture is to be appreciated by all. But alas, it is my fate that I can only be an admirer of such finery. Such riches I will never have. But no pity can there be in this. It is not my way. I am but azmari; humble and poor."

With a great smile and show of smoothing his robes, he announced, "Adiam! Teimbaka! We are ready to repay our hosts for their kindness, their generosity and hospitality! Come, it is time to give these fine people a night they will remember! They will dance and sing to exhaustion! And their dreams will be filled with visions of joy! Let us go and usher them into a peaceful bliss!"

And so it was as Susenyo said: the household became a whirlwind of music and dance and song. And in the hours that followed, the family members, one by one, began to slip away so that they might find rest and solitude within their rooms and in peaceful slumber. It was just after midnight before the last of the family took their leave and Susenyo was able to silence his own weary companions. As Teimbaka, Adiam, and Yolyos followed him to a corner of the great room where pillows and blankets had been set out for their comfort, they could hear the snores and heavy breathing in the quiet of the exhausted household.

"Sleep well, my friends," Susenyo bade them as the three lay down to rest. "Tomorrow we begin our search for Menelik," he added, winking to Teimbaka. "I will see you in the morning."

"But where do you go?" Teimbaka asked when he realized Susenyo was not joining them.

"To breathe some of the night air and allow my thoughts to relish this fine day. Do not worry, Teimbaka. When you become as old as I, sleep does not come as easy as when one is in his youth."

With that, Susenyo departed. It was not long thereafter that the snores and the heavy breathing of the exhausted azmaris mingled with those of the household.

But for Teimbaka, sleep was short-lived, for soft hands caressed his face, enticing him to awaken. And as his eyes fell into the smoldering gaze of Yeshie, she placed one finger to his lips while others touched him where no woman had touched him before. In this dreamlike state he stood, and in the throes of desire, followed her out through the courtyard and beyond.

Down to the river did she take him; one hand stroking his groin while the other took one of his and rubbed it hungrily over her firm breasts. Thusly, they awkwardly headed toward the moon-speckled water without making a sound, save for their breathing, which was short, urgent, and deep. And when they got as close to the water as they dared, Yeshie softly pushed away from him and stared deeply into his eyes. With his lips slightly parted and his mouth suddenly dry, Teimbaka watched her robes fall away, her nakedness capturing him within its alluring, moon-washed splendor.

"You—"

Placing a finger to her lips for silence, she stepped to him and removed his shamma. Drawing their naked bodies together, she ran her tongue along his neck while her fingers stroked his erection. Lowering them to the ground, she mounted his hips and placed him inside her. His skin on fire, unable to think, he welcomed the raw passion that spread through him. As he became lost in the grinding, thrusting motion of her hips, shuddering spasms began to surge through his body, culminating in an exploding moment of overwhelming ecstasy.

In the aftermath of his first encounter with the pleasures of the flesh, Teimbaka stared up at the stars, thinking that paradise had been discovered. With Yeshie nestled against his chest, he welcomed the murmur of the slow-moving water of the river and the beauty of the pre-dawn sky into his thoughts. Closing his eyes, he envisioned everything about the moment, doing his best to capture every detail of it so that it might never be forgotten.

But Yeshie's playful fingers stirred him, and as he readied himself for more pleasures of the flesh, the sound of hurried footsteps broke the spell the two of them had cast. Irritated, he crouched and placed Yeshie behind him. It was Adiam, he could see, hurrying toward the spot where he and Yeshie lay naked. In the waning moonlight Teimbaka could make out the shapes of the kebero and a walking stick in his grasp.

"It is time we go, Teimbaka," Adiam announced in labored gasps. "Susenyo and Yolyos have already left. We must hurry if we are to catch up with them."

"Your intrusion is not welcome," Teimbaka told him, doing his best to shield Yeshie from his prying eyes. "Have you no consideration for this woman's dignity?"

"Any other time, I would. But—"

"Then leave us, Adiam. Before you alert any of the household. We wish to still be alone."

"You don't understand. If you are still here when the household awakens, you will be in great trouble."

The urgency in his voice made Teimbaka stand and place his shamma about him.

"Please come with me," Adiam added. "I will explain everything when we have gone."

"Why are you in such a hurry to leave a house that has offered you both shelter and food?" Yeshie asked as she placed her robes about her. "Why are you so distressed?"

Teimbaka echoed her question with a stern glare.

Adiam rocked back and forth from one foot to the other, his glances between Teimbaka, Yeshie, and the house becoming more urgent the longer he remained silent. When it seemed that Adiam would not respond at all, Teimbaka became angry, and grabbed him firmly by the back of the neck.

"Tell me what you have done. Tell me now or I will carry you back to the house so that all may hear what you have to say."

"Teimbaka," he pleaded, "you must not go there. It would not be wise for you to—"

"My kindness has limits, Adiam. Please do not test me. Even among those who befriend me—"

A fleeting picture of the field of dead elephants and Bawa's insane grin came to him. He gripped Adiam's neck even tighter.

"Susenyo," Adiam blurted out. "He is a common thief."

He looked to Yeshie for some understanding.

"As is Yolyos; as they have made me. As many valuables that could be carried have been taken. They will be sold or traded in the next town or city, or the one after that," he confessed as though he were offering an apology. "So that Susenyo may eat the best food, wear the finest robes, partake of the pleasures of the flesh that he would otherwise never have if he could not pay for them."

Teimbaka released his hold and stepped away. As he listened to Adiam, he realized what had been done and what he had been a part of. A great sadness welled inside of him.

"I do not understand," he heard himself say.

"How were you to know?" Adiam was quick to respond. "Susenyo is convincing, an artist, if you will, when it comes to this game. I should have told you. It was wrong of me not to," he admitted with shame. "You showed us nothing but kindness."

"Thieves! Liars! Seducers!" Yeshie spat, slapping Teimbaka's face as hard as she could. "What atrocity have I allowed to happen? What filth has soiled me?"

She ran a few steps toward the house, but then whirled back upon the two men with rage.

"You will pay for this! You shall not go unpunished!" Her eyes mirroring the betrayal she felt, she took a step toward Teimbaka. "And you," she screamed, pointing at Teimbaka. "You who feign innocence! You shall know pain for what you have done! I will have your sambool cut from you so that you may never defile another who has been duped by your spell!"

Clutching her robes about her, she turned and ran as fast as she could back toward the house.

"Wake up! Thieves! Robbers! They have stolen from us," she cried out as she ran. "Awaken!"

"Hurry, Teimbaka," Adiam urged anew. "We must leave now."

"Why you, Adiam? Why is it that you are a part of this?"

Adiam looked away, saying nothing.

"Come, then. We will take back what we can and ask their forgiveness. We can pledge to recover what else Susenyo and Yolyos have left with. Surely, if we are sincere, they will show us mercy."

Adiam laughed sharply and spit on the ground.

"Mercy," he repeated sarcastically, "mercy does not know of me or care for me." With a sardonic laugh, he shook his head and looked briefly to the sky. "Mercy," he said with disdain. "Others may know of it—perhaps those who can buy it. But mercy does not associate with the likes of me: those who have nothing to give back to it in return for its charity."

He glared at Teimbaka.

"These are the words of Susenyo, not of Adiam. What is it that I cannot see? Why do you follow a man whose company you do not care for, whose way of life is not what you would choose for yourself?"

"I do not know what you are talking about," Adiam stated defiantly.

Lights, one by one, began to blink on within the stone house above them. As Teimbaka and Adiam watched them appear, they could hear the voices of surprise and weariness turn into ones of anger.

"Soon they will come for us," Adiam stated. "Maybe they will show us mercy then, and kill us quickly," he said with a sharp laugh.

Teimbaka glanced back at the house before replying: "I do not believe they will do anything of the kind if we are just honest about what—"

"Be stupid and stay if that is your wish. But I am leaving."

Adiam turned to flee, but Teimbaka grasped him again by his neck.

"Answer me first, Adiam. Why do you go to follow Susenyo? Why do you not flee another way?"

"Let me go!"

"Answer me first!"

Adiam went limp in his grasp. Against the backdrop of shouting voices and torches being lit did he say, "I follow Susenyo for the truth and his miserable death."

"I don't understand."

"I am bound to him, you see, sold to him along with my sister some six years ago."

"Sold? That cannot—"

"Be?" Adiam spit. "Why, because it is unheard of? Unthinkable?" he scoffed. "Tell that to a feeble-minded man who is drunk and has lost in many games of chance to the one I now call Susenyo. Tell that to a boy and a little girl who do not understand, who know no better, who cannot speak or fend for themselves. Tell that to an eight-year-old girl who is traded for a boat four years past so a hasty escape may be made. And tell that to a boy who has grown up being groomed to cheat and steal from everyone he meets so that one day he may learn where his sister might be—if she is even still alive. We spoke of irony once, Teimbaka. Well this is mine: to hope to gain such truth, I must rob and lie and deceive right along with the man I most despise in this life. I would kill him if I could take the chance. I would kill him a thousand times."

In the first light of dawn, Adiam looked solemnly at Teimbaka.

"I will kill him," he said. "When it is right, I *will* kill him."

"There! Down by the river! There they are!"

"The Mother has given you a mighty burden, Adiam," Teimbaka said, releasing his hold. "It would seem our paths are shared. Perhaps we should travel together for a time to find what we have lost."

"I cannot—will not, Teimbaka; too much of me lies in another direction. It is a way I must see through to the end."

"Thieves! Liars!" came the shouts of the men of the village, who had joined the patriarch of the stone house. "Take them!"

"Come, Teimbaka."

"Go the way the Mother leads you," said Teimbaka. "And, Adiam—"

Adiam turned back.

"May She grace you with Her mercy, whatever may come to pass."

With a smile, Adiam lifted the kebero and the dula and threw them to Teimbaka.

"Truly these belong to you," he called over his shoulder as he began to run. "Too bad we left your weapons are on the outskirts of town!"

"One is fleeing! Catch him! Catch him!"

It was only then that Teimbaka recognized how close the mob of angry men was to him, and what threat it posed to Adiam's escape. Without thinking, he charged the closest of them, his dula held out before him as a barrier. He knocked him over, then challenged the remainder with a fearless glare. When he saw that none had the courage to step forward, he glanced at the fleeing form of Adiam and smiled; the fleet-footed youth was already far away.

"Why do you wait? Seize him! He has wronged us! He is a thief! Use the torches! Use the fire!"

Yeshie's shrill voice stirred angry mutterings from the men. Those carrying torches stepped to the fore, closed ranks in the shape of a scythe, and began to move on him. Flames were thrust toward him, forcing him to step back, lest he be burned.

"Force him into the river!" Yeshie screamed from her place at the back of the mob. "Let him drown or be taken by the crocodiles!"

The dark faces of the village men stared at him with contempt as they edged him backward to the water with the fire they brandished. Teimbaka looked to Yeshie with a deep sadness in his eyes and in his heart. But if she noticed him looking, he could not tell, for she had covered all but a slit of her face with her veil.

The sound of the water came to him then. It drew him to look upon it, rewarding him when he did with a dusting of soft yellow light that glittered in a swath upon its surface. It reminded him of the moments when he had first seen the spirit herd upon the lake, when all had finally seemed right, when dawn was filled with a promise that he had never imagined existed before.

Flames licked at his arms and his face. He swung his dula like a club and knocked them away. Once more he heard Yeshie's voice urge the men to burn him. Clutching the kebero, he swung the walking stick out toward the angry mob one more time before he turned and raced for the river.

From the edge of the shallow bank he jumped into the water, holding tightly to the kebero for support. The river welcomed him, drawing him down to where her currents ran swift and cold. Teimbaka wrapped his arms around the drum and held it close to his stomach. With his dula firmly clasped in one hand and the vision of the white bird materializing within his thoughts, he drifted with the flow, allowing the water to take him where it chose. For he was at her mercy and her will, having never learned how to swim.

**T**HIS IS JUST going to be the most perfect Thanksgiving ever! Well, not *ever*," Patricia added, glancing at Martin. "That would have been the one after—"

She let the sentence die, still not comfortable thinking about the days when Martin had returned from Korea.

"Go, Saint Augustine!" she yelled, her red-mittened hands cupped around her mouth. "Win one for Martin!"

"What did you say, dear? I couldn't quite catch what you were screaming." He craned his neck around toward Eleanor. "Did you hear what she was yelling, Eleanor?" he asked, a little exasperated. "The darn band is the only thing I can hear."

Patricia's eyes fell to the cumbersome hearing aid that was attached to Martin's left ear. For the thousandth time, as she thought about what it represented, her heart went out to her husband. She fought back the urge to cry.

"I said, I love you, you big palooka!" she hollered, bending close to his left side. "What did you think I said?"

Martin turned to his wife, the midday sun glinting off the scores of tiny scars that riddled the left side of his face and temple. He tapped the overly large contraption that covered what the shrapnel had left of his ear, running his fingers along the wires hanging out the back.

"Oh, is that all," he teased. "If I had known, I would have turned my good ear toward you. But I guess I don't hear too well out of that one, either."

He laughed at himself and his predicament, the same as he had done since his first day back with Patricia.

She ran a hand across his shoulders, a tender smile on her face. *So brave*, she thought, *always the brave front*. But her admiration was tinged with sadness. For the fact of the matter was that what he joked about his hearing was true: the ear that had no hearing aid attached to it was of little use to him, either. A shattered eardrum, the doctors had told them. In truth, Martin was legally deaf in both ears. But no one who had been in his presence could ever reach the conclusion that he was impaired. For he did not allow his hearing deficiency, as he termed it, to be one. And as he had told her time and again, he would never allow it to become one.

"I do hope Gabriel plays well today," Eleanor said aloud to no one in particular. "Won't enjoy his turkey if he don't."

Eleanor shielded her eyes from the sun as she scanned the backs of the players warming up on the field for her son's jersey number.

"I won't be enjoyin' none either, if he don't. Lord, give him the strength of ten men today."

She glanced sheepishly at the Mathises, hoping they didn't think her too foolish. While Martin hadn't heard a word she had said, Patricia's face was full of thought, her expression displaying her own hopes on the day.

"He'll do fine, " she said, "probably great."

Patricia hoped her words would come true, for even though Eleanor had raised Gabriel from the day they had stepped off the ocean liner, the reality was that he was the Mathis's legal son. It was a secret that they and Eleanor had kept all these years, having told no one, not even Gabriel himself. To all but the federal government and the state government of New Jersey, Gabriel Tate was just who he appeared to be: Gabriel Abraham Tate, son of Eleanor Tate. But where official records were filed and kept, he was, in reality, Gabriel Abraham Mathis, adopted son of Patricia Mathis and Senator Martin Lewis Mathis of New Jersey.

"This is a proud day for Saint Augustine's, ladies," Martin proclaimed, fiddling with the newly fitted glasses that were pinching the bridge of his nose. "I can hardly believe we're only one victory away from our first undefeated season." Martin sighed with joy as he contemplated the implications of what he had just explained.

"Whatever the outcome, however, we should be proud as all get out of Gabriel. Eleanor, he is a fine young man. You have done such a wonderful job with him." Martin patted her on her knee, adding with a wink, "Yup, a fine young man."

"He is, isn't he?" she said with pride. "Come on, son!" she yelled down to the field. "Run hard!"

Down on the playing field, Gabriel could hear nothing of what was being yelled to him from the bleachers. The band, sounding a bit off and a little too loud (as was its norm), covered up any shouts that might otherwise have reached the field. But Gabriel searched the hundreds of faces in the crowd in the bleachers, then did the same with the throng of people who had been too late to get a seat and were left to jockey for a spot along the fence that ringed the school's football field and track.

Out of habit and prompted by his mother's expectations, he waved to the bleachers, knowing she and the Mathises were somewhere there. But what he really was hoping for, as he scanned the crowd who had shown up for the sold-out game, was a glimpse of his girlfriend, Jennifer Stamper. Or the sound of her voice calling out his name.

Gabriel licked his lips and swallowed dryly. Even the crisp, cold air of the morning had not cleared his head yet. He inhaled sharply, wishing he had some water, all too aware that he should not have sneaked out of the house last night after his mother had gone to sleep. But any chance to see Jennifer was one he would always take. It had been that way since they had first gotten together, and he was sure, on this bright, sunny day in late November, that it would remain that way for the rest of their lives.

Just thinking of her pushed everything else aside, even the prelude to the biggest football game in the history of Saint Augustine. *Where is she?* he wondered. *Why isn't she here yet?* He scanned every blond-haired woman he could see one more time, making certain he had not overlooked her.

*Stupid game,* he thought with a little angst, *she's not here and I'm not with her. And even when she does get here—if she shows up—she'll probably be standing next to some jerk trying to put the make on her. Stupid game.*

"All right, huddle up! Huddle up! Kickoff team, sound off! Defense, get ready!"

Gabriel unsnapped one side of his chin guard from his helmet and halfheartedly jogged toward the sideline for the pregame huddle. While his Coach delivered the final pep talk before the game, Gabriel scanned the bleachers for Jennifer again.

Back in the stands, both the Mathises and Eleanor heard Coach Crimmens call the team together near the 50-yard line in front of the home team bench.

"Come on, Scarlet Knights! Come on, Saint Augustine! Come on, Gabriel!" they shouted in staggered outbursts.

The three laughed at themselves for being so excited.

"Pardon, me, ma'am."

Eleanor looked up to find a tall, grey haired, middle-aged man, dressed in a wool overcoat and matching hat, smiling down at her.

"Yes?" she politely responded.

"You are Mrs. Tate, aren't you? Gabe Tate's mother?"

"Gabriel Tate is his given name," she corrected him, "and yes, I am his mother."

The man tipped his hat to her.

"I just wanted to stop by before the game gets underway to say hello and wish you and your son luck. He's had a remarkable year. This will be the first chance I've had to come see him in person."

"Who are you?" Patricia asked straight away, peering around Martin's shoulder.

"My pardon to you—"

"Mrs. Mathis. And this is my husband, Senator Mathis," she told him with a touch too much pride in her tone.

"My pleasure, Mrs. Mathis, Senator. And I'm sorry for not introducing myself before." With another touch to the brim of his grey wool hat, he went on to say, "Jerry O'Rourke. I'm here representing Notre Dame."

"The university?" asked Eleanor.

"The very same, Mrs. Tate," he replied, smiling at her astonished tone.

"Your son's achievements on the field of play have drawn our attention, as I am sure they have for a good many schools."

"And the Scarlet Knights take the field for the opening kickoff!" the game announcer blared over the public address system. "Let's give the team a rousing hand!"

Amid the eruption of applause and shouts of encouragement from the people in the stands, Mr. O'Rourke tipped his hat once more to Eleanor and took his leave. When the din of the crowd subsided, Eleanor found herself still staring at the man's figure descending the bleacher steps. One of Patricia's hands took her own and squeezed.

"Notre Dame," Eleanor muttered, still in awe. "The university."

"Just proves how special he really is," Patricia told her, energized with the implications of what it would mean for Gabriel to attend Notre Dame on a football scholarship. "Gee, what a day this is turning out to be!"

"You know, ladies," Martin offered, his eyes twinkling with excitement, "it's just about going to make my heart explode when he takes the field for Yale next fall." With a wink and a nod, he went on, "Assuming he's accepted, which he will be. Stand aside Dartmouth! Give way, Princeton! And hide your heads in the mud, you vile creatures of Harvard! Gabriel Tate is on the way to Yale! The Ivy League title is ours!"

Patricia cuffed his shoulder and giggled.

"Oh, you! Don't you know who that was? Didn't you hear what university he wants Gabriel to attend?"

Martin leaned toward her and said, "Of course I want Gabriel to go. Yale may be tough, but he'll come out a better man for it. You'll see, Pat. Come on, Saint Augustine! Come on, Gabriel!"

Patricia could do nothing but smile and press her cheek against his shoulder.

As the ball was kicked off into a sky so clear and blue that it threatened to swallow the brown, oblong dot into its seemingly endless expanse, all eyes were drawn to it, mesmerized by each and every twist and turn it took. And as it traveled through the air, all the prayers, hopes and dreams of every parent, student, teacher, and alumnus of the red-and-white-clad Scarlet Knights traveled with it. For never in the history of the school had there been such a season as this: where a win against their arch-rival,

Holy Cross, would not only give St. Augustine an undefeated season, but a berth in the state championship game as well.

The two schools' rivalry game, traditionally played on Thanksgiving Day, had been a joke for much of the past quarter-century. For it had been an easy, lopsided win for Holy Cross for the past twenty-five years, and a humiliating, pounding defeat for Saint Augustine. But this year, the administration, the students, the team, and all who had ever graduated from Saint Augustine's had vowed that that would all change. Victory, in large part due to Gabriel Tate's athleticism and stellar play, was almost a certainty.

Within fifteen seconds, however, the enthusiasm of the Saint Augustine crowd was dealt a crushing blow. A collective "ugh" arose from the crowd of loyal fans when the opening kickoff was run back for a Holy Cross touchdown.

"Not to worry," Martin yelled out with a clapping of his hands. "Only one play. Only one play."

But when he bent sideways so he could speak in confidence to Patricia, he said, "Heck, they looked like a bunch of sissies, the way they were trying to arm-tackle that boy. I hope that's not going to set the tone for the day."

Unfortunately for every Scarlet Knight fan, the first play of the game was indeed a prelude to the bad tackling, bad blocking, dropped balls, fumbles and interceptions that occurred. Any miscue, it seemed, that could happen, did—and with all too much frequency.

For Eleanor and the Mathises, the first two quarters passed in a state somewhere between extreme discomfort and nightmare. Something was not right with Gabriel, they all told themselves in a code of arched eyebrows, deep sighs, and glances filled with dismay.

"Runnin' like he be knee deep in mud," Eleanor muttered at one point.

Martin and Patricia nodded their agreement, for Gabriel was not displaying any of the quickness, the power, or the ability to change direction on a dime that everyone had come to expect from him. He even fumbled the ball in the open field with no one around him, stopping the only drive that the Scarlet Knights had mustered into Holy Cross territory up to that point. By halftime, with the score 16 to 0 in favor of Holy Cross, Eleanor was close to tears, while Patricia sat in stunned silence, her hands covering her face.

"I don't know what in the world is wrong with 'im," Eleanor blurted out soon after the band had taken the field for the halftime performance. "He's not even thinkin' straight. Don't even look like he cares. You saw him after that fumble. Just walked off the field like nothin' happened. And what he be lookin' for all the time he not on the field? Land's sake, he more interested in what behind him than what's happenin' in the game. Lord! I feel like going down there and giving 'im a good shaking."

With the hurt and disappointment plain on her face, she turned to Patricia and Martin, seeking some solace.

"He just don't seem 'imself," she said with a pleading shake of her head. "I don't understand it, don't understand it at all."

"Did he sleep well last night?" Patricia asked.

"Should've. Went to bed the same time I did: 9:30. Got up at 7:00 likes we always do. Cooked 'im a big breakfast, too."

She pursed her lips and furrowed her brow.

"But, come to think of it, he didn't eat much of it."

"Maybe he's coming down with something," Patricia offered.

"I sure hope he not. Not this day. Nope," she stated with a frown. "Ain't the right day for that to be happenin'."

"Maybe the second half will be different," Patricia replied, putting on the best smile she could muster. "Maybe he's just saving himself for a big comeback, a big melodramatic finish."

Eleanor's frown became a little more severe.

"I'll skin his hide if that be what he doin'. No rhyme or reason to put us through somthin' like this just to make 'imself look good."

She paused, waiting for some input. When no one offered any, she continued.

"Don't know what it is. I noticed he been preoccupied lately, but I just chocked it up to a boy growin' into a man. Guess it ain't easy bein' seventeen with no brothers or sisters at home to talk with. People being rocketed into space, Cold War, hydrogen bombs, Russians. Land's sake, seems like there be trouble—"

She shook her head again and sighed.

"The band's not as bad as I remembered," Martin proclaimed, his face awash with a bright smile. "Though, you know my hearing can be a little off sometimes. What do you two think?"

"Martin," Patricia whispered crossly.

"Faith," he stated, looking at each of them. "Where is your faith? You give up too easily. Whatever the outcome, remember? Don't sell him short. Still plenty of game to go."

"Uh, hi."

The three looked up to find a teenage boy with wire-framed glasses and longish, unkempt hair looking down at them as though he knew them.

"Mrs. Tate, Mrs. Mathis, " he said with a nod to each. "And you, sir; might I assume that you are Senator Mathis?"

"Indeed I am, young man," Martin replied while he stood and shook the other's outstretched hand. "And you are?"

"Peter Lyons, sir." Leaning to address the two women more than Martin, he added with a nervous laugh, "I'm sure you probably don't remember me. I went to school with Gabriel in first grade. Chesterbrook Elementary, Mrs. Gallagher's class. I was the one—"

"Mrs. Gallagher, yes, I remember," Patricia said, giving Eleanor a look to see if she, too, remembered. "You know, Eleanor, the boy who was with Gabriel the day the dog—"

"Oh, my, yes! Such a long time ago! I didn't know you and Gabriel still keep in touch."

"Well we don't— Or haven't," Peter confessed with some embarrassment. "But I've never forgotten him or what he did for me."

Peter adjusted the wire-rimmed frames around his ears and tucked in the strands of hair that had fallen out around them.

"I— I—" he said before falling silent.

"Its nice to know that Gabriel has a friend who still thinks of him from so long ago," Patricia hurried to say. "It was very nice of you to have stopped by."

"Will you tell him I said hello? I don't know if he'll remember me, though."

"I'm sure he'll remember you," Eleanor said reassuringly. "And don't worry none, we'll tell 'im you stopped by. I just hope he's in a good mood after this game."

"Gabe will do just fine. Just like in kickball. He'll get it going."

Peter surveyed the field, and then with a hop and few hurried steps, made his way from the stands to field level.

"That was nice," said Patricia.

"Very nice," Eleanor agreed.

"Faith," Martin interjected, "that boy's got it."

Bolstered by Martin's unflappable belief in Gabriel, both Eleanor and Patricia regained some of the confidence they had brought to the stadium. They soon found themselves echoing the rhyming chants that the cheerleaders were hollering up into the stands.

*

A T HALFTIME, WITH most of the team's attention directed at Gabriel, the talk Coach Crimmens delivered to them in the locker room fell on deaf ears. For as all of them could easily see, by the way their star player was staring off into space slumped against one of the lockers, they could tell that Gabriel either didn't care about what had happened on the field during the first half, or he wanted to be somewhere else altogether. Either way, his seeming indifference to everything that was going on, was deflating. Mirroring that state of mind, after Coach Crimmens finished his halftime speech, the team filed out of the locker room in silence with their heads cast down.

For Gabriel, the walk back out to the playing field was as confusing as the haunting dreams he had been having over the past several months. Dreams that made his head throb and left him in a cold sweat. Dreams, that when he would awaken, would leave him with a dissolving glimpse of a small boys face that stared at him in silence, though his eyes were open wide and filled with terror.

It was troublesome enough that he still had a bit of a hangover from the rum and Cokes that he and Jennifer had partied with last night. But the looks he had gotten in the locker room from his teammates and coaches, and now from the faces he dared to glance at as he walked toward the field, were no less unnerving than those of the boy that would linger from his nightmares.

Narrowing his eyes, he tried to block out all the images and distractions, but a picture of Jennifer kissing some other guy, giggling at him when she looked his way, kept flooding into his thoughts. His head began to pound with a jolting, searing pain. Just the idea she was cheating on him was more than he could bear.

"Hey, Gabe! Kick it hard! Kick it straight!"

Gabriel scowled at the guy with the shaggy hair and the wire-rimmed glasses. *What the hell is the idiot shouting?* he thought. *And what the hell does it have to do with football?*

"Hey."

He froze.

"Jen," he whispered.

He turned and pushed his way toward the sound of her voice.

"What the heck?" someone protested as he jostled by.

Gabriel paid him no mind.

"Come on, Tate! Still a second half to play!"

Vaguely, he recognized Coach Crimmens's voice. But he was close to her now. He would be able touch her with a few more steps.

"I'm watching you," she mouthed with rose-pink lips he could still taste from a few hours ago. "Show me what you've got."

She flashed him her sexiest smile, then whirled around and drifted into the crowd. He kept sight of her as long as he could, her shining, white-blond hair holding him within her spell.

"Tate!"

Coach Crimmens grabbed him by the facemask and shook him.

"I don't know what's wrong with you or what the hell you think you're doing, but there's still a half of a game to be played, and I for one am not going to leave this field today without having given it my best shot! I am not going down without a fight, and I won't let this team go down without a fight! So if you don't think you can—"

"Coach!" Gabriel screamed. "Nobody's going down! Nobody's going to lose! We're going to win!"

Coach Crimmens slapped the side of Gabriel's helmet.

"Finally!" he yelled back, smiling when he saw the resolve in Gabriel's face. "Let's go, then! Let's go!"

Just before the two minute warning at the end of the game, Saint Augustine's had clawed its way back to be within two points; the score after fifty-seven minutes and thirty seconds of play: 16 to 14. Gabriel had done his part, scoring on a sixteen-yard screen pass on fourth and goal to go in the third quarter and then again on a thirty-three-yard draw with five minutes remaining in the game. But Holy Cross, who had played a tough, grind-it-out type of ball-control offense all game, had stayed true to its game plan and pounded the ball through the Scarlet Knight defense after the ensuing kickoff. Using their timeouts wisely, and with a bruising physicality, it had methodically worked its way down to the Scarlet Knights' twenty-seven-yard line. With just under a minute remaining, its kicker put a field goal through the uprights from thirty-four yards out to try to seal the win. Things looked bleak for Saint Augustine. It was now 19 to 14.

On the following kickoff, the ball seemed to descend from the sky in slow motion. As Gabriel waited, watching it turn end over end, he caught a glimpse of its shadow hurtling toward him through the grass. Suddenly, other shadows appeared next to it. Gathering, they swept toward him in a mass. With the pain in his head building, he looked up at the last moment to see the shapeless forms surge together to become one. Instinctively, he reached out with both hands and caught it, then cradled the ball into his arms.

As he burst forward—dodging, sidestepping, plowing through, and hurtling over the opposition—the pounding in his head began to throb with more severity. He suddenly found himself gasping for air through his mouth guard as he tried to stay focused on the white lines he was crossing. Off in the distance, he could hear what sounded like thunder rolling down upon him. The swell of the thunder began to reverberate inside his head, growing louder with each churning stride.

When the roaring suddenly burst inside his skull like a thunderclap, he dropped the ball, clutched the sides of his helmet with his hands, and dropped to one knee. The thunder enveloped him. He hung his head, dizzy and weak.

He did not hear what his teammates were shouting, or feel the hugs and slaps that they gave him. The thunder had become a continuous, pulsing roar. He was having trouble breathing. Suddenly, he felt himself being swept upwards, a tangle of arms and hands ferrying him towards an echoing din that both terrified him and filled him with joy. Slowly, as he caught his breath, his head began to clear. The thunder turned into stomping feet and clapping hands. He could hear his name being shouted. He looked up into the bleachers to find a sea of ecstatic faces. His headache disappeared.

Helmet raised, he jumped up on the bench and stared at the celebrating crowd, finding it impossible not to laugh with utter abandonment at the sight of so many cheering, adoring faces. It was a moment he would never forget, he told himself, made all the more special because Jennifer was there to witness it all.

Yet, his moment of complete joy would be short-lived. For as he began to walk off the field after the game had ended, he was drawn to a confrontation that was taking place between some of his teammates and members of the Holy Cross squad at midfield.

"Yeah, well who cares if you won!" one of them was shouting. "You had to use a nigger shit to do it! Nigger shit ain't winnin'! Nigger shit's just the same as cheatin'!"

Gabriel bolted toward the group of taunting Holy Cross players, ramming the ones closest to him. The blow knocked them backward off their feet. Filled with a fury he did not quite understand, he challenged the fallen players and their teammates with a look of sheer defiance.

"Nigger shit on you!" he screamed. "This nigger shit just shit on you! Just beat your white, chicken asses!" he spit, pounding his chest.

Glaring at them, he raised his clenched fists.

"And he'll do it again right now if you've got the stomach for it."

Suddenly, a tackle from behind sent him sprawling to the turf. Furious, he twisted and pulled his assailant beneath him. Without thinking, he started punching, pummeling his assailant with savage blows. Even when the arms of his own teammates began to pull him away, he kept swinging. Slowly, as he got himself under control, he heard voices muttering, "Stupid nigger." The downcast eyes of his teammates gave him a cold, odd feeling.

"Tate," came the pained and sputtering voice of Coach Crimmens.

Gabriel looked down and saw that his assailant was his own coach, his face oozing blood from his nose and mouth.

"Tate," he struggled to say, "you're— off— off the team. Get your stuff out of the locker room before I get there."

Dumbstruck, Gabriel wanted to explain, but the look on Coach Crimmens's face told him there was no point. He glanced around at his teammates, looking for some support, but they averted their eyes and stayed silent. His heart sank. His head started to pound again.

"Really? Not one of you? Nothing?" he asked in disbelief.

"Tate!" Coach Crimmens screamed.

Without another word, Gabriel ran off the field, slowing to a jog when he reached the section of plywood that had been set down to cover the soft surface of the track. The sound of his cleats on the thin, flat boards echoed the pounding in his head.

"Great game, young man."

Gabriel looked up and scowled at the grey-haired man who was standing at the opening of the fence.

"I was hoping, if you had a minute, that we could talk."

"I don't," was his terse response.

"I think if you could spare a moment young man, that you—"

Jerry O'Rourke went silent as Gabriel ripped off his helmet and threw it to the ground.

"Gabriel Tate! What's gotten into you? What's wrong?"

Eleanor's voice was high-pitched and filled with concern as she threaded her way through the crowd. When Gabriel saw her, he cringed, the sight of the old aqua-blue car coat she was wearing sparking a wave of embarrassment and anger.

"When are you going to get rid of that ugly thing?" he asked, the condemnation clear in his voice.

She stopped dead in her tracks and stared at him, bewildered.

"Old, ugly thing. Ought to have gotten rid of it years ago."

"That's enough," she told him, grabbing him roughly by the arm. "This coat's served me well, and I'll wear it till I decide it ain't got no more use."

He felt her trembling hand slide down his arm.

"This is a lovely coat," she went on. "Why, your—"

She caught herself before she lied.

"Gabriel! Gabriel! What happened? We saw the fight on the field! What's going on?"

Patricia's face was filled with worry as she and Martin raced up to him. Gabriel looked away.

"Blows were exchanged," Martin calmly stated. "Nothing good can come of it, Gabriel. Not ideal that it was your own coach."

"But I didn't know it was him!" Gabriel blurted out. "All I knew was that someone tackled me from behind! I thought I was being ganged up on!"

"What started it, Gabriel? Surely there's a good reason," said Patricia.

Gabriel looked at Patricia and said, "Mrs. Mathis." But he could not continue, again looking away and shaking his head.

"How in the world could there be a good reason?" Eleanor snapped. "You just won a football game that gets you into the state championship. What in the world you thinkin'?"

"Not for me," he mumbled.

"What's that?" Patricia asked, her eyes narrowing. "Eleanor, what did he say?" She grasped Martin's shoulder.

"Speak up, son," Eleanor instructed. "I ain't raised you to mumble. You gots somethin' to say, say it so we all can hear."

But Gabriel wouldn't repeat what he had said.

"I believe there will be no more football games played for Saint Augustine. Is that the case, Gabriel?"

Gabriel glanced at Martin, and then, in turn, let his gaze fall to Patricia and Eleanor; he nodded. The disbelief he saw in their eyes could not match what he was feeling.

"That's right, Mr. Mathis," he admitted, his voice barely louder than a whisper. Looking at Eleanor, he explained, "Coach threw me off the team. Told me to get my stuff and get the hell out."

"But—but you just won the game for 'em," she managed to say. "He can't— I mean— He can't be serious."

Eleanor looked at the Mathises with pleading eyes and an air of desperation.

"But how? He can't just— I don't understand, son."

Her face abruptly changing from disbelief to anger, she yanked hold of Gabriel's arms, pinned them to his sides, and squeezed his wrists.

"Now you tell me, Gabriel Tate, just what in God's holy name happened. Make me understand what's goin' on here."

Gabriel tried to pull away from her, but she would have no part of it.

"Now you tell me, ya hear? You tell me now."

Gabriel's face grew fierce, anger briefly flashing in his eyes. Eleanor gasped, stumbled back, and whispered, "What in the—?"

"You ever tired, Momma?" His tone was defiant. "You ever get mad, get angry?"

"Why, course I do. I think—"

"I don't mean just angry; I mean plain sick of everything mad."

He looked past her to include Martin and Patricia, his emotions swelling with each word.

"I'm tired of listening to it! Tired of just being expected to keep my mouth shut and take it!"

"What on earth—?"

"Nigger, Momma. Nigger!"

His brown-black eyes were filled with fury. His jaw trembled.

"You ever get tired of hearing it? Tired of having it used to make you feel like you were born from pig shit, like you're just a scab on a donkey's ass? Damn chicken shits!" He pounded his chest with a closed fist. "Pretend they're all your friends when they want something from you," he spat with a scowl on his face. "But then they're right there with their own kind when the nigger-baiting starts. Can't wait to join in." He pounded his chest again and leaned forward. "Oh, and don't go getting all angry 'bout it, boy," he chided himself, turning his face to the sky. "Cause we don't like that from our Negroes. Oh, no, just can't have that from—"

Eleanor's slap to his face was stunning. He looked down at her with all the pain and hurt that was inside him.

"Forgive me, Lord," Eleanor pleaded, her cheeks streaked with tears. "I— I—"

She searched her son's face for understanding or forgiveness. But there was nothing.

"I'm sorry, son," she cried, falling against him, awkwardly trying to get her arms around his padded body so she might hug him. "I don't know—"

"It's alright, Momma," he gently told her, planting a kiss on her cheek. "Maybe it doesn't bother you anymore. Maybe you're used to it, just accept it as being normal."

"That's not it at all," she told him, pushing off his chest. "Don't ever think that I—"

"Tate! I told you to get off the grounds! Move it, or I'll have you jailed for assault!"

Coach Crimmens was almost sprinting when he reached them.

"And if you think I'm joking," he added, bumping Gabriel with his puffed-out chest and sticking his face right under his nose, "you just keep standing there. I'll have the police here in no time, and they can drag your—"

"I believe it was you, sir, who struck the first blow."

Martin's voice was calm but forceful. Coach Crimmens reacted to it as though a cannon had been shot off behind him. Whirling with a vengeance, he shouted, "And just who the hell are you, mister? Ever hear of minding your own business? Ever hear of shutting up?"

Martin ushered Eleanor and Patricia behind him.

"I propose that neither your tone nor your anger is warranted or appreciated. And as for who I am, what does it matter? A common citizen is all I need be to testify in this young man's behalf." He went on, "And as for you, *coach*, perhaps you are unaware of the penalty for giving false statements to the authorities or committing perjury in a court of law."

Coach Crimmens's face contorted with anger.

"You stupid, jackass," he spat. "Look at my face! Look at the blood! See my split lip, you idiot! And you're going to take the side of this— this—"

"Young man," Martin offered with a smile.

Coach Crimmens's mouth trembled as he scrambled to find the words he wanted to hurl back at Martin. At a loss, however, he was reduced to casting intimidating glances at each of them before stalking off in a huff.

"Lord bless us all," Eleanor intoned. "What's gone wrong with this day?"

"That man ought to be fired," Patricia said with some vehemence. "Can't you do something about him, Martin?"

But Martin did not hear her, or pretended not to, for he was focused on Gabriel.

"Days never seem to unfold as we might like them to" he said to him. "I'm sorry this had to happen on the day we celebrate as Thanksgiving. I fear any thanks will be tempered at best."

He looked over his shoulder at the receding form of Coach Crimmens.

"For some, there won't be any at all."

"Good day to you folks," Jerry O'Rourke bade them with a tip of his hat. "And good luck to you, young man," he said as he walked away, though he did not seek to make eye contact with Gabriel.

"There goes Notre Dame."

"What's that you said, Mother?"

Eleanor smiled, gladdened that he had called her Mother.

"Not important, not important. But what is, is that we all together and that there's a big, juicy turkey waitin' for us at home."

She smiled as best she could, looking to each as she smoothed out her aqua-blue car coat.

"So what say you all to just be puttin' all this to rest for a time and just be thankful? The troubles of the world can wait—even our own. Even the good Lord takes a day off, you know. I think we can spare an afternoon."

"Was that a peach pie I smelled baking in the kitchen this morning?" Patricia asked. "It smelled out of this world!"

"Peach-blackberry it was. I made it special for today," Eleanor stated with pride. "One of Gabriel's favorites."

She hoped the mention of the pie might bring a smile to his face, but Gabriel's expression had not changed: still dour, still pensive.

She looked to Martin, but he seemed as troubled as Gabriel.

"Now come on, you two. Stop actin' like the world won't be movin' till you ready to hop on it. Time's a wastin'. Turkey needs tendin'."

Martin returned her smile and then gave a wink to his wife.

"We'll be along presently. Why don't the two of you warm up the car? I'd say we could all use a touch of heat for our toes right about now."

"Good idea. Come on, Eleanor. Let's give the men a few minutes to chat. We'll come back and pull them by their ears if they're not in the car in ten minutes."

Patricia gave her husband a knowing look.

"We'll be there before you know it," he told them. "Hardly miss us at all," he added as the women took their leave.

He watched them walking for a few moments before turning to Gabriel. He was not surprised to find him still staring at the ground.

"Sucks, doesn't it?"

Gabriel's distraught expression turned into a smile as he raised his head.

"I never heard you say that before, Mr. Mathis," he said with a chuckle. "Didn't even think you knew words like that."

Martin let his eyes drift skyward.

"I've said worse, much worse in my time, Gabriel. And don't you think it's about time we get over this 'Mr. Mathis' stuff?" Martin smiled. "Can you just call me Martin, or Marty, or Deafy?" he suggested with a laugh, tapping his hearing aid. "After all, I've watched you grow up since you were midget, you know. I would have thrown in the name Whitey, because of my hair, but I doubt you could see past the other implication."

Gabriel's smile faded, the lines of troubled thoughts taking its place. He looked Martin straight in the eye.

"Is it always going to be this way? Are white folks always going to try to take away what people of my color do? Try to make me feel like I'm a cheater when I do something good? Call me nigger if I beat them in a game or get a better grade? Stick together no matter what, when there's a Negro involved?"

He paused to gauge Martin's reaction.

"'Cause if things don't change...." His shoulder pads lifted and fell as he took a deep breath. "God help us all, Mr. Mathis—uh, Pops," he said, forcing a momentary grin. "if things don't. People can't just go around sayin' nigger anymore. It ain't right. We, I—I know I'm not gonna let it happen. Already trouble in the South because of it; beatings, Ku Klux Klan, cross burnings, hangings—it's all just gonna explode." With his lips beginning to tremble, he went on. "I just won a football game for this—this—school—and they just all stand around and do nothing when the other team calls me a nigger! You'd think one of my so called teammates would stand up for me!" With his jaw clenching and unclenching, Gabriel fought the tears pooling in his eyes. "It ain't right! It just ain't right!"

"No it isn't," Martin softly agreed.

Gabriel glared at him before running the back of his hands across his eyes. "Bunch of white chicken shits," he hissed. "Bigots." He shook his head and let his shoulders slump. "It ain't right."

"No, as you put it, Gabriel, it ain't right. You'd like to just wish it all to be so that everyone one would just sort of wake up and see that it's time that we all need to get along, move ahead. If it were only that easy."

"Nothing's easy."

"No, no, I agree. Nothing is easy. So where does that leave us?"

Gabriel frowned and said, "That life sucks."

"At times, it does," Martin concurred with a nod. "But here we are, aren't we? We're right smack dab in the middle of it—the good and the bad of it. Almost makes you forget sometimes—all the bad stuff—about all the good things. The nasty side of life makes our mouths sour, makes us spit everything else out, or tries to. Like being called a nigger; now there's a stupid, nasty, sour-tasting word. And for me, an unforgivable one, but there will be worse ahead. There always is."

Martin ran his fingers over each of the scars on the side of his face and head.

"There is a brutality in this world that's hard to imagine."

Martin lapsed into his past, sifting through everything he had been through. To Gabriel, it was an awkward silence.

"No offense, uh, Pops, but that doesn't do a whole lot for me."

"Doesn't do a whole lot for anyone. Just knowing about something doesn't change what it is. Bigotry is bigotry, whether you recognize it or not. Injustice is always injustice, even if everyone who is a witness to it agrees that it is. So, yeah, knowing there'll be worse ahead doesn't do much for anybody."

Martin shivered. Gabriel looked away.

"But here we are, standing right in the middle of what sure seems like a big, confusing, unfair mess. So what should we do? Throw in the towel? Call it quits? Hope that somebody else steps in and cleans it all up?

Gabriel studied the older man for a time before shrugging his shoulders.

"Don't know, I guess."

"Don't quit, don't give up, never stop trying."

"But—"

"Bigotry has been around for a long, long time, Gabriel, and it comes in all shapes and sizes. It'll be around a while longer too, I'm afraid to say. So if you want change, even if you think you won't be able to enact it, you have to try. You have to believe you can. Because you have to hold to the notion that, somewhere down the road, what you do is going to make a difference."

Gabriel looked away with a sigh. His attention drifted to the line of cars slowly exiting the school's parking lot.

"I guess I must sound like, like a— What do I sound like?"

"A mother," Gabriel told him flatly. "And I already got one of those."

Martin laughed. "Been called a lot of things, but never a mother. I'll have to file that one away."

He waited for Gabriel to laugh, but he showed no indication that he found anything amusing.

"What's the sense in tryin', if things are never going to change?" Gabriel blurted out, running an open palm over the clenched fist of his other hand. "And don't try to fool me with that stuff about changing the world. You even said as much. It just doesn't happen."

Martin tapped the edge of his thumb against his front teeth a few times before answering.

"Changing the world takes a cumulative effort. Changing *your* world only takes you."

"Like I can change any of this right now," Gabriel countered, waving his arm to encompass the football field.

"Well don't expect anyone else to do it for you. It's just you and me standing here."

Gabriel's face flashed with anger. He pursed his lips.

"It's hard isn't it, having to grow up before you're ready?"

Gabriel stared at the ground.

"It was for me."

Stone faced, Gabriel looked up and out across the football field.

"Confusing, this thing called life. Not easy to keep a handle on, to see it clear all the time. It has the tendency to spin you around in a lot of different ways. Sometimes it makes you feel like you don't have a clue."

"Like now?" Gabriel grunted, turning his face to Martin.

"Yeah, like now."

Gabriel took a deep breath and grabbed the opening of his shoulder pads around his neck with both hands.

"So what am I supposed to do?" he grudgingly asked.

Martin tapped his head and then his chest. "Believe in yourself. Trust your instincts. May sound overly simplistic, but down the road, that's all there really is to hang your hat on."

"Then I wasn't in the wrong for sticking up for myself?"

"No, not for sticking up for yourself."

"Doesn't sound like you believe it."

"Not the sticking up part, but—"

"I knew it."

"It's the part where punches were thrown. That doesn't need to be part of the deal."

"You mean, Coach?"

"See, you knew it all the time."

"But he didn't have to tackle me. He could've just grabbed me by the arm and just yelled at me or something."

"Yes, he could have," Martin agreed whole-heartedly. "But he didn't. And that's where *he* was wrong."

"So I should still be on the team, right?"

"Unfortunately for you, he has the power—and he used it—to do just what he did. It's a tough lesson to swallow," he added. "Nobody comes out a winner in this. Everyone loses. In this case, your coach has made it worse by making another bad decision just because he has the upper hand. I guess he thinks it's all ended."

"Hasn't it?" Gabriel asked, letting his hands fall away from his shoulder pads to hang by his sides. He took an abrupt step sideways and kicked at the football helmet sitting on the ground.

"He was rash, Gabriel. And there are usually consequences to face when you don't use your head and just act in the moment, on impulse."

Gabriel glanced at the laces of his cleats.

"Guess I fall into that category too, don't I?"

"What do you think?" Martin said with a shrug.

"You ever call anyone a nigger, Mr. Mathis?"

"That's Pops to you, and no, not up to this point, anyway."

"I don't understand. You mean you might?"

"How can I answer one way or the other, yes or no? I'm just like everybody else. I can get angry, lose my head, lash out at someone for no better reason than just to be hurtful. Don't get me wrong—I hope to God that I don't. But," he lamented with another shrug of his shoulders, "I'm no nearer to perfection than you are. And here you referred to folks with my skin color as … chicken white asses, was it?"

Gabriel smiled wryly.

"So much for bigots only being white, I guess."

Martin raised his eyebrows and smiled. "Point well made."

In unison, the two men looked out over the football field and the empty bleachers. It was hard for either of them to come to grips with the fact that, less than a half-hour before, those bleachers had been filled with an exuberant, cheering crowd. Harder still to realize that Gabriel's days as the star halfback for the Saint Augustine Scarlet Knights was over.

"So what now?"

Gabriel furrowed his brow and sighed.

"Guess I take these off for the final time and head home. Slip in and out of the locker room as best I can."

"I should sincerely hope you wouldn't do that."

Gabriel rolled his eyes and shook his head. "Don't tell me. Let me guess. Going quietly is the easy way out."

Martin smiled.

"I should walk in there with my head held high and look everyone straight in the eye, right? Then maybe speak up and tell them it was great to be their teammate for the past three years, that we had a great run, and that I enjoyed every minute of it," he added with a touch of sarcasm. "Or maybe I should say that bigotry has no place amongst teammates, and that, sooner or later, each and every one of us is going to have to come to grips with race if we ever hope that things will be better in this world." Jutting his chin outward, he tilted his head to one side and raised his hands with his palms facing skyward. "Good?"

Martin raised an eyebrow and shook his head no.

"Oh, right. I forgot. And then I should find Coach Crimmens and tell him that two wrongs don't make a right and that I'm sorry for making his stupid chicken-white-shit-ass-face all bloody."

Gabriel allowed himself a smug laugh.

"An interesting perspective, that last part. Exactly what I might have said, had I been in your place, deleting those inflammatory adjectives at the end, of course. Perhaps there is a future for you in politics."

"Don't see that happenin,' Pops," he chuckled with a shake of his head.

"I felt the same way when I was your age."

"Well, if you think—"

"Oops," Martin interrupted, tapping at his hearing aid, "I hear us being summoned."

Gabriel looked over at the parking lot and saw Mrs. Mathis stepping out of the big silver Cadillac the Mathises owned.

"Mrs. Mathis is just getting out of the car," he relayed, somewhat perplexed. "How could you have heard—"

"The intuition of a married man," Martin told him, tapping his hearing aid. "I know she had the doctors plant some of it in here before they attached it to my ear," he explained with a smile. "Clever girl, that one. Never ceases to amaze me."

Martin turned and waved to his wife. She waved back and then got back into the car.

"Want me to come with you? Or would it be better if I wait in the car with the ladies until you're ready to leave with us and go home."

"I think it best if I go alone."

"Yes, I agree. Plus, it wouldn't look very manly, what with your girl looking on."

Gabriel's lips parted. He shuffled his feet. "What are you talking about? What girl?"

"The blonde. The one who got you going in the second half of the game. That same really pretty young lady who is sitting in the driver's seat of that flashy yellow Stingray over there. I suppose you've been sneaking out at night to see her?"

Gabriel did his best to let his face go blank, but his eyes kept flicking back and forth between Martin and where Jennifer was parked.

"I don't know what you're talking about," he weakly protested, offering a half-hearted laugh.

"I may be an old fossil to you, Gabriel, but I'm not blind or dumb just yet. What's her name? I'd like to meet her."

Gabriel stared at the yellow Stingray for a few moments.

"No offense, Pops, but maybe you haven't noticed that she's, uh, the same—got the same skin color as you."

"Oh, much better than mine," he replied. "Makes me lament my youth. She really is very striking. I doubt if I could have ever attracted someone that pretty, even at my best. Don't say that I ever said that around Mrs. Mathis, though."

"She's white and I'm not," Gabriel pointed out.

"Yes, she is. Is that what drew you to her?"

"Time to go, Mr. Mathis," Gabriel abruptly announced, turning to walk away. "You better go to the car, or—"

"Gabriel."

Reluctantly, Gabriel stopped and turned back. Martin drew closer and lightly grasped his forearm.

"Walk carefully there," he told him with a nod to the Stingray. "There are those who will not understand."

*

"AND MAY THE sacrifices of those who gave so much not be made in vain or go unrewarded. Let there be healin' where there be pain, forgiveness, where there be hurt. And where there be blindness, oh Lord, caused by ignorance and fear, we ask that You, by Your light, give those souls the miracle of sight. And lastly, dear Lord, I ask that You bless this house and those round this table for this meal that we 'bout to receive, by the fruit of Thy bounty, amen.

"If I may," Martin hurried to get in before Eleanor began to make the sign of the cross.

"Please," she acquiesced, refolding her hands.

Martin rose to his feet.

"May I add, though it is not often that I invoke the Lord's name to do our bidding, that we ask that there be peace in this world, and that no young men or women will need to sacrifice themselves in wars that make no sense. I ask this of You, Lord, on this Thanksgiving Day, because it must be so."

"Amen," Eleanor added when Martin fell silent.

"Yes, amen," he said.

"Anyone else have somethin' they wish to add? Gabriel? Patricia?"

Patricia glanced at Gabriel with a pensive look before enthusiastically gushing, "Yes; let this food we are about to eat not be cold due to my husband's impromptu speech—as lovely as it might have been."

She giggled at him, her face scrunched up with mischief. But when Martin returned her giggle with a blank expression, she rolled her eyes to the ceiling and asked with a touch of annoyance, "Martin, did you hear what I said?"

"I'm sorry, dear. What's that you said?"

"I said—"

"Food's getting cold, you know," he told her, trying his best to suppress the smile at the corners of his lips. "If you don't finish what you're trying to say pretty quickly, none of us will enjoy our meal."

Patricia's expression went from disbelief to anger to amusement.

"You! I'll get you for this."

"Can't hear a word you're saying," he quipped, with a finger pointing to the plastic blob where his ear should have been.

"Someday that's not going to be so funny."

"Someday, yes, but not today."

They all laughed at the exchange—even Gabriel, they were glad to see—although his laughter was short-lived and without the same joy.

Shortly thereafter, Martin carved the turkey and served each of them their plates. They delved with gusto into the feast that Eleanor had spent hours preparing.

"Delicious," came the compliments after they had sampled each item. But soon after, the meal fell into an uncomfortable silence, save for the occasional clinking of silverware on china.

In time, the uneasy silence drew concerned glances from Martin and Patricia. Finally, with a look from Martin that conveyed "your turn" to his wife, Patricia broke the quiet.

"I think you've outdone yourself this time, Eleanor. Might be the best Thanksgiving meal you've ever made."

"No prizes awarded just yet, dear."

"Martin!" she said incredulously.

"No concrete decision can be reached until dessert has been sampled," he explained with an engaging smile. "But just the sound of a peach and blackberry pie, warmed and served with a touch of French vanilla ice cream, leads me to cast my vote with yours, dear. But I must be fair," he went on, holding up a hand in mock protest. "Rash decisions are never wise decisions, especially where dessert is involved."

Eleanor smiled at the complimentary bantering, but her thoughts were elsewhere.

"And how you like your meal, son? Anythin' to say?"

Gabriel remained silent, engaged as he was in a staring contest with the pool of gravy nestled inside his mound of mashed potatoes.

"Gabriel, I asked you a question."

Patricia dropped her knife on the table, the substantial clang it produced causing Gabriel to look up.

"I'm sorry. Did I miss something?" he asked when he realized the three of them were staring at him.

"President Kennedy just called and invited you to the White House," Eleanor told him. "But he hung up when you wouldn't take the phone."

"Oh, I'm sorry," he replied with sincerity.

Eleanor frowned.

"Would you like some sweet potatoes in your ears, dear? Or how 'bout some green beans up your nose?"

"That's fine, Momma." When he saw the look on her face, he added, "All the food is really good, as always."

Eleanor sighed, exasperated.

"How did things go in the locker room?" Martin inquired as he lanced a piece of turkey from the platter with his fork. "I meant to ask you earlier."

Gabriel shrugged and said, "Okay, I guess. Nothin' that I was surprised at."

"And how did your teammates respond to the little speech you gave them?"

"They never heard it," he relayed without much emotion.

"What speech was that, son?"

Martin eyed Gabriel with concern when he seemed to have nothing further to say on the matter.

"Gabriel was going to go into that locker room with his head held high—as it should have been—and tell the rest of his teammates what he thought about bigotry, and how it has no place on a team or in a school or in any of their lives."

"Why that's wonderful!" Patricia gushed. "It's about time someone spoke out against it. It's such a stupid way to think. I don't understand why some people are like that."

Her enthusiastic smile slowly faded when she saw that Gabriel was not warmed in the least by what she had said.

"Somehow I get the sense that it didn't happen that way, though," Martin interjected. "Is that right, Gabriel? What did happen?"

"Coach invoked a gag rule on everybody before I got there," he said in a monotone, once more engaging in a stare down with his gravy and mashed potatoes. "So nobody would talk to me or listen to me or even look at me. So I said the hell with it."

"Gabriel! We don't use that language—"

"Sorry, Momma. I meant 'the heck with it.'"

"What about Coach Crimmens? Did you get an opportunity to speak with him?"

"He had his office door closed and locked," Gabriel relayed with a swift, sarcastic smile. "Didn't feel much like talking to a door, so I left without saying a word to anyone. And no one said one to me. Segregation at its finest."

"That's disgraceful. He ought to be fired or suspended or something. Martin, can't you, won't you do something?"

"I don't want anybody to do anything," Gabriel stated forcefully, his anger rising to the surface. "I'll fight my own battles."

"Gabriel! There's no call for that tone here. Mrs. Mathis just tryin' to help."

"My apologies," he was quick to respond. "No offense intended."

"None taken, Gabriel. And you're quite right to be angry. Well he is, Eleanor," she said, casting a look of support for Gabriel toward her. "Anybody would be if they had been treated like that. It's just not right. Something should be done. Someone should speak out."

"Somebody is and has been doing so for some time," Gabriel flatly told her. "His name is Reverend King—Martin Luther King."

"Who?"

"A very passionate and eloquent speaker who's been speaking and organizing demonstrations in the South, dear. He's causing quite a stir in Washington, I might add," Martin told her.

"That's all fine and well, but I still think action should be taken against that coach. It shouldn't be condoned, what he's done."

"Mrs. Mathis," said Gabriel.

"When are you going to start calling me Patricia?"

"Patricia, then," he said, giving Martin a quick glance. "I still have to finish out the year there. And I doubt if it would be very pleasant if the coach were fired because of what happened to me. Don't think it would go over too well with the other three of us who go there, either."

"You're not implying that—"

"Sorry to say, but I am, Mrs.— Patricia. Prejudice isn't just confined to the South or buzz-headed football coaches who were born there. May not be as bloody or as vocal as it is in Alabama and Mississippi, but it's hovering around the hallways of Saint Augustine's just the same. Right outside this house too. Good old Rumson's the same as anywhere else."

"I've never noticed any prejudice here," Patricia relayed with an air of shock, looking perplexed.

"Why would you? You're white."

"Gabriel Tate! That most surely is enough!"

Eleanor's face was harsh, unforgiving, and worn.

"I'm just—"

"This ain't the time or place to be talkin' 'bout this. Maybe you forget what day it is, or supposed to be."

"I'm just trying to explain, trying to— After what happened to me today, about how I feel."

"Oh, really?" Eleanor chided. "And just what happened to you today that makes you think that we all—"

"Getting thrown off the team without a second thought! Like I was nothin'!" he told her, his expression harsh. "Do you think that would have happened if I were white?"

"After beatin' up your coach? I should hope so. I'd hope anybody be thrown off of any team for actin' like that. Knockin' them boys over 'cause they called you a name. Punchin' your coach's face till it was a bloody mess. Blind stupid is what it was. Just plain damn dumb—excuse my French."

She trembled as she sat and glared at him.

"You just don't see it, do you?" said Gabriel.

"Oh, I see it all right, young man. See it plain as day. I see somebody makin' excuses for what they done."

She huffed and fidgeted in her chair.

"You got yourself into this. You, Gabriel, not nobody else. And don't go leanin' on the color of your skin for what happened. Land's sake, you start usin' that as a crutch—that you be a Negro—and you be hobblin' on it for the rest of your life. God didn't put anybody on this earth so he have to listen to 'em whine 'bout their lot in life. Person makes their own way in this world. Gotta stand on your own two feet, no matter what. So don't cry to me cause we be Negro," she stated firmly, shaking her head. "Don't be using what you are to excuse what you done. Uh-uh. No, sir. 'Cause it don't fool me one bit. No, not one bit."

Eleanor was at once conscious of the fact that she had become the center of attention. Squirming at the notion, uncomfortable with the expressions of concern on the faces around her, she grabbed the edge of the table.

"Please excuse me," she apologized, stifling the tears that were ready to burst, "I never meant to ruin dinner."

"Eleanor."

She waved Patricia off as she got up from her chair and hurried out of the dining room.

"If you'll excuse me as well," Gabriel added, pushing away from the table. "I don't think I should be here right now."

"Gabriel."

Gabriel left the dining room through the doorway opposite the one that Eleanor had taken.

"This is terrible, Martin. I don't understand why they are fighting."

Martin looked across the table at his wife, mirroring her worried look with one of his own. He took a moment to respond, choosing his words carefully. When he finally spoke, neither he nor Patricia found any comfort in what he had to say.

"I feared this day might come. I never saw where it might take us, you know, when we stumbled across him in that river—that river of sand. Ethiopia seems as if it is an entirely different world now, doesn't it? And it looks as though things are about to change for all of us once again."

*

T HE STINGRAY LEAPT forward as Gabriel pushed down on the accelerator. The sudden surge of power pressed Jennifer farther back into her seat.

"Hey! Slow down! All I need is to have Baby linked to another speeding ticket. Daddy said one more, and he'd take Her away."

But even as the words left her mouth, she put her head back into the leather and closed her eyes; she loved the sensation of speed.

"But go ahead and get stopped by a statey, if you want. It might be fun to see the look on his face when he sees a pretty white chick riding along with a—" she looked at him sideways, her eyes round with feigned shock, "a Negro, of all things."

She laughed while smoothing her long, platinum-blonde hair.

"Shit, I might even say you stole the car and forced me to come along. Oh, God," she went on, her laughter heightened, "that *would* be funny."

The car slowed immediately, the pulse of the roaring engine subsiding as they drove down River Road.

"Not even close to funny tonight, Jen. Not one damn bit funny."

Gabriel tried his best to sound angry, but Jennifer knew better; knew that, even if he was mad, he couldn't stay mad at her for more than a few seconds.

"Then again, maybe it would be funny," he countered. "Might just tell the officer that we had sex countless times and that you enjoyed it each and every time. Might even tell your daddy the same thing when he came to see 'that nigger bastard' in jail. Think that'd be funny, Jen? Huh?"

"Jesus God, Gabriel! Don't you ever let those words leave your mouth. He'd kill us both without a second thought." After a few seconds, she added, "Probably kill himself after that, too. Poor little Daddy, thinking his life was over. Everything he worked for ruined, a disgrace."

"I'll shut up if you'll shut up, then. Deal?" Gabriel chuckled.

"Deal—signed, sealed, and done."

Without warning, Jennifer leaned over and planted a hard, wet kiss on his lips, slipping her tongue into his mouth for a delicious moment. The Stingray swerved sharply. The blare from a car horn forced him to turn his face away.

"You trying to get us killed?"

"Oh, to die in a lover's embrace," she replied in her best Shakespearean voice, "how sweet death would taste."

"Maybe for you, Miss Temptress, but this boy ain't ready to make that crossing just yet. Too many places to go, too many touchdowns to score."

"Shit! I almost forgot! I have something celebrate your," she looked at him with an impish grin, "magnificent display of athletic supremacy."

She giggled like a girl of five.

"I accept your esteemed opinion," he concurred with a nod and a broad smile. "What, therefore, is my reward?"

She turned, tucking her legs beneath her so she could kneel.

"I thought a bit of moonshine was in order," she announced as she reached behind her seat. "Sour mash for the man who mashed Holy Cross."

Gabriel rubbed his head, his expression pensive as Jennifer pulled the pint bottle of bourbon from a brown paper bag.

"What's wrong, Gabe? I thought you liked this stuff as much as me."

"I do, but—"

"Yeah, I'm listening."

He frowned at himself in the car's rearview mirror.

"I've got one of my stupid headaches again. Had it since I scored that last touchdown on the kickoff return."

"Pussy."

Without hesitating, Jennifer broke the seal of the bottle with her thumbnail and screwed the top off. With a hint of wildness in her sparkling blue eyes, she put the bottle to her lips and took a quick swig.

"That one was for me," she announced, holding the bottle aloft. "And this one is for—"

"I'll drink mine myself, thank you," he told her, grabbing the bottle out of her hand before she could drink any more.

"Thought you had one of your mysterious headaches. Thought the hounds of hell were barking inside your head."

The Stingray suddenly swerved toward the curb. Jennifer grabbed the steering wheel with one hand and the bottle of bourbon with the other.

"Hey! You okay?"

"Shit, sorry. Soon as you said it, the barking got louder. And the face of that—"

"Hey, I'm sorry. It was a joke, you know," she apologized.

Jennifer released the steering wheel and gently ran her hand along his cheek.

"Not your fault," he told her, stealing a glance. "Little demons never give me a moment's peace," he added lightly, doing his best to sound upbeat.

"I might have something to quiet them."

"Right here in the car? While I'm driving? Boy, I love the vixen side of you."

"No, not that, big boy. Least not yet," she told him, squeezing his thigh. "That's for later, señor, when my body is afire with love."

"Is that Spanish or Italian? I can't seem to place the accent."

"I am both," she replied seductively. "I am many. I am, as they say, the temptress d'amore."

They both erupted with laughter. Celebrating the moment, Gabriel took the bottle of bourbon from her and took a long, hard swig.

"Hey, don't drink it all! Give me some more of that fire water!"

"I don't know if that's a good idea. I'm not sure I can handle you being any more crazy then you already are."

"Give me the bottle," she said through clenched jaws before growling at him.

When he jerked a hand to his head, she realized what she had done.

"Oh, God, Gabe. I didn't mean to. I really didn't."

"It's okay, Jen." He handed her the bottle of bourbon and massaged his brow with his fingers. "I know you didn't mean nothin'."

Jennifer took another hurried swig of bourbon, hoping to calm herself. She replaced the cap and then stowed it back behind the driver's seat. She shimmied the hem of her skirt down and adjusted her pantyhose.

From the corner of his eye, Gabriel watched as she unbuttoned the front of her blouse down to the bottom of the V of her burgundy V-neck sweater. He felt the stirring in his crotch when her hand reached inside her blouse and slid under her bra. He could almost feel the smoothness of her flesh as her fingers worked their way around her breast and the lace that cupped it.

"Here we go," she giggled. "Thought maybe they had disappeared for a moment."

"Don't ever let those beauties disappear. All of the men in the world will mourn if that day ever comes."

"Not my boobs, dummy. These."

Gabriel squinted to see what she was holding, trying to focus on what was in the palm of her hand every time the car passed underneath a street lamp.

"Cigarettes? Not for me, thanks."

"These aren't Winstons, honey."

"Marlboro, Winstons—doesn't matter what kind. You know they make me sick to my stomach."

Jennifer put one of the cigarettes between her lips and struck a match from a pack she took from the glove compartment.

"This isn't tobacco, Gabe. This is the high-octane stuff."

As the small flame touched the tip of the hand-rolled, pencil thin, filter-less cigarette, Jennifer inhaled deeply. Holding her breath, she offered the smoldering rollup to Gabriel.

"Here," she gasped while trying to suck air in. "Take a hit. But don't inhale a big one till you get used to it. It's pretty harsh."

She exhaled while closing her eyes.

"God, what's that stinking smell?"

"It's what's going to get rid of all those mysterious little demons you have living in your head." She giggled. "It's the dreaded marijuana ciga-rette," she teased. "It will make us crazy. Make us seek out an encounter with a U.F.O."

"Stinks like all get out."

"You going to try it, or just sit there and complain about it? Cause it burns pretty quick. So if you don't want some, I'll have my *joint* back please." Laughing, she added, "That's what I was told to call it."

"Who told you?"

"Later. Right now, let's do this."

She guided his hand to his lips.

"Inhale on it a little, now, Gabe. Seriously, it's not going to hurt you. Promise. It may even really make those little you-know-whats from hell disappear. Go on, now, just a little puff, okay? For me?"

With a slight shrug of his shoulders, Gabriel did as Jennifer bade him to do.

"Hold it in, now. And if you feel like coughing—don't."

She took the joint from his fingers, watching him for any reaction to the marijuana.

"Hey, hey, don't suffocate yourself," she told him, taking another drag. "Exhale. Good. Now take another puff. Do as the doctor says, now, Gabe. There, now, that wasn't so bad, was it?"

By the time they had finished smoking the joint, the skyline of New York City glittered ahead of them. The lights of the skyscrapers seemed to sparkle brighter than they had ever done before. Gabriel drove toward them with a smile. Jennifer touched his hand and gazed up at build-ings with wonder in her eyes. With a heightened sense of anticipation and adventure, they began the crossing into Manhattan via the George Washington Bridge.

"King Kong."

Gabriel heard her voice, but it seemed as though she was speaking through a tunnel. His eyes swept the skyline until he found the Empire State Building. And there, just as she had said, he imagined the mighty ape climbing up the sides, one massive arm swatting at the miniscule air-planes trying to do him harm.

"Do you see him?"

He nodded his head and murmured, "Fighting off an army of lunatics."

"Lizards of habit, seeking flies."

He shook his head, wondering if he had heard her right.

"What did you say?"

"Sounded cool, didn't it?" she asked excitedly.

"What? What sounded cool?"

"What I said; just the sound of it. Just the way the words rolled off my tongue."

"Lizards of craziness searching for bats?" he offered.

"That's even better."

"Better than what?"

"What I said."

Gabriel strained forward to try to see the top of the Empire State Building. King Kong was no longer there.

"He's gone."

"I think we both are," she agreed with a chuckle.

"My mouth's dry," he told her.

"Have some more bourbon."

"No," he told her when she went to reach behind his seat. "I need something to drink. You know, refreshing, like a soda or something."

"Beer?"

"Beer? What about it?"

Jennifer struggled with her navy blue, pleated skirt and the waist of her pantyhose as she bent back and rummaged behind her bucket seat. Smiling like the cat that had just eaten the family's pet canary, she pulled a bulky bottle off the floor and held it up to him.

"What the hell is that? A torpedo?"

"Yeah," she answered with an impish squeal. "A torpedo of suds, a depth charge of foamy fun, a battleship of—"

"Enough, already! To the moon with you, Jennifer! To the moon!"

They both burst out laughing at his terrible impression of Jackie Gleason and kept on laughing until they both forgot what they had found so funny. When their laughter stopped, they fell silent, suddenly lost within the colorful traffic lights and the motion of the city.

"What were we talking about?"

Jennifer giggled.

"What was I saying?" he asked again. "Where are we? What are we doing? How do I stop the car?"

He burst out laughing.

"Beer!" she exclaimed as she bounced the quart bottle she was holding on her knee. "We were talking about beer!"

"That's right! Shit—hey, how long ago was that? What time is it, anyway?"

"Who cares? We've got all weekend. No school tomorrow, stories are straight with the folks, no school tomorrow."

"You said that."

"Hell, maybe I won't ever go to school again. It's such a drag anyway."

"Beer. Concentrate on beer. My mouth feels like somebody stuck a paper sack filled with sand in it."

"Now that you mention it, mine's the same way too. Beer, beer, beer, beer, beer, beer, beer. Whew."

With a burst of urgency, Jennifer rummaged through the glove compartment and, with an "Aha!" came out of it holding a bottle opener. She quickly popped the bottle cap, tilted the bottle to her lips, and drank.

"Save some for me, will ya? It sounds great."

Jennifer almost choked as she pulled the bottle from her mouth. Large drops of foamy beer ran down her chin and landed on the exposed skin of her upper chest, where the buttons of her blouse were undone.

"What do you mean, it sounds great? How can it sound great?"

"Listen," he instructed, taking the bottle from her.

When he tilted the bottle to his mouth, a low, distinct, patterned bubbling sound could be heard.

"Hear it?"

"Yeah, Gabe, I hear it," she said with a dramatic eye roll. "No more funny cigs for you."

"I'm fine. Just like the sound, you know?"

He took another gulp of beer, eyeing the bottle with renewed interest.

"Bourbon, beer, marijuana—where'd you get all this stuff, Jen? I mean, uh, where did it come from?"

"Wouldn't you like to know?"

"Yeah, I would. That's why I'm asking."

"Any howling dogs inside that crazy head of yours?"

Gabriel looked pensive for a moment and then smiled.

"No," he replied with a mixture of happiness and surprise. "Not a one. Say it again just to make sure."

"Dogs, bow wows, bark, bark, bark, grrrrrrrrrrrrr!"

She finished with a coyote howl to his face.

"God bless this stuff! It's rid me of the crazies. I don't even have a headache anymore, come to think of it. This is great! Yeah, this is really great!"

"The turnoff!" she shouted. "The turnoff! Quick, you're going to miss it!"

The tires screeched under the pressure of the turn, but Gabriel held the wheel steady, his eyes riveted to the road. When he managed to get them on the right throughway, he heaved a sigh a relief, nodding his head with satisfaction.

"Not to worry, my dear. Old Gabe Tate's behind the wheel of Baby tonight. She goes as we go, turns as we turn, flies as we fly."

When she didn't respond, he looked over at her. He was perplexed to find her staring out the window. He had hoped for some appreciation for how he had handled the car.

"Whaddaya doin'?"

"I don't know. Thinking, I guess."

"What about?"

"I don't know," she relayed with a shrug. "Nothing. Everything."

"That's pinpointing it."

"Maybe we should smoke the other joint."

"Right now? Right in the middle of the city?"

"What? You can't handle it?"

The challenge in her tone was like a knife slashing his skin.

"I can handle anything. But I thought maybe we should save it. For the ride home, you know?"

"Who says we're going home? Besides, Titus has got plenty of the stuff. Got some other things too."

"Titus," he sneered. "Who the hell is Titus? And what kind of stupid name is that? And what do you mean by other things? I don't think we should—"

"The voice of reason," she moaned. "I would have stayed home with the old grump if I wanted to hear a boatload of that. Probably tell me all about the construction business for the four thousandth time and how he got it all started. Save me."

She turned her face to stare out the side window.

"Holidays always suck," she told him somberly, her nose pressed against the glass. "Not a whole lot of fun being the only kid with a father who can't talk about anything unless it's business or golf."

She fell silent for a moment. Gabriel could see the reflection of her eyes drifting with the passing scenery.

"I wonder where she is tonight? I wonder if she's okay—or even alive," she barely whispered.

"Still never hear from her?"

She shook her head no.

"And he still won't tell you anything?"

Again, she shook her head from side to side.

"Guess we're two peas in a pod. I've got no dad, you got no mom; maybe that's why we're together. Maybe next year I'll get my mom to invite you over."

"Oh, right, and have her faint when she opens the door and sees a white chick on the other side. Not to mention my all too fly-off-the-handle father, who might make a surprise appearance with a shotgun in his hands."

"Yeah, I guess the world ain't ready for the likes of us yet. I wonder when it's going to be. Tired of being, you know—keeping it all hush-hush."

"You eat with Mr. and Mrs. Mathis, right?"

"Yup, just about every night, except when he's in Washington. Been like that since they moved my mom into the apartment over their garage."

"I wouldn't mind sharing a turkey leg with him. Even with that big plastic blob on his ear, he still cuts a hunk of handsome. He nice?"

"They both are. Not like most people like them would probably be. You know, with him being a senator and all."

"He knows about us, doesn't he?" she asked after a pause.

"Not from me. I never said a word," he was quick to say. "I know how much hot water you'd be in."

"Take a right after the Port Authority. And I never thought you did—or would. It's just the way he eyed me in the car when you were talking after the, uh, the game."

Gabriel slammed on the brakes and hit the horn.

"What are you, crazy?" he shouted through the windshield at the meandering, raggedy figure on the street just ahead of them. "Stupid wino! Don't you have a home?"

With one last honk, he nudged the Stingray forward, shooting angry looks at the man through the rearview mirror.

"Man, they ought to do something about guys like him. Sorry, Jen. What were you about to say before Willy Wino stepped in front of the car?"

"It's just that he seemed to know, by the way he was looking over at me. Just a feeling I got."

"Yeah, he's got a knack for that. I don't know how he knows some of the things he does. I guess that's why he's a senator."

"Makes me wonder."

"About what?"

"How many other people might know—or have some idea."

"Come on, Jen. We've been careful. We never go anywhere where it's like we're making some big announcement. He even told me to be careful, and we have."

"Yeah, but Baby's not the most invisible car in the world. Even with us just driving the back streets, someone could easily spot us. Jesus, some nosy busybody could be over at my dad's house right now getting him all worked up."

"Hey, hey, hey—settle down. Stop getting so emotional. You're just being—"

"Being what?"

Seeing the reproachful look on her face, he said, "I can't think of the right word, so don't let your imagination run away with you. Besides, if anybody had a clue about us and what we've been doing, we would have heard about it a long time ago. And it would have been very loud and very clear."

Jennifer frowned at the suggestion.

"Maybe. Guess I might be a little stupid thinking like that. But only this much," she told him flatly, holding up her thumb and index finger together so there was barely any space between them. She softly jabbed him in his side and laughed.

"That's better. We're celebrating, right? Where do you want me to go, anyway? Or should I just drive around Manhattan—or are we in Brooklyn now—until we run out of gas?"

It was close to midnight by the time Gabriel found a parking space close enough to Titus's apartment that their walk wouldn't be too far.

"Hold on a second," Gabriel told her as they started away from the car.

"What?"

Gabriel eyed both sides of the empty street before letting his gaze study the row of metal trashcans that hugged the old brick building they had parked in front of. Leaving Jennifer to wonder what he was up to, he walked to the corner of the building and looked down the alleyway. Dim, wall-mounted alley lamps illuminated the tops of another long row of silver trashcans. Jennifer tiptoed up behind him.

"What are you doing?" she whispered, peering over his shoulder. "Come on, it's getting colder. I didn't dress for alley exploring."

"Let's smoke the other one," he replied.

"Right here? Now?"

"Can't you handle it?"

"You—"

He pulled her to him before she could finish, wrapping her inside the big, navy blue pea coat he was wearing. When he felt her warm body relax against his, he shuffled them forward into the alley. A few feet in, he stopped and checked to make sure that the shadows would at least partially shield them from any prying eyes.

"Light it up."

"Maybe we should save it and smoke it with Titus," she whispered.

"What for? You said he had plenty of it. And what are you whispering for? These guys aren't going to tell us to shut up," he said, nodding at the row of trashcans.

"Think there's any rats here?"

"I know there's at least two big ones," he told her with a playful hug. "Come on. This is the coolest, don't you think? It's like we're a couple of real beatniks on our way to a hip poetry reading in some smoky coffee house."

"Oh, Lord, what have I done? You've gone Looney Tunes on me. Next you'll want to start up some rock 'n' roll group, be the next Chuck Berry."

"Wow, I never thought of that. I could play ball for half a year and be a rocker the other half. It would be like—"

"Oh, shut up and stick this in your mouth."

She lit a match and cupped it in her palm. The flame flickered, casting a wavering glow on their faces. Gabriel inhaled deeply, pulling the smoke into his lungs, his cheeks puffing out when he tried to suppress the cough that was just on the verge of getting out.

"I told you to draw easy," she snorted, a bit of snot shooting out of her nose onto his jacket. "Oops," she chuckled, wiping her hand across the droplet.

"Gross me out," he objected, exhaling. "Nice, Jen, real nice. I wonder what I ever saw in you."

She took the joint from him and put it to her mouth. Cocking her face slightly, eyes full of softness, she gently drew on the rollup, pulling more of the smoke into her lungs than Gabriel had thought possible. With her free hand, she guided his lips to hers. Blowing the smoke from her mouth into his, she kissed him passionately, stirring arousal in both of their bodies. When she broke the encounter, Gabriel's body heaved.

"Oh, yeah. That's what," he murmured.

He kissed the tip of her nose and ran his tongue across her slightly parted lips. A gust of wind caught the lighted end of the joint, lifting tiny sparks into the space between their faces.

"I think it's trying to say that it's your turn."

Out of the corner of his eye, Gabriel caught a glimpse of a snowflake floating through the light of a streetlamp.

"I used to think those were the feathers of baby birds."

Jennifer followed the direction of his gaze and smiled.

"Snow. Makes me feel … soft."

He hugged her tightly.

"When was the first time you remember seeing it?" she asked.

"I guess it was some night—I remember Mr. Mathis carrying me into their house. Weird, huh?"

"Where'd you live before that? You know, you've never said much about when you were a kid."

She saw his brow furrow and noticed his eyes staring into the shadows behind her.

"Don't know, really. Momma doesn't talk about the time before my dad and brother died. And I've never really asked her about it, I guess. But I know I haven't lived here all my life. I don't know why, because I don't remember anything, really, but I know I grew up somewhere else."

Jennifer shivered.

"You cold?"

"Getting there. What do you say we smoke the rest of this on the way to Titus's?"

"Lead on, my little chickadee," he replied, trying to sound like W. C. Fields.

She pulled him to the street, laughing.

"Oh, and I almost forgot," she said a little too loudly, "whatever you do, don't call him Titus."

"I thought that was his name?"

"Would you want to be called Titus, if that was your name?"

"Probably not," he confessed with a chuckle. "What should I call him, then?"

"Call him T or T-man. He likes either one."

"How'd you meet this guy?"

"He used to work for my dad's company. It was just one of those chance meetings when I went to see my dad one time when he was on a site."

"What's his full name? Or am I not allowed to ask?"
Jennifer started to giggle.
"Titus Klinglehauffer," she spit.
"What?"
"Yeah, Klinglehauffer," she laughed.
"German?"
"No," she told him, her laughter growing out of control, "that's the crazy part! He's from Puerto Rico!"
Gabriel laughed along with her, but it was tempered, unsure.
He wasn't going to tell her, or even admit to it if she happened to ask, but his head had begun to pound again, throbbing with the same shooting pain he had experienced on and off for as long as he could remember. He didn't know why it had started up so suddenly, but he couldn't get around the notion that his head had started to hurt when he had tried to remember where he was from.

CRISP. ELEANOR PUSHED her shopping cart down the sidewalk to the corner, pulling her aqua-blue car coat around her. *The air is crisp this morning*, she thought with a shiver. And for some reason, it made her think she had forgotten something while shopping.

"Crisp," she said out loud. "Darn it all."

She pictured the cupboards in the Mathises' kitchen, trying to place the items from them that she would need to make an apple crisp. *What did the recipe call for?* she wondered. *How many apples are in the refrigerator? Are they the right kind? Do I have enough cinnamon?*

She opened her handbag and pulled her shopping list out. It was written on the back of the recipe she had copied from the *New York Times* food section. Award-winning, the paper had deemed it, so she had copied it and decided to give it a try. But she wasn't going to put the recipe on an index card and file it with her own collection of proven winners until she deemed it worthy.

"Granny Smith," she sighed with a shake of her head. "Know darn well there ain't no green apples at the house."

She looked back at the Safeway, wondering if she had time. Raising the sleeve of her coat, she checked her wrist, sighing when she remembered she didn't own a wristwatch.

"Land's sake, you old fool," she chided herself. "Maybe this Christmas somebody get you what you been wishin' for and buy you a nice Timex."

Eleanor jerked her head up with a start and looked around the parking lot for the silver Cadillac that Patricia would be picking her up in. Not finding it, she glanced back at the grocery store.

"Best wait and see if she has time for me to go back in."

She scanned River Road in both directions, looking for the car.

With a shrug, she told herself, "Can't leave all this food unattended, anyways."

Two women hurried past her, giving her a wide berth and uncomfortable smiles.

"People probably thinkin' you be a crazy woman talkin' to yourself," she muttered. "And here you at it again."

She laughed nervously, then was silent. She took the time to reflect on what the coming months might bring. The sudden, pulsating roar of a car's engine broke into her thoughts.

"What in the world?"

The rumbling of the engine drew her attention to the drugstore across the street. The canary-yellow sports car parked in front of it sparked instant recognition.

"Guess she be home for the weekend," Eleanor said, her voice holding an edge of disapproval. "Come to torture her poor father, I imagine."

The double glass doors of the drugstore opened; Eleanor felt her stomach go tight and hollow.

"How could it be? He's got a—"

She couldn't finish the sentence, suddenly not knowing what to say or what to feel. Doubting herself, she squinted over at the young black man, trying her best to make herself believe he wasn't who she knew him to be.

"Gabriel! That you?"

Even as the words left her, the man ducked into the car. She thought she saw him stuff a pack of cigarettes into the outer pocket of his jean jacket—the one she had bought for him last Christmas. The one she had purchased over her own misgivings about letting him wear such a ratty thing.

Eleanor found herself hurrying across the street.

"Gabriel! Gabriel!"

Through the driver's-side window, Jennifer looked up at her with a mixture of surprise and concern. In the next instant, the car pulled away from the curb with a screech of its tires.

"Gabriel!" Eleanor yelled, anger swelling.

Her anger quickly melted into an empty sadness. She watched the car go down the road with tears in her eyes.

"Gabriel," she muttered once more, as though she had just lost a cherished lifetime possession.

A car horn beeped politely behind her, the short, quick honks repeated several times before they registered. Somewhat dazed, she turned to offer her apologies.

"Don't tell me you haven't been to the store yet!"

Patricia's head popped out of the driver's window, her face, as always, adorned with an engaging smile.

"What's wrong, Eleanor? Are you feeling ill?"

Another car horn blared from behind the Cadillac.

"Hold on!" Patricia yelled back. "I'm parking it, okay?"

In the minutes that it took for Patricia to park the car, retrieve the groceries, and begin to place them in the trunk, Eleanor had decided not to say anything about what she had seen. She needed time to sort out her thoughts, she told herself, and to maybe do a little detective work, too. It upset her that Gabriel had been with Jennifer Stamper. He knew all too well what she thought of the young woman, had been aware of it ever since that Thanksgiving four years ago, when that girl and he had stayed out all night doing whatever it was they had been doing. It made her dizzy and a little sick to her stomach thinking about what an uproar it had caused the next afternoon.

"That it?" Patricia cheerfully asked, putting the last of the paper grocery bags into the trunk of the car.

Eleanor stared at Patricia for a moment and then glanced at the Safeway sign.

"Did you need to go to the drugstore too? Is that why you were crossing the street?"

Eleanor kept her eyes on the Safeway sign, feeling as if she was not remembering something she was certain she was supposed to remember.

"Eleanor? You all right?"

"I suppose so," she replied. "Though I feel like I've left somethin' unfinished, for some reason," she confided, deciding to look Patricia straight in the eye. "Can't for the life of me think of what it might be, though."

"Oh, is that all?" Patricia said, stepping over to the driver's door. "Join the rest of us common folk. I still can't remember how to work the coffee pot, even though you've shown me—how many times, do you think? Four hundred million?"

"Four hundred million and twenty," Eleanor corrected her with a smile. "And that don't include this morning's lesson."

Patricia threw her head back and laughed, curls of her auburn-brown, frizzy hair swaying across her shoulders.

"Come on, let's go home. I want everything to be perfect for Martin's return."

"Flight still gettin' in at five thirty?"

"Yes, as I've told anyone who'd listen to me in the past week. If everything goes right—and that would be a miracle in and of itself, trying to get out of the city—he should be walking through the front door between seven and seven thirty."

"Pope Paul comin' caused a big stir, ain't it?"

Patricia turned the ignition key, lightly pumped the gas pedal, and put the car in reverse.

"Any excuse to get Martin home is fine with me. But it'll be short, what with President Johnson wanting him back in the city for the Pope's visit tomorrow. Did you see the day's itinerary in the paper?" Patricia sighed and checked the rear-view mirror. "Too bad Martin can't catch one of Gabriel's games, or part of one, while he's back in the country."

"Probably just as well if he can't," Eleanor relayed with a dismissive sigh. "Ain't even played this season, far as I know."

"His leg still bothering him?" Patricia asked, surprised. "Maybe we should take him to see a specialist. It's been over two months now, hasn't it?"

Eleanor nodded her head in agreement, though she was focusing more on what she had just said than on what Patricia had offered. She wondered just what she did know about Gabriel anymore.

His grades, his football, his attitude—all of them had been in a steady decline since his freshman year. She shook her head at the memory of when he had told her that he didn't want to go to Yale, that he had chosen Columbia instead. She didn't understand it then, and was now having more trouble with her decision to relent and allow him to go to the college of his choosing.

Certainly, his freshman year had been good—excellent, in fact, she had to acknowledge—both on the playing field and in the classroom. But ever since then, something had gone sour.

His sophomore season had been decent, but far below what the coach had expected of him after his stellar freshman year. And his grades had noticeably slipped, she recalled, getting worse as the year progressed. And this past one, his junior year—well, she barely could find the stomach to think about it.

The coach had even called her, asking if there was some problem at home that would explain Gabriel's lack of concentration and dedication to the team. That's when he had told her about his grades; that they had slipped so far that Gabriel was not only close to losing his scholarship, but of being kicked out of school, period.

But the worst of it all, to Eleanor, was Gabriel's total lack of concern about anything related to school or football. He had become so apathetic—cynical almost. She had seen the signs of it over the past year or so, but now it was impossible to ignore. She had to admit that she had been losing him the past few years, but facing up to that fact made no difference in the situation. He was almost a man. And as much as she wanted him to grow into someone whom everyone could admire and respect, she knew it was out of her hands now. There was nothing she could really do about that aspect of his life anymore.

Eleanor gazed out at the fall foliage and the passing, familiar neighborhoods, wishing that she had the answers. Vaguely, she realized that Patricia was still talking.

"… have you? Not a word, I bet." With raised eyebrows, she glanced over at Eleanor. "Good God, I hope I haven't gotten *that* boring as of late. Martin will just turn his hearing aid off altogether if I have," she offered with a laugh.

"I'm sorry, dear. My mind seems to be someplace else today."

They passed the gas station, the butcher shop, the hardware, and the new, cute gift shop that had just opened in Fair Haven. As they rolled on toward Rumson, the reds, oranges, and yellows of the leaves prompted her thoughts to wander, transporting her to days gone by, to memories tucked away in special places.

"How much longer Mr. Mathis gonna be in the ambassador business?" Eleanor asked, trying to put her thoughts about Gabriel aside. "Iceland," she said with a grunt, "don't know what we need an ambassador there for, anyways. Don't seem to hold his interest much, either, if you don't mind me sayin'. And it's keepin' you two apart, for heaven's sake. Be different if you two was together. But I guess he got his good reasons for wantin' you to be here. Always does, that one. Wish more men like him—sensible. Hmmph."

"Where did all that come from?" Patricia scrunched her face up with mischief before adding with a giggle, "You think he's got an Icelandic woman way up there keeping him warm at night?"

"Don't you say that, young lady. That man don't have a cheatin' bone in his body. Shame on you for even thinkin' that way."

"Eleanor! Gosh almighty, I was joking! If I thought for one minute that Martin was—well, you know—I'd be up there so fast it would make the glaciers melt."

Eleanor sensed Patricia staring at her, but she would not acknowledge it.

"Besides, I know why I'm not there. I was a little relieved, as you well know, when he let me off the hook—bleak, boring, and boring—whew! Only reason he's there is to make certain our military bases remain there forever."

Eleanor caught Patricia biting her lower lip.

"But?" Eleanor asked.

"What do you mean?"

"You bitin' your lower lip. Been around you long enough to know a worry sign when I see it."

"I was not."

Eleanor gave her a reproachful look.

"Oh, gosh. All right. Maybe I was."

"So?"

"So if the Democrats don't win in sixty-eight, it won't matter any-way, because Martin will be replaced with some Republican crony. Part of me hopes he will be, in either case. I do miss him terribly, and his hearing isn't getting any better, you know. And you are right, he's not getting much satisfaction from the post. Martin's used to being in the thick of things—and there's nothing *thick* about Iceland. I wish the Party hadn't approached him with this deal. I truly feel they're grossly misusing his talents. He should have been offered the Peace Corps position instead of having to stroke some politician's head."

Eleanor turned almost completely around in her seat when she glimpsed a blur of yellow parked halfway down the street they were passing.

"What is it? What's wrong?

"I don't know, don't know," she hurried to say. "Thought I saw some-thin'. But—"

"I can turn around."

"No, no. We almost home. Probably just nothin', anyway."

As Eleanor stepped out of the parked car, her shoes softly crunched down on the rounded stones of the driveway. She vividly remembered the night she'd stood in the same spot, when Martin had lifted Gabriel out of the car and carried him into the house. She could almost feel the snow-flakes that had fallen that night. "Feathers," Gabriel had called them when he was a bit older, when he had gotten a good grasp of the English lan-guage. She could still see them swirling about their bodies as they made their way from the car to the kitchen door.

"Snow," she heard herself say.

"I don't think so, Eleanor. Not today anyway. A little too sunny, don't you think?"

"I need to make a phone call."

"What is it? What's wrong?" Patricia pressed, her brow furrowed with concern.

"Do you mind if I leave the groceries for a bit? I won't be long. They should be fine in the trunk in this cold."

"Eleanor?"

Eleanor looked at Patricia with troubled eyes.

"I'll take them in. You go and take as much time as you need." Patricia lifted one of the paper grocery bags out of the trunk. "Go on, now," Patricia prodded when Eleanor hesitated. "And don't let the fact that everything will be in the wrong place prey on your mind." Patricia smiled, hoping Eleanor could tell she was being mischievous. "It will be fun for me to try and find where everything is supposed to go, I imagine. Now, off you go. And say hi to Gabriel if you get ahold of him."

"How did you—?"

"I've been thinking about him too."


Patricia bent down and tilted her head sideways so she could peer up and out through the lower corner of the window of the back door. She gazed up at the apartment over the garage for the umpteenth time, her concern growing. The first hour that had passed after Eleanor had gone up to make her phone call had been manageable. But the second had made her nervous. And now, well into the third, she found herself pacing the kitchen floor, biting her lower lip and wringing her hands.

She heaved a deep sigh and shook her head, at odds with herself over her respect for Eleanor's privacy and her right to know what was going on with her adopted son.

She had noticed the changes in Gabriel the past few years. She'd have to have been a fool not to have, she told herself. Ever since that Thanksgiving four years ago. That was when it had all started. *But how can I blame him for changing?* she had asked herself a thousand times over. *Doesn't everyone change?*

The Thanksgiving of four years past had been an awakening. She had been stunned by Gabriel's views of racial prejudice in their own community and felt totally inadequate on the subject of the Black movement that was taking place across the country. Even to this day, in 1965, she still reproached herself for not having any clue as to who Martin Luther King Jr. was back then. A man who would be awarded the Nobel Prize for Peace; how ludicrous for her not have known anything about him.

After that exchange, as her knowledge of Dr. King and other champions of equal rights had grown, so too had her disillusionment over the country's inability to live up to its promises of equality. To her, it seemed America would rather cling to a past filled with injustices and ignorant prejudice than fulfill the doctrine upon which it was founded.

At first, the entire scope of what was taking place in the country of equality had made her furious. But then, as the freedom marches and demonstrations had turned into conflicts and then into riots, and the effort to end segregation brought bombings and death, her fury had changed to sorrow and then to disgust.

The pettiness, the cruelty, and, in many cases, the blind hatred of people that fought "to keep the Negroes in their place" were, to her, unthinkable and abhorrent. How could all people—black, white, yellow, red—not want equality and freedom for each other? Was this not what countless men and women had given their lives for, not only here, but on foreign soils as well? Were truth, justice, equal education, equal rights—and, yes, even freedom, she dared to add—all just useless words, a myth for any person whose skin color wasn't white? Had assassinations, cross-burnings, hangings, murders, lies, and beatings become the new pillars on which America rested?

Often, when she thought of Gabriel, she wondered how he could not be affected by it all. How could it *not* change him or disillusion him? These were questions she and Martin had never imagined having to ask themselves when they had brought him here. And yet, here she was, staring up at the garage apartment where he had lived most of his life, wondering just who he was becoming and what part she was playing in it all.

Jennifer Stamper. Patricia ran a hand through her hair, wishing she was the goddess Athena so she could shift change and wipe away the girl's importance, her lure—even the existence of the girl's name—from his thoughts. Even with all the other distractions the world was throwing at him—school, football, Vietnam, the draft, the race riots—she knew full well what the real cause for the change in him was: Jennifer Stamper.

Love could be as draining to a person as it was uplifting, a ravager as well as a healer, a sin instead of a blessing, she had come to realize. His relationship with Jennifer, as far as she was concerned, had been his unraveling. How strong the girl's hold must be on him, she mused. And yet, how strong their bond must be to have endured over the span of four years, no matter how she might otherwise wish to view it.

But the changes were hard to take.

"I wish he had never met you, Jennifer Stamper," she sadly whispered. "I wish—"

She sat down at the kitchen table and rested her head in her hand. She was running out of patience. Where was Eleanor?

As if on cue, the kitchen door opened.

She pushed herself from the table and embraced Eleanor as soon as her arms could wrap around her. She felt the shaking, sensed the pain, saw the sorrow in the tear-streaked face that tried so stoically to maintain a façade of strength. Only once before had she seen Eleanor so broken and distraught. The mere thought of that memory caused her to lose her balance. Feeling herself beginning to swoon, she stumbled backward.

"Whoa, now. Hold on, hold on," Eleanor stammered, steadying them both before they tripped.

"He's not—?" Patricia blurted out, frantically wiping the tears from her eyes with the back of her hand. "Is he—?"

"What? Dead?" Struggling with the notion, Eleanor blinked her eyes and tried to focus on her surroundings. "Lord forgive us for even thinkin' that way."

"You look so— so—"

"Suppose I do," she confessed, breaking free of Patricia's hold to walk over to the row of cupboards above the sink. She opened one and searched the contents.

"What is it then? What's wrong with Gabriel? He is all right, isn't he? Eleanor?"

"I'll make us some coffee."

"It's in the other cupboard."

"I know, I know. I was just—"

She suddenly laughed, shook her head, and then abruptly stopped. When she turned to face Patricia, her expression was one of despair. Patricia felt her heart racing as she waited for Eleanor to speak.

"I don't know what I'm doin'. Don't rightly know what I've been doin' these four years gone by."

Patricia said nothing.

"I've been sittin' up in that apartment for a good hour just tryin' to find the strength to get out of my chair, tryin' to find a reason to move. The good Lord tests a person, sometimes. Takes 'em to the limit of what they can bear."

Eleanor reached in the front pocket of her floral house dress and pulled out a handkerchief. She wiped her eyes and blew her nose.

"Why don't you come sit at the table with me?" said Patricia.

"Won't do me no better. Won't change nothin'. Didn't think the Lord would put me through somethin' like this again. But I suppose He got His reasons."

She fell silent for a moment, deep in reflection.

"Coffee. That's what I was about, wasn't it? Least that ain't changed, I hope. Good to know there's things you can count on."

"Eleanor."

"Lost a son, is all. That's all I found out on the phone. Been lost for a while now, I has to admit. Just couldn't seem to bring myself to say it."

She broke down and covered her face with her hands. Patricia stepped to her and gave her a hug from behind.

"It'll be all right. You'll see. Everything will be okay."

"Will it?" Eleanor snapped. "I wish to God I could believe it." Eleanor raised her eyes to the ceiling and crossed herself. "Forgive me, Lord," she said. "I didn't mean to use your name so lightly."

"What can be so bad? Tell me. Is he flunking out of school? Losing his scholarship? Because if it's—"

"He ain't in school. Hasn't been there since last March, as far as the school knows."

Patricia took a step back. She could feel the blood draining from her face.

"A dropout is what he is. Would have been kicked out if he hadn't left on his own, they told me. Grade point average so low, hardly room to get worse, they said."

"But that's impossible. His report card said—" She paused. "That's right!" she cried out, her face brightening. "We got his report card from last semester! And it showed he was starting to pull his grades up! So whomever you spoke with must be mistaken! Just a mistake, a misunderstanding! That must be it!"

Eleanor's icy glare deflated her.

"Fake," Eleanor stated coldly. "Just like everythin' else about 'im. Administration told me lots of that happening lately. Figure it's 'cause of the draft. They catch most of the fake ones, they told me. He got mostly incompletes on his real one. One professor gave him an F."

"But why? Why would he—? I mean, what was he thinking? Why would he go to all the trouble? If he wanted to take some time off or transfer or something——"

She sank into a kitchen chair, her head spinning with all kinds of crazy thoughts.

"Didn't want us to know. Don't get much plainer to me. Didn't want us to know so he wouldn't have to hear nothin' from nobody. He just lied and lied like he be doin' all along lately. Just a liar and a fake is what he is. Just a—"

"Shut up! That's enough! I don't want to hear that about my son!"

Eleanor stared at her, dumbfounded.

"Your son?"

"Yes! My son!"

Patricia's face and her voice were filled with defiance.

"All these years," Eleanor said with a sigh. "Bedtime stories, doin' homework, sittin' up with him while he sick or have bad dreams and headaches; never crossed my mind that you saw 'im as yours. Guess I was just foolin' myself thinkin' he was mine. Take some gettin' used to, now that I know."

Eleanor stared at the floor for a moment before looking back at Patricia. Slowly, an odd smile formed on her lips.

"Suppose you be wantin' to change his name. You gonna have 'im go by Martin Junior, now?"

Anger briefly flashed across Patricia's face before it softened into a smile of her own.

"What an idiot I must sound like. What an utter fool. A jackass of the worst kind. An imbecile."

"Some of that did cross my mind," Eleanor said. "But not all," she was quick to add when it seemed Patricia was taking offense.

They shared a quick laugh.

"Oh, God, Eleanor. What are we going to do? We don't even know where he is."

"He's right here," Eleanor told her with a wave of her hand. "Saw 'im comin' out of the drugstore when I was waitin' for you."

"So that's why you looked so—"

"Yes, that's why. Didn't wanna believe it was him, though."

"Did you ask him what he was doing?"

Eleanor frowned. "Didn't have a chance to. He got into that yellow sports car we all too familiar with. And, yes, she was drivin', like always."

Patricia moaned and put her head on the table.

"How many more of our mistakes are going to come back to haunt us?" she murmured.

"I best make that coffee. Looks like you be needin' some poured into your ears again. Just like that time—oh, good heavens, just leave it as a good while ago. Startin' to talk gibberish. Our mistakes? What do you mean, girl? What we done?"

Patricia raised her head from the table, her eyes red and moist.

"Sending him to St. Augustine's instead of just keeping him in public school, for one. He never would have met that siren if we hadn't put him in there. And then to think we allowed ourselves to be persuaded to let him pass on Yale—Yale, for God's sake—so he could go to Columbia! What were we thinking? How could we have allowed that opportunity to go by?"

"Won't be long for that coffee. You be wantin' it in the right ear or the left?"

"Eleanor, this is no time for jokes."

"On the contrary—uh, Momma," she teased. "This is the best time to keep a sense of humor. Not gonna do any one of us any good to wallow in self-pity. Now, which ear you be wantin' it in?"

"Both, then," Patricia told her, forcing a laugh. "And make it extra hot."

Patricia welcomed the sound of the percolator as though it was the footsteps of a long-lost friend walking on her front porch. For a moment, she wrapped herself in the comforting sounds and smells of her kitchen: the soft rattle of china cups being placed upon saucers, the rich aroma of fresh-brewed coffee being poured. Her memory drifted with the wisps of steam rising from the cups.

"Martin will be crushed by this." She looked evenly at Eleanor. "He always wanted children—a son. And seeing that we—that I could never give him one, well, he—"

"I know how he feels 'bout Gabriel. Be a dumber, older fool than I already be, if I didn't see that the boy be like a son to 'im. Think, some-times, Mr. Mathis enjoyed those football years at that school even more than Gabriel did," she said with a soft chuckle.

"I know," Patricia sighed. "He'd be so excited on Friday nights that he could barely sleep sometimes just thinking about Saturday's game. I guess those days are over."

"Hmmm—guess they are. Guess the boy'll never play pro ball like he always used to go on 'bout."

"He's no boy anymore, is he?"

"Always will be, in my eyes. Hard to let go of that, hard to forget that first night he be right here in this kitchen lookin' so weak and lost. Never forget him being so taken with the snow like he was," she wistfully recalled. "Baby bird feathers."

"Maybe we shouldn't tell him, then. Or wait until his day with the Pope is finished."

"Mr. Mathis, you mean?"

Eleanor reached for the percolator and poured a little more coffee into their cups.

"You two ain't ever lied or kept things from one another as long as I know you. Hate to think you'd start now. Make me think things a little worse off than they be, if you do. Wouldn't be right. 'Sides, he'd want to know. He got the right to. He's the boy's father, after all. Might just be that on a piece of paper to everyone else, but he be a father to that boy since day one just the same.”

Eleanor fell silent and sipped her coffee. Patricia did the same.

“Sometimes I wonder if his real mother or father hasn’t been looking for him all these years,” Patricia said. “It makes me feel sad when I do, thinking that maybe I’m the cause for someone’s anguish and worry and loss.”

Her eyebrows twitched as she sipped her coffee.

“Be a lot sadder for everyone if you had left him to die in that hospital you told me about—the one in Akka Babba or whatever.”

“Addis Ababa.”

“Like I said—or if you and Mr. Mathis had never gone on that safari like you did. Boy’d be dead, wouldn’t he? Animals done ripped him to shreds, way you told it. Be nothin’ for no one to look for, then. God sent you there. That’s what I always believed, and that’s what I still believe. He had somethin’ in mind for you—for all of us.”

She sipped her coffee and thought.

“Don’t rightly know where He’s goin’ with all of this now. But it ain’t my place to question, is it? Least not right now, anyways. Maybe when ol’ St. Peter givin’ me the once-over, He be obliged to let me in on it all.”

“Sometimes I wonder,” Patricia mused.

“Wonder what?”

“Wonder if God doesn’t drop His plans sometimes. Like, He just leads a person to a path and then leaves them on their own after that, to see where they go.”

“Can’t be very pleased then, can He? Not the way things be turnin’ out. Must be up there shakin’ his head, wonderin’ why He went to all the trouble.”

“Must be a reason.”

“Hmmph.”

They stared at the white china cups rimmed in royal blue and let their thoughts struggle with what God had in mind. A few moments passed in accepted silence.

“Guess we do what Martin always says,” Patricia softly offered. “Have faith.”

*

A HALF-MILE AWAY, PARKED at the end of a cul-de-sac that overlooked the Navesink River, Jennifer and Gabriel sat comfortably in the yellow Stingray, sharing a joint.

"What a nowhere place, with a lot of nowhere people," said Jennifer. "Home sweet home."

"Yeah, that's a joke. Old fart-brain thinks New York has rotted my brain. Says that if I stayed here and went to Monmouth that I wouldn't be so cynical and sarcastic about everything. Thinks I would appreciate the stability of a place like this. Can you imagine? The square zero."

Jennifer peered out the windshield, blowing smoke out of the corner of her mouth while she shook her head.

"Some sort of upper-middle-class sanitarium, if you ask me. Everybody walking around without the slightest clue about what's going on around them," she managed to say while taking another drag off the joint.

"That include us?" Gabriel asked as he took the joint from Jennifer's fingers.

"Hell no, that doesn't include us. We're almost out. We're hip. We know where it's at."

"Dropout heaven. Everybody ought to experience it. Drone on, little sociology professor. Twit. What you know about life from inside the cover of a book? Dazed little ripple head. Wonder how they ever hired you to teach."

"What the hell are you talking about, Gabe? Did you drop a tab again while I wasn't looking?"

"Don't you remember? That egg-headed bitch I had in one of my last—and I do hope it *was* my last—class. Don't you remember me telling you about her? Thought I was some perfect example of— of—"

"Of what?

Gabriel drew deeply from the joint, smoke curling out of his nostrils.

"Of an underprivileged minority rising above the constraints society has placed upon someone with skin color such as mine," he grunted, trying not to exhale. "I wonder what she'd think if she saw where I was from," he went on, smoke rushing out of his mouth in a furious cloud. "Stupid bitch, thinking she knew what I was about just 'cause I'm black and she's up there teaching slobs who believe every word she says. Going to be a bunch of misinformed morons coming out of that school."

"Oh, right, like you wouldn't have stayed if they hadn't kicked you out."

"What the hell is that supposed to mean?"

"Uncle Sam, baby! He wants you!" she shouted, pointing a finger at his face. "Vietnam and atom bombs!"

Gabriel's face tightened into a scowl.

"First of all," he told her, "go to hell. Secondly, I'm not fightin' in no war that isn't even a war in some hellhole of a place that don't mean squat to anybody. And third, I hope someday they draft women so you can go to boot camp and take orders from some square-headed, pimple-faced asshole who doesn't know his dick from his brain."

"Oooh, the mighty Gabe Tate has spoken," she mocked, rolling her eyes. "Listen up, Government Man: he ain't goin' if you draft him. He's gonna hide in the ambassador's basement until you forget all about him. Maybe get himself smuggled into Iceland and become a whale hunter."

Gabriel looked at her, trying to decide whether he should be angry or laugh.

"You're some kind of voodoo bitch," he ended up saying. "Titus is rubbing off on you."

"It comes natural," she perkily replied. "I used to practice the evil voodoo on a doll when I was little. I imagined it was my stupid father. I even stuck needles in its eyes and heart."

"Did it work?"

"No—but it was fun."

Abruptly, her smile vanished.

"What's that face for?"

She stared out the windshield.

"You okay?"

"I used to think about killing him. Used to dream about it." She shrugged her shoulders and reached for the joint. "Still do, sometimes."

As Gabriel was trying to grasp what she had just told him, Jennifer stuck out her tongue and flashed him a big smile.

"Funner to drive him nuts, though. Drive him out of his tiny little mind. Make him pay for everything he did to—" She took a drag on the joint.

"I always wondered why you hooked up with me. Couldn't figure out why you'd want to take all that grief from your friends, why you were okay with everybody saying you were a slut."

He let his gaze wander to the river, his face brightening at the sight of a sloop in full rig sailing by.

"Guess I know now, though," he went on. "You just wanted to stick it to your dad by going out with a nigger."

"Yeah, that was mostly it," she replied in an even tone. "I just wanted him to choke on his own vomit. But then I got to know you, and from then on—well, here we are, four years later and counting." Her face suddenly took on a blank expression, her eyes glazing over. An instant later, she started to giggle. "Don't think I would have hung with you this long just because you're a nigger, do ya?" she teased, seeing how glum he had become. "You do have some very appealing qualities, you know, baby," she added, reaching over and grabbing his crotch. "Brains and balls— that's what I love about you. Hey! I'm serious, Gabe."

She touched his shoulder, trying to draw his attention away from the river.

"I— I love you, you know. You gotta know that. You got to. I mean, we're going to be together forever, you know. And we're gonna be rich, too. Long as we keep selling for Titus, expand the market like he says. We'll have more money than all the hypocrites who live around here. And down the road, we'll lose Titus and set up our own distribution gig. We'll be the fat cats. Let somebody else do all the leg work, take all the chances."

"Sounds like you got it all planned out. Nice and neat with a big bow wrapped around it."

"You obviously don't think so," she shot back, a little put off. "You got a different take, then let's hear it."

He squirmed in his seat, trying to find a position where he could stretch his legs. He grunted under her scrutiny.

"I don't have no plan," he told her tersely. "Don't want one, either. Don't mean anything if you've got one. Plans never work out, never fall into place. Might as well not even look into the future. Might not even be one, you know? World might blow itself up, with the stooges we got running it. Or maybe—"

He watched the sloop sail out of his line of vision and let out an angry sigh.

"Fuck it."

Jennifer giggled, but quickly stopped. She stared at him as he kept his attention on the river.

"What if we got married? That would keep you out of the draft, wouldn't it?"

"Two months too late," he replied without even looking at her.

"But I thought they weren't taking married men."

"Changed the rule in August. Married is the same as single now. They don't give a shit. See what I mean? You plan; they change it. About the only thing you can count on is them changin' shit to screw everybody," he said.

"Then we'll hide in the city, like T-man does. He could keep us from being found, I bet. We'll just melt into the streets like he does. They'll never find you there."

"Look, Jen—"

"Or we'll go to Canada—Toronto or Montreal. Maybe we could work something out with Titus where—"

"Shut up, damn it! Just shut the fuck up, will you?"

When he saw the lost-in-the-department-store look on her face, he closed his eyes and shook his head.

"I should just let 'em drag my ass to Vietnam so you can be done with me," he muttered.

"Fine with me."

"Sorry," he apologized, taking one of her hands in his. "You know I didn't mean it. I guess I'm a little weirded out, you know. Seems like nothing's working out—except you. Seems like everything is just going every which way. Crumblin', you know?"

Slowly, the look of hurt faded from her face.

"Hey, I was babbling. I would have told me to fuck off, too."

She giggled uncertainly.

Gabriel stroked her cheek, and then pulled her to him. They shared a long and passionate kiss.

"Couple of nut cases, I guess," he said when their lips parted.

"You just finding that out? My dad could have told you that four years ago."

"Your dad," he repeated, looking pensive. "Did you mean what you said? You know, about him?"

"God, which part, Gabe? Which conversation from what year?"

"You know," he said, glancing at the river. "About doing him in."

"You mean, would I kill him?"

Gabriel watched her eyes lose their brightness, her smile fade, the softness of her face grow hard. When she didn't answer him right away, he diverted his attention to the river below, hoping he might catch sight of another boat rigged in full sail. When she spoke, her voice was small, but the words were not.

"Yeah—I'd kill him."

*

NORMALLY, WHENEVER MARTIN arrived home from a trip, the bright glow of the front porch light provided him with a warm welcome. But this night, the glow of the bulb seemed harsh and cold. Not at all what he was used to. Not at all what he had envisioned.

"Looking forward to one of Mrs. Tate's home-cooked meals, I bet, Ambassador."

Although he was slightly aware that his driver was saying something from the front seat, Martin made no reply. He patted the envelope that was stuffed inside his inner suit coat pocket and tapped at his hearing aid.

"Say again, Peter?" he absently asked out of habit.

"I said," Peter's voice close to a bellow, "I bet Mrs. Tate has cooked something special for your homecoming."

Martin politely smiled at the eyes that looked at him from the rear-view mirror. He nodded and said, "Yes, I imagine she has. Wonderful girl, wonderful person."

He glanced away, again, patting the envelope in his pocket.

"Here we are, sir. We made pretty good time, considering the traffic getting out of LaGuardia."

When Martin didn't respond, Peter slid out of the car.

"I'll get the luggage, sir."

Martin's thoughts were a tangle of Eleanor, Patricia, Gabriel, and the letter that he carried. Aware of little else since one of his aides had given the letter to him as a favor from an old friend, he stared straight ahead, deep in reflection, even when the door he was sitting next to was opened.

"Ambassador?"

The title sounded odd to him tonight. The envelope in is suit coat pocket suddenly felt very heavy.

"Is there something wrong, sir? Are you feeling ill?"

"Just a bit of jet lag, I'm afraid, Peter," he managed to say, falling back on one of his standard, practiced responses. "Too much travel and never enough time to regroup."

"Then tomorrow won't be of any help, will it, sir?"

Martin slid out of the car. Arching his back, he let his eyes go to the few stars that were visible.

"No," he confessed. "Tomorrow won't be any help in that department."

"Seven a.m. still, sir?"

"Yes, that will be fine."

Martin crossed the porch to the front door. Peter followed and set down his suitcase.

"And Peter," Martin added in a weary voice, turning the knob and swinging the door open.

"Sir?"

"Good luck on your law school applications. And thank you."

"As always, my pleasure, Ambassador Mathis."

Peter adjusted his wire-framed glasses and tipped his cap as Martin pushed the door closed.

"Martin? Is that you?" he heard.

He chuckled as he strode toward the kitchen. *Already discovered*, he thought. When he saw Patricia standing next to the kitchen table, he beckoned her with open arms to come to him.

"I return on the wings of Hermes."

Their embrace was long and uplifting; their kiss tender, without haste.

"It's good to have you home," she sighed, squeezing him tight. "God knows how much I've missed you."

"Aren't you going to tell me how much you've missed me and love me?" he asked with a laugh, cupping her face in his hands.

"But I just—"

She stifled her tears with a smile while her hand stroked the lobe of his lone ear.

"Of course I am," she told him loudly. "You have to give me a chance first."

She stood on tiptoes and planted a kiss on his cheek.

"I've missed you terribly, you big lug. And yes, for whatever reason, I still love you. I love you!"

"Land's sake. Let me get out of here so you two can have some privacy," Eleanor announced, pushing away from the kitchen table. "Homecomings are for two, and me makes one too many."

"No, Eleanor. Stay," Martin told her.

He stepped to her and bent to give her a hug.

"I've got— I'm—" he stammered, looking pensively to each of them.

"What's wrong, dear? I know that look well enough."

He reached inside his coat pocket and extracted the envelope.

"I was given this by one of my aides," he told them, holding it aloft. "I should not have received it. It should have gone directly to him. But, well, I guess rank still carries its privileges."

Patricia hurried to him and read the return address.

"Selective Service? What are you trying to say? They can't, can they? I mean he's—"

"I'm not quite sure what the letter specifically says. Haven't opened it. But, yes, I'm fairly sure that he's being called upon to serve his country."

"God help me, no!" Eleanor exclaimed. "Not him too!"

"That's not the only problem. There's trouble here for all of us. I don't know what we are going to tell him."

"What do you mean, dear? What are you saying?"

Martin pointed to the address, stabbing at the name with a fingertip. He shook his head and lowered his eyes when her fingers grabbed the edge of the envelope.

"What? Oh, good God," she moaned. "I never thought."

She took the envelope from her husband and handed it to Eleanor. Eleanor took it with a puzzled expression.

"Read the name," Patricia said to her.

"Mr. Gabriel—" She glanced up, startled. "Mathis. Mr. Gabriel Mathis."

She stepped back and steadied herself with the corner of the kitchen table. She stared at the letter, her lips moving as she read over the heading one more time.

"Lord have mercy on our souls," she intoned. "And may He give us the strength to see this through."

Tears welled up in her eyes. Patricia stepped to her when she saw her hands begin to quiver.

"What in the world we gonna say?" she gasped, choking back her emotions.

"We'll just have to—we'll have to," Patricia looked back at her husband before she finished, "tell him the truth."

"The truth?" Eleanor sniffled, wiping her eyes. "Truth's not even clear to me. How's he gonna take all this in? Two mothers lost, a new one poppin' up. Real father gone, the one he thinks was his daddy dead, and now a brand new one pushed at 'im. Land's sake, how anybody supposed to handle all that?"

Eleanor's face quivered. She tried to say more, but found she couldn't manage it.

"I've been thinking long and hard since the letter was given to me," Martin began. "And I feel strongly that I should go up to the city and explain all of this to Gabriel. I'm certain, once I have explained the situation to the university administration and to his coach, that they will allow him to miss a day or two of school so we can try and sort all of this out."

"No, it can't be that way," Patricia said a little too quickly.

"Of course it can, dear. Like I told you, I will just—"

"No. You don't understand. You don't know what's happened."

Patricia looked to Eleanor for support, but Eleanor had her head down, her hands covering her face.

"You might want to sit down."

"Just tell me, Pat."

She glanced at Eleanor one more time before saying, "Gabriel's not in school."

"He left during football season? Why would he do that?"

"He hasn't played football this year."

"What do you mean? I know about the hamstring pull keeping him on the sidelines and all, but—"

He stopped talking when he saw the icy resolve in his wife's eyes.

"His letters and phone calls were lies," she stated, her tone of voice going suddenly cold.

"Lies? Gabriel?"

He stared at the floor for a moment.

"I can't believe it. He's never lied. I mean, well, kept things from us sometimes. But all kids do that from time to time as they grow up, don't they? Didn't we? You know—little secrets about test grades and secret crushes and—"

"Last semester's report card was a forgery. He stopped going to classes sometime last March, as near as we can figure. God knows what he's been doing since then." She softly bit down on her lower lip. "No wonder he was so adamant about not wanting any of us to visit him the past several months. And I've wondered why this semester's tuition check hadn't shown up on the bank statement yet." She rubbed the sides of her face with her hands. "Now I get why he wanted to to mail it for me that day." Patricia eyed Martin and Eleanor with a look of resignation. "And why he's been so interested in the mailman's delivery schedule since then," she added with a short, hard-edged chuckle.

To Martin, the kitchen seemed suddenly cold and filled with memories that he really did not want to entertain. He wiped away the visions of snarling hyenas and burning jeeps with a shake of his head.

"He'll be a fugitive from the federal authorities if we can't get him this letter. We have to find him."

Martin looked to his wife.

"Eleanor saw him earlier today."

"Where? Excellent! Then we—"

"He was in that yellow sports car we all know too well," Eleanor muttered despondently.

"They could be anywhere by now," Patricia added.

"Lost," Eleanor sadly stated. "Probably been that way since the day you found 'im, I reckon."

"We'll find him. You'll see. We'll make it right."

"It's no use, Mr. Mathis—Martin," Eleanor replied. "Still be lost, won't he? This was never his home."

She looked around the kitchen as if seeing it for the first time.

"Never really could be, could it? 'Cause home be somewhere 'cross the ocean in a country I ain't ever seen."

"Where's our faith, ladies?" Martin offered, doing his best to sound enthusiastic. "Faith will—"

"Oh, it ain't faith that's missin'," she told him plainly. "It's facin' up to the truth that's gone and made this a mess. 'Cause rightfully, you gots to admit, it be hard to know what that is right now."

Eleanor looked at them, her expression a mixture of strength and sorrow, confusion and compassion.

"The good Lord has set down a mighty test for us all. And I reckon it ain't gonna end anytime soon."

# JANUARY 2, 1972



*The turning of the calendar has never held more meaning. How exhilarating it is to join hands with time as I travel to my new life and ordained rebirth. Surely it is no coincidence that a new year begins as I, too, step forward upon this threshold that the Lord has set before me.*

CLAIRE ABSENTLY CARESSED the cross about her neck, a smile creeping to her lips as she looked upon the sleeping face of Sister Angelique. From there, she gazed out the jeep's open windows, scanning the terrain they slowly passed. Rugged, bleak, dry, desolate; all these caused her spirit to soar. Nowhere in the parched brown landscape did she find cause for concern. *To the contrary*, she thought, *the Lord has delivered me to a most compelling undertaking, a pilgrimage of divine challenge.* Even within the hardened, dark, worn faces and black-brown eyes she had encountered since debarking in Djibouti from France, she saw only the unbending threads of God's will, and not any of the desperation, poverty, and disease about which she had been forewarned. She closed her eyes and smiled; how glorious it was to be in His service.

*I pray daily that you will cease to harbor fear for my safety. I wish no pain upon any in this world, especially those who brought me*

into it. Although the disappointment in your eyes over my choosing
a life with God still haunts me, through prayer and reflection, I
have come to see that it was only your devoted concern for me that
you were exhibiting, and not any feelings of condemnation. I did
not choose a life with Our Lord Jesus Christ to be a burden to you.
I can only humbly offer that you embrace my faith in Him as your
own, and allow that faith to fortify you. And through the grace of
His blessing, all your fears and doubts will be vanquished.

The jeep bounced sharply, jarring Sister Angelique's head against the unforgiving steel frame of the back seat.

"My apologies, Sisters," the driver offered when Sister Angelique groaned. "An unseen pothole, I'm afraid. And one that I must remember on any further passage this way."

"No apology is necessary, Ali. No harm was done." Claire nodded to the set of eyes that met hers in the rearview mirror. "You see, Sister Angelique still rests."

"This is good, then, for there are many more miles to go."

"How much longer, do you think, Ali?"

"Three, maybe four hours, Sister, if there are no problems. Maybe more, though—maybe more."

"Did I see a sign for Shiket not far back?"

"We most certainly did."

"Then, Mek'ele—did I say that right? I do hope I did—should only be forty miles more or so, should it not?"

"I do not know miles, Sister. Only kilometers. But even kilometers cannot measure time on this road, I'm afraid. You will see how little this will resemble a road as we go farther. But, yes, you did say it very well: Mek'ele."

"Thank you, Ali," Claire replied. "I know you will deliver us there in good time."

The eyes in the mirror blinked their acknowledgement and then turned to the road ahead. Claire went back to her letter.

So please set aside your tireless (albeit welcome) worries for my *safety. The hospital and orphanage in Mek'ele are well established, with many supporters in the surrounding community and region. I am sure what you have heard will prove unjustified.*

*I thought of both of you over the Christmas celebration. It is impossible not to revisit memories of my time in Philadelphia— Chestnut Street, the pipe organ at Wanamaker's, lights on Boathouse Row—whenever the blessed celebration of the Lord Jesus Christ's birthday occurs. And now a New Year has arrived; I am filled with hope and faith that it will prove to be a most special one.*

*I do not know when this letter will reach your hands, but I will write to you soon after my arrival in Mek'ele so that you may have a better understanding of the area I will be stationed at for the foreseeable future. Know until then, however, that I am in God's care and that He will watch over me.*

*As always, if you need word sent to me, do so through the Sisters of the Holy Cross. God bless you and keep you safe.*

*Your devoted daughter,*

*Claire*


Very carefully, Claire tore the sheets of paper from the writing note-book, neatly folding each one before slipping them into the envelope she had placed next to her.

"Keep them from worry, Dear Lord," she murmured before running her tongue along the glued edge of the envelope. "My life with You should not be a source of unhappiness for them."

She sealed the envelope and then sought the cross about her neck. She grasped it firmly.

"I am sorry, Sister," Ali interjected, "I did not hear what you said."

"I was asking the Lord to keep my parents well," she replied, offering a quick smile to the inquisitive eyes in the mirror.

"Oh," he replied with a nod of his head, "I see."

She allowed herself a giggle.

"And may God look after you as well, Ali."

"It is Allah, blessed be He, who looks to my well-being, Sister. Your god need not be concerned. Allah blesses this land."

Claire frowned.

"Perhaps Allah and the Lord could each look after you in their own way," she offered.

She saw his brow furrow.

"Allah needs no help in this, Sister. But what your lord, as you call him, does, I cannot be responsible for."

"Very well spoken, Ali. You should be a politician."

"Yes! I will take the Emperor's place when he is removed!" he quipped.

"Haile Selassie? But I thought all of Ethiopia loved him."

"Not all," he told her with a shake of his head. "Most especially not in these times. From all parts of the country there is dissent. But you will come to see this for yourself. Have you not noticed the parched earth around you? People are in need of food and water. Crops and livestock are withering as we speak. Help is begged for—but none is given. And then there are the conflicts: whispers of independence in the Tigray and the Oromo regions, outright rebellion in Eritrea and in the Ogaden. Indeed, unrest everywhere."

Claire fidgeted in her seat.

"I did not mean to cause you concern, Sister. I was of the mind that you were aware of these things before you decided to travel here, were you not?"

"I— I was told some of this by my order," she admitted, subdued. "You say there is drought and famine where we go?"

Ali responded with a humorless laugh before saying, "Where we go, where we have been, where we are now; all of Welo is a place that the government pretends does not exist."

"And the children, Ali? What of them? Surely the government must see to their well-being."

Ali said nothing for a time as the jeep bounced along on the packed-dirt road. Just as Claire was about to repeat her inquiry, he answered her in a saddened voice.

"May Allah guide them to the oasis of His paradise, Sister. Their cries of sickness and hunger never dim for those who have heard them. Most grievous it is that the young are the first to submit to death's starving hand. Many hundreds, if not thousands, I have heard, have already gone to Allah, blessed be He. And many more shall perish as well, I fear, if rain does not come or help is not delivered in great haste."

"Then, in God's name, why has this help not been delivered, Ali? Why hasn't the government stepped in or called upon the world for assistance?"

Ali shook his head with a heavy sigh.

"The one who has proclaimed himself to be the Power of the Trinity will not admit that tragedy has entered his kingdom. He goes to great lengths to suppress all that is happening. The foreign press is not allowed here, Sister. And what is spoken on the government-controlled radio and television is not the truth."

"That is—"

"It is those who are already in need that suffer the backlash of the Emperor's secrecy."

In a moment of anger, Claire trembled and felt flushed. But the cross she clasped steadied her, God making her calm and strong, as He always did.

"You spoke of the Power of the Trinity, Ali."

"Yes, Sister. The Emperor."

"And he equates himself to this Power of the Trinity?"

"Yes, Sister, as close as it can be interpreted by your tongue."

"No Christian man would allow this to occur," she told him sharply.

"Nor a man of Islam," he reproached.

"I beg your forgiveness, Ali. I did not intend a slight to your religion."

"And none is taken, Sister. I was merely pointing—"

The jeep squealed to a halt, throwing both Claire and Sister Angelique into the frames of the seats in front of them.

"What is it, Ali?" Claire asked while trying to see if Angelique had been hurt. "Why did you stop so suddenly?"

"Qu'est ce que c'est? Pardon—what is it?" Angelique asked, somewhat alarmed. "Did I say well, Sister Claire?"

"Very well, Sister," Claire answered with a heartfelt smile upon her face. "If I could only learn French as easily as you've picked up English, we'd be— Je m'excuse."

Claire took hold of Angelique's small hand and squeezed it reassuringly. The look on the innocent face of the young novice told her she had spoken the English words too fast.

"Boulders in the road," Ali said from the driver's seat. "I do not like this."

"Surely this is a common occurrence, yes, Ali? The surrounding terrain is filled with rocks and stones, is it not?"

"Not here, Sister, and not like these have been placed."

"Devon-nous prier? Pardon—pray?"

"Is there another way, Ali?"

Ali shook his head while his deep-brown eyes scanned the sides of the road ahead.

"We will look around, if you like. Perhaps the stones are not heavy. Some physical exertion may be just the tonic for this weary trip we are enduring. Come, Sister Angelique."

"No! No, Sisters—it is best you stay. We can—"

The windshield splintered as a bullet shattered the glass. Ali's body jolted back from the impact, his head exploding in a spray of blood and tissue. The doors of the jeep flew open. Taut, spindly black arms reached inside from both sides and yanked Claire and Angelique out. Claire heard Angelique's terrified scream.

"Angelique!" she yelled.

The butt of a rifle slammed against her temple.


Claire regained consciousness with a throbbing in her head and something sharp pressed against her cheek. When she tried to move, a strong hand held her face immobile. Confused, blinking rapidly, she was able to focus her eyes on the rough, grey cloth of her blindfold. When she felt fingers on her breasts and others probing her loins, she recoiled.

"Enough!"

Instantly, the fingers left her body. She could hear footsteps shuffling away.

"Bless you!" she called out, near panic.

A boot came down across her chest. She winced when it began to exert pressure.

"Silence," the voice hissed.

"You're—European?" she struggled to say, gasping for air.

She tried to scream when she felt something hard being thrust into her mouth. Gagging, her tongue felt a round opening and tasted the bitter aftermath of sulfur. When she heard the engine of the jeep turn over, her body went rigid.

"Yes—be afraid," the same accented voice told her. "But we thank you for delivering some much-needed medical supplies."

Somehow wrenching an arm free from the hand that was pinning it to her side, she pulled the rifle barrel from her mouth.

"No!" she screamed. "Those are for the orphanage, for the children!"

Laughter erupted next to her, spreading until it seemed to be all around her.

"Children. Orphanage," the European voice mocked. "We are at war. What do I care for useless children? The penicillin, the bandages, the disinfectants—they will go to the freedom fighters who are wounded." She felt a rush of air blow against her face, the pungent stench of cigarette smoke making her wince. "Children," the voice scoffed.

"Your accent. You are German."

The slap was hard and stinging, knocking her head harshly to the ground.

"Know your place."

A boot kicked her side, accentuating the command.

She heard the doors to the jeep being closed, then hastily taken footsteps and men's heightened voices speaking in a dialect she did not understand. She could distinctly make out the voice of the German man, however, conversing with the others in their own tongue.

The back of her neck prickled when she sensed that someone had bent very close to her.

"So, you are a nun."

"Yes," she replied, cowering away from the blow that she was certain was coming. "We are nuns."

"Why were you not dressed in your costumes with your beads dangling from your necks, then? Why the disguise of skirts and simple frocks?"

"You mock us? Humble servants of Jesus Christ?"

The man's laughter was so close and loud that it set her head spinning.

"We are Sisters of the Holy Cross," she stated forcefully. "We are on our way to the orphanage and hospital in Mek'ele. God will show you mercy if you will allow us to proceed."

"Oh, will he now," the man chided. "Perhaps, once you and your companion have tended to the needs of my men for a time, I will allow you continue on your way. For *his* sake, of course."

He laughed coldly and passed a rough finger along her cheek.

"Such pretty, smooth white skin," he whispered. "Our needs are many," he chuckled. "Has it been touched like this before?"

"May God have mercy on you," she told him, her voice tinged with fear, a cold knot of sickening panic growing in her stomach.

"You will find, as I have, that if there ever was a god, he is surely now dead, or at best, finished with this place. So pray to him if you like, if that will make you feel better. I will have my men take your costumes and baubles to camp so you can pretend, if you like. They might enjoy your dressing up. Though I am not so sure your friend will be needing hers."

"Sister, Angelique? What do you mean? What have you done to her?"

She felt the toe of a boot trace the outline of her breast.

"Angelique!" Claire screamed. "Sister Angelique!"

Sharp metal pricked the side of her face, prodding her to silence. The German barked out commands in the language she did not know. She heard his footsteps receding while activity seemed to spring up all around her. Someone grabbed her wrists and yanked her to her feet.

Startled, she gasped when the blindfold was lifted off of one of her eyes. A set of red-rimmed, dull black orbs bulged outward from a slim, dirty, unshaven, sallow brown face. A lecherous smile greeted her gaze.

The man dangled a small silver cross in front of her. Feeling for her own, she realized it had to be Angelique's.

"Why do you have that?"

The man pressed the cross against her lips as she heard the jeep pulling away. He forced her to turn her head.

"Dear God!"

Angelique was unconscious, drooped between the arms of two other men. One side of her face was bloodied, her eye swollen and turning purple. Around her neck, where she had worn the thin silver necklace that held her cross, there were bruises and splotches of red skin with bloody scratches. Her black travel frock had been ripped down one side, as had the white tunic she wore beneath it. The frayed edge of her bra strap dangled loosely off one shoulder. The milk-white flesh around her breast was inflamed.

Before Claire understood what was happening, the two men holding Angelique took a step closer and pushed Angelique to her. Struggling with the weight of Angelique's limp body, Claire fell to the ground with her in a crumpled heap. Claire's heart began to race when she felt Angelique's slight, ragged breath against her neck and heard the soft, pain-filled moans escaping from her lips.

"No!" the man who held the cross yelled, pulling Claire roughly to her feet. "Move! Now!" Pointing a machete toward Angelique, he screamed, "Carry!"

"You— you speak English?"

The man took Claire by the neck and pulled her face to him. He forced his lips against hers, and thrust his tongue inside her mouth.

"No!" she spat, screaming, pushing him away.

His lecherous smile returned. He held up the small silver cross and pointed to the one Claire had around her neck.

"Jesus," he taunted.

Claire's wrapped her fingers around her cross.

"Yes," she replied, confused. "The Lord, Jesus Christ."

"Die?" he asked, pushing Angelique's cross close to her face.

"Yes," she told him, her voice cracking, "He died on the cross."

The lecherous smile widened, the bulging eyes going wider.

"Same," he told her, pointing to her chest. Then, pointing to the slumped body of Sister Angelique, he added, "Move, carry, same."

The smile suddenly vanished, his lips turning into a snarl.

"Now!"

With her head spinning, Claire took a quick look around. For the first time, she studied the dozen or more partially uniformed men who had attacked them and killed Ali. Equipped with machetes, rifles, and an assortment of bags, packs, and ammunition belts, they looked to her to be a ragged, undisciplined bunch. But what uniformity they lacked in dress and weaponry they countered with identical steely, grim expressions and ruthless, cold eyes.

"Now!" the man shouted again. "Or!"

He rubbed the cross across the front of his crotch.

Although Sister Angelique's frame was slight and somewhat diminutive, Claire struggled to lift her off the ground.

"You must help me if you can, Sister," she urgently whispered. "Seek God's strength. He will make us both strong."

When Claire somehow managed to raise her and balance her against a shoulder, the man with the cross came and tied ropes around each of their waists and gathered the ends into his hand. Giving Claire a final chilling smile, he slid her blindfold back down across both of her eyes. Shortly thereafter, she felt a tug on the rope around her waist and heard words shouted at her in the language she did not know. But their meaning was clear; she began to walk, dragging Angelique next to her.

How long they walked in this manner, Claire could only guess. The notion of time was lost within the heat of the sun and the buzzing sound of swarming flies. Struggling mightily with each step, she began to pray in earnest, asking God for His help, holding fast to the belief that, if her prayers were offered in utter sincerity, He would answer them.

After what seemed an eternity, a soft wind eased the sweat of her brow and tousled her short, brown hair. She shivered. The air was cooler now, the sun not as strong as when they had started out. Daylight was coming to an end, she realized. She was unsure if that was something to be happy about or to dread.

When Angelique suddenly fell to the ground, Claire tried to keep them upright. But the best she could manage was to land on her knees, yelping when the rocky dirt dug into her skin. The soft, forlorn weeping of Angelique drifted to her ears. Tentatively, fearing a rebuke, she removed her blindfold and rubbed her eyes.

"The Lord will protect us, Sister," she said, taking one of Angelique's cold, weak hands into her own.

Nearby, one of the soldiers laughed. Claire edged closer and placed Angelique's head to her chest.

"Faith, Sister," she tenderly said, stroking the girl's crudely cropped blonde hair. "Come, sit up with me. We will pray."

Claire righted them somewhat and tenderly squeezed Angelique's fingers. Gently interlocking them within her own, she began to pray.

"Our Father, who art in heaven, hallowed be thy name. Thy kingdom come, thy will be done, on earth as it is in heaven. Give us this day our ..."

While she continued with the Lord's Prayer, she watched the men gather wood for a fire and begin to set up camp for the night. Although the men directed several lustful glances and bursts of laughter their way, they seemed content with readying their meal and cleaning their weapons. She hoped this was the case. Silently, she added that very same request to the Lord, certain that He would see that they left Angelique and her in peace.

Claire looked over at the men and stared at the food being parceled out. She swallowed dryly, suddenly realizing how hungry and thirsty she was. Then she glanced at Angelique. She felt selfish and ashamed.

"Food! Water! Please!" she called out. "My friend!"

A chorus of laughter ridiculed her plea.

Close to tears, she hung her head. Her fingers found the cross about her neck. The image of Christ suffering on the day of His crucifixion flooded into her thoughts. Gazing into her eyes, He said, "I am thirsty." The agony of his voice made her gasp. Tears welled in her eyes. Claire gripped Angelique's hand with renewed resolve and began to recite the stations of the Rosary. She raised her face to the sky. Her voice was strong, every word spoken with conviction.

Slowly, with Angelique leaning heavily upon her, she fell into the trance of her own monotone. The holy words slowly became a whisper, and then a murmur, before stopping altogether. Unable to keep her vigil any longer, she drifted off into the temporary haven of sleep.


Claire's awakening was abrupt and filled with terror: a hand cupped over her mouth, her shoulder grasped and pulled, someone's breath hot against her cheek, a voice whispering, "Come."

Against the backdrop of a clear, star-filled night, she could make out only the silhouette of a robed head and a dark, bare arm. She tried to back away, but the hand upon her shoulder tightened.

"Quiet," the man harshly ordered in a whisper that was barely audible. "The children need you," said the man, his tone softer. "We must go."

The grip on her shoulder loosened; the hand cupping her mouth released. Claire looked up to the face hidden within the robing. She could not see through the shadows to find the man's eyes. The man stood and reached out a hand to help her rise. She shook her head and nodded toward Angelique. He bent quickly and whispered, "Death already calls her."

"I will not forsake her," Claire whispered back. "Help me."

The man stood and stepped away. Claire reached out for him to stop. "Please—"

He was upon her before she could utter anything further, pressing a hand against her lips.

"She will die," he mouthed, his lips brushing against her ear so she could hear him.

Claire shook her head. Trembling, she started to cry.

"Not here," she whimpered.

He lifted her as he rose to his feet. She found that she could barely stand, and she fell against him. Something sharp poked her side.

"Ouch!"

He covered her mouth as quickly as he could. They both listened in silence, hoping. After a few moments, he steadied her and moved to Angelique. Claire gasped and tried not to scream. Angelique's face was a bloated contrast of disfigured darkness and a pale, lifeless white.

*Please*, she begged with her eyes. She prayed he would understand.

In one swift motion, the man in the robes bent and lifted Angelique in his arms. The sudden movement caused Angelique to groan. At the campsite, someone stirred. Grabbing Claire by the arm, the man began to run. A voice shouted out after them.

They had only covered twenty yards when the first rifle shot boomed behind them. Flashlights suddenly clicked on, beams of yellow light fanning out around them in flickering, swaying patterns. Voices called out angry and surprised, rising to a crescendo when a slender corridor of light illuminated Claire's shoulder and head. Another gunshot erupted. Claire bent low. The bullet threw a mound of dirt up in the air five feet in front of her. An instant later, Claire's rescuer pulled her back into the darkness and shoved Angelique's limp body into her arms. The beam of the flashlight searched anew, swinging and arcing, stopping when it found the three fugitives it sought.

For a fleeting moment, a memory surfaced when she heard the arrow shoot through the air. She remembered a similar sound, seeing the formation of Canadian geese passing close over the fields, the air pushing through the feathers of their wings as they passed over her head. With the loosing of the arrow, the beam of light from the flashlight swiftly fell away.

A chorus of screaming voices cursed them, followed by muzzle flashes and a rain of gunshots. As Claire's rescuer tackled her sideways to the ground, Angelique was ripped from her grasp. She watched Angelique's body lurch backward, the bullets making a sickening thud as they imbedded into her flesh.

More flashlight beams skipped about them. A foot came down on the back of her shoulder, pinning her. She heard the whizzing of the air three more times in quick succession: string, shoot—string, shoot—string, shoot. One by one, the flashlight beams arced into the sky or dipped and disappeared. The foot came off her shoulder.

"Come, now!"

"Angelique," she protested.

The darkness hid the blow, the fist catching her behind her ear. She never felt the hand that cupped her head and laid it softly to the ground.

He shot one last arrow toward the soldiers before shouldering his bow. Crouching, he lifted Claire to his free side and shuffled over to where Angelique lay.

From the light of the stars, he saw the oozing bullet wounds in her neck and chest. After looking upon her battered face, her one eye closed in swollen darkness, the other staring blankly at the stars above, he touched his palm to her face and smoothed her tortured features to a calm.

"May the Mother embrace you as one of Her own," he murmured.

Balancing Claire across his shoulder, he raced headlong into the cover of darkness.

*

"WHY IS THAT so hard for you to understand?"

"Pleasing Father is never a chore, Mother, or a burden, as you refer to it. It is the cruelty to the animals that upsets me. Although it is far worse for the fox, you and I both know there is still hardship placed upon the hounds and the horses."

Claire's mother looked away, tired of the argument that always seemed to take place between them before the hunt went off.

"Will you dispute the beauty of it, too, Claire? Or that your father cuts a handsome figure on horseback?"

She looked deep into her mother's eyes, her own growing more serious as she struggled to say the next words.

"It is the end Mother, the purpose of these gatherings, that, for me, strips all of that beauty away. For I have seen—as you are well aware—the hounds at their worst when the day's sport has reached its conclusion."

"You should have never been allowed to see that. It was sheer stupidity on the Whip's part—or too much brandy."

"Regardless, it happened: a cornered, frightened animal ripped apart by twenty frenzied dogs. And all in the name of sport, all for the enjoyment of the dozen riders who had kept up."

The horn sounded as the hounds were sent off. The red-coated Whip cantered down a grassy knoll, keeping pace, shouting his guttural orders to keep the stray dogs with the pack and the leaders on point for the course that had been plotted out.

*Claire turned and watched the riders rein their horses in to follow. Her father, as was his custom, was one of the first to be off on the Whip's tail.*

*"Shall we drive to the hill for a better view?"*

*"May I linger for a while longer, Mother? I thought I might—"*

*"Do as you please," came her mother's terse reply. "But don't make me come find you. I'll be with Mrs. Hannahman, most likely. You know her Jeep."*

*"Yes, Mother. I won't be long."*

*A pang of guilt shot through Claire as she watched her mother walk away. But it was fleeting. She dismissed it altogether when she thought how utterly insensitive it was of her parents to always insist that she join them when they knew full well what she thought about fox hunts since that awful day with the hounds.*

*"Society," she said sarcastically, not caring who might be within earshot.*

*With a singular purpose, she focused on her favorite reason for coming to this estate, making her way to the large, tranquil pond that was set between three grassy hills adorned with clusters of white birch on either end. It was a setting like no other she had ever visited. Like something she had read in a fairy tale somewhere.*

*Claire tried her best not to hurry toward the solitude she sought. She had no intention of drawing attention to herself—or, worse, having some uninvited admirer follow her to try to draw her in to some unwanted conversation. She giggled at herself. If her mother and father only knew what was inside her head. What fainting and consternation it would cause.*

*As the sounds of the foxhunt dissipated, Claire shrugged off her misgivings of the hunt, deciding the setting she was approaching was much too lovely to spoil with such thoughts. Standing atop one of the three grass-covered hills, she gazed down at the pond in the morning's splendor and lost herself within the swaths of sparkling, gold-tinged reflections on the water's surface.*

*To her delight, a flock of some thirty or more Canadian geese was feeding at the far end. Its presence only enhanced the picture she was marveling at.*

*"Surely as God intended," she said in a soft voice.*

*She crossed herself and bowed her head.*

*"What glory You have given to this world, oh Lord. Thy grace is boundless."*

*She looked up to the sky, a heartfelt smile forming on her lips.*

*"Always when I think of You, a peace comes over me. Your touch is this."*

*Stretching her arms out wide, she gazed admiringly at the scene laid before her. "Your presence is not lost on me."*

*A flicker of movement caught her attention. She giggled when she caught sight of a red fox scampering along the pond's edge.*

*"How beautiful," she murmured, captivated by the striking red and white of its fur, her eyes dancing with the movement of the bushy tail that floated behind the animal as it ran.*

*She clapped with pleasure, but then stepped back with a start when the flock of geese suddenly took flight.*

*The honking of the large birds rose up from the dale in a trumpeting crescendo. To her amazement and joy, the flock took to the air in unison, banking briefly across the surface of the pond before lifting higher and taking flight in a path that brought it directly toward her. She covered her ears against the honking thunder as the geese drew near. And then, quite suddenly, the air went quiet. Claire removed her hands from her ears and let out a small gasp as the flock flew over her.*

*Feathered wings pushed through the air, turning the sky right above her head into a symphony of whispers. Her eyes went wide. Her spirit soared.*

*An arrow flew across her sightline. Entranced, she followed its course. When it pierced the surface of the pond, she became confused. For the water rose up and held firm where the arrow had struck. The wavering face of a woman appeared at the apex. The woman turned her face toward Claire; her eyes seemed to be but a foot away.*

"That's it. Open your eyes all the way, now. You've been asleep far too long and taken up too much of my time."

Claire blinked several times and swallowed dryly.

"Thirsty, I bet. Here, lift your head a little. That's it. Now take a sip."

Claire did as she was instructed, drinking gratefully, the sensation of water on her tongue awakening her senses. She blinked a few more times, letting her head fall back to rest with a weary moan.

"A confusing dream?"

"Dream?" Claire hoarsely croaked. "Which?"

"Oh, I'm afraid this is all too real, Sister. It doesn't get much realer than this."

Claire stared blankly upward, questioning what the voice was saying.

When she closed her eyes for a moment, the geese, the pond, and the fox were still there. And then her mother appeared with a stern expression on her face and began to shake her.

"Don't drift back to sleep," the woman said, her face appearing out of the water again, her tone sounding a bit cross. "I don't really have time to keep checking in on you. Stay awake now, okay?"

Claire numbly nodded. She sensed the woman leaving her. She sighed.

"Mother!" she suddenly shouted, wincing when a pain erupted in her head. "Ouch," she murmured, rubbing the lump her fingers found above one ear.

"What now?"

Bewildered, Claire looked around her.

"Where's Mother?"

The woman of the pond shook her head in dismay. She opened her mouth as if to speak, but then stopped. Lips twisting and brows lifted, she gave Claire an odd look.

"Is my mother angry? Did I make her miss breakfast?"

The woman of the pond rolled her eyes.

"Give me patience."

"What?"

"How old are you, Sister?"

"Twenty-two," Claire responded without hesitating.

"Are you trying to tell me that you've come all this way with your mother in tow?"

Claire shrank back at the woman's incredulous tone.

"She hates to miss the hunt breakfast," she meekly offered.

The woman of the pond seemed pained by her answer.

"I don't have time for this nonsense," she sighed. At that, the woman of the pond walked off in a huff, her hands jerking excitedly by her sides as if they were engaged in some desperate, silent conversation of their own. Claire closed her eyes and took a deep breath as she tried to put some order to her jumbled thoughts.

She tried to place the whimpering that quietly seeped into her moment of reflection, her clouded memory laboring as she slowly flipped through pictures of recent events in search of a suitable match. Absently, she reached for the small silver cross about her neck.

"Angelique!" she screamed.

The whimpering grew louder.

"Dear Lord, children!"

Claire jumped up and dashed around the corner of the crumbled wall where she had been lying. Stepping from shade into the harsh glare of the sun, she fell to one knee, placing her hand to the ground to keep from falling altogether.

"Help," a woman's voice weakly pleaded.

A frail, black, withered hand touched her shoulder.

"Save."

Claire recoiled and scurried backward, covering her mouth to keep from screaming. The emaciated woman, not much more than a skeleton with skin, staggered toward her, bearing—by what power Claire could not imagine—what looked to be a child in her outstretched arms.

The child was a girl no more than five. Her legs, hanging lifelessly out of the bottom of a dirty, tattered, purple dress, were disfigured with wide patches of raw skin and burned flesh that had bubbled to a yellowish-orange. The girl's head bobbed listlessly toward the ground. Her eyes were frozen open, staring blindly up into the blazing sun.

"Lord Jesus Christ," Claire whispered.

"Save," the woman croaked, holding the child out to Claire. "Please. Help."

Out of reflex, Claire stood and offered her arms to receive the child. A black cloud of buzzing flies momentarily lifted off the girl's legs as Claire took her, but just as quickly settled back onto the wounds. Instantly, Claire began to choke and gag from the rancid odors.

"What— What happened? How long has she been like this?"

Claire searched for the answer in the woman's bleary, unfocused eyes. The woman could only look at her with a sadness that was etched in the creases and lines that crisscrossed her face.

"What caused these burns?"

With great difficulty, the skeleton woman raised one boney finger upward.

"I don't understand; something from the sky?"

The woman crumpled to the ground.

"Help! Come quick! She's fainted! She's fainted! Quick!"

To Claire's great relief, the woman of the pond came running. She shot Claire an angry glance before bending and attending to the figure lying on the ground. After giving the woman a brief examination, the woman of the pond stood up, her expression unreadable.

"Can you help this child as well? I'm afraid I—"

The woman eyed the girl, felt her wrist for a moment, and then said, "If I had to venture a guess, I'd say the poor girl's been dead for at least a couple of hours."

Horrified, Claire let the body fall to her feet. With a hop backward, she frantically wiped at her arms. The well-placed slap that stung her cheek left her momentarily stunned. She wrapped her arms tightly about her chest and began to sob.

"What kind of pathetic, ignorant—" the woman of the pond hissed with rage. "These people come here for our help. Even the dead deserve respect. Is that so hard to grasp?"

The woman of the pond glowered at her.

"Look! Look around you! See what you have caused because of your—"

Hesitantly, Claire turned her head from one side to the other. Everywhere she looked, she found scores of people—young and old, huddled in groups, sick, starving, tired, listless—all looking right at her, condemning her with stares that made her shake. Covering her face with her hands, she fell to her knees.

"I'm sorry," she sobbed. "I— I— God forgive me. I'm sorry."

"Are you going to be like this the whole time you're here? Because if you are …"

"What?"

Claire wiped her eyes.

"Pick up the girl and follow me."

The woman of the pond crouched and gathered the withered body of the aged woman in her arms. Shooting Claire another angry look, she said, "Did you hear me?"

Guardedly, Claire reached a hand out toward the dead girl's body, but snatched it back when her fingers touched her flesh. Near panic, she searched for help from the woman of the pond. But the woman had already left. Claire caught sight of her as she stepped into the doorway of what looked to be the only standing building in the compound.

A slight push to her shoulder made her gasp. She whirled her head round in terror, thinking the dead girl had come back to life.

"God have mercy," she begged.

A little boy with deep-black sunken eyes was staring at her. Her heart sank at the sight of his bloated stomach and the rows of frail, protruding rib bones.

"I don't understand."

Rocking from one bare foot to the other, the boy pointed to the dead body before turning the finger to his chest. The expression on his face tore at her soul.

Without warning, the boy stepped to her. Before she could react, he clasped the silver cross around her neck between two of his twig-like fingers. The silver of the metal sparkled in the glare of the sun. The boy smiled widely. Claire felt the tears welling in her eyes.

"No," she gently told him, her hand joining his fingers about the cross. "This will not become you," she assured him, nodding her head at the dead body. "You will not die."

The boy cocked his head. Claire brought him to her chest and held him close.

"I knew I'd end up doing this myself."

The woman of the pond had her long, thin arms perched on her slender hips. The look on her face was unforgiving.

"Has it dawned on you what effect that dead girl's body can have on all the other children here? Is it only the living that you have compassion for?"

Stung by the reprimand, Claire screamed, "I will bring her! Don't touch her!"

"Fine!" the woman of the pond shouted back. "Then do it!"

"Will you take the boy, then? He is in need of comfort," Claire added, smiling at him and caressing the back of his head.

"Everyone who is here is in need of comfort, Sister," the woman said, the word *Sister* enunciated as though it were an insult. "Or haven't you noticed?"

Offering no response, Claire gave the woman of the pond the boy's arm. With a firm resolve, she rose, and with a degree of difficulty, gathered the dead girl's body up into her arms.

"Where?"

With a nod of her head back over her shoulder the woman said, "Where the dead are prepared. The house with walls."

Without replying, Claire struck out across the compound. The woman of the pond and the little boy followed.

As Claire walked toward the house with walls, she took in her surroundings: a half-dozen partially demolished mud structures spread out along a line some fifty yards long, a shanty of tents on the opposite side strung from blankets and pieces of metal, smoke rising here and there from fires that only added to the smells, the heat, and the dust.

Children, mostly young, dressed in rags or clothes that did not fit, signs of starvation evident in their bodies and faces, began to line the way where she walked. Their attention was divided between the dead girl and the one who carried her. Claire stopped ten feet from the doorway. The smell of rotting flesh and the sound of buzzing flies was overwhelming.

"Prepare yourself, Sister. It is not a sight for eyes as innocent as yours."

"Has it always been your way to insult?"

"I beg the sister's pardon," came a sarcastic reply. "There is little place for amenities here. Hardly time to breathe deeply, for that matter."

"Then perhaps you should just attend to your duties."

"What do you think I'm doing?" came a curt, laughing response.

"Surely there are others that must need you more than I do. I am quite capable of delivering—"

"Oh, you're not ready for what's in there, *Sister*."

"Claire! My name is Claire!"

"So it would seem."

"And yours?" Claire hotly demanded, close to tears, though she would not look at the woman to give her any satisfaction.

"Lee."

"L–e–i-g-h?"

Lee sighed.

"What could it matter? You are amusing, aren't you?"

Claire jerked her head around and glared at the woman with a steely expression.

"L-e-e, if it makes a difference. And I hope you can keep up that feistiness. You're going to need every bit."

Claire took another step toward the house with walls.

"Are you sure you want to go in there?" Lee asked, touching Claire's arm, bidding her to stop.

With her lips slightly trembling, Claire hesitated, a moment of doubt flickering within her amber-speckled brown eyes.

"Sometimes being stubborn—"

The crying that erupted from Lee's side startled both women. The little boy was shaking and sobbing, his eyes wide and terrified as he looked at the house with walls.

"Here, here now," Claire began in a soothing tone. "There is no need for all of this." Glancing at Lee, she asked, "What's his name?"

Lee responded with a frown, "You ask the most inane questions."

"Do you not wish to help this child? Can you not see he is frightened?"

Lee pulled on her stringy, red-brown ponytail, her light-brown eyes flaring with anger. She lifted the boy with ease and placed him against one of her broad, bony shoulders.

"Nothing would suit me better, Sister. If the devil would take my soul in exchange for but a thimbleful of your God's power, I would sign my name in blood right now and give it to him without a second thought. But the devil doesn't bother with this place anymore, so the deal has never been offered."

A rebuke was on the tip of Claire's tongue, but when she saw that Lee was sincere, she swallowed her urge to preach.

"Then I shall call him John, unless you wish it to be something else," she simply said, offering a smile of peace.

"Like all of them, he is afraid that is what his future holds," Lee replied, her eyes darting to the house with walls. "When one of them is taken there, they see themselves."

"It will not be so with John. Will you tell him that?"

Lee sighed and shook her head.

"You are— I suppose I know enough of Amharic to tell him, if that is even what dialect he speaks. Doesn't seem like he knows any English."

"Then I will teach him."

"Are you going to hold that dead girl in your arms all day?"

Jolted by the question, Claire shifted the weight of the dead body in her arms. She took the final brief, faltering steps to the house with walls. She stopped altogether when the buzzing of the flies grew to a threatening drone.

"I will be fine," she said aloud.

Steadying herself with a deep breath and a silent plea for God's help, she stepped through the doorway.

She instantly regretted her decision.

Swirling clouds of buzzing flies swarmed from one dead body to another, massing to feed on one before lifting to move on to the next. Bloated flesh and excreted body fluids were everywhere, the odor of it all immediately bringing bile up into Claire's throat.

Wanting nothing more than to dump the body and run outside, she searched for an appropriate place to set the girl down. That's when she noticed the withered, skeleton-like body of the woman who had brought the girl to her. *How was it that she had been able to carry the girl when she had been so close to death herself?* she wondered.

Prodded by some sense of family, Claire laid the girl down on the ground next to the skeleton woman, making the sign of the cross in the air above both of them as she rose.

"May God keep you both," she said, blessing their bodies with the sign of the cross..

As she turned to leave, she stopped. *Who is the keeper of the dead?* she wondered. *Was someone in charge? Surely they are not just left here to—* She looked around.

Ribbons of sunlight filtered down through the cracks of the thatched rooftop, the shafts of translucent golden light illuminating the dirt floor and the bodies lying upon it in a macabre display of shadow and highlights. Although the room was not overly wide, it ran lengthwise for some distance.

A large pile of multi colored fabric—some six feet high and just as wide—off in one corner caught her eye.

Thinking the pile could be items that the children of the camp could use, she edged forward. A twitching pair of bony black feet, partially hidden beneath the pile of clothes, disappeared at her approach. The wailing scream she wanted to release remained frozen in her throat.

A hunched form, swathed in robes of scarlet and black, came around the stack of tattered rags and garments.

"Another to bathe, is it?" a zombie-like woman asked, her accent European, her words spoken in English.

The zombie moved toward Claire. She seemed to float through the patches of darkness and the bars of sunlight.

"Pretty," she remarked with a clicking of her tongue.

Two ancient-looking fingers touched the fabric of Claire's habit.

"Pretty," she said again. "But too big."

Claire thought she heard bones crack when the tiny woman shrugged.

"The other's a bit better—but still too big."

She moved on, stopping at the newest arrivals, studying their corpses. Bending, she felt the air above the girl's raw wounds.

"Napalm," she softly moaned, shaking her head. "Not right, not right."

"Napalm?" Claire repeated, peering over the zombie woman's shoulder. "How would she—?" She remembered the old woman pointing to the sky. "They would kill children?"

"Who?" the woman asked, her dark eyes almost invisible beneath her heavy, line-worn lids.

"Those who are making war," Claire replied with conviction. "A child's life should not be lost to war."

The woman's laughter was shrill, her features swallowed up in the wrinkles of her face.

"So you do not know," she said, speaking as though she were casting blame.

She pushed by Claire and made her way to the pile of clothes.

"Bring water and long grass. Must have them for the bath," she added absently. "Make clean, presentable."

The woman's body creaked as she bent to retrieve something from the floor.

"All clean. All ready."

Gathering a bundle of dried grass in her wrinkled, twisted hand, she motioned to several other naked bodies laid out on the floor. Most were children.

"See? All clean, all ready. Go to their gods without dirt or shame. Careful now. Must not spill," she decreed, lifting a small cast-iron pot from the shadowed corner behind her. "Happy they will be. Friends they will be. Friends are the dead."

She cocked her head to one side and smiled.

"Soon for you. Soon for me," she added.

The woman's smile suddenly vanished, her expression pained.

"Who will bathe me?"

Claire looked into the pot and saw the few drops of dirty water it held. She felt both bewildered and sad.

"Maybe you?" the woman asked, her mood unexpectedly hopeful. "Maybe him!" she cried. "Yes!"

She gave Claire a jealous look.

"The drum man," she whispered. "Like he did for you."

She examined Claire from head to toe.

"Too big, too big, but pretty—pretty."

Confused and a little frightened, Claire turned to leave.

"What were they like?" the woman inquired in earnest.

"What was what like?" Claire replied, at a loss as to what the woman was talking about.

"His hands."

"I'm afraid I—"

"When he bathed you—strong, were they? Tender?" she went on, her eyes drifting toward the roof.

With a sympathetic shake of her head, Claire took a few steps away.

"Tell me," the woman pleaded, grabbing the edge of Claire's black habit. "Over there," she went on, pointing to the dark corner of the room. "Where you still lay. What was it like? Tell me—tell me."

*Surely the woman is mad*, Claire thought. *Surely she can see that I am alive. How can she think I am dead when I am standing right here?*

"Come—see for yourself."

With a tug on Claire's habit, she motioned for Claire to follow. Claire pulled back for a moment, but then relented, realizing it would be heartless to refuse such a simple act to one so misguided. With a final, longing glance back toward the doorway, she allowed the woman to lead her deeper into the room.

"See? See how you are? Clean he made you. Very clean."

Claire fell to her knees and pounded a fist against her chest.

"Angelique," she gasped before she gave herself over to great heaves of emotion.

Claire averted her eyes, but the scores of flies trespassing over the stiff body of her dead companion brought them back. In utter sorrow she gazed at the stark, naked form of her dead sister. The bloated, purple, fly-infested flesh caused her to wonder. Why had God allowed this to happen? Was this really what He intended? If it was, she didn't understand.

"Lie down again," the woman suggested, touching Claire's hand. "Perhaps he will come back, bathe you, bathe me."

The woman burst into a feverish cackle. Claire covered her ears in a futile attempt to rid herself of the maddening noise. When the zombie woman leaned forward and stuck her face close, her lost, unfocused black-brown eyes stared up into Claire's.

"The wounds," she whispered, stretching a hand out toward Angelique, "very careful he was."

She nodded as she studied the ruptured, purple-blue flesh on the throat and chest.

"Very clean. Yes, very careful. Look," she went on, her twisted hand shooing the flies from the wounds. "See how good? Ready for her god. Ready for the grave."

The woman took Claire's fingers and pulled them to the edge of Angelique's chest wound.

"Touch it," she bade. "See how nice?"

Pulling her hand out of the grasp of the zombie woman, Claire took a hurried step back, shaking uncontrollably.

"No!" she screamed.

The house of walls accepted her shriek, mixing it equally with the zombie woman's sharp, mocking laughter.

Claire felt her stomach turn when the woman ran a finger along the perforated gash on the side of Angelique's throat.

"Clean," she pronounced, admiring the finger when she withdrew it. "Bathe me, I hope. Yes, drum man."

"Why haven't you buried her?" Claire demanded, suddenly enraged. "Why is she not covered? Why have you done this?"

The zombie woman flinched and scurried away, her wrinkled features caught in perplexed confusion. When she was an arm's length away, however, she abruptly turned, her face brightening with a smile.

"Only sleep with them," she explained, waving an arm to encompass the room. "Clothes," she added, her voice animated as she pointed to the pile in the opposite corner, "I keep safe for them if they want them back, if they ask."

She laughed.

"They never do, though. Always go naked."

She laughed louder, nodding her head.

"No—not ask back, not ask back. Never once."

Claire clutched her cross while her other hand felt along the white collar of her habit. The memory of the bullets ripping Angelique from her grasp suddenly flashed through her thoughts. She remembered what Angelique and she had been wearing when Angelique was shot.

"You say she was wearing this when she was brought here?" she asked, pinching the flowing sleeve of her own habit.

"Drum man—yes, pretty. After he bathed her, dressed her, dressed you," the woman answered, admiring Claire's robes. "But too big. Even hers."

Claire shuddered and ran her hands across her body as if she was wiping something away.

"Do you have it?"

The zombie woman took a step toward the pile of clothes, then turned and eyed Claire with suspicion.

"I did not hear. She asked?"

"Yes," Claire was quick to reply. "She asked."

"When?" the woman asked, edging closer, her eyes turning into slits within wrinkled lines. "And why?"

"While you were sleeping," she offered out of hand. "The flies bother her."

"Oh," the woman said, seeming to understand. "Why didn't she tell me, tell the drum man when he put her down?"

While Claire thought for an answer, the woman's eyes narrowed once more.

"Why bathe her, then?" she wanted to know, her head jerking forward, her lips drawn to a snarl. "Wasted water!" she screamed. "No waste water! Children need! Look. Look. Everywhere dead! No clothes!" she barked. "No waste water!"

The zombie woman began to violently shake, her face filled with rage, her once dull, lost eyes now sharply focused.

Claire grasped her by the upper arms, then quickly let her go, startled by the strength she found in them.

"Calm yourself," she told her in a soothing tone. "I'm sure it is just a misunderstanding. No one wishes to upset you or waste the water. You need not be—"

"What in the world is going on?" Lee huffed, striding into the room of the dead. "Sister Claire, are you all right? The entire camp heard the shouting. It's scaring them. It scared the boy," she said, looking straight at Claire. Lee took a few deep breaths before adding, "John. He ran away."

"Why didn't you tell me that my sister was here? Surely you would think that I would want to know. That I would want to care for her remains."

Lee cast her gaze between Claire and the zombie woman before letting her eyes come to rest on the body of Angelique.

"I know nothing about her," she said, casually shrugging her broad shoulders. "I was not aware that you were traveling with another."

She knelt at the side of the body and placed her fingers above the two bullet holes. She traced the wounds before waving her hands over the bruises and lacerations on Angelique's breasts and loins.

"Eritreans? Government forces? Rebels?

Lee looked to Claire for the answer.

"Or just plain robbers and thieves?"

"I don't know. They blindfolded me. But the ones I did see seemed like they were in some kind of army."

"Do you remember anything else about them?"

"Just a man's voice," Claire told her, shivering as she remembered. "He spoke English, seemed to—"

She shook her head, not wanting to relive it.

"Go on, Sister, Claire," Lee urged her, rising.

Claire stared down at Angelique, tears in her eyes.

"What will her family—? How will they know? How, who will tell them?"

Lee placed her palm along Claire's cheek.

"It is important you tell me about the man, his voice."

"She was just a novice—a child, really. So innocent, so caring. I don't think either one of us knew what—" She stared off into a dark corner of the room and wiped her eyes. "We begged the Mother Superior to let us come," she explained, her voice rising. "We pestered her every day. We just wanted to help where there was a need. It is the doctrine of our order: to teach, care for the sick, see after the orphans—anyone who has no one."

She fell against Lee, her tears flowing freely.

"We begged her. We didn't know," she lamented, rubbing her face on Lee's arm. "This is not what we envisioned," she said, her voice barely audible.

"What was the man's voice like, Claire?"

Claire pushed away, her face filled with confusion.

"What could it matter? A young girl is dead! Do you not grieve? Have you no compassion? Look at her! She's dead!"

"I suppose, somewhere, I do," Lee sighed, resting her large hands on her hips. "If I seem indifferent, I suppose that's what I have become. It's what I've had to be."

She studied Claire's face, wondering if her words were getting through to her.

"There is no dignity in death here, Claire," she added softly. "It doesn't allow for it. It leaves us no time. The blade—it swings too fast. We can't keep up."

Claire said nothing in response. The buzzing of the flies filled the silence.

"He seemed to relish being cruel, seemed to find joy in being brutal."

Claire spoke evenly, without emotion, her eyes fixed on Angelique.

"He hinted at rape and torture as though they were just acts to pass the time. He wanted me to be afraid."

Claire sought Lee's eyes.

"When I said he sounded European, German, he kicked me in the side."

Lee closed her eyes.

"God help us," she murmured.

"You know of whom I speak?" Claire asked, surprised. "He must be brought to justice, then. He must be held accountable for what he has done. We must find him. Take him to the authorities."

Lee's nervous laughter puzzled her.

"You don't understand," Lee started to explain, wringing her hands. "Gunstard is not someone you—"

"Gunstard! No!"

The zombie woman fell to the floor and covered her head with her arms. Like a wounded animal, she pushed herself along the dirt floor to the far wall, sliding along it until she came to the pile of clothes. With a final wail, she burrowed into the mound of clothing, frantically arranging the garments until she was certain that every inch of her body was hidden.

When Claire started to go to her, Lee pulled her back.

"What on earth?"

"Come. This is not the place to talk about this."

"But Sister Angelique is not clothed or properly laid to rest. We must see to her needs."

"There will be time for that later. He will see to everything."

"But she is naked!" Claire protested.

"I don't think she cares," Lee replied. "And we have upset Ella and all the ones she looks after."

"Ella?"

"Yes. Ella," Lee said, glancing toward the pile of clothes in the darkened corner. "Didn't you introduce yourself when you brought the body of the girl in?"

"But she— she—"

Lee awaited Claire's next words with a stern expression.

"She's insane," she finished in a whisper.

"A matter of perception."

"But she sleeps here—with the dead."

"Yes, I know. It saved her once. How long ago that seems now. Sometimes I wish her cleverness had not been so successful. I am given to feel that she would have been better off dying."

"That is for God to decide!" Claire blurted out.

"Is it? Then I suppose you are in agreement with his decision to have—Sister Angelique is it?—raped, shot, and killed? I know I've certainly come to wonder about whose responsibility death is."

Claire turned her head to look out the doorway.

"Who is this Gunstard? And why does the mention of his name cause Ella to hide?"

"Who is he?" Lee repeated, shaking her head. "I don't know who he is or where a man like him might have come from. A mercenary for certain, the way he relishes butchering people. Even when it comes to the men he fights alongside of. Ella had a son. He was a medical student at the time, I was told. He was one of Gunstard's—casualties."

Lee paused, pulling on her ponytail before she went on.

"He hanged him, then slit his stomach open. All because he helped a few fleeing soldiers they had been chasing. He'd followed them all the way from Sudan, I later found out. And everyone was made to watch, including Ella. And then he let his men go wild."

Lee stepped through the rough-hewn doorway. Claire gave Angelique's corpse one last look before following Lee outside.

"I don't think I need to tell you all the things that men are capable of doing when they are filled with the words of the devil. This was once a place of healing, of learning. Now it is—"

She studied the dilapidated, burned-out buildings and the tattered makeshift tents around her. Her laughter was short-lived, sad, and filled with despair.

"People come here with their last hopes. And I have nothing to offer them to keep their hopes alive."

Claire looked around at the desolate terrain.

"Why here? Why a place so bleak, so remote? Surely there is a better location where these people could be offered more."

"Because there is nothing here that anyone wants. And it is where Ella and her son had finally said 'Enough.'"

She fell silent for a moment.

"There was no haven for them—not in Eritrea or in the Tigray. So they fled here. And people followed because they offered help. But there was no safety here."

Lee scraped a bare foot along the parched earth, the swirling dust coming to rest on the bottom edges of her khaki trousers.

"They did not know of Gunstard. Didn't count on having to deal with a man who lives for killing. He was with the government forces at the time, I was told. Hired by some provincial general or colonel or whatever, ordered to find and clean out all pockets of resistance and dissent. That was several years ago. And now he fights against that same government. Though for who, no one really knows."

Lee stretched her long, limber arms out from her sides, her palms facing upward.

"But it doesn't matter who. He destroys everything: steals medical supplies; confiscates rations, water, vehicles; burns anything with a roof; burns books!" she ranted, exasperated. "An incarnation of Hitler," she spat, "set loose upon this land by the devil."

Claire crossed herself.

"God protect us," she soberly intoned.

"Yes, Sister Claire. God protect us, protect *you*."

"Surely there is nothing for him here, though, nothing to bring him back to this place," Claire offered.

"His mind is not like ours. The fact that he has lost something he thought was his," she looked at Claire with concern, "may bring him here to retrieve it."

"But what could he possibly think there—"

"You, Claire. There is you."

The hungry cries from a group of nearby children took Lee away, leaving Claire to grapple with what she had learned. Amidst the crying, the buzzing of the flies rose up from the house of walls, summoning her back. With great reluctance, she retraced her steps, her stomach churning at the thought of stepping back through the morbid doorway to persuade Ella to find and then give her Sister Angelique's habit.

But the vision of her brutalized companion proved to be more powerful than the repulsion Claire harbored toward the house with walls. Angelique would be properly dressed, she had decided, and buried with dignity.

*

C LAIRE CURLED HERSELF into a ball and wrapped the single blanket Lee had given her around her shivering body. She found the ground was hard, unforgiving. *Much like this place*, she thought, *more so than I would ever have imagined it to be.* She closed her eyes for the hundredth time, hoping for sleep. But sleep would not come, even though exhaustion pulled at her very core.

When a breeze had kicked up just before sunset, she had been grateful for its respite—the cool of its touch, its easing of the heat. But now, as she tried to rest, it carried the low, constant moans of suffering upon it, poking at her, rebuking the quiet she so desperately longed for. She pressed her eyelids tight and covered her face with her hands. With a deep breath, she fought to cleanse her thoughts into blankness.

Ali's head suddenly splintered and splattered across the windshield. She shook at the vision, feeling more empty, helpless, and alone than she could ever remember being.

The beating of a solitary drum seeped into her consciousness, keeping time with the pounding of her heart. Little by little, as she listened to her breaths escaping through her fingers, the beat of the drum changed. She sat up with a start.

The child she had named John was sitting at her feet.

"A drum," she whispered. "The drum man. He is real?"

John turned his head and pointed in the direction of the sound of the drum. Claire stood and began walking. John clutched at the hem of her habit, whimpering.

"There, John," she said to him, laying a gentle hand upon his brow. "I—"

She looked down to find his face full of sadness.

"I will come back to you," she assured him. "I promise."

Claire followed the sound of the drum past the house of walls, briefly hesitating before entering the darkness beyond. Although she knew nothing of the area or the terrain around the compound she had been brought to, she strode ahead with confidence, steadfast in the belief that God, as always, would keep her from harm. When the drum fell silent, she stopped, unnerved. Grasping her cross, she peered into the night, turning in every direction. Stretches of emptiness and murky shadows surrounded her.

"She is ready."

The voice seemed both near and far.

"Drum Man?" she asked, shuffling ahead.

The drum beat once in reply. It sounded closer, pulling her forward. She stumbled on a rock.

"She is ready. Be quick."

"I don't— Who's ready? Where are you?"

The flame from a match ignited. In the halo of light it cast, Claire glimpsed a mound of soil. She edged forward. The flame went out.

"Why are you out here?"

"To unite the child with the Mother."

The voice was close. She was almost upon it.

"I— I don't understand."

She felt the mound of dirt at the tip of her feet and smelled the awful scent of rotted flesh. It was a grave.

"Who is it that you bury?"

"The one you came with."

"Angelique?"

Claire froze; the man's face was suddenly very close.

An eerie call floated to them from some distance away. Claire felt her muscles tense. The sound reminded her of ghouls and goblins.

"We must hurry. They will come if the scent is not covered."

"Who will come?"

"Are there any words you wish to say?" he asked, peering down inside the grave.

Claire would not look.

"Words?" she replied, confused.

The voices of the jackals and the hyenas came to them again. Claire shuddered; they were getting closer.

"If there is something you wish to say to her, say it now. The hyenas are almost here."

Claire sought his face, searching through what light the night sky offered to find what lay within his eyes. But his gaze was directed past and over her, set upon the camp.

"They will be scared," he said.

"I hardly knew her," she told him, her voice cracking.

"Stand to the drum, then. Beat on it with strength."

"What? What— I—"

The drum man suddenly grabbed hold of her wrists and jerked her to him. Claire struggled as he pulled her away from the grave. And when he slipped behind her and pressed his body against her, she twisted violently, trying to break free.

He lifted one of her hands and then slapped it down on the drum, the skin of the drumhead stinging her palm. Her other hand pounded the drum as the first was lifted off. The *boom-boom* of the instrument quieted the calls of the animals. Twice more the drum man forced her arms and hands to repeat the beat. When her palms slapped the drum for the third time, she turned to complain. But the drum man was no longer behind her.

With the feel of his hands still strong on her wrists, she played on, delivering an echoing pulse unto the night. Claire looked on as the drum man bent to one knee, bowed his head, and in a soft, weary voice said: "Mother, though this child was not of you, it is to you that I send her. I would ask that you take her into your sky and earth and water so that she may understand why she came here. Let the spirit elephants guide her to your paradise, where the great bulls stand watch."

The drum man took a fistful of dirt and let it drop to the body below.

"Mother, help her find the way," he murmured as the last of the soil fell from his grasp.

Only when the grave was filled in and heavy stones scattered over it did the drum man go to Claire to stop her methodical pounding. Even so, when his fingers pressed her hands to the skin of the drum to prevent her from playing, she did not react to his touch or seem to comprehend that he was even there.

"I will take you back now," he offered.

"What?" she dazedly murmured.

"It is done."

Claire stared down at the grave for a moment and nodded her head.

"God bless you for your kindness," she told him, abruptly sweeping past him, glancing back before crossing herself.

When she knelt down at the foot of the grave, grasped her cross, and began to pray, the cackle of a lone hyena gave her pause.

"We must go," he told her.

Claire gazed up into his face again, straining to find his eyes through the darkness. In the end, her stare settled on the soft outline of his slender lips, the gentle rise of his cheeks, and his brooding brow.

"I must pray for her first. Go on if you'd like. God will keep me safe," she told him.

She raised a hand in gentle protest when she saw he was about to argue.

"He will," she assured him. "He is here."

The drum man stepped away, bending to gather a bow, a quiver of arrows, and a long, metal-tipped spear.

"Wait," Claire said. "I do not know your name."

The drum man cocked his head to one side but said nothing.

"I can't just call you Drum Man. You do have a name, don't you?"

"Teimbaka."

"Teimbaka," she repeated with a slight bow of her head. "Does your name mean something in your culture?" she asked, looking back up to him.

But she was alone. Teimbaka had already gone. And as the calls of the hyenas began to grow bolder, she said in a loud voice, "My name is Claire. Sister Claire."

Teimbaka slipped an arrow from the quiver and nocked it to his bow. Although he was keeping watch over Claire from some twenty yards away, obscured to her by the dark, his eyes scoured the terrain around her while he listened for any sound that might foretell danger.

Steps taken lightly behind him, approaching where he stood, caused him no alarm. Even when the footfalls fell silent, changing to a mischievous hop, he only smiled.

"You have come to watch over her, then?" he asked without turning.

The child lightly took hold of the bottom edge of Teimbaka's tunic. With the other, he pointed toward Claire.

"She prays," Teimbaka told him. "She is a sister."

The boy stared hard at the kneeling figure for a moment before looking up to Teimbaka.

"*Eh-heht*," he said in what he thought might be the boy's language. "Sister."

"Sis— sist—"

"Sister," Teimbaka quietly repeated.

"Sister."

Teimbaka smiled at the boy.

"*Wayzaro?*"

Teimbaka nodded his head and said, "Lady."

"Lay—"

"Lady."

The boy smiled.

"Sister Lady."

"Yes," Teimbaka told him, "Sister Lady."

The animal's eyes were nothing more than the briefest flash of yellow some thirty yards past where Claire knelt. Teimbaka shot his arrow and waited, listening, straining to hear the sound that might tell him it had found its mark.

"Wait," he instructed the boy when the child started to move toward Claire. "They're moving."

"Sister Lady," the boy said, tugging at Teimbaka's pants leg.

"She comes," he told him, watching Claire's figure move away from the grave. "See? Meet her and take her back."

Teimbaka looked down at the emaciated child and rubbed his head.

"There are things I still must do."

FIFTY KILOMETERS AWAY, Peter Gunstard sat at his makeshift desk, staring into the lantern that provided the only light inside his tent. Within the wavering flame, he saw the images of burning Panzer tanks and exploding bombs, of villages set ablaze, and of smoldering mounds of human carcasses, their number too great for a grave. Bursts of sparks from automatic weapons erupted from the edges of the flame. As he gazed at them, the sparks became an inferno, a mass of raging flames engulfing fields of crops doused with gasoline. Emerging from the inferno he saw himself. The cold-hearted expression he saw on his own face made him smile. He well remembered the numerous columns of torch wielding soldiers he had commanded as they marched upon sleeping villages to kill, rape, and steal.

Germany, Algeria, Egypt, Sudan, Rhodesia, the Congo, and now Ethiopia; what had begun in the Third Reich during a war that had encompassed the world had devolved into a succession of bloody rebellions and lesser coups. It had become a regression. Once an elite officer in one of the world's greatest armies, Gunstard was now a forgotten soldier-for-hire with an allegiance to no one. He rubbed his weary, grey-blue eyes.

"My destiny," he muttered to the images with contempt.

He took stock of his bare, meager surroundings, a rueful smile tugging at the corners of his mouth.

"Perhaps I should have remained in Addis," he mumbled.

But even as he entertained the notion that he should have remained as an advisor to the Ethiopian army and its emperor, Haile Selassie, he had known at the time, when he had made the decision to switch alli-ances, that it was the right one. For to remain would have been foolish, and more than likely would have cost him his life.

To be a white officer in the hire of a black man's army came with many benefits, especially when the arrangement was based on a mutual need: normally, money for expertise. And for several years, he had enjoyed the benefits of such an arrangement with the Ethiopian government. But once the United States had begun to withdraw its political support for Haile Selassie and had shut off the free flow of arms to the Ethiopian army, he had sensed the situation rapidly changing. Haile Selassie and those who supported him were in danger of losing everything. The clear signs of deceit and mutiny were everywhere. The upheaval in the political landscape had made the decision to switch allegiances an easy one.

The flame of the lantern flickered, drawing him into it once more. The fire seemed to embody all the killings he had taken part in—from his days in Rommel's army to the present, commanding a ragtag, ill-equipped, loosely organized, undisciplined band of rebels.

"Eritrea," he said with a shake of his head.

A burst of gunfire from an automatic weapon broke his musing. As he expected, shouting erupted from just outside his tent. The sound of run-ning boot heels followed close after.

"Colonel! Colonel!"

Gunstard chuckled; everyone was a colonel nowadays. Generals, it seemed, were no longer in vogue.

A soldier yanked his tent flap open.

Gunstard stared at the black-brown face, trying to decide if he rec-ognized the man. Lately, all the men around him looked the same. Other than the poor excuse of an Eritrean uniform the man was wearing, there was nothing about him that Gunstard found overly familiar.

"What is it, Lieutenant?" Gunstard inquired, noticing the single silver bar on the man's collar. "What prompted the gunfire?"

The man saluted sharply. Gunstard sighed.

"One of the sentries thought he saw a lion, sir," said the soldier.

"Did he, now?" Gunstard replied with an air of sarcasm. "Did he hit it?"

"Unknown, sir."

"Unknown," Gunstard repeated contemptuously. "And why would that be?"

"The men—" he began, his eyes focused on a spot a foot or so above his colonel's head, "they are afraid."

"Afraid," Gunstard grunted.

"With the famine and drought, the beasts are often half-mad," the man went on to explain. "Very unpredictable, dangerous."

Gunstard's laughter shocked the man.

"Orders, Colonel?"

"Orders?"

Gunstard eyed the man with a mixture of contempt and bewilderment. The lieutenant's expression gave him some cause to be concerned; loyalty amongst the soldiers in his commanded was suspect, trust ebbed and flowed.

"Very well, Lieutenant. Double the guard and place two men around the food supply."

The man said nothing.

"Is there something more, Lieutenant?"

"Permission to allow the men to build a fire."

"Permission denied."

"But, sir."

"No *but*, Lieutenant, or perhaps the men would like to hand our position over to the armored column we spotted today?"

The lieutenant's eyes shifted uncertainly from side to side. Gunstard recognized the signs of fear.

"If everyone must stay awake all night to keep themselves alive, then so be it, Lieutenant. Come dawn, we break camp to strike that same armored column that so obligingly sits somewhere close by, ready to be picked clean. A victorious blow against the government forces is worth a lost night's sleep. Wouldn't you say so, Lieutenant?"

Gunstard perceived a grudging nod from the man.

"Good. Pass the word: no fires."

"Sir," the lieutenant smartly replied, saluting.

"And, Lieutenant."

"Yes, sir?"

"Take two men and scout out the area. See if you can locate the lion."

Gunstard took delight at the open fear in the man's face.

"That is all."

The lieutenant turned and quickly left the tent.

"And don't piss on yourself," Gunstard mumbled, chuckling.

The flame of the lantern called to him again. Unconsciously, he fingered the two ivory teeth that hung about his neck, the ones he had taken from Bawa's faceless body. In the base of the flame, the lithe figure of a young man appeared.

"Boy," he whispered.

How many years had passed, he wondered, since he had witnessed the boy fighting off a lion with just a spear? He remembered the morning clearly; the boy had not wavered, even when the lion had leapt to pounce. He had drawn blood from the beast. He had exhibited bravery.

"Teimbaka," he said to the figure in the flame. "And now a lion appears."

He stared into the lantern, wondering, smiling, nodding his head, enthralled with the possibility that Teimbaka was somewhere near.

*

"SISTER LADY! SISTER Lady! Sister Lady!"

"Dear God, John! What have you done?"

John ran up to where Claire and Lee were standing, his face smeared and dripping with blood.

"What on earth?"

"Sister Lady!" the boy exclaimed happily.

John cupped his hands and pantomimed drinking. Smiling, rubbing his stomach, he pointed to his heart, feigned plucking it from his chest, and then took an imaginary bite.

"Dear Lord, child! Tell me you're not trying to say that you've been drinking blood and eating something's heart?" Claire gasped in utter dismay.

John instantly became despondent at Claire's reaction.

Lee bent to him and wiped the blood from his chin.

"Drinking the blood of animals is not so uncommon," Lee said, giving Claire a disapproving look. "It does not evoke the ghoulishness here that it does in the States."

Lee jostled John's head and gave him a warm smile.

"Sister Lady," he responded, offering a sheepish smile to Claire while again rubbing his protruding stomach.

"That's barbaric. It's disgusting. It's—"

"Survival," Lee told her forcefully, cutting her off. "Not to mention a part of all of our histories. *All* of our histories," she repeated, almost inviting Claire to disagree. "Even yours and your God's."

"Do not disparage the name of the Lord in my presence," she scolded Lee. "And may He forgive you for your insolence."

"This is the cup of my blood; the blood of the new and everlasting covenant. Drink from it and—"

"Silence!"

For a moment, Claire shook with rage. In the next, she was falling to her knees, sobbing. At once, John knelt beside her and took hold of her hand.

"I am sorry, Claire—Sister Lady," Lee said, placing a hand upon the crown of her head. "It is no way to begin another day."


As sunset turned to twilight, Claire and John found the drum man sitting upon a flat-topped boulder, holding the kebero between his knees. He took no notice of their approach, his attention cast to the western horizon and the beat he was softly pounding, welcoming the pinks and violets to the evening sky.

The rocky hills around them, bathed as they were in these melancholy, pastel hues, took on an air of timelessness, as though they were part of another era.

John and Claire stood in deference to the mood of the moment and the man seated before them. They, as much as Teimbaka, seemed to want to drink in the colors and the tone of the evening before the fall to darkness changed it all.

"Why have you come?" the drum man quietly asked.

John tugged on Claire's sleeve when she did not immediately reply.

"We wondered— we wondered why you did not come to eat. It was you who delivered the two antelope carcasses to the camp, was it not? It would only have been right for you to be there when we gave thanks."

Teimbaka said nothing, though the rhythm he beat seemed to pound a bit stronger.

"Although I do not agree with you allowing the boy—John—to drink its blood or partake in the eating—"

Claire fell silent as she stared at his features in the changing light, his square jaw and noble brow half cast in shadow, his soft brown eyes alight with the last glimmer of the setting sun.

"Will you hunt again tomorrow?" she tentatively asked. "Can you get more food?"

He silenced his hands, resting them on the drum, his loose-fitting white tunic drooping with his slumping shoulders.

"I only ask because more children wandered into camp today. Perhaps you saw? We fear—Lee and I—that there will be more tomorrow."

She waited for an answer.

"Do you see what I'm getting at? Teimbaka? Have I said something to offend you?"

"The day—will it last forever?"

"The day?" Claire asked, confused. "It— it is ending now," she told him carefully.

"But it does not," he told her flatly. "For years it has gone on. So I ask you again. Will it end?"

He locked eyes with her, binding her to him with his question.

She flinched and looked away.

"Your boy—is he happy?"

"John? Why, yes. Today, anyway. There was food, thanks to you."

"He is small."

"That may be, for now," she responded, taking a step closer to John. "But he will grow. He will become big and strong," she went on, pulling John to her. "The house with walls will not have him."

"Your dreams—the day does not heed them," he said with a tired voice, his words laced with exhaustion.

"Then the day must be made to listen, to see, to understand. It will not take from me that which the Lord has placed in my heart."

Teimbaka sat quiet for a moment before a small smile crept to his lips.

"So much certainty. Does this lord of yours make all his women this way?"

"He makes of us what we make of ourselves. Doubt is not a part of Him. For those who embrace Him—truly embrace Him—there comes the strength of peace, the resoluteness of love, the might of faith. With Him, Teimbaka, all things are possible. All."

"Can he stop the day? Will he end it before it goes on forever?"

Claire hurried to answer, but then stopped herself. Her expression was at first fretful, but then it cleared and brightened as she strongly replied, "Yes."

"Then ask him. Ask him to end it now, before, as you say, the house with walls covers this land."

"I cannot."

"Why?" he asked, seeming suddenly hostile, the muscles tightening in his neck.

"The Lord is not a servant," Claire answered calmly. "His will is His own. It does not belong to us."

"Then what good is he?" Teimbaka asked dismissively.

Claire smiled slightly.

"I have harbored the same thoughts since you brought me here. And for that, I ask the Lord's forgiveness. It was wrong of me. For I could not have wandered further from the truth. He gave us life, you see, Teimbaka. We are His children. He can guide us—nurture us if we allow Him to— but He does not live our lives for us. He does not keep us from finding our own way."

She clutched the small silver cross about her neck before going on.

"Surely he feels the pain of all who are here. Each child that dies draws a tear from His eye. I believe that. I believe that His love is unfathomable, eternal, His faith in us without question. But, like all parents, He can do no more than look on and hope that we find the right path, the right road back to Him. And no, Teimbaka," she hurried to say, seeing the skepticism in his face, "it is not easy, will not be easy. I'm sure it will seem impossible at times."

She looked to John and ran a hand over his cheek. The evening seemed to stand still as she said, "But what price is paradise worth? What will you give of yourself to reach it? What amount of sacrifice are you willing to bear to reach the threshold of His grace?"

John whimpered, holding tight to Claire's trembling body, frightened by the feelings she was emitting.

"Children know nothing of this," Teimbaka stated plainly. "Should their innocence condemn them?"

"It is in our hands that they learn and understand. We can teach them, Teimbaka. With knowledge and faith, they can overcome—no, they have the *chance* to overcome—any obstacle set before them. But we must be—are—the instruments of the Lord. His hands, if you will. We are the ones who must enact change, Teimbaka. We are these children's greatest hope."

In a softer voice, she said, almost pleadingly, "If they are to live, it will be from our strength, our hope, and our faith."

Teimbaka stared at her intently. In return, she opened herself to him, hoping, through her eyes, he could see what lay in her heart.

"Survival is not a matter of faith."

"Isn't it, Teimbaka? Isn't it?"

The roar of a lion shattered the moment, tearing away the calm. Screams of children echoed through the rocky hills. Before Claire could think or speak, Teimbaka was running past her, his long, steel-tipped spear held firmly by his side.

*

WHEN TEIMBAKA REACHED the village, all was in turmoil: children screaming and wailing all around him, running or crawling for a place to hide. He moved deftly, the spear held out in front of him, his hands spread apart along the shaft, his grip balanced from opposite sides. Within the cries of the children, he listened for the beast.

The blanket in the doorway of the house with walls fluttered. A white hand slid along one edge, a finger pointing to the corner of the far wall. Teimbaka edged closer.

The lion backed out from the edge of the house with walls, dragging its kill out into the open by a leg. A small, wrinkled foot dangled from the side of the animal's mouth. Blood dripped from its ankle to its heel.

"Ella!" Teimbaka yelled.

The lion, a gaunt, rangy male, dropped his kill. He turned at the sound of Teimbaka's voice, uttering a low, menacing snarl.

"John! Come back!"

The lion flinched at the sound of Claire's voice, his eyes shifting to her running figure, his ears following every swish of her habit.

"Stop, Sister! Do not move!"

But his warning came too late. The lion loped toward Claire as the last word left his mouth.

"Sister Lady! Sister Lady!"

John ran to meet the lion with only a stick as a weapon. The lion jerked to a halt and swung a massive paw. John froze. Claire screamed hysterically.

Teimbaka thrust his spear at the lion's haunches, raking the tip sideways, luring the animal to turn and face him. Filled with rage, the lion gathered to pounce.

For the oddest of moments, Teimbaka saw the lion emerge from the elephant grass, his eyes afire, his jaws dripping with saliva. As it had been on that morning so long ago, the great spirit-bull was standing right next to him, digging up chunks of earth as it swung its massive tusks from side to side. But the vision fell away when the lion leapt for the kill. Teimbaka stood alone, with only his spear to protect him.

"Teimbaka!"

As Claire screamed his name, he rushed forward to meet the beast's charge, thrusting his spear into the lion's chest as its claws sliced across his own torso.

The piercing cry that filled the air, he could make no sense of.

## NOVEMBER, 1972

T ITUS STUFFED A handful of potato chips into his mouth, wiping the grease off on the sleeve of his peasant shirt before he resumed counting the wad of bills he held in his other hand.

"Good week," he managed to croak as he swallowed. "Business keeps going like this, we can all retire in a few years."

He brushed a few crumbs from his full, black beard and then picked his teeth with the nail of his index finger.

"Oh, man, watching you eat is, like, the pits, T. Shit-a-phoria."

Titus snorted, swallowing what sounded like a throat full of snot.

"Gross, T. Real fucking gross."

"Be cool, Jen babe. Ain't easy countin' all this crumpled up, hard-earned cash, you know. Wouldn't want me to lose count, would ya? Cut you and the Gabe man short."

Jennifer grunted and folded her arms across her chest.

"Why don't you fire up another doob or somethin'? Put some Hendrix on. Mellow out, man."

"I don't want to mellow out, *man*," she retorted.

"What's with her?" Titus asked, his dark-brown, sleepy-lidded eyes shifting to Gabriel. "She on the rag?"

Gabriel pushed his rose-lensed glasses up on the bridge of his nose before adjusting the black-handled hair pick sticking out of the back of his afro.

"Nixon, man; she's still all weirded out 'cause he got re-elected. Don't jive with the woman that the pointy-nosed dude gonna be holdin' court for another four. Bad vibes, you know?"

"Well she ought to lighten up, you know. You should be happy 'bout it, babe. Party hearty. Old putty head is our main man, you know." He held a stack of bills out in front of her. "See this?" he told her. "Dude make it easy, you know? Ain't squeezing down on us. Doesn't fuck with the Heads. So let it be, let it be."

"Let it be," she scoffed. "Be cool—stupid, goddamned pig," she cursed, fingering the tattered holes of her skin-tight blue jeans. "Another four years of napalm and Vietnam while his fuckin' pretend soldiers go around shootin' protesters. Fuckin' asshole probably kill all of us if he could get away with it. He doesn't give a damn about us, our generation. He just sucks in all the power he can get. Gets off on it. Just digs the power trip. He ain't no fuckin' leader. How could he be, when he has his head up his ass?"

"Damn girl, you be acid like. You got vibes that could slice a pie. Hey, dig it: vibes, pie—cool, real cool."

Titus laughed at his play on words, getting a slight smile from Gabriel and a cold, stony stare from Jennifer.

"Come on, Jen babe, lighten up, would you? You're puttin' some bad stuff in the air. When was the last time you had some fun? Gabe, when was the last time you took the lady out and blew off some time in the clouds?"

"We've been busy, T, you know? Like runnin' deliveries for you and scammin' out new deals," Jennifer told him sarcastically.

"Oh, solid, like I'm the uptight bad dude, huh? I don't see my man Gabe complainin'. Nice crib, nice threads. Not my fault if you two don't take the time to mellow. Or maybe you need a refresher course. Maybe old T should show you where it's all at."

Jennifer rolled her eyes.

"Oh yeah, right, T, like you've been outside this cave lately. Like you even remember what the sun looks like. Drawn blinds, black lights, day-glo shit everywhere—I mean, like, where are you coming from?"

"Be cool, Jen. T can't be runnin' round like us. Make the connection man real edgy if he did. Faceless; he gotta be faceless, dig?"

"Right on," Titus agreed with a definitive nod.

"Solid," Gabriel replied.

Jennifer started to giggle. When she kept it up for an uncomfortable time, Gabriel and Titus raised their eyebrows.

"You're losin' it, Jen," Titus told her. "Really losin' it."

Jennifer stuffed a handful of her stringy, limp blond hair into her mouth in an attempt to gain some self-control.

"Oh, man," she spit in a burst of laughter. "You should fuckin' hear yourselves. You're straight out of the *Mod Squad*."

She straightened her shoulders, stuck her chest out, and with a very serious look said, "Solid, Link. Right on, Pete."

Unable to sustain her mock seriousness, she burst out laughing again.

"I guess— I guess— and I guess that makes me Julie, right? Except *my* tits are way bigger."

She cupped her breasts in her hands and jiggled them.

"I mean they are, aren't they? Julie never had anything close to these. Heck, my *nipples* are bigger than her boobs," she chortled.

"Man, what you on today, Jen? You, uh, slip a little Window Pane in your tea this mornin'?"

Jennifer stuck out her tongue while giving Titus a Bullwinkle Moose double-handed antler wave.

"You belong in the zoo, baby. You need some time in a cage."

"Oh, T, yeah, cool! The zoo, man! Let's head down to the zoo! We can go watch the people watchin' the animals. It'd be cool! Whaddaya say?"

Titus absently grabbed hold of his long black ponytail and pulled it up over his head.

"Man, I haven't been to the zoo since I was a kid," he sighed, seeming to lose himself in a memory. "How 'bout you, Gabe? When's the last time you went to the zoo?"

"Ain't ever been," he told them, fidgeting in his seat and playing with his glasses.

He glanced at Jennifer to see if she was picking up on his mood, hoping she was going to remember that animals unnerved him, like the imaginary barking dogs of his past and the headaches they caused. A cold shiver ran up his spine.

"Settled, done deal, then."

"Say what?" Gabriel dazedly inquired.

"The zoo, man, the zoo," Titus told him. "We all gonna trip on down to the zoo, Gabe. You lunchin' on us?"

"Just zoned out for a sec," he replied with a shrug. "No biggie."

Titus arched his thick, bushy eyebrows.

"Man, you're both out there today," he proclaimed, glancing at both Jennifer and Gabriel. "T better rustle up something good to bring you both back in from the ozone. What's good for a zoo trek?" he asked them mischievously. "Ludes, Black Beauties, some Mesc, maybe?" He chuckled. "Or how 'bout—that is, if you can handle it—a little four-way Orange Barrel; one apiece?"

He slapped his hands to his thighs.

"This is gonna be fun!"


Gabriel tried to relax and ride the electric waves the Orange Barrel acid was pushing through his body. But the undertones of anger and confusion tugging at the edge of his thoughts would not quite allow him to give in to the sensations of the acid trip.

"Damn, these fuckers stink," he said, sniffing the air. "They always this noisy?"

But when Jennifer and Titus—walking ahead of him, giggling and holding hands—didn't respond, it made him wonder if he had just imagined speaking. He looked cautiously around.

The animals were staring at him. He could feel it. Some looked at him with sadness; others with contempt. They were sneering and mocking, seeming to challenge him to feel something other than the anxious fear that was building in his stomach.

An old male lion looked out at him from behind the thick steel bars of his lair, greeting Gabriel's arrival in front of the concrete enclosure with an icy stare and an audible snarl. Gabriel felt his heart begin to race. His breathing became shallow, labored.

"Whatcha doin' back there?" Jennifer called to him, looking over her shoulder. "You lost in a lost world?"

He snapped his head around at the sound of her voice, his chest heaving with relief. Feeling their connection, ecstatic with the bond her voice offered him, he smiled back at her like a lost boy who had found his way home.

"We're gonna go feed the seals!" Titus yelled. "Argh, argh, argh!" he added, clapping stiff arms together. "Meet us there!"

"We'll get a plate of—argh, argh—fish for you!" Jennifer laughed as she and Titus skipped on ahead.

A power surge from the acid shot through him, setting his whole body humming. All around him, the animals began to yelp and howl. Gabriel cringed and hurried to catch up.

But the roar of the lion froze him in his place. And when he turned, the large animal was in front of him, staring directly at him. Its jaws were open, its teeth dripping with blood-tinged saliva. He wondered if what he was seeing was real.

Off in the distance, a tiny bell began to ring. The lion shifted his attention in that direction, a hunger in his eyes. Gabriel covered his ears with his hands; ocean waves were pounding within his palms. The lion looked at him and snarled. Gabriel felt the threat of it wash through him.

A little boy tugged at his arm. His eyes were filled with tears.

"Have you seen my mommy?" the boy mouthed.

Slowly, Gabriel lifted his hands from his ears. He stared at the child, wondering if he was real.

"Have you?" the little boy whimpered.

"Have I what?" Gabriel dumbly replied, not recognizing the sound of his own voice.

A white-topped, blue-bottomed blur suddenly swooped in between Gabriel and the boy.

"There you be," a harsh voice hissed, the menace in its tone giving Gabriel a start. "I told you to stay right outside the restroom, didn't I? And where's your brother? Where's your brother?"

An instant later, the voice, the blur, and the child were gone. Gabriel gaped at the empty space in front of him.

Reaching out a hand, he felt the space where the child had been standing; there was nothing. A bell jingled somewhere near. A hyena seemed to answer the sound with a ghoulish cackle.

*Where's your brother?*

The question fell upon him like stones hurled in the dark, the sound of the words crushing him with a painful anxiety.

Wide-eyed, gripped with paranoia, he whirled round.

Strange-looking people stared at him and moved away, their whispered mutterings reaching him as threats. He recognized no one.

*Where's your brother?*

The voice reverberated all around him, permeating his very core. The chemicals in his blood stream began to accelerate, humming at an alarming pitch.

A figure stepped in front of him: a black child, nearing manhood, dressed in an earth-colored robe, leaning upon a thick shaft of wood.

Gabriel eyed the youth suspiciously.

"Why did you not find him and keep him safe as I asked?"

Gabriel blinked several times, certain that the vision would disappear. Tentatively, he felt his own face, sighing with relief when he touched flesh. Then, in the grasp of a stupor, he watched the same hand move outward to touch the figure standing before him.

"Where is he now?" the boy in the robes asked.

Before Gabriel's hand could touch the boy, blood began to stream out from a jagged wound that appeared between the boy's neck and shoulder.

"You must help him," the youth told him, his blood-streaked image beginning to waver. "He needs you."

"Who? Who needs me?"

The youth held the stick out for Gabriel to take, but before he could touch it, the vision drifted into nothingness.

A hyena howled and a bell jingled. A sharp, searing pain shot through his head. He staggered backward.

Small fingers took hold of his hands, steadying him.

A boy, younger than the first, stood before him, smiling. Gabriel racked his memory for his name, certain he knew him. He raced back through the years, trying to place his face. The boy stood up on his toes and ran a gentle finger under Gabriel's eyes.

"Why do you not cry for Tafari? He fought the lion so we could escape. Father will not be happy that you shed no tears."

The child tilted his head to one side, his expression questioning, his eyes filled with concern.

"What is wrong, Menelik? Why do you tremble so?"

"Menelik."

The saying of his name pierced the dark, throbbing pain that had haunted him since his childhood.

"Teimbaka!" he blurted out. His hands began to shake. Tears blurred his sight. "I didn't know! I didn't mean to run!"

The hooting laughter from a pack of hyenas mocked him, their calls awakening the pain hidden in the scars on his leg and arm.

He lurched forward to embrace his brother, stumbling badly when he found nothing to grab hold of. Wild eyed, he righted himself, completely lost between the emotions of his past and present. Behind him, the lion growled. The memory of Tafari's death bubbled inside him, the acid heightening every detail of the gruesome moment. Adrenaline began to surge through his body. His muscles expanded, each fiber seeming to intensify. Rage began to flow across his synapses. When the lion growled again, he did not hesitate.

Leaping over the iron fence that separated the enclosure from the zoo path, he hurled himself at the beast, his body crashing hard against the steel bars. He landed deftly in the space between the fence and cage, then righted himself and unleashed a roar of his own. The lion retreated, ducking into the square opening at the back of its lair. He shook the bars and glared after it.

Some distance away, the hyenas howled again. Their calls were maddening, accentuating the sharp pain of his old wounds. Bent on revenge, he raced off to find them, leaving a score of stunned onlookers gaping after him.

Twisting and dodging, he sped effortlessly forward, his muscles bursting with previously untapped energy. People shuffled out of his way, pulling their children aside, shouting, gasping, and cursing. But he neither saw nor heard what was around him except the river of sand beneath his feet and the calls of the hyenas up ahead.

When he saw them, he came to a sudden stop. Just as it had been those many years before, there were three of the beasts.

He breathed deeply and flexed. His muscles felt like steel. He was filled with a sense of utter invincibility. He moved to the hyenas' enclosure, leaping the waist-high iron perimeter fence with ease. Landing, he grabbed the bars of their cage and howled.

The hyenas eyed him warily before separating. One moved quickly to his left side, another to his right, the one in front crouching down as if to leap. They snarled in unison, their teeth slick with saliva. He growled back, his right hand reaching outward for a weapon that he didn't have.

"Hey, asshole! What the hell are you doing? Get away from that cage! You're not allowed in there!"

Finding no weapon, Menelik rattled the bars of the cage, certain he could pull them apart, the acid driving him into a frenzy, locking him into the need for brute force.

But the bars would not give. The hyenas began a hooting chorus of taunts. Enraged, he thrust an arm inside their enclosure, desperate to reach them. He envisioned choking each one until their laughing voices were strangled to silence.

Hands fell upon him from both sides, wrenching him from the bars, wrestling him to the ground. Grunts and groans filled his ears, quickly transforming into the snarls and growls of ravenous beasts when he felt hot, moist breath on each side of his neck. Gritting his teeth, he snarled, furious that he had not noticed these other hyenas that had been in hiding outside the cage.

Reliving the moment from his past when the beasts had bitten him and torn open his flesh, he willed his strength to gather, then flung his assailants off him with a mighty thrust of his shoulders and arms.

In an instant, he was on his feet, gauging the threat around him. Shifting his gaze from animal to animal, he tensed, waiting for the attack.

"Calm down!" the hyena on his right screamed.

"No one's going to hurt you!" the one on the left yelled.

Menelik heard the words entangled with the hooting of the three hyenas inside the cage.

"Fuckers!" he spit, giving the two beasts that were on either side of him his full attention. "Hyena-men! Killers!"

He hurled his fist into the face of the hyena-man to his right, knuckles smashing bone, the power of his punch sending the man sprawling backward.

Spin-jumping back around, he glimpsed the blur of a short wooden spear swinging down upon him. Stepping forward and under, he clamped the forearm of the hyena-man with one hand and squeezed with all his strength. When the beast squealed, he wrenched the weapon away. The sensation of the smooth wood between his palm and fingers transported him back to the river of sand. In an instant of panic, he searched the ground around him for Tafari's remains. It was then that the hyena-man who had lost the short wooden spear grasped him roughly by the arm. Menelik shoved the spear into the beast's stomach and pushed him away. Lunging after him, he tried to thrust the point of the spear into the hyena-man's chest. But the spear was too short. The hyena-man simply retreated, unharmed. Menelik flung the useless weapon to the ground with an agonized scream.

Behind him, inside the barred enclosure, the hyenas cackled and bayed. The hyena-men on either side of him moved cautiously toward him.

"Don't make me pull my gun, nigger," one of them snapped, slapping his hip.

In an acid-swept moment of clarity, Menelik saw that his situation was hopeless. He could not kill the beasts unless he had a weapon—a weapon that would reach not only the ones hiding behind the bars, but the two that were attacking him on the outside.

With an image of a spear inside his head, he leapt to the iron fence above him and pulled himself up. The growling hyena-men closed in behind him, jumping to reach his legs. But Menelik easily swung his body over the lip of the fence, leaving the man-beasts clawing at air.

His flight out of the zoo was a blend of asphalt and sand, people and animals, buildings and dense thickets of scrub brush that ran along the banks of the dry riverbed. Wild animals hooted, called, growled, and roared—sounds that he had once feared but now welcomed, their familiar voices ushering him home, back to the land his father had called Ethiopia.

Leaving the zoo, he ran straight into the middle of a street. Momentarily confused, he blindly started across the busy intersection. Horns blared and brakes screeched. Ethiopia fell away to a swirling, noisy mass of concrete and metal.

A horn blasted behind him, a big yellow taxi clipping the back of his thighs as it pushed by him.

"Get out of the street, jerk-off!" the driver screamed.

Menelik jumped to the side, weaving through the stream of onrushing cars to the safety of the sidewalk beyond.

"Fuckin' hippie junkie!" a voice yelled when he stopped to turn back to see where it was he had come from.

The shouted insult and the color yellow made a brief connection within his thoughts. He rifled through his memory.

*He saw himself slamming on the brakes, bringing the car to a sudden stop, placing an arm out to protect Jennifer. A black man in tattered clothes had staggered out in front of the car. He remembered sitting in the driver's seat, yelling at the man.*

"What did I yell at him, Jen?"

His voice startled him. He touched his fingers to his lips three times, humming, enthralled with the sensation.

"Jen," he whispered, smiling at the way her name felt upon his fingertips.

He gazed across the street, hoping she was there, a snippet of a thought hinting to him that she might be somewhere back across the tangled mass of cars and concrete.

Hyena-men appeared. They jumped into the street, blowing whistles and stopping cars. They had followed him.

"I need a weapon," he heard his voice say.

With a nod, he took off.

Still pulsating from the grip of the chemicals inside his body, he ran just to run, no intended destination taking him one way or the other. Expanses of brick and glass, concrete, slate, and steel whirred by, all of it familiar, all of it strange, his mind racing between what was real and what was imagined. Only when the maze of streets began to shine with the glow of headlights and street lamps did he begin to slow down.

Breathing heavily, his body soaked with sweat, he crouched, listening; the whistles and shouts of the hyena-men were gone. He had lost them.

A neon sign flickered on and off, catching his eye.

The electric blue and red of it glimmered on a storefront window some fifty paces ahead. Moving slowly, he suspiciously eyed the few people who were on the street. Hyenas were clever, he had come to see—more so now that they were able to walk on their hind legs disguised as men.

The neon was hypnotic. He stood in front of it, absorbing the blinking colors, his body attuning to its rhythm.

Slowly, his attention shifted to the display of iron clubs and balls, uniforms and pennants, shoes and jackets that were arranged behind a large pane of glass. His eyes wandered without a purpose, sifting through the confusing assortment of shapes and sizes, seeing everything and nothing at the same time. He didn't realize he had found what he was looking for until his gaze came to rest upon a long slender shaft with a pointed tip. He smiled, certain that fate had led him there.

The javelin rested upright, taking a spot in a back corner of the display. The decorative, swirling lines of yellow and red running along its shaft had almost concealed it within the blue and orange of the Knicks jacket hanging beside it.

He reached for it; the glass shuddered with the smack of his hand. The street light above him flickered and hissed. The skin on the back of his neck prickled. He closed his eyes and thought of brothers.

In a flash, he leapt backward and then hurled himself forward. Just before he crashed against the sporting goods store window, he lowered his shoulder and raised his arms to protect his face. The glass shattered inward, creating a jagged hole big enough for him to wedge his upper body through.

He looked at the javelin. Without hesitating, he twisted up and in, grabbing hold of it as the front door to the store flew open.

"What the fuck?" a man screamed before slamming and locking the door shut.

Menelik pulled the javelin to him, wrenching it free from the piece of knotted twine that held it.

A siren began to wail. At the end of the street, the reflection of flashing red lights swirled on the corner of the farthest building. Menelik hurried to get the spear free of the window, gashing both of his forearms on the jagged shards of glass.

Raising the javelin above him, he screamed. "Tafari! Teimbaka!"

Blood dripped and splattered his face. He laughed, a raw savagery welling up inside him at the sight of his red-streaked arms. Pressing his face into his skin, he licked the open wound.

Flashing red lights raced along the buildings as the squad car sped up the street with the siren blaring. Menelik raised the javelin above his head and unleashed a mighty roar. The squad car came to a sudden, screeching halt.

The doors of the car swung open; two hyena-men jumped out.

"Put down your weapon!" one barked.

The whirling red lights danced in Menelik's eyes, confusing him.

"Ethiopia!" he screamed.

Javelin firmly in hand, he raced down the sidewalk toward the mass of moving lights at the other end of the block, dodging and jumping over any cars that blocked his path.

When the slow-moving fire river of cars engulfed him, he ran against its current, oblivious to the honking horns, the screaming voices, and the terrified faces behind the rectangles of glass. He began to concentrate on the sound of his rubber-soled feet slapping against the asphalt as the police siren started to slowly fade away.


Menelik shivered as he slipped from alley to alley. The sweat of his body had turned to ice as the night air had methodically changed from cool to cold. He stood still for a moment and wrapped his arms around his shoulders. Blood from his forearms smeared the front of his sleeveless white T-shirt.

A rat scurried over his feet, its whiskers twitching as it smelled the air. He jumped to the side and kicked out at it. Losing his balance, he dropped the javelin and fell against a row of metal trashcans. In the aftermath of the clanging echoes, he held his breath and listened. When he felt safe again, he picked up the javelin and edged forward, trying his best to keep to the shadows.

Up ahead, on the opposite side of the street, where the alley ended, a single streetlight cast an eerie glow on the pavement below it. Wisps of swirling mist gathered at the base.

Gabriel stared at it, afraid. He leveled the javelin, the pointed tip facing forward for protection. A single snowflake drifted through the vision.

"Jen," he said softly, a smile of joy taking hold of his face. "I'm close."

*

HE STOOD AT the door of Titus's apartment, sagging with fatigue. Licking his lips, he swallowed dryly. Placing the base of the javelin to the floor, he grabbed hold of the shaft with both hands. Leaning forward, he used his forehead to give the door a weak knock.

He waited. No one answered. Using a fist, he knocked again. He placed his ear against the door; there was music. He knocked again. No one answered. Confused, he kicked the door just beneath the knob.

"God damn it," he muttered when pain shot up his foot.

"Where are you guys?" he said, suddenly overwhelmed with an acute sense of loneliness. His eyes filling with tears, he crumpled to the floor.

Suddenly experiencing a near incapacitating state of panic, he fumbled for the doorknob. When it turned and the door cracked open, he whimpered and wiped his tears from his face.

Too disoriented to get up, he entered the apartment on his hands and knees, sliding the javelin along the floor as he went. Once inside, he nudged the door closed behind him with his foot. He let his eyes adjust to the darkness. Peering up the entry hall, he could see the faint glow of purple in the living room just beyond.

"Titus and his blacklights," he chuckled.

Shaking, filled with a sense of relief, he stood and walked to the living room.

Hearing a click, he stopped and listened, positioning the javelin so the point of it was well ahead of him. The tip of the spear shimmered with hues of electric green and purple. The click sounded once again, followed by a barely audible threatening hiss. The palms of his hands began to sweat. When the familiar guitar riffs of Santana began to play, he almost fell to the floor.

"Fuckin' eight-tracks," he murmured.

He continued into the living room, half expecting to find Jen and T sitting on the couch sharing a joint. But they weren't there.

He stood in the middle of the room, soaking in its familiarity. The blacklights sparked a surge in his body, his head vibrating with the pounding beat of steel drums and the buzz of Santana's electric guitar.

Running his tongue over his dry, parched lips, he tried to swallow again.

"Thirsty," he told himself.

He made his way around the corner of the living room to the galley kitchen and leaned the javelin on the wall by the entryway. He opened the refrigerator.

A harsh light splashed into the narrow room, revealing a few dirty dishes in the sink, along with a couple of crumpled Budweiser cans and an empty liter of Coke on the countertop. Bending, he surveyed the contents of the shelves in the fridge. He quickly skipped over the containers of Chinese food, the slice of pepperoni pizza, the two lemons and the half of lime before focusing on three Budweiser cans.

"Solid, motherfucker," he sighed, grabbing the beers.

Pulling a can free from the plastic carry top, he popped it open and guzzled the twelve ounces down in a matter of seconds.

With a satisfied *ahh*, he crushed the can with one hand, tossed the pulverized aluminum back in the refrigerator, and pulled off a second beer. Within thirty seconds, he finished it.

Eyeing the final one, he placed it back on the wire rack, saving it for later.

The slice of pepperoni pizza beckoned to him. He patted his stomach, grinning.

"Hungry?" he asked, peering down at his torso.

When he saw the amount of dried blood that was smeared across the front of his T-shirt, he furrowed his brow, not understanding or remembering how it got there. Slowly, afraid of what he might find, he twisted his arms to their soft underside.

"Fuckin' hell," he cursed when he saw the long, thick scabs running from below his wrists to just above the elbow of each arm.

He picked at one of the scabs, lifting a large hunk of it from his skin. Fresh blood oozed out of the wound.

"What the fuck did I do?"

Trying to take stock of himself, he realized he needed a mirror. He headed for the small guest bathroom that was just down the hallway, absently grabbing the javelin as he left the kitchen. Before entering the bathroom, he glanced across to the bedroom opposite him, noticing the door was ajar. A dim, narrow band of light streamed across a slice of the floor.

Leaning the javelin against the frame of the bathroom door, he stepped inside. He closed the door softly behind him and searched for the wall switch.

The sudden light was blinding, the glaring, white light sending needle points of pain through his pupils. He pressed his hands to his eyes and moaned.

After a few seconds, he pulled his hands away and cautiously looked into the mirror above the sink. He waited for the brooding reflection staring back at him to change, certain that what he was seeing wasn't real. Little by little, however, as he and his likeness continued to gaze at one another, he began to comprehend that he was looking at himself. The realization sent a shudder down his spine.

Blood was everywhere. It was splattered all over his shoulders and face, globs of it matting his hair, turning his usually perfect, fourteen-inch Afro into an imbalanced mass of disarrayed tufts.

He bent forward to examine his face, pressing down on his cheeks, studying his eyes, unnerved when he realized that most of the brown of his irises was no longer there. The dark, fathomless pits of his pupils alarmed him. He shuffled back a step, startled when his reflection did the same.

"Fuck," he moaned.

Bending to the sink, he turned on the water, splashed his face a few times, and ran his wet fingers through his hair. When he stood to look at himself in the mirror again, he shook his head in dismay; the few handfuls of water hadn't done anything to change his appearance. Only a shower would do that, he realized. After a final look into his dilated eyes, he switched the light off and opened the door.

Reflexively, he grabbed the javelin and crept the few feet across the hall to the bedroom, stopping to listen before pushing the door slowly inward.

What had been a narrow band of light when he had first peeked into the bedroom from the hall was now a triangular swath. Arcing his upper body inside, he looked back over the edge of the door to see if someone was in the main bathroom that was situated on the far side of the walk-in closet. Through the opening, he could see the toilet, nothing more.

He slipped into the bedroom to the bathroom, leaving the javelin in the near corner of the walk-in closet. Shielding his eyes against the glare from the three bare bulbs burning above the mirror, he stepped inside, shutting the door behind him.

Taking a moment to collect himself, he inhaled deeply, hoping that the acid had about run its course. Exhausted, he wanted nothing more than to get cleaned up and find a quiet place to come down.

When he pulled his T-shirt up over his head, he winced from the pain shooting down his left shoulder and gagged at the odor coming from under his arms.

"God, you reek like week-old bong water," he whispered, partly amused, partly disgusted. "Stink like a fuckin'—."

Jerking his head to the side, he peered into the mirror. Studying the image there, he watched his lips curl and lines of scorn appear at the corner of his eyes.

"Hyena."

The word triggered his memory of the events of the past hours.

A fleeting shadow raced from the back of his reflection out past the edge of the mirror. He felt his balls tighten as an icy shiver swept up his spine. He began to shake.

Suddenly irritated and angry, he clawed the scabs off his arms. The appearance of the oozing blood made him shudder. His eyes flitted to every corner of the bathroom.

*What if the hyenas are already here, hiding?* his thoughts screamed. *Why was the front door unlocked?*

The notion sent him into complete paranoia.

A muffled snort erupted from the other side of the door. Without hesitating, he whirled and yanked it open.

Nothing was there.

Perspiring, with his heart racing, he took a tentative step out of the bathroom and grabbed hold of the javelin.

Snorts sounded from within the dark section of the bedroom; three, four he counted, coming all in succession, followed by a long, whistling hiss. Exiting the walk-in closet, he raised the javelin to his shoulder.

The light from the bathroom gave him a clearer picture of the queen-size bed where Titus slept. The lower section was a mass of confusing ridges and dips, while the upper section remained cloaked in darkness. From within that darkness, he could hear heavy breathing and a series of soft moans. A hyena-man was hiding, he thought. His arm shaking, he gripped the javelin a little tighter and took aim.

The man-beast snorted and coughed. Menelik wavered and stepped back into the walk-in closet. When the string from the closet's overhead bulb brushed the back of his neck, he reached up and pulled it. Instantly, the room was flooded with light. With his chest heaving, he leapt back into the bedroom.

He looked quickly to each corner of the room, expecting a hyena-man to attack. But the corners of the room held no such beast—only an old armchair sitting in one and half-dead, potted decorative trees standing in the others.

Two quick snorts, a movement beneath the blanket, and a hooting chuckle snapped his head toward the bed. In the bright light, he caught a glimpse of a thick, dark, bushy tail slipping back under the covers. As he raised the javelin, the blanket suddenly gathered, shielding the beast beneath it so he couldn't see where to aim. It was then that he noticed the strands of platinum blonde hair fanned out across the near pillow.

"Jen," he whispered.

Bending to her, he sat on the edge of the bed and ran a finger softly along her cheek.

"Jen," he whispered again, hoping she would awaken.

"Jen," he said a little louder, his fingers arranging her hair behind her ear.

It wasn't until he let his hand drop to her shoulder that he realized how cold her skin was. Concerned, he tugged at the blanket, hoping to cover her and make her warm. The blanket yanked back with a snort, leaving Jennifer with less of it than she'd had before. Menelik stared at the sensual lines of her back and the rounded underside of her breast. Memories of their naked bodies joined together flooded his thoughts. When he stretched out to lie down next to her, a surge of conflicting emotions began to swirl inside him.

She had nothing on.

Shivering against the utter coldness of her body, he drew his arms about her and began to rub her. Sliding his palms quickly across her skin, neck to buttocks, shoulders to wrists, he tried to warm her.

"Damn, you're freezing, babe," he quietly told her, his mouth close to her ear.

Renewing his efforts, he swept his fingers over her breasts, down across her stomach and across the tuft of the hair between her thighs before letting them trail back up. Just below her elbow, on the inside of her arm, his fingers rubbed against an object that should not have been there. Confused, he traced its outline: tubular, narrow, a circle on one end, the other end pressed against the skin of her arm, ending in something hard and incredibly thin.

"What the fuck?" he murmured.

He sat up, pulled back the corner of the blanket, and stared at the syringe dangling in the crook of her arm. The sight of it was unnerving, for in all the years they had been together, neither of them had ever used a syringe, or even talked about wanting to.

Slipping a hand to her wrist, he felt for a pulse. When he couldn't find one, he placed his hand to her neck, pressing with his index finger for the faint throb he was afraid he wouldn't be able to find. Using his thumb and forefinger, he opened the lids of her eye, quickly letting them close again when the orb stared lifelessly past him to the ceiling above.

Stomach churning, throat constricting, lungs struggling for oxygen, he pulled the needle from her arm and loosed a guttural scream.

"What, what, what!" a hyena-man growled.

Menelik watched the hyena-man roll off the bed to a crouch, his dark, bushy mane framing a pair of deeply set, dark lifeless eyes.

He thrust the syringe and needle out toward the beast, his jaws grinding with rage.

"She's dead!" he screamed, hurling the needle and syringe at the beast's face. "She's dead!"

The beast slowly rose to his feet, his face going pale. His eyes flicked nervously between the bed and the man standing across from him. The blanket slipped from his grasp, revealing his hairy, naked body.

Menelik watched the beast slowly rising, its eyes searching for an opening, flaunting its balls and penis in a mocking display of contempt.

"Why kill her?" he shouted, shaking. "You were after me! Me!"

"No, no, no," the beast hurried to say, bending to reach for the blanket.

Menelik saw the hyena-man coil to strike. He thrust the spear out in front of him.

"Hey, hey!" the beast shouted, raising a hand in protest. "It's not like it looks, Gabe man! I didn't kill her! She must have done it herself after I passed out!"

The beast eyed Jennifer's ultra-pale body.

"We ran into a buddy of mine after we couldn't find you at the zoo," he started to explain. "We were fuckin' high, man, you know? Weren't you? Fuckin' trippin' our balls off. My main man had some fuckin' smack on him. We decided to score some, you know, for kicks."

Menelik heard the hyena-man weave a trap of words.

"We were waiting for you to show up," he went on, taking a few tentative steps toward the foot of the bed. "But, man," he said, wildly gesturing with his free arm, "this is fuckin' crazy, you know? I told her not to fuck with it. Dude said it was close to pure. Warned us and all, you know?"

Menelik bristled, stiffening when the man-beast began to move toward him.

"And hey, like, nothin' happened, you know, between us," the beast continued, pointing at Jennifer. "Not like I didn't want it to, you know," he chuckled. "We just started to fuck around, is all. But she said no when, well—you know—when it got right down to it. Said she loved you, man. Said she loved you. You, man! Old Gabe Tate," he told him, shaking his head, smiling, rounding the corner of the bed.

Menelik edged the javelin around to keep it pointed straight at the hyena-man, jabbing it outward when the man-beast rounded the foot of the bed.

"Whoa, motherfucker! Why the spear? What the fuck you doin' with that thing, anyway?" the hyena-man asked, narrowing his eyes. "Holy fuck, man, look at you! What the fuck's with all the blood? Shit, man, you look like some fuckin' horror movie."

The beast took a step forward. He reached for the end of the javelin.

"You didn't kill somebody or something, did you, Gabe? Like, where the hell have you been? You're still trippin', aren't you?"

Menelik saw the man-beast's eyes narrow and its demeanor change. When it reached out to take his spear, he blocked the attempt with a glancing strike to its hand, nicking the skin, drawing a thin line of blood.

The hyena man recoiled, snapping its jaws.

"Gabe. Gabe. You're trippin', man! Fuckin' be cool, would ya? Shit! Goddamn it, man, you fuckin' sliced me with that thing! Put it the fuck down! Put it down, Gabe. You're fucked up. You're fucked up!"

The beast began breathing heavily, moving backward, putting the bed between himself and the javelin. Looking down at Jennifer's body, he said, "I can't believe she fuckin' OD'd. But it wasn't my fault, Gabe. You gotta believe that. I mean, like I explained how we were gonna heat it and all, and then shoot the stuff, but like— like I said— I guess I passed out after she—you know—said no, and she just must have went and done it all herself anyway."

The hyena-man glanced at Menelik before letting his eyes rest on Jennifer once again.

"Not the brightest chick in the world, huh?" he offered with a shrug.

"Fuckin' killer body and all—like, you know that, right?" he laughed. "But always was missin' a beat or two inside that pretty blonde head. I'm sorry, man. I really am."

He stared at Menelik and extended an open palm.

"Guess we better move her before she gets all stiff and shit, right?"

Menelik followed the beast's eyes to Jennifer. The sight of her lifeless body froze everything around him.

In the distance, a tiny bell sounded, the faint cling-clang paced at a walking gait, moving ever closer. A delicate mist slowly formed in the far corner of the room. It moved lazily toward him, driven by the whisper of a warm, swirling breeze. A youth emerged, holding a walking stick, his face shrouded within the folds of a white robe. As he stretched his dula out before him, a subtle golden hue materialized beneath his feet. Extending outward, it created a pathway into the hall. For the briefest of moments, Menelik saw the image of a glowing white bird waiting at the end of the path. As the white-robed youth approached the foot of the bed, he lifted his face to look at Menelik.

"Tafari!" Menelik gasped.

Bending, placing a single finger on the back of Jennifer's ankle, Tafari gazed back at Menelik.

"I will take her to Ras Dashen," he said, touching the dula to Jennifer's hand. " We will wait for you there."

Now bathed in the same soft, golden hue that formed the path, Jennifer rose and took her place next to Tafari. She donned the white robes he held out for her. With tears in her eyes, she looked longingly at Menelik for a moment before arranging the robes atop her head so he could no longer see her face. As the two moved toward the hallway, the path behind them began to disappear, the mist dispersing as though it had never formed.

"Wait!" Menelik pleaded, reaching out for them.

Tafari hesitated just outside the doorway.

"Where?" Menelik hurried to say, but then lost his train of thought. "Where—?" He struggled to remember what he wanted to ask. "Where is Teimbaka?" he ended up saying, though it felt all wrong.

The tiny bell fell silent, the golden hue in the hallway dimming to a shade so faint that it was as though it had all just been imagined. With the edges of his white robes disappearing behind the wall, Tafari said, "Waiting for you."

Hollow laughter—low, gruff, and mocking—chased the last vestiges of the image away. The hyena-man, now dressed in a peasant shirt and jeans, held a Smith & Wesson .38 Special in one hand. Glaring at Menelik, he shook his head.

"You are fuckin' tripping, brother, aren't you? Holy fuck. What the hell were you seein' just now? Ain't no one here but you and me, dude. And who the fuck is Teimbaka?"

As he had on that morning so long ago, Menelik saw the hyena from the river of sand, its eyes filled with bloodlust, the haunting cackle of its voice filling his ears. He lifted the javelin above his head.

"Put it down, Gabe!" the beast commanded, aiming the gun at Gabriel's head. "Put it down."

Menelik tensed.

"Earth to Gabe! Wake up! Snap out of it! Time for you and your dead honey to go!" he yelled, waving the gun toward Jennifer's body. "You both need to fucking get the fuck out of here, cause I ain't going down because of either one of you, you hear? You hear me, you stupid prick?"

The intense growling, as it had been on that day long ago, was a warning that the beast was about strike. Menelik coiled his arm and waited.

"Take her and get out! You hear me? Put some fucking clothes on her and throw her over your shoulder like she's passed out."

The beast began to tremble as he gaped disbelievingly at Menelik.

"God, you're a fucking asshole, you know," he spat, frustration scrunching up his face. "Here," he said, bending and grabbing a handful of clothes from the floor by his feet. "Put these on her," he told him, throwing a rainbow tie-dyed T-shirt and a pair of white Levi's onto Jennifer's body. "And get her the fuck out of here before people start to wake up."

Menelik held his breath when the hyena-man bent, certain the beast was about to come hurtling at him. But when the clothes the beast threw landed on Jennifer's body, he realized he was wrong. He sensed the hyena-man was about to attack her first.

Enraged with the thought that the beast would rip into her flesh while he stood by and watched, he jumped up on the bed to protect her. Thrusting the javelin forward, he lanced the beast in the shoulder.

The room reverberated with a thunderous roar as the bullet tore into his side, the force of the impact twisting him backward off the bed. Landing awkwardly on the floor, he struggled to hold on to the javelin. Using it as a crutch, he braced his body upright as the hyena-man circled the bed.

Bleeding from his right shoulder, the hyena-man stepped to the side of the bed, the gun held steadily out in front of him.

"You fucking twisted bastard," he hissed. "Now look what you've done."

The beast glanced down at his shoulder, grimacing when he touched it. Conflicted, sighing heavily, he ran his free hand through his hair.

"Can't trust you with no alibi now. Who knows what the fuck you would say? I guess that's it, then: you attacked me after I came home and found you and your dead bitch in my bed. Just protecting myself in my own pad, you know," he explained, brandishing the gun toward Menelik. "Tight that it's your fingerprints all over the needle she OD'd on. Makes the story straight up. Pigs will be down with it. So—sorry, man."

In the instant that the hammer on the .38 cocked back, Menelik saw the image of the hyena-man fall away. Titus was now standing before him: bleeding, angry, pointing a gun, with Jennifer's dead body lying just a few feet away. It all made no sense. But Jennifer was dead. *Fucking dead!* his head screamed.

Jennifer was dead!

Menelik swayed and teetered and hurled his spear. The blast from the .38 grazed him, gashing open his scalp, blowing off the tip of his ear. Titus staggered backward, the javelin embedded in his throat, blood streaming out from the wound where his artery had been sliced open.

Menelik cupped a hand over his ear, desperate to stop the deafening ringing that was echoing inside his head. Dazed, he caught sight of a blurry figure standing in the doorway.

"Call the police! Call the police! They're all dead! They're all dead!" the figure screamed as it raced away.

The wisp of a faint gold light caught his attention. It hovered in the hallway where Tafari and Jennifer had gone. Wounded and disoriented, he suddenly found himself gasping for air. Struggling to reach the golden light, he stumbled and fell face-down onto the floor.

A tiny bell jingled. He lifted his head, confused. A siren—distant, muffled by the walls of the building—seeped into his consciousness.

"Waiting for you," he heard the voice of Tafari whisper.

He pushed himself from the floor.

*****

THE CLAMOR OF the bells was jarring, each clanging ring pounding on the inside of his eyes. Reluctantly, his lids weak and fluttering, he awakened and numbly looked around.

Rows of grey, rectangular stones rose up behind and beside him. A set of six grey-white marble steps, leading upward to the street, was but a few yards away. Their railing cast shadow bars on the wall to his side. Above him, where the steps in front of him reached their end, an elevated bridge of concrete stairs began, these leading up to another landing of an imposing stone house. He placed his hands on the ground as his eyes followed the bridge of steps upward and then back down. The stone beneath his hands was icy cold.

Shivering, he pulled the front of the faded jean jacket closer around him. He blinked his eyes as he tried to focus on where he was and what he remembered.

With a painful wave of emotion washing over him, he began to rock. He pulled his knees into his chest as tearful sobs began to wrack his body. Snippets of his memories of Jennifer flew helter-skelter inside his head. There she was, smiling, laughing, joking, somber, defiant, tender, scared, carefree—and then ghostly dead. *What had happened? How could she be gone? What will I do?*

Whimpering, he rocked back and forth, the questions left unanswered. The ache of loneliness—hollow, numb, and frightening—burrowed further into his spirit.

The bells continued to ring, slamming his head with jolts of deep, disorientating pain.

Covering his ears with his hands, he found the moist scab on the side of his head and felt the sore, throbbing mess that was the tip of his ear. He quickly checked his side; it was hot and wet. Realizing he was still losing blood, he shivered anew. With the shiver, a wave of pain surged through his body.

The bells kept ringing. He moaned.

The door of the imposing stone house opened above him. Menelik froze when people stepped out onto the bridge of concrete stairs. Holding his breath, he kept his body rigid as a man, a woman, and a little girl began their descent. A surge of panic gripped him when he realized that the steps they were taking shared their ending with the ones in front of him.

Chancing a quick glance, he saw a little brown teddy bear in the hands of the girl. The bear was watching him. Lifting his gaze upward, he saw that the little girl was staring at him too. He offered a smile, entranced by her blazing blue eyes and her honey-colored hair.

As she skipped down the final steps, the sun caught the edges of the gold buckles on her tiny, black leather shoes. Looking up from the girl's sparkling feet, he saw the teddy bear's arm waving goodbye. He caught the nuance of a shy grin pulling at the sides of the little girl's lips.

And then she was gone.

He was alone.

His emptiness grew tenfold.

Although he wanted to fight it, he began to weep again. The past and the present had become too much to bear, the future impossibly meaningless. Images of Martin and Patricia and Eleanor tried to find a place within his thoughts. But he angrily shut them out, reproaching himself for having ever harbored the feelings of guilt he had entertained from time to time about shunning them the past four years. They were liars.

The bells clanged on.

Shadow figures began to sweep across the shadow bars on the wall beside him. Off in the distance, though the sound seemed out of place, he could hear the slow clip-clop of a horse's hooves. Voices began to drift down to him from street level. They were polite, animated, all of them trading adjectives about the morning or bantering about choirs, organ music, and the game being played on the television later that day.

The sound of the approaching horse grew louder. He could hear the voice of the driver—strong, clear, plodding like the horse—describing the area to the beat of the animal's hooves.

"Saint Patrick's Cathedral on your right," a man's voice boomed. "The bells are announcing the nine o'clock mass. After services are completed, everyone is urged to go over to the Holy Apostles soup kitchen and volunteer. It's a sight to behold, if you are interested, as some days the kitchen sees five hundred or more come through its doors."

The shadow of the horse, driver, and carriage drifted across the wall beside him and disappeared into the archway beneath the bridge of stairs. The voice of the driver quickly faded.

The bells began to echo in his head.

He shivered violently.

And then the bells suddenly stopped.

The abrupt silence was distressing, creating a void that pushed him from the stone slab where he was sitting to the edge of the stairs leading upward. Determined, legs shaking, he slowly climbed the steps to the landing above. Leaning heavily on a pillar to catch his breath, he came face-to-face with a black, cast-iron sculpture of a lion's head, its jaws frozen in a perpetual roar.

Taken by surprise, he pushed away from the lion, narrowly missing a passerby. Steadying himself, clutching his side, he staggered to the middle of the sidewalk. He soon found himself caught up in a stream of people. They were all headed in the same direction. Mindlessly, he joined them. Within minutes, he was at the foot of a wide expanse of stone stairs. Stopping, he peered upward; the climb seemed too great.

While gazing up at the massive doors at the top of the steps and trying to gauge the expanse of the stunning cathedral they served as an entrance to, he was nudged from behind. The push moved him forward, forcing him to climb the step in front of him or be knocked to the ground. Although weak and dizzy, he turned in anger, a spate of curse words on the tip of his tongue.

A ghostly baby elephant placed its trunk along his wounded side and flapped its drooping ears.

Stepping backward, he tripped and stumbled. But the baby spirit elephant rushed to steady him. Wrapping its trunk around his waist, it gently pulled him so that he could use its body for support.

Bewildered at the sight of the animal, questioning that it was even there, he fumbled for words to say. In the end, he kept silent, staring at it as though it was a lost treasure.

The baby elephant moved upward, towing Menelik along. He slowly followed, stopping once when a painful spasm doubled him over. When the pain subsided, he righted himself. The crowd of people he had been walking with had gone. The baby ghost elephant nudged him forward.

Trembling uncontrollably, his body wet with sweat, he came to the great brass doors at the top of the stairs. There, without sound or gesture, the baby elephant vanished. Menelik fell against one of the doors with a thud.

The adjacent door swung outward, an outstretched arm motioning for him to enter. Menelik slid sideways and stumbled in. A pair of hands took him by his shoulders and guided him toward the nearest pew. A face suddenly loomed in front of his, a pair of wispy gray eyebrows pinching together as the eyes of the face seemed to be studying his.

"Do you need help?" the face asked him.

Menelik stared at the face, grappling with what the voice had asked. With an odd smile, the face nodded and then moved away. Menelik gazed after the receding figure, watching it until it turned and disappeared into a hallway. Relieved and grateful, he bowed his head and slid into the pew. Slumping forward, he rested his forehead against the pew in front of him.

The first note from the pipe organ jolted him upright. The music coursed through him, his bones buzzing and humming with every pulsing chord. Not fully comprehending where he was or what was happening, he began to look around, his senses beginning to awaken to sounds and smells that seemed strange, yet totally familiar.

Incense lingered in the air, its heady aroma both clouding and uplifting his thoughts. A wispy trail of the scented smoke led his gaze to the altar, where a billowing cloud of the burnt, sweet-smelling spice formed a layered shroud.

Along the floor and across the rows of patrons, he saw sparkling colors of blues, reds, and greens. Hints of yellow glimmered amongst these. The church was bathed in a mosaic of color and sunlight. The bright, shimmering colors brought him a sense of joy. With a smile of relief, he took a deep breath and fell into a trance.

People stood and sang, kneeled and prayed, sat and listened. They bowed their heads, clasped their hands, and lifted their voices in songs of glory and praise. Menelik registered some of this, momentarily snapping out of his trance when he heard voices ask for guidance and forgiveness. The words, the chanting, and the music flowed through him, sweeping his pain away, filling him with peace.

He absorbed his surroundings in silence, chancing glances only when a song would bring the people around him to their feet, or a single voice would instruct them to kneel. Throughout it all, he could feel himself drifting away. He was growing weaker, struggling for clarity. He felt death close at hand. He smiled anew when the vision of the teddy bear waving goodbye came to him. *How did the little girl know?* he wondered.

The sound of distant police sirens chased the memory of the little girl and her teddy bear away. Fragments of what had happened after he had fallen on the bedroom floor of Titus's apartment came flooding back. Grabbing clothes from the walk-in closet, running blindly, lurking in shadows and jumping into a stairwell to escape the flashing red lights: all these fragments rushed into his memory. Struggling with the sudden recollections, he was startled when a voice out of nowhere proclaimed, "Peace be with you."

Cowering away, he looked up. For a moment, he saw Eleanor's face.

"Peace be with you," the middle-aged, brown-skinned woman kindly said to him again, extending a white-gloved hand.

"I— uh—," he stammered.

Raising her eyebrows, the woman placed her gloved fingers to lips. With an expression of shock, she quickly moved away.

"I— uh— yeah," he managed to get out. "Uh, peace."

The woman glanced back at him with frightened eyes. Menelik watched her snatch up her pocketbook and exit the other end of the pew.

A tiny bell rang once from the front of the church. Immediately, he was drawn to it. Sliding out of his seat, he stood up. Slipping back into a trance, he started walking toward the altar.

Tafari was there, dressed in a flowing white robe, his arms raised to the sky, his body enshrined in a mixture of iridescent light and incense. He was standing atop a raised plateau, beckoning him forward, his voice guiding him with a calming song.

He walked straight for him, grasping the edge of each pew as he went, mesmerized by the figure calling to him, unaware of the shuffling feet behind him or the murmurs of alarm that arose and swelled as he drew nearer to the altar.

"He's bleeding!" a voice yelled out.

"There's blood everywhere!" another exclaimed.

Menelik struggled forward, single-minded in his purpose, smiling when Tafari nodded to him and reached out a hand.

A tiny bell rang twice.

The mosaic of colors began to spin.

Menelik hurried and stumbled. Behind him, shoes slapped against the marble floor. They were running, getting closer.

"Hold it right there!" a voice shouted. "Police!"

Menelik glanced over his shoulder. Two hyena-men were racing toward him.

Bouncing off the edge of a pew, he surged ahead. Panic-stricken, knees buckling, gasping for air, choking on blood, he reached the foot of the altar.

"Tafari," he labored to say. "Tafari."

With his arms outstretched, his eyes pleading, he fell face forward, his brow smacking against the smooth marble tile. Frenzied, he rolled over, desperate to see his brother. Above him, hanging limply from a wooden cross, a face both tormented and forgiving looked down upon him.

With the world around him shrinking into a ring of darkness, he lost himself within the gaze of Christ's tortured, loving eyes.

## JANUARY 1973

FEARING SHE WAS about to urinate on herself, Eleanor squeezed her legs tighter and pressed her hands against her lower abdomen. Abruptly she stood, then sat again, knowing there was no point in walking over to the door she had been staring at for the past fifteen minutes. It would only add to her frustration, she knew. Listening to the muffled sound of voices inside wouldn't help. She needed to hear what was being said. Even then, she mused, if she *could* hear what was being said, it wasn't going to comfort her all that much.

And there hadn't been much comfort over the course of the past months, she thought. Telephone calls, newspaper articles, radio broadcasts, and even the evening news had all become sources of distress. The nightmare she had been living—they had been living—since November was spiraling out of control.

Yet, as she sat outside the assistant district attorney's office, staring at the title engraved on the little plaque above the door, she yearned to know what was going on inside. She pulled at the edges of the wadded tissue she was holding.

The doorknob turned. The click of the latch brought Eleanor to her feet.

"What he say?" she asked before the door was fully open. "What they gonna do?"

Patricia stepped out of the office and wrapped Eleanor in a bear hug. She buried her face in crook of the older woman's neck.

"Oh, God, why is he doing this to us? Why?" Eleanor moaned, trembling.

"I don't know," Patricia replied, her throat choked with emotion. "I just don't understand it."

Patricia lifted her face, her tear-filled eyes mirrored in Eleanor's.

"He's still saying he doesn't have any parents. Says his died in Africa. Still sticking with he doesn't know who we are or who we think we are."

Patricia sniffled, rubbing her nose with the back of her hand.

"He still won't see us," she blurted out. "Refused to see our lawyer—again. Sent a message through the D.A. to tell us to stop wasting our time."

Eleanor was not at all surprised by what she was hearing; it had been this way since the first day Gabriel had regained consciousness in the hospital. It was as if all the years she had raised him, all the years the Mathises had given him, had never existed. Nor had Gabriel Tate, either, for that matter.

Although Eleanor had prepared herself to hear the same incomprehensible scenario, she wept. She pressed her hands to her face with the hope of holding on to a little bit more of herself than what was seeping away.

"The district attorney—rather, his assistant—" Patricia went on to say, "says they'll be pushing for a trial date as soon as possible. Says all the media attention is bringing a lot of pressure down on their office."

She went to pull on her hair. Forgetting she had just had most of it cut off, she ending up pinching the air beside her neck.

"Said he couldn't and wouldn't force Gabriel—Menelik, as he is going by now—to accept our lawyer to represent him and that the court has already appointed a public defender to take his case. Says there is nothing more he can do."

"Or will do," Eleanor flatly stated, shaking her head. "Child's gonna be railroaded. I can just feel it. They gonna try and stick 'im in the electric chair just 'cause that girl was white."

"Eleanor!"

"Well that's the drift of the news reports," she answered defiantly, her expression hard, unforgiving. "Don't tell me you haven't heard the same.

Just 'cause her daddy's got money—hmmph! Probably bought off the judge and jury already."

"I don't believe that. I can't. If I thought that was true—"

Patricia bit down on her lower lip and nervously tugged at the fingers of her left hand.

"No offense, but it wasn't too long ago that you didn't think bigotry existed in Rumson, neither."

Eleanor's raised eyebrow stifled the denial on Patricia's lips.

"Naïveté," Patricia sighed, smiling. "That's what it was. Product of a sheltered environment."

"Whatever. Still don't excuse the fact that you thought otherwise. So don't go foolin' yourself again," Eleanor told her, looking her straight in the eye. "Been a lot a niggers—excuse me—black folks sold up the river before."

"Eleanor!"

"Well, what's the point of sugar-coatin' it? That's how white folks see it, see us."

"Not all white people," Patricia reminded her, placing her hands on her hips.

"And thank the good Lord for that, lest there be a terrible mess in this country. But you hear me good, Patricia Mathis: our son's just another nigger boy whose hand's been caught in the cookie jar to them people in that room. A white girl's dead."

"Jennifer Stamper, Eleanor."

"And now he's going by some crazy African name? That ain't gonna help him one bit. Why, if I could just get five minutes with the boy, I'd box his ears real good, knock some sense into that head. Didn't think I'd raised such an all-out fool. Makes me look like some kind of half-witted jackass."

Patricia's giggling took Eleanor by surprise. Her expression swayed between perplexed and unabashedly angry.

"What you find so funny?" she demanded to know.

"You," Patricia replied, putting her hand to her mouth and glancing away.

But as she looked back Eleanor's serious expression, she sighed.

"Nothing. Nothing at all," she admitted. "There's really nothing funny about this whole mess, is there?"

"Nothing that comes to mind right away, unless you be holdin' out on me, keepin' somethin' from me I don't already know."

Staring at each other, they tried to smile, to no avail.

"What's the ambassador up to in there?" Eleanor inquired as she looked away.

"Trying to make certain that due process isn't being processed too soon just to satisfy the reporters," she said. "The politics of politics," she added off-handedly. "Elections are never too far off to be a non-factor, especially in a case like this."

"Nor are the bloodsuckers who come crawlin' out from under."

"What?"

"Look," Eleanor said, nodding down the hallway. "He look like he be somebody you wanna talk to? 'Cause he look like a bloodsucker to me."

A man hurried down the hallway in their direction, waiving his raised arm.

"Oh, God. Don't they have anything better to do?" Patricia said.

"A minute of your time, ladies?" the man shouted. "Off the record, of course!"

"Off the record, my ass," Patricia hissed.

Grabbing Eleanor by the arm, she pulled her across to the door she had just exited from.

"You know I ain't allowed in there," Eleanor mildly protested. "I ain't the boy's momma. Just be the honkey's housekeeper—"

"Oh, shut up, and screw the D.A. I'm not going to let either one of us be fed to this jerk for lunch."

"Ladies, please! Just a quick question on why you think this Menelik person became a murdering drug addict!"

"Jesus," Patricia muttered as she opened the door to the assistant D.A.'s office. "Get a real job, would you?"

Closing the door behind them, she ushered Eleanor into the nearest chair before any protest could be uttered.

"My apologies, gentlemen," she said, nodding to Martin and the assistant D. A. "Please, just continue as if we're not here."

Paul Conley, a slickly dressed, middle-aged man in his late thirties who looked to have just jumped off the cover of *GQ*, eyed Patricia and Eleanor with disdain. But before he could raise any objection to their presence, Martin addressed the man with more of what was obviously their unfinished conversation.

"I am still not convinced that it is in the best interest of the boy for this office—"

"*Man*, Mr. Mathis," Conley interrupted. "Gabriel Mathis—or Menelik, as he wishes to be referred to now—is a man, not a boy," he added, smirking when he said "Menelik." "He's what, closer to thirty than twenty, am I right? Or is that aspect of his life in doubt as well?"

Martin glared at the man, his jaw set tight.

"I'm sorry," Martin apologized, tapping at his hearing aid. "I'm afraid you'll have to speak up. Don't hear too well, you know," he said, the slightest trace of amusement in his tone.

"Get to your point," Conley told him. "I've got a busy schedule."

"My point, sir, is this: not only is Gabriel still recovering from the physical wounds that almost killed him, he is obviously suffering from a great deal of mental stress that is causing him to think unclearly. I don't honestly believe—I can't believe—that he fully understands the charges being brought against him. He simply can't understand them, or he wouldn't be refusing good legal counsel. Or at the very least, he wouldn't refuse to acknowledge the very people who raised him, who love him and only have his best interests at heart."

"And I've told you before, the doctors in charge of this case have given their clearance for him to stand trial. And as for not seeing or acknowledging you, well, that's his right, isn't it?"

Leaning forward, straightening the knot in his tie, he added smugly, "And how do I know how well he was raised or if you really have his best interests at heart? Maybe he turned out this way *because* of his upbringing."

"Watch your tongue, young man."

"Your son, Mr. Mathis, in case you haven't heard, has been charged with two counts of murder, breaking and entering, burglary, assaulting a police officer and a zoo employee, assault with a deadly weapon, public intoxication, public nuisance, cruelty to animals—and let's not forget to top it all off—evading the draft! So as far as I'm concerned, Mr. Former Ambassador, he can go on trial tomorrow and be put away where he belongs as soon as possible. So I don't want to hear any more mumbo-jumbo crap about him suffering from anything physical or mental. He's a killer, goddamn it! And as guilty as any I've ever prosecuted before."

Having spoken his mind, Paul Conley leaned back in his high-backed brown leather chair and ran a hand through his short, sandy hair. In the next moment he was leaning forward, picking up a folder from his desk, opening it with an air of keen interest.

"Presumption of innocence, Mr. Conley, is the steadfast right of every accused, no matter how the public or those charged with carrying out due process and justice may otherwise choose to view it. Your job, sir, is to present the facts, and not, thank God, bring a verdict into the courtroom pre facto."

Paul Conley slapped the folder shut.

"Your time is up, Mr. Former Ambassador. Your rhetoric is beginning to sound like that of every other guilt-ridden failure that somehow feels he can make up all the shortcomings of his life by coming into this office and rattling on about justice and fairness. Perhaps your every word was once given credence, but that privilege is long past and not relevant as to how this case proceeds. In short, you bore me, Mr. Mathis. Now kindly take your leave of this office so those of us who are still trying to make a living can get on with their job."

"A lot of good men and women gave their lives fighting for the very right to be *boring* where it pertains to justice and fairness being served. I doubt very strongly that they would appreciate your attitude toward the very ideals they gave up their lives for. You, sir, are a public servant—"

His jaw beginning to tremble, Martin suddenly stopped and took a deep breath.

"May God help you to find the path of dignity, Mr. Conley, and in the meantime, may God save this country from men like you."

Turning on his heels and donning his fedora, he addressed Patricia and Eleanor.

"Ladies. Shall we?"

Casually, Martin stepped across the room, offering an arm to each woman. Rising from their chairs in unison, they accepted his gallantry and took their leave. But before Patricia could grasp the doorknob, Paul Conley threw a parting jab.

"See you at your son's execution, you old jackass," he muttered.

"Indeed, sir," Martin replied, turning his head back to challenge the man. "That remains to be seen."

"Oh, I see your hearing has made a remarkable recovery," Conley shot back. "I wonder how you heard me at all, what with your back being turned and your hearing aid facing the wrong way."

"Not at all remarkable, Mr. Conley," Martin said slowly, enunciating each word with care. "For you are very much like a common barnyard cock. When the sun comes up, the cock has to hear himself crow, whether anyone is within earshot."

Martin smiled pleasantly and tipped his hat. Patricia, however, shot the man a hostile glance before opening the door and stepping out into the glare of television lights and the blinding flashes of cameras.

*

"Come on, come on," came the usual order with a shove or two to his back. "This ain't no stroll on the beach. Move your butt, move your butt."

"Move your own butt, piggy man. I ain't in no hurry," replied Menelik.

A poke in the kidney from the guard's nightstick brought Menelik to a halt. He bent, pretending to tie his shoe.

"You're just beggin' to have your head cracked open, aren't you? Stupid goddamned nigger. You just don't know how easily that can be arranged in here, do you? Now get your black ass moving, 'cause I'm not gonna get mine chewed out for not having you where you're supposed to be on time."

Menelik stood and gave the guard a hateful glare.

"You're just one dumb-ass nigger, aren't you, boy," the guard spit with another poke of his nightstick to Menelik's ribs. "All full of yourself, full of that dumb-nigger thinking that got you where you are right now." He laughed, pushing Menelik forward. "How sweet it's gonna be to watch you get taught how truly stupid you are. Big house got a lot of real bad-ass dudes that're just gonna love to get their mitts on you."

His face filled with defiance, Menelik stuck out his chin.

"Oh, and don't think I just mean prisoners. Hell, no, boy, I mean the guards too. They're just gonna love to whittle your black ass down to size. Amazing what they can do to you in there. Nobody's ever the wiser, either. They're a fraternity, you know? Nobody sees nothin', nobody hears nothin'." He laughed out loud. "Know what I mean, nigger?"

"Why you keep callin' me *nigger*, man? You're a brother, too. Your ass is just as black as mine."

"Oh, no, nigger; you and me ain't the same at all. Just because my skin is black like yours don't mean shit. Brothers," he scoffed, spitting at Menelik's feet. "Niggers like you—junkies, pushers, pimps, *murderers*— you keep handing whitey all he needs to keep everybody thinkin' that all blacks ought to be sent back to Africa. It's niggers like you, nigger, that keep *me* gettin' called *nigger*." The guard gave him a sardonic smile. "Be a real fine day when your black ass is fried in the chair." The man smiled a little wider and nodded his head. "Yeah—that'll be a mighty fine day."

"I didn't kill her!" Menelik shouted. "I didn't kill her," he repeated, though even to him, it sounded weak and pathetic.

"I didn't kill her," the man mimicked in a feminine, mocking tone. "Well, la-di-da-di-da, nigger. That's some big consolation, isn't it? 'Cause you just might as well have. 'Cause that's how it looks to everybody—but you."

Another shove moved Menelik on his way. He walked the remainder of the hallway in silence, stopping when they reached the door that led to the visiting rooms.

"I don't want to see nobody," Menelik told the guard, almost snarling.

"Nobody gives a damn what you want in here, boy. Or has that fact escaped you, too?"

With a final push, the guard sent Menelik through the door.

Inside the cramped, windowless room, seated in one of the two chairs that were placed on opposite sides of a small wooden table, was a young man with wired-rimmed glasses. His long, dark-brown hair was pulled back in a ponytail that reached halfway down his back. With one arm propped up on the table, the man was fingering the stitching of the brown suede patches that had been sewn to the elbows of his green corduroy sport coat. Upon Menelik's arrival, he rose, a broad smile beaming across his face.

"Gabriel," he said in a warm, friendly tone, extending his hand, "I'm—"

"Don't give a damn who you are," Menelik curtly replied, cutting him off. "And if you're that lawyer that my—those asshole liars—hired, you can take a hike right now."

Menelik turned his back and faced the wall.

"While I might wish I was being paid the sum the Mathises are willing to shell out for your defense, I'm afraid I am not nearly close to seeing a fraction of that retainer. I'm actually the court-appointed public defender, Gabriel. My name is—"

"Menelik! My name is Menelik! Don't call me by that stupid other lie! Menelik!" he shouted, whirling around

Very calmly, the young man pulled a note pad from the inside of his sport coat and placed it on the table.

"How do you spell that?" he asked, clicking on a ballpoint pen.

"What?"

"*Menelik*. How do you spell it?"

"What the fuck does that matter?" Menelik angrily demanded.

"Because, Gabriel," the man explained in a very calm manner, "if you go to court using a different name than the one the legal system recognizes, I will have to petition the court for permission. And in the papers I would submit on your behalf to be able to use that name, I would need to be able to write it down in the exact manner you wish it to be used. So, again, how do you spell *Menelik*?"

Menelik's angry expression turned to one of belligerence. Slowly, however, as he continued to stare at the man, his expression changed to one of frustration.

"I don't know," he confessed, the words rushing out of his mouth.

"I see. So should I put down d-u-m-b?"

"Hey, man, you can go to hell."

"How do you spell *that*?"

Shaking with rage, fists clenched at his sides, Menelik hissed, "Fuck you, flower child. I ain't sayin' another word."

"Well, at least you've still got that stubborn streak in you. Just like in your days at Saint Augustine's. How did the football career work out?" Dismissing the question with a wave of his hand, he said, "Never mind, never mind. And I guess I'll find out the proper spelling of your African name on my own."

"Not African! Just my name. It's just my name!"

"Okay, okay. Jesus, Menelik, relax."

Menelik's lips moved with an unspoken curse word.

"Last name?"

Menelik stared straight ahead, expressionless.

"And the spelling of it too, I'm afraid."

Dismayed by the question, Menelik whirled back around and charged the closest wall, slapping his hands, open palmed, against it.

"Hey, man, I'm sorry. Really."

Sighing, Menelik pressed his forehead against the wall.

"Maybe if you want, we could use the name of the country you're from. Uh, if you don't mind and you remember it. Or we can just wait for a later time on that."

For a moment, there was utter silence.

"I remember— I—" Menelik struggled to get out, his voice somber, barely audible. "Too little. But I remember him saying Ethiopia. I don't remember—guess I never will—where I was born. But, yeah, Ethiopia."

"Menelik Ethiopia. That's a cool name. Okay, we'll start with that."

Menelik shrugged, wiping his nose, sniffing back mucus.

"All right, okay. Why don't we—whenever you want—start at the beginning of what you remember from that day, and we'll get going."

Menelik shook his head.

"I know it's probably hard for you, but we have to go over what you remember, you know, the way you remember it, if we're going to have our say in court."

"Go away, hippie. Leave me alone."

"Sorry, no can do."

"Then make up your own fucking story about what went down, 'cause I ain't sayin' nothin' about nothin'," he emphatically stated, turning back around to glower at the man.

"Well then, we'll just plead you guilty on all counts and ask for the harshest punishment possible. Never thought I'd meet someone who *wanted* to go to the electric chair, but if that's what you want— I mean,

I guess if you need to be punished for killing that girl and the dude. Just admitting to killing the girl would do it, though. Admitting to everything else would just be overkill."

The vision of Jennifer's lifeless, pale body floated to the surface of Menelik's thoughts. He shook his head, not quite able to accept that she was gone.

"I didn't kill her," he whispered, not realizing he had spoken out loud.

"Then why take the blame?"

Menelik mulled the question, turning it over and over, examining it from every conceivable angle. Regardless of why she was dead, the fact remained that she was. And he hadn't been there to prevent it.

"Go to hell."

"No, thanks. I'm already there."

Menelik grunted.

"See, it's my job. I step into it everyday and carry it home with me at night. Most of us public defenders do. Gotta come here and try to make sense out of some asshole's predicament just so justice can be placated. Once in a while, it can be gratifying. But mostly it's just dealing with losers like you, man, asshole head cases who can't get past their own self-serving pity parade to save themselves."

"Your time's about up, isn't it, hippie? Don't you need to go do your hair or somethin'?"

"You know—" the attorney replied, shaking his head, disappointment etched around his eyes.

"You must really wow 'em in court," Menelik chided.

"First grade. Remember that far back? I thought, sometimes, that life couldn't be any worse. Kind of rotten when a kid that age thinks that's how life's going to be throughout, you know?" He shook his head. "I wasn't very good in sports," he chuckled, leaning back in his chair. "Wow, listen to me. I was *terrible* in sports. And I guess because I looked and acted like a geek, I didn't make very many—okay, any—friends."

"You gonna start cryin' now, hippie?"

"Except this one guy. Sort of a de facto kind of thing," the lawyer pressed on, ignoring Menelik's sarcasm. "We were always the last ones picked, you know? Like, for everything. I wasn't picked because I was skinny and uncoordinated. He wasn't picked because he was black in a basically all-white school. Never seemed to bother him, though, being picked last because he was, you know, a nigger."

"Keep it up, whitey."

"But it bothered me. Except this guy, back then—his name was Gabe, Gabe Tate—he would always tell me I could do it, you know? Like, 'Come on, Peter, you got this!' or 'Yeah, Peter, you can do it!' Always had my back."

Peter paused for a moment, staring off into space.

"You remember anything like that? You know, before you switched schools and became the big football star at Saint Augustine? Remember when the dog came after you on the playground and you had some kind of blackout hallucination? Then the teacher told your mom that you were too much trouble, that you needed special help? Remember that? Remember your old school buddy, Peter Lyons?"

"Everything from back then up to now is just one big fucking lie, a sham. Don't count for nothin', don't mean nothin'."

"So you don't remember me, is that what you're saying?"

"I suppose I remember you, I guess, if I wanted to put my mind to it. But you're just a part of the whole lie I was livin'. I wasn't even who you thought I was. That Gabe Tate dude never existed. Weren't never no such dude on the planet."

"Wow, that's a heavy trip," Peter concurred with a nod of his head. "Too bad, though. That Gabe Tate was a pretty cool guy." He paused. "Back then," he added with a wink. "He meant something to me, anyway. Bet he meant something to some other people too."

"You almost done with your head games, boy?"

"Jennifer Stamper mean anything to you, ever, at all? Or was she just a part of that nonexistence that you were living? So the years you had a relationship with her, it was just a meaningless figment of her imagination? Like, it would have had to have been, you know, seeing that you didn't exist."

"Shut up, man! You don't even know what you're fuckin' talkin' about!"

Menelik lunged across the room and pounded his fists down on the table.

"You hear me, white boy?" he snarled. "You shut your mouth about Jen! Shut your fucking mouth!"

"Is that what this is all coming down to? Black and white?" Peter responded, barely flinching at Menelik's outburst. "Just the old bigotry, ignorance, and prejudice game?"

Menelik's laughter thundered through the room.

"What kind of rock you been hidin' under?" Menelik pressed. "You don't think racism exists?" he continued with outstretched arms. "Man, you high? You ought to be black—everybody in America ought to be black for just one day! Then you'd know about prejudice and racism, you stupid honkey."

"Open your ears, boy!" Peter shouted.

Menelik started around the table, muscles tensed, fists clenched.

"That get your attention, did it? One stupid word and you're ready to waste me? So tell me, Mr. Afro-American, who's got the power over whom? That all a white boy has to say, *nigger* or *boy*, and you can't think straight? Can't reason? Can't see that the jerk-off saying it is just trying to do to you exactly what you're doing to yourself right now? 'Cause if that's the case, then you're just letting some damn jerk have a stranglehold on you that he isn't ever going to release."

Peter gazed at him with an air of disdain.

"And I never said racism doesn't exist. I just said I'm sick of people whining about it."

Menelik grappled for a quick retort, but in the end, threw up his hands and muttered, "What the hell do you know? You ain't black."

"No, no, you're right, Gabe. I ain't black. But being black doesn't give you a corner on the pain market, either."

"Go to hell, man," Menelik shot back, waving Peter away. "Just—"

"You just don't want to listen, do you? Don't want to hear anything that doesn't fit into your own dim-witted little brain. Well, guess what." When Menelik covered his ears with both hands, Peter continued to assail him. "Yeah, that's right, plug your ears, baby, plug your ears. You want to talk prejudice? How about the kind that comes with not being cool enough, or not good-looking enough, or not being a man's man in this beautiful world of ours? Or how about being turned down for a date with a girl you've been daydreaming about because your car isn't all that, or your job isn't quite up to her standards, or you don't live in a nice enough place, or you don't have the bucks to take her out to a nice restaurant? Yeah, I know about that kind of prejudice," he said, nervously playing with his glasses. "I even know pain, Gabe, the really cutting kind." He ran a hand across the side of his head, smoothing back his hair. "You know, where you're told that you're not very good in bed, or worse, where you can't get it up even when you're so desperate to get a hard-on that it makes you cry? And you forget, Gabe—or maybe you're the one with some prejudices—about being Hispanic or Vietnamese, or anybody who comes to this country with an accent and skin color we don't necessarily care for. You listening, Gabe?" Peter angrily pressed. "Or try being a woman, Gabe. Maybe a big, fat, ugly one who's trying to get a job when the boss only wants a pretty face and a pair of tits to look at."

Peter paused to catch his breath. Menelik stared over his head at the adjacent wall.

"What was it John Lennon said in that song? "Woman is the nigger of the world"—that ever get you wondering? Ever ask Jen about how she felt about being a woman? You two ever talk about issues like that? She ever whine like you do about what life put on her plate? She ever tell you that your dick was too small? Is that why she slept with that Titus dude the night she died, the night you killed them? Is that why you stuck the needle in her arm, 'cause she dumped you for the Puerto Rican? Somebody who could satisfy her? And then you put a javelin through his throat when he laughed at you?"

Menelik moved in a blur, pouncing on Peter before he could even finish speaking. Thrown against the wall behind him, Peter fell to the floor in a crumpled heap, his glasses flying.

"These yours?" Menelik casually asked, dangling the wire-framed lenses over him.

Dazedly, Peter eyed the glasses.

Menelik dropped the glasses to the floor by Peter's head. With a smirk, he ground his foot into them, crushing them into the linoleum.

"Something else to remember me by," he muttered, walking away.

"Hey! Open up!" he shouted, pounding on the door. "Man's sick in here or something! Collapsed on the floor like he had a heart attack! Hey! Open up! Come on!"

Peter struggled to sit up when he heard the jingling of keys on the other side of the door.

"Hold on," he stammered, weakly raising an arm. "We still need to—"

"What the hell's going on in here?" the guard demanded, rushing into the room, his nightstick raised. "What happened?"

"It's all right, it's all right," Peter said, getting to his feet. "I just fainted, I think," he told him, rubbing the back of his head.

"Whatever," the guard shot back, giving Menelik and Peter a wary look. "Time's up, anyway. I'm taking your client back to his cell."

"Just one last thing," Peter hurried to say, squinting at Menelik. "I'll do the best I can—Gabe."

APRIL, 1973

"HOW'S ELEANOR DOING?" Martin asked, prying his wife's fingers from his arm and placing them in his hand. "She's been in the ladies' room for quite a while now."

"Sorry," Patricia offered, glancing at the wrinkles on his suit coat. "I'm worried about her, to tell you the truth. The trial's taken an awful toll. Hasn't helped that Gabriel—excuse me, Menelik—won't have anything to do with her," she said, shaking her head and pursing her lips. "Unforgivable the way he's treated her. After all the years she gave up for him, it's terrible."

"Sad and ironic after all this time, isn't it?" he mused, eyes half-closed. "I remember those conversations we had back at the beginning about whether we were doing the right thing in bringing him here, having Eleanor raise him," he went on, his bushy grey eyebrows slightly raised. "Have to wonder now. Have to wonder if we shouldn't have just let things go as they were intended."

"By intended, you mean allowing him to be ripped apart by those hyenas and left to die? Is that what you mean by intended?" She smoothed the wrinkles from his coat sleeve. "So let's not delude ourselves. There's nothing to wonder about. And I'm not going to spread any blame for the way his life has turned out." Patricia sat up a little straighter and turned her face so she could look squarely at Martin. "We didn't start him using drugs," she stated forcefully, though, to Martin, there was a touch of guilt in her tone. "And we didn't turn our backs on him. And we didn't pick the person he fell in love with, either."

"No," he softly agreed. "But—"

"But what? What more could we have done?"

Martin rubbed his face.

"Maybe pursued those headaches of his a bit more determinedly," he tentatively suggested. "Maybe told him that he was our adopted son when he was old enough to understand the decision we made. We all did lie to him. I can't say he isn't right on the money about that."

"Hogwash," she told him, rubbing the back of his shoulder. "I'm not going to fall into that trap. And I'm not going to let that big, soft heart of yours break over it, either. We *did* pursue those mysterious headaches, as you should well recall. And what did that get us? A lot of shrugged shoulders, vague explanations, and asinine prognoses pointing us toward exploratory brain surgery," she scoffed. "Medicine in the fifties, dear, was not what it is today. And even if we did have him under a psychiatrist's care—well, who knows if it would have done him more harm than good? I mean, how do you think *that* would have affected him?"

Patricia closed her eyes, offering a nervous laugh.

"And the lie? Which lie? What lie? The lie to ourselves that we could have raised a black child on our own at the time we adopted him? The lie that he wouldn't have been terribly confused or scared that his parents were white? And let's be real, as they say nowadays, dear. Let's not forget that this was before civil rights and Dr. King and Malcolm X and all. Let's not forget that it was 1948 and you were just embarking on your career with the State Department. Oh, don't look at me that way. It's easy to be reproachful about it now—what, almost a quarter of a century later? That's too easy, if you ask me. We did the best we could, and if that wasn't good enough—well, at least we tried. And don't sit there and tell me that Gabe—Menelik—isn't acting like a spoiled child, the way he's decided to take the news that he's *our* adopted son and not Eleanor's. He knows the full story. Don't you think for one moment he could look at the whole picture like a grown man and see that what we did, we did for him? Is that too hard? And just who was it that dropped out of our lives to become a drug dealer, of all things, for goodness' sake?"

She suddenly went quiet, biting her lower lip.

"God, Martin, when I think of everything that has happened. It just, it just makes me sick to my stomach."

She began to cry.

"There now, dear," Martin told her in a quiet tone, pulling her gently to his shoulder. "It will be all right. Everything will turn out okay."

"Oh, don't give me that 'everything will be fine' crap," she replied, sniffing back her tears. "Because it won't, it just won't."

Martin squeezed her to him a little tighter.

"I know it seems that way, Pat. I know it's hard to think that everything will turn out satisfactorily. And I know you're going to slug me for saying this, but it will, you know. I believe that. I have to, really. Wouldn't be able to go through all of this if I didn't think that, in the end, the truth will come out and justice will decree a fair verdict."

"And how is that supposed to happen when that damn fool won't even answer any questions on the witness stand?" she asked harshly, punching his ribs. "I don't know how you can say such a thing, much less believe it, when he won't even speak up for himself in his own defense. God! It's like he wants to be punished for what happened. Like he's begging to be." She shook her head. "The only time he's even said more than two words to Peter is when he wanted his last name changed to Arbagna, or whatever it is."

"That may well be, but—"

"Hell, maybe he is guilty. Maybe that's why he won't deny the charges. Maybe he did kill the girl out of sexual rage like the prosecution said, and then— "

"Enough!" Martin barked, his normally pale, wrinkled face flush with anger. "Our son did not kill Jennifer Stamper!" he proclaimed, his eyes glassy with water. "Peter told us as much! I don't know exactly why she died, but he did not do it! He couldn't! I won't hear of it! He's our son, damn it," he told her. Lowering his voice, trembling, he added, "He couldn't have."

Startled and a little taken back, Patricia eyed her husband with concern. She was starting to realize that there would be no winners coming out of this mess. Everyone touched by Menelik and Jennifer's relationship had suffered, and would continue to. As she gazed at Martin, she felt as if he had aged a good ten years in the past few months. Even a miracle wouldn't be able to change that.

"Our son," she muttered, wiping her eyes.

"Yes, our son," Martin repeated with conviction. "Gabriel Tate Mathis or Menelik Arbagna. Whatever name he wishes to go by, whatever wrongs he has committed, he's still our son." Martin abruptly stood. "Do you hear that?" he bellowed, lifting his head. "He is our son and we are proud of it!"

The members of the sparse crowd that had gathered down the hall-way from the courtroom shot Martin uneasy glances, their hands cupped over their mouths to hide what they were whispering. Those who dared to openly meet his eyes were rewarded with a stoic, challenging, unflinching gaze.

"Please don't get yourself so upset," Patricia implored, grasping his arm. "We don't even know the verdict yet. And besides," she went on, glancing at the gawkers across the hall, "we don't need to prove anything to these people. They're just here for the drama. They're not worth the effort."

"What is it? What is it?" Eleanor exclaimed, half running out from the ladies room. "I heard somebody yellin'. Thought maybe Gabriel was bein' hauled back into court."

Eleanor dabbed her forehead with a tissue, breathing laboriously.

"You haven't missed a thing, dear, except for Martin flexing his vocal chords." Seeing the distraught look on Eleanor's face, she assured her, "Really, nothing has happened."

"Gabriel wouldn't be brought into court from out here, anyway, Eleanor," Martin added. "That would only have been the case if he were out on bail."

"Another brilliant decision on his part," Patricia bitingly lamented. "Even refusing bail because the money was coming from us. Makes me wonder how much hurt he wants to throw our way."

"Can't do no more with me. Boy's already done his damage, there. Hoped I'd never know the ache again like I did when Abraham and George were taken from me. Never thought it would be possible, really. But it is."

Farther up the hallway, voices erupted in shouts among waving arms and the sporadic flashes of light bulbs.

"Is that Peter?" Patricia asked, getting off the bench where she and Martin had been seated.

"I can't tell yet," Martin said, looking at the wave of bodies moving in their direction. "Too many reporters. But it's got to be either him or Mr. Conley, the way the press is acting."

"Bastard," Patricia hissed. "Never seen a man relish being so calculated and cruel. I think he'd hang Gabriel himself if it was legal."

"Political aspirations change people, turn them into cartoon characters of themselves, sometimes."

"Sometimes," Patricia scoffed. "How about most of the time? Just look at the ying-yang in the White House now. Heaven help the future."

"God will punish in His own way, in His own time," Eleanor stated in a monotone. "He punishes us all. Mr. Conley be no exception."

"It is Peter," Martin told them, perched on the tips of his toes.

"Wave him down, Martin, wave him down. Maybe he has a few minutes to spare before he goes into court."

Obligingly, Martin did as his wife asked, raising and waiving an arm, hoping Peter would be able to see him.

*

MENELIK ENTERED THE courtroom with his head held high. But today, like every other day since the trial had begun, he made no eye contact with anyone. Even when he was escorted to the table where his lawyer, Peter Lyons, waited—with Eleanor and the Mathises seated directly behind him in the first row—he offered no greeting, nor acknowledged that any of them were even there.

His continued silence had been a source of joy to the prosecution and frustration to his defense. And here, on the day his verdict was about to be handed down, he gave no indication to either side that anything would be changing.

Although his silence had been a point of contention and heated debate for everyone involved in the proceedings of the trial, it had not been so for Menelik. For in his silence he had found time to reflect, to judge, to detach, and to gain some perspective on everything that had transpired since the Mathises had brought him to America.

His life, from the moment he had been taken from Ethiopia, had been a falsehood, he had concluded. And although he viewed it as such, it had, nevertheless, caused the death of two people, and was now placing him in jeopardy of earning his own. The paradox was complete; he had never belonged here, never should have been taken from his homeland. But although he wished he could denounce his life in America as the farce that it was, he found that he couldn't. Everyone he had ever touched had suffered, he realized, and he was the cause.

He glanced quickly around the courtroom, grunting at his own musings. What more was there to do but bring everything to a close? It was time to shut the lie down. Death would be the path to Ras Dashen, he concluded. He would be reunited with Jennifer.

"Jennifer," he mumbled.

"What's that?" Peter whispered, bending closer. "Is this your way of telling me that you're ready to talk? Because if it is, I'm afraid you're way too late."

Menelik said nothing, his attention fixed to the portion of the table where his hands were resting.

"Look, man, this is it," Peter added, sounding cross and completely spent. "Since you wouldn't testify, you're as good as gone. The prosecution just followed the trail of blood you left for them. From the altercation at the zoo to your stealing the javelin from the sporting goods store to your fingerprints being all over the syringe and the spear you shoved into that guy's throat."

Peter pressed his glasses against the bridge of his nose.

"I wish I could get through to you, man," he went on, taking a quick look over his shoulder to the three people sitting directly behind them. "I wish you would wake up from whatever it is that's got a hold on you. They're going to crucify you, Gabe. And you're the one supplying the nails for the cross. Don't you see? Until you give your side of the story, there won't even be a basis for an appeal. Are you just going to let your whole life end without saying anything? Don't you even want to see Ethiopia again?"

Menelik sat stone-faced, saying nothing.

"Oh, hell, man. Forget it. I don't know why I'm even bothering after all these weeks. Maybe they'll reinstate the death penalty just for you and you can get your wish. What do I care?"

Ethiopia: the river of sand, pretending to be the Emperor's soldiers among the goats, racing Teimbaka to their father, gathering the firewood, running from the lions, shivering among the thorn bushes in the dark, hearing the bell of the goats, watching his parents and Tafari drift by. The images shuttled through his thoughts as soon as Peter said the name of his country. It was the one great loss his silence was costing him: a return to his homeland to find his brother.

He fidgeted in his seat, uncomfortable with the visions parading through his head. If only Jennifer were still alive, he thought, she would know how to help. She'd understand about Teimbaka's appearance at the zoo. She would help him find his brother.

But Jennifer was dead.

"All rise."

"Stand up, get up," Peter said, shaking him by his shoulders, waking him from his thoughts.

Grudgingly, he rose.

The gavel pounded.

Thunderclaps of searing pain shot through his skull.

"Has the jury reached a verdict?"

A trace of incense reached him.

"Yes, Your Honor."

A tiny bell jingled from afar. Cling, clang, cling, clang. He could hear the goat bleating as it drew closer.

"The defendant shall face the jury."

*A bull elephant—crystalline, eyes of reddish-pink, tusks awash in a golden light—smashed through the courtroom doors, trumpeting an urgent, thunderous call.*

*Shaking, Menelik sank to his knees, the floor buckling beneath him as the spirit beast drew near. He bowed his head, waiting. A shuddering convulsion racked his body when a massive tusk swept him off his feet. Falling sideways, he curled into a ball. The wooden floor shifted and then disintegrated. He slammed into a stone outcrop atop a mountain.*

*Stunned, he lay panting and gasping for air. Whimpering in pain, he righted himself. Incense wafted to him again, drifting to him on wisps of clouds that floated across the ledge where he had fallen.*

*A gunshot erupted—booming, powerful—its echo reverberating throughout a sky of sunrise purples, pinks, and reds. As the echo subsided, he heard the agonized cry of an elephant. He crawled to the edge of the cliff.*

*A herd of ghostly elephants, a thousand strong, were gathered on a honey-colored plain, their translucent bodies shimmering with hues of gold. Beyond them, stretching outward as far as he could see, were the sparkling waters of an azure lake, its surface alive with the rays of the morning sun.*

"A gift of the Mother," a hushed voice proclaimed, a soft breeze swaying the folds of Teimbaka's robes.

Teimbaka offered his hand. Menelik took it and rose.

The vast herd of ghost elephants raised their trunks, trumpeting a welcome. The brothers stood in silence, smiling, captivated. When a massive bull split from the herd and lumbered toward them, they marveled at its majesty.

A bullet struck the bull in the center of his head. His crystalline form shattered, shards of light splintering outward in all directions. The wail of his death cry was ear-splitting.

Three more shots—boom, boom, boom—rang off in succession. Three more spirit elephants exploded, droplets of crimson staining the ground where they had stood. Teimbaka touched Menelik's shoulder and pointed; a blonde-haired, white-skinned man raised a rifle and fired. Another elephant exploded, erupting into particles of light that turned blood red as they fell to the ground.

Without warning, Teimbaka leapt from the ledge, clutching a steel-tipped spear. Menelik stared at him in disbelief.

"Wait!" he shouted, terrified that Teimbaka was jumping to his death.

"Will you not help him?"

Distraught, Menelik forced himself to look away from Teimbaka. Jennifer stood next to him, her face half-covered by the hood of her white robe.

"Jen," he whispered.

She neither turned to look at him nor spoke.

Gunshots rang out from below—boom, boom, boom, boom—the death wail of an elephant following each one.

"He needs you," she told him.

But when Menelik turned back to see where Teimbaka was, everything had changed.

A drab grey sky now hung over a field of butchered carcasses, the beasts' severed tusks strewn across the blood-soaked soil. Teimbaka was there, kneeling in the center of the slaughter. The white-skinned man stood behind him, pointing the rifle at the back of his head.

"No!" Menelik screamed.

"Why aren't you there?" Jennifer's question was condemning, her voice cold.

"It— it— it's too—I would die," he stammered, caught between watching what was unfolding beneath him and making her understand.

He looked to her, pleading, but she turned her back on him.

"Won't you even try?"

Frantic, Menelik reached out to her, but a massive spirit bull suddenly appeared and wrapped his trunk around his torso. Raising him aloft, the spirit bull hurled him backward as a rifle shot boomed across the plain below.

"No!" he shouted. "No!"

The sound of the gunshot echoed over and over. Menelik pressed his hands against his ears and screamed. When his scream subsided, the echo of the gunshot had changed.

Distant and solitary, rhythmic and forlorn, the measured pounding of a drum engulfed him. The hollow sound made everything empty. He closed his eyes and began to weep.

A light touch to his cheek lifted him from his grieving. The baby spirit elephant stared down at him, its eyes filled with sorrow.

"I don't understand," Menelik confessed. "Where is Jen?"

The baby spirit elephant tilted its head to the side, inviting Menelik to look.

"Where?" he asked. "I don't—"

The baby spirit elephant placed the tip of its trunk against his lips. With a slight shake of its head, it moved away, dissipating as Menelik stood and watched.

"But where?"

The drum beat louder.

A lion roared.

A woman screamed.

Menelik sprinted toward the sounds, but fell face first into a loose mound of earth, the edge of a large, flat stone having caught the toe of his foot.

The drum went silent.

Again, a lion roared.

Mound after mound of freshly turned soil stretched out and around him, creating a loose pattern of tiny hills, each weighted with a slab of stone. Some of the stones were oblong and flat, others rounded and broken with craggy *edges and peaks. The way between them was haphazard. They seemed to have neither a beginning nor an end.*

*A woman screamed once more.*

*The walls of a building suddenly loomed some fifty yards away. A figure of a woman was crouching beside it. A lion leapt around the corner of the building and pounced. The woman succumbed quickly, the lion finishing the kill with a savage bite to her throat.*

*Menelik ran toward her, coming to a halt as the lion looked up. Its jaws shining crimson, teeth dripping with blood, it snarled.*

*"Why did you not help her?" Tafari now stood beside him, his arms crossed, his face etched in pain.*

*Before Menelik could answer, a boy raced around the corner of the building, holding a big stick over his head. The lion roared and swiped a massive paw, raking the boy across his chest.*

*"No!" Menelik screamed.*

*But the boy vanished. The claws of the lion passed through air.*

*Behind him, carelessly walking across the mounds of dirt and stones, three hyena-men made their way toward him, their laughter growing bolder as they neared.*

*"Help me." Ghostly pale and wide-eyed, Jennifer stared at him, pleading.*

*"Will you just watch?" Teimbaka demanded of him, boldly striding toward the lion with his spear in hand.*

*"Help me!" Jennifer begged again.*

*The hyena-men howled.*

*The clash between the lion and Teimbaka was swift: a blur of tawny fur flashing, Teimbaka thrusting his spear and then staggering back in pain as the lion's claws ripped across his chest.*

*A woman screamed.*

*Teimbaka fell to the ground, blood seeping from his wounds. A woman's voice shrieked his name.*

*"You would let them both die?" Tafari accused him.*

*"No!" Menelik shouted. "No!"*

*"Why do you not help her, then?" It was the little boy who asked. He was looking at Jennifer. "She will die," he told Menelik. The boy gently placed his*

*fingers to her lips "She is dead," he stated, tears streaking his face. "You have killed her," he whispered. "You have killed her."*

*"No," Menelik told him. "No—I would never," he said, his voice rising, muscles tensing. "I would never! It's Jen! I could never! I did not kill her!"*

*"You did!" the hyena-men shouted. "You killed her! It was you!"*

*"No! I didn't kill her! I didn't kill her! I didn't kill her! It wasn't me!"*

*"You did," a voice hissed into his ear. Strong hands grabbed his shoulders. "You killed her."*

*Menelik struck out at his faceless assailant with his fists, striking blow after blow, wanting nothing more than to silence the lie.*

"I didn't kill her! I didn't kill her! I didn't kill her!" he screamed. "I loved her!" he sobbed. "Didn't you know?" he asked, pulling the face to him, trying to focus. "Didn't you know?"

Little by little, the face cupped between his hands began to take shape, evolving from the desolate face of the little boy to the macabre muzzle of a hyena-man to the shocked face of Peter Lyons. His mouth bloodied and his glasses askew, Peter stared at Menelik, dumbfounded.

"Cuff him!" came the order from the bench. "Get him in a straight jacket! Get him under control!"

The bailiffs rushed to Peter's side, pulling Menelik off, twisting him roughly around while they placed handcuffs on his wrists.

Confused and disoriented, he shook his head, unable to comprehend what had just transpired.

For the first time since his trial had begun, he looked at the spectators seated in the courtroom. His eyes found those of Eleanor, Patricia, and Martin.

"I didn't kill her," he told them as the bailiffs were pulling him away. "I need to go home! I need to be free!" he yelled.

As the bailiffs shut the door behind him, the judge banged his gavel and left the bench. But no one else in the packed courtroom moved or uttered a word. Somewhere, near the doors in the back, the flash from a photographer's camera went off.

# SEPTEMBER 1974

*Dearest Mother and Father,*

*The rains of the kremt were little this year. But unlike the rains of
the past two, they gratefully materialized. Any relief is welcomed,
of course. Yet it is disturbing that such a small amount of rain
has fallen in what is supposed to be the wet season. It will change
nothing.*

*Even now, as I write this, my fourth letter to you since my arrival
here, the night breeze holds only the buzzing of flies and the
tormented sleep of the people. There is no moisture. And even
if there were, the parched land would absorb it all and leave us
nothing. And though we too are thirsty, I cannot find fault with the
needs of the earth.*

*Since I have been here, I have received no word from the Order,
nor, alas, from you. I pray nightly that God keeps your faith strong,
for I know, since this land is in the constant turmoil of war and
drought and famine, it would be natural for you to think that I have
perished. So I pray that this letter finds you and relieves you of that
burden. Knowing you both, as I do, I know your hearts must be
heavy. I trust in the Lord, that His will be served.*

*I must confess that I have doubted Him. For what He has placed before me has greatly tested my strength. Wrongly, I have cried myself to sleep and asked that He replace me with someone who is stronger. But then the morning comes and I am shown the weakness of my sin—my selfishness. How trivial my failures are when those who come here only wish to survive, or as it is more often than not, seek only to save the children they bring.*

*Children. They are the reason I am here. I believe it is the reason that this place I have been delivered unto exists. May God give us His blessing—it is all we ask, all we hope, all we pray for.*

*It has been rumored that the Emperor, Haile Selassie, has been overthrown by the military. We are cautiously hopeful that aid may reach us now that he is gone, for there was none while he was in power. It was as though his people did not exist. May God have mercy on his soul for what he allowed to happen here, and may God be swift in His punishment, if indeed that is His will.*

*Are the leaves changing color yet? And if they have, are they as beautiful as ever? I sometimes envision them and see Father riding beneath them wearing his hunt colors. But I stray from my train of thought. (Perhaps purposely.)*

*How dreadful I must sound! How I must make everything sound!*

*Forgive me. Not all is as dour as I have obviously made it seem. If paper and pencil were not in such short supply, I would rip this letter up and begin anew.*

*The village, as I now refer to it, has grown. Because of this, we are stretched to the limit. What little we can give is due to the untiring efforts of the man I have mentioned to you before, Teimbaka. A most compelling man he is, filled with courage and concern, and—though he would protest my saying it—a boundless love for his country and his people.*

*I suffered days of great misgiving after his killing of the marauding lion over the wounds he suffered from the beast. At the time, as you may remember from my previous letters, we had no medicine with which to treat the terrible clawing he received. Lee and I felt certain infection had set in at one point. But through prayer and the will of God, he somehow survived. I am reminded each day of God's grace when I look upon the awful scars that disfigure his chest.*

*But again, due to his efforts, we now have a meager amount of medicine. He comes by this in ways I do not condone—dare I say by theft, or as he says, "borrowing with no return"—but as the village is in dire need of it, we accept it without question. Food and water— always items of scarcity—are mostly hunted for, a skill he excels at. Although at times—again, I do not ask how—canned rations taken from one warring side or another find their way into our hands.*

*As we have pursued these most basic of needs, we have also fashioned more structures so that we may at least offer those who travel here a roof to shade them. John, the boy who has adopted me, has been most helpful in these endeavors, learning the skills of Teimbaka either by direct tutelage or by imitation. Because Teimbaka has, on occasion, brought books back to the village, John and he have talked of erecting a school, and of all things, a chapel of some fashion where the evening prayers could be offered. This, of course, brings tears to my eyes. Often I tell them that their ideas are endlessly heartwarming, a tribute to both God and to them. My tears, you see, they take as sadness and not joy. I suppose, having witnessed only the tears of suffering for most of their lives, it is hard for them to think otherwise.*

*Lately, I have been given to wondering what will happen to all these children who have come to know this place as home. God willing, of course, there will be an end to this, someday. But when that time arrives, what will the future hold in store for them? When my time is served here—as God will surely show me—who in this land will care for them, teach them, keep them with hope? As many are orphans, it is a worrisome point that I tend to dwell upon too much of late. Lee simply tells me to shut up when I go on about this. She is so direct with her tongue! And she says that we can only do what we can, and not what all humanity should be doing.*

*Survival—it is a word I have come to know all too well here. We struggle for it daily. It is the driving force behind all that we do. Never do I hear the word* dream *spoken. And for me, that is the most tragic aspect of this impoverished place. To exist without dreams, or even the will to dream; it is though they have given up on ever finding a way that will deliver them from this misery. As if this is a land where hope does not exist. It is tragic, and as of yet, I have not found the way to show them otherwise.*

*Faith; I have always relied on faith. And therein lies the answer. And so shall it be with them.*

*I believe that I shall see the bounty of the Lord*

*In the land of the living*

*Wait for the Lord with courage*

*Be stouthearted and wait for the Lord*

*Words written a thousand years before my life: how true they are this day and for days a thousand years hence.*

*Dearest parents, be not sorrow-filled if this letter reaches you and within my writing you perceive a daughter bearing hardship. Do not allow this letter to misguide you, for I am filled with faith. How can it be otherwise when God has brought me here? For in me, He has entrusted His will, and He has guided the meekest and the most forlorn to this place so that the power of His love will be known. To know that I am the servant He has placed His faith in fills me with an unmatchable sense of all that life is and what it was meant to be. This is the state of my being, regardless of what my words cannot convey. I pray that I am worthy of the task.*

*Yet, even as I write these words, I realize that I must be worthy of it, for to fail would mean condemning countless of the innocent. This I shall not let come to pass. I cannot. I will not.*

*May God keep you both well.*

*Your loving daughter,*

*Claire*

T HE FLAME OF the low-burning candle flickered in the night's soft breeze. Shadows wavered over the paper and the penciled script. Claire gently placed one hand atop her other, calming the trembling of the pencil grasped between her thumb and forefinger.

Carefully folding the crinkled, tattered sheet of paper, she smoothed the side with the plain face, making certain there was ample space to write her parents' names and address. Like she had the other letters she had written to her parents, she would send this one by way of Teimbaka, without an envelope or stamp. And though common sense and logic told her that a letter sent in this fashion would never reach its intended destination, she preferred not to dwell on that aspect, relying on the will of God—through the kindness of some thoughtful stranger or divine happenstance—that the letter would, eventually, make its way to America and find her parents' mailbox.

With a final wistful touch of her fingertips, she said a silent prayer, staving off the tears welling in her eyes with a quivering sigh.

John stirred at her feet. As was his practice, one of his hands felt for the end of her robe. Claire looked down at him and smiled.

"Beloved John," she whispered. "Always by me."

Claire slid the letter off to the side as she rose from the drum she sometimes used as a table. Wearily, she stretched, rolling the tightness from her shoulders, yawning away the misgivings of the day now coming to a close.

As she bent to blow out the candle, the flame curled and danced, a smattering of its light shining on a row of jagged, pink scars.

"What is it?" she asked in a voice so low the sound of it was barely audible.

"Lee," he softly told her, glancing away as she adjusted the folds of the white shamma she had taken to wearing as of late. "She has fallen."

"Is she badly hurt?" she inquired, stepping closer, crossing herself.

Asking for her silence with a slight shake of his head, he motioned her to follow, extinguishing the flame with his fingertips as he left. The smoke twisted with his touch, swirling with the movement of their bodies.

Claire clutched the silver crucifix about her neck.

"I have taken her from the camp as she asked," he relayed in a quiet tone. "Her skin is afire."

"But you said—"

"Fallen to a sickness I have seen before. She knows, I would think. She asks that you not come."

"Nonsense."

"She forbids you. She wants only that I tell you, she said."

"How can—?"

"Sister Lady?"

John's voice both stirred and quieted Claire's apprehension.

"It's all right, John. Go back to sleep. Teimbaka and I," she looked to

Teimbaka in earnest, "we have to go somewhere for a short time. I will be right back."

"I go too," John proclaimed. "I go where you go, sleep when you sleep."

"It is as she thought," Teimbaka stated.

"John, you must stay here," Claire instructed, kneeling to be level with his face. "I—we—will be right back, okay?"

"No," John told her flatly, folding his arms in front of his chest. "I go too."

"John, you can't," Claire explained, cupping his face in her hands. "Lee is sick. I must go to see her without you so that you won't get sick as well."

Steadfastly, John shook his head, his resolve not weakened by Claire's pleading tone.

"Teimbaka, tell him he must stay. Tell him it is what Lee wishes."

Peering over Claire's shoulder, an expression of mischief on his face, John giggled and asked, "Where he go?"

With a mixture of surprise and resigned frustration, Claire plopped to the ground. Pulling John into her lap, she said, "I don't know."

*

A HORDE OF GHOSTS and goblins slithered along the ceiling and the walls of the cave. Angels of the dark world were also there, hovering just outside the light of the fire, awaiting orders from their soulless master.

Lee shivered and clenched her fists, her body soaked in sweat. Desperately, she tried to blink the images away, but the monsters of her childhood would not go. Spurred on by the fever burning through her skin, they edged ever closer, baiting and taunting her, hoping her end was near.

"Not like this," she begged. "Dear, God, not like this."

When the chills had overcome her two days earlier, she had ignored them, brushing them away as a nuisance. Overtired, she had reasoned at the time, overworked, overburdened, and overwhelmed. Even when the chills had grown into a slight fever and her back had started to ache deep in her joints, she still dismissed it all. The symptoms were nothing more than a nagging, lingering form of fatigue, she had told herself. But as the fever had grown stronger and the ache in her joints had become more severe, she realized she could no longer ignore them. The implications were too threatening, especially to the children.

The sensation of cool water glided across her brow. Droplets of it slid gently down one cheek and then the other. A hand slipped beneath her neck, lifting her head. Water was placed against her lips, leaving her frantic for more.

"Slowly," a voice directed.

Obediently, she tasted a bit of the water and then sipped. Immediately, the smoldering embers lodged in her throat were washed away.

"Lord," she sighed, quivering, "is it you? Is it time?"

"No, Lee, I am not your god. It is Teimbaka."

"Teimbaka," she moaned. "How I have hated you. How—"

"Silence," he said, placing a damp cloth upon her forehead. "Do not waste your words. Save them for when you are stronger."

Lee opened her eyes wide and looked at him.

"I saw the eyes of the devil in yours," she struggled to say, a weak, unsteady smile flashing briefly across her lips. "But they were never there. It was just temptation to see evil in you. The evil was in me. And now you come here and—"

Overcome with exhaustion, she twisted her head away to the side. Teimbaka wiped her brow and then dabbed at the tears gathering on the ridges of her cheeks.

"There is no evil in you," he replied, his tone urgent, but calm. "Do you hear?"

"Water," she gasped. "More."

He lifted the wooden cup to her lips. Tipping it ever so slightly, he coaxed the water into her mouth with care.

"Where?" she asked after she had swallowed twice. "How?"

Teimbaka placed the cup against her lips once more, but she shook her head, refusing.

"Don't waste it on me. You should not have taken it from the children."

"This is not the water from the village," he relayed. "It is some that the Mother saved from the kremt. Even while Her land goes thirsty, She saved this for you."

Lee blinked rapidly, her head rolling from side to side.

"Drink it, Lee," he prodded. "It is a gift to you from the Mother."

But if Lee heard him, she did not show it, for her body suddenly arched in a wave of pain. Her brow was heavy with sweat; the tiny pustules dotting her skin seemed to suddenly burn a brighter red.

"Why must this be?" he asked.

Pouring water from the cup, he moistened the cloth and placed it on her forehead. Yet, even as he did, he knew it would be of little use, for the look of death was already upon her.

Sparks crackled into the air as he placed a few more sticks upon the fire. The fragments drifted upward before arcing toward the endless expanse of the night sky beyond the mouth of the cave. Soon, Lee's spirit would join them, he knew. He hoped the final hours of the smallpox would be merciful.

"As you once told me," he said, staring at the stars, "they are the children of your god. I would keep you from them if I could."

The fire popped and hissed, prompting his thoughts to stray. The flames shifted and wavered, their sudden movement creating a pattern of shadows that took him from the present to the past.

Around the campfire they sat: Matula, the powerful; Untello, the noble; Reta Basa, the steady and silent; Bawa, the babbling teller of tales; and Gunstard, the killer.

Teimbaka saw columns of armies in the braided rows of Reta Basa's hair. And in the blue-black face of Matula, he spied a water buffalo pondering its mood. And when the howling laughter of Bawa arose, his ivory teeth flashed, the fire catching them as he bobbed and weaved his head in the telling of one of his endless numbers of tales. Farther past, just on the fringes of the flames, sat Untello. His eyes were sad, as was the sound of his voice when he spoke of the Africa of old.

An icy chill crept across the back of Teimbaka's neck when he looked at Gunstard. It had been that way since the first moment they had met, he supposed. Not even a fire could keep the feeling away. It was though the shadow of death was at his side, patiently waiting for him to deliver another soul into its grasp.

*Untello*, he mused, picturing the man's face. They were standing at the cave of the tusks. Untello was speaking of the spirit elephants that haunted him, of footprints appearing from beasts that only he could see, of the earth rattling from a thundering stampede that only he could feel.

Where was Untello now, he wondered? And did the spirit elephants still haunt him? Were they waiting for him, as he believed them to be?

He returned to the present with an emptiness building in his chest.

Where had the spirit elephants gone, he wondered? He had not seen them since the morning of the slaughter.

He stared into the flames to see if they would appear, but the visions had already gone, vanishing into the ashes.

"Matt!" Lee screamed, her body lurching upward. "Look out! Matthew, look out!"

Teimbaka reached for her to hold her down.

"Matthew," she cried, her voice filled with a begging grief. "Don't die. Don't die!"

As though the minions of the underworld were taking her heart, Lee's body shuddered in a massive spasm of pain.

"God! Please, God—no!"

Her scream filled the cave with torment, the very air swirling with the emotion. The fire exploded in a shower of sparks.

Sprinkled with cinders, Lee's body suddenly convulsed, then went limp. Fearing she had died, Teimbaka found tears welling up in his eyes. He hugged her tight, trying to keep her in the present.

"Why do you cry?"

"Because I—" he began. Astonished, he wiped the tears from his face. Lee gasped.

"Because I thought you were dead."

Having spoken his fear aloud, he freshened the cloth with clean water and began to cleanse Lee from head to toe.

"What more can I do?" he asked, raising his eyes upward. "Always, here, there is more."

As he continued to bathe her, Lee fell into a rhythmic, shallow breathing. Lulled by the spell it cast, Teimbaka fell into a like calm. Seconds slipped into minutes, then minutes into hours. Gently rocking on the balls of his feet, he was unaware that the night had flowed toward dawn. The fire dwindled to a few sparks and ashes. And as the darkness gave way to light, a chilling breeze entered the mouth of the cave. It sent a shiver across the back of his neck.

With a sense of foreboding he rebuilt the fire, hoping with every stick that burst into flame that the touch of death would be postponed. When he looked upon Lee in the early morning light, he quickly turned away. He did not wish to remember her that way.

"Claire," he wondered aloud, "what more can I do?"

A fleeting smile touched his lips.

"Pray—and have faith," was his whispered reply.

Nodding, he allowed himself to look upon Lee anew.

"But how?" he asked. "What words will your god hear?"

The fire hissed, sending smoke spiraling toward the ceiling. Wistfully, he ran a finger through it, his eyes brightening when it swirled to his touch and gathered about his hand.

"So, you are here, as Claire has always said."

He bowed his head.

"Still," he continued, addressing the fire-spawned veil wrapped around his skin, "Claire would know a prayer that you might better listen to, rather than one that is said in the Mother's voice. Perhaps," he ventured, "if she were here?"

Closing his eyes, he beckoned Claire to him. Envisioning her face, concentrating on her every feature, he willed her image into substance.

She was asleep—John, as always, slumbering close by her feet. Careful not to disturb the boy, Teimbaka quietly approached her. He awakened her with a finger laid softly against her cheek.

Claire's eyes greeted him with tenderness. Her smile filled him with joy. As he motioned for her to join him, she arose and took his hand. He led her to Lee, and they knelt at her side.

Gripping her silver cross with one hand, clasping Teimbaka's palm with the other, she gazed upon him. He felt her faith wash over him.

"Now he will hear?" he asked.

"He has always, Teimbaka," came Claire's solemn response. "Always will He."

"But I—"

"Shhh; do not doubt. Let Him hear you."

The breath of dawn entered the cave, sweeping through the enclosure as a brief, swirling gust of wind. Claire was lifted by the current and spirited away. Teimbaka tried to cling to her fingers, to no avail. Her final words, however, remained in his thoughts.

"I must tell you that I am of the Mother," he began, his voice uncertain. "This woman who lies here, she is of you, you see. It is taught that you are the sun and the moon, the stars in the heavens themselves. Sister Lady, she tells me that you are all: Father, Mother, Child, and Spirit. If this is true, I am confused, for I do not know you as such. But her faith is strong. So I trust that her faith will lead my words to you. So I petition you now, believing that you will hear me."

Her body twitching, her sallow features beaded with a fevered sweat, Lee moaned.

"This woman has known much suffering. She has toiled here for many years, bearing great hardship, while asking nothing for herself. Death she has fought almost daily. And now, this sickness tortures her, punishes her for the work she has done. So I ask you; will you not ease her suffering?"

Although not expecting a response, he paused, so if one was forthcoming, it might be given.

"Perhaps, like the Mother, you are angry with your children, angry with what we have done, or failed to do, or what we will do in the future. I think of this often: what wrong we must have committed that even the land must be punished."

He lowered his head. Doubt was seeping in. He was losing Claire's faith. He felt the presence of a dark entity drifting closer.

"If it is I that you are angry with because I believe in the Mother, then I ask that you place your wrath on me. Fill me with the disease that you have placed upon this woman and release her from its agony. For she does not deserve its pain."

He paused to gather his thoughts. As the first rays of the sun entered the cave, he wished for the touch of Claire's hand.

"Make it not so," he softly pleaded, seeing what the sun had unveiled.

The eruptions of the smallpox had begun to fester, swelling Lee's flesh to the threshold of the macabre. Heartsick at the sight, he trembled, his emotions torn between sadness and anger.

"Mother, and you, Father," he intoned, lifting his face skyward. "Will you not share words together, so that, between the two of you, forgiveness can be given to those who have done no wrong? Please," he begged, his voice rising. "Please."

"Teimbaka."

The voice startled him in a pleasant way, for the tone of it was what he had always imagined the Mother's might be.

"Who is it you are talking to?"

Laughing at himself, he sheepishly looked down at Lee.

"It's been so long since I've seen your smile and heard your laughter," she said. She attempted a weak smile of her own, but failed. Her eyes blinked against the brightness of the sun.

"Morning?" she asked, mustering what strength she could.

Nodding, Teimbaka picked up the wooden cup of water and the cloth he had been using to soothe her fever.

"Save it," she struggled to say, the shake of her head no more than a slight twitch. "We are not fools."

He glanced away, saying nothing.

"I was speaking to the Father," he offered a moment later.

"The—?"

"Your god."

She closed her eyes.

"Claire said that he would listen, that he always listens."

"Yes," he thought he heard her reply, though he wasn't certain.

"And to the Mother I spoke. She— she sometimes does not want to hear, will not listen if you are not of Her."

As the sun rose higher, the fever of the smallpox grew stronger. The sickly, red pustules grew larger. A heavy layer of sweat now covered Lee's body in a slick sheen of moisture. Dismayed, Teimbaka poured some of the water from the wooden cup onto Lee's brow and wiped her face with the cloth.

Eyeing him with rebuke, she moaned, "I told you—"

"Who is Matthew?" he interjected.

The saying of the name seemed to stab her. She jerked her neck away, her expression filled with despair.

"A loved one lost?" he carefully pressed.

"God, how I think you are the devil sometimes," she snapped. "You expose every weakness, open every wound."

Teimbaka continued to wipe away at her fever.

"I told Claire as much," she went on. "Or should I call her Sister Lady?"

"Does the name offend you?"

"No!" she spat, struggling between exhaustion and laughter. "How could it?" She coughed, shaking her head.

"She is devoted to you," he calmly pointed out. "She would be here now, had I not told her not to come."

"She is blessed."

"As you are."

"Perhaps," Lee said. "Perhaps there was a time when I thought I was. Blessed. In this place." She shook her head and licked her lips. "How is it possible?"

He put the wooden cup to her lips; reflexively, she sipped.

"It is her faith," she whispered. "It is why she is blessed. To have faith, here, where there is so much misery."

"One day the Mother will no longer be angry," he replied. "Or your Father, I hope. This is what Sister Lady teaches the children, to give them hope, to keep their smiles. It is why I—"

"So you will stay and help her, then, until there is no need?"

"You speak of eternity. How can I pledge what I do not have?"

"But you said."

"I said I hope there will be a time when both the Mother and the Father will no longer be displeased by us. But I cannot see a time when help will no longer be needed here. An eternity."

"Then this is what you must promise, promise to Claire, Teimbaka. Eternity. It must be eternity, then."

"And if why I was brought here, what saved me from drowning, or placed me on the road when Claire's car was attacked—if it finds me, if it brings my brother and me back together, Lee? What then?"

"Then he too must remain."

"If that were to happen, I could not ask this of him—to lose himself in this as we have done."

"You will!" she cried, gasping for air, shaking.

"Please," he said, trying to comfort her, sliding a hand behind her head, raising the cup of water to her lips. "There is no need to speak of what might or what might never be."

Gently, he pressed the cup to her lips, inviting her to drink.

"It is not right that you go thirsty," he said.

"What is right?" she hissed. "What is ever right?"

"Very little, it seems sometimes," he admitted, drifting to a thought he did not share. "But to those who are eternal—perhaps everything."

To his confusion, she began to weep.

"Why do you cry?"

"How can they embrace any suffering as being right?" she demanded. "How can the taking of children—any child—be part of their wisdom?"

Teimbaka dabbed away her tears.

"It seems so cruel, so senseless, so—" She bit down on her lower lip, unable to finish.

"Matthew—he was your brother? Was he small when he was taken?"

Lee nodded matter-of-factly, as though he had been privy to the knowledge of her family all along.

"My brother, as well," he told her, remembering Tafari. "We were very young."

"He didn't even have the chance to know life," Lee murmured. "He was a cripple—polio. I don't think he ever remembered being normal." She scoffed. "Normal. How I came to despise that word, despise myself."

She fell silent for a moment, remembering.

"That's what killed him: the normal world—me. A cripple's just not quick enough to dodge somebody who's in a hurry, who's busy getting somewhere, who gets behind the wheel of a car."

"You were there?"

"Yes," she replied, her eyes going wide with the vision. "Just trying to be a normal child. That's all he was doing. Just trying to catch a ball so he could throw it back across the street." Her eyes went glassy, her face ashen. "Just wanted to be a child," she repeated. "Like everybody else."

"And you, the memory causes you to—"

"I was talking," she explained, her voice far removed from where she was. "Standing right next to him. Talking to a woman across the street. Her son had a ball. Why was I talking, Teimbaka?" She looked to him, her eyes pleading. "What could I have been saying that I forgot that he was there? What on earth were we talking about? It happened so fast that I didn't even understand. Why didn't I step out onto the street to get the ball? Why didn't I?" she demanded of him, the pitch of her voice nearing hysteria. "Why?"

"Be calm, Lee, there is—"

"Half his head was scraped off! It was just gone! Spread along the street like butter!"

"Stop it, Lee! Stop it. It was too long ago. No good can come of this."

"The blood never disappeared, never went away." She shuddered, her voice growing weak.

"Even when the road was re-tarred, I could still see it."

Teimbaka placed his hands on her shoulders to steady her.

"It seems our paths have run near to each other," he said. "I see blood as well, everywhere."

"Teimbaka!" she screamed, clutching his arms. "You must bring my things! Bring me his book!"

"Quiet," he implored. "Just rest. Save—"

"Where the dead rest. I buried them," she gagged out, "where Ella slept, beneath the pile of clothes. Bring them, Teimbaka. Dig them up. Bring them."

"Do not ask me to leave you now."

"Do as I say," she pleaded, staring him plainly in the face. "Hurry. Let it be a last kindness."

Teimbaka started to protest, but then thought better of it, relenting to her will, hoping to place her mind at ease.

"Drink then," he instructed. "Before I go. Yes?"

Grudgingly she complied, sipping from the wooden cup when he brought it up to her mouth.

"You have earned the Mother's love," he told her, placing her head softly on the cave's stone floor. "And if it not anger the Father, may Her love be with you for all eternity."

Bending to her, with great feeling, he kissed her cheeks and forehead.

"I will bring you what you have asked. Rest now. Rest."

Lee watched him go without feeling or awareness, seeing only a silhouette melding into the sunlight. With his departure, the angels of the dark world returned, as did the ghouls and goblins from the previous night. Their disfigured shapes crept closer.

But Lee did not fear them on this morning, nor try to will them away. She knew full well why they were there. She had been expecting them to come since her brother's death. She had always known that they would be the ones who would take her. It was only a matter of time before a worthless life such as hers came to a fitting end, she reasoned. She was ready now. She had been ready for many years.

In a scream of silence, her body racked in fevered agony, Lee passed from the realm of the Mother and entered the kingdom of the Father, her moment of death witnessed by no one save for the soulless monsters of her own creation.

*

"WHY DO YOU bring my habit?" Claire asked when she saw Teimbaka carrying a bundle in his arms.

Teimbaka tried to speak, but found he could only shake his head.

"I don't understand. Why have you brought my clothes?"

"Lee," he managed to say. "She—" He lowered his eyes toward the ground.

"Why didn't you take me to her?" she snapped. "I would have been able to help."

Teimbaka lifted his face, his eyes filled with grief. He stared at her in silence.

"I'm—I'm sorry," she said. "I didn't mean to—"

"No!"

Claire shuffled away, taken back by Teimbaka's vehemence.

"When you are ready," he told her after a pause. He laid the bundle at her feet. "I will be—" He shrugged and walked away.

"Teimbaka, Teimbaka!"

John took hold of the edge of her shamma, offering a smile when she looked at him.

"John, would you go to him please? Ask him what I'm supposed to do with my habit."

Always willing to please her, John heartily nodded.

"John."

"Yes, Sister Lady," he immediately replied, stopping himself before he had taken but a few steps.

"Would you mind taking my things back to my hut before you do?"

"Yes, Sister Lady!" he told her, gathering the bundle into his arms. "Sister Lady?"

"What is it, John?"

"These are not yours, I think."

"Why, of course they are, John. Who else have you seen—?"

"A cross, like yours," he told her, dangling a silver cross in his fingers. Reflexively, she reached for her own.

"Then whose?"


John sat down on the opposite side of the orange-red flames, offering no explanation to Teimbaka for his intrusion. Teimbaka said nothing in return. For a time, they both lost themselves within the fire, occasionally glancing to the white-blue stars in the sky above them. It was as though each of them, in turn, was reflecting upon which entity held more mystery and inspired more awe. When Teimbaka placed another stick to the flames, the crackling of it interrupted their silence, giving John an opening to speak.

"Sister Lady, she needs some special milk or for— formula? I think that is the word she taught me to say. —A baby was brought to her today. It is hungry."

"Mek'ele, where Sister Lady was heading the day—" he replied, his tone subdued. "That is where to ask or borrow."

"Goat's milk? Is that what she means?"

"No," he chuckled half-heartedly. "Baby formula. And other supplies that babies need."

"I have never been to Mek'ele," John said, puffing out his chest and sitting straighter. "Where would I look for it?"

"There," Teimbaka replied, pointing to the northwest. "Do you see that star?" he asked John, gazing above. "Kokeb," he repeated in Amharic. "There, the brightest one; do you see it? If you keep to it, edging just right of the place it holds in the sky, Mek'ele will be a full night's journey by run, plus a day more if you walk."

"How I know it?"

Teimbaka studied the child for a moment before replying. John had grown, he could see. More a young man now than a boy, he thought. Close to the same age he himself had been when Yeshie— He closed his eyes, not wishing to remember.

"How I know it, Teimbaka?" John asked him again.

Tiembaka opened his eyes and looked northward. "There will be light rising from the ground, like that of a winter moon."

"I will go, then."

"No, it is too far for you, too difficult a journey. Besides, the hospital might only look upon you as a child. They will not entrust you with what Sister Lady wants," he explained, shifting his attention to John. "They will not see that you have come to them as man," he added, seeing John's angry expression.

"I will make them see," the man-child vigorously stated. "I will show them that I am no child."

"It is not that they won't see that you are becoming a man," he assured him. "It is simply that they won't give—"

"Teimbaka? I must speak with you."

Tentatively, Claire stepped into the light of the fire. She clasped a small black book in her hand.

"I'm sorry about earlier," she offered.

Teimbaka didn't respond.

"Must I beg to apologize?" she tersely questioned him, her eyes flashing with the oranges and reds of the flames.

"This night, there will be no useless talk. I have promised this to myself and to Lee. Tomorrow, if it must be, you can say what is not needed," he conceded, casting his attention back to the fire.

"Where is John?" she asked, sitting down where John had been seated when she'd first arrived. "He was right here, wasn't he?"

Teimbaka glanced to the north, but remained silent.

"John!" she called out. "John! Where are you?"

"Proving himself a man," he told her.

"What? What does that mean? Where has he gone?"

"To become a man."

"What are you saying? And why do you sound so troubled when you say it?"

Teimbaka eyed the stars above them for a time, letting his eyes drift from one cluster to the next, one constellation to another.

"I remember another boy," he finally said, his voice subdued. "Another boy who, to become a man—" he sighed, taking his eyes from the sky. "Too soon it is gone forever."

"But where is—?"

"The stars, Claire," he interjected, looking back up at the brilliant night sky, "do you think she is there? Do you think your Father has given her one to be a part of?"

"You're talking in riddles."

"Lee. It would be good to think that she is. I cannot think of a better place to roam for eternity."

Drawn in by his musings, Claire found herself searching through the canopy of twinkling lights in an attempt to find the brightest.

"I was angry," she said to him while she gazed above. "I was mad that you did not take me to see her. I could have helped. I could have—"

"Silence," he softly told her. "It is useless talk. There is no place for it on this night."

Claire hastily wiped her eyes, the flush in her cheeks hidden by the glare of the fire.

"How can you call it useless? I'm not saying that I could have saved her, but between the two of us—between the two of us, it might have made a difference."

Teimbaka sighed and closed his eyes.

"Even in death, her killer may still be with us. There was no champion that could have saved her. She knew this. Even now, the death that took her may lay claim to another."

"Stop talking in riddles! Dear God, Teimbaka, I am not some stupid underling! I am not some silly, adolescent little girl who hasn't seen how the real world is!" she cried, nearly choking in her vehemence. "So don't treat me like a child! Don't tell me I couldn't have helped! Or that I shouldn't have been there with her! Prayed with her! Prayed for her! Or just been there to hold her hand when she cried out for God's forgiveness!"

A sudden gust of wind blew in from the north. The flames of the fire erupted with its touch, the moment emphasized by a deep rumble of thunder and a flash of light.

Claire gripped the silver cross around her neck, her lips moving in silent prayer. When a second echo of thunder reached them, Teimbaka could not help but chuckle.

"So now you ridicule me?"

"You misunderstand," he was quick to tell her.

Claire shrugged and averted her eyes.

"I was wondering who it was that was speaking. The wind, the thunder: Was it the Mother or the Father dismissing our words?"

Claire would not look at him and said nothing.

"But that is useless talk. It changes nothing."

"I am not useless!"

"Smallpox renders us so," he countered, his face stern. "Lee understood."

"Smallpox!" she exclaimed. "God save us all."

"Yes," he agreed, though there was no feeling in his voice. "Save us."

The fire slowly dimmed, the flames drawing down to embers as Claire and Teimbaka sat in silence.

"How well did you know her?" Claire asked when she felt it right to speak. She stared at him while she waited for him to answer. "Teimbaka? Did you hear me?"

"How well?" he quietly repeated. "As well as I know you. By what the days ask of us and not what we say."

"Did she ever talk about faith? Tell you why she came?"

"What is there in talk," he shrugged, "when you are here? She saw this. When there is no end to the day, what use are words?"

"Then she never told you that she was like me, a Sister of the Holy Cross?"

Teimbaka shook his head.

"Why did she never say anything? I would have thought—"

Claire shook her head, a fleeting smile passing quickly across her lips. Teimbaka nodded.

"These things of hers," Claire told him, holding out the small book and a folded piece of paper, "they— She meant them to be given to you."

He stared at the items, but said nothing.

"You were—" she pursed her lips, searching for the right words to say. "Perhaps I should just let her tell you."

She held the book and the folded paper out to him, but he did not accept them.

"They are yours now. Please take them."

"I do not want them," he told her, shaking his head. "They're of no consequence."

"You are wrong!" she shouted, shaking the book toward him. "These are what she believed, what she cherished. They are what she was."

"All that I need to keep of her is here," he replied, touching his chest.

"Useless talk. That is what you are saying. Useless and stupid. Yes, stupid, Teimbaka," she told him, ignoring the look of anger that flashed within his eyes. "As Lee has said to me many times: you can exhibit a good amount of pig-headedness on occasion."

"I can see her saying it now," he laughed, his face brightening. "Though she would say the words without the kindness you give them."

"Yes, I dare say she would have," she agreed, sharing in his laughter. "She would have said it a good deal plainer."

They shared the laughter for a moment more before it ended.

"So you have read her writing?"

"Yes. I read everything she left."

"Then the words will not be a struggle for you."

"You mean?"

"Please. The written symbols. Some I do not know."

"Then you will have to be instructed along with the others." Seeing the hurt her words had brought to his eyes, she quickly added, "I'm sorry. Certainly I will."

As she unfolded the sheet of paper, Teimbaka rebuilt the fire. Ghost shadows danced across his face with each stick that went to flame.

Claire began to read.

*I have stolen a few precious moments to write this. What prompts me to set down my own epitaph on this particular day is at once both a mystery and a right of passage. I do not know if anyone will ever read this, as there is a chance that it will never be found. But it is my hope, or wish, that Teimbaka will find this, and read what I have set forth. Although I know little of how he came to be here, or why he stays, I am grateful that he is here, however odd it may seem to him that I feel this way.*

*I am here for penance, though there will never be enough of it to cleanse my soul. As for Teimbaka, I have yet to see what cross he bears, save that perhaps he is the conscience of God, the way he has made me question my faith, the way he makes me wonder if I am worthy in the least to cling to any semblance of hope and salvation.*

*I first saw him as a devil-angel, but then he made me see that we are all a mixture of the two, an equal share of what is pure and what is evil. It is with this thought in mind that I leave to him a child's prayer book once belonging to my brother, Matthew. What meaning it will have for him I do not know. Yet my desire is for him to have it. Let it stand at that. It is yours, Teimbaka, if you would be open to accepting it.*

*As for myself, I am aware that in the coming days and months and years of turmoil, I will die in this land called Ethiopia. I confess that I fled America in an attempt to leave behind all the darkness I created there, the darkness that haunts me still. There is no leaving it behind, I have discovered. The guilt is always with me.*

*I was wrong to embrace the possibility of salvation through distance and prayer, wrong to hide behind devotion, self-sacrifice, and obscurity, sinful to try to find a place among an order of women who are devoted to God's work and God's will. It is with shame that I recognize my weaknesses, my failings, and my sins. And it is in this vein that I remove my habit and refuse to wear it again for fear that I shall tarnish it even more and insult that which is holy.*

*Understand that it is not the Order of the Holy Cross that I denounce, or the vows of their devotion, or the symbols of the Order's soul-felt beliefs. Rather, it is I, Lee Ann Nelind, who I denounce: a devil-angel who is not deserving of God's blessing.*

*Lastly, to my brother, Matthew: I go through this life with your blood forever on my hands. Asking for your forgiveness is meaningless. I can only hope that when my death does come, that it is painful. I can only hope.*

Claire began to refold Lee's letter, but stopped herself, the notion that she was closing a person away unsettling.

"Away!" Teimbaka shouted without warning. "Leave!"

Abruptly springing to his feet, he picked up his spear and thrust it into the darkness behind them.

"Be gone!" he commanded. "Leave us!"

Claire rushed to him, clutching him for protection. His trembling body scared her; she had never known him to be afraid.

"What is it? Who's out there? Teimbaka?"

"Do you hear? Go! Now!" he screamed, thrusting the spear into the dark once more.

"Teimbaka!" Claire cried, squeezing him closer.

The wind from the north blew down upon them, siphoning sparks from the fire, swirling the cinders about their bodies. Transfixed by the glowing cocoon, Teimbaka smiled and stroked Claire's hair. She felt him relax, then heard a light chuckle escape from his lips. Bewildered, she pushed him away, eyeing the darkness behind him with skepticism.

"I do not find it amusing to be made a fool of," she angrily told him, though there was doubt in her tone. "What kind of joke are you playing?"

"The spirits that wander in the dark—those that fear fire—they are not a joke."

To his surprise, Claire laughed.

"Now you mock me," he stated evenly.

"Oh, please," she giggled. "Surely you are playing a trick, aren't you? I know you don't believe in such things. Goblins and ghosts and such—they are the misgivings of children."

"The spirits of both worlds walk this land. It is not only children who can see them or believe that they are real."

"But spirits are—" Claire held her tongue when she saw that he was perfectly serious. "I don't mean to sound— I mean, you never struck me as one who would believe in, well, ghosts."

He stoked the fire with the tip of his spear while he surveyed the darkness around them.

"The power of the trinity. You know of this?"

"Yes, I know it from my teachings."

"This trinity—"

"The Holy Trinity," she interjected.

"Yes, the Holy Trinity. Lee would speak of it sometimes, in the first days, when faith was not so fragile for her. Invincible, she would say, that union: the Father, Son, and the Holy Ghost. Is this not a belief of yours as well?"

"Of course it is. But that is different. The Holy Ghost is not a figure of haunting or lore. It is the spirit of our Lord; it is the will of God."

"Is it because you are of the Father that your spirit is more real than those that are of the Mother?"

The flames of the fire wavered as he looked to her.

"The realm of each is so vast, filled with knowledge we cannot grasp. Must everything be of the Father for you to believe? Are there not devils and angels in the writings of your beliefs?"

"Yes, but—"

"What is real for the Father is equally real for the Mother. Useless talk does not dismiss this. The spirits of the Mother, of her children, are ever present. Some are permitted to see them. Others are not, but this does not change the fact that they exist. Is it not the same for the spirits of your Father? Is it not so that some can see them and some cannot? And is that a reason to believe in them or not believe?"

Claire thought of the apostle Thomas in the days following Christ's resurrection.

"Not until I have put my hand into his side," she murmured, remembering the passage. "Yes, it is so," she told him, her eyes widening. "Even those of the purest soul are given to doubt when what is true does not manifest itself into a physical form."

An eerie call floated toward them, carried by a stiffening breeze from the northwest. A chill swept through them both.

"What was that?" she asked, startled.

"I do not know. Perhaps it is best not to."

"John!" she suddenly exclaimed. "He is alone!"

"It may be that he is not," he responded.

Claire heard a note of sadness in his words.

"What is it that troubles you? Is it linked to what we have been talking about, John being alone, but not alone? Please tell me. I want to understand."

His expression softening, his tone calm, the fire blazing in his eyes, he said, "There was a river of sand."

He went on to tell her about Tafari and the lions, and how his family had come to their end. So too did he tell her of the early years spent with Untello and the others, including Peter Gunstard. And in his telling of those years, he recounted to Claire the tales of the spirit elephants. In a hushed tone, he explained how the spectral beasts had first shown themselves to him. And with a look on his face she couldn't quite grasp, he described the great bulls he had seen, those who protected the great spirit herd and the one who had come to his aid at times.

His face filled with joy, he went on to describe the numerous nights of great mystery and jubilation that he had spent amongst them. How they had made him a part of their existence until the morning of the slaughter on the plain. With regret he confessed that, in an act of savage revenge, he had taken the life of Bawa as payment for the murder of the tiny spirit beast.

In a voice that conveyed a deep sadness, he admitted that, since that morning, the spirit elephants had not shown themselves to him. He had failed them. He closed his eyes at the memory of that grizzly morning, wondering what he could have done differently, what he should have done so that Gunstard and the others would not have been able to butcher all who had died that day.

"I think of them, always. If I had only known, been able to understand what they wanted from me, what they expected me to do. They have not appeared to me since then. Surely they must know that I miss them. Surely they must know that I hurt. They were a blessing of the Mother that I squandered—one that I may never know again."

The fire took his thoughts for a moment before he went on.

"And so the ache grows a little more each day. For what I once had, what I was, I have lost. And I do not know how to regain it."

Claire stepped to him and slipped her hand into his.

"You will find a way," she whispered, placing her head to his shoulder. "You know this."

*

O N THE OUTSKIRTS of Mek'ele, a score of hours having passed since his journey northward had begun, John the man-child slipped back into the shadow of the building, unaware that the scope of a rifle was focused on the back of his head.

"Wait."

The finger squeezing the trigger loosened.

"He goes toward rebel territory. Perhaps he will lead us to a camp."

A match flared. The end of a cigarette ignited, startling the man steadying the rifle.

"Keep your site on the boy. And what is there in a match that frightens you?"

"He steps behind the building. I can't see him."

Gunstard drew on his cigarette, the smoke blowing from his nose in a steady stream as he exhaled.

"What is your hurry, boy?" he wondered, as he caught a final glimpse of the youth running away. "I think it would be wise to find out what he took, don't you, Private? See to it."

The soldier saluted before hurrying toward the entrance of the hospital.

Peter Gunstard ventured a wry smile. Drawing heavily on the Gauloises cigarette dangling from his mouth, his mind wandered to visions of another time, another life. He could see it materializing within the grey smoke hanging in the air.

Looking to the shadows where the youth had run, he saw the slight frame of another boy, Teimbaka. Saw him rushing from the carnage strewn across a field. His strides were unsteady, almost panicked. Perhaps the faceless corpse of Bawa had been at his heels.

"The last great harvest," he said, recalling the cache of ivory they had taken that day. "The last day for many things," he added, fingering the two ivory teeth tethered about his neck. "Ah, the days of old," he recalled, shaking his head.

"You sound like an old woman," he spat in the next instant, frowning. "And old women are of no use."

Taking a final draw of the Gauloises, he threw the butt to the ground, stepping on it with a vengeance.

"And old men are worse."

With the sparks of the cigarette crushed into the grit beneath his foot, he walked to the back corner of the hospital, where the boy had disappeared. Taking a precautionary peek around it, he moved to the edge of darkness, where the glow from the hospital lights reached their limits.

"As I thought," he congratulated himself, hearing the slippage of rocks to the southeast. "Right to rebel territory."

Hurrying footsteps broke into his train of thought.

"What did you find out?" he asked, turning on his boot heels.

"Baby formula," the man replied, a hint of ridicule in his answer. "The major says you see too much in the thievery of a boy. We are to let him go without incident. Though he was angry that we allowed the child to slip by us with stolen property of the Derg."

"And just whose order was it that you followed when you reported this to the major?"

The soldier shuffled his feet.

"No one's, sir. It was a matter—"

"Silence!"

The soldier straightened his shoulders.

"Didn't you hear that?"

"I heard nothing, sir," the soldier responded, perplexed.

"That's because your tongue clicks too much." Looking straight into the man's eyes, he added, "Fortunately for us—and the major—that I was listening."

With a smirk, Gunstard turned back to the southeast, peering into the darkness as though he could see for miles.

"What is it that the lieutenant has heard?" the soldier boldly inquired.

Gunstard burned with anger at being addressed as a lieutenant. For in this newest version of this Ethiopian army—the Derg—lieutenants were seen as being as worthless as a regular foot soldier. Of little consequence, easily discarded, easily replaced. Even more irritating, however, was the manner in which the soldier had spoken to him. His tone was disrespectful, almost ridiculing.

"Are you now the one giving orders, private?" he icily inquired, his focus kept to the southeast.

There was a long pause before Gunstard heard a weak no.

"Then you won't be averse if I kindly ask you to accompany me a quarter of a mile to the southeast to see if what I *thought* I heard is really there. We wouldn't want to run to the major with information that isn't verified, now, would we?" he challenged the private, turning to stare him in the face.

The private glared at him. Interpreting the man's expression to mean that the soldier saw him as nothing more than an aged, worthless white man who was too free with his advice where it concerned black Ethiopia and too smug about his stature within the army of the Derg, Gunstard glared back.

"No," he casually replied after a long pause.

"I'm sorry?" Gunstard hissed.

"No—sir!"

With a smile and a nod, Gunstard swung out his arm, inviting the private to lead the way. Dutifully, the man complied. Gunstard fell in close behind him.

The darkness had become a treasured home to Peter Gunstard. It was a haven for the demented imaginings born of his twisted mind. In the void of light and in the absence of watching eyes, every nightmare of his creation found substance; every delusion was given its due. The night welcomed him as he followed the private into the darkness. It eagerly awaited whatever lunacy he would enact.

"Do you see the rebel column yet?"

The soldier stopped.

"I can see nothing," he uncertainly replied.

"I heard the squeaking of treads. An armored personnel carrier, I'd wager."

The soldier cocked his head and cupped a hand around his ear.

"I can't hear or see anything," he replied, insolence lacing his voice.

"Perhaps this will help you."

The night's calm betrayed no hint of the sharp steel slicing deep into flesh and cartilage. Nor did it carry the sound of the muffled scream or the gurgling choke of death as Gunstard's blade severed the throat of the man standing in front of him.

Intent on what he was holding on to, John hurried ahead. Even though he had put a good amount of distance between where he was and what he had left behind, he could not seem to shake the feeling that he was being followed.

He shifted the box he was carrying, straining with its bulk and weight. Thinking that something was trailing him made him feel weak. It drained his energy, tiring his arms. Exasperated, he sighed. There were still many more miles to cover before he could even think about setting his package down.

Hearing distant laughter, he stumbled and fell hard to the ground. Not wanting to let the box fall, he landed against a sharp rock, the edges smacking against his ribs.

"Sister Lady," he whimpered, coughing, pain shooting across his chest.

Wiping the tears from his eyes, he struggled to his feet. What lay ahead and what was behind him suddenly seemed equally unsettling.

"Sister Lady," he whispered, trying to bolster his resolve.

A voice called out to him from the darkness, yelling words he could not decipher. Laughter, like that of a hyena, arose as the voice fell silent. With a ball of fear forming in his bowels, John clamped his thighs together stifling the urge to urinate. Hearing a distant rumble of thunder and seeing an eerie flash in the sky, he cradled the box with both arms and began to run.

Behind him, in Mek'ele, Gunstard stood in front of the major, retelling a tale of a murdering band of thieving rebels armed with machetes and automatic rifles. They had stolen medical supplies, killed a guard, and made their escape under the cover of darkness. Smiling with the orders he received upon his recounting of the tale, Gunstard calculated how far the boy might have traveled since having left the hospital. He was certain he would be able track him. Delighted to finally be engaging in some action, he found himself eager to see where the child would lead him. He was looking forward to the prospect of destroying whatever the boy would lead him to.

When John perceived the glimmer of dawn on the eastern horizon, his feet were bloody from numerous cuts, his toes bent and twisted, broken from the rocks and stones he had rushed across. Even his ankles were covered in bruises and lacerations that would make walking extremely painful for days to come. Yet he continued on in stoic pride, intent upon carrying out his quest. His sole purpose was to fulfill Sister Lady's wishes. He was steadfast in his belief that he would be returning to the village as a man—a man that Sister Lady would be proud of and view as an equal.

After the last stars of dawn had long given over to the pale brightness of day, he came upon Teimbaka. The drum man was still seated by remnants of the fire they had shared nearly two days ago.

"Teimbaka!" he shouted, grinning from ear to ear, holding up the box of formula. "Teimbaka! Look!"

Rising with the call of his name, Teimbaka raised his spear and offered John a half-hearted smile.

"You return as a man," he stated, seeing the condition of John's body and the expression of pride on the man-child's face.

"Food for the baby!" he happily announced, lifting the box for Teimbaka to gaze upon. "Sister Lady—she be happy."

"The baby, John—"

"Where is Sister Lady now? I bring her my gift."

John's expression of joy began to unravel as he looked upon Teimbaka's somber face.

"The child passed on to the Mother not more than an hour ago. I—" Teimbaka said with great empathy, "I am sorry."

Confusion, doubt, disbelief, betrayal—all these swept through John as Teimbaka spoke. *Surely it cannot be true*, he thought. Teimbaka was orchestrating some kind of hoax. He was a man now. He had fulfilled Sister Lady's wishes. He would take Teimbaka's place beside her around the campfire. He would be the one she would choose to talk to about things. He was a man now. He would not let Teimbaka make him out to be a fool. He was a man.

"Where is Sister lady?" he demanded.

"The child, the baby—Claire grieves her death," he told him.

"Sister Lady!" John blurted out. "No Claire! No Claire!"

"As you say."

"Yes, I say!"

Teimbaka looked past him, scanning the hills toward the northwest.

"No thing is there," John sneered, seeing what Teimbaka was about.

"There is always something there," Teimbaka evenly replied, glancing at John and then back to the hills.

"No one saw!" he shouted. "No one trails!"

Teimbaka said nothing.

"Sister Lady, she believe me!"

"Sister Lady should be given some time to grieve."

"Do not say what Sister Lady need," John hissed. "I show her that I a man. I bring what she want. I come back with the box."

"The child is dead."

"I do not care! I bring box! More will come!"

Teimbaka searched John's face; his innocence was gone.

"John," he began, hoping to reason with the youth.

But with a sneer on his face, John stomped past him, defiance in the tilt of his shoulders. As Teimbaka turned to watch him go, he saw traces of blood in the youth's footprints. The cuts on his feet and toes were still oozing, leaving a trail.

"John!" he bellowed.

The youth stopped. Reluctantly, he turned his head, offering Teimbaka only a sliver of his face.

"What made you run? What was in the dark?"

John's eyes went wide. His attention left Teimbaka and filtered back from where he had come. Without warning or explanation, he threw the box of baby formula to the ground and ran toward the village.

Teimbaka retraced the trail of John's night crossing for a time, following each blood tinged footprint, searching the outlying terrain for other prints that would explain the reason for John's hurried, careless return. After several kilometers, having found nothing that would explain the youth's haste, Teimbaka returned to where he started, an uneasy feeling building inside him.

The box stood alone near the ashes of the fire, its square brown shape suddenly appearing ominous. Teimbaka shivered at the sight of it, a trace of foreboding racing up his spine.

"What spirits do you bring?" he asked of it. "What darkness are you from?"

Receiving no response, he lifted the box and followed John's footprints back to the village. But as the dozen shanties came into his view, the structures no longer seemed the same. It was as if, in the hours that he had been gone, everything had somehow changed. And as he placed the box of formula down in front of Claire's hut of branches and grass, he wondered if it wasn't true.

Claire pulled back the blanket she used as a door, her expression stern. "You should not have let him go," she told him. "He is badly injured. It was no trip for a boy."

"The boy is a man now."

Claire let the blanket fall back into place.

*

BY EARLY EVENING, Teimbaka found himself besides Lee's grave, holding the small black book she had left to him. Opening it for the first time, he flipped through the pages until he came upon an illustrated card at the end. The card bore the depiction of a lamb resting atop an altar. Around the lamb, there were other objects: a chalice of gold with a flaming heart within the rim; the letters P and X, joined together as if they were one. He stared at the card in earnest, puzzled by its meaning, finding the figures portrayed in it both perplexing and mesmerizing.

Taking the card out to study it further, he discovered another illustration behind it. This one was etched into the inside of the book's back cover.

"The Father?" he wondered aloud, studying the figure hanging limply from a cross.

He slowly traced a finger over the gold and sky-blue carving of the figure, marveling at the artist's craftsmanship.

"You are who Claire wears about her neck. She calls you Jesus. What did you do to be treated so?" he asked of the illustration. He stared at the spikes in the man's bloodied feet and hands, and at the crown of thorns that had been pushed into his head. The image of Jesus stared back at him in silence.

"You need not reply. There is cruelty in all of us."

Once more, he traced the outline of the raised depiction of Jesus on the cross before turning the pages back to the book's beginning. Without haste, he began to study what each page contained.

Holy men, in various stages of performing a ritual, were pictured opposite pages where only words were written. He scrutinized each, trying to decipher what relation the images had to the writings placed beside them. Further in, he saw illustrations of Jesus start to appear; they gave him some understanding of the story of who the man was and how he ended up being nailed to a cross.

That the one Claire referred to as Jesus Christ always appeared in these pictures with a glowing orb of light around his head, though his eyes were laden with sadness, filled him with a mixture of sympathy and curiosity. He did not understand how one depicted as divine could appear so forlorn. And when he came upon the picture of Jesus on a mountaintop standing next to a figure with black wings, he drew his hand back with a start. For the image of evil—a dark angel—was one with which he was familiar, and it rekindled memories of tales he had been told by wandering madmen—tales of their encounters with the ruler of darkness when they had come upon him in the most remote reaches of the Mother's forgotten lands.

With a shiver, he let the pages fall together and closed the book's cover, slipping the illustrated card back where he had found it.


As evening turned to twilight, and then to the full darkness of night, Teimbaka sat once more by the fire from the previous evening. He stared into the flames, trying his best to keep his mind blank. But the cooking fires from the village below kept enticing him to turn his head and look. He found his eyes drifting to the hut where Claire slept. The reproachful look she had given him when he had set the box of baby formula down by the entrance to her hut still lingered in his thoughts. With a shiver, he cast his gaze back to the flames in front of him. Envisioning the box, he felt the same sense of foreboding he had experienced before.

*

IT WAS STILL well before dawn. And although Peter Gunstard had a rough idea as to where he would find the rebel camp—thanks to the scouts he had sent ahead and the trail of blood the boy had conveniently left for them to follow—he was nevertheless using the time to formulate his battle plan. As always, he was counting on the darkness to play an important role.

He envisioned that this would be the first of his many victories in the region. And with each new success, his status within the ranks of the Derg would grow. This newfound standing would allow him to deal with any future factions of rebel pockets as he saw fit. Fighting on the side of the new Marxist regime was going to serve him well, he reasoned. And the glorious road to a new era of unfettered killings was just ahead, only several kilometers away according to the reports he had received.

Gunstard lit a Gauloises and smiled; the unfiltered tobacco tasted exceptionally sweet.


The dying fires of the village burned like beacons in the eyes of Peter Gunstard. He surveyed the outlines of the shanties through a pair of high-powered binoculars. How brazen the rebels were, he thought, and how stupid, to place their encampment in the center of a flat, unprotected plain situated between a pair of rocky hills. How little regard they must have for the Derg forces, he thought, and how they were about to pay for that foolishness.

"We will divide the men into two groups," he informed the sergeant standing next to him, pointing down at the crude map he had sketched in the earth. "Each team will carry two mortars and fan out into a semi-circle on the ridge of this hill," he explained, marking an X in the dirt with the toe of his boot where he wanted each armament placed.

He momentarily swung the narrow beam of light from the flashlight he was using into the man's face and then pointed it back toward the ground.

"When the men are in place, we will commence the barrage upon my firing of a single flare. Understood?"

"Yes, sir, understood. Question, sir."

"What is it, Sergeant?"

"Sir, shouldn't we send out an advance team to reconnoiter the enemy position to take out any sentries they may have posted?"

Gunstard bristled.

"If you feel that is how the operation should be run, Sergeant," came his terse reply. "If you want the sun to rise and expose our position to the enemy. Is that what you want me to put down in the report to the major if we fail to annihilate the rebel scum who murdered one of our own?"

"Major Mengistu—"

"So it is 'Major Mengistu,' is it? How nice it must be for you to be allowed to address your commander by name. Perhaps, one day, I will be as fortunate."

"No offense intended, sir," the sergeant quickly responded, straightening his shoulders. "Of course, the lieutenant is right."

Gunstard eyed the man, trying to gauge how much loyalty, if any, he could count on receiving from him.

"Very well, Sergeant. You have your orders."

"Sir, if I may point out ..."

"Some other objection to the operation?"

"No, sir. Nothing of the kind, sir."

"Then what is it, Sergeant?" Gunstard hissed, anxious to get started.

"The single fire on the opposite ridge, sir."

"Yes, I have seen it."

"Shall I dispatch—?"

"I will see to it myself, Sergeant. Now go. We need to strike before the sun rises."

Claire struggled to fall asleep, her thoughts at odds with the weariness of her body. Several times she had already risen from her bed of dried grass to peer out the entrance of her hut and gaze up at the solitary fire glowing on the hill.

"God keep you," she whispered on each occasion. "And God keep us all," she would add, her gaze sweeping the village.

After each worrisome trip to her doorway, Claire would turn and smile down at John, relieved to see him sleeping comfortably, hopeful that after a night's rest he would be at peace with the outcome of his quest and take back the troubling words he had said about Teimbaka.

With her mind cluttered with thoughts of John and Teimbaka, the death of the infant child, and the welfare of the forty other children under her care, Claire lay herself down once again. She began to repeat the stations of the rosary to transport her to sleep.

*The fox turned on her Father, ripping his throat out with a vengeance. Blood splattered the front of his riding finery while her Mother stood by, babbling on about the fine points of social etiquette.*

*"Father!" Claire screamed.*

*But no one heard or cared. Her Mother stepped away, ignoring the gruesome scene altogether. Absurdly, she pointed out an outfit some young girl was wearing that she found particularly stunning.*

*"But, Mother! Father's dead!"*

*"Hasn't he always been, dear?" her mother cavalierly responded, tossing her head and giggling.*

*The fox pranced about her, displaying its kill. The head of her Father dangled in its jaws.*

*"Please, God, stop," she whimpered. "Please make it stop."*

*"Stop that embarrassing sniveling, young lady," her Mother reprimanded. "Do you want to make a spectacle out of all of us?"*

*"But Father's dead!"*

*"Yes, dear. I know. Hasn't he always been, as I said before?"*

*"Mother!" Claire pleaded in a heartbroken, tear-choked whisper.*

*"Come along, Claire. Come on; get up. We have a busy afternoon ahead."*

*A condescending smile crept over her Mother's face.*

*"We have that brunch menu to plan for the Art League that no one seems to feel is important but me. Then there's the matter of finding you just the right dress for that tea we are attending next week to benefit the Junior League's spring house tour. And then there is the small matter of picking out a suitable escort to—"*

*"Stop it, Mother."*

*"—the Boathouse Ball. You know, July is just not as far off as some would have you believe," she went on. "And of course, there is the—"*

*"Stop it, Mother. Just stop."*

*"Of course, you are right," she patronizingly agreed. "We can best discuss these matters at home. Come along. Let's be on our way."*

*"No! I won't leave Father!"*

*"Come, come. No argument."*

*"But he's dead!"*

*"Of course he is. And quite happy, I'm sure. Now let's go. We don't want to be construed as faux equestrians, now do we? I mean, the Hunt has already gone off."*

*"He's dead!"*

*"As he has always been, dear. Where have you been all these years?" she admonished her. "It's in the book. It's how it has always been."*

*"No!"*

*"Enough, Claire!" her Mother scolded. "That is just about enough. Time to go. Now."*

*"No! Father!" Claire cried out in a panic. "Father!"*

*The fox momentarily paused in front of a pond amid clusters of white birch. It made certain Claire was watching before it dragged the remains of her Father into the water.*

*"No! Stop it! Stop it!"*

"Sister Lady!"

*"Stop it! Please! Stop!"*

"What is it, Sister Lady? What is it?" John asked, terror-stricken.

*Claire reached for her cross, but her Mother's hands grabbed her wrist and then shook her by the shoulder.*

*"Stop it!" she pleaded. "Stop it!"*

"Sister Lady! Sister Lady! Wake up! Wake up!"

Claire opened her eyes, trembling with the notion that she was still being tormented by her nightmare.

"Sister Lady. Are you sick?"

Claire gasped at the piercing black eyes that were staring at her, taken back by the glimmer of orange light that seemed be soaring within them.

"It is John, Sister Lady. Do not be afraid. It's John."

"John!" she gushed. "Oh, dear God, bless you, John!"

Overcome with relief that her horrible nightmare had ended, Claire embraced the man-child with fervor.

"Thank God you are here, John. Thank God."

"I will always be here, Sister Lady," John solemnly told her, reciprocating her embrace. "Always."

As Claire buried her face in the crook of John's neck and squeezed him so tight that the man-child could barely breathe, strong stirrings of manhood swelled to life within him. His emotions teetered between sheer pleasure and an unnerving fear. As a rising flare exploded in a brilliant shower of orange light, John felt as though his whole body was afire, his sanity consumed by a wave of agonizing passion.

"What in God's name?" Claire exclaimed.

The blows from the first wave of the mortar bombardment struck the camp in quick succession—boom, boom, boom, boom—turning the calm of the pre-dawn into an eruption of destruction and death. Shells exploded in a maelstrom of thunder and blinding light. Shrapnel screamed out in all directions; wails of terror followed almost instantaneously.

When the second round of mortar shells hit, the village was engulfed in a wave of hysteria. The crying of the doomed swelled to a deafening crescendo. Children shrieked in horror. Cries of misery and pain arose as the children stumbled in the darkness, scrambling to find a place to hide.

Panic-stricken, Claire raced out of her hut only to be tackled from behind by John. Furious, scared, confused, she struggled to get free, but

John had her legs pinned to the ground. She edged forward, pulling herself along the dirt with her elbows, dragging him behind her.

Another flare rocketed above the camp. The freakish orange glow illuminated the horror that had taken place. Bodies were strewn haphazardly across the compound. Lying twisted and bloodied, some still struggled for life, their fear-stricken faces gasping for air.

Picking her way across the mangled battlefield, a skeletal little girl raced toward Claire, her stick-like legs laboring to keep her upright.

"Here, darling, here!" Claire shouted. "Here I am! Over here!"

Hearing Claire's voice, the little girl stopped. Her quivering face broke out into a smile. She raised her arms high and wide, waiting for Claire to lift her up.

Claire would never forget the smile on the child's face, for in the next instant a mortar shell exploded behind her. Thrown forward, her body tumbled across the ground, landing with a sickening groan just inches from Claire's face. In a spasm of death, the girl's teeth clattered for a moment, and then grew still. Claire's stomach heaved. She tasted the bile rising in her throat.

"Let me go," she pleaded, twisting. "I'm going to be sick."

"No!" John shouted back. "I will—"

Another mortar shell exploded directly behind them. The small shanty that had been their home was blown to splinters.

"Get off, John! Get off!"

Overwhelmed with a frenzied madness, Claire fought to get free. Astonishing herself, she shook John clear, throwing him to the side. Pulling her legs beneath her, she slid over to the girl's body.

In the dwindling light of the flare, Claire grabbed hold of the girl only to pull back in horror when her fingers felt the shredded tissue and the jagged protrusions along her severed spine. Shaking uncontrollably, she vomited what little there was in her stomach.

As another flare sailed into the sky overhead, Claire looked anew at the death beside her; the little girl's arms were still stretched outward in a gesture expecting salvation.

"She is dead. Come, we must go."

"Leave me alone, Mother!" Claire raged.

John reached down and grabbed her by the arm, pulling her. Claire slapped it away.

"Father is dead!" she wailed. "I am not leaving him!"

John staggered back, bewildered. A burst of automatic gunfire sent him back to Claire's side.

"Teimbaka!" he called out, his eyes now wide with terror. "Teimbaka!"

With the onset of small-arms fire, the mortar bombardment ceased. But in its wake, the cries of the victims intensified, their tortured voices washing over what remained of the village in a wave of despair.

"Stop it!" Claire screamed. Her face contorted in agony, she yelled, "Stop it! Stop it!"

As John looked frantically about for Teimbaka, silhouettes of men walking out of the darkness began to appear. Gunfire flashed from the barrels of their weapons.

"Come!" he shouted in a panic, bending to Claire. "We must go! We must go!"

"But Father is dead!" she whined, heaving sobs tormenting her every word.

Without warning, John slapped her across the face. With her lips twisting, she began to choke on a word she was struggling to say. John pressed the sides of his face with his hands as he watched her cheeks turn a ghostly pale. When her eyes fluttered shut and her body went limp to the ground he bent to her. But as he began to pull her away a new surge of panic surged through him. He could not seem to pull her fast enough.

Bullets raked the ground beside them as a shout of "No survivors!" rang out.

Gathering himself, the man-child squatted next to Claire, and with a monumental surge of power, hoisted her to his shoulder. His legs buckled. Steadying himself, he balanced her body as best he could. Somehow managing the first few steps toward escape, he staggered away from the slaughter.


"Surrender, rebel!" Gunstard called out. "I will not hurt you!" He laughed. "Do you not wish to be the only survivor?" His laughter grew, mingling with the sounds of the massacre below. "Come out, rebel. We will not torture you too badly!"

Still laughing, Gunstard fired another round as he methodically advanced.

"I tire of this cat-and-mouse, rebel! I tire of you hiding! Time to face me like a man! Coward!"

Angry that he had thus far been cheated from the bloodletting, he quickened his pace, his attention fixated on the boulder shielding the rebel he had cornered. But as he stalked ahead, the first glimmer of dawn transformed the eastern horizon with a pale strip of yellow-white light. This occurrence compelled him to hesitate. He looked upon the light with disdain.

The arrow struck him just above the knee. The jolt of pain collapsed his leg. Loosing a spray of bullets from the automatic rifle he was holding, he fell back and to the side. As he fell stunned, fumbling to comprehend how he had been shot, the second arrow embedded in his chest. Blood sprayed at the impact. It oozed quickly, dampening his shirt.

Enraged, he slung his rifle outward, strafing the area ahead of him in an arc. His finger pressed tight to the trigger, he fired blindly. Then suddenly, there was nothing. The magazine of his weapon was empty. The screams coming from the camp had also ceased. He smiled. The silence of death was intoxicating. He laid his head back and listened. A cold tip of sharpened steel pressed down on his throat. He laughed.

"Butcher."

It was almost an afterthought that he looked up to see who was about to end his life. When he saw who stood above him, he could barely contain the dark humor he saw in the situation. He choked back the laughter that was racking his body.

"Killer," Teimbaka hissed, pressing the tip of the spear a little harder against Gunstard's throat. "Killer of children, of woman, of elephants."

"So, it is you, boy," Gunstard said lightly, an evil smile taking hold of his lips. "You, the executioner of depraved old fools," he laughed. "Am I to be Bawa now? Will you take my ivory teeth?" he taunted. "Teimbaka, the darky boy. Who would have thought? After all this time, eh?"

Gunstard's eyes twinkled in the first light of dawn. But in the next instant they turned dark, an icy glaze snuffing out the glow from the sun.

"Send me to hell, boy, so that I can come back to haunt your every night."

Gunstard waited, staring up into Teimbaka's troubled face.

"Why do you tarry, boy? Is it suffering you wish to see?" he chortled. "Look down at your camp. See what I have done. See what suffering really looks like."

Teimbaka pressed his spear a little deeper, drawing blood.

"So it's to be slow, boy? Like a downed elephant waiting for its tusks to be pulled? You remember, don't you, boy? Remember hacking away at their faces while their eyes cried with every stroke?"

A gurgling laughter escaped from his lips.

"Teimbaka the elephant killer. Teimbaka the killer of feeble-minded men. Are we so different, you and I?" he asked, smiling. "But you won't find any tears here," he added, looking at the spear pressed against his throat. "I will not cry like the elephants."

Teimbaka pulled the spear back, coiling his arm for one final, massive thrust.

"Swift it will be now? Why the change? Why not enjoy my death? Why not linger over it? Why not revel in the avenging of those pathetic creatures' massacre?"

Teimbaka hesitated, his body trembling.

"Yes," Gunstard said easily, nodding his head in the direction of the camp. "Take a look. Do you not see the souls of the butchered even now being gathered by the one of darkness? How well I have done for him. May their pitiful voices plead for mercy while they burn in hell!"

With his screaming of *hell*, Gunstard lunged. Grasping the spear just above the steel head, he jerked it to the side. But though he was fueled by the madness of a wounded animal, he was no match for Teimbaka's will. Countering Gunstard's attempt at escape, Teimbaka thrust his spear downward and then pulled it to the side. The steel tip dug across Gunstard's chest, slicing open a gash that ran from one side of his ribs to the other.

Gunstard's hands fell away from the shaft of the spear to the wound on his chest.

"Not deep enough, boy!" he screamed, running his fingers through the cut. "You'll have to do better!"

Gunstard watched Teimbaka jerk his head to the side as a bullet whizzed by it and then wince in pain as another bullet grazed him on the arm. With a depraved, evil glint in his eyes, Gunstard began to laugh.

"You waited too long, boy," he mocked. "Waited too long!"

Gunstard's bellowing laughter of insanity rocked Teimbaka backward as several more bullets screamed past his head. Ducking, scurrying sideways, he gathered his bow and arrows. Leaping from the hill, he retreated in a pattern of twists and turns, bullets raking the ground all around him as he ran. Above the din of rifles being fired by his troops, Gunstard slung his words toward Teimbaka with all the energy he could muster.

"Hurry, boy! Flee! They're all dead! Food for the hyenas! Remember me, boy, remember! I will find you! I will haunt you!"

JUNE, 1978

ELEANOR TEETERED HER way across the newly installed carpet, weaving her way toward the lamp she had turned on several hours before. Her hands shaking, she turned her face sideways to lessen the glare of the light bulb.

"Hurt my eyes," she muttered.

Fumbling, her finger found the switch. She turned it off with a sigh. The room went dark.

"Don't need you no more," she mumbled.

Her first step back to her easy chair was a faltering one. Her feet crossed over each other. She stumbled.

"What's wrong with you?" she scolded her wobbly legs. "Y'all desertin' me, too?" When no answer was forthcoming, she scoffed "Regardless, I don't need ya anyways."

The easy chair welcomed her return with a creaking of springs and wood. The sounds were a familiar testament to the years they had spent together. Comfortable once again, Eleanor stretched, her elbow catching the corner of the side table.

"Darn," she said, when she heard a dull thud from the floor.

Bending over the side of the chair as far as she could, she felt around for the fallen bottle. A good whiff of the spilled gin filled her senses before her fingers felt the wet spot on the carpet.

"Land's sake," she sighed with a click of her tongue, "what's Patricia gonna say to this?"

With a shrug of indifference, Eleanor retrieved the bottle. She took a little sip before cradling it to her chest. Savoring the taste of the alcohol in her mouth, she closed her eyes.

"Didn't need no new carpet," she said. "Didn't need new paint, neither, or the new record player."

She nodded, quite satisfied with her answer if the subject of the stained rug ever arose. She lifted the bottle of gin to her lips as a reward.

"Always buyin' needless, an' for what?"

She took a swig of gin before any answer could be rendered. Happy for the quiet, she rested her head back on the cushion.

"She ought to buy that man a new set of ears, is what."

Startled, she sat straight up, searching the depths of the shadows of the garage apartment for the intruder who had spoken.

"Who's there?" she challenged.

She listened intently, waiting for a response.

"Who's there?

She held her breath.

"Ought to buy that man a new set of ears," she heard again. "Ought to buy that man a new set of ears."

She frowned and hissed.

"Old fool. That was you."

The realization eased her apprehension, but only briefly.

"Losin' yer mind now. I'm losin' my mind," she said, holding the bottle of gin to her face. "Should have known it be like this. Done lost just 'bout everythin' else. No reason to think my mind be any different."

Uncomfortable with her thoughts, she fidgeted in her chair, a few tears escaping from the corners of her eyes.

"Lost everyone," she whispered, a cold shiver running down her spine. "I—"

The few tears grew into several, choking off her words, sapping what little was left of her resolve not to think about her past.

"Why, Lord, why?" she pleaded.

"Not the boy's fault, honey. Just a little accident is all."

Eleanor pushed out of her chair at the sound of the voice.

"George? George, that be you?"

It was just a silhouette, just a dark outline of a man sitting on the couch across the room from her. She rubbed her tear-laden eyes, uncertain.

"I mean, it's really no big deal, is it? Just a little soda on the rug? It'll come clean, won't it?" the imagined silhouette said.

"That's not the point."

Eleanor gasped at the reply, for the voice was her own. But what she said and the way she had said it confused her. For it all sounded just the way she had spoken the same phrase some thirty-five years before.

"You know full well, George Michael Tate, that soda is not allowed outside the kitchen when it's allowed at all," she told him in no uncertain terms.

"Such a little thing." It was a silhouette of her talking now. It was standing right behind the imagined shadow of her late husband. She stared at the alter-image of herself and blinked her eyes. Her silhouette was younger. Much younger then she herself was. It was as if Eleanor was looking into a mirror and seeing herself—but as she looked thirty-five years ago. "Let it go. Let it go," her younger self glibly told her.

"Somethin' you don't understand 'bout a simple rule?" Eleanor shot back, dismayed that her alter-image would suggest such a thing.

"The boy and me," the man's silhouette offered, "we, we were just— we just forgot, dear."

Eleanor's heart began to break apart as she listened to her husband speak.

"It's just a few drops. I'll have it cleaned up in no time."

"You won't do no such thing, not on this rug. Uh-uh. No, sir. Now you skedaddle, and take Abraham with you. Like I don't have 'nough work to do already. Hmmph, land's sake."

"Boy's outside."

Her late husband's voice was just as she remembered it: soft, kind, loving.

"I'll take him for a little walk. Maybe go into town and see what's new in the windows that we can't afford."

Even his laughter—easygoing, good-natured, pleasing—was just as it had always been. She wrapped her memories around the sound of it as though it was in the present, hearing it as if her late husband were actually sitting right across from her.

"And that won't be hard," he chuckled, getting off the couch, "seeing as we can't afford much these days, anyway."

"Don't be too long. Supper be ready in an hour. And don't be buying Abraham no hot dog from that Frank's! You hear me, George?"

"Oh, I wouldn't dream of doin' no such thing, dear," he assured her, though there was a hint of mischief in his words. "Like to keep my head on my neck, you know."

"What was that last part? I didn't quite hear what you said."

"Said, I love you!"

"Love you too! Now be careful! Don't let Abraham walk in the street!" Eleanor reminded him, sitting back down in her chair.

A part of Eleanor crumbled as she watched the shadow of her late husband get up from the couch and leave the apartment.

"No!" she yelled, suddenly flooded with anxiety. "Don't go! Don't go! I done lost you before! I don't wanna lose you 'gain!"

"Finally, a few minutes to myself. Maybe I can even get off my feet for a spell."

Eleanor turned in shock, furious with the attitude her alter-image was displaying.

"Stop him," she begged. "Go after 'em. Tell 'em both how much you love 'em."

But her imagined alter-image paid her no mind. Pretending not to hear Eleanor at all, she went about dabbing at the wet spot on the rug.

"Don't you understan', woman? Your man and boy been taken from you once already. Now they be leavin' 'gain. You fool. You'll be all alone."

"A few minutes alone," her alter-image mused. "Just going to sit right down in my favorite chair and rest a spell."

"Wait till I get up," Eleanor protested.

But it was too late. Eleanor's alter-image sat down on top of her, trapping her in her seat. And with the melding of her two selves, the bitter emotions of the past thirty-five years suddenly erupted, ripping apart all the barriers she had erected in trying to forget. Consumed with despair, she loosed a terrifying, tortured scream that no one heard.

"Wait!" she suddenly wailed. Panic stricken, she jumped up from the chair. "Wait for me, George! Wait for me, son!"

Eleanor yanked open the hall closet and pulled out her aqua-blue car coat. Flinging open the door, she raced down the stairway, her slippers barely making any sound on the painted wooden steps. As she reached ground level, she searched in every direction before breaking into a run. After several minutes, she found herself in Red Bank, dazedly staring at the front of Frank's Luncheonette. Exhausted, dizzy, and disorientated, she asked, "Abraham? George? You two in there sneakin' a hot dog?"

Eleanor stared at the front window, oblivious that the inside of luncheonette was dark. She stepped over to the entrance, pressed her face against the glass, and looked inside.

"You two better not spoil your dinner," she warned, scanning the booths and stools at the counter as the aroma of grilled hot dogs and French fries wafted out to her on the sidewalk.

"I done made a peach pie and everythin'," she added with a shake of her head.

Headlight beams swung through the empty diner, the reflection on the glass temporarily blinding her. Befuddled, she staggered backward, coming to a jarring halt when she ran into a metal signpost. The hissing of air brakes and the sound of an automatic door swinging open only added to her confusion.

"Well?" a man's voice said.

"What?" she asked, straightening her glasses, bewildered.

"You waitin' for the bus, lady, or you just startin' my day off lousy?"

"Bus?"

"Yeah, bus. You know, like going somewhere?"

Eleanor stared up into the bus, scrutinizing the driver.

"Well?" he sleepily inquired.

Eleanor stepped closer to the open door with a furrowed brow.

"You ain't him," she stated. "You ain't George."

"No, I ain't no George," the driver wearily admitted, placing his head against the top of the steering wheel. "Man, the sun's not even up yet."

"What you mumblin' 'bout?"

The driver laughed for a second.

"Are you going to get on this bus, ma'am? I've got a schedule to keep, you know."

Eleanor looked up and down the empty sidewalk.

"Have ya seen 'em? Did they get on the bus?"

With a frown, the driver began to close the doors.

"Have you seen them?" Eleanor shouted, sticking her hands between the doors so they wouldn't close. "Have you?" she demanded, her face twisted into a belligerent scowl.

"Look, lady," the driver earnestly replied, reopening the doors, "I don't know what—"

But before he could finish, Eleanor stepped away and began to cry.

"Hey, lady, you all right?"

Eleanor tried to shuffle away, but she tripped and fell hard on the cement sidewalk.

The driver bounded down from the bus and gently touched Eleanor's shoulder.

"Hey, lady, you okay? You hurt?"

Eleanor whimpered.

"Why me, man?" the driver sighed. "Why me?"

With a deeper, heavier sigh, the driver lifted Eleanor up in his arms and carried her inside the bus. As he laid her down on the molded plastic seats designated for the handicapped, Eleanor curled herself up into a ball and pulled at the ends of her pink flannel nightgown trying to shimmy the fabric down to the top of her fuzzy blue slippers. With a final pat to her ankles, she rested her head against the plastic and blew a gin-infused breath out of her mouth. The bus driver tilted his head away and cupped a large hand over his nose and mouth.

"Man, why'd you have to be on this route this morning? Why'd you need to start off my day like this?"

Eleanor stared up at the roof, saying nothing.

"Well you certainly can't lie here all day. Thank goodness there's a bakery two stops ahead, where I might be able to get them to open up a little early and see if we can't get you some coffee and then call you a cab or something."

Eleanor startled the man by pointing to a poster on the wall opposite her.

"Why you got their picture up there?"

The driver glanced at the poster advertising the Big Brothers organization. The picture was of a middle-aged black man with greying hair and a young black boy standing next to him. He looked back at Eleanor and started to speak, but ended up just shaking his head.

"I'll tell you all about it when we get a nice cup of coffee into you, okay?" he told her. "Now you just stay put while I get the bus going, okay?"

She paid him no mind, transfixed as she was by the picture of the man and the child on the wall.

"You okay back there?" the driver called back when he put the bus into drive and started forward.

The driver's voice encroached on the spell she had cast over herself. Rousing herself, she sat up and took a look around. When she glimpsed her own reflection in the window across from where she was seated, she felt uneasy.

"Just another block or two. Coffee sounds good, don't it?"

"Coffee?" she mumbled. "Patricia? That you?"

Eleanor turned her head, uncomfortable with seeing herself staring back. Looking back across her shoulder through the window where she was seated, she caught a glimpse of two faces sliding by.

"There they are," she whispered.

The wavering images of the faces from the Big Brother poster slid to the window next to her, and then the next until the reflection she was seeing suddenly vanished as the bus continued on its way.

"Wait for them," she mumbled, slapping the glass, glancing up toward the driver. "They're right outside," she said a little louder, pressing her face as close to the glass as she could in an attempt to see where the man and boy were going. "Wait for them," she pleaded, her eyes tearing. "Please! Stop!"

The bus hissed as it slowed to a halt. Eleanor smiled, wiping her eyes in joyous relief as the doors swung open.

"Okay, here we are. The owner's a friend of— Hey, where you running off to?"

Eleanor tried to rush by him, but the driver held out an arm to stop her.

"Let me go," she implored. "They waitin' for me. They right outside."

"Lady, I just drove here, and there ain't nothin' out there but an empty street, this bakery, and the ramp to the Parkway twenty yards ahead."

"Please," she begged.

"Who do you think is out there? Who you gonna find?"

"My son, Abraham," she gushed. "And my husband, George."

She gave him an engaging smile, her eyes wide and bright.

"I'm gonna walk home with 'em and we gonna sit down to a nice dinner and have a big piece of my peach pie for dessert."

"Look, lady," he started to say, keeping his arm up, preventing her from leaving, "I really can't see—"

"Please?" she asked, the desperation in her voice mirrored in her face. "Please. It may be my last chance to be with them."

"But I—"

"You need to keep on that schedule of yours."

She patted the arm holding her back, giving the driver her sweetest smile as he let it fall away. And before the man could say another word, Eleanor was gone.



On the sidewalk at the rear of the bus, Eleanor paused and scanned the street behind her. The hope she had exited the bus with began to wane with every passing moment she could not locate Abraham and George.

"Abraham Tate! George Michael Tate!" she called out.

The bus lurched forward with a hiss. The sound startled her, prompting her to turn around. There, in the periphery of the bus's headlights, she caught a glimpse of a man and a boy: two figures walking hand-in-hand into the shadows, hurrying toward a one-lane road that wound up a hill.

"Wait for me!" she yelled, taking a few quick steps to follow.

But the bus made a slow, arcing turn that blocked her view. By the time it rolled on in its new direction, the wispy figures of her son and husband were gone.

"Land's sake," she sighed. "Where'd you two get to now?"

Above her, the rush of cars heading to New York City via the Garden State Parkway had just begun. She could hear the sound of tires speeding along asphalt and saw the flashing beams of headlights whizzing by. Drawn to them, she made her way up the ramp to the four-lane highway above. She was certain that Abraham and George had taken the same route.

Near the top, where the ramp merged with the Parkway, Eleanor thought she saw them, their silhouettes weaving in and out of the headlights of the speeding cars.

"Where you two gettin' to now?" she yelled, exasperated with their ceaseless wanderings.

The blare of a car horn made her hesitate just as she thought she saw George raise a hand and motion for her to follow. The sound of rushing tires and the glare of the lights were confusing. She stumbled back to the guardrail, her backside coming to rest on the metal barrier.

"Why won't you wait for me?" she weakly cried, a sudden twinge of pain shooting through her chest. "Why? Why?"

Eleanor clutched her chest, coughing, slipping to one knee as the whoosh of the cars overwhelmed her senses. Gasping for breath, struggling to keep her balance, she closed her eyes and focused on the faces of Abraham and George. But no matter how much she tried, she could not seem to keep their faces intact. Blinking her eyes open, she looked out across the Parkway. Something was there, she saw. But what was it? She got to her feet.

A small creature she had only seen in pictures and on television stood on the opposite side of the road, its tiny red-pink eyes watching her with interest. Tentatively, she raised a hand and waved. In turn, the baby elephant flapped its ears and raised its trunk.

"Well, ain't that somethin'."

At the sound of her voice, the glowing creature of white and gold turned and began to move away.

"Wait!"

The baby elephant glanced back, as if expecting her to follow.

"I'm trying to find my family!"

As she spoke, Abraham and George appeared on either side of the young beast, their hands joined across its back.

"Dear God, thank you," she whispered, crossing herself.

Oblivious to all but the vision filling her eyes, Eleanor stepped out onto the highway, euphoria building with each taken step.

She never heard the blaring horn or the screaming brakes of the car that hit her, or felt the crushing impact of the steel that ended her life. And as the Garden State Parkway became a snarling mess of slamming brakes and shouts for help, Eleanor Tate placed her hand atop those of her late husband and son. With the baby elephant lighting their way, they began the walk toward home.

APRIL, 1980

T HE LINES OF black ink came slowly together: short and choppy, fluid and curling strokes all creating hollow characters in the corners of letter from the U.S. Passport Agency. Crude images of a hyena and a lion, their faces poised against each other in one corner, counterbalanced a drawing of a hyena-man in another. Above these, a depiction of a faceless spear-wielding man was methodically taking shape.

The pen hovered over the empty face of the spear-wielding man, the point almost marking the surface of the paper several times before it was yanked away. Abruptly, and without warning, the pen placed a large X across the expanse of the paper.

"Go to hell," Menelik cursed, scribbling over the face of the hyena-man. "Go back where you came from."

"Who you talkin' to, Gabe?"

Menelik stabbed the hyena-man's face, punching a hole in the paper. Peter eyed him with an impish grin.

"Another unsatisfactory reply from the passport office, I take it," he said, feigning sympathy.

Menelik crumpled the paper he had been doodling on and hurled it at the wall.

"What do they want from me? Blood? What is it I have to do before they let me out of this fucking country?" he asked, the strain of the past few years showing up in the wear lines at the corners of his eyes.

"You know that's just half—"

"Yeah, yeah, I know. Just half the problem."

"Testy, testy."

Menelik shrugged, his expression of disappointment unchanged.

"Why put yourself through it, man? When are you just going to let it go and get your act together?"

"I have to go home," he told him, his voice solemn, his memory instantly transported to the vision of his brother above the plain of spirit elephants. "I— I have to get there."

"You are home, man."

"No! I'm not home!"

"That's not how either government sees it."

"Don't you think I know that?" he screamed, exploding out of his chair, slamming a fist on top of the metal desk. "Why the *fuck* you gotta remind me of it? Do you do it just to piss me off?"

Peter averted his gaze and held his breath. Gradually, Menelik regained his composure and sat back down.

"Shit. Why'd they have to do this to me?" he grumbled, staring at the pen between his fingers.

"Who?" Peter tentatively asked.

Menelik furrowed his brow, his eyes narrowing to slits.

"You know who. The ones who've made me an exile from my own country."

"Oh. Them," Peter responded, exaggerating the length of the words.

"What's that supposed to mean?"

Peter gave him an innocent shrug and shuffled some papers in front of him.

"Why'd you say it like that: 'Ohhhh. Them'?"

Peter glanced at the floor for a moment before he replied.

"Because it's tiresome, man, that's why. It gets really old listening to you blame a few real good people for everything that's happened in your life."

"I ain't blaming them," Menelik protested. "I'm just layin' the responsibility where it belongs, man. And don't try to tell me that the moment they took me out of Ethiopia and decided they'd bring me up living a total lie, it didn't make them culpable for everything that's gone down with me."

"Bullshit."

Menelik grunted.

"I suppose," Peter continued, "if you are going to follow that line of logic, then you actually owe them big time."

"Owe them!" Menelik exclaimed, exasperated. "Just where the fuck do you get off?"

"For saving your life, man. Like, you always tend to want to overlook that fact. Like it never happened that Martin shot those hyenas that were about to rip you to shreds or that Patricia had to shoot at that maniac guide to keep him from shooting you?"

Peter gave him an angry look.

"Jesus Christ, Gabe, they stood by you when you went to trial for murder. When you wouldn't even give them the fucking time of day! God! And who do you think spent every minute of the past two fucking years of their life getting the state to hear your appeal? Do you know what price they paid for that?"

"Guilt money," Menelik stated without emotion.

"It cost them a lot more than money, you asshole."

"What do you mean?"

Peter glared at him, his lips quivering.

"Never mind. I promised I wouldn't. Shit, you don't even know about—" With a firm shake of his head, he said, "No. I promised. Not until you ask."

"Ask what? Know about what?"

"Yeah," Peter softly replied with a shake of his head. "That's just the point, isn't it?"

"What's the point?" Menelik pressed, his anger rising.

"You tell me," Peter said dismissively.

The two men scowled at each other, a strained air of defiance growing between them.

"How the hell am I supposed to know what you're talkin' about when I haven't the slightest idea of what you're talkin' about?"

"Because you don't want to know! Because you'd rather sit there and sink deeper into the pity hole you've dug for yourself. Not the Gabe Tate that I once admired. Not the kid who stood up for me when— Oh, forget it.”

“So the truth finally comes out,” Menelik spat sarcastically. “The great public defender bares his soul and tells his new partner how he really feels about him. Like I didn’t spend two fucking years in Rahway and go through six months of shock therapy in that fucking loony house. You don’t think it did a number on me? Guess I’m just another poor nigger charity case to make your snowy white ass feel good.”

“Oh, Jesus, man. I wish they *would* let you go to Ethiopia just so I wouldn’t have to listen to your crap!”

“So do I. Then I would be rid of all the lying honkies in this bigoted country.”

“Ooooh,” Peter mocked. “Pulling the big crutch out, are you? The big racist fallback? You gonna start limping now, start hobbling around, yelling ‘Whitey crippled me! Whitey made me the weak, sniveling, can’t-do-nothing-for-myself poor persecuted black man!’”

“Too easy,” Menelik countered. “How easy it is for a white boy to lay that rap down. Make me think it’s all my fault that *I’m* black, while giving a pass to all the lily-white white folks, when most of them would just as soon spit on a black person than offer him their hand.”

“It is easy, man, especially when that black person is *you*,” Peter mocked, though there was a mischievous smile on his face. “Especially when you’re spouting this bleeding-heart routine. You know, it’s not just the blacks that deserve better, Gabe. If you’d ever get your head out of the crying clouds of Mount Menelik, you’d be able to see that.”

“And if you’d stop cleaning your new contact lenses in that everything-is-beautiful-if-you’re-white solution, then you’d see that blacks get shitted on all the time, like it’s an amendment to the Constitution or something. Your slave-owning ancestors might just as well have written it that way in the original, the way things have been going the last couple hundred years.”

“Oh, good one. Blame it on people who’ve been dead for a couple of centuries. Or better yet, why not get a jump on the next administration and blame them too. Reagan and the Republicans—can’t think of an easier target.”

"Well it sure as shit isn't going to get any better, is it? You know as well as I do that the funds that were allocated over the past four years for social programs and urban development are just going to dry up. 'Cause if you think the Republicans are going to go for *raising* any of those levels, or even keeping them at the levels they are now, well, then I *should* have just let those older kids go ahead and beat the crap out of you on the playground when we were in first grade," he laughed.

"Shit. I don't know what to believe, Gabe. Seems like nothing is getting better. Seems like we're all too caught up in our own bullshit to get anything done."

Menelik was quick to open his mouth with a rebuttal, but just as quickly stopped.

"I'll say one thing, though," Peter added, his tone softened, almost apologetic. "The relations between the U.S. and Ethiopia sure as hell aren't going to blossom, what with who's in power in both countries. Reagan, if he's elected, sure as hell isn't going to kiss up to no Marxist military regime. And Carter's been waffling on just about everything else in Africa because of the hostage shit. And I'm sure that Mengistu is going to respond in the typical communist way by embracing the Soviets and all their anti-American propaganda. Just thinking about it makes me think that you'd have to be some kind of diplomat or senator or something to be allowed into Ethiopia right now. And even then, that wouldn't be a sure thing."

"Thanks, man. I really needed to hear that. Now I have to run for office in the land of the honkies just so I can get back to the country where I was born."

Menelik tossed the pen he had been holding in the air and watched it turn in tumbling circles until it bounced off the dingy black and white squares of the linoleum floor.

"Black and white," he sarcastically mumbled.

"Maybe that could be your campaign slogan," Peter offered. "I'd vote for you. Well—maybe."

"Maybe!" Menelik shouted, shooting Peter a faux glare.

"I only qualified my intent on the grounds that, if you were to run on the platform of stupidity and insensitivity—like what you are displaying now—I would have to decline casting my ballot in your favor." Before Menelik could respond, he hurried to add, "But, but, but— If you were to, say, run on the issues and display the upright characteristics of the person I know to be Gabriel Tate, then I would whole-heartedly pull the lever next to your name. Might even actively work for your campaign. Maybe run the entire shebang for you."

"Lord have mercy on my soul," Menelik chuckled.

"Of course, we'd have to start small, work our way up to senator. We've got the state representative seats coming up for election in the fall. And thanks to *me* and my dogged persistence, you finished your college degree in the big house, got yourself a real good last name, and are on your way toward an associate's degree in the field of law with the classes you're taking at night. And you've already lived in this district long enough to qualify as a legal resident. So what do you think?" he asked with a wide smile. "We could get you elected and then you could find some reason to travel to your homeland under the guise of official state business, or some other political angle. Who knows? We might even be able to find some legitimate reason for you to be over there by then."

*

MENELIK DROVE DOWN the Garden State Parkway, having left the small office he and Peter shared in Newark to escape an early heat wave that had turned the poorly ventilated building they were housed in into a sweatbox. Even though he was only an hour into his journey toward his ultimate destination of Cape May, the grumbles and gurgles from his stomach informed him that it was time to eat. Checking the road signs, he saw there was a service area just ahead at the Toms River exit. When he saw that one of the fast food eateries at the rest stop was a Roy Rogers, he smiled. Without a second thought, he maneuvered the car over to the right and exited the Parkway.

"Four chicken wings, two biscuits, and a large orange soda. No— Make that two containers of milk," he ordered.

After paying his money and receiving his tray of food, he found an empty table. With a nod of satisfaction, he sat down to enjoy what had become one of his favorite fast food meals.

"Chicken, biscuits, milk, a day out of the office: mmm, life *can* be good sometimes."

Suddenly conscious that he had spoken out loud, he laughed and sheepishly looked around. Satisfied that no one had taken notice, he settled into his meal, quite happy to be in the strange yet welcoming peaceful anonymity that every fast food chain offered. Soon, however, a loud voice interrupted his solitude. Sounding odd but familiar, the voice spawned a peculiar, uneasy feeling in the pit of his stomach. He glanced over his shoulder when he heard the man speak again.

"No, no mo' co' saw!" an elderly, white-haired man seated at a table across the dining room bellowed to the woman seated opposite him.

Menelik studied the somewhat familiar features of the man, raising his eyebrows when he saw the woman sitting across from him write something down on a piece of paper before sliding it over to him.

"Oh, no," the man loudly complained. "Ot fo' din-r too!"

As the elderly man laughed at this, the woman tenderly grasped his arm. A bright, engaging smile broke out on her face. Then, as if she had something else of urgency to say, she quickly scribbled another note and placed it in his hand.

Menelik could see the man's lips moving as he read the words she had written.

"Ah cahnt hear ooh," he told her, laughing. "Cahnt hear a wurd ooh wit-tan," he went on, tapping the device inserted in his ear while waving the note in his hand. He laughed uproariously.

The woman laughed as well, but seemed distracted, casting a few furtive glances to the tables around them.

"Good, God," Menelik mumbled, catching a full glimpse of the woman's face for the first time.

He quickly turned his head away, hoping she hadn't noticed him staring. He was suddenly no longer hungry.

"Shush, Martin," he heard her say, her voice dredging up memories Menelik had labored to keep locked away. "We're causing a scene."

Martin said nothing as he picked at the food in front of him.

"I'm sorry, dear," Patricia went on, scribbling another note. "People must think I'm talking out of my hat."

"At!" Martin hollered, staring at her lips. "Did I for-get my at?"

"Read the note, dear," she told him, squeezing his hand.

The biscuit in Menelik's fingers crumbled, the layer of unmelted butter in the middle forming a thick glaze on his skin. Visions of hyena-men suddenly invaded his blank stare, rekindling the pain in the scars on his arms and leg. Short of breath, he clutched the side of the table. Sliding his fingers along the edges, he grappled to find a good grip.

"Ut ould I do wif-out ooh?"

Menelik felt his chest constrict with every garbled, out-of-sync syllable Martin struggled to say. The words slithered down his throat until he thought he would suffocate.

Lurching from his chair, fighting to keep his balance, he rushed toward the exit. As he fumbled for the car keys, the taunting laughter of a hyena echoed inside his head.



He had no recollection of getting into his car, nor was he aware that he had decided to head back north. But as a small amount of clarity returned, he found himself driving back the way he had come, the exit for Red Bank looming just ahead.

He changed lanes, moving to the far left, trying to avoid the exit ramp coming up on his right. He wanted nothing to do with any of the reminders the area would surely dredge up. As he put his foot to the gas pedal, the car surged forward with the boost of power.

*"Trying to get noticed?"*

Menelik gave a start at the sound of the voice.

*Jennifer giggled and popped the tiny, pink bubble of gum between her lips.*

*"Get more attention if we mooned them," she suggested, her eyes twinkling with mischief.*

*"No way," he replied. "That's all my mom needs to hear: not only did we skip school, but we're driving around with our pants around our ankles."*

*"Oh, I bet she wouldn't mind all that much. Your mom's got a good outlook on things."*

*"Yeah, like knowing where to land a ruler on the back of my legs."*

*"Come on, Gabe, she's not like that. I bet she'd get a good laugh out of it."*

*"Sure, Jen, just like your old man would, huh?"*

*Jennifer looked away, the passenger-side window suddenly receiving her complete and undivided attention.*

*"Sorry," he immediately added.*

*Jennifer's silence hit him like a stone thrown at his head. He rubbed his temple as though the pain were real.*

*"I'm just an idiot. I—"*

*He glanced over at her, hoping she would at least meet his eyes.*

*"I'm—"*

*She didn't look.*

*"I guess the only thing I can say is, I'm really sorry."*

*He watched her back rise and fall with a heavy sigh.*

*"I—"*

*"It's okay. It's okay," she grudgingly told him, her voice terse. "I mean, it's okay, Gabe. All right? It's okay."*

*The engine of the Stingray pulsed with another surge of power. Their bucket seats started to vibrate under the steady stream of the car's deep rumbling exhaust.*

*"It wears on me, you know?" she added.*

*Her eyes, as she turned to look at him, were those of a child: all wonder and innocence.*

*"You don't have to say anything."*

*"I get tired of not saying anything," she explained, her gaze drifting to the windshield and what lay beyond. "After a while, it's like having a big rock chained around your neck."*

*The green and white sign of Frank's Luncheonette flickered past the window behind her head.*

*"I could kill the bastard, you know? I swear I'm going to find the slowest, most agonizing way to make that asshole suffer some day."*

*The river came in to view as Menelik brought the Corvette to a stop at a light. He took a right onto Rumson Road.*

*"It's not right what he did," she went on, her words taking on more emotion. "It's not right at all what he did to her. There was no need to put her in that place, you know? No need at all!"*

*"Hey, babe, relax. Relax."*

*"No! I don't want to relax!"*

*The smooth white skin of her face became flush. He could see her teeth grinding. He watched her start to tremble.*

*"I swear it, Gabe, even if it kills me, I'm going to make my father wish that he were dead!"*

*Like slivers of jagged ice, Jennifer's words sliced into the skin on the back of Gabriel's neck.*

*"Don't say that!" he yelled.*

*"Why not?" she countered, unfazed by his outburst. "If that's the way I feel, then that's the way I feel."*

*"Just don't say it, is all! Okay? The turd ain't worth it."*

*Jennifer's unabashed laughter was like an old-fashioned, tried-and-true remedy, instantly diffusing the anger that had surfaced in each of them.*

*"Turd," she repeated, relishing the way it sounded. "So simple, but so true. He's just a big bag of smelly shit."*

*They fell silent for a time, letting their thoughts go to the rhythm of the Stingray's engine. They passed through the borough of Fair Haven without so much as a glance.*

*"Five years went by before I found out where she was. He wouldn't tell me where he put her. Said it was better that I didn't know. What did he think I was, a stupid little bimbo? Like I wouldn't realize what he'd done, what had happened? God, the fucker."*

*With a huff, Jennifer pulled a crumpled, half-smoked joint from her jeans pocket and reached for the lighter.*

*"Whoa, babe, not if we're going to see my mom."*

*Her eyes twinkling, she said, "Who said anything about seeing your mom? Is this Meet the Parent Day? You trying to tell me something?" she asked, nudging his arm and smiling.*

*"I thought— Didn't you say— I mean—"*

*He shook his head and laughed.*

*"Then what am I doing driving this way? I must be losing my fucking mind."*

*"And who's saying no?" she teased, placing the joint in the ashtray and shutting it closed. "I mean, even though I know she doesn't like us being together—okay, she doesn't like me—" she admitted with a giggle, "I could maybe use a little motherliness. Maybe have a slice of that homemade peach pie you're always going on about."*

*"Cool. Yeah, okay. That's cool."*

*The canary yellow stingray sprang forward with another influx of gas. He gazed out the windshield and smiled.*

"Wish you could have met her."

The sadness in her voice bumped the joy from his face.

"Well, maybe I can," he offered. "Maybe we can go see her."

Jennifer shook her head.

"Can't see her anymore. She's dead."

"Shit."

"Hung herself last year. Didn't know until the day of the funeral. The fuck didn't have the guts to tell me before then. Asshole."

"God, Jen, you never said a word."

"I know, I know."

She looked over at him then, her expression, her eyes caught somewhere between lost and scared.

"Guess it's a day of confession or something."

He exhaled sharply through his nose.

"What?" she asked.

"Nothing," he told her, shaking his head.

"Go on, ask."

"No, really."

"Go ahead, Gabe. It might be your only chance."

"Why'd she hang herself?" he blurted out.

"Didn't want to live the rest of her life in a mental institution, I guess," she told him with a shrug, surprisingly calm, a peculiar expression passing across her face. "Can't say that I blame her."

"But—"

He stopped himself from saying anything more, pressing his lips tightly together.

"Because she wasn't crazy," she replied, knowing what he was going to say. "She never was—least not any crazier than anybody else, you know?"

"Then why?"

"Because the turd was punishing her for playing around. That, and her making a point of getting totally smashed every time he made her go out with him to some stupid society social function."

"How could he—?"

"Do it? Easy, man. When you're the big, fucking Carl Stamper, and you *own just about half of what's around here— including people—you can do just about anything you want."*

*"Heavy, Jen. I mean, like I knew your old man was a—."*

*"You don't know the half of it, Gabe. You're not even close. Bastard should be hung for murder," she icily stated. "But that's okay," she added, her tone suddenly light, almost carefree. "I'll get him. I'll get him. Even if I have to kill myself to do it."*

*Gabriel gripped the steering wheel's leather covering, sweat breaking out between his fingers.*

*"I don't ever want to hear you say that ever again!" he angrily told her. "You got that? It's enough that your mom's dead because of the creep. Don't you go gettin' all stupid on me."*

*"I'll do what I have to do! Maybe you'd be able to see it better if it were your mom who was dead! I wonder how you'd feel, then?"*

*"Shit, let's just cut this rap altogether, okay? I mean, here we are at my place. I don't want to go in and have us see my mom while we're talkin' about all this suicide shit, okay?"*

*Gabriel brought the car to a stop and turned off the ignition.*

*"All right, Jen? Deal? Jen?"*

The soft hiss of the car's air conditioner winding down was all the reply he received. Slowly, his head spinning, he unwrapped his fingers from the steering wheel of the little blue Chevy Chevette he had borrowed from Peter.

"Damn, Jen," he whispered, "how could I have forgotten? How is it I never thought about that day until now?"

Shaking, he slid open the car's ashtray. The half-smoked filter-less cigarette he found lying in the middle of it loomed up at him. He shivered.

"Why didn't I remember?" he muttered.

Suddenly realizing where he was, he stared out the windshield, tracing each of the exterior steps up to the garage apartment. Nothing had changed, he thought. He wondered if Eleanor was up in the kitchen at that very moment making a peach pie. Finding the notion disquieting, he reached for the key in the ignition.

Behind him, where River Road met the corner of Starling Way, the roar of a rumbling car engine swept over the asphalt. Snapping his head around, he caught a distant glimpse of a canary yellow car and the blond hair of its passenger as the car sped past the intersection. His spine started to tingle.

"I remember now. We never had that piece of pie that day. Just like now. You left me here and sped off. I couldn't reach you for two days."

The last echo of the pulsing engine faded as he finished speaking.

"This is getting weird, man," he told himself, shaking his entire body out in an attempt to break free of the spell he had cast over himself. "You're going to freak yourself right out of—"

The sound of a door slamming shut nearly brought him out of his seat. Looking back up the stairs, he could see the door to the garage apartment open a sliver before it closed. He sighed. Eleanor had seen him.

"Shit," he softly cursed. "Shit."


When he knocked on the door, it slowly swung open, the hinges creaking with rust. He stood still, waiting for the woman of the house to invite him in. When she didn't, he rapped his knuckles on the jamb of the door.

"Mom?" he called out, letting his hand slide down the wood. "What the hell?" he asked.

His palm felt the rough gouges in the door frame where the latch should have connected to the faceplate. Bending to study the area, he discovered that an entire section had been pried off. A crowbar, he thought. What the hell was going on?

He took a step into the apartment and then stopped. The sheets covering the furniture in what he had once called his living room puzzled him. A few more steps inward brought him closer to Eleanor's favorite chair. He stood and studied the sheeted outline of the bulky piece, half expecting to see her sitting in it, her eyes half-closed, watching one of her favorite television shows or listening to music on the radio.

Looking over his shoulder, he saw that the TV and the stereo system were no longer there. All the knick-knacks she had collected over the years and all the photographs of her family that she had so proudly displayed were also gone. Without knowing why, he stepped to the chair and pulled the sheet away. The dust made him sneeze.

Looking at the brown and yellow plaid-patterned cushions, he recalled how ugly he had always thought the material was. He also remembered all the times he had told her the very same thing. With a smug smile on her face and an I-told-you-so look, she would always pull the long wooden handle on the side of the chair to pop the footrest up.

"Comfort don't mean pretty all the time," she had always said. "An when ya find somethin' feels right, you stick with it."

He ran a finger over the chair's wide, flat arm, feeling the raw patches of wood where the finish had been worn away. Noticing a stain on the rug, he shook his head. He recalled what a stickler for cleanliness Eleanor had always been. What had happened?

Creaking hinges squealed once more as the front door swung closed. When it settled flush against the frame, Menelik heard another creak off to his side. Looking to see what it was, he saw that the door to Eleanor's bedroom had come ajar.

"Mom?" he softly inquired. "Mom, you in there?" he called out, taking a few tentative steps toward her room. "Mom?"

He pushed open the bedroom door and stepped inside.

Unlike the living room, Eleanor's bedroom was not covered in sheets. To the contrary, the room looked to have been ransacked, with dresser drawers fully open, some lying atop the cut-open mattress. Gazing through the open closet doors, he was bewildered by how disorganized and messy it was. Eleanor would never leave her clothes scattered across the floor like they were now. Doing a slow turn, he saw that her night tables were askew and out of place. The small desk where she kept her antique jewelry box and personal items was broken in half, as though something heavy had struck it.

"Fuck," he whispered.

A strip of yellow tape dangling between the edge of the mattress and the box springs caught his eye. Drawn to it, he picked it up and read the two bold, black words imprinted on it: "DO NOT."

He turned the tape over, and then looked around for more. *Police tape?* he wondered. He quickly scanned every section of the room.

The crucifix hanging over the broken table caught his eye. The silver figure hung atop of the rosewood cross, seeming to beckon to him. Before he realized it, he was reaching for it. Wrapping his fingers around the wood, he felt a piece of paper wedged behind it. Lifting it out, he saw that it was a clipping from an old newspaper. He unfolded it.

"Eleanor Mary Tate. Shit, man, why didn't—?"

He remembered what Peter had said about asking.

"Died, June 1978. Fuckin' hell. Two years ago."

He stared at the crucifix for a moment, but then quickly looked away. It unnerved him to think that a figurine made of metal could convey such an air of sympathy and understanding.

"I don't get it," he said, shaking his head, crumpling the paper and throwing it to the floor. "Why didn't anyone—?"

He looked back at the figure of Jesus on the cross. The eyes of Christ now seemed questioning. He stared back at the image, not knowing what to say. The creaking hinges of the front door saved him from trying to decide.

"Who's there?" he half-heartedly called out, laying the cross on the mattress and hurrying out of the bedroom.

He walked into the living room in time to see the front door swinging shut.

"Jesus Christ, man," he mumbled.

With a shiver and a furtive glance back at Eleanor's bedroom, he bolted for the front door and took the steps back down to his car two at a time. As he fumbled for the keys, the door at the top of the stairs slammed shut.


He had no intention of going to the cemetery when he pulled out of the gravel drive, but as he drove the car back toward the Garden State Parkway, he found himself making the turns necessary to deliver him to the entrance.

"Turn around, man, turn around," he told himself.

But the car didn't heed his advice, continuing on its chosen course, following the well-manicured lane that ran the length of the cemetery.

He pulled the Chevette to the curb and turned the hazard blinkers on. As he got out of the car, a moist wind blew against his face. Looking up, he saw ominous grey-black clouds darkening the sky. He could hear thunder originating from miles away.

Making certain he was at the right location, he took a quick look around, noting that there were far more graves and markers in the cemetery than what he remembered. The small backhoe parked next to a mound of freshly dug earth reinforced all the changes that had taken place. Last time he was here, it was a wheelbarrow and shovel that had been parked next to a newly dug grave. He wondered if Mr. Brown was somewhere about.

A distant flash of lightning brightened the belly of the dark sky and cast an eerie reflection across the headstones and crosses jutting out of the ground. His head cast downward, careful to step between the gravesites, he weaved his way to where the Tate family had been laid to rest.

Eleanor's headstone matched that of her husband and son: a grey, speckled granite, smooth on the face, coarse and rough on the sides. He gazed at her name, suddenly trying to recall her face, wishing she were still alive. He didn't notice the approaching shadow until it enveloped Eleanor's name.

"You know the lady?"

Startled, Menelik whirled around to find a large brown-skinned man standing right behind him. He stared at the uniform he was wearing; a light blue shirt, dark blue slacks and tie, and polished black shoes.

"I've never seen you here before, is why I ask."

The man pulled a dark blue cap with a black brim from under his arm and ran a big, powerful-looking hand through his grey-tinged, close-cropped, wiry hair.

"I bring flowers every now and then," he went on, his attention shifting to Eleanor's headstone. "Not today, as you can see, but sometimes. Can't afford them all the time on my pay, you understand. You a relative?"

The man's voice was calm, confident, strong, and easy-going. A faint smile passed across his lips as he continued to gaze at the chiseled block of stone.

"She was—" The man shook his head, unable to finish.

"You know her?" Menelik asked, curious.

"In a way," the man replied, shrugging his shoulders. "Last one to know her, I guess you could say."

The wind stiffened; the thunder grew closer.

"Going to be a nasty one, by the looks of it," the man said, eyeing the sky.

"What did you mean, last one? Did you live with her or something like that?"

The big man's brow furrowed, his dark-brown eyes narrowing.

"You don't know nothin' 'bout the lady, do you?"

Menelik looked at the name engraved on the headstone, not knowing how to answer.

"You some kind of weirdo? You here to make some kind of trouble?"

Menelik shot him a confused look.

"I know— I knew her a while back," he told him. "Knew the people she worked for, too."

"The Mathises?" the man said, smiling at the name. "Real nice folks they are—real nice. Too bad about his stroke. That woman's got to be a saint the way she dotes on him. Used to be some kind of politician, right?"

"An ambassador and a senator," Menelik told him with a tad too much emotion.

"Oh."

The wind swirled between them in a sudden gust, the trees on the perimeter of the cemetery swaying back and forth, caught between the push and pull of the approaching storm.

"Won't be long now," the man commented. "Best be gettin' back to the bus," he went on, taking several large steps away.

"Wait."

Lightening flashed within the clouds above them, infusing the greyish-black mass with a pale green hue.

"You said you were the last one," Menelik hurried to say. "Tell me what you meant. Tell me how she was. Tell me how she—how she died."

"Look, man, I got to get back to my bus and check in with my supervisor. I'm late as it is, and he's already warned me once about coming here when my—"

"Please," Menelik bade him. "Please."

The burly, heavyset bus driver stopped.

"You sound just like she did before she got off the bus," he recounted, taking a step back toward him. "Doubt if I'll ever forget," he continued, his words caught in the whispers of the past.

"Forget what? Why are you shaking your head that way?"

The driver looked at Menelik as though he could see right through him.

"Wasn't but a few minutes, you know. Ten, maybe. But it seemed longer than that. Seemed like, well—"

The first drops of rain began to fall. The wind suddenly abated in a brief moment of unexpected calm.

"Thought she was way out drunk, you know," he continued, as though he were explaining that morning for the first time. "I mean, she'd been drinking, that was for certain."

"Drinking!" Menelik exclaimed. "She never had a drop in her life!"

The bus driver raised an eyebrow and shrugged.

"What can I tell you, man? Don't take offense, but she reeked with the stuff."

"That can't be," Menelik stated, shaking his head. "I mean," Menelik lost his eyes in Eleanor's headstone. "I mean, it just doesn't sound like her."

"But over time, I've come to think a little differently about it. I mean, like, I know she'd been drinking, but she was— She was just real focused about finding them, is all. Just real determined, the way she kept coming back to them when she talked."

"Coming back to who? Who was she looking for?"

"Her family, man. Her husband and son."

"But they've been dead for years! Look," he said with a tinge of anguish, pointing to the two headstones next to Eleanor's. "They both died in the forties."

"Well, I know that now," the bus driver explained, sounding a bit defensive. "But I didn't know it that morning. And she sure didn't seem to think that they were dead. That's why she got off the bus, you know, 'cause she saw them walking on the street."

"Walking on the street?"

The man shrugged.

"That's right. Probably would have climbed out a window if I didn't let her out the door. Like nothin' was going to stop her from gettin' to them, you know. Guess that's what I saw in her eyes when she pleaded for me to let her off the bus. Otherwise," he shrugged again, glancing at her headstone, "I guess that's pretty much the reason they finally decided it was an accident and not a suicide."

"Suicide?"

Menelik repeated the word as though he had never heard of it.

"Yeah, like, you know, if I hadn't told them what she said and the way she really believed that they," he nodded at the graves of George and Abraham, "were out walking on the street, they were ready to call it that. I mean, how else they gonna call it, the way, you know, the way she ended up dying?"

A flash of lightning split the clouds directly above them, striking behind the hill not far from where they stood. The ground beneath their feet rattled with a tremendous burst of thunder. Reflexively, the two men ducked and covered their heads with their arms.

"How did she die?" Menelik yelled as the bus driver began to run away.

"Walked out!" he yelled over his shoulder as the rain began to fall in sheets. "In front of traffic! Up on the Parkway!"

"What about me?" Menelik yelled, his eyes burrowing into the back of the man's head. "Didn't she say anything about me?"

The rain became a torrent, driving straight down, driving his words to the ground before they had a chance to carry. His fingers pulled at the sides of his face as the bus driver disappeared around a bend in the lane.

"What about me?" he screamed, fighting off an urge to cry. "What about Gabriel?"

OCTOBER, 1980

EVEN THOUGH THERE were barely any words written upon the sheet of paper Menelik was bent over, he crumpled it up and threw it in the trash can stationed beside his dull grey metal desk.

"Why don't we call it a day?"

"Hmm?" Menelik replied, studying the pencil between his fingers.

"I said, why don't you call it a day? It's close to ten."

"Football?" he grunted as he took another blank sheet of stock paper from the stack piled next to him.

"That's Monday night, dummy. It's Thursday."

"Who's playing?" he asked, rubbing his forehead.

"Led Zeppelin and Aerosmith."

"Sounds good," he muttered.

"Yeah, and they're showing highlights of the best of Rocky and Bullwinkle during halftime."

"Sounds real good," he replied, finally looking up. "But you go on. I've got to get this speech down for Saturday's debate."

"Gee, can't wait to hear it, seeing how your mind is clicking right now."

Menelik fiddled with the location of his desk lamp, trying to coax a little more brightness out of the dingy light it was giving off.

"Come on, Gabe. You can get to it first thing in the morning. I think you're on overload right now."

"No, really, you go on ahead. Enjoy the game."

"There is no game, knucklehead! That's what I've been trying to get across to you. You're not thinking straight."

"Just want to get—"

"Look, man, you're tired, I'm tired, the whole world is probably tired." Tapping the tip of a pen against his desktop, Peter gave Menelik a questioning look. "What are you smiling about?"

"You, turkey. You and the way you—"

Peter swiveled his head around when Menelik stopped talking. He rose from his desk.

"What can we do for you?" Peter asked the heavyset man stepping across the threshold.

The portly, gray-clad figure ignored him entirely as he casually made his way to Menelik's desk.

"You this Menelik Arbagna running to represent district twenty-nine?"

Menelik gazed at the man as though he were some remnant from his haunted past.

"I'm Peter Lyons, Menelik's campaign manager," Peter announced, rounding his desk. "What can we do for you, Mr. …?"

Peter thrust out his hand. The man placed his plump, diamond- and gold-jeweled fingers limply within his palm. They briefly shook, though the man never looked at Peter directly.

"Reverend. Reverend Rue Thompson."

"Reverend?" Peter repeated, somewhat surprised.

"You find it your place to question that a black man be wearing the cloth of God?"

The full girth of Reverend Thompson turned on Peter, the Reverend's plump fingers touching the stiff, white collar ringing his fleshy neck. Pulling a large silver cross out from beneath his gray overcoat, he held it aloft so Peter could get a good look.

"Nothing of the sort, I can assure you Rev—"

"Though *man* may be hindered by the color of skin to find worthiness in those who serve Him, the *Lord* welcomes all who would proliferate his word."

"Your perception of what I meant is way off base, Reverend. I never meant—"

"It is an intrinsic characteristic of your race to be prejudiced against blacks," the Reverend was quick to say, holding up a fat hand for Peter's silence. "The white man's racist character is the root of all problems in this country, if not the world."

"Oh, give me a break. Excuse me, but that's just so much bull."

"It has always been the white man's way to deny his sins against his black brother. Only when he confesses to his wrongdoings and makes restitution to those he has enslaved and repressed will there be God's peace in this world. Surely, you, brother Menelik, must see this as well."

Rue Thompson turned his cold, black eyes to Menelik. For Menelik, it was if the hyena from the sand river were staring at him in the moment before it attacked.

"If you will excuse us, Reverend," Peter interjected. "We do have a good amount of work still to get to tonight."

The Reverend ignored Peter and continued to stare at Menelik.

"If you can't see this as being what has kept the black man from his rightful place in God's creation, then you are no man to represent the people of the twenty-ninth district, or your race."

"I'll take care of this, Peter," Menelik announced, waving off Peter's intention to speak. "Go on home. I'll call you later. It's okay. Go."

Peter glared at Reverend Thompson. The man smoothed his slick, black, duck-tailed styled hair. Peter snorted. The Reverend smirked.

"May this night be an awakening to your sins," the Reverend smugly said. "Although your race is burdened by centuries of iniquity, the Lord is always receptive to honest penance."

"Cram it, asshole," Peter retorted, flipping him off as he left the office.

"A lover of whites has neither the chance to win this election nor any place in the black community."

Menelik heard the statement as though it was the day of his arraignment in court: a simple accusation that left him unfazed and numb. Wearily, he sat down.

"In the country where I was born, the hyena is boldest at night. I've seen little difference between there and here."

"Raised by whites, engaged in a sinful relationship with a white girl that ended in the blood-thirsty jaws of the devil. And an alliance with a white man who embodies all the bigoted traits of his race."

The eyes of Rue Thompson smoldered like a cold-burning flame as he spoke.

"There is no place for you in this election. The black man must be represented by a black man now, and that black man must be ready to wage war on all of his enemies, make the white race pay for all the sins committed against us. And you are not that man, Tom. You do not represent blacks. You must withdraw! You must quit!"

Menelik heard the hooting call of the hyena warning off those who might wish to feed upon the remains of a carcass.

"It is the Lord's will that you renounce your candidacy."

Menelik saw Paul Conley strutting across the courtroom, his accusation of guilt spoken as though it was a holy proclamation.

"Would you blaspheme His will by your self-serving silence?"

Titus and a faceless hyena-man melded into one, their joined hands pointing a gun, preparing to shoot.

"What could you possibly know about God?" Menelik shouted. "Don't you think I know who you are? Don't you think I know who I'm running against? Don't you think I've seen your fat, greasy face on the news or in those cheap, asinine political ads you're running, ranting your extremist rhetoric, filling the people of this city with hate and distrust, inciting them to lash out? You think you're talkin' to some kind of fool?"

"Those of color who do not embrace the revolution against the tyranny we have been and still are subjected to are not only fools, but traitors in the war that must be waged!"

"Hate and stupidity will only produce more senseless violence and killing."

"Blood must be loosed to purge the sins from our oppressors! Blood will be the price of true freedom! Blood will cleanse the path to our future! Blood will be the way!"

"The way," Menelik scoffed, pressing his fingertips to his eyes, the blood of Titus and Tafari pooling on the inside of his closed lids. "Blood has flowed across the past and the present since the beginning of time.

If blood is what God favors to cleanse the world, then surely he can't be much of a god. Only those of darkness would desire more."

"You will not see the promised land! You will not be a part of the black man's reign!"

Menelik slowly rose from his chair.

"I am of the promised land," he roared. "I am of Africa! I am of Ethiopia! I am of the Mother!"

As he intoned Her name, the bond of his origin swelled within him. The Mother was a revelation that he had long forgotten; he stood taller.

Rue Thompson momentarily wavered at the speaking of the Mother's name, but quickly recovered.

"You will not win!" he proclaimed. "You will not confuse the flock with your white-man's tongue! You shall not be heard!"

Menelik found himself laughing.

"Get out, Reverend," he told him, waving him away. "Go peddle your bullshit somewhere else."

"You dare to ridicule?"

Rue Thompson's face quivered with rage.

"You dare mock me? God will see you punished!"

With his foretelling of Menelik suffering a punishment by God's hand, the Reverend Thompson settled back into his customary persona of smug arrogance, his fat lips stretching into a smirk, his fingers lifting the gaudy, silver crucifix dangling atop his portly stomach.

"Enjoy your walk home," he said over his shoulder as he turned to leave. "I'm sure you will find it invigorating."

Wraith-like, the Reverend seemed to glide out the door, exiting the office as quietly as he had entered.


Well past midnight, Menelik paused at the bottom of the steps of the squat, grey stone and glass building, the second floor of which housed the office of the Lyons and Associate Law Firm. As he breathed deeply and stretched, the night's breeze stirred, carrying the scent of the Passaic River to him from several blocks over. He allowed himself a slight smile; the odor of it didn't make him pinch his nose like it normally did. Slightly shivering in the crisp autumn air, he turned up the collar of his jacket and began his normal walk down Union Street to the bus stop on Ferry.

Deep in thought, running through the speech he had been working on since Peter and the Reverend Thompson had left, he didn't notice the three dark figures slipping out of an alleyway up ahead of him until he was almost upon them.

"You Arbagna?"

Menelik stopped.

"You hear me, old man?"

He quickly checked behind him: no cars, no people, not even a foraging rat.

"You don't belong here, *Tom.*"

The three darkly dressed figures spread out and edged closer. Although they each wore a black ski mask to hide their identities, Menelik reasoned they were young from the way they carried themselves and the build of their bodies.

"Best leave this neighborhood, Tom-nigger."

Same voice, he realized: the leader, confronting him head on, talking for all of them as the two others sought to flank him.

"Man says you need to be punished," the leader threatened, a glint of steel flashing in his hand.

"What man?" Menelik calmly asked.

"Why, the Lord, fool," he laughed, the two others nervously joining in.

The leader took a step forward, brandishing a six-inch stiletto. With bared teeth, he lunged.

"Ethiopia!" Menelik screamed, bunching his muscles.

For a moment, his assailant hesitated. Quick to recover, however, he sliced the space between Menelik and himself with his shiny blade. His companions did the same.

"Let's do this," the leader hissed.

"Hyena-men!" Menelik shouted, suddenly enraged. "Scavengers!"

Slipping his coat from his body, he wrapped it about his arm. Using it as a shield, he blocked the knife jab directed at him from the front, while kicking out to his right. The heel of his foot caught the man-beast just below his kneecap. The beast retreated with a yelp.

Using the shifting of his weight to propel him, he pushed off and jumped back to the to his left, bringing a roundhouse punch straight down into the next beast's face. The hyena hooted and cried, falling backward as blood formed about its snapping jaws.

The leader again drove his blade forward, swinging wildly. Menelik slid to his right—the blade just nicking the material of his shirt—and then whipped the zippered end of his jacket into the hyena man's eye. The animal whimpered and cringed. Menelik moved in to finish him off.

The gunshot was loud, out of place, the pain in his shoulder immediate. Blood began to flow from the wound before he stumbled to the street.

"No! Idiot!" the leader shouted. "He ain't payin' if he dead!"

The hyena-men gathered. They shuffled, uneasy, whimpering from their wounds, their heads swiveling in every direction to see if they were in danger. The leader kicked Menelik in the side.

"Fucking cowards," he gasped, grimacing with pain.

"Ain't dead," the leader proclaimed with satisfaction. "Let's go."

Breathing heavily, his shoulder throbbing from the bullet that had grazed him, Menelik crawled to the sidewalk and propped himself up against the frame of a parked car. The street was eerily quiet. *Didn't anyone hear the gunshot?* he wondered. He placed his head against the metal of the car and sighed.

He became aware of footsteps heading his way, sounding like the soft ticking of a slow clock. As he listened to their precise cadence, a sense of relief washed over him.

"I need help!" he groaned, hoping he sounded coherent enough that the person would not mistake him for a drunk or a junkie.

The footsteps didn't change: unhurried, deliberate. Just as he was about to call out again, they stopped.

"Brother Arbagna, what's provoked the Lord to place you thusly on the street?"

Menelik looked up to find Rue Thompson standing above him, his overly large silver crucifix held between his fat, jewel-encrusted fingers. The man looked at him and smiled.

"Some streets in this district are not safe to walk after dark," he casually remarked. "No, not safe at all."

Menelik watched as the man brought the crucifix to his lips and lightly kissed it.

"May God protect you and see you home safe. And may His wisdom enlighten you in your decisions."

"You, fat fuck, you don't—"

"Do not further bring the wrath of the Lord down upon you with insults and cursing!" Reverend Rue Thompson admonished him. "Praised be Almighty God for protecting and showing you mercy tonight."

Headlights briefly illuminated the reverend as a car swerved up Union Street from Ferry.

"That will be your white handler," the reverend said, giving the approaching car a passing glance. "Lucky for you, I was having a late night meeting with some of my—constituents—and saw, from afar, what happened to you." With a smug smile, he said, "Of course, none of us could see anything. Just outlines of shapes."

The little blue Chevrolet Chevette screeched to a halt.

"Ah, the night air. Invigorating, is it not, brother?" Rue Thompson asked, slapping his chest with open palms. "A gift of the Lord. Now you take care."

*

ROWDY, *BOISTEROUS, DISORDERLY*: these were the adjectives the newspaper and television reporters were writing in their notebooks when Menelik, leaning against Peter's shoulder for support, arrived to take part in the first and only debate that had been organized for the state assembly seats that were up for election.

"Where are the other two candidates?" Peter hoarsely whispered as he guided Menelik through the crowd. "I thought we'd be the last to arrive."

Menelik stared up at the hastily erected platform on the corner of Broad and Green streets, his attention focused on the heavyset man dressed all in gray. His eyes slowly drifted to the white ring of fabric that encased the man's fleshy neck.

Menelik didn't directly answer Peter's question, and Peter didn't repeat it. The other two candidates would not be making an appearance, they both knew. That point had been clearly accentuated two nights before on Union Street. The other two candidates had been scared away.

"So, we have ourselves a debater!" Reverend Thompson announced to the crowd, swinging an arm out toward Menelik for the people to follow. "And I say behold, brothers and sisters!" he bellowed, causing screeching feedback in the public address speakers mounted on tripods at the corners of the stage. "Look who leads him here! Look who he has chosen to bring! Look who he aligns himself with!"

Peter's white skin was like a magnet. The eyes of the crowd followed him as he made his way up the temporary steps to the plywood platform.

"Do you not see the hypocrisy?" the reverend chided just as Menelik took hold of Peter's outstretched hand and helped him up the final step. "Do you not feel the affront?"

Rue Thompson eyed both Menelik and Peter with a contemptuous smirk.

"Are you not as incensed as I," he continued, his voice rising with emotion, "that a black man who audaciously calls himself Menelik Arbagna—an African name—comes here, no, not with a fellow African, no, not even with another black man—because there are no black men or women working for his campaign—are you not as incensed as I, as outraged as I, that he would insult us all by bringing a white man—a white man—to a debate where the issues at hand are only of concern to blacks and to the future of this black community?"

The crowd roared its agreement, the shouts of disapproval from the two hundred plus people on hand rolling over the stage like a thunderclap.

"But let us ..." Rue Thompson raised his jeweled hands for silence.

The shouting discourse subsided, eroding into a few catcalls and obscenities.

"But let us not judge too harshly! Let us not condemn before justice is given its due! Let us not cast aside this man of falsehood before we listen to what the white man has told him to say!"

The reverend smiled at Menelik, gesturing him to the microphone as he stepped aside.

"This is a setup, man," Peter angrily whispered, grabbing Menelik's arm. "This isn't how it's supposed to go down. There's not even a moderator."

The throng below the stage surged forward, waving their fists and shouting for "the white motherfucker" to get off the stage.

Unfazed, Menelik smiled at Peter and confidently stepped to the microphone.

With an air of utter calm, even though insults were being yelled out from the crowd, Menelik motioned for Peter and Reverend Thompson to be seated in the row of chairs that had been placed at the back of the stage.

"I am ..." he began, his words spoken softly.

But the crowd drowned him out, unleashing a barrage of insults and ridicule.

"I am African!" he raged, pausing between each word, his eyes filled with defiance. "Yes! I am African!"

He paused, allowing the notion to be absorbed.

"And—I am not!"

The multitude of faces below him frowned, an undercurrent of complaints gathering force.

"I am American!"

Menelik looked knowingly at the faces closest to the stage.

"And I am not! Which of you feels the same? Which of you has felt the sense of not belonging, as I do? African," he stated, striking his fist to his heart. "American," he proudly proclaimed. "Both? Neither? Is it not the same for you?"

The crowd shuffled and fell quiet, their expressions perplexed, but curious.

"So where are we? What are we? Where is it that we are going?" He gave the reverend a fleeting glance. "Questions," he lamented with an expressive sigh, "that the people of this city ask every day. I, as Reverend Thompson has so kindly informed you, am Menelik Arbagna. I am Ethiopian, African. Both my heritage and my family are there. Yet I am here, in this city, running to represent this district, unable to be a part of that to which I was born. So there is an emptiness here," he told them, touching his chest with a finger, "a yearning to go back, my heart crying out for what my life is not. And yet, and yet—time isn't going to turn back to allow me to be African again."

Menelik looked out over the faces of the people, nodding when he could see that his words were being understood.

"American," he continued. "They tell me that I am American. But surely I am the last to understand what that should mean. Surely, I am here," he told them, raising his right arm. "There is no denying that. But this is a land not of my blood, not of my origin. It is though I have no home."

He paused for some length. The crowd became uneasy, whispering, wondering.

"Yet we struggle and suffer," he went on, "wondering when this land that does not acknowledge us will see that we exist. It is though we have been orphans—orphans!—since our freedom was proclaimed."

The crowd stirred.

"Yes, I understand your feelings. Freedom can't be dismissed, or the history of it forgotten. It must be nurtured and cultivated. It must be taught and cherished. Freedom must be protected, as though it were a gift from heaven, given to the very heart of each of our children, a blessing from God."

The outbreak of applause surprised him.

"We have lived as orphans in this land long enough! Even free orphans must have a home! And although this nation does not, as yet, acknowledge us as its children, there is no disputing that that is what we are!"

Again, applause broke out, spreading and swelling until the plywood beneath his feet began to shake.

"Stick to the issues, Arbagna!" The Reverend shouted from his chair. "These people don't need their heads filled with any more meaningless speeches!"

"Issues!" Menelik announced, motioning the crowd to quiet. "The good reverend wishes for me to address the issues."

Looking over his shoulder, he gave Rue Thompson a wry smile.

"The issue is a nation—a country, a city—that we are of, and for. The issue is to take the decaying streets and empty buildings of our neighborhoods and, from them, forge a new city! A city reborn from our labors! A city reborn from our strength! A city built upon the foundation of faith, courage, and dignity! We are pioneers!" he shouted, gripped by the fervor of his own racing heart. "We are the ones who must forge this new community! No one—no one—is going to give us anything! *We* must be the ones to make this city whole again! *We* must be the ones!"

Applause began to swell, but Menelik continued speaking.

"Fear and hope," he said, his voice trailing softer, the crowd hushing each other so they were able to hear. "These are the issues that bind us all. Black" he stated with pride, sweeping his arm out to encompass the entire crowd. "White," he said evenly, motioning behind him toward Peter. "Yellow, brown, red; man, woman, or child: fear and hope, the bond shared by all. Fear kills without bias, maims without thought, blinds without care, turning brother against brother in an endless circle of—fear. We must not fear prejudice, but conquer it. We must not fear poverty, or crime, illiteracy, and unemployment, but squash them. We must meet them on every street corner in this crumbling city and match them blow for blow until they cower, until they yield, until they are no more. But most of all, ladies and gentlemen—neighbors—but most of all, we must not fear the world that the white man has set before us. For we, together, can change what has been put into—"

"Outrageous! Contemptible! The words of a Tom! The delusions of a criminal! The words of the white man hidden in the mouth of a black! Hypocrisy! Blasphemy!"

The fleshy jowls of Rue Thompson shook with every shouted syllable while his hands yanked the microphone stand away from Menelik.

"Go back where you came from, white-lover!" he hollered into the microphone. "Go back and serve your master! You're no brother! You're not African! You're a tool of the enemy sent to keep us in chains! Get off the stage! Get off this street! Get your Uncle Tom ass out of this election!"

The reverend set his gaze upon the crowd, motioning for them to support him. But as he turned to confront Menelik anew, he unexpectedly fell silent, taken aback by what he saw.

Having shed his brown herringbone sport coat and chocolate-brown shirt, Menelik stood bare-chested before the crowd, his muscular frame displaying rippled tautness. Fresh blood seeped through the bandages wrapped around his shoulder. He took the microphone back from a confused Reverend Thompson.

"Fear did this," he told the multitude of faces staring up at him, touching his wound. "As fear causes the reverend's misguided words. This city is in decay, but its people need not be. Right now, as we stand under the light of the sun, there is hope. But at night, fear creeps out of the rubble, skulking in the alleys and gathering in packs on the street corners because we have allowed it to. We have forgotten what strength there is in hope."

Menelik blotted the trickle of blood dripping down his arm and raised his red-stained fingers to the crowd.

"A gang of faceless boys—hyena-men, I call them—did this to me. Attacked me out of fear: fear that their city might change, or perhaps fear that it cannot change, that they will never be able to escape the rot they find themselves falling deeper into."

"And who's to blame for that rot?" Rue Thompson shouted, pushing Menelik to the side and taking the microphone. "The white man is to blame! The white man is the cause! And it is the white man who wants to keep us here! He doesn't want us to claim what is ours! Nor does he want us to succeed! We have a destiny to reach! And only war will lead us to it! A war against the whites! War against this oppressive society! War on the government that wants to keep us enslaved!"

The reverend glanced toward the back of the crowd and hurried on.

"Enough slavery! Enough talk of change! Enough of the white man's words! It's time for blood! Time for war! Time to rid ourselves of any who are not for the ascension of the black race in this country! Rise up, I say! Rise up! Rise up and take that which is rightfully ours, brothers and sisters! God is with you! God is on our side!"

There was a surge from the back of the crowd as several young men made their way toward the stage. Trying to whip the mood of the gathering into a frenzy, they screamed, "Rise up! Rise up!" while pushing and shoving their way to the front.

"Be calm!" Menelik yelled, getting as close to the microphone as he could. "This is no place—"

Rue Thompson shoved him away. Menelik's plea for restraint was lost in a blast of feedback.

"I warned you," he hissed, glaring at Menelik. "And now you will know the power of the Lord." Leaping backward, "He's got a gun! He's got a gun!" the reverend cried out, a terrified expression on his face. "God have mercy!" he wailed into the microphone, pointing a diamond-adorned accusatory finger at Menelik. "God have mercy! He's got a gun!"

The cry caused instant pandemonium. Panic stricken, the crowd scattered in every direction. At the reverend's unspoken signal, the young men in his employ leapt to the stage. Almost simultaneously, a gunshot exploded. Splinters of wood burst upward as a bullet blew a hole in the plywood.

"He's got a gun!" the gang of youths screamed. "He's got a gun!"

So fast did the subsequent events transpire that Menelik would not have a clear picture of what had actually taken place until two days later, when he was shown a video feed from a news camera while being interviewed at the police precinct. Even after he had watched the video played over and over until he had it memorized, he found it difficult to make sense of, the ending leaving him shattered.

In the split second it had taken him to open his hands to show that he was not armed, a gun flashed forward from the gang of youths. The hand that held it was level and steady, a finger already pressing the trigger. Then came the blurred image of Peter jumping in front of him as the gun flashed, followed by the awful spasmodic lurch of his body as the bullet ripped a hole into his chest.

No matter how many times he viewed the tape, Peter always crumpled to the stage, the pack of hyena-men scattering in every direction as he fell. Then in a moment that seemed surreal to him, he would watch himself kneel at the side of his friend as a pool of blood formed around Peter's body. It was at this point in the tape, no matter who was in the room with him studying the video, that the person or persons would ask him why he suddenly looked up from the body to look back across the stage.

"The hyena-men," he would relay in an emotionless voice. "The fuckers were laughing."

That was where the video feed always ended. Then the screen would go blank.

# DJIBOUTI, OCTOBER, 1980

HUDDLING WITHIN THE soiled, tattered shamma he had worn since arriving in Djibouti, Teimbaka rested the back of his head against a wood piling, his weary, bloodshot eyes fighting to see through the sea mist rolling in off the waters of the Gulf of Tadjoura. Although he had no reason to suspect that something out of the ordinary might happen this night, he willed himself to stay awake, hoping that the reason he had traveled here might eventually make itself known.

It was two in the morning: the hour of the smuggler, of the black market; a time when drugs and weapons and people were shuffled on and off swift, silent-running boats. It was a time when it was in one's best interest to be as invisible as possible.

As an unkempt beggar who had taken up residence on the dock two years earlier—playing his ancient drum for tourists and petitioning those of wealth for whatever they wished to toss his way—Teimbaka had become a familiar piece of the pier's setting: a thin, bearded, harmless castoff who was both accepted and ignored by the captains, crews, dockhands, and customs officials who made their living there. Even the merchants who came to do business on the docks, who had first looked upon him and treated him with disgust, now gave him not a second glance, seeing him as nothing more than a permanent fixture amongst the crates of cargo. To them, he was just another sea bird perched on the edge of a piling, squawking for a piece of fish.

At night, however, especially now, when only those who did not wish to be seen were conducting business, it was not wise to beg or be noticed or wander about uninvited. He had learned this on the very first night he had arrived. Witnessing the throat of a begging teenage girl slit open from ear to ear, simply for being in the wrong place at the wrong time, had left its imprint. He did not wish the same fate to befall him.

Pulling his shamma closer about him, concealing his head within its folds, he let his eyes wander. Determined to keep his vigil, he struggled to stay awake, all the while acting as though he was in a state of fitful rest. To those who might wish to give him a closer look, he was nothing more than a feeble-minded beggar troubled by dreams that afforded him no peace.

The fog, when it came, as it did on this night, brought with it images of Claire and John and Lee. He could not escape them. Their presence would drift down upon him without notice or sound, seeping into his thoughts, swirling inside of him until he felt as if he might go mad. And try as he might at times to forget those years and all the feelings they would dredge up, he found that a part of him did not want to let them go. He found himself clinging to them, as if somehow, someday, they might return. But in his heart, he could not see the path that would lead him to such a reunion.

So too, when a caravan or a single trader would travel to the port from Ethiopia, he would hear Peter Gunstard's name uttered. Gunstard, deemed the "Red Terror" by the people of that country. He who had risen to a powerful place within the inner circle of the Mengistu regime, a commander who had overseen the killing of over thirty thousand opponents of the new government. His victims included as many as a thousand students, Teimbaka had heard, put to death for doing nothing more than handing out leaflets critical of the new government's policies. Gunstard's name was always spoken in hushed tones by fearful voices, as eyes constantly flitted from one face to the next, wondering who might or might not be one of his spies. It was as though the man's last words to him had become a prophecy. He had followed him, was hounding him, torturing him with tales of his unspeakable butchery. His name was a constant, painful reminder of the morning on the hill. The dawn that was the ending of all he had cared for. The time of Sister Lady had been obliterated in a handful of minutes.

It had taken him several days and countless miles to find his way back to the camp after that morning, for Gunstard had sent several men after him in pursuit. But the Mother had watched over him, leading him to shelter and water and food while impeding his pursuers with heat and dust and scorpions. Lastly, She had led him to a passage through an Eritrean rebel–held ravine. It had been the final end of Gunstard's soldiers.

He had come to wish, at times, that he had discovered Claire's body amongst the carnage and the ashes when he returned to the camp. For it would have offered him an ending, given him a chance to say goodbye. But with the passing of so many days, and with the work of the scavengers and the flies, recognition of any remains in the camp had been impossible. In the end, he had simply dug a grave for each lump of rotted flesh he had found and buried them all with a plea to the Mother that each would find peace amongst the hills that bordered the plain of the spirit elephants and be reborn within the pure, glittering waters of the lake that stretched to an endless horizon.

When he had finally taken leave of the camp, he had left with three items that had somehow managed to survive: his drum, the child's prayer book that had belonged to Lee's brother, and the small silver necklace and cross that she had once worn. These were now his only link to that time in his life, to Claire.

Within the folds of his shamma, he felt the cover of the book pressed against his chest. His fingers clutched the smooth surface of the cross that hung around his neck. The drum, as always, stood next to him.

"Sister Lady," he murmured. So hushed was his voice that it was instantly lost within the mist. "Claire."

Below him, endlessly lapping against the pilings that had become his home, the water seemed to whisper to him in return. It murmured his name over and over, repeating it in a steady, rolling rhythm, spoken neither as a greeting or a farewell. Yet, the sound of it always left him with the feeling that there was something more to the voices of the waves that they wished for him to hear. If he were only able to learn how to listen to them, he thought, what might they tell him?

The sea mist closed in around him, wet and clammy. The cross suddenly felt cold. He wrapped his shamma closer about him and closed his eyes. Soon afterward, something slid across his ankles.

Jerking awake, he pulled his legs into his body. The mist briefly parted as his hands whipped the air.

"Zanzibar," he whispered, a smile replacing his anxiety.

The sleek, slate-gray cat wound her body between his ankles, softly purring at the sound of her name.

"How is the night?"

Without warning, Zanzibar bolted across the pier, the mist barely troubled by her hurried passage.

Then, Teimbaka heard a sound.

Uneven footsteps—one heavy, one light and scraping, as if one foot was being dragged across the planks of wood—were steadily coming his way. Through narrowed eyelids, he observed the mist billow forth and then swirl to a tangled current as a hooded figure stepped through.

The limping person drew nearer.

Teimbaka held himself rigid, head downcast with his chin resting on his chest, hoping the person would pass him by, when the footsteps slowed and then stopped.

But the mist parted and then closed again as the figure moved on, leaving him to consider what little he had seen. A metal box carried tightly in both arms, a set of ugly scarred feet with gnarled toes, shuffling by in a pair of worn and frayed sandals. A feeling, as well, lingered for him to mull, an unnerving pang of queasiness brought on by the sound of the hobbling feet. That the figure was clutching a box only sparked his imagination further. He looked to the wooden planks of the pier for traces of blood.

"John," he mouthed.

Zanzibar returned, her claws lightly pulling at the uneven edges of his robe.

"So you return," he quietly stated.

A sudden gust of wind came in off the water. It carved a path through the center of the sea mist, opening a narrow passage from the pier to the city.

"As if . . ." he murmured, gazing at the newly formed path.

For a moment, Zanzibar searched Teimbaka's eyes. Her own, a candle-flame yellow, seemed to widen and glow. Without warning, she cuffed his ankle with her paw and bolted off, running full tilt down the wind-forged corridor.

Below him, the water suddenly splashed against the pilings with urgency, his name now whispered in a burst of white-capped spray. Getting quickly to his feet, he gathered his drum and hurried after Zanzibar.

Staying true to the wind-hewn course, he felt more than saw his way along the uneven roads that took him past mist-shrouded warehouses, shops, and dwellings. Several times, with the growing feeling that he was lost, and having found no sign of Zanzibar or the hooded figure anywhere, he turned to go back to the pier, only to find that the fog had closed the way behind him. Left with little choice, he continued on.

Lights began to appear around him, illuminating veiled silhouettes within kitchens and bathrooms: fishermen, bakers, and dockhands all starting their workday well before dawn. The sound of waves—stronger now, crashing against a shoreline—reached him, carried by a breeze of a different origin. The wind now caressed his face, where before it had been at his back.

He stopped and turned in a slow circle.

"Where?" he wondered.

The fog began to thin. The breeze stiffened. The sound of the waves grew louder. "The other side of the peninsula," the swells seemed to be saying as they rolled in from the Gulf of Aden and the Arabian Sea.

Teimbaka turned to face the easterly wind straight on, his eyes opening wide as he took in what glimmer of light the sky now held. Drawn to it, he moved onward, lured by the sound of the churning sea and the prospect of watching the sunrise over its clear, turquoise waters.

From an unseen alleyway, a blur rushed toward him, a bolt of darkness against the backdrop of a waning night. Taken off guard, he only had time to stop and steady himself. He winced as Zanzibar's claws latched on to the scars on his chest.

"Zanzibar," he gasped. "What are you doing?"

He said nothing more as she sunk her claws deeper, her flaming eyes gazing up at him as though he were supposed to understand what she was telling him.

He heard the slight scraping sound of the dragging foot first, then recognized the weighted step of the other. With them came the premonition of a shadow heading toward him. It was coming down the alley Zanzibar had just run from.

Moving swiftly, he rushed to the corner of the building and sat down with his back to the wall. Placing Zanzibar in his lap and his drum to one side, he covered his head within the folds of his shamma and pretended to be asleep. As the limping steps drew closer, Zanzibar extended and retracted her claws into his upper thighs.

The cat exploded from his lap when the limping figure came out of the alley. To Teimbaka's dismay, she careened into his drum, knocking it sideways to the ground before scampering down the street and out of sight.

He held his breath at the noise it caused.

The limping steps stopped right beside him.

"You!" a man's voice hissed. "Is that your animal?"

Teimbaka shut his lids tight, fighting back the tears that were building in his eyes. For though the voice was gruff, cold, older, and unkind, there was no mistaking whose voice it was.

"I'm talking to you!"

As Teimbaka grappled with what to do, John's foot slammed the back of his head into the wall.

"Speak, filth, before I—"

Disoriented and dazed from the blow to his head, Teimbaka struggled to make sense of what he was hearing. There came a loud slapping of skin, followed by the frantic gasp of someone gripped by fear. Then came a whimper and a stifled cry, and the sound of several feet shuffling away.

Teimbaka rubbed the back of his head and opened his eyes. A faint smell of lavender lingered in the air. He slid to the edge of the alley.

"I meant nothing," he heard John weakly protest in a hurried whisper.

"Silence, idiot!"

Teimbaka could make out the silhouettes of three others dragging John back up the alley. He moved a few steps to follow.

"I must see her," John said, almost begging. "I must. She is mine."

Teimbaka's head jerked back when he saw John's head snap sideways from a stinging slap to his ear.

"Please," John sobbed. "Please let me see her!"

Teimbaka winced as he waited for the next blow to be struck. But no blow came. Only an uneasy silence ensued.

"As I have made clear to you many times, my young friend—"

The sound of the man's voice quickened the pace of Teimbaka's heart. He felt his stomach churn.

"—only when you can pay. Only when you can pay."

"Susenyo," he mouthed.

The revelation left him cold.

"But I brought the box," John whined. "And it was I who brought her to you!" he complained, sounding like a spoiled child.

"You brought her to me," Susenyo sarcastically scoffed. "Were it not for my underlings, you would be dead and she would be— Why do I bother? Business, John, as I have tried to teach you. Nothing begets you nothing. However, money—or something of substantial value—will bring you your beloved for an evening. You bringing the box was simply part of your job, nothing more."

"That's not—"

The slap to his face was clear and loud.

"Bring him. The streets awaken. Already too much has been said that others might have heard."

Teimbaka slipped farther down the alley as the others moved away. Muscles tensed, senses heightened, he traversed the alley in a crouch, careful to move without making a sound. When he reached the alley's end, he stopped. John, Susenyo, and the two others were nowhere to be seen.

The street where the alley came to an end ran north to south. Another alley was situated directly across from where he stood, the opening some fifty feet away. He looked in each direction, trying to decide, listening intensely for anything that might give him a clue. But he heard and saw nothing.

Heart racing and stomach churning, he ran across the street and scampered up the second alley, discarding caution for speed. Seventy-five yards later, with the sky above him taking on the pale light of dawn, he stopped again; the passageway emptied into a small courtyard. Along the opposite wall, four doors stood in greeting.

As he took a tentative step forward, he could smell the faint scent of lavender. He approached the four doors, studying each.

"Which?" he whispered.

The heady scent of perfume grew stronger the closer he moved to the doorways. Closing his eyes, he stepped to each, inhaling deeply, trying to discern which held the strongest remnant of the fragrance. Choosing the one to his far left, he grabbed hold of the knob and turned it.

A massive forearm clamped about his throat, lifting him off his feet and jerking him away. For a sobering moment, he was unable to breathe. The thought of death flashed through his mind. As dark angels began to flutter about his face, he was thrown roughly to the street.

Struggling to rise, gasping for air, he felt his torso explode with pain when two well-placed, powerful kicks struck him in the stomach and ribs. Rolling with each kick, he backed farther away, hoping for the slightest opening to make his escape.

A deep, mocking laughter assailed him as he lay panting. Dazedly, he tried to focus on his foe.

"You should have stayed on the pier, beggar."

The words were said to him without feeling.

"But I am grateful that you didn't. I've had little to do as of late."

He tried to take stock of the man, blinking at his massive form.

"Matula?" he moaned, confused.

The man spit close to his face and shook his head. Teimbaka saw that it wasn't Matula, but someone very similar. Like a great water buffalo, the man was a massive hulk of blue-black muscle; broad rounded shoulders connected to a tree stump neck, a wide protruding forehead overhanging a pair of deep-set, coal-black eyes. His expression was impassive, almost bored, as he stared down at Teimbaka over a flat, flaring nose.

And then the water buffalo–man bent to grab hold of him. As the man reached for his neck, Teimbaka could see that his hands were a mass of twisted knuckles and long, thick, scar-laden fingers.

A spitting hiss preceded Zanzibar's eruption into the air, a screaming bolt of savagery that flew at the water buffalo–man with claws and fangs extended. The cry of pain was instantaneous. Zanzibar inserted her nails into the flesh of his face and raked them downward. Blood began to stream from the scratches, staining the man's white silk shirt.

Zanzibar hissed again, clawing at his eyes. The water buffalo–man stumbled backward, frantically trying to get his hands around the feral beast. Finally able to get hold of her neck, he flung her off to the side with all the strength he could muster. Zanzibar met the wall of the alley with a sickening thud, her legs twitching, her chest heaving before a body-length tremor laid her still.

"No!" Teimbaka screamed. "Zanzibar!"

"I will crush you!" the water buffalo–man roared.

Enraged by the wounds that the cat had inflicted upon him, the water buffalo–man lowered his head and charged.

The massive frame of the man struck Teimbaka square in the chest. The force of the collision carried them across the small cobblestone courtyard, their bodies tumbling head over heels. When they stopped moving, Teimbaka rolled sideways, springing lightly to his feet while the water buffalo–man labored to rise. Wiping the dust from his silk-adorned shoulders, the man stepped toward Teimbaka with a menacing smile etched across his bloodied face.

The roar of a lion—deafening, earth-rattling, fear-provoking—reverberated through the courtyard. Shutters shook and doors rattled. The water buffalo–man jumped at the sound, his small, dark eyes frantically searching for the killing beast.

Zanzibar stared up at him, her flame-yellow eyes shining and bright. She held the tip of her tail high, calmly twitching it back and forth.

"Zanzibar!" Teimbaka shouted with joy. "Truly you are a gift of the Mother!"

It was a chilling, surreal moment for both men when Zanzibar arched her back, bared her fangs, and loosed the roar of the mighty *negusa negast* once more. Even Teimbaka, who had walked amongst the spirit elephants, wondered how such an intertwining of entities could be so. He looked upon Zanzibar in awe, overwhelmed with amazement and pride.

Above the courtyard's stone floor, a woman's voice called out, "There is a lion in the city! There is a lion in the city!"

Wooden shutters drummed open against the surrounding walls. Stunned mumblings and cries of surprise rose up, sounding like the chattering of a flock of frightened birds taking flight.

"What sorcery is this?" the water buffalo–man hissed. "What evil have you brought, beggar?"

But Teimbaka neither heard the words of the water buffalo–man nor the cries of the people above, for he had been swept into the flaming gaze of Zanzibar, and now wandered in a realm between what is possible and what is thought not to be so.


*He walked between fires that raged along both banks of a river. Zanzibar scampered ahead of him. Looking up, he saw a great rock looming—a single, mountainous stone rising up from the river of sand. A figure lay atop it. Snakes slithered near the rock, with heads of white attached to bodies of shimmering black.*

*Zanzibar growled and looked to the sky. Dark angels were descending, black wings fluttering, their hollow eyes fixed upon the figure that lay atop the rock, the body robed in scarlet and white.*

*A lion roared.*

*Teimbaka looked to Zanzibar, but she was no longer there. In her place stood a lion from his past, its side disfigured by a jagged scar, its chest marked by the gaping hole where his spear had lanced its heart.*

*A pack of hyenas emerged from behind the stone, cackling as they stalked, hooting to each other as the person within the robes began to stir.*

*A gargantuan spirit bull elephant came crashing through the flames. Embers burst outward, showering the mountainous stone with fiery ash.*

*"Teimbaka!" Claire screamed out his name from the pinnacle of the rock, her hand extended.*

*"Claire!" Teimbaka cried.*

*Zanzibar leapt upon his shoulder.*

*"What must I do to protect her? What beast must I fight?" he asked, gazing into her flame-yellow eyes.*

*A calm spread through him as the baby spirit elephant appeared out of the fiery ash and took hold of his hand with the tip of her trunk. Together, they started toward Claire.*


The water buffalo–man blocked his path.

"Where is the lion?" a woman called out from a window above. "I see no lion!"

"Only a beggar and a cat!" a man shouted with a mocking laugh. "And Susenyo's henchman caught in between!"

A chorus of laughter echoed against the walls of the cobblestone courtyard.

"You and your cat shall not leave this alley," the water buffalo–man snarled. "No man or beast shall make me a fool." Incensed by the taunts, the water buffalo-man struck, lifting Teimbaka up by his neck and hurling him against the alley wall.

His breath knocked out of him, his body throbbing with pain, Teimbaka struggled to his feet. He looked to Zanzibar, hoping that she would help.

The water buffalo–man moved toward him.

Zanzibar slipped through the legs of the huge man and headed out of the courtyard to the alley beyond. Stopping briefly, she looked into Teimbaka's eyes. And then, with a flash of flame and ivory, she was gone.

"Zanzibar!" he cried.

A rock-like fist crashed against his skull, sending him spiraling down the alley like a feather caught in a strong gust of wind.

"These walls will be your coffin," the water buffalo–man snorted, stalking toward him, his face twisted with anger.

"Roar!" someone jeered from above. "Become a lion!" another chided. "At least put up a fight!" a third laughed.

The howling voices reached him as if they were a pack of hyenas lusting for a kill.

*She appeared before him, her expression fearful. Once more she reached out to him. The dark angels hovered nearby. A hyena leapt from the sand to the low-hanging ledge of stone, the serpents striking at the air beneath its paws. Tears began to fall, one by one, a slow parade of sadness sliding down the sides of her cheeks. He whispered her name: "Claire." The hyena laughed. A serpent bit down on the ledge of stone and hoisted its slithering body up.*

"No!" he wailed. "No!"

The courtyard seemed to burst as the roar of the *negusa negast* was unleashed, a terrible paralyzing scream that made the onlookers above close and latch their shutters and run to place their shoulders against their doors.

Half out of his mind, Teimbaka shredded the shamma from his body, his fingers tearing at the jagged scars etched across his chest. Drawing blood from his wounds, he loosed a torturous cry, his shriek melding with the death roar of a lion. In the eerie silence that fell over the courtyard, he watched the blood of the lion pool with his own.

The water buffalo–man lifted Teimbaka by the throat and began to squeeze.

"This is your last—"

Filled with a lion's fury, Teimbaka raked his fingers across the man's neck, tearing at his flesh. With an inhuman strength surging through him, he drove the hulking mass backward, pushing and choking him until they both smashed into one of the wooden doors. It burst inward. Teimbaka and the water buffalo–man crashed through and fell into a murky passageway.

Overcome with a killing rage, Teimbaka gripped the man's windpipe. Squeezing and pulling, he tried to wrench it from his throat. Little by little, the water buffalo–man began to falter. Teimbaka looked down at his contorted face. The face of Bawa was looking back at him, a twisted smile on his lips.

"Kill him," Bawa hissed. "Kill him too."

Teimbaka recoiled. A section of the floorboards erupted in a spray of splinters and dust next to the water buffalo–man's head.

"Release him! Or the next bullet—"

Still fueled by the lion's spirit, Teimbaka leapt away from the hulk beneath him. Tumbling sideways and then rolling to his feet, he reached the open courtyard as the next bullet ricocheted on the cobblestones beneath him. Sprinting for the alley, he bounded into the entrance and ran, leaving his kebero and the child's prayer book behind.

*

AFTER HIDING ALL day and through the first part of the night, Teimbaka returned to the alley and slowly made his way to the courtyard. Having clothed himself in a stolen black shamma, he kept to the shadows to hide his approach. When he came to the alley's end, the kebero was waiting for him, standing upright next to one of the middle doors.

Eyeing the darkened corners of the enclosure, he listened for the soft movement of feet within them. Closing his eyes, he sniffed the air, searching for any trace of lavender. Satisfied that he was alone, he quietly stepped across the cobblestones and placed his hands atop his drum.

"Lion of Djibouti."

The dull, metallic muzzle of a handgun emerged from the dark slit of an opening door.

"You will make no sudden movements; understood? The bullet is quicker and more deadly than even *negusa negast.*"

"Will you not join me, Adiam? Will you not retrieve your washnit, so that our music might rekindle the past?"

"What? Who? Teimbaka?"

Adiam slipped through the crack of the open door. Teimbaka backed away with his arms raised as the weapon Adiam held motioned for him to do.

"I cannot believe this. Remove your hood so I may look upon the hunter, the mystical Lion of Djibouti."

"Will you kill me, Adiam, if I refuse?"

"Even faces from other times must be secured," he explained without apology. "The city and our business dictates this, you see. It is not unlike the jungle of your youth, Teimbaka. Threats take many forms. Your sudden presence in this alley has sparked many questions, to say the least. Are you the hunter once again? Or, perhaps, the hunted?"

Teimbaka took stock of the man before him, trying to separate what Adiam once was and what he had become. No longer a poorly dressed, poorly fed azmari living from one handout to the next, Adiam now boasted a fleshy roll of skin which hung above a richly colored silken tie, and a portly stomach which he took great gains to hide by fastening the three front buttons of the expensive western suit coat he wore.

Teimbaka moved to lower the folds of his shamma from his head.

"Be not sudden with your movements, my old friend. You have not said which you are, the hunter or the prey."

"As it has always been, Adiam," he replied, slowly lowering the covering from his head and face, "I am both and neither."

"I must know which you are, Teimbaka," Adiam replied after an uneasy silence passed between them. "I cannot allow you to leave here until I do."

"So if you are the hunter, Adiam, what does this allow me to be?"

"Why are you here?" Adiam pressed, his tone a mixture of anger and anguish. "Why have you come? What is it you seek?"

Teimbaka stared at the unwavering gun.

"The Mother. She led me here."

Teimbaka paused, his brow creasing into a deep furrow as he sifted through his thoughts.

"Two years have I been here. I did not know why, until," he glanced at the doorway that had been repaired, "yesterday."

He saw the gun being raised to his heart.

"Susenyo, do you remember him?" Adiam asked in a hushed voice. "He feels you are a demon unleashed to devour him. There is a price already on your head. The Lion of Djibouti. You are to be killed, Teimbaka, killed."

"Was it not so long ago that you saw him as a beast of the darkness? And now you do his bidding?" said Teimbaka. "Your sister—were you ever able to find her?"

Adiam lowered the gun slowly, in increments, following its descent with haggard eyes.

"She was … no longer?" Teimbaka asked in a whisper of respect.

"If it had only been so," Adiam muttered.

Adiam holstered the gun inside his suit coat.

"The day I— When she—"

He moved away from the door and walked across the courtyard.

"Who I found, what I found, was not my sister," he managed to say, grunting the final phrase. "Better that she had been dead, as I had prayed."

His laughter was bitter, hollow.

"I prayed that she would have died ten years before, or twenty, or even the day before I found her."

He fell silent then, staring, it seemed to Teimbaka, into a dark spot on a wall.

"Does she still live?"

"No," he was quick to say, without a trace of sadness in his voice. "She no longer suffers the sins of this—" he left off, casting his gaze downward. "She was dead. What I had held her to be when we were children no longer existed. I could do nothing," he said, speaking as though he had repeated the same phrase to himself a thousand times over. "There was nothing left to comfort."

The kebero spoke soothingly as Teimbaka touched out a beat that sought to relieve the bitterness of Adiam's words. The old instrument, giving forth a sweet and tender timbre, echoed along the walls and cobblestones in a patter of shifting, hypnotic rhythm.

"Drum man," Adiam quietly said with a nod of his head. "Lion of Djibouti. What more is there of you that I do not know?"

The drum kept on.

"So long ago does it seem," Adiam whispered, enraptured by the beat. "If it were only—"

"What madness?"

The distinctive sliding click of an automatic weapon being primed to fire accompanied the voice of Susenyo.

"Adiam? What stupidity has befallen you?"

"The years have not softened your scorn, Susenyo." Teimbaka stepped forward. Susenyo's eyes narrowed.

"It is he," stated the voice of the water buffalo–man from the depths behind the door where Susenyo stood. "It is the lion, Master. He is the lion."

The water buffalo–man appeared as a dark silhouette behind Susenyo's shoulder. Teimbaka nodded a greeting, but the man would not meet his gaze.

"Bring him," Susenyo commanded. "Shoot him if he resists."

Susenyo slipped back into the doorway, the pungent scent of lavender lingering where he had stood. The water buffalo–man stepped out into the courtyard, the Uzi clutched between his massive hands looking like a toy.

He stared at Teimbaka, uncertain, nervous.

"There is no reason for your fear," Teimbaka told him. "I am but a man like yourself."

The water buffalo–man said nothing in return. The Uzi beckoned Teimbaka inside. He took a step toward the door, then hesitated.

"Go. Enter. Go," the water buffalo–man ordered, shoving the short muzzle of the Uzi into his lower back. "Now."

Teimbaka stepped through the doorway.

He stood at the front of an arched entranceway of stone, some ten feet in length, a soft, semi-transparent curtain hanging halfway through it. Pressed to continue by the impatient grunts behind him, he parted the curtain and walked ahead. When he reached a second curtain of deep-red velvet, he stopped.

"Go."

Teimbaka pulled the heavy curtain aside and stepped through.

He found himself in a cavernous, oblong, rock-hewn room, the walls of which were stacked high with bolts of brightly colored silk and exquisitely detailed rugs. Along the floor, basking under the glare of industrial lights, crates of all sizes and shapes were stacked in neat rows. Some were open. These, he saw, held an assortment of weapons and artwork and an array of gold and jewels that dazzled the eye. But what made him stagger and gasp was the cache of tusks he saw piled from floor to ceiling at the far end of the room. The mountain of ivory was a testament to the deaths of many hundreds of elephants. His heart sank into despair.

"Spirit elephants," he said. "What have they done to you?"

"You are one of the few outsiders to have ever laid eyes on this room, Teimbaka. Is it not a wonder to behold?"

Adiam pushed by the water buffalo–man and swept his arm across the expanse of the room to include each and every item it contained.

"Everything one dreams of having is here," he gushed, his face beaming with pride. "And if it is not, then we will get it for you." He looked at Teimbaka and winked. "For a price, of course," he laughed. "A very high price."

"Yes!" Susenyo heartily agreed as he appeared in the room with two other Uzi-toting men. They, like Adiam, were dressed in sand-colored, western-style suits with white shirts and brightly colored ties. "Anything for a price! Anything!" he emphasized. "Have you not found this to be true in your lifetime, stranger?"

"Stranger? Do you not know me, Susenyo?"

"Oh, I am certain that I do," he quickly said, waving his fleshy hands about in a gesture of mock apology. "Or I did. I must have, at one time, yes? Seeing that, as you say, my scorn has not—how did you say it—*softened* through the years?" He added, giving Teimbaka a cursory glance, "But what does it matter? I have known many in my time. And none seem to hold a place in my memory."

Susenyo smoothed the lapels of his dark blue suit and fiddled with the half-dozen gold chains hanging loosely about his neck. Contentedly, his eyes drank in the riches around him.

"And your son?" Teimbaka inquired. "What of Yolyos? I do not see him. Is he with you still?"

"Oh, quite dead," he casually replied, waving the question off as though it were but a speck of dust on the shoulder of his suit. "Stupid at birth, stupid at death."

He shrugged.

"What could one expect otherwise? Idiot hanged himself in jail the day before he was—by way of a very substantial bribe, I might add—to be released. Ah well, stupid to the end," he sighed. "But he did save me from paying. I did thank him for that at his funeral."

In the silence that ensued, John entered the room from a doorway that Teimbaka had not noticed, hidden as it was behind an intricately patterned Persian rug that was hanging on a wall. John's face showed only a troubled doubt as he set his eyes upon Teimbaka.

"How is it you would like to die, Lion of Djibouti?" Susenyo asked in a pleasant manner.

"In peace," Teimbaka responded. "With the Mother's blessing."

"I am afraid that is not a choice I am prepared to offer you," he replied with the faintest of smiles. "Though, you may—"

"There is a woman here, a woman brought by him," Teimbaka said, nodding at John. "I would see her now."

Susenyo's face flickered with an array of different expressions before settling on a depraved grin.

"She is important to you? Your heart is tied to her, perhaps?"

"I had thought her dead. We once shared—" he fell silent, not certain what words to say.

Susenyo furrowed his brow for a moment, studying Teimbaka's face.

"Then you must see her! For her beauty brings pleasure to all who have been blessed by her smooth, white skin! A reunion there will be! A reunion!"

Teimbaka looked at each man in the room, searching for clues that might explain Susenyo's perplexing words. But none would meet his eyes, save John. And in his, Teimbaka saw, there was nothing but a blankness that sent a chill up his spine.

"Show him the woman, Adiam. Take him to her room of ..." he chuckled, "pleasure."

"No! She is mine! She is mine!"

John lunged toward Susenyo, his face twisted in a fit of rage. At a nod from Susenyo, the water buffalo–man smashed John's forehead with the butt of his Uzi, sending him to floor.

John, blood seeping from his head, struggled to get to his hands and knees. Incoherent, he crawled in several directions before finally coming to rest at the base of one of the rugs stacked against a wall.

"Not the rug, idiot! Off the rug!" Susenyo yelled, kicking John in the side until he scrambled away from it.

"If you have spoiled that treasure with one drop of your worthless blood," Susenyo glared at the man-child, "I will—!"

The anger on the obese features of Susenyo abruptly vanished, changing to a devilish glee that seemed no less threatening.

"I will sell your precious Claire to one who has coveted her white skin for some time. Surely you know of whom I speak, John," he taunted. "The one they call the Red Terror."

Although stunned and in pain, John instantly clutched his temples as if they had been skewered by a thin rod of hot steel. His face quivering uncontrollably, tears suddenly streaming from his eyes, he whimpered with the tormented spirit of broken heart, as though he had been made to watch his true love thrown into a pit of ravenous wild dogs.

When Susenyo spoke of the Red Terror, Teimbaka saw scores of hollow-eyed, starving, skeletal children. A gathering of withered, broken, blood-drenched orphans, all crying for survival. Their voices swelled inside his head until he could not contain them any longer.

"Gunstard!" he bellowed.

The mountain of ivory trembled with his voice, each tusk seeming to quiver before a few at the top came tumbling to the floor.

"You know of him?" Adiam asked, his voice hushed and fearful.

Susenyo looked at Teimbaka as if seeing him anew. His eyes narrowed as he contemplated who—or what—the man really was.

The children in Teimbaka's head pleaded for him to help.

"It would seem that you are of the same blackness from which he was dredged, Susenyo."

"Take him, Adiam! Take him to his beloved whore! Look upon her, oh great lion! Let *her* tell you what she has become! Then come back to me and dare to speak!" Susenyo glared at Teimbaka, his face quivering with rage. "If there are words left for you to say," he hissed.

"Take me, Adiam."

"Yes, take him, Adiam," Susenyo tersely ordered. "So we can end this."

The crying children clamored for Teimbaka to hurry.

"Show me," he told Adiam.

Adiam led Teimbaka out of the room through another passageway that was hidden behind several bolts of silk. Entering an antechamber heady with the fragrance of myrrh, Adiam took Teimbaka down a narrow hallway that ended at a thick door of dark polished wood with gold-plated fittings, secured from the outside by a long, thick sliding bolt. Adiam reached to slide the bolt when Teimbaka gently stayed his hand.

"Before you enter," Adiam started to say.

Teimbaka shook his head and slipped the bolt from its mooring.

The children in his head wailed.

"She will not be as you remember," Adiam warned as Teimbaka pulled the door open and stepped through.

"He has made her—"

Teimbaka pushed the door shut, blocking out the words Adiam would have him hear.

Teimbaka had not yet turned around before the children inside his head became a choir of somber pleas, each voice resonating with an infinite sadness that tugged at the frayed edges of his spirit. Seeing Claire, he was shamed to tears. He turned his face and averted his eyes so he would not have to see what he could hardly bear to look upon.

She was asleep, lying on a circular bed of white silk sheets, her head resting on a red satin pillow. A bare leg, slender and milky white, was exposed below her waist. A soft, rounded shoulder, a flawless, supple arm, and a hint of a breast showed above the sheet that was draped across her naked body.

Taking a step closer, he could see that her face had been decorated. Her cheeks had been tinted with a dusting of rose-petal pink, her eyes adorned with thin lines of black that highlighted the pale shade of blue that had been painted on her lids.

Staring at her, he felt a sudden foreboding. The children in his head whispered some unintelligible warning, their voices unnerving and confused.

Shivering with the sensation of a cold wind wrapping around his feet, he shifted uncomfortably, raising a hand toward Claire as if he was seeking her help. Slowly, the coldness slithered higher, growing stronger as it twisted around his legs. When it wound about his chest, his breathing became labored, his neck constricting from an icy pressure he could not see.

The Serpent raised its milky head, baring its fangs, while the upper coils of its shimmering, black body rose away from his chin. The deep orange of its flaming eyes gazed into his.

"She is mine," it hissed with a flickering tongue.

Fear-struck, Teimbaka staggered back, recoiling from the creature. The stench of sulfur and the taste of his own rank bile made him gag.

"It cannot have her!" the children screamed. "Save her! Fight for her, Teimbaka! You must fight!"

Taken off-guard by the wailing voices, the Serpent renewed its death grip on Teimbaka with a fury. The coils around his neck tightened until he began to choke.

"You cannot have her!" they shouted. "Release her!"

The Serpent hissed at the clamor, furious at the defiance the voices carried. Poking and thrusting, feigning a strike, the Serpent sought an opening for a quick end.

"She is mine," it proclaimed. "As will he be," it hissed.

"Take me instead!" cried a girl, her voice no more than a whisper.

Teimbaka saw her, a crawling tangle of arms and legs, her spine sliced in two.

"No, me!" shouted a boy no more than three, his side shorn away.

"Take us all!" the voices of the children shouted in unison, an orange light illuminating their terrified faces. "Take us all!"

The Serpent eyed Teimbaka coldly, its head swaying from one of Teimbaka's ears to the other. It studied the openings of his nose and examined the pupils of his eyes, as if it was deciding if there was a clever way inside, an easy way, to reach the voices that were tempting him.

Momentarily resting its white head on Teimbaka's shoulder, the Serpent relaxed its constricting coils and let its eyes drift slowly closed. And then, in a blur, it attacked.

Striking at Teimbaka with fangs extended, it angled its head so they might tear open Teimbaka's eyes. Three times it struck at him. Three times it failed, each failure driving it further into madness. Hissing with rage, the Serpent tightened its coils again. Teimbaka gasped for air.

"Wait!" the children shouted. "We will come out! We will come to you!"

*The Serpent wavered, the flaming, vertical pupil in the middle of its orange eyes widening as it relaxed.*

*"If you deceive … " it hissed.*

*"Release him and we will step into your waiting jaws."*

Teimbaka placed his hands over his mouth, hoping to silence the children. For although he had witnessed and heard all that had transpired between the Serpent and the souls of the children that had taken refuge inside of him, he felt powerless to act, to defend them as he would want.

*One by one, the souls of the children left the haven they had found within him. Those that Peter Gunstard had massacred stood quietly, awaiting their fate, as did those who had passed through the house with walls, their souls having drifted to Teimbaka after he had buried each of their bodies. A multitude they became when they were all gathered, the room where Claire now lay barely able to contain their number.*

*Though their innocent eyes reflected what was about to befall them, the children stood fast, tiny hands joined firmly together, their bond aglow with a golden white light.*

*"Come, Serpent," they said. "Release the ones you covet. We are ready."*

*The Serpent slowly unraveled, leaving Teimbaka's neck to slither around the room and peer into each child's face.*

*Teimbaka sagged to his knees as one weary of battle might do.*

*"Teimbaka," they called out. "Rise up. Rise up and witness our sacrifice. Rise and be strong so that this may never come to pass again."*

*Teimbaka seemed not to hear.*

*"Rise up, Teimbaka!" the children cried. "Lift her from this pit!"*

*Teimbaka looked to the children in despair, struggling to find his strength, blinking back the water welling in his eyes so that he might find a way for them to survive.*

*The seemingly endless black Serpent hissed impatiently and then opened its jaws. The closest child let go of the hand it held and stepped into the Serpent's waiting mouth. Teimbaka shuddered.*

*"No more!" he shouted.*

*Teimbaka's voice having left his throat as a tortured whisper, the Serpent gave him only the briefest of glances before gnashing its jaws and sliding to the next child in line.*

*Greedily, the Serpent moved from one child to the next, swallowing them whole, gorging itself until its body was swollen to a grotesque obesity. And as the last child crawled calmly toward damnation, she looked at Teimbaka and said, "Blessed are you, Teimbaka. Blessed are you who walks with the spirits."*

*Nodding to Claire, she added, "Save her. Reclaim the one who belongs to both the Mother and the Father."*

*The Serpent rose up and plucked the girl where she knelt, devouring her before Teimbaka could respond.*

*Tears of sorrow flowed down his cheeks, his body heaving in spasms of sickened disbelief, his heart darkened by all he had seen. And in his state of grieving, while his strength faltered and paled, the Serpent slithered to where Claire was lying, the wicked flame in its eyes burning brighter.*

*"No!" He screamed, leaping to Claire's side. "You will not take her!"*

*The eyes of the Serpent turned upon him, holding him spellbound. Rising above him, growing in magnitude until its coils filled the room, the one of darkness released a suffocating cloud of sulfur from its jaws while flames spawned from hell spewed forth from the pupils of its eyes.*

*Teimbaka gazed upon the beast unafraid, his flesh protected by a force that covered him in a shield of shimmering, golden white light. Grasping the Serpent by the neck, he yanked it roughly down until their eyes met.*

*"We do not fear you!" he roared.*

*The flames within the Serpent's pupils faltered.*

*"Leave this place and do not return!"*

*The Serpent opened its jaws to show Teimbaka the souls that now rested within its bowels. And then, in flash of fiery, blinding light, the room reverted to what it had been when he had first entered. In the stillness that ensued, he roused himself from what others would say to him was a dream.*

"Claire," he whispered.

Her half-naked, unmoving form wounded him deeply. And as he gazed upon her in sorrow, looking anew at her body, he saw what he had been too blind to see before. Ugly, red bumps and broken, reddish-blue veins disfigured her inner arms as well as the milky skin of her inner thighs. Bruises and cuts of various shapes and sizes ringed her ankles and wrists, and along her backside, near her buttocks where the fabric of the sheet left her bare, he saw jagged scratch marks.

Tenderly, he placed a finger against her chin.

"Claire," he whispered.

When she did not stir, he gently raised the lid of her eye. There, where had once shone the joy of the day, where the soft brown and amber speckles of her iris had radiated with hope and faith, he saw a lifeless void, a dull, bloodshot orb that held no hint of what he remembered.

He lifted Claire into his arms and held her close to his chest, trembling with an emotion that lay somewhere between rage and heartbreak. Looking down into her face, he was tempted to cry. But the echo of the little girl's parting words reverberated in his head.

Covering her as best he could with the sheet from the bed, he moved quickly to the door. Pulling it open, he carried Claire across the threshold.


"No!" Adiam shouted. "Teimbaka, you must not."

Looking anxiously behind him, Adiam blocked Teimbaka from going any farther.

"If you wish it to be so," Teimbaka replied, holding Claire out for Adiam to receive, "then take her, Adiam. Take her back to the misery of that room."

Adiam swallowed nervously, his eyes darting everywhere at once.

"Susenyo will—"

"Is this not your sister, Adiam?" Teimbaka calmly asked of him. "Should I pray that she is dead too? What have you done to her? To what place did you condemn her spirit?"

Unable to reply, Adiam could only look upon Claire with an open mouth and a lost expression.

"But she is not yet lost, Adiam. She is in need. If she were your sister, would you deny her the chance to live?"

"I," Adiam began, harshly wiping at his eyes, "it is too late. I do not know how."

Teimbaka smiled.

"Then I shall show you," he said.


"John."

The man-child stirred at the saying of his name, jumping to his feet at the sight of Claire. But seeing her in another man's arms stirred the jealousy that bubbled inside him, and in a blur, he flew toward Teimbaka, his lips curled into a snarl.

Susenyo laughed.

"Stay!" Teimbaka commanded.

A strong gust of wind burst against the wooden doors out in the courtyard. The red velvet curtain fluttered in the currents that slipped through the cracks.

John stopped, his face a mass of confusion.

"See me, John. Do you not know me?"

"He sees only lust!" Susenyo bellowed. "Lust and the needle are their bond, you see. It is a shackle I have given them both to wear."

John eyed Claire hungrily.

"John, remember. John, do you remember yourself?"

John's attention swayed between Claire's body and the eyes of Teimbaka.

"A simple shamma, John. For Sister Lady," he told him, lifting Claire a little higher in his arms.

"Sister Lady?" John mumbled, confused.

"Yes, John, Sister Lady. Do you remember?"

John furrowed his brow and stared at Claire's face. And then, in an instant, he was gone, scampering between the rows of crates before anyone could stop him.

"I tire of this," Susenyo interjected, sounding utterly bored. "Shoot him, Adiam. After all, it is you who has allowed him to bring the whore this far."

Adiam stepped out from behind Teimbaka, the Beretta held loosely in his hand.

"I— I can't," he stammered.

"Very well," Susenyo sighed with a shrug of his shoulders. "Kill them all," he instructed the water buffalo–man and the two other men who carried Uzis. "And take the carcasses to the dock so the fishermen can cut their livers out for bait."

Upon Susenyo's final word, the doors rattled and shook, the wood groaning and creaking to the point of breaking. As all were drawn to the commotion, the tremendous roar of a lion rushed down the hallway, ripping the velvet curtain from its anchors.

"The lion!" the water buffalo–man cried. "It returns to him! It is a sign! It is a sign!"

"Oh, stupid oaf, perhaps you have outlived your usefulness as well."

Grabbing the Uzi from the man's hands, Susenyo turned the weapon on Teimbaka.

"Back to your mother you go," he mocked.

The explosion of the gunshot was deafening, the bullet itself nothing but a blur. Susenyo stepped forward and then stopped. He placed a hand to his face, disbelieving of the blood that was pouring out of the center of his skull. In the next instant, he was dead, falling to the floor with a thud.

"Wait, Akmir!" Adiam shouted, pointing the smoldering Beretta at the man before he could raise his Uzi. "A new partnership, yes?" he hurried to say. "A new arrangement that would bring us all an equal share?"

Akmir gave Adiam a calculating stare before pointing the muzzle of his Uzi to the ground.

"And what say the two of you, Bin'ka and Amare?"

The water buffalo–man stared at Teimbaka with fear in his eyes.

"The lion, will you protect me from him?" he asked, looking at Teimbaka and then toward the hallway where the curtain had been torn away.

"Need we fear you, Lion of Djibouti?" Adiam probed, the Beretta still held waist-high.

Teimbaka looked at Claire and then at Susenyo's dead body.

"I did not come as the hunter, Adiam. I wish only to take her away from this …" he looked around the room, "place where evil resides."

"It is decided then," Adiam proclaimed, nodding to Akmir, Amare, and Bin'ka. "Go now, Teimbaka. Go before we change our minds."

As John returned with a plain white shamma in his arms, Teimbaka looked to Adiam, and then to the mountain of tusks.

"The ivory. You must stop trading in it."

"It is one of our most valued commodities," Akmir countered. "And no concern of yours," he added, lifting his Uzi.

"It is the Serpent's market you deal in, and its price is all-consuming."

Akmir met his gaze with a cold, unforgiving stare.

"Perhaps Adiam is wrong to allow you to leave."

A cold wind howled through the hallway where the velvet curtain had hung. It filled the treasure room with a swirling, icy chill. Bin'ka bent and took the Uzi from Susenyo's hand and pointed it toward Akmir.

"Do not bring the lion to life," he warned. "Let them go."

"Do not misjudge those of the Mother," Teimbaka stated, looking directly at Adiam. "Her children will not endure wrong forever."

With a final look to the mountain of tusks, he said to John, "Come, John. Bring me the shamma."

John began to tremble as he approached Teimbaka. He held the plain cotton robe out before him.

"I can't leave," he whimpered. "This is our place," he wept, his fingers trembling in the air just above Claire's body.

It was then that Teimbaka saw the multitude of raised, red-tinged bumps running along John's forearms.

Teimbaka gave Adiam a harsh glance.

"They are both slaves to it," Adiam told him, looking to Susenyo. "They are both addicts, Teimbaka. It will be—"

"She is mine!" John screamed, his face breaking out in sweat. "She can't leave!"

"We go, John," Teimbaka replied, undeterred. "You are of the Mother. She will help you."

John's body shook, then seemed to crumble inward. Whimpering again, he wrapped his arms around his body in an effort to ward off the chills.

"This place has stolen her," Teimbaka told him as he looked to Claire. "Come, John. I must get her away from here."

"Where will you go, Lion of Djibouti?" Bin'ka asked as Teimbaka carried Claire from the treasure room.

Teimbaka looked back at the water buffalo–man and said, "Where her spirit waits."

*

ANZIBAR'S EYES GLITTERED with sprinkles of ivory and gold, the radiance of the light illuminating the gray fur and twisting whiskers of her face.

She directed a pointed *meow*, a sign of her impatience, at Teimbaka. He, with Claire in his arms and John shuffling on his damaged feet, struggled to keep pace with her as she led them out of the city proper to the open landscape beyond.

Where the final clusters of homes gave way to rock-strewn hills and arid swaths of flatlands, Zanzibar leapt atop a dilapidated wall made of stones and waited for Teimbaka to approach.

After setting Claire down with care, leaning her against the rocks, Teimbaka placed a hand upon Zanzibar's head as the last twinkling of the stars gave way to the rising sun.

"Keep you safe, Zanzibar," he said with great affection. "If there is ever a way to repay what you have done …"

Zanzibar purred and rubbed her face against Teimbaka's hand.

"Why do we stop?" John tersely demanded. "Who are you talking to?"

"Zanzibar," Teimbaka replied, lifting his hand so John could see.

"There is nothing there."

Zanzibar stretched her neck into Teimbaka's palm.

"Keep you safe," he told her, a touch of sadness in his eyes.

Zanzibar leapt down from the wall and headed back toward Djibouti.

"I am in your debt," he called after her.

"You are taken by madness," John spat.

Wearily, Teimbaka lifted Claire into his arms and started off.

"We must stay!" John yelled, grabbing hold of Teimbaka's shoulder.

From somewhere in the hills around them came the roar of a lion.

John cowered in fear.

Teimbaka smiled and walked on.


Not long after sunrise had given way to the full of the morning, Claire awoke in distress. Her body was feverish, her stomach nauseated, her muscles cramped with painful chills. Teimbaka took her to the shade of an acacia tree and gently laid her to the ground.

"We must go back," John whined, clutching his stomach.

It was then that Teimbaka realized that John was also feeling the effects of the heroin withdrawal.

He looked at both of them with sadness, uncertain of what he could do. They had not brought food or water or medicine. He looked back toward Djibouti.

"She is mine," John whimpered, his fists clenching open and closed. "We must go back."

Seeing Teimbaka's stony, unrelenting expression, he looked longingly at Claire for a time before turning his gaze toward Djibouti. Without a word, he loped off and headed back the way they had come.


When Claire opened her eyes, Teimbaka recoiled, for where he had expected to see gratitude, there was hate; bitterness where he had hoped to find faith; anger where he wanted compassion to be. But as frightening as the feelings she conveyed were, they were nothing compared to the vileness that spewed from her mouth. Her filthy, raging curses made him shudder.

As the hours passed and he listened to and looked upon the vulgarity she had become, he became uncertain. Was the heroin stronger than his will? he wondered. Had taking her from Djibouti condemned her to a slow and torturous death?

"Courage," the spirit children whispered. "Courage."

Heeding their words, when Claire was given to fever, he fanned her and told her soothing tales of the spirit elephants and the glittering lake near the plain of gold. When she was given to chills, he held her close and placed the small silver cross he carried to her lips. When her mood turned violent and wild, with her fists and legs striking out against him, he absorbed all her blows without rancor, accepting them as penance for the years she had suffered. And when her body was wracked with convulsions, gagging on dry air or heaving forth waves of vomit, he held her close and cleansed her, using his own teardrops to moisten the sleeves of his shamma and wipe her face.

In this way—with Teimbaka offering what little comfort he could, and Claire suffering the demons of the heroin that Susenyo had made her a slave to—the first day of Claire's freedom passed into night, and then back again to a different day.

Near the end of the second day, the two had succumbed to the ordeal of her withdrawal. Exhausted and dehydrated, they were close to delirium. Her body twitching and twisting, Claire drifted into a coma. Unknowingly, Teimbaka fell asleep, unable to keep his vigil.


"Teimbaka," a calm voice said as a gentle hand nudged his shoulder. "We have come."

Confused and disoriented, Teimbaka could only nod.

"Mary," the man said, beckoning someone to step closer.

Squinting at the hooded face peering down at him, Teimbaka struggled to comprehend what he was seeing. For although it had been a score of years since he had last looked upon her, the woman looking down at him seemed not to have aged since they had met on the side road leading to Nairobi.

"It is she," Mary said to him with a smile, her hazel eyes wandering to where Claire lay. "We will tend to her needs."

Mary turned as a young boy appeared at her side.

"I am here, Mother," the boy said in a voice that seemed ageless.

"I— I know you," Teimbaka stammered.

Mary placed a finger to his parched lips.

"It is time," the child said.

Teimbaka stared at the boy, unable to respond.

"Come, Teimbaka, take hold of my hand, and we will walk," the man who had awakened him suggested.

When Teimbaka hesitated, looking toward Claire with concern, the man said, "We will not go far. She will come to no harm."

They had only taken a few steps when the man offered him water from the goatskin pouch that he carried about his neck.

Teimbaka drank deeply.

"Forgive me. I drink more than my share."

"There is enough for all, Teimbaka."

"How is it you know my name?"

"Was it not you, yourself, who told us?" the man replied. "I had wondered if we would meet again."

The anguish in the boy's scream shot a gripping fear into Teimbaka, causing him to shudder and swoon. Grabbing hold of his arm, the man steadied him.

"Behold," he said, nodding to the acacia tree.

The boy was on his knees, Claire's hands held tightly in his own. Kneeling across from him, Mary had unwound Claire's shamma to reveal her nakedness, her fingers tracing the track marks on her arms and inner thighs. She looked into the eyes of the boy as she touched each one; the boy would nod, then gasp and scream. Mary kept her fingers in place until each sore disappeared.

"But how?"

"There is no need to speak, Teimbaka. It is as the children have asked."

"The children?" Teimbaka questioned, perplexed. "You know of the spirit children?"

The wind stirred, carrying the faint ringing of a bell. The man looked to the sound and nodded.

From beneath the acacia tree, Mary rose and walked toward them.

"She is weak, Teimbaka, in both body and spirit. She will need you."

"How is it—what the boy and you did?"

"Where will you take her?" Mary asked.

The jingle of a small bell sounded from the western hills.

"Back to the Mother."

"You will need sustenance, then. Husband, please, what bread and water we can give," she said.

With a simple nod, the man took a round of *injera* from his shoulder satchel and gave it to Teimbaka.

"Keep the goatskin and what water remains," he told him. "Perhaps, if you are sparing, it will last."

"I am indebted to you," Teimbaka replied with a slight bowing of his head. "And to your wife," he added, turning to address her.

But Mary was no longer standing where she had been, having walked past the acacia tree toward the hills beyond.

"Be strong and have courage, Teimbaka," the man told him as he moved off to follow his wife.

"I will come in a moment, Joseph," the boy said to him. "You need not wait."

Joseph nodded and continued on, briefly pausing to look upon Claire as the child made his last adjustments to the folds of the shamma around her head.

Rising, the child approached Teimbaka.

As though earth and sky were joined in celebration, the western horizon silently exploded into varying hues of violet and fire, the wisps of clouds caught in between coated in crimson and a shining gold. It was a glorious spectacle that both the boy and he gazed upon in awe.

"Are they not beautiful when they are one?" the boy asked, taking hold of Teimbaka's hand as though they had watched many such sunsets together.

"So brief it is," Teimbaka lamented with a nod.

"It is forever, passing over this world and then out into heaven."

"And then where?" Teimbaka whimsically inquired, squeezing the boy's hand.

"To a realm not known to those of this world," the child told him.

Losing themselves in the glory stretched out before them, they fell silent, content to share a moment of beauty that words could not describe. And as the first stars began to appear and the sky paled to muted shades of rust and slate, Claire began to stir.

"Go to her now. This night you shall both need comfort. For what is yet to come to pass—"

"What is it you see?" Teimbaka asked of the boy when he did not continue.

A flash of gold and ivory peeked out from the edge of his robe before the child turned his head away.

"What are you called?"

Even before Teimbaka asked, the boy had already released his hand and had drifted away.

*

"KILL ME."

Her voice was utterly cold and devoid of feeling.

Teimbaka roused himself from sleep and pulled his head back so there would be room between their faces.

"I am sin. Kill me."

"I— cannot." He sought some semblance of what she had once been. "You are—"

"Don't!"

He trembled, taken aback by her rage.

"Do not," she hissed. "Do not say that word." Overcome with a sudden fit of sobbing, Claire covered her face and turned away.

Teimbaka held his arms out toward her, but then let them fall away. Uncertain, he sat next to her, listening to her sobs, watching her body shake. Drifting back through his memories, he recalled all they had been through. In the end, he was left to wonder how they had come to be huddling next to a single acacia tree on the fringes of the Ethiopian wastelands.

When he offered her bread and water, she refused them. When he repeated his attempts, she met each one with a determined quiet. Giving up, he hung his head. In that moment, sounds found their way into his consciousness. He scrambled to his feet.

"Come, Claire!" he exclaimed with utter joy, slipping his arms beneath her to lift her. "I have heard them! We must go!"

Though she would not look at him or speak, Claire made no attempt to struggle. Walking as though she had foreseen that she was embarking on her final journey, she dutifully followed, her gait slow and plodding. To Teimbaka's dismay, she kept silent throughout the days and nights that followed. At times, he was tempted to turn back to Djibouti. But when Claire finally began to accept food and water, hope kept him going.

On the morning of the seventh day, they stared out across the barren wasteland of the Danakil plain. It was as if some cruel hoax was being played upon them. As they came face-to-face with the prospect of crossing over searing deserts, beds of sulfur, and bubbling volcanoes, the path forward appeared suddenly daunting, if not nearly impossible.

"Must this be the way?" Teimbaka asked, his faced filled with doubt.

Claire looked out upon the desolate terrain and smiled grimly.

"Fitting that this shall be the place of my death."

"Death is not why we are here," he told her, hesitantly extending a hand to touch her cheek.

Recoiling at his advance, she quickly looked away, her gaze shifting to the desert.

"Leave me here, Teimbaka," she told him. "Leave me to my punishment."

"Our path does not end here."

"What path?" she snorted, shaking her head.

"They have brought us here. It must be that we are to cross, to follow what course they wish for us to take."

"They?"

"The spirit elephants and the bell of the goat."

Her harsh, condemning laughter was like a slap in the face.

"Go, then," she goaded him. "Go and follow the ghosts and farm animals that guide you." She giggled cruelly.

"And while you chase your precious illusions across the wastelands, please leave me to rot in the hell you have brought me to," she spat, her voice as cold as the expression in her eyes.

"You will not—" he began, but retreated under her savage glare.

Her hardened expression dared him to say more.

"You will not throw away the sacrifice that saved you," he stated. "The children's pleas will not go unanswered. You will not invoke the Serpent to return."

"What nonsense do you babble?" she blurted out, both bewildered and angry.

"Perhaps when the poison Susenyo placed within you is—"

Screaming at the abhorrent memories that the saying of Susenyo's name triggered, Claire suddenly bolted ahead with her hands cupped over her ears to block out her own shrieking. Teimbaka leapt after her, but then stopped. Slowly, as he watched her figure diminish into the desolate terrain, a smile found its way to his lips.

"The way is set," he murmured.


Hours after he started out after her, he found her white shamma discarded in the sand. After retrieving it and moving onward, he came upon her naked figure. She was lying on her side, her head tucked between her knees.

Although the day was hot, he saw that she was shivering. Her fair skin, already burned by the unforgiving sun, was slick with sweat. When he bent and laid the white cotton fabric over her, she grasped it in her fists and threw it to the side.

"You will burn without covering," he said to her, replacing the garment across her. "Even now, the sun has already injured you."

Grasping it roughly, she brought it to her face and began to weep. An instant later, she pulled the fabric away, her face a picture of ferocity.

"I will burn, then!" she screamed. "Let hell punish me for my sins!"

"Yes!" he screamed back. "As the Serpent wishes you to do! Inflict its evil upon yourself! Embrace its darkness! Smother yourself in your sins until you choke on your own wickedness!"

Teimbaka looked quickly away, seeking solace in the mountains that suddenly seemed so very far away.

"Should I not revile myself for what I have become?"

Her question caught him off guard. He wiped the tears from his eyes and looked down at her.

"I am defiled. I—" she heaved, a great sigh escaping her body, "I am a whore. A filthy whore."

"It was not you," he quickly said, bending to one knee so his voice was near to her. "It was not you."

He placed a hand atop her head. And though she shook her head so he would remove it, he kept it there and said, "You are of the Mother and the Father, a child of the two. That is what you are, Claire. You are Sister Lady. You have been blessed by both heaven and earth. Do not let the Serpent steal this from you."

"Just— Just leave me alone!"

"They see what is within you, Claire," he told her with great conviction. "You are hope."

"No!" she yelled. "There is nothing here!" She pounded her fist into her chest. "There is nothing! Nothing!"

Teimbaka stood.

"Cover yourself. We have far to go."

Defiant, she shook her head.

"It is not for you to decide. I will not have you waste the spirits of the little ones. Even now, they suffer for you."

As if she were being strangled, Claire looked up at him in anguished disbelief.

"Why must you torture me?" she demanded. "Let me be. Let me be!"

Unyielding, Teimbaka replied, "Take strength from them. Do not forsake them. It is not your pain they seek, but rather your hope and your faith."

Claire wailed against his words, unleashing a pain-filled, ear-splitting shriek.

"I am sin!" she wailed. "I am sin! Kill me, Teimbaka! Kill me!"

The cloudless, pale blue sky above them reverberated with a tremendous clap of thunder. The ground began to shake as though an earthquake had struck.

A whirlwind of sand swept the air up as the shuddering of the earth swelled.

"Elephants," she gasped. "But where? How?"

Clutching her head as if it might split, she looked in every direction. With a look of terror, Claire thrust her hands out for protection.

With a second booming thunderclap, the maelstrom ended. The earth and sky became still. Claire scrambled to her knees.

"What?"

"The spirit elephants," he told her, his face awash with joy. "They have said their piece. Come. See the path they travel."

Claire stood to look where Teimbaka was gazing, uttering a soft gasp when she saw a dust cloud moving swiftly toward the mountains.

"Dress yourself. It is not right for me to look upon your nakedness."

Claire looked at the plain white shamma at her feet.

"I am not fit to wear the color."

"Robe yourself in this, then," he replied, removing the black shamma he was wearing. "I will take yours until you are ready."

He met her eyes with a fiery compassion.

"It's time we return to where we began."

*

THE TRAIL OF the spirit elephants veered northward, the westward mountains they had thought to be their destination becoming nothing more than a border to the track the spirit elephants had left for them to follow. Every so often, they heard sporadic bursts of thunder ahead of them. Looking to the sky, they hoped for rain.

As they stopped one night to rest and share what remained of the water and bread, they heard the thunder again. But it had changed. The booming they heard was now quickly followed by the sound of an explosion, with fire flashes lighting the belly of the cloudless sky with each echoing rumble.

Claire huddled next to Teimbaka, her hands clutching the fabric of his shamma.

"We must be close to the warring regions," he offered as a fire flash lit up the mountaintops ahead of them. "I had heard talk of it on the docks. The people seek their independence. The government fights to suppress it."

Claire sighed and placed her hands between her knees. Saying nothing, she burrowed her head into his chest and fell asleep. Sharing her exhaustion, he wrapped his arms around her and closed his eyes.

He awakened with a start, his heart pounding, his mind whirling with shadow figures. His body tensed. He bolted to his feet. Cocking his head to one side, listening intently, he took a tentative step forward when he thought he recognized the sound that had awakened him.

"Don't leave me," Claire whispered.

"I heard— There. Do you not hear it?"

Claire got to her feet and stepped next to him.

"I don't—"

The whimpering drifted to them from out of the darkness.

"A child cries," Claire said.

"More. I hear several."

Unknowingly, Claire crossed herself.

"I will go."

"No!" she exclaimed, almost to the point of panic. "They can only be ghosts. They will harm you."

Teimbaka gently took her hands in his.

"If they are spirits, they will not bring me harm. Whether they are flesh or wind, their voices cry for help. I will find them."

"It is a trap," she protested, grabbing his arm.

Teimbaka shook his head.

"The path of the spirit elephants has brought us here. Perhaps this is the reason."

Gently, he pried her fingers from his arm.

"Don't be afraid. What more can there be that we must face?"

"Teimbaka."

The hurt in her voice stopped him.

"Please. Please."

"I will return to you," he told her. "We will no longer be apart."


Teimbaka crouched low to the ground, choosing to cross the remaining distance with caution. Stopping, he listened for a moment, but found there was nothing to hear.

Looking behind him, he suddenly reconsidered leaving Claire alone. It was dark. She would be afraid. He wondered if she hadn't been right. Perhaps this was a trap.

A muffled cry, near to where he crouched, brought him to his feet. He raced ahead. Suddenly, the ground gave way, causing him to fall headlong into a break in the earth. Briefly stunned, he fought to regain his senses.

As he blinked his eyes, he found the steel blade of a machete poised above him.

The weapon edged menacingly toward his throat.

Instinctively, he reached up for the hilt of the weapon, his fingers grabbing on to a skinny wrist. As he pulled the arm and the weapon across his body, a child's voice wailed into his ear.

"What demon?" yelled Teimbaka.

He struggled to get to his feet. A rain of fists fell upon him, hitting him about his waist and knees. The point of the machete whistled through the air, scraping the fabric on his hip.

"Stop!" Teimbaka shouted, wrenching the machete free from the hand that held it. "Get back!"

Crying erupted all around him.

"Silence!" he commanded, raising the machete.

The crying grew louder.

"Stop! I cannot think!"

"Do not hurt us," a weak voice beseeched.

Vaguely, the dark silhouettes of children began to take shape all around him. He lowered the machete to his side. As he dropped to his knees, he saw pleading eyes staring back at him wherever he looked.

"Food. Water," a boy begged.

"Yes, please. Food, water," another joined in.

"Yes, food and water," they clamored.

"Where is your home?"

"Food. Water," they said, their voices filled with despair.

"Who brought you to this desolate place?"

One by one their voices fell silent. Their eyes drifted to the sand when they realized he had nothing to give them. Their faces etched in defeat, they began to drift apart, some sitting where they had stood, others turning away to hide their distress.

Teimbaka counted twelve: all young boys, emaciated, poorly clothed, their faces haggard.

"Food!" came an excited shout.

The call came from some distance away. What looked to be the smallest child of the group was pointing to where the first hint of dawn was showing.

Teimbaka followed the boy's finger.

Against the backdrop of the muted browns and grays of the distant mountain range stood a large male impala, its gaze focused squarely on Teimbaka. As the other children caught sight of the magnificent beast, some screamed with joy while others offered blessings to Allah.

"Food," the smallest of the group repeated as he walked back toward them.

Approaching Teimbaka with the confidence of a man, the little boy came to stand next to him. Tapping the machete Teimbaka held at his side, he pointed back toward the impala and said "Food."

Teimbaka looked at the animal and then to the child. Rising to one knee, he pressed his head to the hilt of the weapon, saying, "You do not understand, little one. The animal will not—"

"Go," the child commanded. "It waits."

A small hand on his shoulder nudged him to act.

"It will not just—"

The boy placed a finger to his lips.

"Go," he repeated. "Go."

Shrugging with resignation, Teimbaka rose and walked toward the animal, holding the machete aloft.

Knowing the impala would not allow him to get near enough to be able to use the blade, Teimbaka made no attempt to hide his approach. But as he drew nearer, the impala stood fast, seemingly oblivious to his presence.

When he was a leap away from the animal, he stopped, suddenly mesmerized by its grandeur. He could not recall having ever seen a stag so beautifully formed. Looking closer, he could see his own reflection in the beast's eyes. The vision reminded him of one from his past. His arm turned cold.

Lowering the steel in his hand, he gazed into the eyes of the beast once more. The hapless, butchered faces of the elephants he had once helped to kill looked back at him. He turned to leave.

In a whirl of rushing hooves, with its horns lowered to the level of

Teimbaka's chest, the impala charged. Without thinking, Teimbaka stepped to the side and swung the machete upward. Blood sprayed as steel sliced through skin, muscle, and bone. The impala crashed to the ground. Its end was swift.

The boys descended on the fallen beast with squeals of happiness, cupping their hands beneath the gaping wound in the impala's neck to drink the blood that flowed.

"Food!" one of them shouted, his eyes wild with the kill that lay before him.

Looking to Teimbaka, the same boy took the dull side of the machete into his bloodied hands and pointed it to the impala's underside.

"Food!" he cried, crouching, running his hand along the animal's belly. "Cut!"

Others joined him, their bloodied mouths chanting, "Cut! Cut! Cut!"

Having forgotten what the insanity of starvation looked and sounded like, Teimbaka stared at the children, feeling empty and confused.

"Aye-yah!"

The boys fell silent, turning at the call.

Arms held out from his sides, standing where Teimbaka had left him, the smallest of the group waited near a hastily built fire. The smoke from the flames curled about the smile on his face. He beckoned the others to join him. Teimbaka stood in dumb fascination as the boys filed by him in an orderly line.

"Bring," he told Teimbaka, gesturing at the impala.

Teimbaka looked at the animal and then the boy and shrugged.

With a look of disapproval, the child sent four of the bigger boys to help. With some degree of difficulty, they dragged the impala over near the fire.

As Teimbaka prepared to gut and butcher the animal, the small one held back his arm.

"What is it?"

Following the boy's gaze, he saw the dust cloud drifting from the south before he heard the sound of the engine.

"Claire!"

Teimbaka leapt to his feet.

"No need weapon," the little one told him, grasping the arm that held the machete.

Wrenching his arm free from the boy's grasp, Teimbaka pushed him away.

"No!" the boy shouted, defiant, blocking his path. "Do not take! Do not take!"

Confused and enraged, Teimbaka raised his arm to strike. But the little one would not back away, meeting his wrath with calm. Teimbaka swung the steel blade down with all his strength.

With a savage scream, he threw the machete to the ground and grabbed hold of the horn he had cleaved from the impala's head. Leaping away, he raced after the dust cloud in tears. A feeling of uselessness began to overcome him, numbing his mind and slowing his muscles. When a dark bundle loomed ahead, a sinking feeling shot through him, almost bringing him to his knees. It was the black shamma that Claire had been wearing.

Panting, he reached down and gathered it in his arms. The needle and the syringe that lay atop it fell quietly to the sand. He unleashed a tormented scream.

Reason having left him, he renewed his pursuit, focused on revenge. He saw blood—the color, the smell, even the feel of it taking over his senses. Its essence was intoxicating. He wanted more.

Lost in his delusion, he was slow to notice that the dust cloud was dissipating and that the engine had gone quiet. When he saw John struggling to free a canister of gasoline, a trace of reason returned. But then he saw Claire slumped in the front seat of the vehicle, and his anger swelled. The sight of her limp, unconscious form drove him toward madness.

The flash and the explosion from the gun in John's hand did not slow him. Nor did the whir of the bullet as it screamed by his head. With the twisted horn of the impala quivering in his hand, he fell upon John, smashing him across his temple with one brutal swing.

Breathing heavily, he stared down at the man-child, his eyes drawn to the gore pooling in his ear. Hypnotized by the sight of the blood oozing onto John's neck, he grasped the horn of the impala with both hands and drove the pointed tip toward the middle of John's throat.

His arms were knocked sideways, the horn plunging into the sand a foot from where he was aiming. Growling with frustration, he set himself to strike again, only to feel himself being pulled backward by fingers gouging into his eyes.

Dazed, his vision blurred, Teimbaka blinked against the glare of the sun. A moment later, a small form was upon him, a tiny hand smothering his nose and mouth with warm, wet blood. Gagging and spitting, he slapped the hand away. He blinked at the little one, confused. The look of anger on the boy's face made Teimbaka flinch.

Then, just as quickly, the boy's expression changed. Tears began to roll down his cheeks as a grave sadness took hold of his face. Raising his bloody fingers for Teimbaka to look upon, he then took them and placed them on Teimbaka's ear.

"No hurt," he whispered in a tear-muffled voice. "No hurt."

Teimbaka looked to where John was lying. There was no movement. He dropped the horn of the impala in the sand and hung his head.

"Care," the little one said, lifting his chin. Nodding to the slumped figure of Claire in the jeep, he said again, "Care."

"By the heart of the Mother, let it not be so."

Claire's breathing was slight, coming in brief gasps and sighs. Although the weeks in the sun had tinted her skin the color of sand, the flesh on her face was now a pale, lifeless shade of ash.

Her eyes, in recent days having just begun to show some of the spark they had once held, were vacant. It was as though he was seeing them as he had found them in the room of the Serpent. Dejected, he pressed his forehead against her shoulder. He could not help but wonder if she were about to die.

"Water."

The little one's voice pierced Teimbaka's sorrow.

Standing on the driver's seat, he thrust the dented canteen in his hand out to Teimbaka.

"Care!" he yelled with a stern look.

Teimbaka placed the canteen to Claire's mouth, relieved when her lips and tongue reacted to the water.

While he tended to her, the little one went back to John and looked over his injury. Muttering a few words above the man-child's bloodied ear, he gently massaged the bump that had swelled on the side of his head. Soon, John began to stir.

"Be—" John blubbered. "Beloved."

Confusion swept across John's eyes as his lids fluttered open.

"Beloved!" he shouted, sitting upright, his face a picture of anxiety. "Beloved!"

Suddenly, he lurched to his feet and began to laugh. He staggered to the jeep with his hands gripping the sides of his head. Almost instantaneously, his laughter turned sour, shifting to scorn. And then a desperate sobbing took hold of him. He began scratching his body and plucking invisible parasites from his skin.

"John," Teimbaka said.

As though a demon had called his name, John looked at Teimbaka, his body beset with uncontrollable spasms. And when the little one took hold of his hand to try to calm him, he jumped away as if the boy were a leper.

Yelping like a wounded dog, John pushed away from jeep. With the look of madness in his eyes, he sprinted away. Teimbaka and the little one watched him run back into the wastelands of the Danakil plain.

*

"WHEN WILL SHE wake?"

Three days had passed since John had fled into the Danakil, three days in which Claire had not regained consciousness. Three days of traveling that had taken them from the fringes of the wasteland to a more forgiving terrain of ridge-framed grasslands and shallow gorges dotted with trees.

Teimbaka had not left Claire's side. He gave her water when she would drink it and forced her to eat by placing a paste of the impala meat to the back of her mouth and massaging her throat until she swallowed.

Yet, even with his efforts, Claire was waning. He did not know what else he could do. She would not wake up.

"Perhaps a story," the little one suggested.

Like the buzzing of a fly, the suggestion filled Teimbaka's head with an unwanted noise.

"A fable of wonder to help her in her dreams. Would it not help her to return?"

Teimbaka stroked Claire's hair and cupped her sallow face in his palm.

"What name were you given?" he asked the little one, having been so obsessed with Claire's diminishing state that he had not thought to ask the simple question before.

"Orphan," the boy lightly replied.

"That is not a name."

The little one tilted his slender, bone-edged face to the side and shrugged.

"It is all I know."

He looked at the other boys.

"It is the name given to all of us."

Teimbaka said nothing, immersed in Claire.

"When the killing neared, when the big guns kept us from sleep, they would tell us a story or say the words."

"A story," Teimbaka mumbled, "words, I do not have."

"In the hills. I think they are there. She has them. Find them."

The little one waited minutes for him to reply, but Teimbaka said nothing.

"When you are ready," the child told him, taking his leave.

So forlorn was Teimbaka that he did not notice the little one depart. The faint ringing of a bell sounded from one of the ridges to the north. Lost within Claire's deteriorating state, Teimabak did not acknowledge it. When the bell jingled once more, he jolted upright, gazing in the direction from where it had come. Turning to see if the boys, too, had heard the bell, he saw that their faces were downcast, heavy with sadness. Until his eyes came upon the little one, who was staring into the shadowed gorge that led to the nearest ridge.

The little one smiled.

"In the hills," he quietly stated, meeting Teimbaka's eyes. "Find them. Bring them back."

The little one pointed.

For the briefest moment, when Teimbaka turned to follow the little one's finger, he glimpsed a figure of light moving along the top of the nearest ridge. But in the blinking of an eye, it was gone. Yet the little one continued to point, his gaze apparently fixed upon the vision.

"The words. She needs them, Etiyopiya," he told him, anxious. "Bring them to her," he said, looking to where Claire lay.

His face lined with worry, Teimbaka looked upon Claire and then toward the top of the ridge. Darkness was coming.

"She will not change, Etiyopiya. Do you not see this?"

Teimbaka bent and gently stroked Claire's face.

"She waits. She needs the words."

"What words?" Teimbaka asked, not understanding.

"The ones you left," the little one said, giving him a curious look. "She has them for you. Go," he instructed, pointing his finger at the ridge once again. "Go. Now."

By the time Teimbaka reached the first ridge, the fire from the camp where he had left Claire and the boys was but a tiny beacon. But seeing it made him linger. He wondered what fool's errand he had undertaken. He did not like leaving Claire again. Even more unsettling was the notion that he had left because of what a child he barely knew had told him.

But he continued on.

Night was now fully upon him. He felt for his path, rather than chose it. His steps were slow. What small amount of light there had been from the sliver of moon was now gone, hidden by clouds that had been pushed across it by a brisk, chilling wind. Hours had passed since he had started out. He was cold and tired. The path was taking him upward and then downward. He was wandering in a place he did not know, with no beacon to keep sight of.

When he saw the shimmering, wavering reflection of a fire, he felt both relieved and angry. He welcomed the thought of sitting next to it and getting warm. But he was irritated to think that he had been traveling in a circle and was now back to where he had begun.

But after drawing closer, he saw that this was not the camp's fire. For the fire in front of him was burning inside a cave. A cave whose walls were alive with the dancing shadows cast from the flames.

Teimbaka crossed a stone ledge to stand at the entrance.

The figure of light lay close to the fire, radiating from the heat, particles of reddish-gold rising from her body. Swept upward by the smoke, the sparks swirled against the ceiling of the cave before drifting out into the open.

A man with skin of brown and shadow-cast black, dressed in a white shamma, came to kneel by the figure of light, a simple wooden cup held in his hands. Gently raising her head from the floor of the cave, he placed the cup to her lips, inviting her to drink. With a shake of her head, she refused.

His body shaking with the vision unfolding before him, Teimbaka fell to his knees, remembering.

The fire grew brighter as the man fed it more sticks. A breeze blew outward toward the opening, the rush of it carrying whispers to his ears.

"You promised," the figure of light struggled to say.

"I remember."

"The words, the missal."

"I lost it."

"Zanzibar brought them."

"Zanzibar?"

"They are here."

"Zanzibar," he repeated.

"Yes, she brought them."

The figure of light seemed to dim as the particles of reddish-gold began to multiply. The man began to weep, his hands frantic as they tried to wipe away the fiery dots before they could completely cover her.

"Say the words," she pleaded. "Say the words. Please, say them."

"I do not have them."

"Say the words so I may know peace."

Caught between the whispers, Teimbaka struggled to understand, his feelings torn between awe and fear.

And then she screamed.

The radiating light, nearly obliterated beneath the smothering blanket of flaring dots, bucked and thrashed, pulsing with a final burst of energy in an attempt to break free.

"Say the words!" Teimbaka heard himself shout. "Teimbaka, say the words to Lee!"

An eruption of air exploded within the cave, the fire extinguished in a swirling force of wind that swept past Teimbaka and out into the clouds. In its wake, there was nothing except darkness and quiet and the notion that something had been lost.

"Say the words," he whispered. "Say the words."

A spark glittered on the cave's floor, capturing Teimbaka's gaze. Drawn to the glowing point of fire, he walked toward it, though the path before him was utterly black.

Standing over it, he wondered if it was real. But the ember dazzled and beckoned him, floating just above the cave floor, waiting to be held.

As he kneeled to it, the cinder seemed to melt, sliding into the darkness, the last glimmer of it blinking away as though it had been siphoned through a crack in the rock.

Behind him, he sensed shadows beginning to gather. He heard the whirling of wings as an icy touch swept across the back of his neck. The dark angels had come. The cave seemed suddenly both endless and claustrophobic, a fathomless pit of the blackest black.

The dark angels slipped inside.

Crouching, he placed a hand to the stone floor. When a portion of floor began to slide away, he grappled with it and tried to hold on. Clamping his palm around something rectangular, he pressed down on it, hoping to keep it from moving any further. It was somewhat soft and textured. He ran his fingers along the edge, feeling each of its pages.

"Can it be?" he murmured.

Just outside the mouth of the cave, Teimbaka heard a shriek that brought to mind a wraith from the old tales. The dark angels inched closer.

Teimbaka flipped through the pages. A shard of light radiated near the book's end.

A shrieking form entered the cave.

Teimbaka opened the book to the light.

The tiny spark burst into a flame.

With a piercing wail, the shrieking form fled. As Teimbaka watched the flame burn, the dark angels slithered away.

Teimbaka lifted the small card from the book's back cover. Captivated by the flame dancing atop it, he could not understand why the paper was not burning. From the light of the tiny fire, he looked upon a lamb lying peacefully atop an altar. The image gave him joy.

He placed the card back inside the book and closed it.

"Bring them back," the little one had told him.

"Claire," he whispered. "Wait."

*

"ETIYOPIYA!"

The little one smiled, nodding at the book in Teimbaka's hand.

"In the hills, yes? The words, she needs them. She will not wait much longer."

Seeing Claire, Teimbaka's hopeful steps turned heavy and slow. She seemed closer to death than he had remembered. Her face was now ghost-like, almost translucent. He fell to his knees, letting the book slip from his hand.

"You must say them now, Etiyopiya."

The voice of the little one intruded upon his despair. Teimbaka's reply was quick and angry.

"Silence!"

But the little one knelt opposite him and accepted his anger with calm. His face bright with joy, he motioned for Teimbaka to be quiet.

"Good are the words, Etiyopiya," he said. "Listen."

Opening the small prayer book, the little one began to read. Wide-eyed, slow with his pronunciation, he enunciated each word with care, repeating them as they had once been said to him.

"Blessed are the poor in spirit, for theirs is the kingdom of heaven.

"Blessed are the meek; they shall inherit the land.

"Blessed are they that mourn, for they shall be comforted.

"Blessed are they that hunger and thirst for holiness; they shall have their fill.

"Blessed are the merciful, for they shall obtain mercy.

"Blessed are the clean of heart, for they shall see God.

"Blessed are the peacemakers, for they shall be called the children of God."

The little one paused, his deep-brown eyes drifting to Claire and then to the eleven who had gathered behind Teimbaka.

"Blessed are they that mourn," he continued, making eye contact with Teimbaka, "for they shall be comforted."

Holding out his hand to Teimbaka, he nodded to the small silver cross that hung about his neck. Slipping it over his head, Teimbaka placed it in the little one's palm. The little one transferred it into one of Claire's, pressing her hand into a fist before resting it upon her heart.

"Blessed are the clean of heart, for they shall see God."

Touching her forehead, he said, "See him now. Tell Him you are still needed here." Then, looking to Teimbaka and the children around him, he said, "Blessed are the poor in spirit, for theirs is the kingdom of heaven."

The mighty roar of a lion resounded through the hills around them. The echo traveled from ridge top to gorge until the proclamation of the beast had encircled them.

"Negusa negast," the little one said. "What would you have us know?"

It was a fragile moment as they waited for the king of kings to speak to them again. With their faces turned upward to the ridge tops and their eyes darting to the depths of the shadowed gorges, the boys held expressions of wonder and confusion. The reason that the lion had spoken to them was unclear. Whether he had come to punish or protect them, they did not know.

But for Teimbaka, the roar of the lion meant nothing. Nor was he concerned with what the presence of the beast meant. For Claire—even upon hearing the words that the little one had been so certain were all that was missing from her recovery—was showing no sign that she was better. Not even fluttering an eyelid when the child had touched her forehead. Despair wound its way deeper into his heart.

Beneath his knees, the sand swelled and rippled, shifting from some slithering form he could not see. Darkness settled over his eyes. The rippling sand surrounded Claire's still body. The blackness of the Serpent returned.

When the muffled voices of the spirit children cried out in his head, Teimbaka clutched the fabric of Claire's black shamma and began to weep. Upon the back of his neck, he felt the foul breath of the Serpent's hiss upon his skin.

He hung his head. The Serpent had come to claim her.

"Etiyopiya! Etiyopiya!" the little one shouted, shaking him by the shoulders. "Say, Etiyopiya!" he screamed into Teimbaka's face. "The words—you must say them! You, Etiyopiya! You!"

The spirit children echoed the little one's cry, adding their haunting pleas to his anguish.

"Look upon the words," the little one urged him, thrusting the open book into Teimbaka's hand. "Say."

Teimbaka stared at the words written on the pages as the little one gently guided the book toward his face.

"Blessed," Teimbaka rasped before his throat constricted. "Blessed are," wild-eyed, he stared at the glimpse of silver within Claire's hand. "Blessed are—the children! For they—for they are the will of God!"

With an air-shaking, booming clap of thunder, Teimbaka collapsed. The boys behind him cowered away.

"Omens! Signs!" they shouted before the little one held them to calm with a simple gesture of his hand.

Jumping lightly across Claire's body, the little one knelt by Teimbaka's side.

"The words, good are they," he told him, lightly touching the pulsing vein on Teimbaka's temple. "She has heard. Look."

A great shadow moved across the ridge tops and gorges from a cloudless sky. Spellbound, the children looked on as the woman they had thought to be in the clutches of death began to stir. And as her lips parted to speak, they drew back as if witnessing a miracle.

"Teimbaka," she whispered.

The little one smiled.

## MAY 1983

66 "THAT BETTER NOT be cigarette smoke I'm smelling!"

The lazy stream of smoke drifted outside from the screened-in front porch, hurried along by a waving hand.

"Like a bloodhound she is, that one."

Menelik stared at the sign on the road fifty yards from where he was seated. The elderly man who shared the porch with him chuckled.

"Be as far away as the Safeway and she'd know. Probably *was* a bloodhound in some former life."

Again, he chuckled. He did not extinguish the cigarette that was perched like an extra appendage between two of his fingers. Instead, he lowered it beneath the seat of the rocking chair.

Menelik politely smiled, not certain what to say.

"Probably should give 'em up, you know. Doctor said, if I don't, they'll probably do me in. But what's a man supposed to do?"

The question came with a shrug of the shoulders.

"Baby himself till he dies? Or enjoy the few simple remaining pleasures that this crotchety old life has to offer?"

Again, Menelik's reply was a polite smile. When the front door of the house opened, he breathed a sigh of relief.

"How you two getting along?"

"Just fine, Belinda. Just fine."

"It's Yutanda now, Dad."

"Says Belinda on your birth certificate. And since your mother and I are the ones who named you, it's still Belinda to me. Still don't see what in Hades difference it—"

"We've been through this a hundred times, Dad. Let's not subject Menelik to it, too, okay?"

With an irritated grunt, the man shrugged his broad, square shoulders.

"And put that cigarette out before Mom comes out and gives you the what for."

Yutanda's father laughed, his aged, chocolate-brown face crinkling into lines that seemed to have been carved into it.

"I've gotten the what for so many times, I do believe I am the what for."

His walnut-colored eyed sparkled as he spoke, matching the playful tone in his voice. Yutanda shook the yellow and white plaid dishtowel she was holding at her father, an expression of mock scorn etched across her smooth, square face.

"You're incorrigible," she scolded, sending a quick wink to Menelik as she went back into the house.

To Menelik's surprise and awkward discomfort, Yutanda's father broke out in song, adding his own lyrics to the melody of the old Nat King Cole classic.

"I'm incorrigible. That's what I am. Just incorrigible. Da, da, da, da. Pretty lousy singer, hey? Guess it was a good decision on my part to stick with rail roadin'."

Menelik stared at the same sign down by the road.

"You all right, son?" the man asked, touching Menelik lightly on the arm. "You feelin' ill, or am I just boring you to death?"

"I'm sorry, Mr. Taylor. I was just—"

"That's, Ed, son. And you were just …?"

Menelik kept staring at the sign, focused on but not really seeing the words: "Windy Hill Restoration Project."

"I was just—just— I don't know, really."

"We don't have to talk, you know. I told Belinda we were getting along just fine 'cause I see she's got some feelings for you. But we can sit here and daydream if that's more suitable to you. Downright pretty, ain't it, May in Virginia? Least ways, that's how I see it. Mrs. Taylor—Lizbeth—she likes

the fall a bit better. Says the leaves changin' to fire and gold is the most—"
Ed sighed. "Sorry. Here I am, talkin' again. We'll just stay quiet. Enjoy the early evenin'."

"No, really, Mr. Taylor, it should be me apologizing. Here I am, a guest in your home, and I—"

Menelik paused when he saw the look on Ed Taylor's face. Or rather, the way in which the man's eyes were glaring at him.

"Did I say something to offend you?"

Gradually, as Ed furrowed his bushy, grey eyebrows, Menelik smiled, and then began to chuckle when he guessed his error.

"Ed," he offered, hoping he was right.

"Not as slow as some of the others she's brought home for supper. Most times, the boys gotta get up out of their chair and go ask her why her daddy's giving them the evil eye."

Ed laughed as his thoughts drifted to scenes in the past.

Below them, fifty yards or so down the hill from where they were seated on the screened-in front porch of the Taylor home, traffic began to pick up with the start of rush hour. The evening commute out to the country from Tysons Corner or Arlington or the District of Columbia had begun, never varying in the time it started or the number of cars it brought with it.

Although separated in age by some twenty-five years, the two men watched the procession in a like manner, garnering a curious sort of comfort from the moving caravan of painted steel.

"What is it about that sign that you find so hypnotizing?"

The question was asked so quietly, so matter-of-factly, that Menelik found no harm in the asking.

"Windy Hill," he commented. "I'm sure it is an apt name for the area when the wind is kicking up."

Ed nodded.

"But Restoration Project? I mean, is it necessary to have that printed on there too? Seems insulting. Like all those cars down there are supposed to pass by and know that the people living here—black people—had to get outside funding of some sort to get their little houses respectable-looking."

Ed eyed Menelik for a moment and then grunted. "Darn it all," he suddenly hissed, recalling the cigarette he was still holding. Since it had burnt down to the filter, Ed ground out what was left of his smoke into the heavily calloused skin of his hand. The remainder he placed into his shirt pocket.

"Can't be littering, you know."

He smiled and almost sheepishly looked away.

For a few minutes, the passing cars became the focus of the two men's attention.

"What do you know about these parts and the people who have lived in 'em?" Ed asked after the long pause.

"Don't really know about either one. But what does that have to do with what I was saying?"

"Just the simple fact that it's wrong to assume that people round here think like you do, or feel like you do, or harbor the same prejudices as you. Perhaps I'm wrong—and I say perhaps 'cause I rightly have no idea—but maybe you like to project, so to speak, your own mindset on people, like some of the other young folk from your era like to do. This isn't a 'burb of New York City or Detroit or L.A. And as close as we may be, this ain't no Washington, D.C., neither. I can only imagine what it must be like living in one of those prisons. I'd think it'd be the same for a city person like yourself when it comes to how folk out in the country live; you can only imagine how it is. Simple fact is, it'd be impossible for you to know, wouldn't it?"

Menelik stroked his newly grown pharaoh-style goatee before responding.

"Prisons," he grunted. "That how you see the big cities?"

"Don't you? Heck, you'd know better than me. But every time I've been to one, I get that closed-in feeling, you know, like the concrete and the steel and the noise is just like a big jailhouse keepin' everybody from feelin' what it really is to be free."

"Black people, you mean."

"Certainly they're a part—a big part, I suppose. But it's too easy to say it's just black folk. More in all those cities than just black folk."

To Menelik's surprise, Ed began to snicker.

"Always put in terms of black and white, isn't it? Like those are the only two colors on earth, the only kind of people that exist."

"In some ways, in this country, they are."

"Well, you be wrong if you think so," Ed stated emphatically, the soft lines of his face suddenly going rigid. "If you can't see past black and white, then you'll never get past it, never move on to see what the world really is. Hmph—black and white—too much damn time wasted on the damn subject," he grumbled, reaching for the pack of cigarettes in his shirt pocket but finding nothing there. "Act like two adolescents who ain't ever going to grow up. Tiresome, if you ask me—which you didn't," he added, lightening his tone. "Get sick of hearing people go on and on and on about it, like it— Already said that."

Menelik shifted his weight, the old wooden rocker beneath him creaking with the motion.

"Don't mean to make you uncomfortable, son. I apologize for runnin' off at the mouth."

"Oh, no need to apologize Mr. Taylor—uh, Ed. I've always respected a man who speaks his mind. But I can't say I've ever run across a black man who sees things quite the way you do."

With an easy laugh, Ed again reached for a nonexistent cigarette.

"You haven't gotten around much, then," he said, the tip of his thumb and index finger pressing the air between them in the absence of a cigarette. "Don't talk to older people much, either, do you? Probably like my daughter—and I don't mean no disrespect—but she's of the habit of only surrounding herself with people of her own age and color and—to her fault—with the same viewpoint as hers."

"Your daughter, sir," Menelik began with a hint of testiness in his tone, "is a strong leader in the battle of race relations."

"That battle was fought 125 years ago," Ed replied with severity. "So many died." He grappled for the right words. "Died for us. Died because of our color. Whether it was for or against. White men—the worst this country had to offer, and most certainly, some of the very best this nation is ever going to see again—laying down their lives. Good Lord, it seems like sometimes that war never existed, the way we never, ever put it in perspective. You wish that God Almighty had only taken the bad: the sinners, the unrepentant. But that ain't His way, is it? You'd think that we'd all be satisfied. Hundreds of thousands of white men killed each other—" He shook his head, lamenting what he would say next. "But there's those that aren't—and probably never will be."

"Different era, different war," Menelik countered without too much thought. "Different measures are required now. The lines of conflict aren't so clear-cut in this day and age."

"Hogwash. 'Lines of conflict aren't very clear'. Always over something that don't really matter much in the scheme of things: color, religion, lines on a map. Can't say personally that I deem any of those as being important enough to give your life up for." As if he didn't want to lose his train of thought, he hurried on, "Second world war, that'd rank up there as being worthy to die for. Freedom—that smacks me as being a darn good reason to fight. Whole lot of men and women put their lives on the line for that."

"Is the fight not to be enslaved any longer worthy in your eyes? Not to be kept down as a race? Not to be looked upon as just—just another nigger?"

"Don't be handin' me any of that 'nigger' shit. Ain't no nigger here inside this," Ed decreed, emphatically poking his chest with his finger. "Never was, never will be."

Ed eyed Menelik square in the face, giving the younger man no room to escape.

"Nigger's a state of mind. You think you're a nigger, then that's what you are. So if you're trying to blame somebody for your being a nigger, then blame yourself. Cause there ain't nobody made you one but you."

Menelik struggled with Ed's powerful stare.

"Nigger—the self-knotted hangman's noose of folks who ain't got the courage to take off their own chains and walk the way God intended them to. You be proud and free by your own making. I got no sympathy for those who just want to hate and wrap themselves up in their own self-serving pity."

"You going to sit there and deny that prejudice and bigotry exist, that they're used to keep the black man oppressed, weapons to keep a race of people under another's thumb, to keep us segregated, a separate nation within a nation, deprived and impoverished? Hell, maybe it's you who hasn't been around much! Maybe it's you who can't or won't see things as they really are!"

To Menelik's astonishment, Ed laughed in his face.

"Spoken like a true pupil of the times. Only one thing wrong with all that mumbo jumbo, regurgitated garbage these leaders—as you call them—like to spit out every chance they get."

Menelik gripped the arms of his rocking chair.

"And what might that be—sir?"

"Africa."

Plain and simple, the word tumbled from Ed's tongue. But the power of it was awesome, nearly throwing Menelik backward off his chair.

"Who's doing the oppressing there, the segregating, the cultivating of poverty, disease, and starvation?"

"The whites of South Africa are re—"

"I'm not talking no South Africa. I'm talking Africa: Ethiopia, Uganda, Zaire, Ghana, Nigeria, and so on and so forth. People in power there are black. Governments are black. Population is black. So who you want to pin their problems on? All too many black people are in such a goldarn hurry to embrace Africa, proclaim themselves African, but I don't hear none of them—none, and that's including my own—" he said, nodding toward the house, "talk about the problems over there or what could and should be done to help. Like the continent doesn't exist when bad news comes out of it. Stench of hypocrisy. If you ask me—which you haven't—ain't a damn thing African about anybody's who's American. This is our country, black or whatever color you are. And that's what we are: Americans, for better or worse."

Ed reached for another cigarette, his fingers seeming a bit more animated in their movements.

"Darn stupid game," he grumbled. "Can't have a damn cigarette when I really want to. Excuse my French."

The distant whirs and swooshing of the passing cars filled the interlude that ensued. Grateful for the respite, Ed and Menelik took refuge in the soothing motion of the sounds.

"About a half-hour till supper."

Yutanda's announcement jolted the two men back to the present.

"You two still getting along? Dad's not boring you with old railroad stories, is he, Menelik? Because if he is—"

"Your father's anything but boring, Yutanda," Menelik told her, forcing a smile. "Just let us know when to wash up."

"Momma! Something's wrong out here!" she shouted as she went back into the house. "He didn't ask me why he was getting the look!"

Though their moods weren't very receptive to humor, both men chuckled at what Yutanda said.

"Don't know how we got on all that, son, 'cause I know that's not what you were really thinking when you were eyeing that sign down there. Weren't no anger in your face—something closer to sadness. So what is it 'bout it that's really got hold of you?"

So much of what Ed had been saying he had not wanted to think about since his speech the day Peter had died. The man's words about freedom being gained by blood, and one's own effort in attaining it, had opened an old wound that he was not certain would ever heal. And the dilemma of being African—but not African at all—of feeling neglected by a government that only exhibited a measure of caring about the blacks of the country when it was politically correct to do so, had placed him back on that stage again, trying to explain who he was and finding out what he truly believed in.

Restoring an inner city—what had Ed called them, prisons? Guns and gangs and the faces of the hopeless. Maybe Ed had it right. Maybe the inner cities were prisons.

Even though three years had passed, he could still not watch the evening news without visualizing the videotape of Peter's death. The media had played it over and over until they got bored with the whole subject, dropping it altogether when the investigation had finally been closed for lack of any tangible evidence.

"Restoration, restore."

He was barely even aware that he had spoken.

Menelik gazed longingly at the speeding cars, watching the words on the sign disappear with each one that passed.

"What is it you yearn to bring back?" Ed softly prodded, he too following Menelik's line of attention.

Minutes later, Menelik answered. "A life."

"Oh," Ed nodded. "Willing to trade?"

"Trade?" he asked, confused. But when he met Ed's eyes, he said, "In a breath."

"I see."

Ed set his chair rocking to an easy motion, a continuous rhythm that soon had Menelik following suit.

"And who'd that leave behind to be wishin' it was someone else, like you are?"

"No one," he replied a bit too forcefully.

"Didn't have no parents, then?"

"Parents?"

Menelik used the term in an odd tone, as if he were learning a foreign language and still not quite comfortable with the way it sounded, a bit uncertain if he had even said it properly at all.

"Family, son," said Ed. "Don't you have any bothers or sisters?"

For a split second, the passing cars became the sound of the wind moving down the banks of the river of sand. Ed's voice became his father's, instructing Tafari to gather the wood. Inevitably, as it had always been, the snarling jaws of a hyena jumped out at him in his memories. He jerked his head back and put an arm out to fend off the attack.

"Whoa, there," Ed muttered, grabbing hold of the rocking chair's arm before Menelik took a spill.

Ed's voice became Patricia's. Over the snarls of the hyena, Menelik heard her pleading for Martin to shoot.

"Martin!" she had screamed. "Shoot! Shoot them! For God's sake, shoot!"

Quick with his hands, Menelik rubbed the areas on his arm and leg where the hyena had bitten him. When he felt no pain, he sat back and dabbed at his forehead, where a cold sweat had formed.

Seemingly oblivious to what had just transpired, Ed set himself to rocking, humming some unintelligible tune.

"Martin ever shoot?" Ed asked after a minute or so.

Only just realizing he had uttered what Patricia had screamed that day, Menelik soberly replied, "Yes. But one got away."

"He, the one that got away—he ever come back to finish you off?"

"Many times."

"Like now?"

Nodding, Menelik said, "Like now. Sometimes in a disguise."

"What is it about you that it needs to kill? Or is it that it's just a killer?"

Menelik opened his mouth to respond, but found himself at a loss. The notion that there was something specific, some particular reason that the hyenas and the hyena-men had pursued him since that day, had never occurred to him. The revelation troubled him.

"Killers," he ended up answering. "It's their way."

Ed kept his rocker moving, his head nodding with the motion.

For Menelik, however, the creaking of the old wood from Ed's rocker became the click of the camera shutters when he was first arraigned for the murders of Titus and Jennifer.

"Was it them, the ones who killed your friend?"

Dazed, Menelik nodded yes.

"I tried to explain," he blurted out unexpectedly, his words laced with guilt. "Tried to make them know that the bullet was meant for me. The coffin, the grave, the hole in his chest—but I couldn't."

"Because it wasn't you."

"It wasn't me."

"So, you'd trade."

"I wish— No, I don't wish anymore."

Somber, but at ease with the notion he had harbored since seeing Peter's blood pooling on the plywood platform, he explained, "I'd die for him if there was a way."

"But yet," the rocker ceased its creaking as Ed bent toward Menelik, "you want to live," he whispered.

Menelik struggled with the statement in silence.

"From the time Martin took the shot, you've struggled to keep going. Perhaps he—your friend—perhaps he understood that."

A car horn blared from the road as Yutanda stepped out onto the porch to announce that dinner was ready. Neither man moved.

"Can it wait a few more minutes?"

Yutanda eyed Menelik with severity.

"No, it cannot wait a few more minutes. Momma's only spent the better part of the day preparing it special for us. How rude of you to—"

"That'll be quite enough, Belinda."

It was a father's voice that spoke, one which Yutanda knew all too well and understood.

"Your man and I will be right in."

"But—"

"Run along now, child," he told her with a wave of his hand. "And don't be pickin' the crust off the corners of the corn bread like you always do," he added, his face beaming with a warm smile.

"Oh, Daddy," she giggled, waving the dishtowel at him again as she went back into the house.

"Girl will have the edges of the pan picked clean if we don't get ourselves to the table."

As Ed rose out of his rocker, Menelik grabbed his arm.

"Could we talk some more? I haven't been able—"

Even though Menelik couldn't finish his sentence, Ed gave him a knowing nod.

"Maybe after supper?"

"We best wash up now. Not wise to disappoint the lady of the house."

"Could we make the time?" Menelik pressed.

"I'm not the one you want to be talking to, son," Ed told him, looking over his shoulder.

Menelik was spellbound, waiting for his next words.

With a snap of his fingers, Ed quietly exclaimed, "Darn it all! Now, where did I hide them 'fore you all arrived?"

He chuckled and gave Menelik a wink.

"Be wanting that evening smoke before bed."


Halfway through supper, Yutanda received a phone call from New York

City. When she returned to the table some ten minutes later, she seemed to glow, a luster of sheer satisfaction radiating from her rosewood-colored skin.

"That phone call rekindle your ill-mannered ways, young lady?" Ed asked after watching her move her food around her plate with her fork for a few minutes. "Seemed you were enjoying your Mother's corn bread at a pretty good clip before you left the table. So if you've had enough now, then you're excused to go into the kitchen and start cleaning up. Leave the rest of us to enjoy this wonderful meal your Momma's made."

"Sorry, Daddy," was all Ed got as a reply. That, and a sheepish grin.

"Ever had snapper fritters before, son?" Ed asked, shifting his attention between Menelik and Lizbeth.

Elizabeth Taylor—oddly silent since meeting Menelik—exchanged a quick glance with her husband.

"Delicious, just as everything is, Mrs. Taylor," Menelik said, giving the woman a brief acknowledgement before averting his eyes to the food on the table.

"Trapped the monster just yesterday," Ed went on, filling the slightly disquieting silence with some animated chatter. "Almost pulled me into the pond. Thought I had hooked the one who was gonna have me for dinner, instead of the other way around. Give you some to take back with you if you want. Froze more than half of it." Ed patted his ample stomach and smiled. "Course, Belinda, she's not half the cook my wife is." Ed winked, staring at Lizbeth, as he called her. "She can make turtle taste so darn good. Ah, my," he sighed with exaggerated contentment, spiking another fritter on his fork, "just about bust me open at the seams how good this is." He paused, the snapper fritter poised in front of his mouth. "But I'll just take that chance."

Fifteen minutes later, when everyone had eaten their fill and Ed had run out of small talk, Yutanda and Elizabeth Taylor cleared the table and left the two men to each other's company.

"Ever had a good pie, Menelik?"

Menelik closed his eyes and let his head fall to his chest.

"They at you again?" Ed asked in a hushed tone.

"I really do apologize, Ed. I don't understand what's— I mean, I don't think I've been a very good houseguest."

Wanting Ed to know he wasn't normally so preoccupied and distant, he searched the man's face. But oddly, and to Menelik's disappointment, Yutanda's father was looking out the dining room window, seemingly not having listened to a word that he had said.

"Excuse me, Ed."

Menelik pushed away from the table, pausing as he stood to ponder Ed's aloof manner.

"My, yes, run along, son. Lizbeth dearly loves it when a man helps her with the dishes."

"How—?"

Menelik furrowed his brow, his mouth still open with his unfinished question.

"You just keep 'em busy for a little while," Ed said to him in confidence, peering past Menelik to see if the women were looking in from the kitchen. "Give me a chance to wander off and have me an after-supper— Well, you know," he said, holding up his index and middle fingers and flicking them back and forth.

Abruptly, Yutanda came back into the dining room. Ed sighed.

"Yutanda, why don't you sit yourself down and keep me company and let Menelik here help your mother finish cleaning up?"

Yutanda's eyes flickered with a trace of disapproval.

"I'm not sure Momma wants any help from someone who hasn't had the courtesy to say more than ten words to her since he first arrived."

Menelik winced under her glare.

"That phone call make you this surly, girl, or is it just bein' back in this house that's got you acting to your old ways?"

"Oh, my god, the call! Menelik, we need to— Menelik? Menelik!"

Yutanda was about to follow him into the kitchen, but Ed grabbed her hand and motioned for her to sit down.


The ghosts of his past had always been with Menelik. But never had he felt so close to them as when he walked into Elizabeth Taylor's kitchen and saw two freshly baked pies resting on a large wooden cutting board sitting off to one side of the countertop. The woman herself—her back turned toward him, her grey-streaked hair pulled back in a bun—was washing dishes by hand, a blue and white checkered apron tied around her sturdy frame. He allowed himself a slight smile when he heard her humming.

"Would you like me to dry?"

Elizabeth's face—broad of nose, high of brow, her full mouth seemingly born with an ever-present smile—wavered when she turned to look at him and realized he was seeing her as someone else. But with a gesture of her hand and nod of her head, she welcomed him.

"Don't seem right to put company to work," she replied with utter kindness. "But it's truly hard to refuse the offer. All these dishes and pans and such—just not used to having them all sitting in a pile anymore. Just Ed and me now, most nights. Sometimes, though it's not as often as it used to be, we have one of the neighbors over, or the reverend. But when it's just the two of us, well, it's a simple meal, most times, and doesn't call for," she looked at the pile soaking in the sink, "all this clutter."

"Make a great cup of coffee, don't you?"

Embarrassed to have just blurted the question out without so much as a comment on what Elizabeth had said, Menelik grabbed the nearest dishtowel and started drying what plates and utensils she had washed. Unfazed, Elizabeth went about washing what still remained submerged in the sink, humming the chore away while her attention was fixed upon what she could see through the kitchen window.

"Just missed seeing the dogwoods in bloom," she remarked. "Prettiest trees in the spring. Nothing else quite like 'em. I'm especially fond of the pink."

"I remember," Menelik replied. "Rumson Road had its share. Quite a few of those Japanese cherries, I think you called them. Of course, you always said God made everything pretty so there'd be no need to play favorites."

"What did you call me back then?" Elizabeth asked, her voice soft, her tone matter-of-fact.

"Mom, when I was little. Ele—"

Realizing what he had done, Menelik could only offer a foolish, awkward laugh.

"Ella? Mom? That who you've been seeing all this time you've been here? Don't know if that's a compliment or something bad, the way you've been trying not to look at me. Though it's obvious you feel compelled to look, just the same."

Menelik turned away from her and wiped his eyes with the back of his hand.

"I do consider my coffee to be a good cup, by the way. But I wouldn't go so far as shedding a tear over it."

She laughed at the idea, feeling a bit better about saying it when Menelik laughed along with her.

"That's why Ed smokes cigarettes. Never did before Korea—least, that's what he tells me," she said, raising an eyebrow. "Reminds him, you know. Only opened up about it once, many years ago. Don't know if he even remembers now." She chuckled. "But, well, it reminds him of someone he wishes he didn't have to remember. And I mean that in the way—like—well, I'm just not so good at explaining it. Guess I mean the cigarettes remind him of a certain time, a certain place. And because that person is from that particular time and place, it's like they never left it, so his memory is stuck there too."

She sighed.

"But still, he needs to remember, so it's cigarettes for him, taking him back, you see. Is it coffee for you?"

"I never gave it much thought before now, before you—before you explained it so it makes sense."

He eyed the two pies.

"Pie more than coffee." He smiled with a fleeting touch of sadness. "Makes me feel— Her name was Eleanor." He shook his head. "Seems like I'm belittling her to equate her with pie."

"She put a lot of love in them, did she?"

He nodded.

"Then she'd be happy. She's probably smiling down from heaven just hearing you say it."

"I wasn't there when she— Didn't even know for a long time. I feel like I—" He sighed, not able to finish.

"What was your favorite? And just start stacking the dishes over there, and lay the dry silverware flat in a row so they can get some air."

"She used to make peach. Once in a while, peach and blackberry," he told her, his eyes watering with the telling. "Fresh. Always fresh fruit and homemade crust. Think I could have eaten a whole one if she had let me. Probably did once or twice."

"Sounds delicious. Peach and blackberry; I'll have to give it a try sometime. Ed, now, he loves to sink his teeth into a good strawberry-rhubarb." She laughed, her head tilted back to let it get clear out. "That man loves to sink his teeth into anything! Ah, but I don't let him. Be like a balloon if I did," she went on, giving Menelik a knowing wink and nod. "Part of our game, you see. Keeps it interesting."

"You both are so happy. I hope, someday—"

Leaving the thought unfinished, he gave an extra rub or two to the white china plate he was drying.

"So, your daddy—he take a liking to those peach pies, too?"

"I'll say!"

The wide smile at the fond memory twisted to a troubled frown. He watched Martin's beaming, smiling face wither to the mostly deaf, aged creature he had last seen him as. The image was deflating.

"He passed?"

The plainness of her inquiry jolted him.

"One is," he confessed. "One—" he looked to her, hoping she would understand, "I don't know. He may be."

"Which one had a liking for pie?"

Menelik couldn't help but laugh as he pictured Martin's face when the man would walk into the kitchen and smell one baking in the oven.

"The one that I hope is still." He stopped laughing. "The one that I haven't seen or spoken to in years."

"Well I'll be. The good Lord blesses you with two fathers, and you're squandering one away? I can see that you're fond of him by the look of you. Excuse me for prying, but what did he ever do to you to make you spurn him so?"

If Elizabeth had asked him that question a year or two earlier, he would have been quick with an answer. But standing next to her in her kitchen, every reason and emotion that he had used as a way to distance himself from those who had tried to care for him no longer seemed to make any sense.

"Nothing but save me from death. Nothing but help—" He turned away.

Elizabeth started humming again and turned the water spigot on to rinse off a shallow pan.

"The pans you best dry with another cloth. You'll find them in that drawer next to you. And then just turn 'em upside down so what drops might be left will just drip out."

Her eyes focused on the dwindling light outside, she added, "So you'll be needing to move those pies to the top of the range to make room. Mind you, don't drop them. Ed might get the idea of using you for snapper bait if you do."

Her whimsical giggle was light, reminding Menelik of another woman. A wisp of a smile touched his lips.

At that moment, Ed sauntered into the kitchen, his eyes drifting until they came to rest on the pies.

"They're not in here," Elizabeth said, though she didn't bother to turn around from the sink.

"What do you mean, woman? I'm staring at them right now."

"You know that's not why you came in here."

Ed shifted from foot to foot.

"Why else would I be here?" he asked defensively.

"Oh, how you do like to play," she sighed. "What you've been trying to remember since I started cleaning the table are out in what's left of the woodpile—two logs in and one down. I should probably let you make yourself crazy trying to remember what you did with them on your own, but you'd just drive me to my wit's end if I did."

"I don't know—"

"Land's sake, Edward Taylor, why else would you mutter some nonsense about, 'it might get chilly enough tonight to burn some wood in the stove this evening'? Seventy-five degrees today, in case you hadn't noticed.

Besides," she turned to look him straight in the eye, "I watched you from the kitchen window."

The three of them shared a heartfelt, spontaneous laugh.

"And why wasn't I invited? Is this a private dishwashing and pie-eating party?" Yutanda spoke up as she entered the kitchen.

"You can certainly take over my part of the party duties, dear," Elizabeth laughed, though she was still looking at Ed. "I'd be happy to surrender my sponge and dishwater to you!"

In the hallway, the phone rang again.

"Saved by the bell!"

"Just like when you were a teenager, Yutanda, when one of your many admirers would call at just the most inconvenient moment. Though I suppose it can't be one of them, seeing that you've already made your choice."

"Mother!"

Yutanda sent her mother a look of mock astonishment, giving Menelik a sheepish grin before she hurried to catch the phone before it stopped ringing.

"So Yutanda had a good many men wooing her?" Menelik asked with a bit of mischief in his tone.

"I wouldn't go so far as to call them all men," Ed interjected before his wife could answer. "But—"

"But Yutanda—" Elizabeth interjected.

"Belinda."

"Now, Ed, she's done had it legally changed for some time now. We're just going to have to accept it."

"Phooey! Belinda. Always was, always will be."

"Now—"

"I suppose if she changes her name to something else African, you'd go along with that too, huh?"

Ed's scowling face brought another good-natured chuckle from his wife.

"And what do you find so amusing, woman? You'd think our daughter would have a little pride in the name she was given at birth."

Waving him off, she said, "Well, Menelik here has a very interesting last name. Why don't you ask him about it? Or maybe you just didn't want to acknowledge the African sound of it when your daughter introduced him to us."

"Arbagna!" Menelik exclaimed with a wide grin. "It means 'patriot,' 'Ethiopian patriot.'"

A squeal of delight came rushing down the hallway, quickly followed by a shout of "We'll be there! We'll be there!"

"Should have pulled the phone out as soon as she drove up the hill. All these years, Lizbeth, and we still haven't learned."

"Menelik! Menelik! We have to go! We have to drive back to Newark!"

Yutanda dashed into the kitchen with such force that the pies shook. She looked at Menelik, hardly able to contain her joy.

"Come on! Get your things! We've got to drive back right now! We've got to be there by—"

"No."

"You don't understand! Thompson's just resigned his seat in the state assembly! That's what both phone calls were about! One of my friends working at the *Times* told me the Feds have evidence—concrete evidence—proving that he's been taking bribes since he's been in office. Guess he's throwing in the towel before it all goes public. They must really have him," she gushed. "Must have him by the—" she glanced at her parents, "uh, the seat of his pants. Damn if justice doesn't rear her head in her own time and in her own way."

Yutanda's enthusiasm was tempered as Menelik walked by her in silence. It left her altogether when he shook her arm free of his and headed for the front porch.


As Yutanda took a step to follow Menelik, Ed took hold of her hand and gently spun her around.

"Thompson," Elizabeth said. "Isn't he the one you volunteered for a couple years back when you got interested in politics and he was running for office?"

"The very same, I'm sorry to say."

"If memory serves me, you once thought he was the second coming, or some such thing," Ed added. "Didn't you almost put yourself in the hospital working so hard to get him elected?"

"I was just so caught up in being a part of an election, Daddy. Just a naive volunteer." Ed watched her brow furrow as her eyes closed for a moment. "Caught up in the movement, I suppose," she said with a sigh. "Going from being a volunteer to Thompson's—But that was before—" her face turned to follow Menelik's path out of the house, "before Menelik. Before that god-awful day, before I realized what a total fool I had been to believe in a candidate who was running on a platform of race hate. Some reverend he turned out to be."

"My Lord, child, now I remember. Your Menelik is the man who was running against him the day that young white boy got killed, isn't he?" Lizbeth gave her husband a concerned look. "You remember Ed. The poor boy on the news some years back? Shot dead on the stage during a debate by a gang of black teenagers who never went to trial because—"

"They never found the weapon or any of the boys who jumped up onto the stage," Yutanda finished.

"My word, girl, why didn't you say something?" Elizabeth whispered.

"That explains a good deal about our—" Ed remarked, shaking his head.

"You don't have to whisper, Momma. And what would I have said? It's done a number on him already. No need to dredge it up all the time. It's time for him to move on."

"Maybe he ain't ready, girl."

"I realize that, Daddy, but he's got to try."

Ed reached for a cigarette, hissing with disgust when his thumb and forefinger found nothing to latch on to in his shirt pocket.

"That why you with him, Yutanda? Because you feel some of the guilt from that day?"

Turning her face away to avoid her mother's probing stare, she sighed.

"Yes and no. I mean," she said, looking back to face both of her parents, "I'll always feel some guilt, just because I was the one who did all the leg work: the press invitations, getting the permits for the stage and the audio equipment, contacting potential candidates, getting news coverage. If I had known it was all going to be a setup— God, I saw a man shot not ten feet from where I was standing and watched him bleed to death on a plywood platform that I had erected! How can I not feel guilty?" Her tone faded to sadness. "Watching Menelik, helpless and lost with his friend dying in his arms. And then again at the funeral, when you could tell by his face that he felt responsible, that he was shouldering it all like it was some sort of penance to try and make up for those boys killing Peter instead of—"

"Killing him," Ed finished.

"Sounds to me like—" Elizabeth started to say.

"I'm not with him just because of guilt!" Yutanda stated, anger flashing in her eyes, her square jaw jutting forward. "I'm with him because— because— Sweet Jesus, if you could have heard him that day! He was like something out of one of those fairy tales you used to read to me, Daddy. Full of courage, undaunted by anything that might stand in his way. His words, his convictions—it was like he was riding one of those great chargers, moving the crowd with, well, with words that I—that we—that we had all been waiting to hear, to feel, for our entire lives."

She paused, her voice soft when she continued.

"And he wasn't a politician—maybe still isn't. And he wasn't a face on some old newsreel, a Dr. King or a Malcolm X or somebody else who's buried. God, if they'd have let him finish, he would have had that street corner that day, probably taken the election right then and there, and we'd be in the middle of healing a city where everything's been allowed to rot."

Shaking, Yutanda wrapped her arms about herself and stared at the floor.

"I— It's probably very selfish of me, but I want to be there when the man I saw up on that stage that day comes back from the place where Peter's death sent him to. And if I have to prod him out, force him out, or bring him out of wherever that is by pulling or pushing or even kicking, then that's just what I'll have to do."

"Sometimes a push can move things the opposite of what you want, Yutanda. Might be pushing the door closed instead of open."

"I know, Momma. But I have to try. I can't let him wait any longer."

"Even if the opening you're pushing him toward might swallow him up?"

As it was apt to do on occasion, the truck siren from the volunteer firehouse located some two miles from the Taylors' residence broke the peace of the early May evening.

Reacting out of habit, Ed looked quickly out the window, searching the sky for any flares that would precede an attack. The sound of the siren always triggered his memory of that night in Korea, the night when the airbase he was stationed at had been infiltrated and hit with mortar and small arms fire. Because he had done as he was ordered and stayed with the Sabre Jet he had been working on, he had remained out of harm's way. But one of his buddies, an M.P. named Ramone, hadn't been so lucky.

Unconsciously, Ed rubbed his thumb and index finger against one another, still able to sense the warmth of the smoldering cigarette Ramone had given him when he raced off and jumped into a jeep to counter the attack. It was the last he ever saw of him. The heat of the cigarette still lingered on his skin.

"Dessert in five minutes?" Elizabeth gently probed, approaching her husband from behind to rub his shoulders.

Ed just nodded, saying nothing.

"I'll make some coffee."

*

B Y NINE O'CLOCK the next morning, Yutanda and Menelik were crossing the Delaware Memorial Bridge over to New Jersey, making the drive up I-95 with thousands of other cars and trucks. Although they had both been subdued since leaving her parents' house, Yutanda was not overly concerned with Menelik's sullen disposition. Having been exposed to his mood swings since the day Peter had died, she attributed his silence to the fact that the firehouse siren had gone off two more times in the middle of the night. It had given everyone in the Taylor household a fitful night's rest.

She raised an eyebrow when Menelik asked her to exit the New Jersey Turnpike and take 33 East when they got near Freehold. But she kept her silence. Although it would take them a good deal longer to get to Newark by going east and then taking the Parkway north, she figured he either needed or wanted the extra time to prepare for the campaign she had laid out for him. But she soon realized she was wrong.

"Pull over, please."

"I think there's a gas station at the next—"

"No, pull over here."

"But—"

"Pull over, Yutanda. Right up here on the overpass."

Shaking her head, frowning, she slowed her silver Mustang II down, putting on her hazard blinkers as she swung the car over to the shoulder. Taking stock of where they were on the Parkway, she asked, "The cemetery? Is that what this is all about?"

"To a degree, I suppose. Sometimes it all seems to start with death, doesn't it?"

"What on earth are you doing?" she demanded as he opened the car door and got out.

"This is where she—"

"Menelik, get back in the car. You're scaring me."

Crouching to peer through the open car door, he sought to soothe her frightened expression with one of calm.

"Go. Do whatever you need to do to lay the groundwork for the campaign. I'll be home sometime tonight. I have some things that I need to do."

"I'm not leaving you out here on the side of the road," she told him, her tone incredulous. "You just get your black ass back in this car right now."

He shook his head and smiled. Innocence, beguilement, mystery, power, a beckoning—she found nuances of each in the corners of his lips and in the sparkle of his eyes. But she was at a loss as to what he was trying to tell her. Abruptly, he stood and swung the door closed.

"Away now!" he shouted, slapping his palm on the roof. "You have much too much to do if we hope to carry the district! Go!"

With another slap of his palm to the metal roof, the car lurched forward as Yutanda accelerated into the flow of traffic.

From a distance, as he walked the familiar sidewalks to the home where he had been raised, the house looked as stately and as well maintained as ever. It was only when he drew nearer and stood on the threshold of the walkway to the front door that the areas of peeling paint became noticeable, as did the weeds in the garden beds and the old leaves piled high against the foundation.

Glancing over toward the garage apartment, he saw that the door at the top of the stairs had been boarded up. Reminded of an old poem he had read in high school, he couldn't help but wonder whether the boards were there to keep something in or to keep something out. With a deep breath, he reached to ring the doorbell.

At the last second, he hesitated and pulled his hand away. Momentarily losing the courage he had found over pie and coffee in the Taylors' kitchen, he moved round to the back of the house. When his feet crunched the gravel of the driveway, he was transported back to the night when Martin first carried him in through the kitchen door.

As he had done on so many occasions in the past, he entered the back of the house without knocking. He didn't recognize her at first. Believing he had made some terrible mistake, he turned to leave. But when he heard the frail figure at the counter hiss a curse at the ancient coffee pot she was attempting to put together, any doubt about the identity of the person standing on the other side of the kitchen was erased. The timeless scene he had walked in on made him laugh.

The coffee pot fell to the floor with a bang as the terrified older woman turned around.

"Mrs. Mathis," he said with affection, hurrying to pick up the fallen appliance.

Patricia's expression turned from one of fear to curiosity.

"You know me?" she asked, her voice quivering.

"I— I—" he stammered. "I was, am—"

Patricia, squinting out of necessity, took Menelik's face into her hands. She lightly brushed each of his features.

Studying her furrowed brow as she sifted across his time-swept skin, Menelik was forced to acknowledge that the years had not been as kind to her as he might have hoped. Her once smooth, fair skin was now a pallid shade of white, with age spots of yellow and brown. Once, her green eyes had vibrantly flashed with the lushness of emeralds. He now looked into eyes that were a diluted shade of pea green. In place of her crown of curly auburn were strands of silver, thinning hair—a perfect match, he thought, to the wrinkles and creases that had taken her youth.

"Gabriel!" she gasped, holding firm to his face, urgently gazing into his eyes as though all the time that had been lost between them could be found in that one moment.

Slightly trembling, her head coming to rest on his chest, Patricia wrapped her arms about him and held him tight.

"I'm sorry," he blurted in a rushed whisper, gently hugging her with arms that suddenly felt weak.

She said nothing in reply, only shaking her head, rubbing her forehead against his chest.

"I'm sorry," he repeated.

To his surprise, Patricia burst into tears, her body shaking, her breathing becoming labored and uneven.

"Here now, why—?"

Fragile fists beat against his chest.

"You," she gasped, struggling to get the word out.

Menelik tilted her head back from his body. He cradled her face as though it were made of the finest, delicate porcelain.

"I can only imagine what I've put you through," he said, trying to see past the tears that were clouding her eyes.

Pushing away from him, Patricia briefly laughed, ending the sound almost as soon as it had started. Somewhat unsteady, she stepped over to the counter and clutched the coffee pot.

"Put us through," she said, her voice clear and strong.

Straightening, smoothing the years of wear away from her hair and body with her hands, she stood before him, exuding an air of strength.

"There's no imagining what we've put you through, Gabriel. It's all too clear what we have done."

"What I've been, what I've done—" He shook his head. "It has nothing to do with what you and Martin—" He lowered his eyes to the floor. "God have mercy on me. And Eleanor, if there was—"

"Oh, if I can only get this contraption apart, we could have a fair cup of coffee."

He could only smile as she turned back to the counter. He did his best not to chuckle when she struggled to remove the lid from the percolator.

"May I?" he asked, stepping next to her. "It was one lesson, Eleanor—Mother—drummed into my head," he joked, taking the coffee pot from her grasp. "Never let Mrs. Mathis make coffee if it can be helped, she always said."

To his relief and joy, Patricia giggled.

"A lost cause from the very beginning. I believe tea would have been much better suited to my talents."

The familiar look of family passed between them.

"You look so good," Patricia gushed, changing the subject. "Except for that awful beard, or whatever that is, on your chin."

Menelik stroked his goatee, half laughing.

"Wouldn't have gone over too well at Saint Augustine's—least not back in those days. I wonder, though, if they wouldn't allow it now."

"Go back and see," she offered mischievously.

"Oh, no thank you to that. One go-round of those years was plenty," he told her, shaking his head. "No need to venture back there again."

Patricia averted her eyes, offering a brief, indecipherable grin as a response.

Sensing the wound he had unwittingly scratched open, Menelik went about the task of making coffee, finding what he needed in the places where Eleanor had always stored it. As he plugged the percolator cord into the outlet with a sigh of satisfaction, he tendered a probing glance toward Patricia. The dark circles beneath her eyes, half hidden by the poorly applied makeup, and the deep, drooping lines running from the corners of her mouth said more to him than all the words she would never utter herself.

"And Martin. How is he?"

The image of the man eating at Roy Rogers flashed through his thoughts. The mostly deaf, withered figure he had seen that day made him wonder if Martin's state of health had gotten worse. Patricia's expression seemed to intimate that it had.

"He'll be glad to see you," she replied after a pause. "There were some good years, if you recall," she solemnly added.

"More, if I hadn't been such a, such a—"

"Humbug?"

"You're too forgiving."

"Am I?"

The percolator began to bubble and hiss.

"Who's to say?" she offered, her face brightening a bit. "But do go in and see him," she added quickly. "Sometimes he naps in the— He would be very upset if he missed you. You go ahead, there'll be time for us to talk. I'm not going anywhere. Besides," she glanced at the coffee pot, "someone's got to keep an eye on our old friend, here."

Menelik rolled his shoulders as though he was shifting a heavy burden. "Where?"

"In the room that looks out over the back yard and the river. His old office. You know the way."

"Should I not say anything about—?"

"Go on," she told him, shaking her head. "Just be yourself. Say whatever it is you came to say."

Suddenly feeling as though he were a little boy, Menelik went to find the man who had stood by him since the day their paths had crossed on the river of sand.

No sooner had he left the kitchen than Patricia went to the table to sit down in a chair. Barely a moment had passed before she covered her face with her hands and tried to suppress the sobs that were wracking her body. It was in this very state that Menelik found her when he came back into the kitchen not two minutes after he had left.

"Hey, hey," he tenderly said, bending to gently hold her.

"He's not good, is he?" she whispered, biting her lower lip.

"He—" Menelik lowered his gaze, unable to bear the weight of the desperate eyes that turned to search his. "I spoke to him, but— I stood right in front of him."

"He didn't know you were there."

Menelik nodded, his face a conflict of confusion and sadness.

"They call it some horrible sounding name: Alzheimer's."

Menelik furrowed his brow.

"They, the doctors, they just came out with it." She breathed deeply. "Some new prognosis or condition that they say affects the elderly." She laughed haltingly. "Something to look forward to," she added, trying to be flippant, though the trace of fear in her voice was clear.

"Does it have something to do with the shrapnel that he took to the head in Korea?"

She shrugged, wiping her eyes.

"They don't—" She looked at him hard, her face flush with anger. "I don't think they know what the hell causes it." She began to pull on her fingers. "Genetics," she spat. "Inherited, they think."

"Is he on— I mean—"

"Medication? To do what? For what?" she bitterly asked, the harshness in her tone forcing him to back away. "Nothing they can do," she added with a bite of sarcasm. "Research. That's the stage they're in. Until they find the—"

She cut herself off and turned away.

Menelik stood helplessly by, wondering what he could possibly say or do.

"Sometimes he's just like he's always been, you see," she mused aloud, her words soft, caring. "He's Martin, my husband. One of the finest—" She bit her lower lip.

"Shouldn't he be," Menelik ventured, struggling with what he was feeling as he watched her wringing her hands, "in a hospital?"

Smiling politely, she asked, "To what end, Gabriel?"

"To what end? So that he can get the proper attention."

"And what is the proper attention for someone who can sit for days on end without knowing who you are or how to dress himself or—" She exhaled sharply. "What nurse or doctor or volunteer is going to care if his hair isn't combed the way he likes it or that he has snot running out of his nose or that his favorite part of day is when he looks out the window at the three white birch trees we planted and sees the sun shining off the bark? Or don't you think that he'd rather be home with his wife than be left to sit in some sterile, god-awful box of a room waiting for whatever ending this damn disease will finally bring to him?"

"I didn't mean to—"

"Nobody means to, Gabriel," she snapped. "We didn't mean to, you didn't mean to, nobody means to." Swallowing hard, she said, "But no matter what we all meant to do or didn't mean to do, we all got what has come to pass."

Menelik shifted uneasily under her stony glare.

"Coffee sounds like it's ready," she said, getting up from the table. "How do you take yours now? It's been quite a while since we've had a cup together."

"What about a specialist? Surely there has to be some physician some-where who's—"

Her shrill laughter was like a sharp knife being thrust into his ears.

"Do you know that the neighbors," she threw at him, whirling upon him as she grabbed a coffee cup hanging from a brass hook beneath the cupboard, "are complaining because our house isn't properly manicured to suit the neighborhood we live in?"

Menelik's expression reflected his uncertainty.

"Not right that a house in Rumson should have peeling paint or weeds in the garden or unraked leaves, or grass that isn't mowed for weeks on end."

Her stare was defiant.

"Times are not what they were," she said. "Money," she went on, giving an odd emphasis to the word, "is not what it was. Medical bills, taxes, lawyer's fees, utilities—" She gazed at the floor, seemingly hypnotized by something. "Everything has taken its toll." When she raised her face to him, she seemed so fragile that he was close to tears. "We're not even hanging on anymore. There's just no— It's not like it was. Martin's not an ambassador or a senator anymore. And the people he knows that could help—the ones who owe him some favors—well, they just don't want anything to do with him."

"But why?" he asked, dumbfounded.

Patricia looked at him in silence.

"Good god. I never thought—" He hung his head, unable to meet her gaze.

"A troubling evolution of our world, I've noticed," Patricia offered without acidity or rancor. "No one thinks, no one means anything, no one does anything."

When Menelik lifted his face to reply, she had her back turned toward him as she poured coffee into a cup.

"Your mother taught you well," she giggled, tasting a sip. "I, on the other hand, must have been her worst pupil."

"You were her dearest friend. Both you and Martin. Neither of us could have hoped for better. It's taken me too long to realize."

"Go on back in," she gently prodded, motioning with her cup for him to leave the kitchen. "I believe that sometimes he hears us, even though he may not show it. Go on."

Steadying her cup with both hands, she shuffled back to the table and sat down.

"I'll just sit here and enjoy your coffee."

Wiping a tear from his cheek, he smiled as best he could and left the kitchen.

*

MARTIN MATHIS WAS as Menelik had left him: sitting statue-like in a high-backed, red leather chair that was edged with brass tacks. It was the only piece of furniture that remained in a once impressive office. The stately walnut desk that had once claimed the honored place in front of the chair was gone, as were the law books and hardbound copies of great literature that had once filled the built-in walnut bookshelves that had served as the background for many a late-night meeting.

To Menelik, Martin seemed to be a photograph frozen in some awful stage of partial exposure. It was like he was a troubled artist's impression of a man in decline: slightly surreal, his features heavily exaggerated, the onslaught of age pronounced. Menelik approached him cautiously, studying him from front to side.

Martin's face twitched with a spasm as he seemed to grimace in pain. Menelik put out a hand to comfort him, but then withdrew it. Even though he had winced, Martin had made no sound. Perhaps it was a symptom of the disease, Menelik thought. He had forgotten to ask Patricia if Alzheimer's was contagious. He waved a hand in front of Martin's eyes. Martin didn't respond. It was as though he was keeping watch over something out the window he was facing.

Following his gaze, Menelik saw the three white birch trees. Thirty years tall, he realized. He watched for a moment as the wind swayed their wispy, delicate leaves to show glimpses of the blue river just beyond. He sighed, remembering the days when Martin would toss him a football and he would run with it, dodging the three trees like they were would-be tacklers.

He would score a touchdown every time, of course, and he and Martin would laugh. And then they would do it again and again.

It was only when he turned away from the window that he noticed the tasseled ends of the curtain cord that had been tied around Martin's waist. His eyes followed the braided, gold rope to the chair legs below, where it had been looped so that Martin was unable to rise. A pang of guilt and sadness surged through him. He bent down on one knee.

"Martin," he whispered. "Father."

The once keen, blue-grey eyes of the man did not react. Blank, glassy eyes stared back at him.

"The hyenas," he found himself saying, briefly glancing out the window before looking back into Martin's eyes, "they followed us here. I wondered if you knew. I wondered if they've haunted you, as they have me. I've wondered why they still do, after all this time. I wish you had killed them all."

He paused, his gaze drifting to what was left of the ear that had been decimated by shrapnel in the Korean War. Slowly he realized that Martin no longer wore the bulky hearing aid.

"They're more clever here. They can become people. It's almost impossible to see what they really are."

Martin stared impassively out the window.

"It is hard for me to understand. Most of that day is a blank for me." He rubbed his arm where the hyena had bitten him. "The river of sand seemed endless." Menelik paused, thinking back. "I ran away. I thought I had lost everything." His tone growing urgent, he said, "I have seen my brother, though. He looks nothing like me, yet our ways seem mirrored somehow." Remembering the vision in the courtroom, he went on, "It scares me. He's been wounded. But he fights."

Menelik took hold of Martin's wrists, probing deeper into the opaqueness of his eyes.

"What can I say to him? So much blood—too much spilled and given, lost. What can I do? How do I tell him that I am alive?"

Once more, a silent grimace shaped Martin's features. With his lips twisting, tears began to form in his clouded eyes. As Menelik looked for something to wipe them away, he saw a dribble of urine slide down the front of the leather cushion. The crotch of Martin's pants grew dark.

"Did I cause that? Am I upsetting you? What is it I can do?"

As abruptly as it had appeared, Martin's grimace vanished. Menelik sighed.

"It's always been *I*, hasn't it? Never about you or Patricia or Eleanor. Not even Jen—or Peter."

He looked to Martin for comfort. None was offered.

"What can I say about my past, my failings? That I'm sorry? It is not nearly enough. Maybe if I had your faith and courage, I would have been a different man. But I came here today to tell you that I will try to become one, a better one. Perhaps one you can be proud of."

There was more he wanted to say, but his thoughts became jumbled and he was unable to put them into words. For a moment, he lingered in Martin's gaze, wanting nothing more than to be recognized. He would be happy with just being a snippet of a memory that created a flicker of movement in the man's eyes, but there was nothing. No glimmer, no hint, no promise that there would ever be one.

With a squeeze to Martin's limp hand, Menelik said his silent goodbye. Rising, he took one last look at the three white birch trees down by the river's edge.

"Gabriel."

The word spun him instantly around. He felt his heart racing. And yet, when he looked to Martin, he wondered if he had heard anything at all. For the man was as he had been when Menelik arrived, a blank facsimile of someone he once knew.

Eyeing his surroundings with suspicion, Menelik stepped across the room to take his leave.

"Gabriel."

It was but a whisper this time, prompting him to reluctantly look back.

As if time had reopened the past, he found Martin looking straight at him, face beaming. For a moment, they stared at one another, father to son. Menelik felt the warmth of his own tears as Martin's steel-blue eyes took stock of him.

"I love you too."

When the phrase swept over him, Menelik wiped the tears from his eyes and moved to embrace Martin. But the moment had passed. Martin was once more sitting impassive and unaware, staring blankly out the window.

Menelik raced out of the room.


He entered the kitchen breathing heavily, his head filled with spinning images of both the past and the present. His heart racing, he placed a hand to his chest to ward off the sense of panic he could neither calm nor pinpoint the cause of.

"You've seen it too?" Patricia casually inquired, her focus fixed on the coffee in her cup.

"What?"

She eyed him thoughtfully for a moment, seemingly perplexed that he did not immediately understand what she had meant.

"That he'll die soon."

She turned back to her coffee and took a sip.

"I didn't—" he started to say, bewildered.

"I won't be able to—" She stopped and stared into her coffee. Offering a polite smile, she said, "Not for you to worry."

"What do you mean, you won't be able to? Won't be able to what?"

"Your brother—how is he? Have you been able to make contact with him?"

"My brother?"

"Yes, the one whose name you called out in the courtroom during the first trial. Don't you remember? What was his name? Telba? Tembasa?"

"Teimbaka."

"Yes, that's it. How is he?"

"I— I've— They've never granted me a visa," he managed to get out. "My prison record and the draft issue."

"You'll find a way," she assured him, oddly cheerful. "Even if you have to will it."

He said nothing in response. Patricia sighed.

"I didn't get to say everything to him that I wanted, that I had planned on," Menelik said.

Patricia seemed not to hear him.

"Makes me think we should be having pie," she muttered after a long pause. "Peach, of course."

"I—" he forced himself to say, looking lost and out of place, "I guess I'll get going."

"That you were there was worth more than any words you might ever have said to him," Patricia told him, her expression holding him in place as her eyes seemed to absorb every part of him. "How meaningless they become in silence."

"He spoke."

Her face seemed to unravel before him, emotions of every kind fluttering for a moment and then drifting away. The lines of her face softened at the notion of what he had told her. When she looked at him, he could almost feel the innocence of her hope. It was overwhelming.

"Say it again," she whispered as if not to break the spell he had cast.

"He said my name as I was leaving."

Part of him did not want to say anything further, for he could see that his every word was affecting the innocence he did not wish to hurt.

"He said, 'I love you too.'"

"'I love you too,'" she repeated, saying the words as though the grace of God had been placed upon them. "Bless you, Gabriel. Bless you."

With a swiftness and agility that belied her frailty, Patricia bounded from her chair and threw herself against his chest. She squeezed him with such ferocity that he staggered back from the force.

"It is you who—"

A hand to his lips stopped him from speaking. In silence, he absorbed her embrace, letting her innocence spread through him.

"Go now," she bade him, her voice soft. "There is still Eleanor to see. What delivered you here has been discharged."

With a slight shake of her head, her fingers lingering upon his lips, she gave him what he had hoped he would find when he stood at the front door.

Their eyes misting over with all the hopes they had once shared, they kissed as mother and son, recovering what they both thought had been lost.


Menelik stepped out of the kitchen door feeling quite fatigued, at odds with his decision to leave. But there was another stop to make, he knew, another destination to reach before the haunting calls of the hyenas could be put to rest.

With that purpose in mind, he started off toward the cemetery, only to be halted by some inexplicable whimpering coming from the tiny grove of white birch trees. Pausing, searching, seeing nothing as he stared at the trunk and branches of each tree, he shrugged his shoulders, wondering if he had heard anything at all.

Yet, as he began the lengthy walk to the cemetery, making his way across the familiar streets he had grown up on, he could not shake the feeling that he was being followed. Whenever he would turn around to check, there was not a sign or hint of anyone or any creature behind him.


The shadows of early evening grew long, creeping by Menelik as he stood and stared at the graves of Eleanor and her family.

"Eleanor."

It was the only word he had spoken since his arrival an hour before. His gaze lost within the encroaching veil of darkness, he was suddenly filled with an urge to convey what he didn't quite understand himself. Grunting, sighing, he felt the words he wanted to say rush up into his throat, only to lose them just as quickly when his feelings pushed them back down. Suddenly exhausted, he felt his thoughts start to splinter. Tears began to fall. They came easily.

The shadow of the evening crept over Eleanor's grave. Stepping closer, he took a teardrop on his fingertip and placed it in the grass where he thought her heart might be.

"What does one say to a mother who loved her son?" he asked, his face tilted to her headstone. "I love you too," he whispered. "I love you too."

# NOVEMBER, 1983

THE SOFT GLARE of the television screen made Patricia squint. But she would not look away, riveted by what was being broadcast. "Isn't it exciting, Martin?" she whispered, her face alight with anticipation.

She raised her husband's hand and placed it against her cheek. Caressing his cold flesh with her face and fingers, she said, "I knew we weren't wrong. I knew that, in time, everything would work out. Wait, I think this is it. Yes, yes, look. There he is."

Menelik Arbagna stepped into the picture, taking a position next to a reporter who was holding a microphone. Patricia leaned forward in the bed, wanting to catch every word that was being said.

"So how does it feel, Mr. Arbagna?" the reporter asked, glancing into the camera and then back to Menelik.

"There's a sense of joy, of course," Menelik replied without hesitation. "But there's also one of relief and accomplishment. Running for office is—well, it can be exhausting."

"There was an awful lot of dirt thrown your way by your opponents in the election. Does this victory give you any sense of vindication?"

"Vindication?" He slowly shook his head. "It is as I have said through-out: my past is my own doing. I do not deny or excuse it. It is part of me. Yet it is done, and will affect the future only if I allow it."

"The Reverend Thompson still insists that you are not qualified to be a representative of this district because you are not of the people who reside here. What's your reaction?"

"I need not be anything more than a human being," Menelik slowly articulated after a brief pause, "to both serve and represent any other individual or group. The way of humanity is not restricted by boundaries set forth by men."

"Which brings us to another of the Reverend's objections: Since you were born in Africa—and recalling how fondly you spoke of your homeland, its people, its problems—is the Reverend Thompson not justified in his contention that your efforts will be geared more toward the needs of the people there than the ones here in your own constituency?"

"As the people of these streets and houses, businesses, and churches are fully aware," Menelik responded, looking squarely into the television camera, "poverty, disease, illiteracy, bigotry, and most certainly starvation are evils that ravage the world without regard to borders. I have, as Mr. Thompson has stated, spoken frequently on this subject, and it is one that the people of this community have both been included in and share in. They, as I, know that the ravagers of the world can and do leap through time and across impossible distances, making it imperative that we engage them on whatever stage it is in our power to do so. Here is where the fight begins. But if we have the means and the courage to lend ourselves to those who do not have the strength to combat these forces with their own hands, then, by all that is held true in this world, this is what we must do, what we will do!"

"He wears the mantle he has grown into very well, doesn't he, dear?"

Out of habit, Patricia glanced over to her husband. Quickly, before the tears could overcome her, she threw her attention back to the television.

"It is certainly quite apparent by the speech you just gave us, Mr. Arbagna, why you carried the day with such a convincing margin. I thank you for your time and wish you—"

The reporter suddenly halted his closing remarks, holding a finger up to the camera.

"Just one more question as it comes in from our studio, Mr. Arbagna," he said. "Yes, Jim, I've got it," he relayed, pressing his earpiece. "The question, Mr. Arbagna, is that throughout the campaign, either by oversight or design, you have referred to the Reverend Thompson solely as Mr. Thompson; is there any particular reason for this?"

"The fabric of any man, any person, is not worn about one's neck or draped across one's shoulders. The cloth we wear is woven by actions and intent. Those who align themselves with God strip away His robing by their own hand if they spin their way on a loom of wrongs. One is not of Him if one is not devoted to Him and His teachings."

"Are you saying, then, that the Reverend Thompson himself has stripped away his own standing in the church by what he, in your opinion, has done in the past?"

"I have spoken what is a personal belief. I will add, however, that while I do not wish to put myself in place of judgment, I will not be fooled by the hyena's ruse of confusion."

"We are out of time it seems, so back to—"

Patricia flicked the television off, her hand shaking as her fingers let go of the knob. Sitting on the edge of the bed, she took a moment to gather her thoughts, letting her eyes and her mood adjust to the darkness.

After a moment, she roused herself and, without hurry, stepped across the room to the dresser that she and Martin had shared for over thirty-five years. In what little light there was from the stars and the sliver of the moon shining through the blinds, she opened the top drawer and grasped the service revolver she had kept since the final days of World War II.

"The same day as the hyenas," she murmured, holding the Colt .45 aloft. "I wonder if he knows," she mused, glancing at the television. "Odd that he would mention them if he didn't. Ah well, perhaps it is—"

With a shrug, she went back to the bed and slid in next to Martin. Lovingly, she took his cold, stiff hand into her own.

"So like you not to have said anything," she teased.

Her eyes began to tear.

"You knew all along, didn't you? Even when those stupid doctors said it was Alzheimer's. Even Gabriel mentioned the shrapnel when he was here. They never even checked."

Patricia began to weep, steady and soft, the butt of the gun pressed against her forehead.

"All these years," she choked in a whisper. "The pain must have been terrible. No wonder your face would get that way. How did you not cry out?"

Bringing his frozen hand to her lips, she kissed it tenderly and then looked at her husband's ghostly, lifeless face.

"Only that last time. I hope I'm as brave."

With a deep sigh of resignation, she placed Martin's hand atop his chest and took firm hold of the Colt .45 with both of hers.

"What was it Gabriel just said? The ravagers of the world know no boundaries?"

The silence in the room was like a vacuum, a cubicle where nothing existed, not even thought. Minutes passed before she awoke from the stupor she had fallen into.

"So too is it the time of the protectors," she said, continuing on as though her train of thought had never paused. "I hope he knows."

The revolver, now heavy in her hands, mirrored the weight of her tired eyes.

"I know, dear," she said, briefly squeezing Martin's icy flesh. "I'm rambling again."

She looked over at her husband, seeing not the ghost of the man that was lying beside her, but rather the image of him when they were first married: young, handsome, brave, and filled with the spirit of a giving heart.

"Even death does not part those who are bound by love," she told him, her voice as soft and as tender as the day they had exchanged vows. "I love you," she whispered. "I love you."


From the tiny grove of white birch trees behind the Mathises' house, the baby spirit elephant wailed at the loosing of the bullet, heartbroken over the loss of a life so rich in innocence. Stomping its feet to show its sorrow, the shimmering, ethereal beast raised its trunk to the sky and trumpeted the passing of Patricia's soul.

Seven thousand miles away, separated by oceans and seas, by deserts, mountains, and plains, the great spirit herd took up the call, petitioning the stars for Patricia's spirit to be placed in their care. So great were their voices, so thunderous their plea, that all the Horn of Africa would quake that night, the very sky shaking from the din.

And in the camp of Sister Lady, the clamor of the heavens jolted Teimbaka from his slumber. Fearing the worst, he looked to the ridges, expecting to find the fire shadows of war. Yet, as he gazed from horizon to horizon, he found no traces of bombs or the fires that would lick the darkness from the peaks of the mountains when they fell. Only the brilliance of an African night welcomed his gaze: a million stars twinkling with clarity, one glittering more than any other.

Across the encampment, not far from where Teimbaka lay gazing upward at the night's beauty, another had been awakened, though the tremors the little one had felt and the thunder he had heard did not startle him or give him reason to fear. For he had wondered when the cry of the great spirit elephants might again be heard, had wondered when the Mother might let her feelings be known.

Smiling with the notion that there would be good dreams this night, he rested his head back upon the ground and began to count the stars that filled his eyes.

ETHIOPIA, 1985

*Dearest Mother and Father,*

*Where do I begin? I am well. If this letter happens to reach you, I know that will be the first thing you wonder, so please know that I am well and still doing God's work.*

*To say that I am sorry that several years have elapsed between this letter and my last seems trivial, almost cruel. Understanding now what silence can do to people who care for one another, I know I have caused you both great pain and worry. And for that—for placing your emotions, your lives, in turmoil—I am deeply and truly sorry. I humbly beg your forgiveness.*

*Where do I begin?*

*War is all around us—and has been for what seems to be forever. I remember Teimbaka—you remember, I have spoken of him— asking me once if God could bring an end to the endless days of suffering that have blanketed this land. With great piety and confidence, I replied He could, but that it was not His way to bring closure to what men have brought upon themselves. I now pray that God will change His mind on this and will bring an end to these wars, for the people of this land have withered beneath the pain these endless conflicts have wrought. It has become almost too much to bear.*

*As God had intended, my faith in Him was shaken, even lost for a time to a darkness I do not wish to recall. If it were not for Teimbaka, I would be dead—or worse—and though much of what I was subjected to I do not clearly remember—or wish to—I know that without his strength, Hell would have surely claimed me. He is blessed, but would be the last to ever acknowledge it.*

*I have spent years in mourning for the children in my care who were murdered in a vicious attack by the forces of Mengistu and his government mercenaries, but I have found hope again in the faces of those who have helped me regain myself: young children of this land—orphans—who have given me faith that God's will is still at work. Yet, the cries of the dead echo in the hills and gorges around us. It is worse for Teimbaka, who carries their voices in his head.*

*If I am not speaking in a way that reassures you that I am of sound mind and body, know that, like all who struggle with faith, I have changed. I must admit that, when I left America to undertake this post through the Sisters of the Holy Cross, I was naïve—and that the two of you had every right to ask me if I wasn't out of my mind the evening I spoke with you about my devotion to God. I see now what you meant. Now that I am old enough to look back, I might question the direction of my life. Even so, though the Lord has tested me with many trials, I cannot say that I am not exactly where I should be. My sacrifices have been little compared to what the children of this land have been subjected to. If only I were stronger.*

*We found twelve boys in the desert. Or perhaps I should say that they found us. Orphans each one. All without names. So I have named them after the apostles. Judas, for obvious reasons, I did not use, nor John, who I will not speak of. In place of these, we have named one Damien, after the leper saint. The littlest one, who refused all other names we offered, insisted on the name of John Too. He, the latter, is an ever-inspiring child of hope and joy. There is something truly—dare I say—holy about him.*

*Teimbaka tells me that we are somewhere in the northern area of Ethiopia, between the provinces of Tigray and Eritrea. We are nomads, moving often, dodging the warring armies and bombs, staying hidden when at all possible. Sometimes at night, when we dare to huddle about a fire, the mountains around us seem to be engulfed in flames. West, north, and east of us, there is bloody fighting. And south, the drought and famine have robbed the country of life. They spread toward us. It is a miracle that we survive.*

*I am running out of paper, and I have said so little.*

*I do not know how this will end—if it ever will—if there will come a time when I can say my work here is done. Perhaps this is God's greatest test of me: that there is to be no ending, only a constant trial of faith that I must endure. I asked Teimbaka once what price he would pay to reach paradise. I sit here now, my hand trembling as I scribble on this piece of wrinkled, torn paper, and know that the question was really not meant for him. Looking back, I see it was meant for me.*

*May the grace of God be with you, and be with us all.*

*Your loving daughter,*

*Claire*

CLAIRE WIPED THE mist from her eyes while she smoothed the wrinkles from the tattered paper Teimbaka had brought to her. Folding the paper, she placed it in the folds of her shamma along with what was left of the pencil she had used to write with.

"Goodbye," she whispered, her fingers lingering atop the letter. "I am sorry."

The sound was faint, still far enough away so as not to cause immediate alarm, but the all-too-familiar squeak and squeal of sprockets and treads meant that at least one tank was on the move somewhere near. Claire hurried her movements.

"Sister Lady!" a voice called in a whisper.

A wiry boy of seven or eight, his cheek disfigured by a scar made by someone's whip, hurried to stand next to her.

"I hear it, Bartholomew. Are we ready to move if need be?"

"Always." He nodded, smiling broadly.

"Where is Teimbaka?"

Bartholomew's smile grew more mischievous.

"Hunting?" he offered, cocking his head to one side.

"You mean foraging."

Pretending he did not understand, he shrugged.

"When will he stop— Oh, never mind. Gather everyone together, then, just in case."

Bartholomew looked suddenly pained.

"What is it?"

The boy looked westward. Following his gaze, Claire asked, "Who?"

"John Too," he replied, not meeting her eyes.

"Hunting? Again? Who is with him?"

Bartholomew shook his head, keeping his face downcast.

"No one," he mumbled.

"No one? But it will be evening soon and—"

The squeal of the tank seemed louder, causing them both to look northward.

"And Damien," Bartholomew guardedly added.

"And where is he?" she inquired, her frustration evident.

"He is sick."

*

THE TRAIL HAD been long, leading John Too far from the area he was comfortable with, far from where Sister Lady and the others would be waiting for him. She would be angry, he knew, as would Teimbaka, if he were to find out. It would be evening soon. The land would not be safe.

When his arrow had pierced the gazelle, he had been overjoyed, but he had not calculated the animal's will to survive or the lengths that it would go to try to escape. The trail of blood from the wound of the beast had been easy for him to follow. It would be easy for others as well. He hurried.

When the gazelle lay at his feet—finally succumbing to loss of blood—John Too knelt to the animal and brushed away the flies that had already settled on it.

"Bless what you have been and what you give. May the Mother set you free to run with the wind and the Father grace you with a path to the stars."

Taking a stout-bladed army knife from the sheath about his waist, John Too gutted the animal with a practiced hand. Absorbed in his work, his mind drifting to the image of the meat roasting over a fire while the voices of the twenty odd others said the blessings that Sister Lady had taught them, the sound of sandaled feet moving amongst the rocks was covered by the work of his blade.

After cutting up the gazelle and placing the hunks of meat into a small tarp that he tied at the ends, John Too wiped his knife clean in the sandy soil, sheathed his blade and shouldered his bow and arrows. Hoisting the tarp across his back, he set off toward camp, hoping to reach it before night set in.

Above him, crouching from one boulder to another, the hides of the hyenas bobbed and swayed as sandaled feet shuffled and leapt. The hyenaman held the twisted horn of the impala outward for balance as his crazed eyes intently watched the path John Too was taking.

*

TEIMBAKA LEFT THE camp of the government forces with as much medical supplies as he dared to carry if he wished to remain swift of foot and able to outlast a prolonged pursuit if one arose.

Although the camp had sentries posted along its perimeter, and lookouts placed farther out along the region it patrolled, Teimbaka had become adept at blending in with the almost constant stream of refugees fleeing Eritrea, joining the procession of the misplaced and the forgotten southward before veering off and doubling back to the ridges and valleys to the north where Claire and the children would be waiting.

Keeping his black shamma pulled close, he hugged the stolen bottle of rubbing alcohol and the packages of gauze, tape, and aspirin close to his body. Keeping slightly bent, careful not to overplay the slight limp he was fond of using from the old gash on his thigh, he hoped to remain unnoticed as he drifted toward the back of the exodus he had joined. Taking a quick glance about him, he breathed a sigh of relief; no one, it seemed, had given him the slightest notice. Pulling the fabric of his robes back over his face, he allowed himself a quick smile. He would be back in the hills by early night.

THE SMOKE FROM the Gauloises escaped from the side of Peter Gunstard's mouth as he focused the binoculars on the black-robed figure limping slowly within the parade of refugees.

"You certain, Lieutenant? This is the same?"

Gunstard's wrinkled, sunbaked hand held the binoculars out for the man to take.

"The one with the limp? Dressed in the black garment?"

"Yes, Colonel," the man replied with a nod after looking through the binoculars. "The very one: dress, limp, time of day."

"And you say he comes from the north each time?"

"Yes, Colonel. One of the sentries remembered seeing him two days in a row. He reported his suspicions to me. We have kept a count since then. At least a dozen times he has been through here."

"A spy?"

"No, a common thief, more like it. Bits of food, medical supplies, knives—even pencil and paper once."

"Pencil and paper, you say?"

Gunstard's pale, watery eyes surveyed the lieutenant with scorn.

"A mapmaker perhaps, or making written accounts of the strength of our troops or tanks or what roads we patrol and which we do not. Did you not think of this, Lieutenant?"

The man squirmed under the scrutiny.

"And where does he go, this thief, I wonder?"

"We don't know, Colonel. I thought it best to inform you before taking any action, in case—"

"Then we'd best find out, Lieutenant, don't you agree?"

"Of course, Colonel. By all means."

"I thought you might," Gunstard mocked, taking the binoculars back and focusing them on the black-clad figure.

"Two of your best trackers, Lieutenant. Let us solve this mystery."

As the Lieutenant saluted and took his leave, Gunstard rubbed the weariness from his face before taking one last look at the man they had been discussing. When the figure in the binoculars glanced upward, Gunstard's lined face broke into a smile.

"Boy," he whispered. "You return."

*

"SHE IS YOURS."

John turned the muzzle of the hyena that had spoken away from his face.

"We can have her."

Wild-eyed, John looked to the hyena muzzle perched on his other shoulder and saw the piercing, fire-orange eyes of the Serpent staring back at him from the cavity of the dead beast's mouth.

He closed his eyes and covered his ears. But the voice would not cease.

"Take her back. Take her back," it hissed. "Have her again. Again."

John clutched the horn of the impala tighter, turning the sharpened tip toward his body. Running his fingers along his arm, he felt for a patch of smooth skin amongst the many scabs that disfigured it from shoulder to wrist. Locating a small scab-free area, he inserted the tip of the horn into his flesh. As Susenyo had taught him with the needle and the syringe, he pushed on the base of the horn, pumping it with his thumb until he felt the rush of the imaginary drug entering his body. Momentarily stupefied, he sat back on his haunches, relishing the euphoria.

"Keep watch," the hyena muzzles told him. "Don't let him get away."

John stroked the fur of the hyena heads as they stared at him.

"Not to worry," he told them, his body twitching as it struggled to adapt to the feelings surging through him. "Blood lingers where he has walked. Do you not smell it?"

The hyena heads chuckled.

From the mouth of the one, the Serpent slithered forth and raised its coiled body so it could look into John's eyes.

"Do you share?" it whispered. "What will you do with the others?"

John pulled the tip of the horn from his arm and licked the blood from it. Pushing the Serpent back into the mouth from which it came, he stood and adjusted the hyena pelts that clothed him. Raising the twisted horn of the impala above him so the last rays of the sun burnished it gold, he leapt down from the ledge of stone he had been perched upon and began to follow the trail that John Too had taken.

*

"LET US PRAY."

"Let us pray," the children responded.

"Our Father who art in heaven, hallowed …"

Claire looked upon the bowed heads with the same hope that she had clung to every night since the day she had been reborn: that tomorrow would bring an end to their sufferings and welcome peace back to their land. But though she clung to hope, she could not help but be afraid.

"… on earth as it is in heaven. Amen."

"Amen, Sister Lady, amen," John Too said when Claire did not join the others in the closing of the prayer.

Teimbaka squeezed her hand, offering her a tired, knowing smile when she turned to look at him.

"Forgive me, John Too, amen."

"Amen," the children responded, their faces fixated on the gazelle haunch roasting over the small fire.

"Blessed are we. Is this not so, Sister Lady?"

"Yes, of course, John Too," she responded, as she always did when he asked, though this night found her eyes flitting to the wavering shadows on the rocks they had taken refuge amongst.

"What worries you, then?" he asked, seeing her apprehension. "We have food, and water from the wells that the soldiers cannot find. And now, Etiyopiya brings medicine."

Claire wrung her hands, trying to cleanse her fingers of the feeling of the little girl's severed spine. She had never been able to forget. Drifting from the silhouettes on the rock formations, her gaze turned upward to the horizon, searching for the all-too-familiar glimmer of fire on the belly of the sky. The shadows of war seemed closer each day that passed. Soon, she thought, there would be no escape from them.

"Sister Lady looks to the Father," Teimbaka offered, "to thank him for bringing us to all of you."

Teimbaka smiled at the boy and then looked to Claire in the hope that she had understood the track of his words. But the look of worry did not leave her face.

"I must see to Damien," she abruptly stated, rising to her feet. Barely meeting either of their eyes, she brushed by John Too and Teimbaka.

"And you have me!" John Too exclaimed to the amusement of the other children.

But Claire, if she heard him, did not look back. John Too sought Teimbaka.

"The tank and the soldiers that followed it, I think," Teimbaka offered as an explanation for her silence. "They come closer each day. She is simply tired of running and hiding."

"But we are home," John Too said. "Where else should we be?"

Although the children had taken to trimming Teimbaka's beard—a practice started by John Too—and went to great lengths to cut out the silver and grey whiskers that had begun to show more and more of late, several glittered in the light of the fire as he thought about what John Too had asked.


"How is he?"

"Weak," she softly relayed. "Feverish," she added after a pause.

"Rinse this for me," she said to the boy who was kneeling next to her. "And bless you, Thomas."

Touching his forehead with his fingertips, Thomas bowed his head and did as he was asked. In complete silence, he accepted the cloth that Claire held out to him and left.

"I wonder if he will ever speak," she mused, watching his slight, gangly form depart.

Teimbaka did not answer, for there was nothing to say about Thomas's muteness that they had not spoken of before.

"What I brought this evening—the pills, the liquid, will they be of help?"

Though Damien shivered beneath the blankets Claire had covered him with, his light brown skin was awash with sweat. In the interlude before she replied, the quiet was filled with the gurgling wheeze of his breathing.

Claire shook her head.

"He has always been sickly," Teimbaka offered. "Perhaps this will also pass, as it has done the other times."

"This is different. I—" She looked at him then, removing the folds of her shamma from her head.

Teimbaka couldn't help but smile when he noticed that the children had obviously been cutting her hair, for they had cut it as though she were a boy and had missed several strands that stood out from her temples like the sprouts of new leaves.

"I don't know what to do," she confessed, distressed, her focus falling to the skinny boy that lay at her feet.

"Do not lose faith. Perhaps the Father sees him right now and makes amends."

Shuddering with emotion, she whispered, "But what if I have?"

She opened herself to him, but then changed her mind, unlocking her gaze from his. "What if—?"

"What medicine does he need? I will get it."

"No!" she said a little stronger, a little louder than she had intended. "Every time you leave—" She turned away, unable to finish.

The voices of the spirit children stirred in his head.

"Tell me what it is called. I will find it."

"Steal it, you mean," she replied, her words laced with bitterness. "It's not right that you—"

"Survive? Do what I must to help these children?"

Eastward, the sky above the mountains began to flicker with the shadows of war. Only a few seconds passed until the stuttered rumble of the exploding bombs reached them.

Claire crossed herself.

"Tell me what he needs. Claire, say what it is called."

"We should go," she mumbled half-heartedly. "We should join the rest and head for a refugee camp. We could get help there."

She hung her head, unable or unwilling to look at him.

"And wait to be slaughtered, or to starve, or to be sold? Or to wither away from both inside and out?" he asked, speaking the words with tenderness and care. "You have heard as much from the many we have crossed paths with. The spirit elephants brought us here. This is where we are to be. Do not ask me to walk back to the Serpent. Do not ask it of yourself."

Venturing a solemn glance, she placed the cloth of her shamma back over her head.

"Penicillin," she said. "When will you go?"

                                   *




THE EYES OF the male Ethiopian wolf followed the movement
of the hyena heads with only a mild interest. It had no intention
of getting near the beast. He had seen the brutality of the animal before, having observed on more than one occasion the large horn it
wielded slash open the side of a jackal or crush the skull of a hyena that
dared step into its territory. Pausing to take one last look, it trotted away.


The night-vision scope followed the movement of the wolf as it made its
way down from the rocky hills to the flatter terrain below it. Shifting the
infrared device back toward the small fire the two trackers had located
some two hours earlier, the soldier peering through the lens tried his best
to focus on the oddly shaped form that was edging closer to it. But no
matter whether he zoomed in or out, he could not get a clear sense of
what the beast was.

"What is it?"

"Some sort of animal, but—"

"And? Why do we care?"

"It has three heads."

The man without the night scope covered his mouth and laughed.

"I swear it is so," his partner said. "By all that Allah holds true. Look
for yourself."

The man waved him off and pressed the illumination button on his
watch.

"I do not care if it has three heads or twelve. I am getting some rest. Orders are to follow the black-clad man. Not some deformed beast. Do you still see him?"

"He moved behind a stone grotto. But I have been watching either side of it in case he leaves it. I am certain he is still there with all the others."

"Good. Keep watch on him, do you hear? Forget your monster. The colonel is far worse than any three-headed beast if we let him out of our sight."

The man with the night-vision scope grunted his agreement.

"Wake me in two hours. I will take over then. And you can rest."

"And what if the three-headed beast comes looking for us? What if it can smell us?"

The man sighed and said, "You have a gun. Use it. Kill it if it comes near."

*

JOHN TOO SAW a faint blink of a light amongst the hills but gave it little thought, imagining it was nothing more than a reflection of the moon bouncing off the horn of a passing mountain goat. Dangling his legs over the side of the rock ledge where he had come to rest, he marveled at the size of the herd that had gathered in the valley below him, overjoyed that so many spirit elephants had come together.

"Truly the Mother must be happy to have so many here," he said with awe.

His smile faded, however, when he turned and saw the sad eyes of the baby spirit elephant.

"I see that now," he admitted, his words tinged with the same sadness. "The more that are here, the less that are still living."

The lips of the spirit beast's trunk pressed his shoulder.

"Why do they kill for ivory? Can they not wait until you have no more need of it?"

The baby spirit elephant shimmered in the light of the moon, its pink-red eyes fixed on those of its kind.

"I worry for Sister Lady."

A white rock dove settled on the stone beside him, the current of air from the flutter of its wings buffeting his side. He giggled. The rock dove cooed. The moon silently bathed the cliff face where the three were sitting in a soft sheen of translucent white. The stars suddenly twinkled a little brighter, as if they had harnessed a force of throbbing energy.

"Etiyopiya says she is tired of running and hiding. But look where we are! Even the spirit herd has found peace here. Where is it she would rather go?"

The baby spirit elephant flapped its ears and raised its trunk.

"It is not time," John Too said. "She is where they want her."

The rock dove softly pecked at his hand.

"Soon, before morning, he will find what Damien needs. Perhaps Sister Lady will feel better then. I wish she could see this. You."

The great spirit herd sparkled in the blue and white light of the moon and stars. They grazed peacefully, moving to their own rhythm. Even the mammoth spirit bulls guarding the perimeters seemed at ease.

The rock dove hopped and perched atop John Too's thigh.

"Yes, I have been watching him. Lost he is. Hungry for Sister Lady. Following for months now. Disappears at times, but always returns." John Too paused as if listening. "A killer? Yes and no. He watches out for her and has not harmed us. But not so for the scavengers that have strayed too close. I have seen the savagery."

The baby spirit elephant moved sideways and stomped its feet. John Too looked toward where they had set up camp.

"He is leaving now. Foraging, he calls it."

*

"WHERE WOULD YOU go if the Mother and the Father granted you a wish?"

Claire couldn't help but smile, but Damien's fevered brow pulled the joy from her lips. After cutting a piece of cloth from her white shamma with the scissors Teimbaka had borrowed on one of his trips, she poured clean water from the canteen onto it and placed it atop the child's forehead. John Too, squatting on his haunches, awaited her answer.

"I— I don't really know, John Too," she replied, though her tone of voice informed him that she had given the question little thought. "Where would you go?"

Damien's lips were cracked and dry, a white paste caked around their edges. Claire placed the canteen just above his mouth and let the water dribble out. The drops seemed to evaporate as soon as they touched his lips.

"I would go everywhere," he said, the words coming easy and with confidence. "But I would always end up here with you and Etiyopiya."

He smiled when she glanced at him.

"Why do you call him that? His name is Teimbaka."

"Because he is Etiyopiya," John Too explained with a shrug. "He is of the Mother. Everyone can see this. He hears Her voices, feels Her moods, and protects Her children. It is why the spirit elephants watch over him. Why they are here," he relayed, looking all about them, his hands showing her that they were everywhere. "It is why I would return—always. The Mother is happy that we are here. Is it so with the Father, do you think?"

"I don't know what the Father thinks, John Too. I wish I did. Then maybe—" She stopped, her thoughts roaming into nothing.

"Maybe you would know where you would go?" he offered, his smile widening. "Maybe America?"

Claire's eyes glazed over with visions of Philadelphia during the Christmas holidays: Locust and Walnut Streets garnished with lights and garlands, flurries of snow falling lazily from the sky as she did her holiday shopping, looking in store windows all lit up and decorated with the season's finest gifts and cheer. Then she saw herself sipping a mimosa, feeling all grown up, the Whip's horn being sounded, the hooves of fifty horses answering the call, the pageantry of the riders and steeds all turned out in their finest, taking to the trail of the hounds. A toast offered and glasses raised by the ones who were staying behind. The crisp autumn morning, awash with the reds and golds of the trees, transforming the scene into a time when life seemed to be so much simpler.

"You are there now?" John Too asked.

Claire shook her head, quickly wiping the water from her eyes before it rolled down her cheeks.

"It is alright to cry, Sister Lady. It is why the spirit elephants love you: because you are not afraid to feel."

"You and Teimbaka with your spirit elephants," she hurried to say, bending closer to Damien so John Too could not see into her eyes. "I doubt that they know I even exist—if they even do."

She tried to laugh, but the sound that came out of her throat did not translate into happiness.

"Do not doubt, Sister Lady," John Too told her, his voice filled with concern. "For that is when fear takes hold."

A chilling, tormented howl suddenly erupted not far from where they were. Claire's hands began to shake as the echo reverberated off the hills around them.

*

J OHN RAN THE sharpening stone across the point of the impala horn until the edge of it was razor sharp. Testing it, he pressed it with a fingertip, smiling when a red splotch of blood immediately appeared.

"Their throats will open without their even being aware."

The flame-orange eyes of the white-headed Serpent flared when they looked into John's. John said nothing, focusing on the picture of Claire that he had kept in his thoughts since the day Teimbaka had taken her from him.

"And then she will be yours. All yours."

John glanced at the hyena head lying on his left shoulder. The Serpent wasn't there, though the voice, he was certain, had come from that direction.

"Then to Djibouti," it hissed, appearing from the beast's jaws on his right. "Why do you wait?"

"They are children," he heard himself reply, although he was sure he had not spoken at all.

"All the more reason to give them to me."

The Serpent slithered from one hyena head into the next, its voice taking on a melodic tone, entrancing him with a soothing calm that filled him with a sense of purpose. He nodded.

"They only get in the way. Always they want, always they need. No reason you should worry. She will be yours."

John thought of Djibouti: the turquoise waters, the breeze off the Red

Sea, the ships making port. They would book a passage on a great sailing vessel to Cairo. Claire would rest on satin pillows. The cabin they would share would gently rock with the waves of the open water. But there was something wrong. The black coils of the white-headed Serpent were wrapped around Claire's feet.

"No! Why are you there? It is just to be us! Just me and her!"

"Hush. Look again. I am only there to bring you what you need. Nothing more. Look again."

John saw them, lying on a small table near the bed: a spoon, a lighter, bags of white powder, a piece of thin rubber tubing, and the needles and a syringe. His stomach churned and his muscles bunched. Fighting tears, struggling with his obsession with Claire and his addiction to the drug, his thoughts turned to blackness, his body growing suddenly cold. He raised his head and howled into the sky.

*

NORTH AGAIN. HE would reach camp sometime after nightfall, he reckoned. Sooner if he felt it was safe enough to run. But there had been something in the look of the sentry's eyes when he had passed him as part of the procession of refugees heading south: a familiarity—almost a smile, he had thought—as though the soldier had been expecting to see him. It had made his palms sweat. He could not shake the feeling that something was wrong. But the soldier had let him pass without incident. He was being stupid. Damien was sick. He needed to hurry. He quickened his pace.

Clutching the pills he had finally located after a long and somewhat dangerous search of the camp's supply tent, he again hoped that he had taken what Claire had asked for. Though she had taught him to read, he still found that some words were very difficult to understand. Withdrawing the box from the folds of his shamma, he studied each letter: *Procaine benzylpenicillin*. He shook his head. What if he had taken the wrong kind? She just said *penicillin*. Would Damien die? And then what would happen to Claire?

He could sense she was troubled and confused. Nothing seemed as clear as it once had. Even when there had been the house with walls and scores of children and adults to tend to, it had been as simple as survive or perish. But that had seemed different somehow. He shook his head, not understanding why it did. He hurried. The first ridge tops of the northern hills were getting closer.

*

GUNSTARD LIT ANOTHER Gauloises, deeply inhaling the unfiltered smoke of the tobacco before allowing it to stream slowly from his nostrils. He coughed slightly and wheezed a second breath before lifting the binoculars to his sunbaked, leathered face. With the cigarette smoldering between his fingers, he adjusted the magnification.

The black-dressed figure was still a dot, but the man was moving at a swift pace. He would reach the first wave of hills before sunset, Gunstard thought. Plenty of time to get his men stationed where the approaching man would be unable to escape, plenty of time to receive a detailed secondary report from the tracker on the destination he was traveling toward and the people that were waiting for him.

"Where have you been these years, boy?" he wondered aloud. "And where is it that you go?"

"The colonel spoke?"

Standing on the passenger seat, Gunstard glanced down at the driver of his jeep. The Gauloises found his mouth. Without replying, he looked through the binoculars and muttered, "Boy."

JOHN TOO STUDIED the hyena heads and hides as they swayed with the shuffle of the man who wore the pelts, taking note of the state of the decaying fur and the unseemly odor they gave off. He wondered why the one Teimbaka had called John would dress himself in such a way. And he wondered, in a more troubling vein, why this man had followed them for over a year without showing himself.

It was near sunset, and the shadows were long. The jutting faces of the stone buttresses had doubled in size with the addition of their silhouettes on the valley floor. John Too stiffened when he saw the hyena-man crouch along one of the shadows. Thomas and Thaddeus had come in to view to begin the nightly forage for firewood. Having left camp with just his knife sheathed about his waist, he quickly and quietly bounded down from rock to rock. He stopped when he was a few feet above and behind where John was poised.

He saw the arm holding the spiral impala horn tense. And then he saw, to his amazement, John speaking to the hyena heads perched on his shoulders. John Too crept closer. He heard John's voice.

"Kill them and drag them away for the jackals."

"But they will scream."

"Not if their throats are cut before they see you."

"And then?"

"Then she will send two more to find these."

"And I will kill them too."

"Yes, you will kill them too."

"And she will send more."

"Yes, until it is only her that is left."

"And then she will be mine."

"Yes, she will be yours."

"Why would you kill those who you once were?" John Too asked. "They do you no harm."

The muzzles of the hyenas opened and closed, bouncing in lifeless mockery as John whirled round. For the briefest of moments, the little one glimpsed a spark of orange within the cavities of the dead beasts' rotting mouths.

He pulled his knife.

But it was too late.

The horn of the impala stuck him across the side of his head.

CLAIRE MOVED DAMIEN closer to the fire. Taking hold of Simon and Peter's hands, she nodded for them to do the same to the ones who were seated next to them.

"We should pray," she said, gazing round at the solemn faces lost to the flames.

"Why has Etiyopiya not returned?" Bartholomew asked her, making known the question the others were too afraid to ask.

"Has he not always returned to us, to you? Perhaps he will be here by sunrise when you awaken."

"What if the three-headed beast has eaten him?"

It was Matthew who asked this of Claire, a normally quiet boy of eight or nine who spent much of every day reading the books Teimbaka had brought to the camp or drawing pictures in the sand with the tip of a stick.

"There is no such thing," Claire assured him. "I am certain Thomas and Thaddeus were mistaken about what they saw," she said. "Besides," she hurried to add, "have you not seen for yourself, all of you, that Teimbaka—Etiyopiya, as you call him—can take care of himself? I have seen him kill a lion with only a spear. He is a great warrior and hunter, is he not?"

"But he has no weapons with him," Peter whispered, squeezing her hand. "He only carries a knife when he goes to forage."

"And where is John Too, Sister Lady?"

It was Philip who asked this, the largest of the twelve, sitting directly opposite her, his broad, black face half hidden by the hood of his deep-red robe.

"Yes, where is John Too?" James asked.

And then they all asked, their voices clamoring for her to answer. Close to tears, feeling that all was beginning to unravel, she kept a tight hold on the hands of Peter and Simon and bowed her head.

"Dear Father in heaven, and you, Mother, here on Earth," she began, squeezing the hands she held until they squeezed back. "We humbly ask, as your children, that you hear us this night, for we are without two of our family, two loved ones who we wish to bring home safe."

Glancing up, she met the eyes that were upon her and smiled. Small hands were wiping away tears.

"I would normally say the Lord's Prayer or beseech the Blessed Mother to protect our souls, but this night, this night I ask …" She paused. "We ask," she corrected herself, gladdened when she felt both Simon and Peter reaffirm their grasp on her fingers, "that you grant those we love—John Too and Teimbaka—safe passage through the darkness and bring them here to the light of our fire. I will not barter with You as to why You should do this for us—for them—nor will I list the sacrifices we have made to try to earn Your grace. You see what we are. You know how we live our lives. We are orphans."

She gazed around the flames, acknowledging each face before she continued.

"But we aren't, really, for we have each other, and we have the two of you, the Father and the Mother. Blessed are we, the poor in spirit, for ours is the kingdom of heaven. When I say this, I realize You have already given this to us: heaven, or something close to it."

She lifted her eyes to the stars.

"We strive to help each other, to do what is right, to survive in the midst of chaos and war. We endure these days in Your name. And are humbled in our hope that our efforts are worthy of your blessings. Perhaps it is hard for some to see, but I know that *this* is Your kingdom, the kingdom of heaven."

She bowed her head, falling silent for a moment, letting the twisting of the breeze amongst the wood-born flames soothe her thoughts.

"There are those of us who are worried. Some who are afraid. But we will not doubt You or the ways in which You see fit to guide us. For to doubt is to allow fear to take hold, and we will not fear that which You have placed within this kingdom. Teimbaka and John Too—they are both Etiyopiya, treasures of this heaven. Guide them to us. Bring them back. See them safe. For we have need of them and love them. Amen."

"Amen," the children solemnly agreed.

"Our Father," Claire began, the children immediately taking up the familiar prayer, as had become their practice, "who art in Heaven, hallowed be thy name. Thy kingdom come, Thy will be done, on earth as it is in Heaven. Give us this day—"

"Look!"

Philip was pointing skyward, mesmerized by what he saw. All looked to the stars in unison, their eyes widening, their mouths forming smiles.

Shooting stars raced across the night sky, burning like flaming arrows shot across an infinite canvas of blue-white jewels. They were just a few at first, traveling east to west, easy to follow, their tails seeming to bend as they reached the western horizon. Then, in a burst, there came a dozen or more, filling their eyes with blazing, pulsating lines, some staying intact until they dipped out of the sky, others fizzling and disintegrating, the glory of their existence ending in a silent glittering explosion. And then it was over, one final flash of rushing light streaking right above them, their upturned faces tracking it across the sky until it passed out of sight.

"It is a sign," Philip proclaimed, other heads nodding in silent accord. "Surely the Mother and the Father have heard."

"Good words, Sister Lady," Bartholomew added.

"Yes, good words," they all agreed.

It was just an undercurrent at first, a low, steady snarl that sounded like nothing more than a dozen empty stomachs yearning for food. But little by little, the undercurrent grew louder and stronger, until one by one the faces of the children turned to peer into the darkness behind them.

Matthew choked on his scream, his spindly arms trying to propel him backward when the three-headed beast leapt into the light of the flames. John, holding the twisted horn of the impala in one hand and the stout army knife of John Too in the other, his arms streaked with blood from the puncture wounds near his elbows, his face etched into a scowl, challenged any that dared to look him in the eye. All the while, the heads of the dead hyenas sat atop his shoulders, smiling with their blackened teeth.

"She is mine," he proclaimed from a frothing mouth. "And you must die."

*

THE SPIRIT CHILDREN screamed. Teimbaka lifted his hands to try to keep his head intact; the butt of the rifle clipped him across the back of his neck. The rope tied around his wrists was jerked roughly downward.

"Would you ever have thought, boy, that we end as we began—you a frightened child, waiting for me to decide your fate?"

Gunstard took a puff on his cigarette and then motioned for the two soldiers who had bound Teimbaka to the grill of the jeep to leave.

"Speak, boy. There may not be many more occasions for us to share a conversation."

"Then let there be silence," Teimbaka said, struggling with the pain from the blow to his neck.

"Between two such as us? Really, boy, have you no interest in what the next hours will hold for you and the ones who wait?"

"The ones who wait?"

"So, you do want to talk? This is good, very good. Perhaps you can help me with my plan."

"Plan," Teimbaka spit, testing the strength of the knot in the rope with a tug.

"Yes, my plan," Gunstard casually replied, smoothing the wrinkles from his khaki-green uniform.

Teimbaka eyed him with contempt as the aged creature fluffed the maroon ascot about his throat and straightened the matching beret on his head. Seeing he had an audience, Gunstard drew deeply on the Gauloises and smirked.

"Is this part of your plan?" said Teimbaka. "To be consumed by the Serpent? To wither in a land where the screams of starving children race through the rocks like the wind? To ferment in the blood of the innocents that you have killed?"

"A riddle?" Gunstard mocked. "Or, perhaps, a lesson taught by an old fool?"

Gunstard reached beneath his ascot and clicked something that was hanging around his neck.

"Bawa?"

"Yes, boy, Bawa. You remember the sound of ivory teeth. How I wish he were here now. But," he sighed, "that isn't possible, is it? Because you killed him, didn't you? Butchered him as though he was nothing more than a poor, dumb animal."

Teimbaka closed his eyes and looked away.

"Nothing to say about that, I see," Gunstard chortled, the butt of the cigarette drawing circles in the air.

"I do not deny what I have done. It will be with me forever."

"Then it is your lucky day, boy! For forever is here! Your burden will be lifted soon enough."

Gunstard laughed.

"And for you, Gunstard? What does forever hold for you?"

The deep lines of Gunstard's face bunched and smoothed as he licked his lips.

"When the war—" he spat, "the second Great War—when it ended, my forever fell between some miserable lines of some irrelevant treaty signed by cowards that knew nothing of the sacrifices of the men they supposedly led. Worthless fools. North Africa is filled with ghosts who walk in the hell of their creation. So many dead—so many, and yet their treaty allowed me to live."

Gunstard ground the remains of his cigarette into the ground with the heel of his boot, his gaze drifting past the mountains to the north.

"What a mistake that was, eh, boy? A glorious, blood-choking screw-up. The price of peace."

He chuckled at the concept, his face twisting into a sneer.

"I should have died then, when the world was at war. But I am still here. I think, boy, that sometimes I will be here forever."

Teimbaka laughed.

"Why you are not dead, Gunstard, I do not know, but do not fool yourself. There will always be a hand that will, in the end, smite those who are of the Serpent. So do not fear."

"Fear? I am the word!" he declared, taking a step back and standing at his full height. "From Kenya to the Sudan, from the Red Sea to Uganda, as far as Zaire, I am the blackness that makes others tremble, a nightmare that turns blood into ice."

Gunstard drew closer, bending to one knee to peer into Teimbaka's face from a foot away.

"What you should fear, though, boy, is what I will do with the nun when we reach her."

Teimbaka's face went rigid, his eyes narrowing to slits.

"She means something to you, yes? But have the years brought the lines of age to her face? Made her frame frail? If it has, it will lessen the price I can get for her. Of course, she still has white skin, does she not? So that itself will bring a hefty sum. Perhaps I shall keep her for a while. Yes, why not? I shall fatten her on elephant meat and beer and have my time with her."

Teimbaka heard the snickering jeer that followed as though it was the cackling depravity of Bawa on the morning of the great harvest.

"I will not let it be so," he spat, caught between a vision of Claire in Gunstard's possession and his memory of the field of carnage.

"Of course it will be," Gunstard whispered. "But you will not be around to see her life ... changed." He smiled. "I will kill you myself after you have watched your second brood of babies killed. Oh yes, I know about them, too. I thought you might like to see it this time—instead of just hear it."

He stared at Teimbaka for a moment before offering a simple laugh of resignation.

"Death, boy. It's what I do. Even your old comrades realized this in the end. Bawa, of course, was your doing."

He reached beneath his ascot again and jiggled the ivory teeth tethered about his neck.

"You will have to tell me, when you join him, if the slicing of his face made it easier for him to talk, or impossible."

Gunstard winked and smiled. Teimbaka looked past him, drawn to the lightening of the sky on the eastern horizon.

"Yes, look to the break of day, boy," Gunstard chided, following his gaze. "Look to the sun as Reta Basa did the morning he was hung."

Teimbaka flinched.

"Killed two game wardens, they say he did," Gunstard said. "Of course, they never found the rifle he used," he went on, nodding to the weapon he had propped against the far fender of the jeep. "But that didn't seem to concern the authorities. Because they had captured a notorious poacher, so they said at the time."

Gunstard fell silent for a moment.

"He said nothing when they put the noose around his neck, I'll give him that. Just kept staring at the rising sun, as you do now. I applauded with the rest of the scum when they pushed him from the platform and his body jerked like a fish taken out of water. The elephants would be safe now, the government official declared when they cut him down. He told me the very same thing two days later when I led his VIP party on an ivory hunt."

Gunstard's laughter was dark and ominous. Teimbaka shifted his body to try to escape it.

"It is though a part of them is in you, boy. Matula, he squirmed just like you do now when he saw his future in the barrel of my gun. But there was nowhere to go. It amused me to watch one so large and strong piss himself. He thought he had retired," Gunstard went on in a matter-of-fact manner. "Thought a certain cache of tusks were his to keep for his years of service. Like I would have forgotten that we had once hidden ivory in old caves." He chuckled. "Did he not understand that greed slows one's reactions and burdens one's prospect of escape? You see, boy," he explained in a hushed manner, as though he were divulging a secret, "it is never for the gain, the treasure, the money. Don't you see? If it is forever that you wish to exist in, then you must simply revel in what you are, what makes you tick. Am I not proof of this? Do these hills not murmur my name even as I walk amongst them?"

"The hills," Teimbaka muttered, his gaze still fixed upon the lightening sky. "There is much in these hills. Much more than you or I will ever know."

"But my name, boy, my name. It is in them."

They fell silent for a time: Teimbaka working the knot about his wrists to see if it would loosen, Gunstard peering off into the hills as though he were watching himself walking there.

"And Untello?"

Gunstard turned his head westward, where darkness still lingered.

"Is he still alive?"

"No, boy. He is not".

"And what hand did you have in his killing?"

"None," he replied, his face suddenly looking old, void of color and emotion.

"Near the lake of the English queen," he went on, his voice lapsing into the memory, "not many years after that morning on the plain, your last with us. It was a great herd we had been following, dust clouds stretching for miles. Three days we followed them, three days of hurrying to overtake them. But we never could. It was as if they knew we were behind them or sensed that death was closing in. Across the water they came, their voices, howling over the lake like a gale, rushing toward us, breaking over us like thunder when they reached our shoreline. And as the night wore on, the clamor of it seemed to fill the very air we breathed. Suffocating it was, like the great beasts were standing on our chests. Even the campfire," Gunstard paused, remembering, "died on its own. Dwindled to a single spiral of smoke. Though the wood was dry and there was plenty still to burn. And then it started: the shaking of the ground, the deafening pounding that ripped the bottom right out of the sky. And then there was dust swirling all around us. Reta and Matula were like whimpering children; huddling together, shaking, invoking the names of stupid gods, using stupid words."

Gunstard shook his head, an odd smile forming on the corners of his mouth.

"But Untello, he was not afraid. In fact, he walked right into the dust and the pounding and the shaking. We found him in the morning. He was crushed like a fly, splattered and flattened, all of him. Except his head," he remarked, his features scrunching, "not a mark on it. His eyes were wide, like he had seen—"

Gunstard shrugged.

"Their tracks were everywhere, yet we never saw one, never found one elephant for days to come. Just tracks, everywhere, but no droppings or trees stripped of bark or the sound of their calls on the wind. As though they were—"

"Spirits," Teimbaka said. "The great herd. It was they. Untello foresaw this. So he is with them."

Gunstard rubbed the weariness from his face and sighed.

"And now, now it is only you who are left, boy. The last of the group. Perhaps the five of you can sit together as ghosts around a fire and tell each other hoodoo stories from this accursed land."

Gunstard stood and stretched as the first hint of the sun began to appear on the eastern horizon.

"Lieutenant!" he shouted. "Time to move! A woman—a woman, Lieutenant—waits for us!"

Shouldering his rifle, he took a long look at Teimbaka. He smiled and then winked.

"And we mustn't keep her waiting."

*

DAMIEN DRIFTED IN and out of consciousness. As he grappled with the fever that had decimated his body and clouded his mind, the nightmare he could not seem to wake up from continued to torture him, pulling at him whether he slept or woke, wringing emotions from him that he did not have the strength to either withstand or combat.

As the campfire had dwindled to smoke and the darkness had passed into light, the whimpering and the cries of his family had been constant and everywhere. And the snarling of the beast—that had been the most disturbing aspect of the dream. It was erratic and unbalanced, a bizarre mixture of pleading howls and terrifying growls. It made his body shiver and his chest ache.

He had asked for her once, had called out "Sister Lady!" His effort was rewarded with a blow to his side and a spitting snarl in his ear. But still the nightmare would not disperse. Eyes open or closed, he could hear the sounds. Eyes open or closed, he could still see the three-headed beast paw and cuff at Sister Lady.

Anger coursed through his fevered body.

Claire looked upon John, trying not to remember, fighting to save what dignity she had reclaimed. She cowered away as he pressed himself to her, turning her face and holding her breath to get away from the stench of his breath and the putrid odor of the decaying hides tied around his body.

Snarling, he licked the side of her neck and rubbed his hardened penis against her thigh. Pinned against a large boulder, she could not move.

The roar of a lion made him hesitate, the echo of it in the hills momentarily drawing him off of her. Claire sighed and looked to the children. As she had instructed them, they were huddled together at the base of a massive outcrop of stone. They were staying quiet, but their faces were awash with worry and fear.

"It is a warning, John," Claire said, seizing the opportunity to create some doubt in the man-beast and gain some time. "The *negusa* is telling you to let the children go."

John turned to the children, his face filled with anger. Taking a menacing step toward them, he suddenly stopped. He bent his head to the mouth of one hyena head and then to the mouth of the other. Nodding, chuckling, he turned back to Claire. His eyes were brimming with lust.

"Like before," he uttered in a hoarse whisper. "In the room."

Claire looked to the hills, waiting, hoping for the lion to roar once again—but there was nothing. John came for her.

She slapped him hard, stunning him. His face went blank, his eyes showing his confusion. But then he was on her again, pawing at her chest, thrusting his groin into hers.

She slapped him again, harder. With tears in her eyes, trembling, rigid, she prayed he would stop. And then she slapped him a third time, putting all the fury into the blow that she had suppressed since Teimbaka had led her into the Danakil. John staggered back, shaken. But then his eyes went dark and his mouth hardened to a thin line. Slowly, he took the impala horn from the twine tied around his waist and pointed it at her.

Stepping toward her, he ran the tip of it over the scabs and scores of puncture marks on his inner arm and then grabbed her wrist. Before she could think or knew what was happening, he pushed the fabric of her shamma away from her arm and inserted the tip of the horn into the soft flesh at the crook of her elbow.

She tried to turn away, but he grabbed the back of her neck, holding it with such force that she could not move. He pressed the tip of the impala horn into her arm a little farther.

She cried out.

He slapped her across the face with the back of his hand. Before she could fall, he grabbed her throat and held her in place.

"Now you will be mine," he growled, his eyes flashing with anger. "You will be happy again. Just like in the room. Remember."

When he howled, her heart went dark. She could feel herself losing consciousness. But then he was off her, hopping to the side, pushing her away as Damien bit viciously into his ankle and held on with his teeth.

The children cheered Damien, their faces alight with the hope that the three-headed beast would flee. But their cheers turned to screams of horror when John lifted Damien up by the scruff of his neck and plunged the horn of the impala into his heart.

Again and again and again John stabbed the boy in the chest. Each demented strike hit at the same spot, leaving the area of Damien's heart nothing more than a mutilated, gaping hole of bloody tissue and pieces of splintered rib bones.

When John was done, when he stood heaving and gasping and covered in blood, he dangled Damien's body away from him with one hand and then tossed it to the ashes of the campfire with a terrifying, gut-wrenching scream.

Claire covered her face in her hands, unable to comprehend what she had witnessed. But the wailing of the other children made her look again. She fell to her knees numb and broken, her soul nearly shattered.

For a moment, all was calm. The sunlight crept over the rocks, casting everything in a warm, soft glow. The horrid changed into the surreal.

"Now!" John bellowed. "Mine!"

Darkness—a strange swooshing, moving blackness—swept across the sun. A flock of quelea, two thousand strong, shaded the day back to night. And though the sudden appearance of the birds was frightening to Claire and the children, John neither noticed nor cared. Claire was reduced to a state of utter anguish as she watched him stalk toward her.

When he touched her, his hands wet with Damien's blood, she felt the vomit churning in her stomach and felt her loins turn dry and cold.

"Etiyopiya!" cried one of the children.

Panic stricken, her eyes blurred with tears, Claire struggled to see Teimbaka. As John stepped away from her, she wiped her eyes and looked.

Something was terribly wrong; Teimbaka was there, but his head was downcast and his wrists were bound.

"Ah, our nun."

"No!" John barked as Gunstard appeared behind Teimbaka. "No!"

Before Gunstard could get his rifle to his shoulder, John was running away. When Gunstard fired, the bullet clipped John near his shoulder, blowing the head off one of the dead hyenas. Before he could fire another round, John fled into the twisting crevices of the rocks and made his escape.

Gunstard shouldered his weapon and looked around. Meeting Claire's stunned gaze, he smiled.

"Lieutenant," he said in a raised voice, "send two men after whatever that was. And kill it."

Eight soldiers stood at attention off to the side while Gunstard paced in front of the prisoners huddled at his feet. The two that had been sent to kill John had not yet returned.

Damien's body had been dragged into the sands and left for the scavengers. Already the skies were thick with circling vultures. Not far off, jackals yelped.

"It is messy, isn't it?" Gunstard asked no one in particular, though his eyes flitted between Teimbaka and Claire.

He ran the toe of his boot through the pool of drying blood where Damien had been lying.

"Killing. Death. Always so much blood."

He smiled.

Looking to the vultures descending from the sky, he said, "A busy day ahead for them. A feast." He chuckled, eyeing the children.

"Please," Claire begged. "They have—"

The two soldiers who had been sent to find and kill John returned. Their faces were downcast.

"And?" Gunstard inquired.

The two men stopped and saluted.

"I'm waiting."

"We could not find him, Colonel," one reported, his voice unsteady. "It was as if he vanished. There was—"

Gunstard silenced him with a wave of his hand.

"No matter. He'll be back."

Looking down at Teimbaka and then to Claire, he said, "Just another man who cannot bear to stay away from you."

He nudged her leg with the blood-stained toe of his boot.

"Another in a long line, eh, sister?" he laughed. "A very long line. You do remember, don't you?"

Claire looked away.

"I am certain the sailors and dockhands in Djibouti will be happy to hear of your return."

"You will not take her!" Teimbaka screamed, jumping to his feet.

Gunstard slammed the butt of his rifle into Teimbaka's gut. Teimbaka doubled over, gasping for breath.

"And who will stop me, boy? You? These whelps?"

He dismissed the notion with a grunt.

"Come, whore," he commanded, roughly lifting Claire to her feet. "It is time to go."

"No! No!"

She struck out at him with her fists, landing a punch to his cheek before he could take hold of her wrists and get her under control.

"I won't go with you!" she spit. "I belong here!"

Wrenching free of his grasp, Claire reared back and aimed a crushing kick at Gunstard's groin. But the ancient German reacted quickly, blocking her foot with a forearm and pushing her leg to the side. In a rush of anger he took hold of her and raised his fist to strike her face. But an instant later, he lowered his arm, his anger replaced by an evil smile.

"Lieutenant!" he bellowed.

The lieutenant immediately stepped to his side.

"Hold her. And hand me your side-arm."

Without question, the lieutenant complied. Gunstard checked the gun's magazine clip and clicked off the safety. He stepped to where the children were massed and kicked four of them apart from the others. Looking to Claire, he said, "Let me know when you change your mind."

Four bullets, four children. Blood, tissue and bone sprayed the rock behind them and the screaming children seated near them.

"God in heaven!" Claire shrieked. "What have you done?"

She fell to her knees, horror and disbelief in her eyes. With the screaming of the children as a backdrop to her misery, she cried out, "Teimbaka! Save them! Teimbaka!"

"So it is he you call for!" Gunstard bellowed. "Then let's have you watch!"

As two soldiers yanked Teimbaka to his feet, Claire realized what was about to happen. Gathering herself, she sprang up and rushed to Teimbaka. Before the soldiers could stop her, she flung herself upon him and wrapped her arms and legs around his torso.

"How touching," Gunstard sarcastically remarked. "If that is how you wish it."

As Claire desperately clung to Teimbaka, Gunstard fired another bullet from his gun.

"You filth!" Teimbaka shouted. "May you burn in hell!"

Claire slid from his body, her face without color, her eyes darting from side to side, her lips opening and closing as if she were uttering words that no one could hear. Though she did not want to, she turned to see whom else Gunstard had murdered. There, beside the bodies of Andrew, Bartholomew, Peter, and Simon, Philip lay lifeless at the base of the buttress of stone, half his face gone.

"No more, Gunstard!" Teimbaka shouted, stepping to the side so Claire would not be in the way. "Let them go. You have me."

Gunstard laughed and nodded his head.

"Yes, boy. I do have you," he managed to get out between fits of laughter. "I have all of you! But since you are offering a clear shot...."

Gunstard slung his rifle off his shoulder and took aim. Claire moved to get in the line of fire, but a soldier held her back.

Gunstard smiled.

The ground began to tremble.

Thomas ran to Claire's side. Pulling on her shamma, his face alight with joy, he spoke for the first time since Claire had known him.

"Mother has sent Her children," he said. "The protectors come."

Claire clasped his face between her hands and kissed him on the forehead. "The light that shines in the darkness," she murmured.

Looking at Gunstard, she finished the proverb, saying, "And the darkness does not understand."

The soldiers shifted from foot to foot, trading whispers amongst themselves as they peered up at the sky and looked through the openings between the rocks. When they saw the ring of dust moving toward them from every direction and observed the vultures suddenly departing, their whispers became frightened mutterings of "evil" and "witches." Though they hadn't flinched even when Gunstard had shot the five children, their faces were now a gallery of frightened awe.

"What are the men babbling about, Lieutenant?" Gunstard demanded, lowering his rifle.

The trembling of the earth became stronger, reaching up through the ground to grasp feet and ankles and rattle them with a power that sought to topple and upend. And when the first blaring calls of the beasts trumpeted across the sands and the rocks began to shake, the soldiers started to break ranks and move away. Their cries of "witches" and "evil" were now shouted in fear. Even the lieutenant began to run to where they had left the jeeps.

"Hold your positions!" Gunstard commanded.

The dust cloud raced toward them, the banks of swirling sand rising hundreds of feet into the air. The trumpeting became deafening. Cracks appeared in the stones as the sound cascaded over them. Hunks of rocks began to break off and tumble to the ground. The soldiers, now in a panic, began a frantic run to the waiting jeeps.

Gunstard pointed his rifle and fired. A soldier fell to the ground, the bullet having blown a hole in his back.

"They come for you!" Teimbaka shouted over the din. "The spirit elephants come!"

"Let them come, boy! Let them come!" Gunstard bellowed firing his rifle into the onrushing sandstorm and into the backs of what soldiers he could locate.

The dust cloud became a raging torrent of biting sand and ear-splitting wails. The ground rocked. Boulders tumbled to the earth. A million stampeding feet rushed toward them, threatening to shatter the bones of all who stood in their path.

As the death cries of the soldiers who had run into the wall of dust rose to a crescendo, Claire gathered the children about her and began to pray.

Crazed but efficient, Gunstard fired round after round into the oncoming maelstrom, reloading when needed, turning to every opening in the rocks to shoot. And when the trumpeting call of a mammoth spirit bull broke open the din like a clap of thunder, Gunstard whirled to the sound and took aim.

Shimmering tusks of gold-hued ivory suddenly appeared, thrashing the earth and smashing boulders into stones. The glowering pink-red eyes of the spirit beast bore into Gunstard from some thirty feet above him. They were ablaze with vengeance.

Gunstard took aim and fired and fired and fired. When he stopped to reload, everything became suddenly still.

*

T O ALL BUT Teimbaka, the forlorn whimpering that arose out of the thinning dust-cloud seemed out of place. But he remembered the sound, recalling the sad cry of the baby elephant when it had come out from behind its mother's carcass to mourn her death. The memory of the pitiful, hollow voice of the creature had never left him.

As a small shape began to materialize within the settling veil of sand, Gunstard began to laugh, the barrel of his rifle taking aim at the diminutive form.

"It is but a baby elephant," Teimbaka hurried to say. "It can be of no threat to you."

Gunstard fired a bullet into the midst of the dark silhouette. The vague image disappeared.

"I am forever!" Gunstard proclaimed.

He swerved the muzzle of the rifle toward Teimbaka.

"No more hurt!"

John Too walked out of the remnants of the dust cloud where the last bullet had been fired. The side of his face was clotted with dried blood. He put up his hand, gesturing for Gunstard to stop. A hole was in the center of his palm, which oozed blood where the bullet had passed through it.

"No more hurt," he repeated, his eyes locked on to those of Gunstard. "No more."

"What is this?" Gunstard chortled, looking to Teimbaka. "Is this the one who will smite me?" he taunted. "Just another boy who will shortly have no face?"

Before Gunstard could take aim, Claire rushed to John Too and thrust him behind her.

"You will not take another child," she spat. "May God send you to hell!"

"Take a look around, Sister," Gunstard coldly responded. "Where do you think we are?"

With a smile and a wink, he raised the gun to her face and said, "I shall show you."

"Bouda!"

As John Too shouted the ancient word, John, with the hides of the hyenas flowing behind him, fell upon Gunstard from the rocks above. Wrapping his knees around Gunstard's waist, he plunged the horn of the impala into one of Gunstard's eyes and the thick-bladed knife he had taken from John Too into the other. Before Gunstard's scream of agony could be fully realized, John extracted the weapons and thrust the horn into Gunstard's mouth, shoving it until the tip ripped through the back of his throat. With his other hand, he savagely raked the knife across Gunstard's neck. Gunstard fell forward in a pool of his own blood. As his face settled into the gore, the trumpeting call of a spirit bull sounded throughout the hills.

In the stunned silence that followed, John rushed to Claire and began to pull her away. Teimbaka stepped to her side and smashed the side of John's face with his bound fists, knocking him to the ground.

"The knife!"

Though numb and in shock, Claire grabbed the bloodied knife from John's hand while the man-beast struggled with consciousness. With a flick, the rope fell away. Teimbaka took the knife from her hands.

John leapt to his feet with a snarl, his muscles taut with rage, his face twisted in a spit-frothed sneer.

John Too hurried to get between them. Looking into Teimbaka's angry face, he shouted, "No hurt! No hurt!"

John raised his fist as if to strike. Claire took hold of his wrist to stop him. Teimbaka lunged forward, brandishing the knife.

"No, Etiyopiya!" John Too yelled, pushing him back.

Teimbaka looked down at John Too, his brow furrowing when he saw a twinkling of ivory and gold flash within the child's eyes.

"No," John Too repeated, his voice softer, the word filled with concern. "No."

"But he was—" Teimbaka angrily countered.

"He was once us," John Too said. "Just lost," he told him, softly patting Teimbaka's chest.

Placing his wounded hand on the knife, John Too lowered it to Teimbaka's side. Searching his eyes, he held them with his own for some time. When he spoke again, it was in a voice without age.

"Just lost. In a place where you have never been."

ETHIOPIA, 1986

MENELIK EXHALED WITH the sigh of a man who had been carrying the burden of elected office for three contentious years. His efforts to reclaim the twenty-ninth district from decades of neglect had taken its toll, he realized. And although he, with Yutanda's support, had made significant progress in the areas of inner-city housing, education, and job training, none of that seemed very important at the moment.

Focused on the briefcase resting in his lap, he studied the unsettling photograph atop the stack of papers and other photos he had packed. The image of the rows of dead children, their naked bodies laid neatly side by side, their skeletal faces frozen in misery, had changed the way in which he now saw the world. The photograph had made everything that had once seemed so important almost trivial. He clutched the edges of it, holding it in place as the jet took a slight, shuddering dip.

When the page had come over the public address system at La Guardia for him to pick up the nearest courtesy phone—only moments before he was to board his flight overseas—he had been certain that his visa had been revoked at the last minute. Just another frustrating ploy by the Mengistu government, he had assumed, a continuation of the game of cat and mouse the Ethiopian bureaucrats had been playing with the U.S. for the past several months. But it had been Yutanda who had paged him. Even now, though she was thousands of miles away, and scores of hours had passed since he had spoken to her, her voice was still fresh and clear in his mind.

"I'm pregnant," she had told him.

The word conjured images both joyous and worrisome.

"I was going to wait until you got back," she had blurted out. "I've only known for a few days. I couldn't keep it to myself any longer." Teasingly, she had asked, "Are you okay with it?" And they had both laughed. "I thought it might give you something to do," she had gone on, still joking. "Maybe have a list of names for me when you get back. And don't just make them all boy names either. You better get used to the idea that she could be a girl."

Yutanda had been so elated, yet the photograph was pulling at him, erasing some of the joy the moment had given him. Children, a child; the visions of birth and death seemed suddenly intertwined. How would it be to be responsible for a child? he wondered. How would it feel to be a father?

His thoughts drifted to the two men he had called Father: one nothing more than a vague figure in robes following a herd of goats along the banks of a river of sand; the other a mixture of a tall, silver-haired politician and the frail, speech-impaired facsimile he had turned into. Even as he thought of the two men, he could not picture their faces. Why? he wondered. Why?

The photograph of the rows of dead children pulled him to it once more. A father, he thought.

"A father."

Not realizing he had spoken out loud, he touched his lips as if to lightly reprimand them. With a troubled expression, he closed the briefcase and took what refuge he could in the banks of clouds below the wings of the plane.

"Are you part of the news media?"

Menelik watched the tip of the wing rise toward the empty blue sky as the plane began a slow turn.

"Which aspect are you going to concentrate on? Although it is a non-story now, isn't it? Or is that the angle you will pursue?"

A flame flickered within the midst of the blue expanse. Menelik pressed his face to the window, not understanding how the flame could be there.

"If the cigarette is bothersome to you ..."

The flame disappeared with a click. Menelik smelled smoke.

"If you would care for one ..." the man seated next to him said, offering the open pack as Menelik turned. He looked pleasantly at Menelik while the smoke of his cigarette drifted lazily upward.

"Oh, uh, no, thank you. I haven't had one since—"

"Ah, a reformed indulger," the man said with a knowing smile and nod. "We will be in Djibouti within the hour, I think," he continued, his voice lively and animated. "Were you looking for familiar landmarks just then?"

"No," Menelik had to confess. "I'm afraid I wouldn't know any."

"Your first time, then? In Africa?"

"I was born here," Menelik quickly replied. "I am from— I mean, I am looking forward to seeing some of Ethiopia."

"Yes, so I had gathered," the man responded, eyeing the briefcase. "Though I thought you American by your dress, your accent, and the way in which you carry yourself. How long has it been since you've been back? You return at such a difficult time."

The man drew on his cigarette and sighed.

"And yet," he continued, his tone changing, taking on a wistful air, "when has it not been so? When has the Mother not wrung her hands in grief?"

"The Mother?"

"Excuse my informality," the man said, placing his fingers to his forehead. "Ethiopia, I mean, or rather all of Africa. It is an expression of a man who I— Who was once an acquaintance."

Menelik looked at the man anew, studying the finely chiseled features and sand-colored skin, wondering what thoughts lingered behind the light-brown eyes that were assessing him.

A flash of gold swept across Menelik's vision as the balding, slight but somewhat portly gentleman switched his cigarette into his other hand. Menelik was not certain how long he had been staring before the man interjected.

"The ring. Some say it is spellbinding."

"I didn't mean to."

"To stare? Nonsense. It is a compliment, a testament to the crafts-manship of the artist who created it."

Passing the cigarette to his other hand, he placed the ring against the backdrop of his deep-blue silk suit. The face of a roaring male lion, molded from the finest grade of polished gold, looked out at Menelik with mesmerizing eyes made from diamonds, a stream of rubies flowing from its jaws to signify its roar.

"It is quite—"

"Yes, it is," the man agreed with a touch of humility. "Of all the trea-sures I have handled," he said, admiring the ring himself, "I would not trade this ring for all of them combined."

"It is the jewelry business you are in, then?"

"In a way. Many items are held as being valuable in this day. Even food," he commented, his gaze resting on the briefcase for a moment. "Perhaps that is the story for your readers."

"My readers?"

"Yes. Would they not," he asked, tapping the top of the brown leather briefcase, "be interested in knowing how it is processed to reach those who are in need of it—or not? But perhaps that is a story that has already been reported on. Or again, as it is with the press these days, perhaps the subjects of starvation and civil war in what the world sees as a third-rate country are no longer of any interest to your audience."

"On the contrary. I would be most interested in learning all there is to know about how the relief aid flooding into this area is processed—and by whom. But it would not be for any story, as you say. I am here on a fact-finding mission on behalf of the United States government."

"I see," the man said, taking a long draw on his cigarette.

The man offered Menelik a weak smile before shifting in his seat and looking away.

"Please, don't turn away," Menelik carefully added, sensing that he had said something to offend the man. "If you know who these people are that are holding up these shipments, perhaps I can do something about them."

"It is only that I wished to seem more important than I am, is all," the man sheepishly offered in reply. "The chattering of someone who would see his name in a newspaper or magazine. Please accept my humble apologies for leading you to believe otherwise."

With a touch of his fingers to his forehead, he nodded in deference and then turned away.

"The ring," Menelik found himself asking. "How did you come by it? Does it hold some special meaning—or do you just value it for its beauty?"

Having closed his eyes as if to rest, the man grudgingly opened them, glancing at Menelik and then to the ring on his finger.

"It is nothing but a symbol of what it depicts," he offered with a reflective smile. "But I have not seen or heard of the Lion of Djibouti for many years. And yet, there are stories," he went on, his voice close to sounding sad. "Always, there are stories."

He shrugged.

"Now I must rest," he said.

And he closed his eyes.

*

THE DEFLATING DISAPPOINTMENT he was feeling was no different at the airport in Djibouti than it had been in Tripoli when they had changed planes for the final leg of the flight. Having waited and struggled for so long to return to Africa, Menelik had envisioned a rebirth of sorts upon his arrival, a surge of belonging and pride. But when he had placed his feet upon the soil of his ancestors—his homeland—he had felt nothing, as though Africa had taken no notice that one of Her own had ever been gone, and had now come back. It was nothing like he had envisioned it to be. He felt empty.

He exited customs like any weary transatlantic passenger, tired and out of sorts, half wondering why he had made the trip at all. Realizing he was supposed to be met by a representative of the U.S. embassy, he scanned the faces of the scores of people moving about in all directions at the terminal, trying to picture what a representative might look like. While his eyes flitted from face to face and head to head, they came to rest upon the passenger that had been seated next to him on the flight out of Tripoli.

Ringed by several men of varying builds and dress, the man in the blue silk suit appeared to be holding court. As Menelik continued to openly stare at them, each of the men turned toward him, their expressions none too friendly. For a moment, he felt a sense of danger. Especially when one individual—a huge mass of a man, black as night and built like a water buffalo—scrunched his face into a scowl and rolled his massive shoulders.

Unexpectedly, Menelik was bumped from behind while a blurred shape in tattered robes pulled the briefcase from his grasp and ran off.

"Thief!" Menelik bellowed, lunging for the crook.

But the robber was swift, running a twisting course through the throng of bodies. No sooner had Menelik started to give chase than he bumped into a startled stranger. The collision caused him to lose sight of both the thief and the briefcase.

"Not the homecoming you had expected?"

Menelik whirled to the voice, somewhat surprised when he found the man in the blue silk suit standing next to him.

"And yet, it is no different in your country than it is here, I would think. These times," he relayed with a slight bow of his head, "have spawned many creatures that do what they must just to survive. Is this not so?"

Before Menelik could respond, the imposing frame of the water buffalo–man loomed next to him. Without acknowledging Menelik's presence, the man handed the man in the blue silk suit the briefcase that had just been stolen. Bowing slightly, the larger man stepped back.

"Well done, Bin'ka! You see, Mr. —"

Bin'ka bent and whispered in the ear of the smaller man.

"Mr. Menelik Arbagna. Still there is some hope for justice, yes?

"How is it? The briefcase, it is—"

"Secure," the man in the blue silk suit assured him, handing the briefcase to Menelik. "Whatever was inside, I can assure you, is intact. You see? It has not been opened."

"Then how is that you—or your colleague, here—" he said, eyeing Bin'ka, "know who I am? I do not recall that we introduced ourselves on the plane."

"This is Djibouti, Mr. Arbagna. Secrets—there are none here. Unless it is safer that one should be kept."

Menelik was left to shrug his shoulders and offer a polite smile.

"Then I owe Mr. Bin'ka, here, a debt of gratitude. Thank you," he said offering his hand. "Thank you for recovering what I could hardly afford to lose."

As Bin'ka took hold of Menelik's hand, his passive features slowly changed. Creases appeared on his smooth, rounded forehead. His lips became a tight line. His eyes seemed captivated by something that he found within Menelik's. Abruptly, he pulled away, looking shaken and confused.

"Please excuse my friend's awkward way with—"

"The— The Lion," Bin'ka stammered, his voice hushed, "he is— I see him in his."

"Do not make mockery of—"

But what the smaller man would have said, he did not finish, for he too was now gazing into Menelik's face, searching his eyes. Suddenly, he clasped Menelik by his upper arms.

"Menelik," he said as though it was a word he had long forgotten. "How could I not see?"

"I don't understand. Yes, my name is Menelik. What does that have to do—"

"Adiam!" a voice shouted from a short distance away. "Adiam! Come! We must go!"

Reluctantly, Adiam looked to the caller.

"Already we are late for our appointment!"

"Be at peace. Akmir!" Adiam called back to a man wearing a checkered kufiya. "I have just found—"

"But Adiam," Akmir protested, walking quickly to him.

"As-salaam alaikum, my friend," Adiam bade him, slightly bowing, his hand placed in front of his eyes with the tips of his fingers nearly touching his brow. " There can be no concerns this day. The Lion of Djibouti—his presence has returned," he told him, looking to Menelik.

Akmir, a dark-brown man with a close-cropped beard and deep-brown, almost black eyes, scrutinized Menelik with a frown.

"The days of the Lion are no more," Akmir stated with a dismissive air. "No use can this be to us. No use can this one be."

"Nay, Akmir, the days of the Lion have always been for him to choose. His roar still lingers in this city. There are many who still believe."

"Then let those who would believe in myths take comfort in their stories. But this is talk for another time. The business at hand will not wait any longer. The buyers have already arrived."

Adiam seemed ready to argue, but Bin'ka stepped to his ear once more and whispered a few words.

"Excuse our abruptness," Adiam said with a slight bow. "It seems that Akmir is correct that we must depart."

With the gesture of the adab, he added, "May the way to your brother be clear."

With that, the three men swiftly took their leave.

"My brother? The way? Teimbaka?"

Coming to understand what he had just been told, Menelik started after the group, only to be held back by a hand to his elbow and a voice saying his name.

"Mr. Arbagna?"

Menelik turned, a surge of anxiety shooting through him.

"You are Mr. Arbagna, are you not? The man at customs pointed you out."

"Yes," he managed to say in a calm voice to the middle-aged, bespectacled white-skinned man dressed in a light-blue cotton shirt and cream trousers. "I am Menelik Arbagna."

"Jim Stokes," the man said with some relief and a nervous smile. "I'm here to take you to the embassy."

Menelik felt himself nodding, his gaze drifting to the area where Adiam, Akmir, and Bin'ka had gone.

"Those three men you were speaking to," Jim Stokes carefully ventured, "do you know them?"

"No, we only just met. Though the one, the smaller man in the blue suit, he was on the flight with me from Tripoli. I believe his name is Adiam."

"I see."

"Why do you ask?" Menelik inquired, catching the curious nuance in the man's tone.

"Its just that they— They are believed to control—"

Jim Stokes fell silent for a moment before continuing.

"I think it best we speak about this with the ambassador back at the embassy. I'm sure you will find it interesting, at the very least."

*

W ITH HIS EYES closed, Menelik perceived dawn on the Gulf of Aden as very much like dawn anywhere else in the world where the ocean and the land share the same sunrise. The cry of sea birds, the lapping of waves, the glitter of sunlight on the water, the sounds of sails being hoisted or engines being turned over, the smell of salt on the moist air, the warmth of the sun on a face turned to the east; all were as he remembered them or imagined them to be, eliciting a sense of the familiar and inclusion within him.

If he had known that Teimbaka had stood on the very same dock, he might have given the tattered gray cat that had followed him from the moment he had stepped out of his taxi a more serious study. Or perhaps tried to befriend it with a scratch behind the ears. But he only gave the animal a few passing glances, assuming that the creature was merely hungry and looking for a handout.

"There is a story that tells of this place, that this is where the Lion of Djibouti first came to be. But there are many stories of him. So many, in fact, that even the ones I know to be true I sometimes doubt."

"And what does the story say of him?" Menelik replied, taking the sudden appearance of Adiam in stride.

The gray cat hissed at the asking, swiping the air with a paw. Having made its feelings known, it scampered into a maze of stacked containers.

"Forever does it seem that cat has been here," Adiam remarked. "I would not doubt that it was here when the world came to be."

"Perhaps it was," Menelik replied, taking in the beauty of the rising sun over the water.

"The mystique of the Mother," Adiam said. "All the secrets She holds that we will never be privileged to know."

The morning was calm—sky, sea, and shore all imbued with a sense of ease, as though all was as exactly as they had intended it to be. The two men took refuge in the spell, relishing the sights and sounds and smells. They spoke no words for a time, but when words were once more exchanged, the gift of peace that the morning had offered them quickly vanished.

"I have been told—warned, rather—that you are a criminal of sorts. That it is you who are responsible for the relief supplies not leaving the docks."

"It is as I have said before," Adiam responded without rancor. "Many items are bought and sold by dealers who see value in one item, but perhaps not in another. There is no gain, no profit, to simply hold an item for the sake of holding it. Everything comes or goes with a price."

"But you control the docks, or so I was informed."

Adiam pulled a pack of Camel cigarettes from his suit coat pocket, tapping the edge until the filtered end of one jutted out a little farther than the others.

"Would it be enough if that were so," he casually replied, placing the cigarette between his lips, "to keep something from leaving here, if all else who have a hand in its concern wished for it to go."

"But you are—"

"I am simply what I am," Adiam told Menelik as he put flame to tobacco. "A dealer of items that can be bought or sold or bartered for. There is no politics in this. Simply business."

"But even as we speak, children are dying. Old people, babies who have no part in this. It is not a business to them. They are trying to live, to stay alive. There are tons of food and water in your warehouses. Won't you release it?"

"The sorrow of the Mother is great. In this, I am of the same heart as you."

"Then how can you keep food from reaching them? How is it you can casually talk of buying and selling when you are affecting human lives? Would you rather see rodents gorge themselves on what you hold than release it to your own people?"

"Your anger is shared by many. But you place it awry."

"Then tell me, Adiam, tell me where to put it so that it strikes the faces of the ones who should be punished!"

"To reach those who are misplaced and starving, how would you proceed?"

"By the love of—"

"How is it you would transport tons of an item?"

"By any means possible! Trucks, planes, ships—anything!"

"And the permits needed to cross borders, to leave the docks and the warehouses, to obtain the trucks and drivers for this journey—what if these papers were not issued, or were delayed, or buried within a maze of politicians and bureaucrats who have been instructed not to comply?"

"What are you saying? Are you telling me that this government is responsible for the relief aid not getting through to its own people?"

"I tell you nothing, brother of him. Only questions do I ask. Only questions can there be."

"If you know something, you must tell me! It's unthinkable not to. Don't you see that, Adiam? Don't you want this starvation and misery to come to an end?"

"You speak the ways of the *ferenji* and see as they would see their own countries. Africa," he said, closing his eyes and breathing deep, "the Mother, you are not of her. She is not like any other on this earth."

"Will she turn her back on those who starve, who are too weak to care for themselves?"

"You wish to judge an ending that you and I will never see. What purpose is there in this way of thought? Your perception is born from another land. Always it is those who are not of Her who puff out their chests and proclaim that there must be an ending." He laughed, dismissively. "And yet, there has been no ending since the moment of creation—even for those of whom we speak. Always is an ending just a beginning. What purpose does it serve to speak of something that does not exist?"

"Because we can end starvation," Menelik quickly and definitively replied. "Because hunger is something that we can and must put an end to."

"Where, Menelik, where?" Adiam pointed out. "One refugee camp, two perhaps, and for how long? And to what sacrifice to those who choose not to huddle together in squalor or wait like lines of ants as they beg or fight for a cup of flour or a spoonful of rice? Is this how the West comforts itself, to feed some while it is fashionable to do so, but not all? I am of the Mother. And from the day I was born, there has been starvation and misery in this land. Do not confuse the Mother with what you think She should be. She cries the tears of Her children and wrings Her hands with the ache of their suffering. And those who are not of Her, to those who come only when it suits them to do so, or see profit in their travel here, She does not believe in you or hear your words or concern Herself with your self-righteous thoughts."

Adiam stared hard at Menelik, his finely chiseled features hardened with resolve.

"Nor do Her children believe in you, the West. We neither believe nor care."

"But there are lives to be saved," Menelik gently responded. "Children who are not old enough to know what they believe who can be saved."

"Then fly to Sudan and ask the border guards why the trucks from Khartoum are not permitted to cross into Ethiopia! Go to Addis and ask Mengistu why he wages war on the very children you speak of, those who will starve to death like so many have done already! Go! Go to the governments of your world—your own, Menelik—and ask them why politics forever takes precedence over the cries of those in need. Why is it that those who are not of Africa blame Her for all Her wounds when it is they who have cut Her and enslaved Her, raped Her and spilled Her blood? And still, still they will not allow Her the peace She deserves. You say I am the force that is keeping this food from moving? Better that you ask who pays me to keep it here and how much they pay and for how long a time they have paid for it to remain. Better that you ask those of the relief organizations who it is who holds the keys to the trucks that do not move."

"You talk as if there is a conspiracy in all of this," Menelik stated, his face heavy with the troublesome thought.

"There is no need for conspiracy when the heads of the dog are many and each barks for its own needs. When millions die of starvation, when thousands die from exposure, on whom do you cast the blame? On whom, Menelik, whom?"

Menelik looked to the water, his emotions rising and falling with the white-capped waves.

"But you can make a difference here!" he shouted. "You can release this food and allow it to be dispersed!"

"The courage of one becomes the courage of many. Yes, this I have seen. Yet I am not the one you seek. You must find this courage elsewhere. I am not fooled by what I am."

"What must I say to make you see?" Menelik asked, his words heavy with frustration. "To make you understand?"

"It is not for me to understand. I am just a businessman. It is those of the Lion who you need to find. Those," he said, lifting his hand so the sun flashed against his gold ring, "like him, these are the ones you must find. Those whose roar can splinter wood as though it were glass, whose claws have sent the Serpent to its hole. These are the ones you must gather and unite. Your brother, Teimbaka, he is this," Adiam told him, nodding to the ring. "Perhaps he will hear you call his name as he has called yours."

Menelik placed his hands to the sides of his face and let them slide down his cheeks, pulling on his skin.

"There is so much pain, Adiam. And you speak in—"

"Yes, there is pain. Even for those who are not of Her, yet walk in Her lands."

"I am not certain I know what you mean," Menelik confessed with a shake of his head. "All I know is that—"

"Come," Adiam interrupted, taking Menelik by the elbow. "We have spoken enough of this. The day passes without regard to what you bargain for. Soon you will be leaving. Already the helicopter you have hired is being readied."

"How did you—"

They both smiled.

"Then, if there are no secrets, you must know where I can find him—my brother."

Adiam's smile slowly faded into long lines of sadness.

"It is known that when he left here, he struck out across the wastelands of the Danakil. From there—" Adiam shook his head. "The struggles in Eritrea and in the Tigray have been long and bloody. And the famine has erased hundreds of thousands more."

"Are you saying that he is dead?"

"I only speak of what those places hold for you if you go there, what they held for him when he went. But the Lion— It is as I have said: many stories there are of he and the woman."

"Woman?"

"Like jewels are the tales. Coveted, spoken of in whispers, as if they were heard by too many ears, the treasure that they are would disappear."

"Why must you speak in riddles? Can you not just tell me where I should search?"

Adiam leaned closer. In a hushed voice he said, "I speak the way of the Mother. The voice of Her children is Her own. When you are of Her, you cannot be otherwise."

The blaring of a car horn invaded their conversation, drawing their attention to the end of the dock. Standing next to the driver's-side door of a long, white Mercedes limousine were Akmir and four rather ominous-looking men.

"Again we must part."

"But you haven't told me—"

"There is a tale of a valley within the hills and rocks to the northwest. Some call it the palm of the Mother's hand. It is where the children speak of a woman who is known as Sister Lady, where the souls of the most forsaken are made whole again. It is said they are kept safe by a great gathering of spirits. It is in this place, they say, that the Lion of Djibouti still roams."

"But where? Where?"

"It is said that where the shadows of war are darkest, where the laughter of the hyena still haunts the night, that this is where the Lion can be found—where the paths of the Mother and the Father have intertwined."

With the gesture of the adab, Adiam turned and walked quickly to the waiting car.

*

B IN'KA SET THE kebero down in the corner of the hanger. Peeking out from behind the massive doors to the airstrip beyond, he watched José usher the American into the passenger's side of the stripped-down, Soviet-made Mi-24 helicopter before he jogged back toward his office.

"José," Bin'ka grunted.

Startled, José stumbled to a halt, the white Panama hat he wore nearly toppling from his head.

"A word."

"Look, friend, I have a— Bin'ka! To what do I owe the pleasure?" he inquired, somewhat fearful, looking quickly past the large figure to see if there were others lurking about.

Bin'ka motioned him over.

Hoisting the waist of his pants up over the roll of fat hanging from his stomach, José cautiously complied.

Placing a massive black hand on his shoulder, Bin'ka thrust two folded brown and red banknotes into José's hand, each worth 10,000 francs.

"From the consortium, to see that you give the American these," he instructed, holding a folded piece of paper between his thumb and forefinger while he nodded to the drum by his feet. "This note—do not allow it to return here, or I will be back. Understood?"

José nodded, eyeing the paper as if it held the plague.

"And the drum?" he asked.

Bin'ka shrugged, his face impassive. "The Lion's."

"The Lion?"

"He wants to find him."

"A myth," José said out of hand, turning to look at the waiting passenger. "But they are paying U.S. dollars for me to fly him wherever he wishes, so what do I care?" He half chuckled. "I wonder where he thinks we will find this ghost?"

José turned back to Bin'ka, a broad smile on his face. But his smile disappeared when he found that he was alone.

*

THE WHITE PLUMES of the jets crisscrossed the sharp, blue expanse of the sky in a pattern of squares and rectangles. It was if the very air was being divided. On the flatlands below, watching from his vantage point on the eastern edge of the Ethiopian highlands, Teimbaka followed the trails of dust being kicked up by the columns of tanks and trucks. Most of them were heading toward him, northwest, away from Afabet and the fighting taking place there. Like giant hornets, two bulky gunships hovered just above them, air support to repel any rebel assault while the government forces withdrew.

He shook his head, disheartened. The war in Eritrea was coming to some kind of climax. The fighting had become ferocious.

Westward, the mountains and the plateaus stretched for miles. It would be a difficult journey for the children and Claire. Even if undertaken, it would only lead toward more war in the Tigray. And from what he had been able to learn from the several camel caravans he had run across as the traders took their beasts into the Danakil for salt, Tigray was equally as violent as Eritrea. Neither region faced the prospect of an end to the fighting any time soon.

Farther north was Sudan, where a brutal civil war still raged. Famine there was widespread and devastating. Entire villages had been wiped out or displaced. The fortunate—the forgotten—huddled in squalor and begged for the world to help. He did not know if anyone was listening. North was not an option.

To the south lay the government of Mengistu in Addis Ababa with his vast military, his terror squadrons, his spies, and his torture. Food and water were acutely scarce. The refugee camps were fast turning into way stations of misery, disease, and death.

There was nowhere to go.

*

JOHN TWISTED THE fibers of the dried grasses into the shape of a bracelet, measuring its circumference against his wrist, glancing from time to time to where Claire was tending to the needs of a group of youngsters in the shade of an acacia tree. Tying the ends together, he studied the hole it made, and then held it up to his eye so he could look through it as he gauged the slenderness of Claire's arms. When she happened to look up, he turned his face.

"When will you let her forgive you?" John Too asked as he dropped a vibrant green beetle in the pile John had been collecting and drying. "When will you allow her into your eyes?"

John shrugged and pursed his lips.

"It wasn't you."

John looked at him and shook his head.

"It wasn't her."

John wiped at his eyes and pulled the ends of the grasses taut.

"How many more will you need?"

John looked at him, confused.

"Beetles," John Too said, pointing to the mound of colored shells.

John began to weep.

*

*BROTHER OF HIM,*

*It will be buried in the back pages of* La Nation, *in tomorrow's edition, that a warehouse on the docks was broken into, ransacked, and then set aflame. The building will be completely destroyed, and the tons of relief aid stored there will be lost. It will be a devastating act of arson committed by persons unknown.*

*That the food, medicine, and water were delivered to a refugee camp across the border in Ethiopia the night after we spoke is a secret known only by the Mother.*

*May the way to the Lion be safe, and may Allah, blessed be He, guide your way.*

*The drum belongs to the Lion. He was once azmari.*

*As-salaam alaikum*

Menelik folded the note into fourths and stuffed it into the back pocket of his Levi's. In the lantern light, he could almost make out the hand stains on the animal hides that were stretched across the old drum José had given him. He tapped it and smiled. A musician—what else would he learn of his brother?

Across from where he was seated, at the edge of the light emanating from the lone lantern he had lit, José puffed on a cigar and rested his back against the body of the imposing helicopter. Menelik studied the face of his pilot.

"How do you know this place?" Menelik inquired, glancing all about him and seeing nothing but darkness.

"When I was training pilots," José replied between draws on the cigar, "certain ranks of the air force were given knowledge of these," he waved the cigar in the air, "refueling outposts. They come in handy, yes?"

"I feel like we are out in the middle of nowhere."

"That's because we are, my friend."

"I thought we would have set down for the night at one of the camps or at an airbase."

"That would not have been a wise decision, my friend. Best that we stay to ourselves. The people of Ethiopia are desperate—as is the military. Best not to tempt them, yes?"

"You've been here a while, then."

"Several years," José replied, savoring the taste of the tobacco smoke. "Long enough to have learned."

"What we saw today—the camps—it's tragic."

"It has been that way for some time. I suspect it will continue until—" he shrugged.

"Until?"

"Until they are all satisfied who's running things."

"And when do you think that might be?"

José puffed a few times on the dwindling stub between his fingers.

"Maybe never, my friend. Maybe never."

Menelik's fingertips found the taught hide of the drum. He tapped lightly, suddenly wondering how Teimbaka might have come to learn how to play the instrument. The thought made him chuckle.

"That is a very old instrument, my friend," José remarked. "It might fetch a fair price with the right collector."

"A fair price. I don't even know what a fair price might be."

Menelik strained to see José's features through the dim light.

"Is that a side business for you? I thought you ran a transport service."

"I transport many things—not just people. The old warhorse here can go just about anywhere and carry a good deal. She has a presence about her, no?" he said, rapping his knuckles on the metal frame. "You should have seen her when she had her guns. Aye-yah, she was something! The motherfuckers would throw down their weapons and run just at the sight of her."

He laughed, coughing on the smoke caught in the base of his throat.

"I would like to go north tomorrow."

Jose stopped laughing and leaned forward.

"That would not be advisable, my friend."

"I was told I could find someone there."

"There are no well-organized relief camps to the north. And it would be dangerous to just fly around without a destination. Rebels might easily assume that we are air force."

"But you are clearly carrying the Djibouti insignia. It's plastered as big as a billboard on each side of your helicopter."

"A flag," José grunted, his face going dour. "Like that would mean anything to a trigger-happy lunatic with a surface-to-air missile launcher strapped to his shoulder." He scowled. "Besides," he went on, his expression becoming filled with doubt as he talked, "north means what, flying blindly across thousands of miles, trying to find a person in the valleys and the mountains? The highlands are a living maze: twisting gorges and valleys stuffed in between plateaus and mountains and hills. There are cliffs and rivers, deserts and forests. I could set this bird down into a ravine and an army could search for months and not find me. And you want to find a man? Please, my friend, please let us just continue to fly above the camps and observe so I can get you safely back to Djibouti."

"It's my brother. I was told he is to the north, with a woman and some children."

"Ah, a woman! Then we should leave him to his *paraíso*, yes?" he laughed. "It sounds like he does not want to be found."

"The last time I saw him—in the flesh—was almost forty years ago. A lion ripped the neck off our older brother. We ran in opposite directions."

José's silver eyebrows pinched together.

"I need to help him."

"So you have spoken to him, then."

"Not in the way you are thinking."

José stared up into the night sky, the smoke from the cigar mingling with the clouds drifting overhead.

"Don't you have family?" Menelik asked. "And if one of them were in need of help—no matter where they were or how long it had been since you had seen them—wouldn't you try to find them, help them?"

"I had a brother once," José replied evenly, studying what was left of the cigar. "But he was killed defending the country he loved."

"I'm sorry to hear that, but—"

"Fighting to protect his homeland from the invading fascists at the Bay of Pigs. It is why I joined the Cuban air force, to fight Americans."

José threw the stub of the cigar into the darkness and gave Menelik a hard, cold stare. Menelik shifted uneasily.

"But that is ancient history," José sighed, scratching the roll of fat at his waist. "Now I am here, in this lovely place," he added, opening the palms of his hands and raising them upward. "When I am able, I send money to my brother's family and their children. Cuba is still struggling to find its way. I do what I can."

"But I need—okay, I came here to find my brother. I have to find him. It's been my life's— It's important."

To his dismay, José chuckled.

"You say you are from here, but you seem to know nothing of this place, my friend," José told him, rubbing his eyes. "Did you listen to what your eyes told you today?"

"What do you mean?"

José grunted and then stood and stretched.

"They all want to find somebody: parents, a brother, a sister, a husband or a wife. It's been that way since I can remember. They stream in from the north from Sudan or Eritrea and from Somalia in the south. All lost and forgotten, looking for a loved one, but looking to stay alive even more," he explained. "And here, in Ethiopia, they are separated by famine or disease or war, or by all three. Everyone, it seems, has lost someone, someone who they can't find—and probably won't. It's almost laughable to say it is important that you find a person, my friend. This whole country is looking for someone."

"But my brother."

"Your brother is not lost, my friend. You say he has a woman and children with him? Then he has a life. Better than most. You should be happy for him. *Paraíso.*"

Menelik ran his fingertips along the edge of the ancient drum, his thoughts immersed in a tangle of splintered memories and twisting emotions. Even though he had spent a lifetime getting back to Ethiopia, it now felt as if he were no closer to reaching his destination than when he was behind bars in Rahway State Prison. What had Adiam said? Where the shadows of war were darkest? He shook his head to clear his thoughts, the tapping of the drum soothing his anxious breathing. Perhaps José was right, he thought. He had a child of his own to think about now, and Yutanda, and a city still in need of him. Perhaps this had been all just a foolish dream. Perhaps it was more than he could have hoped for just to learn that Teimbaka—the Lion of Djibouti—was alive and living in some sort of paradise, as José had said. He wondered if Teimbaka saw it that way too.

The tinkling of a lone bell was almost imperceptible, a faint, jingling rhythm of sound drifting slowly away. Menelik set the drum to his side and got to his feet. As he stepped forward, the laughter of a lone hyena arose nearby. Reflexively, he reached for his dula.

"We'd best turn in, my friend. We'll be safe in the *pájaro,*" he said, taking a step toward the helicopter. "Tomorrow we will visit the remainder of the camps in the south."

"We're going north," Menelik replied, staring at his empty hand.

"No, no, no, my friend. It is as I have said—"

"How much will it cost?"

José's eyes grew a bit wider, a smile creeping to the edges of his lips.

*

KNEELING, HEAD BENT, her fingertips running over the edges of each point of the cross, Claire finished saying her final Hail Mary. The moonlight shimmered off the links of the silver necklace as she let her hand drift down to her side. Slowly, she arose and wiped the sandy soil from her knees.

"How long have you been here?" she asked, seeing someone's shadow appear next to her own.

"I followed when you left," Teimbaka quietly replied, the edge of his face coming into her vision. "John Too insisted."

His features were changing, she saw. The lines of worry were deeper and constant, the greying of his beard—though the children still did their best to keep it free of the color—unrelenting. Even when he smiled, as he did now, the expression no longer brimmed with the confidence of unwavering strength that it once held, but carried an uncertainty to it, a fleeting hesitation that gave her pause.

"Nonsense," she said, running her fingers across the skin of her cheek to see if she could feel any age lines on her own face. "He worries too much."

"He says it is not safe."

She looked at him quizzically and then began to laugh. Touching her hand, he joined her in laughter, their eyes sharing the same unspoken thought.

"What did you pray for tonight?" he asked, pressing her fingers between his.

She lowered her head for a moment, but then looked to him anew. The soft brown of her irises held just a hint of the moon in the amber flecks.

"Something you have wanted for some time," she replied, her tone wishful. "For this to end."

She tried to smile, but found her lips would only tremble. Placing his fingertips gently upon them, he smoothed them to stillness.

"I cannot see that far any longer," he admitted, his thumb moving to caress her jaw. "But I would welcome the day."

"What would happen then, do you think, to them—to us?"

"I," he began, but then stopped.

His hand found the back of her neck. He closed his eyes.

"Would you go home?" he whispered.

When a shiver ran through her body he looked away. He gazed at the moon-swept landscape as he waited for her reply.

She took his chin in her hand and turned his eyes back to her own.

"Where would you have me be?"

He gently guided her face to his and kissed her mouth. Emotions swirled within them, each pulling away from the power of their passion, then finding each other again, the salt of their tears passing between their lips.

"I am broken inside," she whispered in a rush of emotion. "I—"

He kissed her once more, tenderly, allowing the moment to linger until the enchantment of it was complete.

"You are the strength of this land. There would be nothing if you were not here."

"But I—"

He brought her head to his chest and held her. They fell silent, each feeling the beat of the other's heart, the moon casting their embrace in a heavenly light.

*

JOHN TOO EASILY traversed the final length up the face of the cliff, resting for but a moment before seating himself on the ledge and dangling his legs over the side. Looking eastward, he scanned the line where the sky and the land became the same. There was an orange glow toward the north. It was the fires of war wavering against the canopy of night.

Far below him, down on the valley floor, a dark silhouette moved in his direction. He smiled, knowing it was John. His smile grew even wider as he saw the distant flicker of the camp's fire. Etiyopiya was there with Sister Lady. It had gladdened him—and everyone—to see them so at peace when they had returned to say the evening prayers.

"There is hope again," he explained as the white dove set down on his shoulder. "This is home now."

He giggled, pushing the trunk of the baby spirit elephant away from his face when the ethereal beast laid it atop his head. The wings of the dove fluttered against his cheek, the dove cooing into his ear.

"It is John," he said, seeing him start the climb to the top. "He needs to see you. He needs to feel whole again."

The dove flew down to peck at his thigh.

"He is almost better. The hold was strong."

A shimmering, crystalline droplet fell against his dark skin, twinkling for a moment before disappearing. When the second one fell, he caught it in his palm.

"Yes, he will be sad. But we will be here. It is as they told me."

The spirit beast rubbed its face against his shoulder, the remaining tears sparkling into his shamma.

"Two nights ago. Heading toward the Red Sea. They would have the fishermen take them across, and then on to where the Father guides them."

With a flutter of wings, the dove lifted off his thigh and came to rest on his forearm.

"His eyes shine with the light of the moon and the sun. He is everything. He is the Father's son."

They heard a rock falling. They listened as it dropped to the valley floor in a succession of echoing bounces. All three peered downward over the ledge. John was making good progress. The baby spirit elephant tapped its front feet on the ground. John Too got up and looked west. The dove flew back to his shoulder.

"Yes, home," he said, placing a hand to the base of the spirit elephant's trunk.

"The Mother is happy here. She has brought everything here."

The dove nibbled at the lobe of his ear. He laughed at first, but then became somber.

"We do not speak of him. It serves no purpose. Etiyopiya and Sister Lady agree that peace can be found where hate has walked. It is not the fault of this place that the Serpent once sought power here. Others will try."

The cry of a sentry bull trumpeted across the mountainous terrain, the glistening shapes of spirit elephants materializing on the tops of the plateaus that stretched westward.

"Both the Father and the Mother have given their blessings to this place. We are their children. This is their kingdom."

"Who are you talking to?"

John Too smiled as he turned to see John pulling himself up over the edge of the cliff.

"What do you see?" John Too asked.

"Nothing but you and the night," John wearily replied, rubbing the dust from his gnarled feet.

"Why did you follow?"

John placed a finger to his neck and worked the necklace out from underneath the cloth draped about it. The dried carcasses of the green beetles he had collected glowed in the moonlight.

"Ah, you have finished it."

Reaching into the folds of his shamma, John brought forth two other loops of decorative green beetles. He held the smaller of the two out toward John Too.

"For Claire," he humbly stated. "I mean Sister Lady," he said, his tone touched with regret.

"And the other?"

Timid with the showing of it, he held the other, the bigger of the two, aloft.

"Etiyopiya," he quietly said.

John Too's smile was wide and joyful.

"To return as you began," he remarked with happiness. "This is good." Glancing upward and then to the side, he added, "You see? Nearly healed."

Silent of wing, the white dove hovered in the air above John Too. Beside him, the shimmering form of the baby spirit elephant appeared.

John, seeing the visions, fell to his knees as the great spirit herd trumpeted his return.

TEIMBAKA HAD BEEN awakened by the touch of the baby spirit elephant. It was before dawn when it had appeared and laid its trunk to his cheek. There had been fog, a dense, still mist that would only part when they moved through it.

When he had sought to bring his long spear and bow and arrows, the baby spirit elephant had stayed his hand, offering only the sad look of the departed when his expression questioned it. Bowing to its wishes, he had followed weaponless, a sense of the past stirring within him as the small spirit beast led him on a path he could not see.

When he had stumbled and heard the rocks he had dislodged fall into a deep chasm, the baby spirit elephant had turned and placed a walking stick into his hand. When he felt it, the skin of his palm and fingers finding all the familiar nodules and the grain of the wood, there was no questioning that it was the dula of Tafari. And though it had been lost to him for many years, he no longer doubted the ways of the spirit elephants or what was possible and what was not. The power of the Mother and the Father were strong here—here in the place where evil had been dispatched—so he accepted the young spirit beast's gift without question and walked dutifully onward.

First light found them at the edge of the highlands. Teimbaka stood on a great outcrop of stone overlooking a parcel of desert that stretched south and eastward, bordered on the north by a series of rocky, uneven ridges.

The helicopter appeared as dark speck against a backdrop of cerulean blue, its form growing incrementally larger as it flew a westward course.

Like the two gunships he had seen before, the helicopter flew low in the sky, some two hundred yards above the ground. Faintly, the dim roar of its engine reached him, the sound seeming to surround him as it bounced off the ridges to the north and the highlands at his back.

His hand clenched around the dula as the airship drew near.

"Should I not seek cover?" he asked the spirit beast. "I am in the open."

The surface-to-air missile streaked out from a crevice in the first ridgeline and struck the helicopter in its midsection, exploding in a fireball just aft of the cargo door. Immediately, the helicopter swerved hard and away from where the rocket had been launched, but then tilted back again, leaning at a severe angle as the pilot tried to gain control.

Large-caliber automatic weapons fire erupted from the ridgeline, strafing the airship near the main rotor assembly. The ping, ping, ping of the bullets bouncing off the armor-plated panels could be clearly heard even as the engine driving the massive blades began to sputter and smoke.

The helicopter began to spiral and sway, its nose dipping down and then jerking up. It picked up speed as it began to hurtle sideways toward the ground. With another burst of heavy weapons fire, the helicopter took a sudden drop, a section of the tail rotor breaking off in pieces where the bullets hit. Within a matter of seconds, it crashed nose first into the desert floor, flipping forward and then to the side. For a moment, the massive titanium blades continued to rotate, gouging out streams of sand and rocks, sending them churning skyward. Then came a flash and a shuddering explosion as the main rotor assembly blew apart. The ridgeline erupted in cheers. The baby spirit elephant wailed. Teimbaka stared in disbelief. And in the moment of dreamlike silence that followed, he heard the cling clang of a tiny bell.

Teimbaka scrambled down the great formation of stones, reaching the ground in a half run, the smell of diesel fuel and smoke assaulting his senses. When flames began to shoot up from the rotor, he broke into a sprint.

The first bullets exploded into the sand some twenty yards ahead and away from him. Out of the corner of his eye, he saw two vehicles emerge from the base of the nearest ridge, shapeless blobs spitting flashes of white, some half-mile away. Ahead of him, the baby spirit elephant appeared near the wreckage of the airship. The ringing of the tiny bell, like the ticking hands an old clock, beckoned him forward, offering him a steady course to follow while his thoughts fragmented in a dozen different directions.

Bullets strafed the ground again. They were closer to him now, the sound of the weapons reaching his ears a second or two after the sand erupted in plumes. The burning airship was a score of yards away; the men with the guns would arrive within the minute. He slowed, hesitating. The baby spirit elephant cried out. He raced ahead.

The nose of the massive helicopter was a bubble, a collection of tempered, reinforced panes of glass held together by a framework of forged-steel crossbeams. Teimbaka saw the face of a man pressed against a section of the glass, cheek flattened, nose askew and bloody, a white hat pinned over his eyes. A slick pool of deep red covered the back of his neck. More bullets sprayed across the front of the bubble as he raced by. They ricocheted wildly in all directions. *Why am I here?* his thoughts screamed. *Why am I here?*

The kebero caught his attention first, sitting upright, balanced on the smaller of the two ends, the worn, dirt-stained hide stretched taut across the top, as if the drum were waiting to be played. When the ancient drum began to bounce and teeter, he thought he was delusional or on the verge of madness. But then the quaking of the earth reached his feet, and, with it, the thundering sound of the stampede as the great spirit herd raced down from the highlands and onto the desert floor.

He turned to watch them, their crystalline bodies shimmering in the glow of the morning sun, the brilliant gold and white of the light's reflection creating a blinding wall of chaos. As indistinct shouts of fear arose from the men in the jeeps, the vehicles made a sudden turn and headed back to where they had come from. In a shuddering implosion of light and sound, the great spirit herd vanished.

The pungent fumes of diesel fuel lured Teimbaka back toward the downed helicopter. The baby spirit elephant whimpered and touched his arm. When he looked to console her, she had moved some distance away, standing in the opening between two of the massive blades where they connected to the rotor. With her trunk, she lifted up someone's arm.

*

T HE CLING CLANG of the tiny bell was drawing closer. He could almost feel the cleft hooves of the goat stepping into the sand. He was cold—not icy, but the chill was growing, extending to every part of his body. He tried to wrap his shamma around him, but found he wasn't dressed in one. He rubbed the fabric of the shirt he was wearing between his fingers.

The tiny bell was almost upon him. He struggled to turn his neck to see. There! There was the lead goat, he saw, brown with a white beard and a white star on its forehead, its black-socked hooves lifting and falling in methodical precision as it ambled across the river of sand. And beside it walked a lithe form swathed in a brown robe, a boy on the verge of becoming a man. His head was held high and proud, his dula placed to the ground with conviction.

Menelik attempted to raise his arm in an effort to greet him. But he was weak, and faltered. Some force lifted his arm for him. The boy saw him. Approaching him with a smile, he took hold of Menelik's hand.

Teimbaka grasped the man's hand and felt for any sign of life. To his amazement and relief, the man gently squeezed his fingers and fluttered his eyelids. Jerking with the effort, the man opened his eyes.

Teimbaka saw a figure in the deep brown of the man's unfocused gaze. It was a boy, a dula in his hand, a goat ambling by his side. A small bell hung about the animal's neck. Hypnotized by the images, he peered deeper.

The tiny bell jingled as the goat moved past. He could hear the solemn cling clang of it. The boy raised his dula and called his name: "Teimbaka!" And then the boy stared right at Teimbaka and called out, "Menelik, come! Father has a task!"

Dropping to his knees, he clutched Menelik's upper arm.

"Menelik," he half shouted. "Menelik!"


Menelik felt a hand take hold of his. It was warm and strong, giving him a sense that he was safe. He pressed it to let whoever it was know that he was aware. With difficulty, he was able to open his eyes. What he saw confused him.

The dula was standing upright, though he saw no hand holding it in place. A white dove hovered near the top, its wings slowly beating, its presence radiating a light that was a marriage of the sun and the moon.

A face appeared above him. And though the features were those of a small boy, they struck him as familiar. He could feel the recognition pulling at him, grasping his arm. The boy was saying something. The dula was in his hand now. He held it out from his side as he shouted a name. It was his name. He could see the word forming as it passed from the boy's lips. Then he remembered and wanted to cry. The boy's face was that of Teimbaka. It was Teimbaka calling him.

"Teimbaka." His lips moved with the saying of it. The face above him became that of a man. They smiled at one another. He could hardly breathe.


Teimbaka felt the tears well in his eyes when he saw his brother's lips forming his name. How this moment had come to pass—how Menelik had returned to find him after so many years, where he had been, how he had come to be here on this very morning—he did not know or understand. But it was his brother. The jingle of the tiny bell, the appearance of Tafari, the goat, the river of sand, the spirit elephants; somehow they had made it possible. Menelik had found his way back.

Blood trickled out the side of Menelik's mouth, turning his smile into a grimace of pain.

"Menelik," Teimbaka said with urgency.

The sight of his brother's body half-crushed beneath the weight of the burning frame of the airship seized hold of him. In a moment of panic, diesel smoke hanging like a black storm cloud over his head, he looked wildly about.

The baby spirit elephant wrapped its trunk around the dula and placed it at the base of the steel shell. Teimbaka slid it forward, wedging as much of the sturdy wood as he could underneath the frame. With all the strength he could muster, unleashing a furious roar, he pushed down upon the lever, straining every muscle in an effort to lift the smoldering hulk off his brother's body. It didn't budge. He screamed.

As the flames began to spread and grow in height, the smoke swirled and grew denser. Breathing became difficult, the air choking. Heat singed the hair on his face. Below him, next to his side, his brother gasped in agony. Frantic, Teimbaka bore down upon the lever once more. Nothing. Overcome with his failure, he shut his eyes and wailed. Behind him, shattering the air with a blaring rejoinder, spirit elephants answered.

Four gargantuan spirit bulls lowered their heads and placed their immense tusks beneath the smoldering hulk.

"By the Mother, lift!" he shouted. "Lift!"

With the screech of straining metal joints, the wreckage began to move off of the ground. With diesel fuel leaking and pooling on the sand, and with the flames jumping to follow, Teimbaka pulled Menelik free. Moving swiftly, he stepped around him and grasped him underneath his shoulders. Racing the fire, he began to drag him away.

Behind them, hissing, cackling, and dancing, the flames found their way into the fuel tanks. A moment later, the burning wreck of the Mi-24 exploded in a massive fireball, sending a powerful shock wave and shards of shrapnel flying outward in every direction. The ground trembled and shook.

Teimbaka felt a stinging heat cut across his chest, forehead, and shoulders. He watched as the sky began to spin and shrink into black. Dark angels appeared, drifting slowly downward, descending through the slender column of blue sky that still remained intact. And then all went gray.

*

JOHN TOOK THE needle from Claire's unsteady hand. When their fingers brushed, he glanced into her eyes. Checking the length of the thread, he bent over the first of Teimbaka's several wounds and slipped the needle beneath the skin. He calmly guided the thread under, across, and up.

"Just like the beetles," John Too giggled, glancing at Claire.

But Claire seemed not to hear him, staring down at Teimbaka.

"Sister Lady, Etiyopiya will be all right. You will see. John will make him whole."

Claire looked ashen, her expression distraught, the dark circles beneath her eyes hinting at the sleepless vigil she had been keeping since John and John Too had returned with Teimbaka and the mangled body of his brother. She gazed at John Too but did not see him.

"He would have said," she heard him saying. "Only for his brother, did he say, was it time. Not Etiyopiya."

Claire blinked her eyes and shook her head.

"Who?" she asked, though she couldn't quite understand why she wanted or needed to know. "Who said?"

"Him," John Too replied as if she were supposed to understand of whom it was they were speaking.

Claire rubbed her face and pulled at the tufts of her hair. She lowered her head with a heavy sigh.

"Him," she wearily repeated, "I don't know any—"

"The boy," he told her, his eyes widening, nodding his head. "The son."

Claire snapped her head up.

"John Too."

Her tone was stern, her voice tired. The words however, when she was able to speak them, were pleading.

"I don't know what you mean. I don't, John Too, I don't."

John Too reached across Teimbaka's prone body and took hold of Claire's hands.

"The son. Him," he earnestly explained. "The son of the Father. You speak of him always in your prayers. The one who they put to the cross. Him."

His face, as it had always been, was bright, his eyes twinkling with joy. He offered her a knowing smile.

"John Too, the man you speak of, the Son of the Father …" She hesitated. "He died on the cross many thousands of years ago."

She shook her head.

"And rose again, yes? It is what you have told us."

"Yes, but John Too, Jesus was a grown man when he was crucified. And now He sits at the right hand of God, of the Father."

Torn between Teimbaka's struggle for life and making John Too understand, Claire felt all the exhaustion of the past few days pushing down on her. She hastily wiped the tears sliding down her cheeks.

"He has come back," John Too gently told her with a slight shrug. "He says it will happen again. It is why, sometimes, he cannot be as happy as he should be. He sees it."

As Claire stared at John Too in disbelief, John tied the ends of the thread together over the deep gash from the shrapnel that had narrowly missed slicing open the artery in Teimbaka's neck.

"A clean needle and more thread," he stated. "And rubbing alcohol."

John Too and Claire bent to their respective tasks.

*

THE KEBERO WAS somber and forlorn, the beat following the mood of the one who played it. The sky was dark, gray with low-hanging clouds, heavy with the smell and feel of rain. He would welcome it if it came, he thought. Perhaps it would wash away all that he did not wish to remember.

Absently, he took his fingers from the drum and ran them over the stitches on his face. He lingered over each of the sewn seams as though they represented a measurement of time. How little of it he had spent with his brother: the early years of tending to the goats, of playing soldiers with their walking sticks. Even the day of gathering wood along the banks of the river of sand seemed so distant, as though he had only imagined it. And then to be given but a moment to share in the lives they had both followed since that fateful day. He gave the drum a solitary tap.

A drop of rain reached him, carried by a stiffening wind. It rustled the two sheets of paper that he had placed by his side. He glanced down at them and then picked them up before they blew away. He held them for a time, just staring at them. There was no need to read them. He had done that a score of times over the past several days. But they were trea-sures now, nonetheless. He would keep them forever. They would be the memory he would carry of his brother. They would be the words and the feelings they would have shared with each other if Menelik had lived.

Teimbaka had felt enormous pride when he had read the note from Adiam telling of the relief aid being delivered to the refugee camp in eastern Ethiopia. It meant that Menelik had been working to help the people of their country. It would be a story he would tell over and over when the children asked for a tale to take with them into sleep. It gave him great peace of mind to know that his brother had been fighting for their people. He was a child of the Mother. She would be the bond they would forever share.

The short letter to Yutanda they had found in the other pocket of his jeans had evoked both sadness and joy. He fingered the folded sheet, deciding he needed to read it once more.

*Dearest Yutanda,*

*Tomorrow we are flying north to find my brother. It is with a great sense of pride and wonder that I found he is known here as the Lion of Djibouti. It makes me feel as if I am seeking a ghost. I am hoping he is still of flesh and blood. José, my pilot, says we will be taking off well before dawn so that our position can't be so easily tracked. We hope to reach our destination—the "palm of the Mother"—just at daybreak. José says he has heard of such a place. Again, I feel as though I am traveling to some holy place. We shall see.*

*The refugee camps are a tragedy. But the people continue to struggle to survive, and the relief organizations are working as hard as they are able and allowed. I will explain in detail when we speak.*

*Give my love to our child! I am overjoyed with the thought that we will be bringing a new life into the world (boy or girl). I hope you are taking care of yourself. Eat right! And don't let your dad feed you any of those blessedly good snapper fritters when you go to visit! We want our child to be lean and mean! I am laughing. I hope you are too. I love you. I miss you. I am well. I will see you soon.*

*Menelik*

A raindrop splashed atop of Menelik's name. Teimbaka wiped it with a fingertip and placed it on his cheek.


"Will you be much longer?"

Claire studied him, noting the carriage of his body: worn but strong, bent but not yet ready to rest. The line of his jaw was well defined, unblemished by the explosion, shaved smooth by Thomas after she had cleansed the lacerations on the rest of his face. The wounds that John had stitched closed above his left eye and beneath the ridge of each cheekbone were still red, with traces of blue, black, and orange. But the swelling was gone. And soon, she hoped, so would be the barrier he had raised that was blocking his spirit's resurgence.

"John and John Too will be returning soon," she offered, hoping the saying of their names would spark some sort of reaction.

He looked at the sky and then looked to her. The brow that had once seemed so noble and fierce was now tempered and questioning.

"I did not know they had gone," he quietly stated. "Where were they?"

"At the grave of your brother. John made him a necklace of beetles. The same as ours," she told him, holding her wrist aloft so he could see she was wearing her bracelet.

He smiled. She returned it.

"They know you will be ready to travel there soon. They—I—know you will be pleased. The view, it is beautiful from sunrise to sunset. And the stars, Teimbaka, wait till you see the stars. They are so close you can—"

She half giggled, blushing when she saw how amused he was at listening to her talk. It gave her pleasure.

When he struggled to get up from the flat-topped slab of stone he was sitting upon, she moved to help him. But he waved her off, using the kebero to steady himself. Gingerly, he placed the folds of his black shamma across one shoulder. She could see how stiff and sore his arm still was. *Stubborn*, she thought. It made her giggle even more.

Teimbaka lifted the drum by the twine stitched around its frame and ambled down the natural rock path. The wind gusted for a moment, bringing a few more drops of rain. Claire extended her hand. He accepted it with warmth.

"Now, tell me again how my brother was carried to Ras Dashen," he half teased. "The spirit elephants, you said, would not place him anywhere else?"

"The biggest, most majestic I have ever seen," she gushed, tenderly pulling him to her side. "Like glittering mountains they were. John Too says it is where they have been waiting."

"They? Who has been waiting?"

"He only smiles when I ask."

Gently touching each scar on his face, she gazed deeply into his eyes for a time before lightly kissing his lips. Taking each other's hands, sharing a wishful sigh, they walked back toward camp as a steady rain began to fall.


*THE END*